Cut The Deck

B Baskerville

Hyem Books

The DCI Cooper Series Books 1-3

Cut The Deck

Rock, Paper, Scissors

Roll The Dice

B Baskerville

Hyem Books

- CHAPTER 1 -

UNTIL LAST YEAR, RACHEL Pearson had never considered her own mortality. Now she thought about it twice a week, every week. The fifteen-year-old attended yoga classes to rebuild her strength after an accident left her with fractures to her C4 and C5 vertebrae. She'd been bed-bound for four months; the physiotherapy to get her walking again had been brutal.

Yoga class always ended in *shavasana*, or corpse pose. Twice a week, Rachel would lie on the yoga mat, exhausted, sweaty and frustrated. The old Rachel would find yoga tediously easy. The new Rachel struggled to stand on one leg.

"Empty your mind," said the instructor in a voice that was supposed to be soothing but made Rachel feel like she was back in primary school.

She could never empty her mind in *shavasana*; instead, she thought of the day she'd fallen and couldn't get back up. It was the day Great Britain's hot prospect for the next Olympics spectacularly dropped out of contention. Literally.

Rachel rolled up her mat, gathered her things and braced herself for the climb down the stairs.

"Take care, Rach. I'll see you next session."

Rachel tucked waist-length plaits down the back of her sweatshirt and waved over her shoulder. She rarely said a word to anyone at yoga. After all, what did she have in common with these women in their forties and fifties with cardio butts and incessant talk of daytime soaps and PTA meetings?

It was a bitterly cold night at Prior's Haven. The little beach on the North Sea coast was home to Tynemouth's rowing and sailing clubs. Yoga class was held above the sailing club, and it had the most beautiful views of the mouth of the Tyne. The frosty ground cracked beneath Rachel's feet as she made her way up the slope towards the main road. The first snowfall of the year had begun, and snowflakes clung to the fur trim of her coat.

If Rachel Pearson had known tonight would be her last, she would have stopped to appreciate the beauty of a thousand stars twinkling above the North Sea. She would've called her parents and told them that she loved them. She would've called her boyfriend and forgiven him for the horrible things he'd said.

She would have stuck to the main road instead of taking a shortcut.

Rachel pushed headphones into her ears and selected a Christmas playlist. It was still November, but as far as Rachel was concerned, once Guy Fawkes night was out of the way, Christmas tunes were fair game. She loved anything festive, and she was currently halfway through hand-making Christmas cards for her friends and family. Standing at the crossroads between the steep bank up to Tynemouth village and a deserted, unlit car park, Rachel weighed up her options. It would take twenty minutes to walk home through the village but eight minutes tops if she took the shortcut. She had promised her dad that she wouldn't, but the sooner she got home, the sooner she could shower, get into her pyjamas and finish her stupid biology assignment before calling Will to see if he was ready to apologise.

The shortcut won.

Rachel activated the torch on her phone and scanned it back and forth over the frosty ground as she carefully made her way across the car park. Despite the joyful music that made her bob her head and tap her candy-pink nails against the inside of her pocket, prickles ran down the back of Rachel's neck. This route home always gave her the heebie-jeebies. Perhaps it was the pitch-black or the chilling sea breeze, or maybe it was the unshakable suspicion that she was being followed.

A well-worn path connected the back of the car park to a large field dominated by the Collingwood Monument, a tribute to local-born Lord Collingwood, Nelson's partner in the Napoleonic wars.

Rachel was careful of her footing where the ground changed from asphalt to mud. She dug her toes into the frozen earth and pushed herself through the narrow gap between the bushes. She couldn't wait to get home and back into the warmth.

Baby, It's Cold Outside began to play. She loved this number as a little girl, but the older she got, the creepier it sounded. Rachel skipped the song. The lull in the music happened just in time to hear the crack of a twig behind her. It was not in time to stop the plastic bag from being pulled over her head.

- CHAPTER 2 -

Terry Parke shook his head at his wife.

"You're stark raving mad. It's brass monkeys today, or haven't you noticed?"

Gwen smiled at him as she removed her coat and jumper. He was right about the weather, and though she'd never admit it, he was probably right about her; she was an absolute lunatic for wanting to go for a swim in the North Sea on a day like this. To be fair, she'd thought the same thing when she first saw Doris strip off and run straight into the sea wearing nothing but a polka dot bikini.

The Ageing Disgracefully Club liked to meet every Wednesday morning come rain or shine to have a quick energising dip, boost their endorphins and get the blood flowing. There were eight of them in total, all women, all in their sixties and seventies, and all of whom had husbands who thought they were completely bonkers.

Terry threw a tennis ball for his daft-as-a-brush Patterdale terrier and watched him shoot off across the beach, his tail wagging with every step. It was three below zero and even the sand was frosted over. Terry blew into his hands, desperately trying to warm them before shoving them deep into his pockets and walking in pursuit of the dog. The little dafty was more than happy to chase the ball but would never bring the damn thing back.

"Should've got a retriever," mumbled Terry.

Behind him, Gwen was running gleefully towards the water's edge, knees high, arms flailing, and all Terry's favourite bits wobbling. Doris and the others weren't far behind. He could hear their excited squeals as their feet touched the bracing North Sea for the first time that week. Only toddlers and women over forty could reach that pitch. Terry was surprised the terrier's floppy ears hadn't pricked up.

"Come on, Jasper. Get over here. Good boy. How's about when your mother's finished playing silly buggers we pop to the café in the village and get ourselves a nice cup of tea and a bacon butty? Sound good, lad?"

The terrier sat and wagged his tail. Terry was convinced the dog knew exactly what he was saying. He puffed out his breath and watched it condense in the icy air.

"Then it's a deal. Bacon butties it is. Now FETCH!"

The dog hightailed it across Prior's Haven, kicking up plumes of sand in his wake. Tennis ball in mouth, he turned and considered a return to his master only to become distracted by something in one of the sailing boats. Terry tutted, the boats should've been moved to storage for the winter, and in fairness, most of them had been. Some people, however, had more money than sense and had left the laser dinghies to face a north-eastern winter unprotected from the elements.

"Leave it, Jasper."

The dog scurried up to the edge of the laser, his nose peering into the boat, his tail rigid.

"Jasper, whatever it is, leave it alone, ya daft mutt. Get your ball. Come on, for once in ya life, fetch the damn ball."

Wendy, the eldest member of the group, was out of the water now; the quick splash had been more than enough for her. She wrapped herself in a thick white towel and giggled as she watched her friends bounce in the gentle waves.

"Jasper, leave it! Honestly, I've never known a more disobedient dog."

Terry huffed under his breath. He needed to get Gwen's towel ready and pour her some coffee from his flask. Jasper had better not be nose deep in a dead seagull like he had been the last time. Disgusting flying rats. The mangy thing had been full of maggots.

Oh dear God.

Terry fell over backwards and cursed as his behind hit the cold, hard sand. *Dear God.* He tried to yell, but no sound escaped his lips. The girl was young, a teenager most likely, and thin, painfully thin. Her long spindly legs were pale and folded into the boat at such an angle she appeared knock-kneed. She wore shiny black stilettos but no trousers or skirt. Above the waist she was dressed in a white, bloodstained shirt and a black blazer. Bizarrely, a top hat was perched jauntily atop her head, and a magic wand stuck out of her blazer pocket. Long, dark plaits that reached her waist were crossed over her chest. It took a while for Terry to notice that a white rabbit, its pink eyes foggy from death, had been tucked into the crook of her arm.

"Oh sweet Jesus," he stammered, trying to push himself back to his feet. The scream finally came and he bellowed, "POLICE. We n-need to c-call the POLICE."

Terry grabbed Jasper's collar and pulled him into his chest.

"Terrence? Is everything all right?" called Doris. She shuffled out of the water, a goosebump-covered woman with rapidly reddening legs.

Gwen frowned and followed her friend. "What's going on, Terry?"

Terry turned as eight shivering ladies in their swimwear plodded up the beach to see what all the fuss was about.

"Police, you say?" asked Susan, who was rapidly approaching seventy. "What's the fettle?"

Terry's protective instincts kicked in. He had been raised in an age of chivalry, a time when it was good manners - not offensive - to offer your seat on the bus to a pregnant lady. But times were changing, and only last week he'd been called a sexist for telling a young lad off for swearing when there were ladies present. Sexist or not, Terry didn't want his wife or her friends to see what he'd just seen. He was old-fashioned and proudly so.

"No. NO!" He ran towards them. "Don't look. Please, Gwen." His arms were extended as he tried in vain to shepherd the women away from the scene. "You don't need to see that. You don't need—"

"Holy Mary, mother of God."

Gwen collapsed to her knees; sand clung to her damp, pink skin.

"Poor child. Poor, poor child."

"Please, Gwen," begged Terry. "Please get dry. Get dressed. There's nothing we can do. The poor bairn—"

"CPR. Start CPR." Susan's voice was shrill - as high-pitched as it had been only minutes earlier when she'd raced into the sea - only now it was with horror, not joy.

"She's gone," said Terry. He felt helpless, a feeling he was experiencing more and more since shifting to the wrong side of sixty-five. "Please darling, we can't do anything... Oh Gwen, you're turning blue. Please, you'll catch your death."

- CHAPTER 3 -

"But Mum."

"But nothing, Tina. I said no, and I mean no."

Tina sighed. Her eyes were locked on her mother's. She didn't want to give an inch, didn't want to back down.

"I'll be in the spare room. Josh's parents will be there."

"It's still a no, Tina."

"You can call them; they're called Reg and Lucy. They said it's fine."

"And I said it's not. There's no way on Earth I am letting my fourteen-year-old *crash* at her boyfriend's house. Spare room or not. Ask again in two years."

Tina's face crumpled. "Honestly, you are such a BITCH." She stormed upstairs, slamming her bedroom door behind her.

DCI Erica Cooper closed her eyes. This was all she needed. In other homes, one parent would turn to the other for backup, but this was a single-parent household. Tina's father had been nothing more than a monthly child support payment for twelve years. Two years ago, he'd flounced back onto Tyneside after eight years in the south and four years in Qatar and had expected to instantly bond with his estranged daughter. Both Cooper and Tina had understandably been less than impressed at the idea, but lately, Tina had agreed to weekly visits.

Cooper heard Tina's bedroom door creak on its hinges.

"It's 'cause I'm an aspie, isn't it? If I was normal you'd let me."

Cooper propped her elbows on the kitchen table and lowered her head into her hands. As much as she wanted to tell herself that Tina's ASD had nothing to do with this, it probably did. Her daughter wasn't slow; in fact, the opposite was true.

Academically, she was gifted. The term *prodigy* had been bandied about by more than one of Tina's teachers. But Tina struggled to make friends, and her longing for acceptance meant she was easily led. She'd do anything to fit in. Anything to be liked.

"Mum!"

"I heard you," shouted Cooper. She hated talking through walls. "And one, no, it has nothing to do with that. Two, there's no such thing as normal. And three, I'm not going to keep repeating myself. Come down and finish your breakfast."

"I'm going to ask Dad."

The door slammed shut again. Cooper took a deep breath and counted to ten. "Yeah, good luck with that," she muttered through clenched teeth.

Tina had timed this tantrum to perfection, thought Cooper as she looked at her reflection in a stainless steel kettle. The wig wasn't convincing. It was made from real hair, and the light brown colour matched her own. Still, the cut wasn't quite right, nor was the texture. Cooper's hair had a natural kink to it and it fell in gentle waves to her collarbones, or at least it had done until chemo caused it to fall out. Then there was the fringe. Cooper tilted her head back and forth and tried to convince herself that she quite suited a fringe and poker-straight locks, but it was no use, she didn't look like her old self, and she hadn't for many months. A tailored suit that had previously hugged her thirty-something curves was now baggy and hung off the edges of her shoulders like an adult-sized shirt on a child-sized hanger. Cooper's belt was fastened two notches tighter, and her energy levels had dropped from bordering on hyperactive to being in desperate need of recharging. Had she been naive in thinking her first day back at CID after four months of sick leave was going to go smoothly?

Cooper checked her watch. Perhaps she could salvage the day once Tina had been packed off to school by treating herself to a Starbucks and a pastry en route to HQ.

Her phone rang.

"Have you lost your mind?" It was Kenny, the monthly child support payment. "Telling our daughter she can have a sleepover at that cretin's house? No daughter of mine is going to become another teenage pregnancy statistic."

"Like I was, you mean? I seem to remember you playing a minor role in that debacle."

There was a snort at the other end of the phone.

"Besides," Cooper continued, "I never told Tina she could stay at Josh's. In fact, I told her the opposite. Let me guess, she said that *I'd say yes if you said yes,* and she buttered you up by saying she'd spend the whole weekend with you so you two could have some quality daddy-daughter time?"

"How'd you know that?" he asked, a bark still in his voice.

"Because I've lived with her for fourteen years, Kenneth." Cooper's voice was harsh, she hadn't intended to snap at Kenny, but he made it so bloody easy. She ran a hand over her forehead and played with her new fringe. "Sorry. Look, our daughter is a sneaky little genius. Now don't blame me. She gets it from you. I have to go, Kenny. I'm back at work today; I need to get off."

"That's today?"

Cooper could hear the guilt in his voice.

"Right, well, best of luck. Not that you need it. Sorry about going off on you. Should have known."

Cooper ended the call and took a long gulp of coffee. It was cold and bitter but she needed the caffeine.

"Tina, time for school," she called up the stairs.

The door creaked. "I'm not going." Then it slammed again.

It was a bluff - Tina was a stickler for routine - but it was a bluff Cooper could do without. She was about to march up the stairs when her phone rang again.

"Cooper. You live in Tynemouth. How quickly can you be at the Priory?"

Detective Chief Superintendent Howard Nixon was a gruffly spoken man with little time for *hi, how are yous*. The Priory, Cooper knew, was the ruined remains of Tynemouth Castle and a Benedictine monastery where the old kings of Northumberland were buried. It sat atop Ben Pal Crag, sporting views of King Edward's Bay to the north and the river Tyne to the south.

Cooper pinched the bridge of her nose. "I can be there in under ten, sir. What do I need to know?"

"Body of a young woman found in one of the boats at the sailing club. She's in fancy dress and cuddling a dead rabbit."

Cooper's brows knitted together. "Sir?"

"Aye. Might be some student initiation gone wrong. Got drunk, got separated, fell asleep in the cold. But the gent who called it in reported the woman had no trousers or skirt on, and there's blood on her shirt. You still got a field kit, Cooper?"

"Yes, sir. I'm looking at it right now."

Cooper got to her feet; she tucked her phone between her ear and shoulder and pulled on a thick woollen coat.

"Good. Uniforms are securing the scene. Forensics are on the way."

"Who's the SOCO, sir?"

"Atkinson," replied Nixon.

Cooper nodded. She had a good relationship with Justin Atkinson. He was the first scene of crime officer she'd dealt with upon joining the force. He was there when she saw her first dead body, and he was the only one not to take the piss because she'd thrown up all over her own shoes at the sight of it.

"I'm putting Daniel on this. He'll meet you there."

Cooper was about to respond when Nixon hung up.

"*How are you feeling, Cooper?*" the detective drawled in a facsimile of Nixon's voice while she cleared her breakfast items into the dishwasher. "*Good to have you back, Cooper... Let us know how we can ease you back into the swing of things, Cooper.*"

"Tina!" she called, more loudly this time. She picked up her field kit and pulled sheep-skin gloves over her hands. "Got to go. You'll have to walk to school."

A grunt of annoyance echoed down the hallway, but if Tina had anything else to say to her mother, it would have to wait until dinner.

- CHAPTER 4 -

COOPER PARKED HER BEAT-UP old Mazda in a short-stay car park near the sailing club. She pulled up the collar of her coat to protect her neck from the icy wind and stepped out into the crisp morning air.

"So much for a Starbucks and a pastry," she grumbled to herself.

She wrapped her arms around her torso and shuffled down the bank towards Prior's Haven.

Police tape cordoned off access to the beach. As Cooper approached, she flashed her warrant card at two uniforms who stood aside and held up the tape for her to manoeuvre herself under. Steep cliffs overlooked both sides of Prior's Haven. Numerous nosy parkers had already gathered on the Spanish Battery to the south. They were angling morbidly to catch a glimpse of the victim. They'd be disappointed; a sizable forensic tent protected the young woman's dignity.

"Morning, Tennessee," greeted Cooper to Detective Sergeant Jack Daniel.

Tennessee was a statuesque young man with an angelic face that would be better suited to modelling Armani than to patrolling the streets of North Tyneside. He had unruly blond curls and the sort of healthy complexion Cooper would've killed for, even before her illness.

"Ma'am! It's good to have you back." He clasped her gloved hands in his and beamed at her. He looked like he wanted to hug her. Cooper instinctively took a step backwards. Hugging officers at a possible murder scene would not go down well with the crowd of onlookers.

"Ma'am?" asked Cooper with raised eyebrows. "Surely I'm not old enough to warrant the ma'am treatment? You know it's Cooper. Any more ma'am nonsense and I'll have you transferred to Sunderland."

Tennessee nodded formally. "Yes, ma'am. I mean Cooper. Ah, please don't transfer me to Sunderland. My dad will never let me hear the end of it, ma'am. I mean Cooper. Ah, shit."

Cooper held in her giggle and remained poker-faced.

"Bring me up to speed, Tennessee."

"The vic looks to be in her mid to late teens. She's dressed in some sort of magician's outfit with a top hat and magic wand. Uniforms are taking statements from local residents, but most of them have already left for work. Atkinson's in the tent, and his assistant's scouring the beach for evidence. We've been trying to get hold of someone from the sailing and rowing clubs. Both buildings have CCTV on the entranceways. There's no street lighting down here, but the clubs have movement-activated lighting on the doors. I'll let you know when we've tracked down the committee members who have access to the cameras."

Cooper nodded and looked around. She knew this area well. When Tina was an infant, Cooper would bring her to the secluded beach for picnics. They'd amble hand-in-hand along the kilometre-long pier keeping their eyes peeled for dolphins.

Tennessee's phone buzzed and he retrieved it from his pocket.

"DS Daniel," he said. He paused for a second while the person on the other end of the call spoke. "Cooper," he covered the microphone on his mobile. "It's one of the geezers from the sailing club." He put the phone back to his ear and strode towards the water's edge. "Yes, we'd appreciate your help on this matter... As soon as possible, sir."

Cooper readied herself as she pulled on a bunny suit and gloves. She still hadn't grown used to the sight or smell of death, and part of her hoped she never would. She didn't want to become one of those jaded old coppers who could look at a corpse and make an inappropriate joke. Nixon came to mind.

Taking a deep breath of sea air, Cooper bowed her head and entered the forensics tent. Justin Atkinson was crouched next to the body of what had once been a beautiful young lady. She had stalk-thin legs and her brown hair was styled in two long braids that reached her waist. From where Cooper stood, she could see a patch of blood on her white shirt and bruising around the girl's neck. She watched as Atkinson worked, taking samples from behind the girl's fingernails, bagging and labelling as he went. To the left of the boat, a collapsible table was set up. Atkinson's equipment and storage boxes were laid out in perfect right angles, and five pens lay precisely parallel to each other.

Only when Cooper spotted the dead rabbit, bagged and sealed, did she let out a gasp. "Bloody hell."

Atkinson looked up. "Well, if it isn't Erica Cooper."

"Good to see you, Justin." And it was. "I just wish it were under better circumstances."

"Yes. Same here." Justin Atkinson's frameless glasses perched on the tip of his nose, and his pronounced Adam's apple bounced as he talked. He straightened up to his full height of six-foot-four and looked down at Cooper with sadness in his eyes. "I try to stay professional, you know that, but it's hard when they're so young. So much wasted potential."

"How old was she?"

"I'd guess fourteen to seventeen. The pathologist will be able to narrow it down if she's not identified."

Cooper bit her lip and looked at the bruising. "Strangled?"

"Looks that way. Again, Margot will tell us more."

"Margot Swanson? They're taking her to the Freeman?" she asked, referring to a hospital in Heaton where Cooper had undergone most of her cancer treatment.

"Yeah," answered Atkinson. He deposited a swab into a little transparent tube, tightened the lid and removed his gloves. "She's on her way. The Royal Victoria's overrun at the moment. Big multi-vehicle in the West End last night. Anything new's being directed to the Freeman until we're told otherwise."

Cooper swallowed and stuck her head back outside the tent under the guise of needing some fresh air. Rumour had it Margot Swanson was romantically involved with Detective Neil Fuller. Fuller had been Cooper's on again off again lover for over a year; he'd become permanently off again two days after Cooper found the lump in her right breast.

Dealing with Margot Swanson was the last thing Cooper wanted to do. She ran the back of her hands over her mouth and stared out to sea. In the distance, a score of seagulls chased a fishing trawler that was returning to port and headed for the Fish Quay.

"Okay," she said with artificial pep. "What do you have so far?"

Atkinson rubbed the grey stubble on his chin. "Bruising to the neck, probable strangulation. Additional dark powder residue on the neck and ankles. Charcoal perhaps. Samples are off to the lab this afternoon. I was hoping to lift prints from the ankles, but the marks are heavily smudged; I can't get a thing."

Atkinson used tongs to lift the girl's shirt back and revealed a cut to her chest. "She's been sliced open and stitched back up. I shudder to think. I've taken hair samples from the jacket and examined her nails."

Cooper's eyes darted to the victim's nails. They were painted Barbie pink, and all but one were talon-long.

"There's no blood under the nails from what I can tell," continued Atkinson, "but there's plenty of mud, a few blades of grass too."

"Mud?" Cooper met Atkinson's eyes.

"Indeed. Mud, not sand."

"Suggesting she was killed elsewhere and then dumped in the boat?"

"I wouldn't say she was dumped," said Atkinson. "I think *displayed* would be a better term."

"You're right," sighed Cooper, wondering what sort of depraved individual she was dealing with. "The outfit? The rabbit? Whoever did this wanted her to be found; otherwise, he could have pushed her off North Pier, and she'd never have been seen again."

"Or he could've rolled her off the clifftop and made it look like an accident."

"Any prints on the boat? Her clothes?"

"The boat's riddled with prints. Every sailor in the club will have helped haul it up the beach. Then you've got all the kids and dog walkers who come down here. As for the clothes, there are partial prints on the shoes. They're a few sizes too big for her. Look." He pointed to where the shiny leather gaped behind the girl's heels. "And there are numerous mismatched fibres and hairs on the jacket. Hong has started checking the field directly behind us, but he hasn't found signs of a struggle there. There are tyre marks where cars have clipped the edge of the field. We'll take impressions, of course. Just in case."

"Right," said Cooper. The beach may have been tiny, but it had a high volume of traffic between the two clubs and the dog walkers. There was likely to be over a hundred different cars using this stretch of road on any given week.

The sub-zero temperature was beginning to affect Cooper's body. She started to shiver; under the wig, her scalp was itchy.

"Good start, Justin. Keep me in the loop."

Atkinson bobbed his head, then he pushed one of the pens on the table a millimetre to the left.

Cooper stepped out of the tent and found Tennessee talking to Hong, Atkinson's assistant. He held a condom with a pair of tweezers and dropped it into an evidence bag.

"Detective," she called, grabbing Tennessee's attention. "We need more manpower. Request a team down here to scour the area. Have the uniforms extend the perimeter to cover the fields on the Spanish Battery and around the Collingwood monument. We're looking for the victim's clothing. Those clothes aren't her own. For one thing, the shoes don't fit. And look for any signs of a struggle, including evidence of nails being dragged through mud or grassland. She's missing a nail. Pink varnish."

Tennessee closed his notepad and tucked it into his inside pocket. "I'll get on it right away." The young man's eyes darted over Cooper's face. "You doing okay? I am allowed to ask that, right? It's just, you look a little pale."

Cooper felt chilled to her bones. "Just hitting the ground running, Tennessee." She reached out and patted the man on his arm. "And yes, you're allowed to ask."

- CHAPTER 5 -

THE HEADQUARTERS FOR NORTHUMBRIA Police were housed in Wallsend. An area three miles east of Newcastle upon Tyne and so named for being the end of Hadrian's Wall, the seventy-mile fortification that marked the northern boundary of the Roman Empire.

Cooper paced back and forth along a magnolia corridor. She clutched a file to her chest and wished she'd worn her navy suit; navy commanded more respect. Beyond the double doors at the end of the hall, her team were waiting to be briefed. She hadn't seen some of the people in the room for months. Would they treat her differently? Cooper didn't know how to play it. Cool and calm? She could go in with all guns blazing, but that would be obvious over-compensation. She thought honesty was the best policy, but Cooper couldn't bring herself to tell the team she wanted to go home and get into bed. She could barely admit it to herself.

Cooper tapped her feet and looked at the strip lighting on the ceiling for inspiration. When none came, she pulled her shoulders back and strode into CID.

"Right, take your seats. Phones down, eyes up."

The room fell silent. Cooper quickly scanned the place; it looked just as dreary it always had. She hadn't expected banners and balloons, but some cake would have been nice.

"The body of a teenage girl was discovered at Prior's Haven this morning by a...." She checked her notes and took a breath to steady her voice. "Terry Parke. She was dressed up to look like a magician, complete with, I'm sure you've heard, a dead rabbit."

Cooper paused to make eye contact with some of the group.

"Initial impressions indicate strangulation. The SOCOs have an overabundance of prints and DNA from the boat, as well as the clothes she was dressed in. It's going to take Atkinson a while to sift through his findings, so in the meantime, we need to need to get down to business. Who is she?"

Cooper stuck a photo of the girl's face to a whiteboard and turned to face the other detectives.

A man with a middle-aged hairline and a middle-aged spread coughed and got to his feet.

"I might be able to answer that."

"Go ahead, Sutherland."

Sam Sutherland opened his notepad and spoke with a heavy northern accent. "Fifteen-year-old Rachel Pearson of Oxford Street, Tynemouth was reported missing at nine-thirty last night. Parents reported it after she didn't come home from yoga. Guess where her yoga classes were held?"

"The sailing club?"

"Bingo. Physical description matches the victim. Long dark hair, slim build, five-foot-three. When she left home at ten past six, she was wearing cloud-print leggings, a blue Adidas sweatshirt and a black, knee-length winter coat with a fur trim hood."

Tennessee raised his pen in the air. "I have a girl in a fur trim coat and blue and white leggings on CCTV leaving the sailing club shortly after seven-thirty."

"That's our girl," said Sutherland. He walked around his desk, opened a file and flicked through some papers for a moment. "Yes. When she didn't come home, the parents called her friends and her boyfriend, but no one knew where she was."

Cooper perched herself on the edge of a desk and crossed her legs. "Do we have more from the scene? Keaton?"

DS Paula Keaton was round-faced with an upturned nose. At five-ten and a former rugby player, Keaton was built - as Superintendent Nixon would describe - like a brick shithouse.

"We have, boss. A pink yoga mat was found in the bushes at the back of Haven car park."

Cooper looked to Sutherland.

"Aye," he answered. "The girl's mother said she'd be carrying a pink mat."

"Any sign of the clothing?"

"Not that I've heard, boss. But Atkinson's just been on the phone. The uniforms have possible clawing marks in the ground at the back of the car park. Photos should be in your inbox within the hour, and they're taking casts."

Cooper unlocked her phone and opened Google Maps. "Oxford Street?" The map showed a corner of green where the river met the sea. The southern end of Oxford Street connected to a pathway that, if followed west, would reach the Fish Quay, and if followed east, would reach the Spanish Battery. "She might have been taking a shortcut home. There looks to be worn trails crisscrossing the fields between the coast and her street."

Keaton shuffled and began clicking the top of her pen. "The lighting down there's atrocious. Gives me the creeps at night time. Be a miracle if anyone saw anything."

Cooper couldn't help but agree. "What's the media situation?"

"The switchboard's been inundated," said Tennessee. "We've asked the press to keep a lid on things until we inform the family."

"The mainstream press might hold the story," started Sutherland, "But social media's already swamped with photos of the forensics tent down at the Haven."

"Right," said Cooper with a sigh. "Well, we'd better get a wiggle on, hadn't we? Sutherland and Keaton, head back to Prior's Haven and check in with the guys doing door-to-doors. Get hold of the yoga instructor. We need a list of everyone at the class last night. Track them down, find out who saw what."

Sutherland was already pulling his coat on.

"Tennessee, you're with me. Get an FLO ready," she added, referring to family liaison officers. "We need to tell the Pearsons."

Tennessee's shoulders slumped; his eyes lowered. It was part of the job every officer dreaded. Keaton patted the younger man on his back as she passed. When she reached the doorway - which she filled - Keaton turned to Cooper.

"Welcome back, boss."

"How's Hayley?" asked Cooper.

"Eight months gone now. Turn left here." He pointed right.

Cooper had learned long ago that Tennessee's verbal directions were never to be trusted. Left meant right, north meant south, and *it's a seventy* almost always meant *it's a fifty and there's a speed camera up ahead.*

"Hard to believe I'm going to be a dad in a few weeks."

"Tell me about it," answered Cooper. "You look barely old enough to drink. Do you know if you're having a girl or a boy?"

"A boy. Left again. Hayley wants to name the little guy Alfred after her pa, but I think it's too old-fashioned."

"And let me guess. You want to name him after United's starting eleven?"

Cooper parked the Mazda in front of a semi-detached new-build in a small cul-de-sac and killed the engine. Immediately the temperature inside the car began to drop.

"I was thinking Bobby."

Cooper chuckled. Bobby Robson had been a local hero, a great manager and an upstanding gentleman. There were worse people to name your kid after.

Tennessee doubled over, and Cooper swore she saw his eyes darken a shade. "I can't stand this bit."

"None of us can, Jack. But it's nothing compared to how Mr and Mrs Pearson are about to feel." Cooper exhaled and watched her breath fog in front of her face. "Is the FLO on the way?"

Tennessee's knees bounced up and down. "ETA's ten minutes."

Cooper exited the vehicle and walked up to the house. Tennessee lagged behind by two steps. The Pearson's front door was dusty and covered in cobwebs, the paintwork around the window frames flaked, and a large crack ran through the doorstep. Cooper gave her DS a supportive look as she rang the doorbell. The young man had a great future ahead of him in CID, and Cooper recognised her responsibility in helping to shape his career. She had to lead by example.

There was a rush of footsteps before the door swung open. An exhausted-looking woman with frantic eyes and smoker's lips looked expectantly up and down the street.

"Rachel? Is she with you? Did you find her?"

"Mrs Pearson? I'm DCI Erica Cooper," she held up her warrant card. "This is DS Daniel. May we come in?"

Mrs Pearson must have read something in the expressions on the detectives' faces because she crumbled, folding herself in two, arms cradling her stomach.

"No, no," she began to wail. "It's her, isn't it? I saw on Facebook. The body? Please say it's not her."

The slim woman began to hyperventilate.

"Sally?" A heavy-set man emerged in the Pearson's hallway. He pushed his phone into the back pocket of his jeans and rushed to his wife. "What's happened?" he asked Cooper. "Haven't you found her yet? Where's Rachel?"

"Mr Pearson." Tennessee's voice had a stillness to it. "We really need to come inside."

The man pulled his wife to her feet. "Right," he said. "This way."

The Pearsons led Cooper and Tennessee to their living room, and Cooper motioned for them to take a seat. Their sofa was covered in protective plastic sheeting; it emitted a squeaking noise as Mr Pearson sat and adjusted his weight. He squeezed his wife's hand and looked up at Cooper with bloodshot eyes.

Cooper knew there was no sense in delaying the inevitable or trying to soften the blow. "I'm afraid the body of a young woman matching Rachel's description was found at Prior's Haven early this morning—"

"It's not her," snapped Rachel's father. "She's at a friend's."

Sally Pearson's eyes were red with tears. "She's not at a friend's, Lou. We tried all her friends. We called them all. We Facebooked everyone."

"It's not her," he repeated.

"We can't know that for certain, Mr Pearson, but given the location and the discovery of a pink yoga mat nearby...." Cooper's voice trailed away for a moment. "We're going to need you to attend the Freeman Hospital to make an identification." She checked her watch; the FLO should be there soon. Sally and Lou Pearson would need all the help they could provide. "If you don't feel you can perform the identification, please let us know, and we can arrange for someone else who was close to Rachel to attend. An aunt or uncle, perhaps."

Sally Pearson clutched a cushion with both hands. "No. It should be us. I need to see."

Lou Pearson wrapped an arm around his wife. "It won't be her," he said. "You'll see. It'll be some other poor lass. It won't be her."

Cooper's stomach was turning over. The denial mixed with grief and dread was hard to watch.

"I'm very sorry," said Tennessee. He straightened his posture and removed a notepad from his coat pocket. "But we need to ask you some questions. I know you went over a lot of this when you reported your daughter missing, but it would really help us if we could go over a few things again."

Lou Pearson's brows lowered half an inch, and he removed his arm from his wife's shoulders so he could fold his arms across his chest. "Hold on a minute. Are you saying we're suspects? You have a nerve, lad."

Tennessee hadn't said that. Not even close. But Cooper noted how quickly Lou Pearson jumped to that conclusion.

"No, Mr Pearson. But I do need to get a gauge of Rachel's movements."

Sally Pearson placed a calming hand on her husband's knee. When he swiped it away, she got to her feet and began pacing the room, wringing her hands. "I need a smoke," she declared before heading to the back door of the home.

"Mr Pearson," said Tennessee. "Can you go over the events of last night for me?"

The man's eyes returned from following his wife. He clenched his hands into fists and hid his face behind them for a moment. "Rachel goes to yoga every Tuesday and Thursday," he started. "It's part of her rehab. She fell down the stairs, you see. Last year. She couldn't walk for a long time, needed surgery and physio, the works. She can walk again now, but with a bit of a limp, and she still struggles on uneven ground. She won't accept lifts. Very independent girl. Always has been."

His eyes flicked to the front window as he saw Pru Wilson, the family liaison officer approach.

"I'll get it," said Tennessee.

Lou Pearson's tone began to relax. "She was wearing leggings with clouds on them and a blue sweatshirt. Adidas, I think. Her coat is black with a furry hood. It's one of those padded ones, like a quilt."

Cooper nodded. "This is good, Mr Pearson. You're doing really well. Can you tell us the timings? When she left, what time she'd usually be back?"

"The class is six-thirty to seven-thirty," he looked up and watched Tennessee guide the FLO towards the back of the house to introduce her to Sally Pearson. "She usually sets off from here at ten past six, a little earlier if she wants a spot at the front of the class. Most of the time, she's back home by eight, but sometimes she'll pop by Will's, so we didn't worry at first."

"And Will is?"

"Will Harper. Rachel's boyfriend." His voice was tinged with objection. "We called her at half eight, but it went straight through to her answerphone. I called Will shortly after. I was in two minds 'cause Rachel doesn't like being checked up on. Typical teen, right?"

"Very typical," said Cooper. She could relate.

"But her dinner was getting cold, so I called. Will said he hadn't seen or heard from her since school."

"Which school does Rachel attend?"

"Tynemouth Academy."

Cooper's back tensed. "How was Rachel's demeanour yesterday?"

"She was quiet. She can be tetchy. Never used to be, mind you. The accident changed her. She gets frustrated easily, very sarcastic, can fly off the handle."

"It must have been difficult. Learning to walk again."

Lou Pearson's hands formed back into fists. "Gymnastics was her life. She wanted to go to the Olympics. I know lots of kids say that, but Rachel was actually on track for it." He motioned to the mantlepiece where rosettes and trophies surrounded framed photos of Rachel in her leotard. "She was on the under sixteen's England team. Got a silver medal at the junior Europeans."

The Rachel in the photographs was lean and muscular. Her thighs were thick, a stark contrast to the stalk thin ones Cooper had seen that morning. The atrophy after her accident must have been immense.

Cooper's eyes flicked to the coal fire underneath the mantlepiece. It was beginning to die down. The sound of the back door clicking back into place preceded Tennessee, Sally Pearson and Pru Wilson's return to the living room. Sally Pearson was a broken woman. Her body shook as she walked, and she supported herself on the furniture as she passed. She looked as if she might collapse at any moment.

Cooper acknowledged the newcomer with a nod. "Mr Pearson, this is Pru Wilson. She's a family liaison officer with Northumbria Police. Her role is to support you and Mrs Pearson, act as a point of contact and keep you updated with the case."

Pru was young and blonde, with a spread of freckles across her cheeks.

"I'm going to make us all a cup of tea," said Pru. "Then it would be a great help to us if you could make a list of all of Rachel's friends, including the ones you contacted yesterday evening."

Lou Pearson nodded.

Cooper followed Pru to the kitchen and had a quick chat with her to make sure she was up to date with everything that had occurred. Then Cooper and Tennessee let themselves out, catching a glimpse of Lou Pearson adding a few lumps of coal to the fire.

The winter air hit Cooper's chest, knocking the wind out of her. "Did you get anything from the mother?" she asked, her voice wheezy.

Tennessee jumped into the car and buckled up. "Not a lot. She was hysterical. Understandably. I've got an address for the boyfriend, a William Harper. Apparently, the father didn't approve."

"They never do."

"I asked if she knew of anyone who would want to harm Rachel, but the mother says she was a popular girl. Had loads of friends. Always invited to birthday parties, shopping, the usual. The mother didn't know of any fallings out and is adamant her daughter never touched drugs.

Cooper's phone buzzed. She selected speakerphone before answering.

"Cooper here."

"Erica, it's Margot Swanson from the Freeman," her voice had a sing-song Highlands lilt to it.

Cooper's teeth ground as she started the engine and put the car into reverse. "You received the body?"

"Yes." There was a pause. "Erica, erm... You might want to see this."

- CHAPTER 6 -

THE THIN HAIRS ON Cooper's arms stood on end. The cooling system in the morgue was somewhat excessive on a winter's day such as this. Keeping her coat and gloves on, she held the door for Tennessee and followed the route to the post-mortem room where she'd been told Margot Swanson would be waiting in room B.

Rows of stainless steel drawers reminded Cooper of filing cabinets, only these housed the recently deceased rather than folders of accounts and reports. The morgue had a stench made up of death, bleach and anti-bacterial gel. Every time Cooper encountered it, her mind conjured up an image of vomit-splattered Kurt Geiger shoes.

"Erica." A side door leading off from the morgue opened, and Margot poked her head out. "This way, please. Jack, good to see you. Is it still snowing out there?"

"Just a dusting," answered Tennessee. "More forecast for later."

Margot shuddered dramatically. "Only one cure for this weather. A roaring fire, a bottle of port and an epic cheeseboard. Am I right?"

Cooper didn't answer, but Tennessee's eyes drifted to the right. Presumably, he was picturing the curvaceous pathologist lazing by an open fire. Margot Swanson was Scottish, fifty-something, voluptuous and a known flirt. She had double D's, full lips and a penchant for younger men. Cooper believed the technical term was: *Cougar*.

"Shall we get this over with? What couldn't I be told over the phone?"

Margot bristled and ran her hands down the sides of her lab coat. How she made it look like a designer dress, Cooper would never know. She pulled the sheets back from Rachel's face and waited a moment for Cooper and Tennessee to gather themselves.

"Well, I'm not nearly done, and we're going to be waiting a few days for toxicology - they're backed up - but I'll run through what I have so far. We have ligature marks on the neck," she pointed to red and purple marks that looped around Rachel's neck like a macabre necklace. "Justin found some shredded plastic under the victim's nails in his initial assessment and I've found more of the same in her throat."

Tennessee swallowed. "She was suffocated with a plastic bag?"

"That would be my assumption," started Margot. "However, we also have finger and thumb-sized bruises to the neck. I would suggest there was an attempt at suffocation. When she clawed through the bag, our lad or lassie changed their MO to strangulation."

Cooper was sceptical at Margot's use of the word *lassie*. Females rarely conducted this sort of crime. It wasn't sexism; it was statistics. "You think a woman could have done this?"

"The size of the bruising would suggest male, but a larger female would be a possibility." Margot pointed to the girl's neck. "It's also worth noting that her larynx is fractured. Whoever did this didn't just stop her from breathing; they completely throttled her."

Tennessee turned away from the stainless steel examination table and wrinkled up his eyes.

"But moving on," continued Margot. "Taking account of the temperature last night, which would have delayed rigor and algor mortis somewhat, I'd put an estimated time of death at eight p.m. last night."

"That fits with our timeline," confirmed Tennessee, his back still to the table.

Cooper ran her gloved hand over the back of her neck. "Any evidence of sexual assault?"

Margot steepled her fingers. "Well, as I said earlier, we're not done yet." She moved to her left and rested her hands on the edge of the table. "But I can say at this time it looks unlikely. There is no sign of trauma to her pelvis, and we haven't found any semen on the victim." Her eyes moved to Tennessee. "Are you doing all right, sweetheart? Need some fresh air?"

"He's fine," said Cooper, cutting in. "Keep going."

"It's just... it's not going to get any easier."

"Whatever you need to show us, just show us." Cooper was losing patience. She didn't want to be in this refrigeration unit any longer than necessary, and frankly, everything Margot had told them could've been handled over the phone.

Margot's lip twitched. "Okay," she said, pulling the sheets that covered Rachel further down to reveal her shoulders and upper chest.

"Bloody hell," said Tennessee, his voice weaker than Cooper was used to hearing.

"As you can see, she's been cut open and stitched back together. From what I can tell, the tool used to do this was a flat, very sharp blade. Something akin to a Stanley knife or even a scalpel. The accuracy would indicate that this was conducted by someone with a steady hand."

"What was she stitched back together with?" asked Cooper, leaning in for a closer look at the wound.

"We can run some tests," answered Margot, "but to be honest, it looks like standard sewing thread, the sort you could buy anywhere."

Cooper's hand moved to her chest without thinking. A subconscious show of empathy to Rachel. It was a disturbing truth that some killers got a thrill out of taking a memento from their victims. Usually, they took photographs to preserve the memory forever; sometimes, they'd take an item of jewellery or clothing. Now and again, a special breed of psychopath would take something from the victim's body. Last year Cooper saw a murder victim with all of her fingers and toes removed. And Yorkshire Police dealt with a killer who took teeth from his victims: *The Dentist*, they'd called him.

"And why?" she asked Margot, her hand still on her chest. "Tell me this sicko didn't cut out her heart."

"Actually," said Margot, pausing to pick up an evidence bag from a shelf behind her. "They put something in."

Cooper took the bag and turned it over in her hands. She could sense Tennessee join her, his shadow falling over her shoulder.

"What the actual—?"

Cooper stared down at a small laminated business card. Cream-coloured and texturised, it was plain apart from two words printed in black ink: *The Priestess*.

- CHAPTER 7 -

THE PRIESTESS? NOT PRIEST. Priestess. That's why Margot said, *lad or lassie*. That's why she said a larger female could have been responsible.

Cooper opened the front door to her Georgian terrace and was relieved to feel that the heating had come on automatically. Tina's shoes and backpack were in the porch area and sounds from the living room suggested Tina was watching television.

The calling card wouldn't leave Cooper's mind. She pulled her wig from her head and ran her nails over the fine hair on her scalp. *Heaven*. She'd dealt with all kinds of offenders since joining Northumbria CID. Still, she'd never come across a killer who'd left an actual calling card. This was a first. Who the bloody hell was The Priestess?

"Is it true?" Tina was stood in the doorway to the living room. Still dressed in her school uniform, she looked dishevelled.

"Have you brushed your hair today?" asked Cooper with narrowed eyes.

"Of course," lied Tina, hastily pulling her locks back into a ponytail and securing it with a bobble from her wrist. "So... Is it true? Is Rachel Pearson dead?"

Bad news obviously travelled fast through Tynemouth Academy.

Cooper exhaled and filled the kettle. "Who told you that?"

"No one. But there's obviously something big going down at Prior's Haven; the pictures of the tent are all over Twitter. Then Rachel didn't show up to school this morning, and Chloe said Rachel's mum called her last night because she hadn't come home." Tina motioned for her mother to sit down while she took over tea-making duties. "Then Will Harper was called out of art class this morning," she said, wagging a teaspoon about, "and he never came back. Not to mention Linda's been running about like a headless chicken all day and looks like she's about to start tearing her hair out. No offence."

"None taken."

Tina might well have a future in CID.

"Thank you," said Cooper when Tina handed her the warm mug. "Sit, and please don't call her Linda. It's Ms Webb."

"When she's at Dad's, I have to call her Linda."

"We're not at Dad's."

Tina sipped her tea but kept her eyes lowered to the table. Cooper reached out and placed a hand over hers.

"Look, Tina, this morning, someone found a body on the beach. Rachel's parents visited the morgue this afternoon and confirmed it was Rachel."

"Fuck."

"Tina!"

"Sorry, Mum, but I can't think of a better word right now."

Cooper's mouth curled at the corner. She had a point. "No, I'm sorry. Were you and Rachel close? We'll need to speak to her friends over the next few days."

Tina huffed and got back to her feet. "As if someone like Rachel would be friends with someone like me."

Tina began to rummage through the kitchen cupboards.

"What do you mean?"

Tina's eyes scanned over a cupboard that was bare apart from a tin of chopped tomatoes and half a pack of spaghetti.

"Tina."

"Can we have fish and chips?"

Cooper had to hold her tongue when it came to Tina's lack of focus. "Yes, if that's what you'd like. Now, what did you mean by *someone like Rachel?*"

Tina closed the cupboard door and rested her back against the worktop. "She's beautiful and popular, and I'm a grade-A weirdo. We don't exactly move in the same circles."

"You're not a weirdo. Don't talk about yourself like that." Cooper's heart broke a little each time she heard her daughter self-deprecate. "Did you have classes with Rachel?"

"Just music, art and PE. We're in different sets for science and English and stuff." Tina opened Cooper's purse and removed a tenner. "This'll be enough, right?"

Cooper nodded. "You and Rachel never chatted during the classes you shared?"

Tina made a noise that resembled *pfft* and started to lace up her shoes. "I mainly keep out of her way. She's the kind of girl who can turn the whole school against you if she wants. Or she was. Anyway, back in ten. Curry sauce?"

Cooper shook her head.

WITH A BELLY FULL of complex carbs, and Tina settled for the night, Cooper poured herself a glass of pinot noir. She wasn't one for midweek drinking, but today had been no ordinary day. She lay down on the sofa and propped her feet up over the armrest. She opened her laptop, rested it on her bloated stomach and began searching Rachel Pearson's social media profiles.

Sally Pearson said her daughter was popular. Cooper thought back to her own teenage years and distinctly remembered that there were two types of popular: the type where everyone loves you, and the type where everyone secretly hates you. From speaking to Tina, it was possible that Rachel fell into the latter category.

Rachel's Twitter feed was an endless commentary of how annoying her teachers were and how the wrong person had been voted off *Strictly*. There were occasional messages to celebrities, with Ariana Grande being a clear frontrunner for Rachel's approval. She was, by all accounts, the *GOAT*. Cooper had to google that one; it was an acronym for the *greatest of all time*.

Rachel's Instagram was set to private, as was Rachel's Facebook profile. However, a few photos had been uploaded to the public. Cooper scanned these photos but didn't see any connection to a church. Rachel was never pictured wearing a crucifix or a cross. Under her *About* section, she described her religion as *fundamentalist atheist*. Cooper clicked on a photo of Rachel surrounded by school friends. They were all doing what Cooper believed were *trout pouts*. Could one of the posing girls be The Priestess? Some of the taller ones certainly looked strong enough to throttle the stick-thin, five-foot-three Rachel. The following picture showed Rachel with two friends. They'd used a filter to give themselves bunny ears and whiskers. The girls looked like Disney cartoons. She clicked right, and a photo of Rachel in her gymnastics leotard appeared. She had a medal hanging around her neck, and she was being carried on the shoulders of two muscular young men. There was a string of comments attached to the photograph, mainly congratulations messages for her medal-winning performance. Will Harper's comment caught Cooper's eye. He'd posted a red, angry-faced emoji. It would appear Will Harper was the jealous type.

- CHAPTER 8 -

Tennessee was halfway through a Gregg's steak bake when Cooper picked him up en route to the Pearson's house on Oxford Street.

"Want a bite?" he asked with his mouth full.

Cooper ignored the flakes of pastry that fluttered into the car's footwell. When she'd first bought the car, she'd vowed to keep it clean and take it for weekly valets. Her vow had lasted less than a month, and these days it wasn't unusual for the dashboard of Cooper's car to be under a thick layer of dust.

"Please," she answered. "I'm famished."

Without thinking, Cooper finished the steak bake and looked apologetically at Tennessee. "Oh."

"Eyes on the road," he replied, "and it's fine. We'll grab some real grub when we're finished at the Pearsons'."

"Good shout," she said, crumpling up the paper bag packaging and shoving it into a cupholder. "So, were you all right last night? Manage to switch off when you got home?" Cooper was thinking back to the morgue and remembering Tennessee's face when Margot revealed the card that had been stuck inside Rachel's chest.

"Truth be told, I didn't have a moment to think about it. Had to finish painting the baby's room. Hayley's picked out this hideous shade of purple."

"I thought you said you were having a boy."

"We are," grunted Tennessee, folding his arms over his chest. "She started banging on about not conforming to gender stereotypes. Anyway, when I was done with the painting, I had to put the crib together. Guess what colour that is."

Cooper parked the car and put it in neutral. "Not pink?"

"It might as well be, ma'am, sorry Coop. The damn thing's covered in purple and yellow butterflies."

Cooper chuckled. "Well, if I know you, and I think I do, you'll repaint it in black and white stripes the first chance you get." Black and white being the home colours of Newcastle United FC.

"You read my mind," answered Tennessee as he stepped out of the car.

When Cooper and Tennessee knocked on the Pearson's door, it was answered by Pru Wilson, the FLO.

"How're things, Pru?" asked Cooper.

"As you would expect," answered the petite blonde in a hushed voice. "Come on through."

Pru led the pair of them to the living room, where Sally Pearson was sat on the sofa with her legs pulled up to her chest. She was smoking as she stared out the window. An ashtray balanced on the armrest overflowed with cigarette butts. Since her daughter's death, Sally Pearson's smoking had moved from the back step to the sofa.

"Good morning," said Cooper. Of course, there was nothing good about it.

Lou Pearson stomped through from the kitchen with an armful of freshly laundered clothes. He dumped them on an armchair and began furiously folding.

"I can take care of that," said Pru, taking a step towards him.

"I can manage the bloody laundry. Please stop your infernal fussing," he snapped.

Cooper's eyes caught a large bouquet of lilies on the dining table. They were still wrapped in cellophane, yet to be put in a vase. She opened the card and read; *To Sally and Lou, I'm not sure what to write. I'm so sorry for your loss. Our loss. I loved Rachel. I'm lost without her. If you need anything, please call. Will.*

"He dropped them off this morning," said Rachel's father. "He didn't look well, truth be told. Doubt he got any sleep, not that we did either." Lou's jaw clenched. "Said he's not going to school today. His mum's taking him to the GP." He turned back to his pile of laundry and started pairing socks.

Pru laid a blanket over Sally Pearson's shoulders and nodded to Cooper and Tennessee to follow her to the kitchen.

The three of them huddled close to the back door while Pru began to make some toast.

"She won't eat," started Pru, "but I'll keep trying. It was brutal at the morgue. It was a positive ID."

"Nixon told me," said Cooper. "Do you know about the card?"

Pru nodded. "That's some fucked up shit," she hissed. "Leaving a calling card inside the victim? Never in all my days... Margot didn't show it to the parents."

"Good," said Cooper. "We're keeping that under wraps for now. What did she tell them?"

"She kept it brief. Once they ID'd her, they asked how. They always ask how." The toast popped, and Pru fetched a plate from the cupboard and some spread from the fridge. "Margot explained that it was strangulation and that there was no evidence of sexual assault."

Cooper's stomach rumbled. "Okay," she said.

"It was dreadful, as you can imagine. Sally had a panic attack. She was shaking uncontrollably, started talking about running into the road, poor woman. She had to be given a sedative; I've made an appointment for her with Talking Therapies at eleven."

Pru picked up the toast and took it through to the living room. "Here you go, Sally."

Sally Pearson didn't look up.

"I'll just leave it here on the windowsill, tuck in when you're ready."

"Mr Pearson," said Cooper. "I know this is terribly difficult, but I need to ask you some more questions. Perhaps we should move to the dining room?"

Lou Pearson looked at his wife with concern, then he nodded. "Yes, yes, we'll go through to the other room."

He sat down and rummaged through a pile of papers on the dining table. "Here," he said, handing a piece of paper to Tennessee. "You asked for a list of Rachel's friends."

"Thank you," said Tennessee. "This will be very helpful."

Cooper glanced at the paper. It was a long list. Every girl in the year must be named. All but Tina, she noted.

"Mr Pearson, can you tell me where you were on Tuesday evening?"

His face reddened. "Are you having a—"

"It's routine," said Cooper in a quiet, calm manner. "I'm not implying anything."

"I was here. At home. All night. Worried sick." He spoke in quick bursts like a dog barking at a postman. "And so was Sally. Rach went off to yoga then we had our dinner. Spaghetti bolognese. Rachel's was kept in the pan, ready to have once she got home and showered. We watched television, and when she wasn't back by half eight, we started making phone calls."

"Thank you," said Cooper, keeping her voice neutral. "Apart from yourself and your wife, who else knew Rachel's routine?"

Lou Pearson sat back in his chair and slowly exhaled. His eyes darted back and forth across the table as he thought. "Well, Will, obviously. I was never too keen on that lad, but the kid's in pieces. We all are. I don't know how many other friends she told about yoga; you'd have to ask them. The yoga teacher, I guess. She had Rachel's details from her sign-up form. Have you spoken to the other women in the class? Someone must have seen or heard something?"

Cooper leant forward and interlaced her fingers. "We have a list of everyone who attended the class. Our colleagues are taking statements from all of them."

Her answer seemed to satisfy him as his shoulders lowered and the colour started to fade from his cheeks.

"This might seem like an odd question, but did Rachel own a pair of black stilettos?"

His eyes flicked to Cooper's. "She always wore flats. Walking was hard enough for her as it was. She had one pair of heels, not big ones though, just little ones. What are they called?"

Cooper shrugged. "Like a court shoe?"

"Oh, I've no idea. They'll be in her wardrobe. Don't think they were black either. Pretty sure they're navy."

"And again, this might seem like a strange question. Did Rachel own a top hat or enjoy fancy dress?"

Lou Pearson's eyes narrowed. "No."

"And did she have a pet rabbit?"

"A pet rabbit? No. What's going on? What haven't you told me?"

Cooper lowered her voice. "Mr Pearson, I don't want you to read about this in the papers, so I think it's important I let you know a few details about how Rachel was found."

"Oh, God." He raked his fingers through thinning hair. "Okay, go on."

"When Rachel was found yesterday morning, she wasn't wearing the outfit she'd worn to yoga. She was discovered, dressed in a magician's outfit, with a top hat, black stilettos and a rabbit."

Cooper kept her eyes on Mr Pearson. His face was a picture of pain and confusion.

"I don't understand."

"We think whoever hurt Rachel decided to dress her in a different outfit. We don't know why."

Lou Pearson swallowed and began picking the skin around his fingers. "They said she hadn't been... They told me no one hurt her in that way... But you're telling me someone undressed her and...."

"The pathologist confirmed there's no indication—"

"It makes no sense."

"Mr Pearson, was Rachel interested in magic?"

"No," he shook his head. "Wait, she liked those blokes on the television. The Americans. One of them doesn't talk."

Cooper looked at Tennessee.

"Penn and Teller."

"Aye, that's them," said Lou Pearson. "She liked the stuff they did. Other than that, no, she wasn't into card tricks and that."

Tennessee slowly pushed his chair out from the dining table. "We'd really appreciate it if we could take a look in Rachel's room now."

Lou Pearson lowered his eyes. "All right." Then he turned to Pru. "Would you stay with Sally?"

"Of course," she answered, and she got to her feet and returned to the living room.

Rachel's room was immaculately tidy. The first thing to catch Cooper's attention was the bookcase, where all the books had been turned around so that the pages faced the room and the spines faced the wall.

"Unusual," she said, pointing to the shelves.

"Aye. The latest trend on Insta-whatsit, she told me. Turn all your books around so the colours match and look pretty. Course it means you can never find the book you're after. Style over substance."

Cooper opened Rachel's wardrobe and found her clothes organised by colour. On her desk, make-up was arranged in the order she would use it, and her brushes were arranged by size.

"Most parents have to hassle their kids into tidying their rooms," started Lou Pearson, reading Cooper's mind. "I had to tell her to stop at times. She was always a tidy child, but it got worse after her fall."

"Is this Will?" asked Tennessee, holding up a framed picture of Rachel and a young man."

"Yeah, that's him." Lou Pearson took the photo in his hands and sat down on the edge of Rachel's bed. "This was the end of year awards presentation, before the summer holidays."

Cooper's instinct was to comfort the man, but she was here to do a job. She opened the drawers of Rachel's desk and pulled out a leather-bound notepad. Opening it up, it revealed itself to be a diary. Cooper began to read the latest entry while Tennessee opened a laptop and asked Lou Pearson if he knew the password. He shook his head.

Tennessee closed the laptop again. "We're going to need to let the computer forensics team take a look. We'll check if anyone was communicating with Rachel online."

If Rachel had arranged to meet anyone after class, had been threatened online, or received unwanted advances, the computer forensic analysts would find it.

Lou Pearson stared at the framed photograph and traced his fingertip over Rachel's face. Goodness knows what was going through the poor man's head.

Cooper let out the faintest of coughs. Just enough to get Tennessee's attention. He looked up and saw Cooper motion for him to come and take a look at the diary.

Tennessee drew in a long breath and exchanged a meaningful look with Cooper.

"Mr Pearson," he said. "Did Rachel mention arguing with Will Harper on Tuesday?"

"No. Why?" The man was instantly on his feet.

"It says here that Rachel was annoyed at Will about something that happened at school that day. It reads: *Will was a complete dick to me all day. Making me feel like some sort of slut because Nick said my arse looked good in the skinny jeans I wore at the weekend.*"

Lou Pearson's fingers tightened on the photo frame as Tennessee read.

"*He wasn't mad at Nick for not being able to keep his pervy eyeballs in his head. No, he was mad at me for wearing what every girl in our year wears. What does he want? Am I supposed to live my life in joggers and baggy jumpers? Would a burka make him happy? What a dick. If that's how he wants to play it. I'll show him.*"

Tennessee closed the diary just as Lou Pearson slammed the frame on Rachel's desk, shattering the glass.

"That little... He didn't mention any of that when he was round here this morning with his crocodile tears. Wait till I—"

"Mr Pearson," Cooper cut him off. "Your job is to stay here with Sally. She needs you. This doesn't prove anything. Not yet. We're going to need to take the laptop and the diary."

"Want me to call it in?" asked Tennessee.

"Yes," Cooper picked the diary back up. "We needed to speak to young Will Harper anyway, but this certainly moves him to the front of the queue. Call Sutherland. He and Keaton can pick him up."

"On it, boss."

When Tennessee left the room, Cooper had another glance around Rachel's spotless room. She removed books from the bookcase, read their spines and returned them one by one. None of the books concerned magic, fancy dress or religion. As her father had described, Rachel's shoes were all fashionable flats apart from one pair of navy kitten heels with a glittery finish to the fabric.

"Ma'am," gasped Tennessee. He was running back up the stairs, panting as he spoke. He moved close to Cooper. Close enough to whisper. "We need to go. Another girl's been killed."

- CHAPTER 9 -

"ERICA! IT'S SO GOOD to see you."

Bloody hell. That was all she needed.

Detective Inspector Neil Fuller scurried across the lobby of Northumbria Police headquarters. He was a stocky man with a Napoleon complex, a pointed nose, and thick auburn facial hair. Cooper had at one time been quite fond of his beard and how it tickled. It used to look distinguished. Now, he reminded her of a rodent of some kind.

"Neil," she replied, purposely not adding, *it's good to see you too.*

"We'll have to catch up soon. Rushed off my feet at the minute; someone's targeting posh hotels up the coast. Last week two blokes in a white van stormed Langley Castle and Slaley Hall. They arrived at dinner time, held up all the guests, took their money, jewellery, they even nicked the designer heels off the women's feet."

He scratched a scab on his jaw where he must have cut himself shaving.

Cooper's mouth formed into a thin line. "I saw the Slaley case on the news," she said. "The guests were shaken up."

"The bastards are at it again this week. Doxford Hall was done over on Tuesday night. They even nicked a lawn ornament."

Cooper's patience was wearing thin. Neil Fuller wasn't the only one who was busy. She had two murders on her hands. She pinched her nose, but Rat-Face continued.

"Anyway, we don't have much in the way of forensics. The gun they used has been identified as a Smith and Wesson—"

"Really? We're making small talk, Neil?"

Fuller recoiled. He looked genuinely hurt. Cooper might have felt sorry for him had she not remembered how things ended between them.

"I know we're not seeing each other anymore, Erica, but I thought we could be civil, be professional."

Fury flickered in Cooper's eyes. "Okay, have it your way. Let's make small talk. How have you been?" She didn't wait for him to answer. "I'm well. I've been super busy with chemotherapy. That was tonnes of fun. Remember? You were there holding my hand, supporting me, keeping my hair off my face while I vomited. Oh, that's right, you weren't there."

People were beginning to stare, but Cooper didn't care one bit. Fuller, on the other hand, was casting nervous glances left and right.

"You weren't there because you dumped me less than forty-eight hours after I found the lump."

"I... Well... Our relationship was coming to its natural end, Erica." His face was flooding with colour.

"Save it," she said. Cooper turned on her heel and parted the sea of onlookers so she could take the lift to CID. Only when the lift doors closed did she wipe away the tears that formed in the corners of her eyes. Undeterred, Cooper powered into the briefing room just as a wave of nausea swept over her. Grabbing a window ledge, she blinked her eyes a few times and waited for her vision to come back into focus.

Down on the street below, a hunchbacked lady pulled a shopping cart across a zebra crossing. The elderly woman seemed to sense she was being watched and turned her gaze up to the windows of CID.

"Boss?" Keaton's voice made Cooper jump. "Everything all right?"

"Skipped breakfast," replied Cooper by way of an explanation. She turned back to the window, but the woman and her cart had gone.

"I can nip to the vending machine—"

"Thanks, Paula, but we don't have time. Best crack on." Cooper was grateful that Keaton didn't press the matter. She had more important things to worry about than Neil Fuller.

"Right, butts on seats, people," announced Keaton with the authority of someone who used to play fullback. She patted Cooper on the arm and took her own seat beside Sutherland.

A hush fell over the room as all eyes turned to Cooper. She picked a piece of lint from her sleeve and flicked it to the floor before removing a photograph of a smiling, blonde teenager from her file and sticking it to the wall.

"Michelle Smith. Known to friends as Shelly. Fifteen years old, found dead at her home on Belford Terrace just before ten this morning."

Cooper paused and added another photograph to the wall. This time it was of Shelly's body. Horrified murmurs rippled through CID.

"As you can see, we have many reasons to suspect this case is connected to the murder of Rachel Pearson."

Sutherland shifted and rubbed the back of his hand over his mouth. "A serial killer?"

"It's looking that way," said Cooper as more sounds of unease spread through the room. There was no use in denying it. Cooper wasn't one for sugar-coating things.

"We have another case of suffocation," she continued, pointing to the photo. It depicted the blonde with a plastic bag over her head and secured to her neck with duct tape. Cooper stared at the picture silently, allowing the image to burn itself into her memory. She was never going to forget this image so there was no use in trying. The more she looked at it, the more she craved the sweet taste of justice.

"And she's been dressed up," added Sutherland. "Like Rachel was."

Cooper's eyes were still on the photograph. "Yes, as a priest. Or a priestess, to be precise." Her eyes darted over the outfit: black robes, a white dog collar, a purple satin scarf with golden tassels, and a large golden crucifix. "Justin Atkinson has already confirmed that another card was inserted into the victim. This one reads, *The Empress*."

Keaton was on her feet and pacing the length of CID. The sound of her thick-soled boots thudding against the flooring echoed around the room. "The Priestess wasn't the killer? The priestess was the killer's next move? He's telling us what's next."

"That's my understanding," said Cooper.

Disbelief flashed in Keaton's eyes. "What sort of psycho are we dealing with?"

"Believe me, I'm asking myself the same question."

Tennessee took a mouthful of water from a paper cup, crumpled it and tossed it effortlessly into the bin. "Is there any chance this is copycat?"

Cooper perched on her desk. "I doubt it. We kept the card from the press. They knew about the fancy dress, but we didn't tell them about the calling card. Of course, we can't rule out leaks."

Cooper thought of Margot Swanson. Would Margot blab to some handsome journalist who offered his affections or money? No. Margot was many things - a flirt at best and a home-wrecker at worst - but she was no sellout.

"Okay," said Tennessee. "What's the timeline?"

Cooper used her teeth to pull the lid from her pen. She drew a line across the board and began marking times on it as she spoke. "Shelly's mother, Lisa Smith, left for work at six a.m. Shelly would usually get herself ready for school and make her own breakfast. She'd usually leave at eight-thirty and walk to school."

"Which school?" asked Sutherland.

"Tynemouth Academy," answered Tennessee.

Cooper already knew this, but the fact that both girls attended the local secondary made her blood run cold.

"At nine twenty, the school called the mother to enquire about the unauthorised absence. Standard procedure. Lisa Smith picked up her voicemail during her break at nine-thirty a.m. and called her daughter immediately after. When there was no answer, Lisa drove home, assuming her daughter was skiving. When she got to the property, she found Shelly's body posed like this on their front step."

"Christ," said Keaton. She scraped her chair across the floor and sat down again.

Sutherland unbuttoned his blazer and loosened his tie. He looked a little redder in the cheeks than usual. "My girl goes to Tynemouth Academy."

Cooper met his eyes. "I didn't know Caroline had started secondary school?"

"She's twelve now. Started in September."

The last time Cooper had seen Sam Sutherland's daughter, she'd been knee-high to a grasshopper. She had been bawling her eyes out because little Jimmy "Poo-Head" Ashman had spilt cherry cola on her yellow dress at the department barbecue. She couldn't have been more than seven or eight. How time flies.

"If the school's being targeted—"

"We can't jump to conclusions. We need to find out everything that connects these girls. Who did they hang out with? What clubs did they go to? Where did they spend their free time? But Sam," Cooper nervously tapped her pen off the edge of her desk, "my daughter goes there too. It might be worth taking some extra precautions."

"Aye. I'll call the missus and the grandparents. I don't want Caroline left alone for a second. Not until we catch this sicko."

With no parents or extended family in the region, Cooper realised she would have to put some faith in Kenny. She wasn't used to relying on anyone else, especially not him.

"Right," she said. "Where are we with Will Harper, Rachel's boyfriend? Keaton?"

"We called by the school to pick him up. The admin told us he wasn't at school today."

"The Pearsons told us he was taking the day off and had a GP appointment," said Tennessee.

"Yeah," said Keaton. "We assumed something like that. We were on our way to his home address when we got the call about Shelly."

"Okay," said Cooper. "I want you and Sutherland to find him and bring him in. Don't mention Shelly. It's not public knowledge yet. See if he incriminates himself. He'll need a juvenile cell and an appropriate adult."

Keaton tapped her pen to her temple then pointed it at Cooper. "Gotcha."

"Now, back to Rachel Pearson. How are we getting on with the yoga ladies?"

Sutherland opened a spiral-bound notepad. "It's not just women. There were two men at the class on Tuesday."

"Really? New, or regulars?" asked Cooper.

"Regulars. Neither of them even knew Rachel's name, which goes for a fair few of the group. She seemed to keep to herself. Almost everyone in the class parked their cars by the sailing club and drove up the bank and through Tynemouth village to get home. A few reported seeing Rachel walking up the bank, but no one saw anyone else. No one noticed if there were any cars in Haven car park."

"They all went straight home after the class?" asked Cooper.

"Mostly," confirmed Sutherland. "One of the gents stopped for a takeaway in the village, and one of the ladies called by her sister's to pick up her dog. They all have people who can confirm what time they got home."

"Okay. And what about the instructor?"

"She left after the rest of the group. Takes her around fifteen minutes to tidy the mats away and secure the building. CCTV has her leaving the club at nineteen forty-five. All the other cars had left at that point. She didn't see Rachel, but she did see a man walking two Siberian huskies on the Spanish Battery."

Cooper turned to a trainee detective who sat at the back of the room. Oliver Martin was only five-eight, but he added at least three inches to this by gelling his hair into an impressive quiff. Despite his best denials, the team were also convinced he liked to wear make-up. L'Oréal, to be precise. This led to Sutherland and Keaton telling the youngster he was *worth it* whenever they brought him a coffee or helped him on a case.

"Martin, put out an appeal. Our dog walker's a potential witness. Find him."

"I'm on it," he replied. "I've been following the white rabbit," he added, "though that's a line I never thought I'd say. No reports of stolen or missing pets. I've been to the local pet stores and asked them to check their records for sales of white rabbits over the last week or so. I'm keeping an eye out for sales where a customer bought a rabbit without a hutch or much in the way of bedding or food. I figure, why would our man buy the whole kit and caboodle if he knows the rabbit won't be around for long? I'll let you know if anything comes from it."

"Thanks, Martin, and good thinking." Cooper began to pull on her coat. "Keaton, Sutherland, once you've found Will Harper, find out who the FLO with Lisa Smith is and get someone over for a statement. Find out if Shelly was friends with Rachel, touch base with Atkinson, and see what else he's found. Tennessee and I will head to the school. It's time to speak to some of Rachel and Shelly's friends and teachers. Let's find out what or who connects these girls."

- CHAPTER 10 -

Tynemouth Academy was a modern school having been rebuilt three years ago. The building resembled a giant cube with red brick and black and grey cladding. Surrounded by sports fields, bike sheds and an impressive sports hall, it was clear the students of Tynemouth Academy were keen athletes. The school motto: *in omnia paratus,* was emblazoned across the school gates. Many moons had passed since Cooper had studied Latin, but Tennessee's mumble of, "Ready for anything," confirmed her suspicions. Sadly, she didn't think there was a school in the country that could be ready for losing two students in a manner such as this.

"DCI Erica Cooper and DS Jack Daniel, here to see Linda Webb."

Both detectives held up their warrant cards for inspection by an eagle-eyed school administrator with a pinched face and a sniffly nose. The admin officer sneezed into tissue and led them to a small office just off the foyer.

"Erica," greeted the headteacher, who had never dealt with Cooper in a professional capacity before, only as Tina's mother.

Linda Webb looked like she hadn't slept for a week. Was it the stress of the job? Or, was it Kenny - Tina's father and Cooper's ex - who was keeping her awake until the early hours? Cooper put the thought from her mind. It was none of her business what Kenny Roberts and Linda Webb did behind closed doors.

Cooper and Tennessee sat down opposite Linda's desk. It was piled high with paperwork and management manuals.

"You're here about Rachel," she said, taking deep breaths. Her shoulder pads rose and fell in time with her breath. "Terrible, terrible business."

"Yes," answered Tennessee. He folded one long leg over the other and stared at the headteacher with dark, serious eyes. "And, we're here about Michelle Smith."

Linda's brow lowered. "Shelly? Don't tell me she's somehow caught up in this. She wouldn't hurt a fly."

"No, Ms Webb, that's not what we're saying—"

Cooper cut in. "Linda, I'm sorry to have to tell you this, but Shelly Smith was found dead this morning."

Linda's hand flew to her mouth. "No!"

"She was killed in the same manner as Rachel Pearson. We have reason to believe it was at the hands of the same person, but we're not ruling anything out at this stage."

"I don't... I don't believe this...." Linda's voice trailed off, and she got to her feet to open a window. It was barely above freezing, but Cooper understood how trauma could make you feel as if all the air had been sucked out of the room.

"This is going to be a very stressful time for students and staff," began Cooper.

"Stress? Stress doesn't come close." Linda was shaking her head, causing her long, chestnut bob to swish back and forth across the collar of her blouse. "I've had parents on the phone every five minutes. The press too. Kids asking questions I don't have the answers to. Rumours spreading like wildfire. The governors won't get off my back. The art department are pissed I cut their funding in favour of science; I didn't have a choice given our latest OFSTED inspection. And now Michelle. It's going to be twice as bad."

Cooper shot a sideways glance at Tennessee. He was masking his revulsion well but the way his eyes wrinkled at the corners let her know that he was thinking the same thing as she was. Linda Webb was more concerned about how this affected herself than about the safety of her students.

"I think," said Cooper, bringing Linda's attention back into the room, "that the safety of students should be paramount. I'm going to arrange for a police presence at the school gates to act as a deterrent. We don't know yet if the school is a target, but it certainly connects Rachel and Shelly."

"We'll also arrange for an officer to address the students tomorrow morning," said Tennessee. He uncrossed his legs. "They can speak to the whole school or go class to class, but either way, they'll need access to the entire student body. They'll recommend students walk to and from school in groups, that sort of thing."

"And I can recommend agencies to deliver workshops on online safety," added Cooper. "It's imperative that the children aren't giving any personal details out online. It might also be a good idea to bring in some professional counsellors."

Linda Webb was still pacing and shaking her head, but she'd had the good grace to close her mouth and listen to what the detectives had to say up until that last comment.

"Professional counsellors? We don't have the budget for that. We have an excellent peer-to-peer student counselling system. I set it up last year, and the feedback from the parent and teacher association has been very positive. It'll do for now and then perhaps in the future—"

"No, Linda. It won't do for now." Cooper's voice had hardened. "Two girls have been murdered. There's going to be a lot of grief and a lot of fear. Peer-to-peer is all well and good when someone doesn't get the grade they wanted, or someone's crush hasn't called them back, but this is different. Your counsellors are going to need counselling."

The headteacher took on the look of someone who was used to dishing out scoldings rather than taking them. She pouted - actually pouted - and folded her arms.

"Well, we'll see what we can do."

"Make sure you do," said Cooper, getting to her feet and wishing for the love of God that Linda would close the window again. "For now, we need a room. Somewhere we can chat to Rachel and Shelly's teachers, as well as their friends."

"The staffroom is up the stairs and on the left," said Linda. "There's tea and coffee if you want to help yourselves. I'll send a few of Rachel's friends along once the bell goes for the next class."

Cooper thanked Linda before following her directions to the staffroom. Once out of sight, Tennessee ran his fingers through his curls and shook his head at Cooper.

"Talk about a face like a smacked arse."

"Tell me about it. Two dead girls and she's talking about budgets, and governors, and funding."

"Mum!"

Tina Cooper walked hand-in-hand with a lanky, bespectacled boy who hastily pulled his hand away and tucked it into the pocket of his green school blazer.

"Tina. Nice to see you again, Josh."

Josh turned a deep shade of beetroot. "Ms Cooper," he said with half a bow.

"Are you here because of Rachel?" asked Tina, looking over both shoulders.

"Yes," answered Cooper, though she couldn't tell her daughter about Shelly Smith just yet. "Listen, Tina. I'm going to have your father pick you up from netball tonight."

Tina frowned and then raised an eyebrow. "Why? I'm not supposed to see him until the weekend."

"I just don't want you walking home alone in the dark."

"But..." Tina stopped herself and surveyed her mother's face for a good five seconds. "Fine."

Cooper's insides relaxed. She didn't want to argue with Tina, not with everything else that was going on.

"Thank you," said Cooper. "I'll see you at home. Text me later and let me know what you want for dinner. Right, off to class. You too, Josh."

The two green-clad teenagers walked away, whispering about homework and murder.

The staffroom in Tynemouth Academy felt like a giant corkboard. Every wall was covered in posters and flyers, covering everything from sign up sheets for the next school fundraiser to recognising signs of female genital mutilation.

Under the watch of a few staff members, Cooper found herself a seat and opened a file on her lap. Tennessee made two cups of coffee that looked strong enough to power the next mission to Mars and joined his superior.

"Hello." A man in a paint-flecked shirt held his hand out to Tennessee. He wore beads around his neck and had thick-framed glasses perched on a head of bleached hair. "You're with the police, aren't you? I'm Brian Hutchins," he said by way of introduction.

"And I'm Todd Carpenter," announced another man, one with a hooked nose and possibly the worst posture Cooper had ever seen.

Both men shook Tennessee's hand and seemed surprised when he introduced the skinny woman sitting to his left as the senior investigating officer.

Brian Hutchins took a seat opposite. "I was Rachel's art teacher. I just can't get my head around all of this. It's knocked the faculty for six. Todd here was Rachel's form tutor. If there's anything we can do to help the investigation, please let us know. All the staff feel the same way."

Not *all* the staff, thought Cooper.

"Do you have time for a quick chat, gentlemen? Can you tell me about Rachel?" she asked, turning her eyes to Todd Carpenter.

Todd checked his watch. "She was a popular girl," he replied. "It'll be quiet without her, that's for sure."

"Quiet?" asked Cooper.

Todd sat down next to Brian Hutchins and he nodded in agreement. "Quite the chatterbox was Rachel. She could never chat to the person next to her either; she always had to shout across the room to the person sitting furthest away."

"How did the other students feel about that?"

"I guess it was annoying for the ones who were trying to concentrate," answered Brian. "But those are few and far between. These days, kids are all about their *on-demand* whatnots. Skip this, swipe that, three-second memes and nine-second Vines."

"I can appreciate that," said Cooper, though she didn't know what a Vine was. "Other than being a bit on the noisy side," and noting that it was opposite to how her yoga classmates had described her, "what else can you tell me about Rachel?"

"She was, how's a polite way to say it?" said Todd Carpenter. "Erm... An underachiever? She was bright, but she didn't apply herself."

"I think she did in English, Todd," countered Brian. "I remember Catherine saying she had a talent for poetry."

"Catherine says that about all her students. She's a soft touch."

"And who were her closest friends?" interjected Cooper. "Did she have any enemies?"

"Enemies?" Todd Carpenter's eyes widened. "Goodness, I wouldn't have thought so. All the girls wanted to be friends with her. All the boys... Well, as I said, she was popular."

Brian Hutchins removed his glasses from his head and cleaned them on his shirt. "As for her closest friends... Will Harper was pretty much her shadow. Wherever Rachel went, he wasn't far behind. She was friendly with Tess Livingston as well, and Mackenzie James and Michelle Smith."

Cooper looked to Tennessee. He opened the list of names Lou Pearson, Rachel's father, had given him. The top four names were Will, Mackenzie, Shelly and Tess.

"Brian, and... Todd, was it?" Cooper sat more upright in her seat. "I need you to tell me more about Michelle Smith."

- CHAPTER 11 -

Cooper cursed. She was utterly useless in the kitchen, and the fact she couldn't even fry an egg without bursting the yolk was testament to that. She scraped up the sorry looking egg, laid it on a slice of sourdough, sprinkled a little salt and handed it to Tina.

"Thanks, Mum."

"You won't be saying that once you've tasted it," said Cooper, her nose wrinkling at her failed attempt at breakfast.

"It's the thought that counts." Tina grabbed her knife and fork and began slicing. "Aren't you having anything?"

"I'll have some toast once I finish getting ready."

"No, you won't," said Tina, pointing her knife at her mother. "You know, you look like a total badass without your wig on. You should go to work like that. Very Mad Max."

Rolling her eyes, Cooper tried to laugh it off. "I don't think so."

The truth was, without hair, Cooper felt like her femininity had been stripped away. Where Tina saw "total badass," Cooper saw prepubescent boy. She felt weak and victim-like whenever she looked at herself without her wig. She was the one who sought justice for victims; she couldn't face being one herself.

"Did you finish your homework?" asked Cooper, changing the subject.

Last night, Tina had asked for help with her maths homework, which was a rarity. Given how gifted Tina was with maths, she couldn't help but think that Tina just wanted her mother's company, and homework was simply an excuse.

Having broken the news of Shelly's death to several teachers and pupils, as well as Tina, Cooper's mind was fuzzy and in need of rest when she'd returned home.

Unfortunately, she'd been unable to switch off and was less than incompetent when it came to equations.

"Yeah," replied Tina, taking a bite of egg on toast. "I finished it before my show started."

Cooper kissed her daughter on her head. "You're a bright young thing. No idea where you get it from."

Both ladies swivelled their heads in unison at the sound of knocking on the front door.

"Will you get that, Tina?" asked Cooper, rushing from the room to make herself presentable.

She only took a few moments to change from pyjamas to a suit, pull her wig on and slap on a layer of red lipstick.

"Oh, it's you," she said to Kenny as she re-entered the room.

"Were you expecting the Queen?" grinned the wide-shouldered man whose body had been built through a lifetime in the construction industry.

"No. It's just—"

"Thought I'd swing by and give Tina a lift to school."

"That would actually be—"

Tina's knife and fork clattered off her plate. "I'm walking to school. I'm meeting Josh at the corner."

A vein in Kenny's forehead pulsated at the mention of Josh's name. He turned to Cooper in the hope of backup.

"Coffee?" she offered instead, watching the cogs whirl behind her ex's eyes.

"Please," he answered before turning to his daughter. "Okay. How about we give Josh a lift too? There's plenty of room in The Beast," he said, referring to the monstrosity that was his Ford pickup.

Tina cleared her plate and tried to bargain for her freedom. "Fine. We'll drive to school, but I'm walking home tonight."

"No, you're not. I'll meet you at the gates."

"But Dad..."

"But nothing. Go get your school bag."

Tina let out an almighty groan and stormed from the room. Cooper counted the seconds until she heard doors slamming. It was six.

Kenny warmed his hands on the coffee mug and leant forward over the table. The steam from the hot drink danced in front of his round, clean-shaven face.

"I spoke to Linda last night," he said with a hint of trepidation in his voice. "Another girl was killed?"

"Yeah. 'Fraid so."

"And there's going to be a police presence at the school? The kids have to attend safety workshops? Erica, is our daughter safe?"

Cooper opened her mouth to give Kenny a well-deserved earful. He'd never wanted a daughter. When Cooper fell pregnant, he'd wanted her to have an abortion. When she'd been unwavering in her decision to keep the baby, he'd promptly ended their relationship by running away to Devon. Being concerned for Tina's welfare now did not make up for twelve years of turning a blind eye to his responsibilities. No wonder Tina spent as little time as possible with him.

Cooper held her venom back long enough to take a sip of coffee and calm her thoughts.

"We're doing our best to find whoever killed those girls, Kenny." Her voice was cold and businesslike. "It's true that both girls went to the same school, but that might not be the connecting factor, if indeed there is one. We need to find out what else the girls have in common."

Tina appeared in the doorway to the kitchen. Her face was still thunderous, but she had her school blazer on, and her backpack was over her shoulders. "You mean, what they have in common other than Will Harper?"

- CHAPTER 12 -

"Where's Harper?" barked Cooper down her phone as she buckled up in the old Mazda.

"We couldn't find the slippery little eel yesterday, boss," answered Paula Keaton. "Picked him up this morning on Front Street. He looked rougher than a badger's arse. We've put him in juvie cell three while we wait for his appropriate adult. Think his uncle's coming in."

"Uncle?" asked Cooper. Usually minors acted all tough until the second the cell door closed, then they'd cry for their mummies like they were still being breastfed.

"Yeah, he was adamant he wanted his uncle and not his mum or dad. Sutherland's doing the Starbucks run on his way in. Want me to tell him to get you owt?"

Cooper started the engine. "An Americano, please."

"Food?"

"A muffin, one of those poppy-seed lemony ones."

"I know what you mean. See you in ten, boss."

Cooper started the engine and headed towards HQ in Wallsend. Ten minutes was wishful thinking. Maybe before they started digging the blasted tunnel for the A19 to pass under the Coast Road, but not now.

When Cooper crossed the threshold of CID, twenty-five minutes later, Sutherland was waiting with coffee and muffin in hand.

"You're an angel," she said, removing her coat and laying it over the back of her chair.

"Will Harper's uncle just arrived. I've put him in interview suite one. Are we still keeping the Smith murder under wraps?"

"No point," Cooper answered. "It's been public knowledge for over twelve hours now."

"Well, let me know when you're ready and I'll move Will from the cells."

Cooper took a deep inhalation of comforting caffeine. "I'll be ready the second I finish this muffin."

THE STENCH OF WEED and cigarettes almost overpowered Cooper as she walked into the interview suite. She brought her coffee to her nose to try to cover it and looked Will Harper up and down.

He was a big lad for his age, a teenage boy in an adult's body. A triangular frame suggested he lifted weights but regularly skipped leg day. A dusting of acne covered his jaw, and he either hadn't washed his hair in a while or he was wearing far too much product. He looked a world away from the photograph Cooper had seen of him in Rachel Pearson's bedroom.

Cooper took a seat and waited for Sutherland to do the same. Pushing a button on an audio recorder, she began the interview.

"Northumbria Police Headquarters, Friday fifteenth November. The time is ten-fifteen a.m. I am DCI Erica Cooper. Also present is DI Sam Sutherland and Walter Harper who is acting in the role of appropriate adult."

"It wasn't my weed."

Will's eyes began to dart around the room; his uncle laid a hand on his shoulder.

"I mean, I wasn't smoking. I don't do drugs. It was a friend. I was next to him while he was smoking. That's what you can smell."

Sutherland placed his hands on the table face up in an attempt at open, non-threatening body language.

"Listen, son. I don't give a monkey's what you smoke, snort or swallow, but this interview is under caution, so I suggest you listen carefully when my colleague speaks."

"Will Harper," continued Cooper, "you are being questioned in relation to the murders of Rachel Pearson and Michelle Smith. You do not have to say anything, but it may harm your defence if you do not mention when questioned something which you later rely on in court. Anything you do say will be given in evidence. Please state your full name, address and date of birth."

The young man looked at his uncle with eyes like saucepans. It took an encouraging nod from the older man for Will to open his mouth.

"William Harper. 162 Knott Memorial Flats, North Shields. May thirtieth 2003."

"Thank you, Will. Can you tell me where you were on Tuesday evening?"

"I was at home."

"All night?"

"Yes. I didn't go out."

"Can anyone verify that, Will?"

Will looked away and pushed his hands under his thighs. "My parents. We had dinner together, then they went—"

He realised too late what he had said.

"Will? Where did your parents go?"

"To the pub. The Lodge."

"What time was that?"

Will swallowed and kept his eyes in his lap. "About seven, I think."

"When did they return?"

"I don't know. I'd gone to bed."

"Will, do your parents often leave you alone to go to the pub?"

He shrugged.

"I need an audible answer for the recording," pressed Cooper.

Will looked up. "I guess so," he said in a quiet huff.

"And where are your parents now?"

"Me da's probably hungover. Ma'll be..." he paused to find the right word. "Working."

Cooper frowned. "What does your mother do?"

Will shuffled and looked to his uncle.

"Will's mother works in the entertainment industry."

There was something in the way Walter Harper said *entertainment* that made Cooper think he didn't mean she was a singer.

"Can you be more specific?" asked Sutherland.

"I don't think it's relevant to your investigation," replied Walter, and he had a point.

"She's a whore." Will's face hardened. "I'm not supposed to know, but I'm not an idiot. She's a smack-head whore."

Cooper made a mental note to contact child services once the interview was over. "Moving on," she said, leaning back in her chair. "So, you were home alone on Tuesday evening?"

"I'm not lying."

"I'm not saying you are." Cooper stopped to take a drink of coffee and to allow a moment of silence. Silence had a way of making people feel uncomfortable.

"I played on my X-box, had a shower and went to bed. I didn't go out."

"Okay," said Cooper. "How about yesterday morning. Where were you then?"

"I... I was in school."

"From nine a.m?"

"Yes."

"That's not true, is it, Will? Our officers went to your school but you hadn't shown up for registration. You told the Pearsons you had a doctors appointment."

"I... I did."

"But you didn't show."

Will's face crumpled.

"We checked," explained Cooper. "Your appointment was at nine but you didn't show."

"Are they allowed to tell you that?" asked Will's uncle. "Isn't that a breach of patient confidentiality?"

"We didn't look at his medical history, Mr Harper. This is a murder investigation, and I'm trying to establish if your nephew has an alibi for the times when Rachel Pearson and Shelly Smith were murdered. So far, he doesn't seem to."

Cooper turned back to Will. "Where were you yesterday morning?"

"I... I couldn't face school. I'd just lost Rachel. I loved her and I..." his voice started to crack as his eyes glassed over. The child in the adult's body was beginning to surface. "I went to the park for a bit. Smoked until I ran out of cigarettes, then I went home and got into bed. Rachel meant the world to me. I still can't believe she's gone."

"Let me guess," said Sutherland. "No one else was home?"

Will said nothing. Cooper decided to change tack.

"Tell me about the argument you and Rachel had on Tuesday?"

"What argument?"

Sutherland slapped his hand on the table. "Don't play innocent with us, boy. We've read Rachel's diary. You're quite the domineering boyfriend, aren't you? Telling Rachel what she can and can't wear. Blaming her when other guys looked at her."

A tear rolled down Will Harper's cheek. Fear? Guilt? Cooper wasn't sure of either.

Sutherland handed the boy a tissue. "Will, we have statements from others in your class who can corroborate Rachel's version of events. You might as well tell us."

Will dabbed his eyes. "She liked the attention. She did it on purpose to wind me up."

"Did what on purpose, Will?" asked Cooper.

"Flirted and shit. She'd rolled her skirt up at the waistband to make it shorter. Then she asked Nick Davies if he thought it suited her, and he said he thought her arse looked better in skinny jeans." Will's face reddened. "She was testing me, trying to make me jealous, and it worked. When we were alone I told her she was making a fool of me."

Cooper leant forward. "And did Shelly ever make a fool of you?"

"Shelly?"

"Michelle Smith. We know you two dated. A bit odd that two girls you dated end up murdered and you don't have an alibi for the time of either of their deaths."

"Very odd," echoed Sutherland.

Panic was etched on the young man's face. He looked back and forth between the detectives and his uncle. "But... No... I didn't do anything, I swear. I'm being set up. I must be." Will's breathing became erratic. "I'm not the only one who had Rachel and Shelly in common. That freak Xander Wright has it in for me. He fancied Shelly, but she only had eyes for me, then he started seeing Rachel. When Shelly and I broke up, Rachel dumped him for me."

Desperate actions, thought Cooper, deflecting the attention on to someone else. She would speak to Xander Wright as soon as she could. In the meantime, Will Harper was headed straight to the cells. No alibi. No bail.

- CHAPTER 13 -

"THE SNOW'S BACK," OBSERVED Keaton. She handed Sutherland a biscuit to dunk and moved away from the window.

"The bairn'll be happy. She loves snow," he said before playing a game of chicken between his biscuit and his coffee. A look of regret passed over his face when the biscuit gave way and fell into the drink. "Ah, crud."

Cooper's eyes followed an unusually large snowflake as it fluttered past the window. "Well, I'm sure we all want to get out of here before the snow buggers up the school run traffic. So let's get down to business. Alice in Wonderland," she said, turning to young Oliver Martin, "Did you find the white rabbit?"

"Still stuck in the rabbit hole, ma'am. I've hit a bit of a dead-end with the major pet stores. I've had no sales of rabbits without hutches in the past month. Pets At Home have three white rabbits sold in our timeframe, all with the full set-up. Hutches, hay, food, the works. I've got them all on CCTV. An elderly couple who paid cash, a family with five kids who paid cash and a James King who was alone and used his credit card."

"Have you looked into King?"

"Briefly. He lives in Gosforth with his wife and two sons. No priors, and no connection to Tynemouth Academy from what I can tell. I can look deeper?"

Cooper rested her back against the window. It felt like a sheet of ice, so she pulled away again. "Put it on the back burner for now. Move on to the smaller Mom and Pop pet shops. They might not have as sophisticated cameras as the bigger stores, and they might be cash-only, but hopefully someone will remember something."

"You got it," said Martin.

"How are we getting on with the appeal for the man with his huskies?"

Martin shook his head. "Haven't heard a peep."

"I might have something on that." Sutherland flipped through a notepad until he found the page he wanted. "Earlier today we got a report from Tynemouth Academy of a man walking around the perimeter of the school and staring at some of the girls through the chain-link fence at morning break. Freaked a few of them out, so they fetched a staff member. When approached by a Mr Hutchins, he took off." Sutherland paused to dunk another biscuit. "He was walking two dogs."

"Huskies?" asked Cooper.

"Yellow Labs. The lighting down at the sailing club's a crock of shit. If you ask me, two yellow Labs could be mistaken for two huskies in the moonlight."

Cooper agreed. "Follow it up, Sam. The school has cameras by the main entrance. See if he walked by them. Where's Tennessee?"

Right on cue, Tennessee walked into CID looking out of breath. "Sorry, sorry. Had one of those Lamaze classes."

"What's that when it's at home?" asked Keaton.

"Prenatal classes," answered Cooper while Tennessee got himself settled at his desk. "You practice giving birth."

Keaton's mouth fell open. "How does that work? Actually, never mind, I don't want to know."

Keaton crossed her legs - unconsciously protecting her womb - and addressed DS Jack Daniel. "You finished your reports from the school?"

"Yes. Though there's not much to report. By all accounts, Rachel and Shelly were not the brightest, and they were a little on the disruptive side. However, they were very popular, said to have good hearts, regularly did charity events, that sort of thing. The words that kept cropping up were: funny, sweet, kind, pretty. Everyone thought the world of them."

"Not everyone," said Cooper. Her mind returned to what her daughter had told her. "What about the underclass of kids? The ones who aren't popular. The ones whose lives are made miserable by the cool kids?"

Sutherland tilted his head towards Cooper. As a fellow parent, he picked up on the tension in her voice. "Has Tina said something?"

"She told me she tried her best to avoid Rachel. Said she was manipulative and could turn the whole school against you if she wanted to."

"I spoke to some of Shelly's classmates this morning." Keaton leant back in her chair and propped her feet up on the edge of a waste paper basket. "The name Greg Mason kept popping up. It was his house party where Rachel broke her back. Apparently, he was trying to kiss Rachel on the first-floor landing. Rachel wasn't interested, and when she pulled away from him, she fell down the stairs."

"Jesus," said Cooper.

"Indeed. Shelly saw it all and told the entire school it was his fault. He went from the top of the pecking order to the bottom of the heap in one night."

"That sounds like a motive to me," said Cooper. "Someone find out if he has an alibi for Tuesday night and Thursday morning."

"I'll do it," said Sutherland. "Paula?"

Keaton nodded. "Sure thing, partner."

"Tennessee and I will speak to the Xander kid that Will Harper mentioned. Oliver, can you get in touch with Margot Swanson at the Freeman—" Cooper thought of Margot getting her hooks into the impressionable young man and changed her mind. "Actually, you speak to Atkinson, see if the SOCOs have anything for us. I'll get an update from Margot."

Cooper checked the time and watched the snow for a second. It was starting to flurry around the car park beneath them. "You know what to do. Finish your reports and get home to your families. I can think of better places to get snowed in than CID."

- CHAPTER 14 -

By Saturday afternoon Cooper was utterly exhausted. Thankfully, her brilliant but stroppy daughter was spending the night at her useless but willing-to-babysit father's.

Tina had been reluctant initially, especially since Josh had asked her to go to the cinema. Kenny had won her over with the promise of Chinese takeaway and the double promise that Linda Webb would not be the centre of his attention for the entire evening. Cooper couldn't blame Tina on that front. What teenager wanted to spend their free time with their headteacher?

After a morning spent catching up on the laundry and housework that had been neglected over the last week, Cooper braved the shops. Predictably, the good people of Tynemouth had panic-bought staples such as bread and milk and now everywhere was out of stock. It was strange how people panic-bought bread - something that goes mouldy in a few days - but not flour. Cooper couldn't talk. The last time she baked bread - when Tina was six - she almost burnt the house down. Domestic goddess, she was not.

Cooper dumped her shopping bags on the kitchen table and tuned into BBC Radio 2. At the first hint of Ed Sheeran she switched to Absolute Classic Rock. Much better. Given her complete lack of aptitude in the kitchen, Cooper's shopping consisted mainly of tinned goods, ready meals to stick in the freezer, and jars of pasta sauces.

Now in her pyjamas, with make-up removed and her wig stored on the mannequin head in her bedroom, Cooper examined her replenished kitchen. What could she cook that even she couldn't balls up? Cheesy beans on toast - easy peasy.

Here's the plan, she told herself, *eat, get in the bath, read a good book, get an early night.* Ten minutes later and her culinary masterpiece was complete. She was about to sit down and eat when someone knocked on the door. *Ignore it.*

"Erica. Open up. It's Justin."

Justin Atkinson, the senior scene of crime officer, peered through the letter-box.

"Come on, Erica. My glasses are frosting over."

Cooper squirmed and ran her palms over her head and looked down at her baggy, faded pyjamas. *Shit.* She unlocked the door and stepped backwards, embarrassment flowing from the top of her head to the tips of her toes.

"Casserole," he announced, stomping his feet on the mat and leaving white snowy prints. "And wine," he added, lifting his elbow to reveal a Waitrose bag, weighed down with a glass bottle.

"I..." Cooper was confused. What was he doing here? "I'd just made dinner."

Atkinson looked at the plate of beans on toast and then looked at Cooper over his glasses. "That's not food. That's what students eat when they're thirty grand in debt and have spent their loan on hipster cocktails served in jam jars. You're wasting away. I've seen more body fat on an anorexic whippet."

He strode past Cooper and placed a heavy, white casserole dish on the oven hob. He handed Cooper the carrier bag. "Hope you like lamb."

"I love lamb."

"How about Tina? I know kids can be fussy."

"She's at her dad's stuffing her face with spare ribs."

Cooper opened the wine and poured two glasses. It took every ounce of strength she had not to run upstairs, do her hair and reapply make-up. Atkinson hadn't even done a double-take. He was either very polite or very unobservant. Either way, Cooper appreciated it. But, it didn't stop her from feeling self-conscious.

"Oh well," said Atkinson. "More for us."

He picked up Cooper's plate, opened her pedal bin and slid the beans on toast straight into the rubbish. Grabbing two plates from a shelf, he dished up and handed Cooper a portion that was steaming hot.

"You've cooked enough to feed all of CID," she said.

The smell of lamb was so delightful that Cooper began to salivate.

"Empty nest syndrome," said Atkinson. "I'm so used to cooking for four that I'm incapable of cooking single servings."

Cooper gave the man a supportive smile. It was common knowledge that his wife had run off with a waiter she'd met on a family holiday to Spain. He was twenty years her junior. Atkinson was suddenly a single father to twin boys who had left for Edinburgh University at the start of September.

"It must be quiet at home?"

"Too quiet," he replied. "I've spent two days sifting through the Smith house. That poor girl had been in her home - where she should have felt safe and loved - and some bastard broke that safety and took her life."

He removed his glasses and rubbed his eyes on the back of his wrist.

"She let him in. Did I tell you that?"

She bobbed her head; there'd been no sign of forced entry during the initial walkthrough. The killer had even closed the front gate after himself.

Cooper took a sip of wine and a mouthful of succulent lamb and vegetables. In an instant, she felt the vitamins and nutrients flood her body.

Atkinson let out a long, low sigh and took a sip himself. "Anyway, I couldn't switch off. I went for a run along Longsands but it didn't help, so I busied myself in the kitchen, and before I knew it, I'd cooked up enough food to last me till Christmas. I thought you might be in the same boat. This case is seriously messed up."

"That's an understatement," said Cooper. She took another bite and crossed her legs under the table. "I haven't switched off either. I can't let it go. I won't let it go until I've caught the killer and sent him to Frankland."

HMP Frankland was a maximum-security category-A prison in County Durham. It housed the worst of the worst; Charles Bronson, Harold Shipman and Peter Sutcliffe had all done time there. Cooper had been responsible for sending at least thirty men through their doors on convictions for murder, GBH and rape. Often it was Atkinson's evidence that helped her secure those convictions.

As talk of the case eased off and small talk of Christmas preparations, their children, and TV talent shows took over, Cooper found herself beginning to relax. She was enjoying Atkinson's company. She was also enjoying the wine, which had almost run out.

"I'll open another one," she said, getting to her feet and finding a bottle of red at the bottom of the wine rack. "If you fancy?"

Atkinson's Adam's apple bounced as he swallowed the last of his wine. "Oh? Well yes, of course, if you don't want rid of me, that is?"

Cooper raised her eyebrows. "Don't be ridiculous." She opened the bottle and topped up their drinks. The notion that she liked Atkinson and wanted more than a professional working relationship hit her like a bus. And why not? He was a hundred steps up from Kenny. Or Neil Fuller, now she thought about it. A man who ran away when she fell pregnant and a man who ran away when she got ill. *Wow, Erica, you really can pick 'em.*

Atkinson was ten years older than Cooper. Did that matter? Her mind flooded with questions as she found herself looking at the man through new eyes. They were both single parents, lonely, and came with a tonne of emotional baggage.

The pair retired to the living room, sat a safe distance away from one another and began to swap stories from their youth. It turned out Justin Atkinson was born in the same hospital as Cooper and they'd even attended the same tennis club as kids. Cooper had lessons when she was six but hated it, so her parents gave up forcing the sport upon her after only eight months. Atkinson had played until his mid-twenties. Funny how their paths had crossed without them even realising.

"You don't believe in this nonsense, do you?" asked Atkinson, holding the horoscope section of a newspaper.

The newspaper had probably been down the side of the sofa for weeks, but Cooper was feeling daring – and tipsy.

"Maybe," she said with a playful giggle and a coy tilt of her head. "I'm a Gemini. Does it say a tall, handsome man will deliver cooked food to my door?"

A look of shock passed over Atkinson and he stammered for a moment before reading out, "*As autumn fades into winter, it's time to be your own cheerleader. Venus syncs up with the moon and your sixth house of self-care.* Who writes this stuff? *Numero uno should be your top priority, and Mars...* Yada, yada, yada. Listen to the tall man bearing food—"

"Tall, *handsome* man."

Atkinson's face flushed a few shades lighter than the wine he was sipping. "Listen to the tall, handsome man bearing food."

He shifted closer to Cooper. Close enough for her to smell his aftershave. "He doesn't believe in horoscopes or crystal balls."

His voice was low and soft, and he edged closer still.

"Or tarot cards. Or Ouija boards."

His lips grazed Cooper's. Her heart jolted, but not from lust.

"What did you say?" she gasped, pulling away.

"I... Oh, I'm so sorry, I completely misread the situation. I'm such an idiot."

He was on his feet and moving away.

"No, you didn't," said Cooper. She pulled him back onto the sofa and stared at him. "Tarot cards. You said *tarot cards.*"

"Well, yes I did, but—"

Cooper pulled her phone out and frantically started typing. "Magician, Priestess, Empress. Oh God, they're all tarot cards. Why didn't I see this earlier? They're in order."

The colour drained from Atkinson's face as he realised the scale of what they were facing. He shook his head in disbelief. "How many cards are there?"

Cooper did another quick search, her fingers moving at lightning speed over the keys. "In the major arcana?" Her mouth fell open. She turned to stare at Atkinson. "Twenty-two." She felt sick. "There's twenty-two, and I bet he wants the whole deck."

- CHAPTER 15 -

"THE TAROT CARD KILLER," said Tennessee, taking a look up and down Millview Drive on Monday morning. "Has a ring to it."

Cooper almost choked on her coffee. She was not impressed. "Who came up with that?"

"No idea, but it's caught on throughout the department."

"Well, stop it. It's unprofessional. Besides, the last thing we need is for the press to get hold of it. He'll become some sort of macabre celebrity, an urban legend."

"Roger that."

Tennessee pulled his coat around him and waited for Cooper to finish the Starbucks he'd brought her.

"Nice area," he observed.

Millview Drive backed onto Tynemouth Golf Course; it was lined on either side by large, semi-detached mock-Tudor homes. Audis, BMWs, and Bentleys occupied the driveways. Cooper wondered if any of the cars were worth more than her house.

She drained the last dregs of caffeine and crumpled the cup into her car's drinks holder. "How much do you know about tarot cards?"

"Next to nothing. I know there's a death card, but I don't think it means you're about to pop your clogs. Think it's supposed to mean new beginnings or something. You don't think the killer had their fortune read, got the death card, and thought it meant they should become Death?"

Cooper locked the car behind her and approached number sixteen. The house boasted bay windows and an extension over the garage. A privet bush in the front garden had been trimmed into a perfect rectangle, and someone in the household had taken the trouble to clear the drive of snow and scatter rock salt.

"No idea," she answered as she knocked on the door. "But it's a possibility. If tarot's important to the killer, it's important to us. We need to do some research."

A young man with blue-black hair opened the door. He wasn't much taller than Cooper, and given his age and the green blazer he wore, Cooper assumed him to be Xander.

"Alexander Wright? I'm DCI Erica Cooper, and this is DS Jack Daniel. We're from Northumbria CID."

Xander blinked at the pair while Cooper took in his appearance. He had four earrings in his left ear, expertly applied eyeliner and his nail varnish matched the colour of his hair. His blazer sleeves were rolled up to reveal several woven bracelets around his wrists. Cooper, who knew the school's dress code inside out after Tina fell foul of it a handful of times, could tell Xander Wright was not one to conform.

"I thought it was only a matter of time before you stopped by," he said to Cooper's surprise.

"What makes you say that?"

"Rachel and I used to be a thing. We went out for a while. Aren't something like ninety per cent of female murder victims killed by their partner or their ex?"

Cooper did her best to keep poker-faced. "That's correct," she answered, thinking of how many women were scared of strangers and of walking alone at night. It was a disturbing truth that women who were murdered were most likely to be killed in their own home and at the hands of someone who claimed to love them.

"Suppose you'll want to come in." Xander stepped aside and called for his parents. "MUM. DAD. Told you the police would want to talk to me."

Within thirty seconds Mr and Mrs Wright had joined their son on their impressive leather sofa. Mrs Wright clung to her son's hands in a sign of support as Mr Wright scrutinised the detectives through steely eyes. Three overgrown rats - a Chihuahua, a sausage dog, and a pug - snarled at Cooper and Tennessee from behind a baby gate.

"Was it Will Harper?" asked Xander. "Was it Will who threw my name in the hat?"

Cooper preferred to be the one asking questions. "What makes you ask that?"

"I don't like him. He doesn't like me. He rules the school. You've seen him; he's a right gym monkey. Probably sprinkles steroids on his cornflakes."

"Xander," said his mother with a hushing tone to her voice. "Behave."

"I am. Is it true he was released?"

Cooper leant forward. "I'm not here to talk about Will Harper. But yes, we released him. Tell me about your relationship with Rachel Pearson."

He let out a small snort. "There's not much to tell. We went out a while back, before she hurt her back. She was one of those ridiculously busy girls. Went to the gym before school, had a private tutor some nights, gymnastics the others. At weekends she'd travel to Manchester or Shropshire for competitions. She was nonstop. So, our relationship wasn't much more than handholding at lunchtime. If I was lucky, we'd get to hang out on a Sunday evening after she got back from training or competing."

"How did things end?" asked Cooper.

"She said we'd drifted apart, which was a bit of a joke, I thought. How could we drift apart? We were barely together?" He flopped back on the sofa. "A week later, I saw her in Will Harper's arms."

"That must have been difficult for you?"

Xander looked away for a moment. "I wasn't heartbroken or anything. Like I said, we barely had time for each other. My ego was pretty bruised, though."

Cooper realised her leg was twitching. Too much caffeine on an empty stomach. "Thank you, Xander. Now I need to ask you about your movements on Tuesday evening."

Mr Wright folded his arms. "You can't possibly think—"

Tennessee cut him off. "This is a standard line of questioning, Mr Wright. If Xander is to be ruled out of our investigation, we need to establish his alibi."

"I came straight home after school," he started. "I had games last lesson. We played rugby. We're supposed to shower at school, but no one does. So, I showered when I got home at about three forty-five."

"Thank you, Xander," said Cooper, wanting to encourage his honesty. "Then what?"

"Mum was home," he turned to look at his mother; she nodded in agreement.

"I'm a full-time Mum."

Cooper hated that term. As if going to work to provide for her daughter made her... What? A part-time Mum? No, she was as full-time a mother as anyone who had the luxury of staying home. Now, however, was not the time to voice that opinion.

"And you didn't go out again that evening?"

"I walked the dogs," said Xander, nodding his head towards the pack of snarling pups in the kitchen.

Cooper's mind returned to the man with two huskies. Was there any chance someone could mistake those three dogs for two huskies? No, she decided. Definitely not.

"What time was that?"

He puffed out his cheeks and shrugged. "Dunno. About six?"

"Did anyone see you?" she asked.

"Half of Tynemouth. If they didn't see me, they'd have heard me. Well, not me but the dogs. They've all got small dog syndrome, like to bark at every dog we pass. It's annoying."

Xander ran his palms down his thighs and began to tap out a rhythm on his knees. "Oh, I saw the lady from number twenty. She was walking her poodle."

Cooper looked to Tennessee, and he made a note.

"And I called into Gibson's. It's a paper shop. The son was working. I bought a Red Bull."

Mrs Wright shook her head. "No wonder you don't sleep. Those things are poison."

Xander rolled his eyes. "Then I came home and finished my homework."

"What time did you get home?"

Xander shrugged and sighed, then his eyes popped as a lightbulb illuminated in his mind. "Wait," he said, pulling out his phone. "I have it on here. My Fitbit'll know." He opened the app and handed his phone to Cooper.

A red line snaked around a map of Tynemouth but didn't go anywhere near Prior's Haven. The screen read that Xander had walked from ten past six to twenty past seven. There was no way he could have made it back from his house to the sailing club by half seven to meet Rachel as she left her class. Not on foot anyway.

"This is very good, Xander. Do you mind taking a screenshot and forwarding it to this number?" She handed him a card, and he did as she asked. "Now, what about Thursday morning?"

Xander scrunched up his face as he thought. "Ah, that was just a typical morning really. Had breakfast, left about eight forty, met Callum and walked to school."

"Who's Callum?"

"My cousin. Callum Chester. He lives at number forty-three, he's in the year below, but we get on all right. His parents are my Godparents, so we say we're cousins even though we aren't really. Want his number?"

"No, that's okay. We have his address," said Cooper. "And you got to school in time for registration?"

Xander nodded. "Yeah."

Cooper elected to end the questioning there. Xander Wright's movements were accounted for, and she suspected that Will Harper had sent them on a wild goose chase for his own amusement. She thanked the Wrights for their time and turned to Tennessee once they were outside. "What do you think?"

"I think the alibi's solid. I can chase up the poodle lady and the bloke from the paper shop if you like."

"I'll put Martin on to it."

As Cooper got into her car, started the engine and pulled away, her phone vibrated in her pocket. She shifted her weight and handed it to her DS. "Read that, will you?"

"What's your pin?"

"Nine, nine, nine, nine."

"Original." Tennessee unlocked the phone. "It's from Tina. She says she's going to Woods for hot chocolate with Josh after school, and she'll be home by five. Ah, this is interesting. She also says Xander Wright hasn't shown up to school yet."

"That's not interesting. We've just left his house."

"Yes, but Tina says Will Harper is telling everyone that Xander killed Rachel and Shelly and that's why he's not in."

"Little weasel," growled Cooper.

"She goes on. Apparently, the headteacher has - and I quote - done her nut. She's put Will in isolation for spreading rumours."

Cooper chuckled. "Good. We might not have been able to hold him any longer. But Linda Webb can. I'm going to drop you at HQ. Can you type up our report from the Wrights?"

"Sure. You got somewhere else to be?"

Cooper slowed the car to let a cat sprint across the road. "Yeah," she said. "I'm going to gather some intel."

- CHAPTER 16 -

COOPER PRESSED THE DOORBELL of a house in the quaint village of Earsdon, but there was no ringing sound. She raised her hand, but before she could knock, the door swung open. A frail, elderly woman in a pink nightdress looked up at her through thick lenses. She blinked twice.

"Hello. I'm DCI Erica Cooper. I'm looking for Charity Mae."

"You found her, dear." Charity Mae's voice had a raspy rattle to it, suggesting anything from the start of tonsillitis to chronic emphysema.

Cooper took in the tiny woman. She was hunchbacked, and her pale skin was flecked with age spots. "Wait," said Cooper, recognising a strong sense of deja vu. "I know you."

"Oh, I doubt that."

"No. I've seen you. You were walking outside police headquarters in Wallsend. You stopped and looked up at the window."

Charity Mae ran her tongue along the edge of her top teeth and chuckled to herself. "To see is not to know. You may have seen me, but you do not know me. How can you know me when you hardly know yourself?"

Taken aback by that comment, Cooper stood quite transfixed.

"Well, don't just stand there, dear. Come in. You'll catch your death." She turned and began to walk along her hallway. "Follow me."

Cooper gathered herself and shut the door behind her. "Mrs Mae," she said to the back of the woman's head as she walked. "I wanted to talk to you about a case I'm working on. I found your address in the Yellow Pages under *psychics and clairvoyants*. I don't know if you caught the news, but two teenagers have been murdered. We think the person we're looking for has some connection to, or fascination with, tarot cards."

Charity Mae's home smelled of cinnamon and cloves, and the chintzy decor took Cooper back in time to a period when she lived with her grandmother. Pastel table cloths covered side tables, floral tiebacks secured heavy curtains. Pictures and figurines of birds decorated every shelf and sideboard.

"Sit," she said, pointing to a comfortable looking armchair. "I'll make tea."

As the woman shuffled towards her kitchen, Cooper called after her. "It's okay, Mrs Mae. I'm not thirsty. I just wanted to find out about tarot cards and what they represent. Especially the major arcana."

Charity took no notice and returned a few moments later with two cups of peppermint tea served in antique china cups. "Now, what can I do for the girl who sees but does not know? You want to know your future? Or, perhaps contact someone who has passed on?"

"No, Mrs Mae." Cooper took the cup of tea and gave a slight nod of appreciation despite explicitly saying she didn't want any. "As I was saying, I'm not after a reading. I'm working on a case involving tarot cards... and I wanted... to..." Cooper's voice slowed as she realised the woman wasn't looking her in the eyes; she was staring at her mouth. For a moment, she considered she had something in her teeth, then it dawned on her. "You're lipreading?"

"Yes, dear. Deaf as a post. Do go on," she said, taking a seat on the other side of a small, round table covered in lace.

"Ah, well. Yes. I work for Northumbria Police. Two teenagers have been murdered, and the perpetrator appears to be working his way through the tarot deck. The first victim was dressed as—"

"A magician. I saw the news. And a priestess, I believe?"

"Yes."

"Truly awful. Are you sure you don't want a reading, dear? The Hanged Man looks down upon you, you know? The sacrifices you have made are written on your face. I can see you work hard to provide for a child, but the harder you work, the less you get to play the mother. Love can not be bought, no matter how hard you work. Nor can time."

Cooper warmed her palms on the cup of tea and considered what Charity had just told her. She'd never given fortune-telling much thought, but she supposed she considered it guesswork; she certainly hated the idea of her life being mapped out or determined by fate. But how did Charity know she was a mother? The comments about working were easy enough. No one got far in the police, let alone CID, without hard work, but she definitely didn't mention Tina in the two minutes since she arrived.

"Moving on," said Cooper, putting the question to one side. "The major arcana. Why is it special?"

"Ah," chuckled Charity, "the big secret."

"What secret?"

"The cards themselves, dear. Major arcana is a Latin term. It means the big secret, and in answer to your question, the cards are not special. They are merely cards, inanimate objects. It is what they represent that is special."

Cooper crossed her legs and tried to keep her expression neutral, but the old lady was frustrating her, and she had places to be. She thought hearing from an expert would be quicker than trawling through Wikipedia, but on second thoughts, she was probably wrong.

Charity opened a wooden box, took out a deck of cards and spread them, face down, over the table. "The tarot is made up of five decks: cups represent love and relationships; swords deal with consciousness and intellect; pentacles are of work and wealth; the wands stand for inspiration and intuition; and finally," she rested her chin on steepled fingers, "the major arcana, which takes our souls on the journey to enlightenment."

Journey to enlightenment. Cooper could imagine Atkinson's face when she no doubt repeated this to him.

"Turn over the card nearest to you, dear."

Cooper did as she was asked and was faced with the Fool. Feeling somewhat insulted, she met Charity's eyes and waited.

"Don't take it personally. The major arcana tells the story of our spirituality as we travel from the naive wonder of the Fool, to..." Charity turned over another card. "To the fulfilment of the World. We are all on a journey, dear. You are, I am, and the man you hunt most certainly is."

Cooper uncrossed her legs. She may be getting somewhere now. "Tell me more."

"He is transforming. With each death, the killer moves closer to his destiny." Charity reached across the table and turned over the king of wands. She smiled to herself as if sharing a private joke. "Energy can not be created, nor can it be destroyed. It can only be transferred or transformed. Am I right in thinking that the man you seek only kills the young?"

"So far, yes."

Charity cocked her head. "And who has more energy than the youth?"

Cooper ran a hand over her face. "You think he kills the young to stay young himself?"

Charity sipped her tea and stared at an embroidered picture of two blue tits. For almost a minute, it was as if Cooper wasn't there. Eventually, she shrugged and turned back to her. "You see but do not know, and I know but do not hear. Perhaps the wise monkey is what we need. Behind you, dear."

Cooper turned. Behind her, on the windowsill, were three jade monkeys. Cooper picked up the one covering his mouth with his hands and handed it to the old lady.

"Speak no evil," said Charity Mae.

"A sentiment people rarely subscribe to these days," said Cooper. She got to her feet and brushed her coat with her palms. The Tarot Card Killer was on a journey. His actions were about more than just dressing up his victims. Although cloaked in some Rosa Lee theatrics, Charity's comments gave her a potential insight into the killer's mind. If she could work out his journey, perhaps she could intercept him along the way.

Cooper extended a hand. "Thank you for your time, Charity Mae. Your ideas about a transformation or the transfer of energy are really quite interesting."

As the pair shook hands, the lights in the room flickered. Cooper's eyes darted to a dusty chandelier above her.

"Oh, that'll be the postman." Charity let out another rattle of a laugh. A second later, Cooper heard the sound of letters dropping through the letterbox.

Astonished, Cooper's mouth fell open. "NO!" she gasped. "There's no way."

Psychics aren't real, she told herself. They're actors, aren't they?

"Relax, dear. Did you not consider how I knew you were at my door when I can't hear the doorbell? There's a pressure pad under my doorstep. It makes the lights flicker when someone stands on it. My son installed it."

Cooper relaxed, but only a touch. Something about the little old lady made her feel strangely on edge. She might not have predicted the postman, but it still didn't explain how she knew Cooper was a mother.

Charity interlaced her fingers and rested them over her small round stomach. "Allow me to read for you."

"Thank you, but no. I just wanted a better understanding of the cards."

"You're not a believer. That's okay. Not many are. But did you know the FBI have often turned to clairvoyants? Desperate times push people to expand their horizons."

Cooper checked the time on a gold clock on the mantlepiece. It was stuck on five past four.

"Indulge an old lady."

Cooper sighed and wondered what the harm would be. The old lady was right about the FBI; their most well-known psychic, Troy Griffin, worked on over a hundred cases. Although, it was usually as a last resort and his success rate was under twenty per cent. "All right," said Cooper. "But let's keep it snappy."

The smile on Charity's face pushed her glasses up an inch. She collected the cards, shuffled them and placed them on the table. "Cut the deck, dearest."

Cooper halved the deck and placed the top half under the bottom half. Charity dealt the top three cards and laid them face down on the lace. She pointed to each card in turn.

"The past, the present, the future." She motioned to Cooper to turn over the first card. "Ah, the nine of wands. Look here, dear. You see the old man carrying the wand? You see the eight wands stuck in the ground around him? The wands in the ground represent the battles he has faced. The wand in his hand is the battle to come. If you look closely, you'll see the man looks weak and injured, but his face is determined. There is still fight in the old man, and he still desires the win."

Turning her eyes to admire a collection of decorative plates, Cooper thought about Charity's interpretation of the card. According to Margot, the person who strangled Rachel and Shelly had to be a man or a large female, given the size of the bruise marks on Rachel's neck. Could a weak or injured man have overpowered the girls? Perhaps he could, especially in the case of Rachel, who was herself weak from injury.

Charity blinked her magnified eyes at Cooper. "The present?"

Cooper turned the card; it read *Strength* and depicted a woman battling a lion.

"Interesting." Charity leant forward in her armchair. "The lion is strong, but the woman in the card is stronger. Her face looks calm and collected despite the terrifying act she is engaged in."

Two options popped into Cooper's mind. "Is the killer the woman? Or, is he the lion?"

"If he were the lion, who would be the woman?"

"Well, me, I suppose." Cooper tensed. "I'm the one battling him."

"See how the card is rotated towards me rather than you?" asked Charity. "The lion is a symbol of courage and passion. But reversed it depicts a lack of inner strength, fear, and a lack of conviction and confidence in one's own abilities. Perhaps he is questioning how far he can continue on his journey? Maybe he has forgotten the fulfilment he feels from doing what he loves?"

"No," said Cooper. "I don't think he'll stop after two. I think he plans on seeing this through. He'll not stop until he has the full set or I put him behind bars.

Right. Last card." She turned over the final card. "Two of swords. What does that mean?"

"This card depicts the future in our spread. There is a woman, blindfolded, holding a sword in each hand. In the background, you can see a sea filled with crags and rocks. The rocks are obstacles to ships; they stall progression."

Cooper's mind went straight to the Black Middens, a reef in the mouth of the Tyne that had claimed several boats and hundreds of lives before the days of lighthouses and radar.

"Are the rocks the police? Are we stalling the killer?"

"Or?"

Cooper sighed. Did Charity Mae have to be this exhausting, or was it all part of her act? "Or he could be the rock, hindering my investigation?"

Charity merely smiled. After a few seconds she added, "The blindfold signifies a situation which prevents the woman from seeing clearly, and the swords show two choices that lead in different directions. It may seem like an impossible choice, but choose she must."

Scepticism flowed through Cooper, and she wondered how much money the FBI had spent on psychics over the years. "So," she said to humour Charity, "the murderer had a troubled youth. He's faced adversity, and his killings are his way of taking back control? He's lying low until he can harness his strength, and in the future, he has to make a choice. A choice between two victims?"

"Very good," said Charity. She pointed an arthritic finger at Cooper. "Did you ever hear the story of Esmerelda Day?"

Cooper stood up and shook her head.

"Once, there was a young man in York who visited a travelling fair. He wanted to fool the fortune teller, so he put on a wig, a dress and a pair of women's shoes, and he knocked on the door of Esmerelda's wagon. Esmerelda looked into her crystal ball and told him he would marry a fair man with dark eyes. The young man laughed and removed his wig. He handed her the sixpence that he owed and called her a fraud. Guess what happened to that young man?"

Hoping to find a polite moment to make her escape, Cooper had begun to edge herself towards the door. "I don't know," she answered. "She put a curse on him?"

"No, dear," laughed Charity. "Curses aren't real."

Nor are psychics and clairvoyants, thought Cooper, *and yet here we are.*

"The next year, he met a beautiful woman, fell in love and married her. Her name was Lucy Fairman, and she had eyes as black as night. You see, child, there are always two sides to every prediction. You thought we were talking about the killer, but it was you who cut the deck and you who turned the cards. It is you who is weak from battle, you who questions her abilities and you, my dear, who will need to make a choice."

- CHAPTER 17 -

Cooper paced back and forth in the glass-fronted lobby of Northumbria Police headquarters. Charity Mae's words wouldn't leave her head. For a hunch-backed wannabe gypsy, she'd really gotten under Cooper's skin. Had Cooper forgotten the fulfilment she should feel from doing what she loved? Was she suffering from a lack of confidence and conviction? Yes. As much as she hated to admit it, Cooper still hadn't settled back into her role as Chief Inspector.

"Screw her," muttered Cooper. She turned and paced in the opposite direction. Cooper wasn't just going through the motions. She loved her chosen career; she was sure she did. This role wasn't for someone who didn't care. Cooper cared. Her pacing and tormented inner monologue stopped dead when she spotted a blue Citron C1 pull up in the car park and watched as Lisa Smith, Shelley's mother, got out. Cooper greeted the petite, fragile woman at the door. Unlike her daughter - who was blonde and fair-skinned - Lisa Smith had dark features with almost black hair, brown, bloodshot eyes, and a ruddy complexion.

"Thank you for coming in, Mrs Smith. We could have come to you, you know?"

She replied by shaking her head. "No. I needed to get out. Sitting around doing nothing's tormenting me. It's torture. I'd much rather come here. At least this way, I feel like I'm doing something."

Cooper placed a hand on the lady's upper arm and guided her towards one of the family rooms. She felt it would be less intimidating and more appropriate than an interview suite.

Cooper got Lisa Smith settled and had Oliver Martin bring her a cup of camomile tea. She gripped the mug between her palms. Her whole body was shaking. It wasn't cold in the family room, the temperature was centrally controlled to twenty degrees, but Cooper knew from her own experience that trauma and stress could make you shiver even with the heating set to maximum. She thought back to a time when she hadn't been able to warm up for two days straight, no matter how many blankets she wrapped around herself.

"I understand you're staying with friends, Mrs Smith."

The small woman looked up from her tea. "Please," she said, "call me Lisa. And yes, I'm staying with Isabella Lopez, a colleague of mine. I can't go home. I'm going to get the house on the market as soon as possible. I don't think I'll ever be able to step through that front door again."

Cooper was sympathetic. She couldn't imagine living in her home if something like that happened to Tina.

"Lisa, the gentleman in charge of the forensics team has informed me that there's no sign of forced entry at your home. I'm led to believe that Shelley either let her killer in, or he had a key. Would Shelly be likely to open the door to someone she didn't know?"

Lisa shook her head. "Absolutely not. She hated answering the door to anyone; she was always convinced it would be Jehovah's Witnesses or someone trying to sell us something. Rachel was her best friend. She cried all night after we heard the news about her. And I mean, all night. We had a big chat about safety. I just can't believe she's gone," her voice cracked. "Why my Shelly? My baby. Someone killed my baby girl."

She placed her tea on a small side table and buried her head in her hands. "I told Shelly I'd meet her after school that day. I'd booked for her to speak to a therapist because of what happened to Rachel. But..." Her voice trailed away because they'd never kept the appointment.

"We were quite open with each other," continued Lisa. "She didn't keep secrets from me. She wasn't the best behaved child, I know that, but she was always honest with me. For instance, she went to a party a little while back, and she told me about being asked out by this boy that she liked. She was so happy. She also told me that one or two of the kids there were doing coke. She said she had nothing to do with it. But she wanted me to know that it was there in case I heard it from someone else."

"It sounds like you two had a good relationship."

"We did."

Lisa took out a hanky and blew her nose.

According to Atkinson and the team of SOCOs, Shelly had been killed in her living room. The perpetrator then changed her clothes and posed her on the doorstep before leaving and closing the gate behind him. Officers had spoken to several residents on the street, but so far, no one reported seeing anything unusual.

"Who has a key to your home, Lisa?"

"Just myself, Shelly, her grandparents and my ex-boyfriend."

"Is that Shelly's father?"

"No. He died when she was just an infant. He was killed in combat. Iraq."

"I'm sorry to hear that," said Cooper, and she was. Lisa Smith had faced more than her fair share of sorrow. "I'd like someone to contact your parents and make sure that they still have their key, check that it hasn't been stolen."

Lisa nodded. "Of course. I'll give you the number."

"Your ex-boyfriend. Can you tell me his name?"

"It's Ralf. Ralf Bennett."

Cooper felt the tiniest of tingles in the base of her skull.

"Is he local?" asked Cooper.

"Yes. He lives in Tynemouth."

"And have you been separated long?"

"About six months. I never got around to getting my key back. I was putting off seeing him. I should have just told him to put it through the letterbox."

"Can you tell me how things ended between you?"

"He hit me," said Lisa. She picked her tea back up and took a sip. "Only the once. It only needed to be the once. I was knocked out cold and unconscious for over a minute. Shelly saw the whole thing. I'm no idiot." She sniffed. "I wasn't going to stay in that relationship, no matter how many times he said he was sorry and promised to change. I grabbed Shelly, left for my parents, and told him I wanted him gone before I got back. You don't think he could have—?"

Cooper had misjudged Lisa Smith. She might be small, but she was far from fragile. Cooper spent a further twenty minutes with the grieving mother, trying to gather all she could about Shelly's personality, friends, routine, and the things she did every week. Afterwards, she found Tennessee as quickly as she could.

"I need you to get on to the tech team. Find any connection between Shelly, Rachel, and a Ralf Bennett. He was in a relationship with Lisa Smith, and he has a violent streak. He hit her; that's why they broke up."

"Piece of shit," grumbled Tennessee. "They should lock men like that in a room with men like me. See how they like it when someone their own size hits them back."

"He still has a key to their house. I recognised the name as soon as she said it, but it took me a while to place where I'd seen it before. It was on Rachel's Facebook page. He was one of the people who liked her photo in her gymnastics leotard. Why would a grown man befriend his girlfriend's daughter's friends on social media? That doesn't sound right to me."

Tennessee lowered his eyebrows. "That doesn't sound right to me either. Not in the slightest. Do you have an address?"

"I do. Rodney Street."

Tennessee's eyes widened. "That's literally around the corner from the Pearsons. This is promising. Right, I'll speak to tech, then I'll get us some vests and we'll get over there."

"We could do with some backup," said Cooper. "I'll get Paula and Sam. Meet me back here in ten."

RALF BENNETT LIVED IN a standard red-brick two-up-two-down semi-detached. A dirty white van was parked in the driveway; someone had smudged the words *clean me* in the muck. Through the front window, a fifty-inch flat-screen was playing The Jeremy Kyle Show.

Cooper and Tennessee approached the house while Keaton and Sutherland waited in an unmarked car at the end of the street. Tennessee rapped his knuckles on the front door, when there was no answer, he did it again.

Cooper heard huffing and grumbling and the sound of heavy feet shuffling towards the door. It opened ajar, and a man with shaggy blond hair and a stubbly jaw peered out behind the chain.

"What?" he asked in a thick Geordie accent.

Tennessee held up his warrant card. "Mr Bennett? I'm DS Daniel from—"

He didn't get to finish. Bennett slammed the door in Tennessee's face. The detective's nose exploded with thick, scarlet blood. He swore at the top of his lungs before throwing his weight into the door and knocking it off its hinges.

Bennett dashed along the corridor. He wore a dressing gown, black pyjama pants and a pair of slippers.

"He's going out the back," yelled Tennessee, his voice muffled with pain.

Cooper darted along the narrow alleyway that divided the sets of semi-detached houses. She scrambled over a wooden gate and landed in the back garden in time to see Bennett scaling his back wall.

"Stop! Police!" she called out. Cooper grabbed her hand-held radio and directed Sutherland and Keaton towards the main road. "Stop where you are!" she shouted again.

Bennett dropped over the wall and disappeared from sight. Cooper wasn't going to give in that easily. She might be small, but she was agile. It was how she got through all those bleep-tests when she first joined the force. She was never the fastest in the sprints, but she could turn on a sixpence. She grabbed the top of the wall and heaved herself up. Tennessee emerged from the back door and sprinted across the wet grass. The wall grazed Cooper's hands and tore at the fabric of her trousers but she managed to swing her body over it. Being light had its advantages. She landed like a cat and went in pursuit.

As adrenaline surged through Cooper's body, she realised these were the moments she lived for. Thoughts of cancer and chemotherapy faded away to nothing. The title and pay increase that came with being DCI was all well and good, but she loved the chase. She loved the pursuit. This is what she was meant to do. Insecurities about returning to work after four months seemed a distant memory. That upside-down Strength card could bugger off. Erica Cooper was back.

The unmarked car screeched around the corner. Bennett narrowly dodged a speeding Audi as he weaved his way across Tynemouth Road. His dressing gown billowed behind him like the cape of the worst superhero imaginable. Cooper was hot on his heels, and Tennessee wasn't far behind her. Bennett turned into a bridle path that cut away from the main road and headed to Tynemouth Metro station.

"Take Station Terrace," she shouted into her radio.

With only two strides separating her and her target, Cooper launched herself at the back of the man's legs. She wrapped her arms around his calf and pulled him off balance. He hit the ground with a bang and a string of swear words. There was no way Cooper could control him by herself, but Tennessee arrived in the nick of time. He flattened his weight on top of Bennett - drips of blood falling from his face - and secured his arms behind his back with handcuffs. Cooper took a second to get her breath and check that her wig was still in place. Boy, she had missed this.

"Ralf Bennett, I'm arresting you on suspicion of the murders of Rachel Pearson and Michelle Smith," started Tennessee.

"No. Let me up, ya bastard. I didn't do anything."

"You do not have to say anything—"

"Dirty pigs! Let me up. Now."

"As you wish." Tennessee yanked on the handcuffs as hard as he could and roughly pulled the man to his feet. Bennett squirmed and pulled against the cuffs like a dog fighting his leash. He was covered in a mixture of mud and Tennessee's blood.

The unmarked car pulled up at the end of the bridle path. Keaton got out and opened the door to the back seat. She gave Cooper a searching look and Cooper responded with a subtle thumbs up. She was fine. No need to worry over her.

"I'll leave this one in your capable hands, DS Daniel," she said. "Mr Bennett, your chariot awaits."

COOPER LET BENNETT STEW in his cell while she took a shower and changed into a clean suit. She treated her palms with antiseptic and threw her old trousers away. She doubted even an experienced seamstress could disguise the fact both knees had been shredded.

"How's your nose?" she asked when she emerged from the shower room.

Tennessee lightly pressed his face with his fingers. "Tender, but it's all right. I'd have been miffed if he'd broken it. Paid five grand for this nose."

Cooper laughed. "I knew that bone structure was too good to be true." She searched his face. "What else have you had done?"

A delicate flush formed over Tennessee's cheeks. "Just the nose," he said, and then, much quieter, "and maybe the ears."

"I knew it. I bloody knew it. Where is he anyway? Still in the cells?"

"Sutherland has him in interview suite two. He's refusing a lawyer."

Cooper frowned. "Really? Not the brightest move."

"He's not the brightest of bulbs, that's for sure."

"Did Sutherland find any evidence in Bennett's home? Anything relating to the occult?"

Tennessee shook his head. "A team's still raking through the place, but from what I last heard, it's just a typical bachelor pad."

A few minutes later and Cooper was dragging her chair across the floor of the interview suite. The action created a nails-on-chalkboard sound, causing Bennett to wince.

"I'm sorry, Mr Bennett. Was that annoying?" asked Cooper. "Not nearly as annoying as ruining a good suit by having to drag myself over your garden wall, I bet."

He scowled and bore icy blue eyes into her. "No one made you chase me."

"No one made you run."

Cooper turned on the audio recorder and stated the date, time and venue of the interview. She introduced herself and DS Jack Daniel and began her questioning.

"Tell me how you knew Shelly Smith."

"I was seeing her mother, Lisa." His voice was low and gravelly.

"Did you get on with Shelly?" asked Cooper.

"I guess so. She was a good kid. A bit lippy at times."

"A bit lippy, you say? She was cheeky? Answered back a lot?"

"Yeah, that was Shelly."

"Did you ever hit her for her cheek?"

"What? No, course not." He folded his arms.

"But you hit Lisa."

"No. I never."

Cooper leant back in her chair and waited.

"Well, just the once," he mumbled after thirty seconds of silence. "That doesn't mean I killed Shelly. I was as shocked as anyone by the news."

Cooper blanked him. "Do you have a key to Lisa and Shelly Smith's home?"

He shuffled his weight around on the cheap plastic chair. "Might have. I'm not sure, can't really remember to be honest."

Tennessee turned his eyes to the ceiling and tutted. "Listen, Mr Bennett, we pulled a set of keys off you when we brought you in here. They're currently bagged and in evidence. There are six keys on that keyring. Two for your front door, one for your back door, and one for your van. What are the other two keys for?"

He shrugged.

Tennessee leant forward and rested his elbows on the table. "Think hard Mr Bennett, because if that key fits the lock at Lisa Smith's home, you will be in a world of trouble."

"That still wouldn't prove anything."

"It would prove that you like lying to the police. And I can tell you now that's not a very good look."

Bennett chewed the inside of his mouth but said nothing. Cooper decided to move the conversation forward. She tapped her finger on the table four times and asked, "Have you ever had your fortune read?"

The change in topic confused Bennett. "No," he said with a questioning tone. "I'm not into that shit."

"Do you believe in a higher power?"

Bennett frowned. "No, not really."

"What about a lower power? Satan, perhaps?"

He looked from Cooper to Tennessee and back to Cooper. "What are you on about? No, I'm not a Satan worshipper. And I didn't kill Shelly. Are you going to let me out of here or what?"

Cooper narrowed her eyes and decided to switch topics again. "Tell me about your relationship with Rachel Pearson."

"What relationship?"

"Well, you knew her. You were close."

"No, we weren't." A line formed between his eyebrows. "Who told you that?"

"You're Facebook friends with her. Isn't that right?"

"Yeah. So what? I'm friends with loads of people on there. I've got like six hundred friends."

Cooper wanted to make air quotes with her fingers when he used the word *friends*. "And how many of those six hundred friends are fifteen-year-old girls?"

"Woah! Hang on a minute! First, you try and pin these murders on me. Now you're making me out to look like some kind of nonce. I'm no murderer, and I'm no paedo."

Cooper opened a file and spread a selection of photographs over the desk. "For the record," she stated, "I am showing Mr Bennett photographs of Rachel Pearson taken from her Facebook page. They include a picture of her in a gymnastics leotard and two pictures of her in bikinis. Do you recognise these photos, Mr Bennett?"

"Should I?" His tone was angry now. He was struggling to control his temper.

"Yes," replied Cooper. "You liked all three of them. And on this one," she tapped the photograph to her right, "you left the comment: *Looking good, Rach*."

Bennett jumped to his feet. Tennessee matched his speed and stood between him and the door. "Don't even think about it."

"Sit down," snapped Cooper. "Or we'll cuff you to the chair."

Bennett clenched his jaw and reluctantly sat back down. "Liking photos isn't a crime," he grumbled. "I didn't kill Shelly, and I didn't kill Rachel."

"Then prove it," said Cooper. "Tell us where you were at the time of the murders. Let's start with Tuesday evening when Rachel was killed. What were you doing then?"

Silence.

"Okay," said Cooper with a sigh. "And Thursday morning?"

More silence.

"Mr Bennett, you don't need me to remind you that you have been arrested on suspicion of murder. When we came to your home, you ran. When questioned about—"

"I didn't kill those girls," he growled through gritted teeth.

"So, where were you?" Cooper sat back in her chair. "I'll wait."

Bennett rested his head in his hands then ran his fingers through his messy hair before folding his arms again. "I was at home."

"With?"

"No one. I was alone."

"Can anyone confirm that? Did anyone pop round? Did you make any phone calls?"

Bennett shook his head.

"For the record", started Cooper, "the suspect is shaking his head. And we will check your phone records, by the way. We'll know if your phone was on Rodney Street."

Across the table, Cooper saw Bennett swallow.

"Right, so when Rachel Pearson was being strangled to death, you were in your house, alone?"

His lips pursed as he looked to his right. "Yes."

"And what about Thursday morning? Where were you when Shelly Smith, your ex-girlfriend's daughter, was suffocated?"

Bennett's gaze darted around the room before finally coming to rest on Cooper. "I was home alone."

Cooper took a long, slow breath, placed the photographs back in the file and got to her feet. Bennett may be an expert in playing the fool, but Cooper was far from convinced he was on a journey to enlightenment. "Have it your way," she said, thinking she'd at least give the forensics team some more time to sweep his house for traces of the murdered girls. "A good night's sleep in your cell might help jog your memory. I'll speak with you again tomorrow."

- CHAPTER 18 -

COOPER YAWNED. HER AFTERNOON had been spent speaking to the owners of fancy dress stores. She and Keaton had called every store within a ten-mile radius of Tynemouth. They'd asked the owners and managers if they had sold any outfits that matched up with the cards from the major arcana. Almost all of them had priest, magician, death and devil outfits, and a fair few of them had sold costumes matching those descriptions in the past month. Cooper requested any credit card information and any CCTV footage that the stores had. It would take a while for Martin to sort through it all, but needs must. She also sent Bennett's image to all the stores in case the owners recognised him. It wasn't exactly scintillating work and it in no way compared to the thrill of chasing a bad guy down a lane and dragging him to the mud in a tackle Keaton had described as "gnarly."

"Ten quid says he got his outfits online," Keaton put the phone down on the latest shop owner and swigged from a can of full-fat cola.

"That's a safe bet. He'll have used a VPN, paid in bitcoin and had it delivered to an InPost locker." Cooper balanced her chair on its back two legs. "But he's flat out denying any involvement, and frankly, we need more evidence than we have if we're going to charge him. So, until then, we're not leaving a single stone unturned."

"What's your gut saying?" asked Keaton. "Did Bennett do it?"

"All my gut's telling me is that last night's ready meal was a bad idea. As for Bennett, I think he's fishier than North Shields Fish Quay. Whether he's a murderer or not remains to be seen."

"And you think the killer's obsession with tarot means he's on some sort of journey?"

Cooper let out another yawn and covered her mouth with her hand. "Apparently that's the point of the picture cards; a journey from cluelessness to knowledge. The psychic thinks he might be harvesting the kids' energy in some sort of bid for immortality."

Coke spluttered from Keaton's lips. "That's messed up. Sounds like this guy's more than your average bed-wetter with an Oedipus complex. So, what was the psychic like? She give you the lottery numbers?"

"Creepy," Cooper answered, "and I forgot to ask." She checked her watch. It was almost half three, and she was due at Tynemouth Academy to conduct additional interviews with Rachel and Shelly's teachers and to check in with the two uniforms who had been watching the school.

"I can take over here if you need to get off," said Keaton. She shifted her chair back so she could rest her ginormous feet on the standard-issue desk. Cooper should tell her to sit up straight and respect her surroundings, but the posture rather suited Keaton. The woman had an air about her; she exuded the sort of confidence that didn't come easily to those under five-foot-five.

"Thanks, Paula." Cooper pulled on her coat and grabbed her files. She walked past Tennessee's desk where he was furiously scrolling through the database for any previous crimes related to the occult. "Come on. We'll go via the burger van."

Tennessee's eyes lit up, and he practically flew out of his seat and out the doors of CID.

Five minutes later and the detective sergeant was stuffing a greasy burger down his throat.

"Brilliant. Thanks, Coop. Hayley never lets me eat junk food."

Cooper held back a snort. Her sergeant shouldn't be worrying about what he ate. He was at that age where he could eat anything.

"Well, I'm not your wife, and I'm not your mother. I'm your chief. And I don't care how much junk you eat as long as you pass your physical."

"The bleep test?" he said with his mouth full. "I can do it walking on my hands."

"Now that I'd like to see."

Cooper pulled into the only parking space available at Tynemouth Academy. It happened to be the space furthest from the front doors.

Tennessee stuffed the last few bites of his burger into his mouth, swallowed and gave himself the hiccoughs.

"Looks like a - hic - bit of trouble at the gates there." He slapped his hand against his chest a few times in an effort to make his diaphragm cut it out.

Cooper followed his gaze. A small group had gathered to watch an argument between two students and an adult. One of the girls was gesticulating wildly.

"Oh, for crying out loud," muttered Cooper as she got closer. The students were Tina and her boyfriend, Josh. The adult, if she could call him that, was Kenny.

"I'm walking."

"No, you're not."

"We agreed. We're going to Woods café, then Josh will walk me home."

Kenny folded his arms, making his upper body seem even bigger. "You expect this little dweeb to keep you safe?"

"Hey!" Josh's shoulders rounded and his jaw tightened.

"Give over, lad. You couldn't punch your way out of a wet paper bag."

Josh shoved a hand into Kenny's chest. It was probably akin to trying to push over a house and judging by the way Josh staggered backwards, it was a move he instantly regretted. Luckily Cooper, who had hurried over, was now only two steps away. From the opposite direction, Linda Webb was also hightailing it towards the melee.

"Kenny," they both snapped in unison.

Linda was first to say her piece. "Lower your voice. You're scaring some of the children."

"I'm just trying to get my daughter home in one piece, Linda," he grumbled, his lip protruding.

Several students began to giggle when they realised there was something between the headteacher and Tina Cooper's father.

"Then compromise," hissed Cooper, lowering her voice so the crowd couldn't continue to eavesdrop. "Let her go to the café and pick her up from there. I shouldn't say anything yet, but we have someone in custody. The danger might be over."

"Might?"

"We're still gathering evidence."

Kenny shook his head, but Tina burst into tears before he could say anything. Half her year group had watched the scene play out. The poor thing must be mortified.

"I wish you'd stayed in Qatar," Tina spat. She turned and walked away, her head lowered, allowing her hair to fall over her face and hide her tears. Josh took off after her.

Kenny turned on Linda. "Look what you did."

"Nice try, Kenny." Cooper wasn't Linda's biggest fan, but she wasn't letting Kenny pin this on her. "This is your doing. If you want to keep your daughter safe, maybe start by not pushing her away. She never met you until she was twelve, and you expect her to hug you and call you 'Daddy?' I don't think so. She's known Josh longer than she's known you. That girl barely knows you, let alone respects you."

Kenny bristled, unfolded his arms and shoved his hands in his pockets. He looked back and forth between Cooper and Linda before stomping off himself.

Like father, like daughter, thought Cooper. Sometimes nature well and truly trumped nurture.

"Right." Cooper straightened her posture and plastered a fake smile on her face. "Linda, let's head indoors. I'd like to speak to the teachers who taught Rachel on Tuesday afternoon and those who taught Shelly on Wednesday afternoon. Sergeant Daniel," she turned to Tennessee. "Clear the rubberneckers and speak to the patrol officers. I want to know if the man with the dogs has been back. Show them Bennett's photo while you're at it. When you're done, come find me."

"Roger."

LINDA SHOWED COOPER INTO the staffroom.

"Brian," she called. "You remember Erica Cooper? She needs to speak to you again if you have five minutes."

Brian Hutchins turned around from the sink where he'd been washing a coffee mug. He removed his glasses, tucked them over the collar of his t-shirt and checked his watch. "Five minutes is all I have, I'm afraid. Culture club starts at quarter to."

"Culture club?" He couldn't possibly mean the band.

"Catchy name, isn't it?" He motioned to the chairs, and Cooper took a seat. "I run the group with Phillip Dunn, the music teacher and Catherine Grainger, who teaches English literature. Each week we do something different: pottery, poetry, a new song, that sort of thing. Last term we took the group to the Theatre Royal to watch an opera. I was worried they'd misbehave, but they were enthralled. Some of the girls loved seeing a larger female as the star of the show. They said it was refreshing. The club's becoming rather popular, and tonight's activity is sculpting, so I'll be leading the group."

Cooper thought back to the after-school options she'd had as a teenager. If you weren't into hockey, netball or choir, your options were limited. She folded her hands in her lap and lifted her eyes to meet Brian Hutchins's. "I understand you taught Rachel last Monday afternoon?"

"Yes, that's correct." He sat opposite Cooper.

"How did she seem that day?"

"What do you mean?" asked Brian.

"Did she seem worried about anything?"

Brian sat back in his chair and brought a finger to his lips. "No, not really. There was tension between her and William Harper, but you've already ruled Will out of the investigation, haven't you?"

Will Harper was still a person of interest. Cooper, however, didn't feel the need to share that information with a member of the public - she'd already shared too much by mentioning Bennett to Kenny - so she moved on.

"Did Rachel talk about her routine during class? Can you recall if she mentioned where she'd be going after school?"

He thought for a second. "I don't think so. Not that I remember. She used to. I mean she used to talk about gymnastics at length, how hard she'd trained and where she was off to next. Since she stopped competing she became more of a girlie girl." He paused to pick some paint from his watch strap. "Oh my, that's not very politically correct, is it? What I mean is, lately, she was always chatting about boys and make-up and parties. She started to gossip more. But knowing Rachel and how she conducted herself in class, if she'd told anyone she was going to yoga that night, the whole class would have heard. I mentioned before that she could be a bit of a foghorn, didn't I?"

Cooper nodded. "So, just to confirm. She didn't seem anxious or stressed?"

"Not at all. She was more angry than anxious. Like I said, she was a bit short with Will."

Cooper got to her feet. "Thank you, Brian. I won't keep you any longer. Could you tell me where I'd find Pete Parke?"

"Are my ears burning?"

Cooper turned to the door to see a rotund man in head-to-toe Adidas approaching.

"You must be Detective Erica Cooper? Linda sent me to talk to you about Shelly Smith."

Cooper thanked Brian Hutchins again and shook the newcomer's hand.

"I've been told you taught Shelly on Wednesday afternoon." Cooper's eyes flicked to the door as Tennessee entered the room. He introduced himself to Pete Parke and sat next to Cooper.

"Yes," he confirmed. "She was in my PE class. Dreadful thing to happen to her and Rachel. Just dreadful. Please tell me you're closing in on whoever did this?"

"I can't comment on that just yet, but I can tell you we're doing all we can."

"I couldn't believe it when Terry called me. In a right state he was."

"Terry?" asked Cooper.

"My brother, Terrance. He was the one who found poor Rachel. He and his wife, Gwen. They're torn up. Gwen's refusing to go back to the beach and she loves the sea. It's not the kind of thing you can un-see though, is it?"

Cooper gave him a sympathetic look. It was true. She'd seen countless dead bodies since joining the force, and she'd yet to forget a single one of them.

"Mr Parke—"

"Pete, please."

"Pete, tell me about that PE class on Wednesday afternoon. How did Shelly seem?"

Pete tugged at the hem of his sweatshirt. It was slightly fraying and in need of a trip to the washing machine.

"She... she seemed her usual self, I guess."

"And what was her usual self?" asked Cooper.

Pete's lips folded inward while he thought. "Bubbly," he said once he found the word. "She was bubbly with her friends. She was a bit annoyed at me, like."

Tennessee wiggled out of his coat. "Why was that?" he asked.

The PE teacher took a deep breath. "She didn't want to do PE that day. Told me she had her period. She hoped I'd be, I don't know, grossed out, tell her to sit and rest, send her home, who knows. Anyway, I told her if she needed sanitary products, she should pop to the school medical room and be back in the shed within ten minutes. I don't think she was impressed."

Cooper could empathise. She'd used that old chestnut once or twice in her day. What girl hadn't?

"The shed?" she asked.

"That's what we call the sports hall," answered Pete. "The big wooden building across the other side of the field. The kids started calling it the shed and it stuck."

Tennessee removed the lid to his biro and held it between his lips. "You said Shelly had been bubbly with her friends. How was she with the other children in the class, the ones she wasn't close with?"

Pete pulled his lips in again and let out a low hum. "She could be a little..."

"You can say it, Pete," said Tennessee. "I understand people don't wish to speak ill of the dead, but it's important we get a clear picture of Shelly and how she was in the days leading up to her death."

He hummed again. "Okay. She was a little bitchy. That's such a terrible way to describe it, but I can't think of a better way."

"Bitchy in what way?" asked Tennessee.

"Well, she'd make fun of some kids if she didn't approve of their clothes or hair. You know what I mean?"

"She was a bully?" asked Cooper, thinking about how Tina had almost sounded scared of Rachel Pearson. Shelly was beginning to sound the same.

"Sometimes," replied Pete, his lip curling in disgust at himself for talking about his former student that way.

"Please think carefully," urged Cooper. "Did she bully anyone the last time you saw her?"

He shrugged. "It's a big class. Thirty-two unruly teenagers, one teacher and a load of shuttlecocks flying about. Sorry. If she did, I didn't notice."

BACK IN THE WARM serenity of her Tynemouth terrace, Cooper frowned at the empty casserole dish. She'd have to return it to Atkinson at some point. Social etiquette would dictate that she should cook something for him in return, but there was more chance of pigs flying over the Tyne Bridge than her subjecting someone she liked to her feeble excuse for cooking. She'd take him to a restaurant. She'd wait for this awful case to be out of the way and for her hair to grow into something resembling a cute pixie cut, then she'd ask him to join her for dinner.

Upstairs, Tina was still not speaking to either parent, and loud music had been blasting from her room for hours. She'd hung up on Kenny and refused to open her bedroom door to Cooper. An offer of takeaway pizza couldn't even tempt her out.

She doesn't even like music, thought Cooper. She never listened to the radio and rarely watched music videos on YouTube. The only reason for Tina's sudden interest in Slipknot was to annoy Cooper by making the house too loud for her to watch television.

It had been a productive day, so Cooper smiled as she sat down on the sofa. The joke was on Tina. Little did her daughter know, Erica Cooper had been quite the metalhead in her youth. That's how she'd met Kenny. Cooper hadn't been able to see a damn thing from the back row of the Metallica concert, but after a third beer, she'd had the bright idea to crowd surf to the front. Hundreds of hands guided her towards the band, and when she finally dropped, she landed straight into Kenny's arms. He'd been broad and strong and his aftershave had sent her into a blushing mess.

Cooper kicked off her shoes and bobbed her head back and forth to the music while she thought back to her younger years. It took her three songs before she realised she had eight missed calls from Chief Superintendent Howard Nixon.

- CHAPTER 19 -

SUPERINTENDENT HOWARD NIXON'S VOICE was twenty decibels higher than usual. "Cooper," he barked, "where the bloody hell have you been? Two kids never made it home from school."

Cooper got straight to her feet and plugged a finger in her free ear to dull the music coming from Tina's room. "From Tynemouth Academy?"

"Yes. Jasmine Lee, fifteen, and Reuben Jones, sixteen."

"Fucking hell." Cooper's heart was already racing. "But we have Bennett in the cells."

"Calm down, Cooper. I need you focused. We know fine well the evidence against Bennett is sketchy at best. The killer might still be out there."

"Or Bennett has an accomplice?"

"That's a possibility. Now chances are these kids are fine. Just two kids arsing about and giving their parents the runabout, after some attention, you know."

"We can't take that chance, sir, not if the killer's still on the loose. Not if there's a chance he's targeting the school."

"Exactly, but we're not going to panic. I've approved the chopper. It should be airborne within ten minutes."

Cooper pulled on her boots. "I need numbers, sir. As many uniforms as you can spare."

"I'll do what I can, Cooper. There's been a major disturbance in town. A pub brawl's got out of hand and knives have been drawn. It's a blood bath. West Yorkshire and Cumbria have offered support, but it'll take an hour at least for their units to arrive—"

"Dogs?"

"Already prepped. Handlers are at the homes getting items of clothing so the dogs know the scent. They'll then follow any trail from the school." Nixon paused for breath. "Cooper, you know how I feel about relying on neighbouring forces. It's embarrassing. It makes us look weak and ill-prepared."

"There's no shame in asking for help, sir."

"I beg to differ. Commissioner Begum's breathing down CC Davison's neck and he, in turn, is breathing down my neck. Davison's requested a meeting with me tomorrow. We need to find those kids tonight, Cooper, or someone's head'll be on the chopping block, and it won't be mine. Do I make myself clear?"

"Crystal." Cooper checked her watch. "We should notify the media. We've missed the six o'clock news, but I want those kids' faces all over the local press's social media. I want the news channels ready to run an appeal at ten o'clock if we haven't found them by then. I want everyone north of Durham and south of the border out looking."

Nixon coughed. "I'll get the guys in the press office onto it; they'll want a press conference. You know the tabloids are going to want a face to go with the story, and you're the SIO."

"There's no time for that." Cooper grabbed her keys. "If they want me, they can come and find me. I'm joining the search."

"Cooper—"

It is you who will have to make a choice. Was this what Charity Mae had warned her about? Cooper was not interested in playing the media darling to appease her boss, even if it would be a sign of strength for the department. She could drum up more publicity by speaking to the press, but she preferred to be more hands-on. Surely her time was better spent doing what she did best.

"Sir, I live in Tynemouth. I grew up in Tynemouth. These are my streets. These people are my people, and if two kids are missing, I'm going be out there helping to find them. Potts can handle the press. Now, where's my team?"

There was a moment of silence from Nixon. Cooper assumed he was biting his tongue after his DCI cut him off. She heard a sigh, and then, "Daniel's with Martin. They've just left the Lee household in Cullercoats and are on their way to the Jones's on King Edward's Road. Keaton and Sutherland are briefing a search party on Front Street."

"I'll meet them there," Cooper said before hanging up. She spun on her heels. Her instinct as a member of the force was to get out there as soon as possible, her instinct as a mother was to protect her child. She stormed upstairs and walked into Tina's room without knocking and pulled the stereo's plug from the wall.

"Hey!"

"Hey, nothing," snapped Cooper.

Tina was sitting crossed-legged on her bed with textbooks fanned out around her. Her hair was a mess and she'd clearly been crying, but Cooper would have to put the parenting on hold.

"Listen. Two kids from your school have gone missing. It'll be on the news soon enough. I need to join the search—"

Tina sat up and straightened her posture. Her brows knitted together, and her eyes scanned back and forth over Cooper's face. "Can I help?"

"No. Absolutely not. I need you to make a choice and make it quick. I can drop you at your dad's, or you can lock the doors from the inside and promise to not let anyone in other than me."

Tina wiped her eyes and left a trail of mascara across her face. "I'll stay here... If you're sure I can't help."

Cooper wrapped her daughter up in a bear hug and spoke into her birds-nest-hair. "I'm sure. I love you so much, Tina."

She released her and quickly checked the latches on all the upstairs windows and motioned for Tina to follow her downstairs where she double-locked the backdoor and checked the kitchen window.

"Here," said Cooper, handing Tina a paring knife. "Take this. Lock the door behind me and secure the chain and bolts. I want you to text me every fifteen minutes, no exceptions. Do you understand me?"

Tina nodded. Her face had tightened and she suddenly looked five years older. "Yes, I do. But, Mum, the knife...."

"Just in case," Cooper said. She gave Tina a meaningful look. "If you need to use it, don't hold back. Okay?"

Tina swallowed and let the thought mull around her mind for a moment. "Okay," she replied in less than a whisper.

"Every fifteen minutes?"

"Every fifteen minutes."

Cooper closed the front door behind her and waited until she heard all the locks click into place before running in the direction of Front Street. As she ran, she pulled her phone out and called Kenny. The call went straight to voicemail.

"Kenny. It's Erica. I might be wrong about that suspect. Two kids from the academy have gone missing; I'm joining the search party. Tina's at home, the house is secure, and she has strict instructions to only answer the door to me. Can you call her every half hour? Text me when you get this. Oh, and don't go round there unless she asks you to; you might get stabbed."

Cooper found Sutherland and Keaton outside Marshall's fish and chip shop. A row of men and women in reflective gear were fanning out across the street, torch lights sweeping back and forth. Front Street was the centre of Tynemouth village. At its western end, a village green sported a statue of Queen Victoria, and at its eastern end, you'd find the North Sea. In between, the street played host to wine shops, pubs, bars, seafood restaurants and quaint B&Bs.

"What's the score?" Cooper asked, clutching her chest. She hadn't expected to need to run twice in one day. Sutherland watched the search party split in two, half heading north onto Hotspur Street and half heading south through an alleyway between two bars. He guided Cooper inside the fish and chip shop where the warmth from the heaters and the friers helped restore feeling to her extremities. They took a seat at one of the tables near the door.

He opened his notes. "Jang-Mi Lee - known as Jasmine - and Reuben Jones stayed late at school for something called culture club."

"Yes," said Cooper with a nod. "Artsy stuff?"

"Aye," confirmed Sutherland. He slid two photographs across the formica tabletop. "The club finished at four-thirty, and the teachers who run the club walked the students to the front gates. From there, they were in sight of the officers stationed at the front of the school. Some of them were met by parents, others walked off. The officers at the school this afternoon were Andrews and Kowalski; they haven't reported anything unusual."

Cooper looked down at the photographs. Jasmine Lee was of far-eastern descent, with poker-straight black hair, a heart-shaped face and ears - that unfortunately - could rival those of Prince Charles. Reuben Jones was a slim boy with pale skin, grey eyes and a trendy sculpted hairstyle that Oliver Martin would approve of.

"Jasmine and Reuben left on foot?" Cooper asked.

"Yes, with Freya White," said Sutherland. "Jasmine suggested fish and chips, so the three of them cleared it with their parents and came here. I've spoken to the staff and they have confirmed the three arrived here at around four forty. Freya tells us that Jasmin and Reuben were courting, and she felt like a third wheel."

Keaton rolled her eyes. "Courting? All right, grandad."

"Less of your cheek," he retorted. "Courting, dating, gannin' oot, an item, whatever you call it. They were a couple. Anyhoo, this Freya lass was feeling awkward 'cause Jasmine and Reuben spent more time snogging than talking to her. So she left."

Keaton had tipped a small pile of salt onto the table and used her fingers to swirl it around. "No one says snogging anymore either."

Sutherland scowled but remained on task. "Freya got home at ten past five. They'd all agreed to be home by six, so when Jasmine didn't show by six twenty, her mother called her. Jasmin's phone is either turned off or out of battery. Same for Reuben's parents. His phone's off as well. They got hold of Freya at six-thirty and by seven they'd called the police."

Cooper checked her watch; it was gone eight. "What time did Jasmine and Reuben leave here?" she asked.

Keaton broke free from her daydream. "Best estimate they could give us was half five."

"And no one's seen them since?"

Keaton shook her head. "Not that we've been able to ascertain. We have people checking with everyone who went to the culture club - a lot of them are out looking - and we've shown their pictures to all the businesses on Front Street."

At that moment, a canine unit entered Marshall's. An older woman with platinum hair shouted from behind the counter, "Sorry love, no dogs allowed apart from guide... Oh."

She blushed realising the dogs were here on business and not pleasure.

One dog sniffed the air; the other had his nose glued to the ground. They headed straight to the third table on the right and let out yelp-like barks. It was amazing; the dogs could still pick out Jasmine and Reuben's scents over the smell of vinegar and batter. A handler fed them both a treat as they turned out the shop and headed west up Front Street.

"I take it, that's where the kids were sat?" asked Cooper.

Sutherland nodded. "Aye. Let's hope they find those kids safe and sound."

"If anyone can, the dogs can." Cooper stood. "But that being said, let's get out of here and help. Where are the volunteers?"

Keaton opened her phone. "They're in groups of about ten to fifteen and spread out over Tynemouth as well as Shields and Cullercoats," she said, referencing the town to the south and the village to the north. "They're using *hashtag find Jasmine and Reuben* on Twitter to organise themselves. Let me see, ah yes, here we are. A group just finished combing Longsands beach and are moving onto King Edward's Bay. Another group are zigzagging up and down the back lanes around Preston Grange. They have a WhatsApp group too, they've added me, so I'll know straight away if anything comes up."

Cooper was impressed. "What about the teachers?"

"The three who taught the club are with a bunch of other staff members and were scouring the Fish Quay last I heard."

"Right, let's start with them. Then I want to meet Freya."

THE FISH QUAY ON the north shore of the River Tyne was the industrial hub of North Shields, a proud fishing town famous for its crab shacks and smokehouses. Cooper, Sutherland and Keaton jogged down Ropery Stairs - 120 steep steps that connected the old lower and upper towns - and found the search party on the quay.

Cooper discreetly checked her phone and was relieved to find three messages from Tina. The most recent read, *I'm fine, or I would be if Dad stopped calling.*

Brian Hutchins was on his knees, shining a torch under parked cars. "Oh, thank goodness you're here," he said when he spotted Cooper and company. His glasses were perched on his head, and he was wrapped up as if ready to trek to the North Pole. He shook Cooper's hand and introduced himself to Sutherland and Keaton.

"I can't believe it. I just can't," he said, his voice trembling. He drew the attention of two other teachers who came over to flank him on either side.

"I'm Phillip Dunn, this is Catherine Grainger," said a short man in a flat cap. Catherine Grainger had wild, red curls and was as small and thin as Cooper.

"I feel awful," said the slight redhead. "Just awful. We should never have let them walk home. It's all our fault."

"Don't say that," said Brian, a hand coming to rest on his colleague's shoulder.

Phillip agreed. "We walked them to the gates, Catherine. The police were there. We can't very well drive them home ourselves. You know the rules."

"Yes..." she sniffed and began to wring her hands together, "but the rules shouldn't apply now. These are special circumstances."

"Child protection rules are in place for a reason," started Brian, but Catherine cut him off.

"Well, they haven't done an outstanding job tonight, have they? The rules haven't kept them safe tonight. Oh lord, what if something's happened? What if they've been killed?"

"Let's not get ahead of ourselves," said Cooper, though she felt the same way. Her gut churned round and round and filled her with the overwhelming feeling that they were already too late. "Please take a moment and then talk me through this afternoon. Tell me about Jasmine, Reuben and Freya."

Cooper waited a few seconds whilst the troubled teachers gathered their thoughts. Around her, other staff members were checking behind bins, shining their torches over the side of the dock to look into the fishing boats, and were popping in and out of the establishments that lined the quay. As someone entered an Italian restaurant, the smell of garlic temporarily overpowered the scent of the river, and a surge of laughter erupted from a pub named the Salty Sea Dog. All around them, people were going about their business and enjoying their evening, unaware that something diabolical could be happening at this very moment.

"Let's walk and talk," suggested Keaton, an idea which seemed to please Brian, Phillip and Catherine. It helped them feel useful.

Brian turned his torch back on and scanned the ground. "We were sculpting in class this afternoon."

"I remember you telling me," said Cooper, taking a second to count how many people were in the search party. There must have been at least twenty-five of them.

"They did well. The whole group, I mean. They seemed to enjoy it," he continued.

"Well, Freya enjoyed it," said Phillip Dunn. "She was very keen on culture club. Jasmine was, I mean is, her best friend. They're inseparable. Reuben isn't exactly a natural at music or art. I think he feels he's a bit on the cool side to be there. He comes to the club because Jasmine does, and Jasmine comes because Freya does. You get the idea."

Sutherland and Cooper gave each other a look. As parents of secondary school pupils, they most certainly did understand.

"But they tried their best," said Catherine. "Jasmine's sculpture turned out rather well tonight. We were recreating Henri Moore pieces. In miniature, obviously."

"How did the three of them seem tonight?" asked Cooper.

"Happy," answered Brian. He strode away for a moment to check in with another member of the search team and returned.

"Yes," said Catherine, "happy, giggly, the usual. Some clay was thrown about at one point, but it was in good jest."

"Who threw it? And at whom?" asked Cooper.

"Reuben threw it at a young chap named Greg."

"Greg Mason?" asked Cooper.

Catherine nodded. "Yes, that's the one."

Cooper's face betrayed nothing, but she could see Keaton making a note and showing it to Sutherland. This wasn't the first time they'd heard that name.

"Did Greg walk home?"

Catherine looked down as she thought. "Hmm. I think so." She looked to Phillip.

"I can't remember, sorry."

"What time did the club finish?" Cooper said, moving on.

"Just before four-thirty," answered Brian. "As Phillip said, we walked the children to the gates. Then we returned to the art studio to tidy up. That took about ten, maybe fifteen minutes."

"Then what?"

"We said our goodbyes, signed out at reception and headed home ourselves. I was halfway through making dinner when I heard. There was no way I could sit down and eat a meal knowing two of our flock were missing. I called Brian, and he called Catherine."

"Yes, and before long we were all searching. The caretaker is here," she pointed further down the quay towards a vast, white cuboid of a lighthouse that jutted up into the dark sky. "So is Pete from the PE department and some of the admin staff."

"What's really interesting," started Brian, turning to look at his two colleagues. "Is who *isn't* here." He raised his eyebrows at Cooper.

Keaton's radio crackled; she moved away from the group.

"Now, now, Brian. This isn't the time to question—"

Brian cut Phillip off. "This is precisely the time to question her leadership... Or lack of it."

"Boss." Keaton bobbed her head to the left, drawing Cooper away from the bickering teachers.

"What you got, Keaton? Tell me it's good news."

"A hotline's been set up. Calls have been coming thick and fast. Mostly anonymous time wasters."

"Yeah, yeah, it's the same every time."

"Two stand out, though. First, a pretty foul call came in earlier from someone claiming to be the killer. Described what he was doing to Jasmine in horrific detail."

Cooper's heart jolted. "Have they traced it?"

"A payphone in Sunderland. A local unit's following it up. My gut says it's a fake. For one, he didn't mention suffocation or strangulation. Two, he didn't say anything about fancy dress or costumes, nothing about cards. And three, the things he was saying he was doing weren't done to Rachel or Shelly, if you catch my drift."

"I do," said Cooper, hoping Keaton didn't feel the need to elaborate. "What was the second?"

"A possible sighting. A lady who works at the estate agents at the top of Front Street called the hotline to say she saw a boy and girl in green school blazers getting into a car shortly after five-thirty while she was locking up."

"Any further details?"

"She reported the girl as having long dark hair. That's all I've been told."

Cooper sucked her lips in; they were becoming chapped from the cold. Over the smell of the Tyne, Cooper could sense the subtle aroma of imminent snowfall. "Right. Here's the plan. You and Sutherland find Greg Mason."

"You got it. But Mason's just a boy. Aren't we looking for an older geezer who thinks he'll become immortal from killing kids?"

"Perhaps," Cooper answered. "Or, perhaps we don't put too much stock in a walking fortune cookie. I'm inclined to say the perp's older, but I'm not chancing it. I don't want a hiding from Nixon, or Davison for that matter, because we didn't follow up on a lead."

"The CC?" Keaton's face was etched with concern.

Cooper sighed. "Nixon's feeling the pressure. It's nothing for you to worry about. It'll be me they come after if we can't stop this guy. Anyway, I'll meet up with Tennessee and have a quick chat with Freya White and the woman from the estate agents. I need a better description of the car before the additional units arrive. Let's meet at HQ in an hour."

Keaton brought her hand to the side of her head and saluted. "I'm on it."

- CHAPTER 20 -

ETHAN REED TRAILED AT least five paces behind his classmates as they walked to school the following day. Hassan and Miles talked about football – as usual – and if Ethan tried to join in, they would remind him that he was a soft southerner who should stick to rugby. Ethan had, on more than one occasion, tried to tell them that rugby players were tougher than football players, but they'd given a wedgie and pushed into a pile of dog shit for his efforts. He'd learned his lesson after that.

Ethan bowed his head to the wind and let his thoughts drift to Phoebe-May Corrigan, his eighteen-year-old neighbour who, praise the lord, had forgotten to close her curtains before changing last night. He knew he shouldn't have watched, but he was only human, and he'd never seen you-know-whats before. Not in the flesh, anyway, only in the dirty pictures Miles forwarded from his big brother's WhatsApp group.

"My money's on the caretaker," said Hassan, kicking a rock along the dirt road that led out the back of Northumberland Park.

"Ol' Pickett?" laughed Miles.

"It's always the caretaker. Haven't you seen Nightmare on Elm Street?"

Ethan's brain kicked back into gear when he realised his friends had given up discussing the missed penalty at last weekend's game.

Miles shook his head. "It's rated eighteen."

"I've seen it," said Ethan. "It's proper ancient. But I doubt Ol' Pickett killed those girls."

"Yeah," echoed Miles. "He's like a hundred and five. He hasn't got the strength to wring out his mop, let alone wring someone's neck."

Ethan wrinkled his nose. "Miles!"

"What? I'm just sayin'. It'll be that Will Harper anyway. My brother says he was arrested."

"And released," said Hassan.

"Whatever. It'll be him. Mark my words."

Ethan stifled a shriek as he walked through a spider's web. "Eugh. Gross." He dusted his blazer and tried to change the subject. "Did you finish the physics homework?"

"Yeah. And what a waste of time that was. What am I going to need physics for? I'm going into the army like me da and his da before him."

Miles finished a can of soda and tossed it into the bushes. Ethan wanted to say something, but he didn't want another wedgie. Instead, he promised himself he'd come back after school, pick it up and bin it.

The trail out the back of Northumberland Park connected the park with Tynemouth metro station. It didn't see much footfall, not in the winter anyway. Each side of the track was lined by grassy verges, nettle bushes and bare sycamore trees. As the three boys approached a dog turd the size of a cow pat, Hassan shoved Miles in the back. The youngster stumbled but managed to avoid getting his feet dirty.

"Tosser," said Miles before the pair began to play fight.

"Guys," said Ethan, trying to get their attention.

Miles and Hassan's play fight descended into some elaborate, choreographed kung-fu scene that incorporated all the cheesy lines they loved from action films.

"Guys," Ethan tried again.

Hassan repeatedly punched the air. "Yippee ki-yay!"

Miles removed his backpack and swung it around before flinging it at Hassan. "Hulk smash!"

Hassan grabbed the backpack and bellowed, "Do you feel lucky? Well, do ya, punk?" before hurling it towards the nettle bushes.

The boys watched the backpack fly through the air and land at the base of a tree, where the bodies of a boy and girl they recognised were propped up against the trunk.

- CHAPTER 21 -

THE TRACK BETWEEN NORTHUMBERLAND Park and the metro station was closed at both ends. Cooper met Tennessee at the station end and was shepherded under the police tape by a uniform who noted her arrival in the scene log. They were both handed covers for their shoes and asked to walk on thin boards that had been placed on one of the grass verges so they wouldn't disturb any prints on the track.

"Did you sleep?" asked Tennessee.

"Not really," said Cooper. "I joined the search again at around eleven after we'd finished at Freya White's house. Must have been about half two when I got to bed. Even then, I don't think I really slept."

"Same here. Hayley wasn't impressed at how late I got home. Said I'd take her out at the weekend to make up for it. There's some new vegan place she wants to try. It's not my cup of tea but if eating rabbit food gets me back in her good books, then just call me Bugs." He stifled a yawn and rubbed his eyes. "I could do with a jug of coffee and a cold shower."

As the pair followed the track, the white forensics tent came into view. "Well, Bugs, both of those will have to wait."

"Do you know what to expect?"

Cooper stopped for a moment and looked to the ground. "Only what Nixon relayed. Three year-nines found two bodies on their walk to school."

"Fancy dress?"

Cooper's eyes had glazed over. She wasn't looking at the ground, more through it. Her vision was unfocused, and she had the same feeling of dread in her stomach that she'd felt last night. She nodded. "Yes, an empress and an emperor." She could hear her voice quiver.

Tennessee placed a hand on her back and let out a long breath. "It's not your fault."

Cooper straightened up. "I know." Her eyes were red, and her stomach turned over as if she were on a roller coaster. "But I wish we'd saved them. I mean, the whole town was out looking for Christ's sake. We had the chopper. We had the dogs..."

Tennessee ran his fingers through his short blond curls. "We did our best."

"It wasn't good enough." Cooper fastened the top button on her coat and mentally counted to three. "Sorry. I don't mean to snap. I'll pull myself together."

Tennessee shrugged and watched a seagull fly overhead. "No need to apologise, Coop."

The seagull cawed loudly and soared to the chimney of one of the terrace homes that backed onto the park. Cooper wondered what she had done in a past life to be assigned such an understanding DS. She patted Tennessee the way he had done to her, and together they approached the tent.

Paula Keaton was standing sentry. "Morning, boss."

"Paula."

"Here's what I've pieced together so far. Three boys were walking through here on their way from Linskill Terrace when they found the bodies propped up against a tree. A male and female matching the description of Jasmine and Reuben."

Cooper's eyes darted over the tent. It was actually two tents, fashioned around a tall tree.

"Where are the boys now?" asked Tennessee.

"A couple of uniforms took them back along the track and into the park. They're waiting in the café for their parents to arrive. We found some blankets for the little tykes. They were pretty shaken up. Trying to act tough, but I could tell. I've got three little brothers, I know when a boy is struggling to keep it together."

A train rumbled past; Cooper waited for the noise to finish before she continued.

"Did they recognise the victims?"

"Yeah. They're adamant that it's Jasmine and Reuben."

"Did they see anything suspicious? Anyone hanging around?"

"Negative. They'll give full statements once their parents arrive."

"Who's breaking the news to victims' families?" asked Cooper.

"Sutherland and Martin are on it."

Cooper ground her teeth together. "How did we miss this? The park was checked."

"Tell me about it," said Keaton. "A volunteer group came through at about nine or half nine last night, and I was here with the police team at eleven-ish."

Tennessee snorted. "Right under our effing noses. Could we have missed it?"

"I doubt it," said Cooper. "My guess would be they were brought down here after the searches finished for the night."

Keaton blew into her palms. "Do we let Bennett go?"

"Not a chance," said Cooper. "He can stay there until he tells us where he really was during the other two murders. He had a key to Shelly's, and he had an unhealthy obsession with Rachel."

"Tech called me," said Tennessee. "It wasn't just Rachel's Facebook pictures. He followed her on Instagram too and had saved over twenty of her pictures to his phone."

Keaton's nose wrinkled. "Urgh," she grunted. "That's disgusting."

Cooper stifled a yawn and turned back to Keaton. "You been in yet?" she asked, pointing to the forensics tent.

Keaton swallowed. "It's not pretty."

"It never is." Cooper took a small tub of Tiger Balm from her coat pocket and rubbed a little under her nose. It was a trick Atkinson taught her over five years ago; it would help, but it wouldn't completely mask the smell. She offered the tub to Tennessee, and he gratefully accepted.

"After you," said Tennessee with an extended arm.

Cooper jutted her chin towards the tent. "Nice try. Get in there."

"Ladies first?"

"Get in, or I swear to Kevin Keegan, I'll transfer you to Sunderland."

The corners of Tennessee's mouth turned down; he bowed his head before slipping beyond the white fabric. Cooper followed. Her eyes widened and her mouth fell open as she took in the scene.

The girl was slumped against the trunk of the sycamore tree. She wore a full-length dress of red silk, with golden embroidery and an elaborate headdress decorated with gold flowers, red beads and red tassels. Under different circumstances, the dress would have looked beautiful. As it was, it looked horrendous. Mud and blood covered the delicate fabric, and a trail of blood ran down her arm. Cooper's eyes followed the trail to the source and found a deep wound to the girl's bicep; poking out of it was the corner of a laminated card. She could make out the *eror* of *emperor*.

Cooper brought the back of her hand to her mouth and suppressed her need to vomit.

A slain Roman emperor lay with his head on the Chinese empress's lap. There was nothing delicate or elaborate about how he was dressed. The boy was clothed in a cheap polyester costume consisting of a white tunic and red sash. The tunic was gathered in the middle by a plastic gold belt. The same plastic formed a laurel wreath around his head. Brown sandals with long straps that snaked up his calves completed the look. At least eight patches of red blood had seeped into the white fabric of the boy's tunic.

The magician, the high priestess, the empress and the emperor. The killer was progressing through the tarot deck at an alarming pace. Four down, and unless Cooper could do anything about it, eighteen to go.

Justin Atkinson approached Cooper. "He changed his MO. The boy was stabbed."

Cooper met his eyes and looked away again. She desperately wanted to talk to him about Saturday night, but it would have to wait. "What about the girl?"

"I think she was strangled." His tone was low; he spoke slowly. "There's bruising around her neck. We'll get them both to the Freeman as soon as possible so Margot can confirm it."

"Any sign of a murder weapon?"

Atkinson shook his head. "We'll go over this place with a fine-tooth comb, but I'd be surprised if we find a weapon down here. There isn't enough blood." He pointed to the boy's chest. "He has multiple wounds to the torso," then his hand moved towards the thigh, "but this one, this would have made him bleed out. The ground's frozen solid. If that had happened here, there'd be more blood. A lot more."

Cooper shuffled her feet and silently mulled over the information. "What else?"

"He messed up. In choosing that Roman outfit, I mean."

"In what way?"

"I couldn't find a shred of evidence at Shelly Smith's house, which suggests our guy wore gloves. With Rachel, there was a tonne of different prints because who knows how many people had touched that boat. We're still running them through the lab to see if anything matches the database, but it'll take a while to sift through them all. But with this young man, we have some beautiful prints on the plastic belt."

Tennessee folded his arms and turned to face Atkinson. "No chance they're the boy's?"

"Unlikely. I'm no pathologist, but I'm fairly certain the boy was killed before he was dressed this way. Besides, the prints are quite large, and the victim is on the slender side."

Cooper agreed. "Do you have any idea how the bodies were brought down here?"

"There's no access for cars," said Atkinson. He looked around as if looking for somewhere to sit. With no chair available, he sighed and squatted down, removed his gloves and hid his face behind his palms for a moment. "There are several footprints and animal prints in the mud, but they're not fresh. The ground was too hard last night to leave prints. Under the bridge was more sheltered. Hong found some wide tyre tracks under there. An off-road bike, perhaps?"

The pressure was getting to Atkinson. His eyes were sunken, and he looked to be shaking. Cooper tilted her head towards the tent entrance, a signal to Tennessee to step outside. Alone with Atkinson, she extended her hands and pulled the much taller man back to standing.

"I thought I'd seen it all, Erica. I've worked on child murders before, but this is something else."

"Yeah." She let go of his hands and looked back at the bodies of Jasmine Lee and Reuben Jones. "This is new territory for all of us."

"Listen, Erica..." Atkinson's voice wavered. "I'm sorry again. About Saturday. If I misread the situation, or I made you feel uncomfortable—"

"Jesus, no," she hushed. "I like you, Justin. You didn't misread anything. It's just..."

"It's just we both have a lot of baggage?"

"A lot of baggage and..." Cooper swept her arm outwards. "And a child killer to hunt down."

"I understand."

Cooper sucked her lips in for a moment. "I don't think you do," she said quietly. "I think we need to escape this for a while. We all need to switch off." She thought of Tennessee returning home to his pregnant wife and Keaton returning home to her partner and their three cats. She loved Tina, but she wanted companionship too. "Tomorrow night. Do you want to have dinner? No work talk?"

His face lit up. "I would like nothing better than dinner and no work talk."

"I'll text you," said Cooper. She couldn't bring herself to smile. Not in her current surroundings.

Back outside the tent and pleased to have fresh air in her lungs and sunlight on her face, Cooper found Tennessee and Keaton under a stone bridge watching a bunch of SOCOs conduct their business. There was a rumble of a car passing over the bridge and a rustling in the bushes. Cooper's eyes moved fast enough to see a rat disappear into a shrub.

"Oi, you two!"

Tennessee and Keaton approached. They both looked older. This case was ageing them all.

"Right, this is our timeline: Jasmine Lee and Reuben Jones left school at half four with Freya White, and they arrived at the chippy at four forty. Freya left shortly after five, and from what we can gather, Jasmine and Reuben stayed until around half past."

Cooper took a deep breath. "At around the same time, a woman named Sandra Pickering reported seeing two kids in green blazers getting into a car at the top end of Front Street. One male, one female. She couldn't confirm if it was Jasmine and Reuben, but she described the girl as having long, straight, brown or black hair, and she described the boy as slim and pale."

"Did you get a make of car?" asked Tennessee.

"Not quite. It's an estate car. Dark blue or black and had a round logo on the front grill. She thought it was probably a Vauxhall or a VW."

"Well, that narrows it down," he said with a sarcastic drawl.

Keaton adjusted her ponytail and smoothed her palms over her hair. "A volunteer search party came through here at around nine last night, and we covered the same area at eleven."

"The search was called off at two," said Cooper, stomping her feet in the hope of bringing some feeling back to her toes, "and the boys found the bodies at ten past seven."

"Ten past seven's pretty early for kids to be heading to school," said Tennessee.

"They were going to the school's breakfast club," said Keaton. "I've called the school to check, and they were all registered. The three of them go every day."

"So, the bodies were transferred here at some point between two and seven this morning. Margot should be able to narrow it down."

"They locked the gates to the park after the search," said Keaton. "How'd he get them in here? I can't see the perp carting two bodies in fancy-dress down here at six when the gates are reopened. This track might be quiet, but the main park would have dog walkers coming through as soon as the gates opened. He must have done it in the dead of night."

Cooper nodded. "You're probably right. Okay, Tennessee, you're up. How'd he get in here when the gates were locked?"

Cooper liked to test her detectives. She had no desire for a flock of yes-men. She wanted independent thinkers who could forge their own theories and come to their own conclusions.

Tennessee glanced around the scene. "I doubt he abseiled off the bridge. There's allotments up that way, though." He gestured up the steep bank. "They back on to the park. He could've broken into an allotment, or..."

"Or, he has an allotment," said Keaton. "I'll check who the leaseholders are when we get back to HQ, and I'll get a team up there to inspect every square centimetre."

"Good," said Cooper. "See if there's any sign of breaking and entering, trampled cabbage patches, damaged fences, you get the idea. If anyone objects to you poking around, get a warrant and get back in there. We're not going to be pissed about by a bunch of green-fingered old-fogies, especially if there's a chance one of them's our man. He could've stashed the bodies in one of the allotment sheds and moved them after the search was called off. I want every shed and storage box inspected."

She turned to Tennessee. "What else?"

"There's the change in MO." He shrugged. "Something changed last night. I don't think it all went to plan. Something makes me think he saw an opportunity to get Jasmine, but she was with Reuben, so he took them both."

Impressed, Cooper urged him on. "Good. Keep going."

"Or vice versa," he said. "They must know the killer, or one of them does at least. Teenagers aren't complete idiots. They'll have known not to get in a stranger's car. You're taught that from the minute you're out of nappies."

His eyes darkened, and Cooper wondered if the younger man was thinking about his soon-to-be son and how he'd have to warn him about the dangers of this world.

"Anyway," he continued. "He wouldn't have been able to strangle them both because while he strangled one, he'd have to fight off the other. I don't want to be sexist here," he looked at Keaton, "but he was probably safer killing the lad first."

Keaton's shoulders lifted for a second or two. "You're right. He probably stabbed Reuben to get him out of the way. He did it quickly and violently. Even if Jasmine leapt to his defence, it would be too little, too late. Then, he would have easily overpowered her."

The three stepped aside as Hong, Atkinson's assistant, shuffled past with potential trace evidence in sealed tubes.

"Which means," continued Keaton, "he either killed them in the car then took the bodies somewhere and hid them. Or, he took them somewhere and killed them wherever that somewhere is. Then he dressed the poor kids up and somehow brought them down here."

Cooper looked behind her. "They've found tracks in the mud. Justin suggested an off-road bike of some kind, but I'm thinking—"

"Wheelbarrow?" asked Tennessee, eyebrows raised.

"Bingo. It wouldn't have been easy to move two teenage bodies. Not over this terrain. Given the allotments up there, it would make sense. So, what's next, Paula?"

"I'm going to put out an appeal for further witnesses. Someone else must have seen them getting into the car. Let's see if we can get a better description."

"Good. Tennessee?"

"There's not a lot around here, but there's a few shops near the back of the park and some industrial units across the road from the front entrance. I'll have a word and see what they have CCTV-wise. I'll check in with the incident room too and see if any other calls have been made to the hotline."

Cooper sighed. "There's always the possibility he was caught on camera at the metro station. But one, I don't think this guy's that daft, and two, we're not that lucky. I'm going to get a team together and start the door-to-doors. Hopefully, some of the locals have door cameras. If not, I'm certain someone must have seen, or more likely, heard something."

"He might come back," said Tennessee. "They often do. I'll have the guys guarding the entrances watch out for anyone who cranes their neck a little too much."

"Coop," Keaton had folded her arms; they looked thicker than Cooper's legs.

"Yes, Paula?"

"That's four kids. All from Tynemouth Academy. Do we close the school?"

Cooper turned to walk back up the track towards the station. Keaton and Tennessee followed her. "I don't know." She let out another long sigh and felt anxiety flood her stomach. "I just don't know. I'll talk to Nixon, but I think the kids are safer in school than home alone while their parents are out at work. I mean, look at Shelly Smith. She was at home. I'll tell the officers stationed at the school to be on the lookout for dark estates, and," she paused, "I'll have young Oliver find out what type of car every member of staff drives. From Linda Webb to the admin staff, to the caretakers, cleaners and God-damned dinner ladies."

- CHAPTER 22 -

AFTER A FEW HOURS of conducting door-to-doors with the team, Cooper decided to head west towards the Freeman Hospital to see if Margot Swanson had any initial findings for her. Chatting to the locals who lived near Northumberland Park had produced some positive results. Cooper looked forward to discussing them when she got back to CID.

Margot was waiting for Cooper at a bus stop just outside the grounds of the Freeman hospital. She was wrapped up in a glamorous red duffle coat that accentuated her curves and perfectly matched the heeled boots and expensive-looking lipstick she was wearing. For someone who worked predominantly with dead people, she was remarkably stylish.

"Morning, Erica," greeted Margot in her soft Scottish accent. "Thought I'd meet you out here. I haven't had a smoke all morning. Where's that lovely Jack Daniel? Did you not bring him with you today?"

The corner of Cooper's mouth twitched. "DS Daniel is busy following leads."

Margot lit a cigarette and blew a billowing plume of smoke around her. "Pity," she proclaimed before extending an arm and indicating that Cooper and she should walk towards the park across the road.

Freeman Park was a popular area in Newcastle. It housed football pitches, a basketball court, a pond filled with mallards and sticklebacks, and a children's play area. The park was quiet at this time of the day; there was no one around save for a man with a black Labrador puppy and a woman pushing twin babies in a stroller.

"Shall we start with the girl?" asked Margot.

Cooper nodded.

"Cause of death was strangulation. There was bruising around her neck and damage to her larynx. She also had some nasty cuts to the palms of her hands. They look like defensive wounds. I suspect she tried to grab the knife as it was being used on the male. There's evidence that she's had sexual intercourse in the last twenty-four to thirty-six hours. However, there's nothing to suggest that it was non-consensual, no bruising or damage to the genital area."

"And Reuben?"

"The boy died from cardiac arrest following massive blood loss. He received twelve major incisions in total, nine of which were in the torso, including a puncture to his liver and his left lung. He has a slashing wound to his lower abdomen and another on his right thigh. There's a deep wound to the left thigh which went straight through the femoral artery."

Cooper winced. The bastard hadn't held back. Not one bit.

"There's slight fish-tailing to the entry wounds," continued Margot, "that suggests a single-edged blade. The depth of penetration indicates a blade of around twenty centimetres in length and three to four centimetres in width."

Cooper watched the black Lab jump into the pond and send the mallards skywards. The owner shook his head and shouted for the dog to get out of the water.

"A kitchen knife, perhaps?" asked Cooper.

Margot shrugged. "Something like that. He put up a fight, mind you. He has bruising to his knuckles and defensive wounds on his arms."

Cooper stopped by a bench and took a seat. The cold of the wood seeped through her trousers and made her shiver.

"Good," she said. "Hopefully, he hit the bastard hard enough to leave a mark. What about the cards?

Margot took a long draw on her cigarette. "The cuts were made by something very short and sharp. It was an extremely straight blade, like a scalpel or an exceptionally sharp Stanley knife. I'm more inclined to say a scalpel. Whoever did this had a steady hand; the cuts were perfectly straight. Jasmine's card was in her upper arm next to her bicep muscle. The killer inserted the emperor card but didn't stitch the wound back up."

Cooper looked sideways. "In a hurry?" she asked.

Margot shrugged. "Could have been, but the precision of the wound would suggest he wasn't. Reuben's card was inserted into his right forearm. I've removed the card, and it's bagged, ready for you to take. Forensics might be able to lift a print from it. You never know."

Cooper folded her legs. "We have a print from his belt. Hopefully, we can get another from the card, and fingers crossed, they match. How about the stitching?"

Margot stared ahead. "Reuben was stitched back up very neatly. And again, just like with Rachel, it appears to be regular thread that you could buy anywhere."

"What did the card say?"

"Heirophant."

"That fits the pattern. Do you know the time of death?"

"It's harder to tell with Reuben due to the lack of blood. However, extensive livor mortis on the back of Jasmine's legs and torso suggests she was laid supine after her death. The rigor mortis in her upper body indicates a time of death of between five and eight last night."

Cooper pursed her lips. "We believe they were taken shortly after five-thirty."

Margot took another drag on her cigarette. "Poor bairns didn't have very long. Additionally," she continued, "there was very little animal interference with the bodies. I'd estimate they were placed outdoors a maximum of three hours before they were discovered."

Cooper slid her hands into her pockets. "That ties in with what I suspected. Thank you, Margot. Do you have anything else for me?"

Margot shook her head and got to her feet. "Not at this time. Obviously, I've only just scratched the surface with these two. I'll run toxicology and some other tests, and I'll get back to you as soon as I can."

Cooper got to her feet and shook Margot's hand. Margot turned and walked away, following the path around the duck pond. Her bright red coat shone out on the bleak winter's day and made Cooper think of a lighthouse for some reason. She looked down at the grey coat and black boots she had opted for and felt dowdy in comparison.

Get a grip, she told herself. *You're a detective, not a fashion model.*

Cooper turned and walked in the opposite direction. She hoped that the little café would be open so she could grab some caffeine. She had a feeling she would need it.

- CHAPTER 23 -

THE INCIDENT ROOM AT CID headquarters had the distinct aroma of Nando's chicken. Tennessee had brought a boatload of the stuff in from the nearby retail park having said he was *hangry* and ready to hulk out at the next person that wound him up.

Cooper could hardly imagine her mild-mannered, baby-faced sergeant hulking out at anyone. He was always professional, a real gentle giant. Although, to someone Cooper's size, most people were giants. Thank goodness the days when the British police had a minimum height requirement were long gone.

Keaton unfolded a napkin and laid it across her lap. "Thank the lord for flame-grilled chicken," she said with a smile on her face.

"Hear, hear," agreed Cooper. "I feel like I haven't eaten in a month."

"And you look like it too," said Sutherland.

Cooper raised an eyebrow. The man could do with losing a few kilos.

He patted his belly. "Yeah, yeah. I know what you're thinking."

Cooper picked up a chicken piece using a napkin and tore a section off with her teeth.

"Have you heard from Tina?" asked Sutherland.

"Yeah. Kenny dropped her at school this morning, and she sent me a text during morning break. How about Caroline?"

"The missus and I decided to keep her off school. Sue had to go into work today, so the grandparents have come down from the farm to stay with her. Her grandad – Sue's pop – gave me the fright of my life when he pulled his hunting rifle out the backseat of their Land Rover. I started reciting the Firearms Act, but it was like talkin' to a brick wall. I made him lock it in the garage in the end.

Caroline thought she would have a day of sitting on her arse watching Netflix, but her grandmother has other plans. She's printed off a bunch of GCSE sample papers for her to work through today.

"Oh, Caroline's going to love that."

"She'll be begging to go back to school tomorrow, mark my words."

Cooper pulled her phone from her pocket; she had another message from Tina. "Listen to this," she said to Sutherland. "Tina says OFSTED inspectors have shown up. Linda Webb's flipped out and done a runner leaving Hutchins as acting head. Apparently, over a hundred parents turned up to take their kids home and the ones who are left are being forced to do tree-hugging-hippy exercises."

"Tree-hugging-hippy exercises?"

"Bonding. Share your feelings stuff."

Sutherland pulled a face and let out a harrumph.

Just then, Oliver Martin walked in carrying a bunch of files. He dumped them on the nearest desk when he spotted the haul from Nando's.

"Brilliant," he declared, scooping up a box of chicken and a portion of fries. "Who brought this in?"

Cooper pointed to Tennessee.

"Thanks, big man."

"No bother," replied Tennessee. "You're worth it," he added with a wink.

Martin stuck two fingers up at him and cleared his desk of empty soda cans, a tub of hair wax, and half a dozen notepads, and sat down with his lunch.

Cooper considered telling the guys to grow up, but a little banter and some lightheartedness wouldn't do them any harm. She gave the team ten minutes to complete their meals and get themselves ready for the briefing. Turning to face the murder wall, Cooper pinned photos of Jasmine and Reuben next to those of Rachel Pearson and Shelly Smith. She felt her heart split in two when she thought of the four lives that had been cut short. Who would these kids have grown up to be? What would have become of them if some psycho hadn't killed them? Doctor? Sports star? Banker? Journalist? Mothers? Fathers? Grandparents? Who knows where their lives could have taken them.

After ten minutes, Cooper threw her rubbish in the bin and waited for the rest of the team to do the same. Keaton announced her approval of the meal by burping loud enough for the whole building to hear.

"Charming. Let's get on with things, shall we?" asked Cooper. "The good news is we have a fingerprint from the belt Reuben was wearing. It also matches a partial print that Justin Atkinson pulled from the boat that Rachel was found in. The bad news is, it doesn't match anything in the system."

"So, we don't have a name?" asked Keaton.

"We don't have a name," Cooper replied, before adding, "yet."

"And Bennett is still snug as a bug in custody?"

"That he is, and making a right song and dance about the quality of food he's getting by all accounts."

Keaton stuck out her lower lip. "Aww, poor baby."

Tennessee let out a little chuckle. "He might not have wanted to give us an alibi, but I've got the ANPR results for his van for the times of Rachel and Shelly's murders."

Cooper met his eyes. ANPR stood for automatic number plate recognition. "Let's have it then."

"He was pinged headed north on the A1 last Tuesday evening. He passed Alnwick at seven-fifty and came off the A1 somewhere before Brownieside. He pinged again when he headed back south shortly after nine. He made the same journey on Thursday morning."

Cooper picked at her nails while she mulled over the information Tennessee had given her. "Why wouldn't he want us to know he was driving around Northumberland?" she muttered to herself. "This puts him forty miles in the clear." Her mouth fell open, and she clapped her hands together, not caring that she looked like a circus sea lion. "Oh, that little shit! A white van, A1 north, came off before Brownieside? Tuesday evening? That's when Doxford Hall was done over."

"The hotel heists! What else was going on at the time of Shelly Smith's murder?" asked Tennessee.

Sutherland did a quick search on his computer, but it didn't take him long to check the records. "The robbery at Newton Hall."

Tennessee slapped his hand on his desk and laughed at the ceiling. "Ha! We've only gone and solved Fuller's case for him. I can't wait to see his weaselly little face when you tell him."

The thought of telling Neil Fuller that not only did she have a plausible suspect for him but that she already had said suspect in custody made Cooper want to break out the dance moves.

A slow smile crept over her face as she imagined the scene. "I can't bloody wait, either. In the meantime, let's find out who's killing the teens of Tynemouth Academy. We have a number of statements from locals who reported noise at around half four this morning. One lady said her dog started barking at four thirty-seven after something activated her security light. We also have a gentleman with a motion-activated door cam that recorded a car rolling by very slowly with only its sidelights on. That was at four thirty-eight. The car looks to be an estate, but the footage is dark and grainy. Tech are going to see if they can work some magic with it."

"Did Margot give you anything useful?" asked Tennessee.

"Her timings fit with ours. Time of death between five and eight last night but not moved outdoors until at least four a.m."

Tennessee nodded and made a note.

"She also says the weapon used on Reuben was a single-edged blade, around twenty centimetres long and four centimetres wide. He fought back, so our guy might have a couple of wounds of his own. As suspected, Jasmine was strangled. The same scalpel style blade used on Rachel and Shelly was used for the calling cards. The card in Reuben read: *Heirophant.*"

"What's one of those when it's at home?" asked Keaton.

"It's like a pope," answered Cooper. "Tennessee, what do you have?"

"He definitely came into the park via the allotments. There're signs of disturbance including a broken lock on one of the gates and a tyre track going through a vegetable patch. It looks the same as the track we saw under the bridge. Justin's team are taking impressions to compare, but they looked identical to me. There's a hole in the fence at the back of the allotment and a partial trail coming through the bushes."

Cooper was pleased. They were getting somewhere. "Brilliant. Paula, did you find out who the allotments were leased to?"

"Sure did, boss. There are a few worth noting. First, there's a Frederick Webb."

"Related to Linda Webb?"

"That's what I wondered. Haven't checked yet, but I'll get right on it. Second, there's Victor Pickett. You recognise his name?"

"Yes," answered Cooper, "But I can't place it."

"He's the caretaker at Tynemouth Academy," said Keaton.

"Interesting."

"I thought so," said Keaton. "The last one we should look closer at is Isabella Lopez."

"I know that name too."

"When we arrived at the scene of the Smith murder, it was Lopez who Lisa Smith requested we call. She's a friend and colleague of Smith's."

"Whose allotment was damaged the worst?" asked Cooper.

"That would be an Alistair Goodwin. He's out of the country. On holiday in France for two weeks. I've spoken to him and he was very cooperative, had no problem with us poking about. Wanted us to catch whoever broke his gate."

"Not bothered about us catching a murderer, though?"

Keaton laughed. "Not so much. I heard from Hong earlier. He had some updates from the forensics team. Justin got a good set of footprints from the bushes behind the allotments; they match some from under the bridge. They haven't identified the specific brand of shoe, but they're size tens. There was a very small amount of clay under Jasmine's nails and some trace amounts of something called poly... polyvinyl...poly-vinyl-pyro-something. I can't pronounce it, but it's usually shortened to PVP."

"What's that?" asked Oliver.

"I looked it up and it's used in a tonne of stuff. It's a binding agent. It's in medicines, foods, make-up. The shit you put in your hair? That'll be full of it."

Martin's hands went to his head, and he checked that his style hadn't budged.

"We can probably assume the clay under her nails was leftover from the sculpting class," said Cooper. "But we should ask for some samples from the school to compare. Anything else?"

"Grey denim fibres," said Keaton. "On both Jasmine and Reuben's clothing."

Tennessee lifted his pen in the air. "That Xander kid had a grey denim bracelet around his wrist when we went to see him."

Cooper nodded. "Yes, I remember. But he had a solid alibi. Besides, so many people wear denim, it'll be tough to follow that one up. We'll bear it in mind, though. You have the floor, Tennessee. What have you got?"

"I have sweet FA. The lumber yards near the park have CCTV, but they only cover their front gates. I've taken a look and there's no activity in the early hours. Same story at the car wash. There's a Chinese takeaway around the back of the park with cameras on their door. It's closed now, but I've left a message asking the owner to get in touch as soon as they can. It opens at five. If I haven't heard by then, I'll go round myself."

"I've had more luck with the car," said Martin, flipping open a spiral-bound notepad.

"Go ahead," Cooper replied.

"Well, you asked me to find out what car every member of staff at the school drove. There's four that I would call dark-coloured estate cars, and all four are driven by people whose names we'll recognise."

Keaton sat up a little taller. "The plot thickens."

"Parke, the PE teacher. He was the last staff member to see Shelly alive and was part of the search party for Jasmine and Reuben. He drives an old grey Skoda. Phillip Dunn: music teacher, part of the group who run the culture club, and also out searching last night. He has a black Volvo V60. There's a blue VW Passat driven by Victor Pickett, school caretaker and allotment owner."

Ears pricked up and eyes darted about CID as everyone read each other's faces.

"And the fourth?" asked Cooper.

"A grey Mercedes E class, driven by a Ms Linda Webb."

Cooper raised her eyebrows. "Bloody hell."

"And Webb was notably absent from the search," said Sutherland. "The other teachers were miffed about it."

"I think we have enough to seize the cars. Oliver, make the arrangements. Paula, go with him. Give Justin's team a call and have them conduct a sweep for any forensics."

Martin picked up his phone. "Right away, Coop."

"Last but not least," she turned to Sutherland. "Tell me tech came back with something?"

"They're still working through the laptops and phones from the four kids. One thing they did mention was that all three girls had secret Instagram accounts."

"What do you mean by secret?"

"They had two accounts each. A nice, polite one for their families to follow. Wholesome pictures of family gatherings, cute pictures of pets, you get the idea. Their second accounts were followed by school friends and the pictures were not so wholesome. Drinking, smoking weed, less clothing, more skin."

Cooper knew the second she got home, she'd check Tina's phone for secret social media accounts.

"There's some private messages between Shelly and Jasmine regarding a 'Dunk the Hunk', whoever he is."

Cooper shook her head and wracked her brains. "I can't recall a Duncan from the lists of classmates and friends."

"Me neither. There's also some text messages between Reuben and Xander about Rachel and Shelly. They were sent after the girls were killed and they weren't exactly kind. I've printed them off."

Sutherland handed out the copies and Cooper watched faces wrinkle as they read. She took a deep breath and tried to keep her thoughts under control. They were supposed to be eliminating suspects, but the list seemed to keep on growing. Right now, it felt like everyone was a suspect.

"I want alibis for everyone," she told the team. "I want to know where our four estate drivers were between five and eight. While we're at it, I want to know where they were at half four in the morning. According to my daughter, Linda Webb has done a runner from the school."

"Will Kenny know where she is?" asked Sutherland.

"Hopefully. I'll pay her a visit. As for Xander Wright and Will Harper, let's find out what they were up to last night and early this morning. If they have alibis, they'd better be airtight."

Tennessee stood up and smoothed his hands over his shirt. "But first?"

"First, you and I need to practice our smug faces. Neil Fuller awaits."

"RIGHT, YOU TIME-WASTING PIECE of dirt." Cooper marched into the interview suite where Ralf Bennett sat. He'd been handcuffed to his chair and an officer with a sense of humour had placed a chocolate bar and a can of coke just out of his reach.

Bennett's eyes flicked to Cooper's. "Let me go. I didn't kill them," he spat. "And what have I got to do to get a toothbrush around here? My mouth tastes like rabid badger vomited in it."

"Delightful imagery." Cooper leant against the door frame and folded her arms. "Mr Bennett, the good news is I am releasing you without charge."

"Ha!" His eyes lit up. "I told you I didn't do nothin'. Daft cow trying to pin—"

Tennessee slammed his hand on the table and pointed a finger in Bennett's face. The sad, bitter man shut his mouth and he swallowed anxiously.

"As I was saying," continued Cooper, "before you rudely interrupted me. The good news is that I'm releasing you. You are no longer a suspect for the murders of Rachel Pearson and Michelle Smith."

A satisfied look passed over his face, closely followed by a look of confusion as Detective Neil Fuller shuffled into the room and took a seat opposite him.

"The bad news," said Fuller, "is that I'm arresting you for illegal possession of a firearm and the robberies of six Northumbrian hotels. You do not have to say anything, but it may harm your defence if you do not mention when questioned something which you later rely on in court. Anything you do say may be given in evidence."

"This is bullshit."

"No," said Cooper. "This is justice." She turned to Fuller and placed her hand on his shoulder. "I'll leave you to it. Pleasure doing business with you, Neil."

Cooper maintained her professional composure as far as the double doors at the end of the corridor. When they closed behind her, she turned to Tennessee and they slapped each other's palms in triumphant high-fives.

- CHAPTER 24 -

It had been a long day, but it was far from over. Cooper took a window seat in The Lock café at Royal Quays Marina and watched Themis, an impressive thirty-five-foot yacht, manoeuvre from the Tyne towards the jetties. A slender woman with long, dark hair dropped anchor while a dashing man at the helm guided her in. He leapt from the mid-ship and secured the warps to a cleat.

Must be nice, thought Cooper, to have the freedom of sailing. Another day, another bay. She ordered a bacon and sausage sandwich that appeared big enough to feed a small nation. It took Cooper almost twenty minutes to eat it, and when she was finished, she felt bloated, a little nauseous, and in need of a nap. Sadly, she had work to do. She paid the bill and began walking around Royal Quays towards a modern apartment block where she understood Linda Webb rented a penthouse.

A gaggle of reporters lurked around the entrance to the building. Cooper thought she recognised one or two of them from press conferences, but before she could say 'excuse me,' she had a dictaphone shoved in her face.

"Do you live in the building, madam?"

"Do you know Linda Webb?"

"Do you think she killed those kids?"

The questions came thick and fast before a man with a bushy, auburn beard bellowed over the hubbub. "That's Erica Cooper, you daft shite." He held a microphone with one hand, and with the other, he held an ice pack over his temple. "She put Eddie Blackburn in Frankland. I'm Vince Shepard, Evening Chronicle. Is Webb a suspect? Is Webb the Tarot Card Killer?"

Cooper groaned inwardly. Did someone from the department leak the nickname, or did the press come up with it on their own? She pinched her nose for a moment and took a deep breath.

"The investigation is still ongoing," she said. "Any questions can be directed towards the press desk. Now, please let me through. And if I hear of you pestering anyone else who's trying to access this building, I'll have you arrested faster than you can say *extra, extra, read all about it.*"

Cooper pressed the intercom and waited.

"I told you to bugger off," came the reply.

"Kenny, it's me. Erica."

In less than a second the intercom buzzed and the door clicked open. Cooper turned and gave the reporters a stern look before making her way to the lifts.

"Are those vultures still down there?" asked Kenny as he opened the door to the penthouse. He pulled her in for a quick hug. The stress must be getting to him; Kenny Roberts was not usually the hugging type.

"They are," said Cooper, breaking free. "And one of them's holding an ice pack over his face. Did you have something to do with that, by any chance?"

Kenny didn't say a word, but he briefly glanced at his knuckles; it was the only answer Cooper needed.

Cooper stared at him and looked aghast. "For goodness sake, Kenny." She sighed before continuing, "How's Linda doing?"

"About as well as you can imagine. Come on through to the kitchen. She's making some horrendous looking health drink. Says she needs the vitamins."

Linda's kitchen was vast and sported sweeping views over the marina and the Tyne. White gloss doors were accented with copper trim and the appliances were all top of the range. The room screamed *high-end.*

"They think I did it," said Linda as she peeled a banana and threw it into an expensive blender. She was dressed in a silk dressing gown and fluffy slippers. "I heard them muttering in the staffroom. How dare they," she rambled to herself.

Linda opened a cupboard and pulled out a bunch of plastic tubs containing vitamins and supplements. She took a scoop of spirulina and added it to the blender along with a multivitamin, a calcium tablet, some activated charcoal, and a pinch of wheatgrass powder.

"Me? Me? That school was rated inadequate before I turned up." She pointed at her chest before hitting the button on the blender and whizzing its contents into a dark green sludge. She poured the contents into a glass and then held her nose as she drank. She rinsed the blender and popped it into the dishwasher before announcing, "I'm going back to bed."

Cooper let Linda get as far as the kitchen door before she said, "Your absence was noted last night, Linda. I'm sorry to do this, but I need you to tell me where you were. We can do it here or at the station."

Linda stopped in her tracks and placed her hand on the doorframe. She stayed motionless for a good ten seconds before slowly turning and looking back and forth between Kenny and Cooper. She folded her arms and stuck out her lower lip. "This is unbelievable," she hissed.

Cooper opened her notepad and poised her pen above the paper in a posture that suggested she would wait all night if she had to.

With a noise that reminded Cooper of Tina's teenage tantrums, Linda began pacing back and forth in front of her floor-to-ceiling window. "Fine. I, I left school at around three forty-five yesterday."

"That's rather early," remarked Cooper.

"I had a salon appointment. I got a haircut, not that anyone noticed." She flashed Kenny an annoyed look.

"Which salon? And how long were you there for?"

"Serenity Lounge. I was there about an hour, maybe an hour and a half."

Assuming that the appointment was at four o'clock, that took Linda's alibi up to around the half five mark, the same time Jasmine and Reuben went missing.

"Did you drive?" Asked Cooper.

Linda turned to face her. "Yes," she said with a clenched jaw.

"And can you confirm that you drive a dark grey Mercedes E class?"

"I do. How do you know that?"

Cooper ignored the question. "And what did you do after your hair appointment?"

"I came home and did some paperwork until Kenny came over at about nine. Was it nine?"

Kenny nodded.

"I didn't have the TV on, so it was a shock when Kenny told me about the kids."

Television or not, Cooper knew the news had been all over the internet and social media sites. What were the odds that none of her colleagues sent her a text message or picked up the phone?

"Did you speak to anyone when you arrived home? A neighbour? A doorman?"

"We don't have a doorman. And no, I don't think I saw the neighbours. You'll have to ask them."

"What did you do after Kenny told you about Jasmine and Reuben?"

Linda thought for a moment. "We had dinner. Thai food. Then we," she paused, "went to bed."

Cooper got the idea. She thanked Linda and asked Kenny to walk her out. Once they were alone, she lowered her voice and turned to Kenny.

"How did Linda seem when you told her about the missing kids?"

He shrugged his broad shoulders. "Dunno. She was shocked. She didn't cry or owt. Think she was stressed more than anything. That's understandable, right?"

Cooper did her coat up, ready to face the November winds. "I know on a personal level it's none of my business, but I'm here on business. Did you spend the night?"

"No." His brows furrowed, and a deep line appeared between them. "I left at midnight, or thereabouts. I didn't have a change of clothes with me so I went back to mine. Why? Is there something I should know, Erica?"

"I'm doing my best to eliminate her from the enquiries, Kenny, but she is a person of interest." Cooper saw concern etched on Kenny's face. "I'll keep you posted if that changes."

Kenny opened the door. "Do you still need me to pick Tina up?"

"Please. That would be great. But Kenny," she lowered her voice to a whisper, "no Linda, okay? Just you."

He nodded and gave her another quick hug. Two in one day. Wasn't Cooper a lucky girl?

"I think Tina wanted to spend time with Josh," said Cooper. "If you could pick them both up and bring them to mine, they can hang out there until I get home."

Kenny's mouth thinned.

"Come on, give the girl a break. No Josh bashing. They're allowed in Tina's room as long as the door stays open. I should be back by five."

"You're killing me here, Erica. But okay, I'll see you at yours at five. Stay safe."

"Same to you," said Cooper.

It was a pleasant surprise to be home at the time she'd promised to be. Such days were a rarity since Cooper had returned to work. But, she'd done all she could for one day and her pyjamas were calling. After a warm shower and a full exfoliation, Cooper changed into her favourite PJs and joined Tina in the kitchen, where she found her reading the case file on the Tynemouth murders.

"Tina, you know you shouldn't be looking through that."

Tina didn't even look up. "Why not? It's interesting."

"For a start, there are details in there that haven't been released to the public. And second, it'll give you nightmares."

Tina rolled her eyes.

"How are you coping with all of this?" asked Cooper, aware that she hadn't checked in with Tina other than a few text messages here and there.

Tina finally looked up. "I'm fine, I guess."

"You guess?"

She shuffled into a seat at the dining table. "Well, it's a bit weird, isn't it? Having four people you go to school with murdered."

Weird wasn't the word Cooper would have chosen.

"But I wasn't close to any of them," she continued. "It's still horrific, mind you. No one deserves to die like that. I don't think anyone has the right to take someone else's life."

Cooper reached across the table and took Tina's hands. "Are you worried?"

Tina averted her eyes. "Hmm. Not really. I keep looking over my shoulder, but the only one following me about is Dad."

"It won't be forever, T. We will catch whoever's doing this. Anyway, I wanted to talk to you about something. I invited a colleague over for dinner tomorrow night. I wanted to check that it was okay with you."

Tina brought her eyes back to her mother's but removed her hands from hers. It was either eye contact or physical contact, never both.

"A man?"

"Yes. If that's all right?"

"Oh, not Neil?"

Cooper laughed. "No, not Neil."

"Good, because he was a total wanker."

"Tina!"

Tina raised an eyebrow. "He was. Admit it."

"You might have a point," conceded Cooper. "Well, this guy isn't a *total wanker*, as you put it. His name is Justin, and he works in forensics. He's a few years older than me—"

"Do you like him?"

Cooper thought back to all the interactions she'd had with Atkinson. "He's a nice guy. Yeah, I like him."

Tina shrugged and got to her feet. "Then I like him too. You deserve a little romance after everything you've been through this year."

Tears formed in Cooper's eyes. It was a struggle to hold them back. She got to her feet, pulled Tina in for a hug and spoke into her hair. "You're brilliant, you know that?"

Once she released Tina, she removed a cookbook from the kitchen shelf. Until that moment the book's only use had been to act as an occasional doorstop. "Right, come on then. Help me choose what I'm going to make."

Tina froze for a moment. "Oh no," she said, her eyes widening. "No, no, no, no, no. You said you like this guy."

"I do."

Tina snatched the book from her mother's hands. "Then there's no way in good conscience that I can let you cook for him. He's not going to stick around if you give him salmonella."

Cooper scrutinised her daughter. "Nice to know you have so much faith in me."

"I have faith in *you*," said Tina, "just not your cooking. Look, I got an A in food tech. Leave it to me; I'll make something. All you'll have to do is serve it up when he gets here. He'll never know."

Grateful, but perplexed at how her daughter could out *adult* her, Cooper agreed. It wasn't that long ago that she'd described her daughter as a 'sneaky little genius.' She'd been right.

- CHAPTER 25 -

After what happened at the school gates with her father, Tina asked to be dropped off two streets away when Cooper drove her to school on Wednesday morning. Cooper couldn't blame her; the poor thing had been thoroughly humiliated. Josh was waiting on the corner as Cooper pulled up. He was playing keepie-up with an empty can of Pepsi. He threw the can into the nearest bin when he saw the car approach.

"Morning, Josh."

"Morning, Ms Cooper."

"Are you ever going to call me Erica?"

He looked at his feet and then broke into a huge grin when Tina jumped out of the car and took his hand.

"I might see you at school," called Cooper as Tina and Josh began to walk away. "I need to speak to a few people. Otherwise, I'll see you back home tonight. Your Dad's picking you up. Tina? Are you listening?"

Tina looked over her shoulders and hissed. "Yes. Be cool."

"Be cool?" muttered Cooper under her breath. "I wouldn't recognise what passes for cool these days if it slapped me in the face." She restarted the engine, tuned into Absolute Radio Rock and was pleasantly surprised to hear Guns and Roses playing. "Now this is what I call cool."

Cooper easily found a parking space on the road outside Tynemouth Academy. She was reluctant to turn off the radio until Sweet Child O' Mine finished, but duty called.

"Drew," she said as she approached PC Andrew Underwood, who was one of the uniforms stationed at the school gates.

"Ma'am," he replied, "the man with the two yellow Labs was back yesterday."

"Oh, really?" asked Cooper, letting the *ma'am* go, for now.

"We got the name and address. The bloke's called Nate Douglass. Lives in the village. I called Oliver Martin with the details so he can run a background check."

"What was your impression of Douglass?"

He scrunched up his face. "Told me he was only talking to those girls because his dog's ball had gone over the fence, and he was asking them to throw it back to him. He certainly didn't seem shifty."

"They never do."

"Yes, ma'am."

Cooper winced. There was something about that word that was like nails on a chalkboard to her. "Anything else to report?"

Drew Underwood shook his head. "To be honest, it's pretty quiet. A lot of the parents are keeping their kids at home."

"So I heard," said Cooper. "Thanks, Drew. I'll check in again with you later."

The glass doors to Tynemouth Comp slid open and Cooper entered the lobby. The atrium seemed sterile, cold and clinical. It was as if the cleaning staff had worked overtime to scrub away the horrors of the last week.

"Chief Inspector. Good morning." Brian Hutchins approached and took Cooper's hand in both of his. The art teacher stood with impeccable posture, he fixed a welcoming smile on his face, but his eyes were red and gave away the stress he and the other staff must be feeling.

"How are you this morning, Mr Hutchins?"

"It's Brian, please, and we're coping the best we can. I've brought in a team of eight counsellors, but we have around twelve hundred students today. If we're lucky, they'll make it round all the most vulnerable by the end of the day."

"What's the usual attendance?" asked Cooper.

"Almost two thousand," said Brian. "Did you hear we have OFSTED inspectors in?" He glanced at an antique clock that hung over the reception area. "Due at any moment. Talk about timing. I don't think it's a coincidence."

At that moment, a group of surly-looking men in business suits arrived.

"Oh, speak of the devils," said Brian. He removed his glasses from his pocket and popped them onto his face. His eyes appeared to double in size. He took a deep inhalation and held it for several seconds before finally breathing out. He turned to Cooper, "I'll assist you in any way that I can. The rest of the staff feel the same. Just let us know what you need."

"I need to speak to someone from the culture club. I understand you're busy so I won't keep you. Perhaps you can direct me to Phillip Dunn or Catherine Grainger?"

Brian raised his hand in greeting to the inspectors. "Of course. Catherine is on the third floor so it will probably be easier for you to find Phillip. I believe he has a free period first thing. If you follow this corridor," he motioned to his left, "right to the end, it's the last office on the right."

Cooper nodded her thanks and set off down the corridor, leaving Brian Hutchins to turn on the charm offensive for the box-ticking, paperwork-loving henchmen of the Department of Education.

When she found Phillip Dunn, he was slumped over his desk. His head rested on his forearms and his back rose and fell in a slow rhythm that suggested he was asleep. His flat cap and coat had fallen off the peg on the back of his door and lay in a heap on the floor.

"Mr Dunn?"

He didn't stir so Cooper gave a loud cough, jolting him back into consciousness. "Huh? What?"

"Mr Dunn. It's DCI Erica Cooper. We met—"

"At the search. Yes." He ran his hands over his face. His cheeks had the permanent flush of a man who consumed too much alcohol and he had two days' worth of stubble on his jaw. "Tell me, detective. Why was my car taken as evidence last night?"

Phillip sat back in his chair, his eyes running up and down Cooper in a manner that made her skin crawl.

"Jasmine and Reuben were seen getting into a dark-coloured estate car on the evening of their disappearance. A number of cars have been—"

"I helped try to find those kids and now I'm being treated like a suspect!" His voice took on an aggressive tone and his fingertips turned white where they gripped the wooden arms of his chair.

"They came to my house," he continued. "My wife was home. My kids were home. My daughter goes to this school. You know that? You should have seen the way she looked at me. Like she didn't know who I was anymore."

"Mr Dunn, it's important that we—"

"We're a one-car family. I had to take three buses to get here this morning. My wife had to get a taxi."

"Mr Dunn," Cooper's voice hardened. "I'm sorry that our quadruple murder investigation is an inconvenience to you, but if you're quite finished interrupting me, I need you to take me to the art department so I can collect some samples of the clay used during Monday's culture club."

"Why?" he asked with lowered brows.

Cooper didn't answer. "Then I need you to show me where I can find," she checked her notes, "Leroy MacDonald. He was Jasmine and Reuben's form tutor. Correct?"

Phillip nodded and got to his feet with a number of groans. "This way," he said. There was still no warmth to his voice. "So, who else had their car seized?"

Cooper followed but said nothing.

"Victor drives a blue Passat. He arrived on foot this morning. In here." He opened the door to a large open space that smelled of white spirit and body odour. Wooden desks were splattered with bright paint and covered in ink doodles, making each table a work of art in its own right. Paintings hung to dry on lengths of string that zigzagged across the ceiling like a clothesline.

A handful of children who looked to be twelve or thirteen removed their green blazers and donned coveralls. They rummaged through drawers and collected their materials for the lesson. A woman with thick, postbox-red curls and heavy jowls took a seat at the teacher's desk.

"This is Henrietta Winters. Substitute teacher. Stepping in while Brian is acting head," explained Phillip. "Henrietta, this is DCI Cooper. We'll be out of your hair in a moment; we just need some clay."

Eyes followed Cooper and hushed whispers flitted around the room as the students recognised Cooper as a detective.

Phillip entered a store cupboard at the back of the room. Cooper declined to enter the confined space with a man as grumpy as Phillip, so she waited by the door. He emerged after a few seconds of annoyed searching.

"Here. This is the clay we used."

He dropped a brick-sized lump of clay wrapped in clingfilm into Cooper's hands."

"Thank you, Mr Dunn. You've been very helpful." The temptation to use a sarcastic tone was strong, but Cooper's professionalism held it at bay. "Now, where will I find Mr MacDonald?"

"Upstairs. He shares an office with Pete Parke. Room thirty-eight." And with that, Phillip Dunn walked away with his arms folded over his chest. He didn't seem like the same man Cooper had met during the search for Jasmine and Reuben. His mood was understandable if she considered his daughter's reaction to his car being searched by forensics. Tina had called Cooper many names over the years but she'd never suspected her of violence, or worse.

Once upstairs, Cooper knocked on the door to room thirty-eight. A prompt reply told her to "Enter."

Leroy MacDonald and Pete Parke's office was a cramped affair with two desks that were too big for the room squashed in with filing cabinets and piles of textbooks. One half of the room was cluttered: papers, half-drunk cups of coffee, a newspaper, and at least six pens littered the desk. This was the side of the office where Leroy MacDonald sat. He pushed himself to his feet when he saw Cooper was not a student.

"How can I help you?"

"DCI Erica Cooper. I'm investigating the murders of Rachel Pearson, Michelle Smith, Jasmine Lee and Reuben Jones."

"Of course. Come in, come in. Please, take Pete's chair. He's in the shed teaching basketball to the year tens."

By contrast, Pete Parke's half of the room was sparse and tidy. His desk was clear save for two framed photographs and a bottle of Evian water.

Leroy MacDonald was a portly man with a thick beard and a bald head. He wore a crisp white shirt tucked into faded black jeans.

"Awful times. Just horrific." His voice was quiet and soft with hints of an Irish accent. "Do you have children, detective?"

"Just the one," said Cooper. "She goes here. Tina Cooper."

"Oh, of course. I thought I recognised you. I only ask because I have two myself and I'm finding the whole thing just so..." His voice trailed off. "I keep having nightmares."

"I can imagine," said Cooper, and she could. Only last night she dreamt someone was taking a scalpel to her chest as someone had done to Rachel.

"My two are younger. In the primary school in Monkseaton. Ben's nine and Julia's eight. I've enrolled them at the boxing club. Not sure what good it'll do against an adult but I want them to be able to throw a punch if needed." He turned and stared out of the window.

"You were Jasmine's form tutor?"

"Yes," he answered without turning back to Cooper. "And Reuben's. Joined at the hip, they were. Freya too. Poor lass hasn't returned to school yet. Can't say I blame her."

Cooper swallowed. The situation was horrible for everyone involved. "Can you tell me about Jasmine and Reuben?"

Leroy turned his back to the window and pushed his thumbs into the belt loops on his jeans. "They were sweet kids. Rebellious, yes, sometimes, but they weren't bad kids."

"Rebellious in what way?"

"Hmm." He mulled over his words. "Well, Jasmine acted like the rules didn't apply to her. She was put in isolation more times than I can count for uniform violations. Make-up, skirt too short, heels too high."

"Lots of girls like to dress older than their age."

"Oh, I know. I'm not trying to shame her, or whatever they call it. I'm just saying she didn't like following the rules. Reuben was the same. He liked to wear trainers, wouldn't tuck his shirt in or tie his tie correctly. What I'm saying is they liked to test their boundaries, see what they could and could not get away with. Then they were suspended for two weeks each last term."

"What for?"

Leroy sat back at his desk and began to run a biro between his thumb and forefinger. "Smoking marijuana on school premises."

Cooper's brow lifted. "Weed? In school?" Never in her metal-head youth of underage drinking and fooling around with boys would she have ever taken drugs during the school day.

"Yes. Caused rather a stir."

"Leroy. Can I call you Leroy? Shelly Smith's mother mentioned Shelly had been to a party recently where coke was available." Her mind also turned to Will Harper, who had reeked of weed whilst he was being questioned. "Is there a drug problem at this school?"

Leroy considered the question. "Yes and no," he said. "Yes. Some of the student body definitely use drugs. But, no, I wouldn't say the school has a problem. We're doing well in the league tables. It's incredibly rare something like that happens on school grounds. With Jasmine and Reuben it was a one-off, and as awful as it sounds, I think Jasmine was the instigator. I always got the impression that Reuben just went along with anything Jasmine suggested."

Cooper leant back in Pete Parke's chair. "It does make me wonder, who's dealing to these kids? Are drugs, or drug money, part of this?"

Leroy closed his eyes for a moment and pressed the heels of his hairy hands into his sockets. When he opened his eyes again he said, "If I find anyone trying to sell anything like that to my kids..."

"It's probably best you don't finish that sentence," said Cooper, though she felt the same way. "Can you recall if Jasmine or Reuben seemed worried about anything, or anyone, lately?"

"Not at all." Leroy shook his head. "They appeared not to have a care in the world. Very *que sera sera* kids."

"And their attitude didn't change in the last few days?"

"Not that I noticed. Not even with everything that's been going on. But to be honest, I'm only their form tutor. I only saw Jasmine at registration or if there was a problem. I saw Reuben a little more as I had him for biology three hours a week."

"Okay," said Cooper. "I won't keep you much longer. You said Jasmine and Reuben weren't bad kids. Tell me about their positive attributes."

"Well, by all accounts, Reuben could be a very sweet young man. Despite his rule-breaking, he'd often help teachers carry things, or he would hold the door open for others, that sort of thing. He was raised to have good manners. I could tell. He had decent grades in most subjects. He actually had a bit of a gift for biology. He told me he wanted to go into marine biology when he finished school."

Cooper had wondered where the lives of the four victims would have taken them. The world was now down a marine biologist. Perhaps he would have rid the oceans of plastic or brought a species back from the verge of extinction. She'd never know because Reuben Jones never got to follow the path he'd chosen.

"Jasmine wasn't academic, despite pressure from her parents. Mrs Lee was a bit of a tiger mum. Tried to push Jasmine into piano and violin. She had private tutors for maths and science, but it didn't help. Her heart was never in it. She loved sport, though. Pete thought the world of her."

"Pete Parke?"

"Yes. He said she was a born runner. Said she was like a gazelle on the track."

Cooper spun on her chair and faced Pete Parke's desk. Neither of the framed photographs was of his family. The first was a picture of the school's athletics team. Jasmine Lee was front and centre in a fitted running vest and tiny shorts. She was gripping a trophy and smiling from sticky-out-ear to sticky-out-ear. The second framed photograph featured the netball team. The seven first-team players sat on a bench with the seven reserves standing behind. The girls wore short netball dresses in the same shade of green as their school blazers. Cooper recognised two faces: Michelle Smith, wearing a captain's armband and cradling a netball under her arm, and fresh-faced, bare-legged Tina Cooper.

- CHAPTER 26 -

An uneasy feeling settled in the pit of Cooper's stomach. What sort of teacher had photos of his teenage students, rather than his family - or at least a pet - on his office desk? She put her concerns to one side so she could make a quick phone call to Tennessee.

"DS Daniel."

"It's Cooper. How are things at your end?"

There was unusual silence from Tennessee.

"Talk to me, Jack."

He sighed. "I'm not sure how to say this, ma'am. Shit. Sorry. I'm not sure how to say this, Cooper, but the Chief Constable's shown up. Looks a right flashy git in a designer suit and Rolex. He's been holed up in Nixon's office for an hour."

Cooper had to steady herself against a wall in a corridor of Tynemouth Academy; she felt as if she was falling. She knew Nixon was under pressure; she just hoped he wasn't throwing her under the bus. She felt small and feeble and vulnerable. She had to move quickly and solve this bloody case before it was taken off her.

"Coop?"

"Just processing everything. Do you have any good news?"

"Justin's been on the blower. He's finished with some of the cars."

"And?"

"And Dunn can collect his car later today. There're five sets of prints in the car, but none of them match Jasmine or Reuben. No blood or sign of a struggle. There's also no sign of the car being cleaned recently to rid it of evidence. No bleach or anything like that. There were green fibres. The same green as the school blazers but we know his daughter attends Tynemouth so they probably came from her."

Cooper walked along the school corridor, occasionally glancing through a classroom door and seeing a number of empty chairs. The school had an eerie silence to it.

"What about Pickett?"

"Only one set of recent prints. There's plenty of mud and soil in the driver's footwell, which ties in with him leasing an allotment. There's a muddy print as well, a size twelve."

"Too big. Unless he squashed his feet into a smaller shoe before dumping the bodies."

"Is that likely?"

Cooper puffed her cheeks. "Anything goes with this case."

"Have forensics started on Webb's car? Or Parke's?"

"Parke's car was immaculate. Must have had a full valet within a few hours of us picking it up."

"Hmm," said Cooper.

"Hmm, indeed. Anyway, Justin says they need to run more thorough tests to get to the microscopic level. It will take a little longer, but if there's evidence, they'll find it."

"Webb?" asked Cooper. She paused outside the girls' toilets.

"Well..."

"Spit it out, Tennessee."

"Linda Webb hasn't surrendered her car yet."

Cooper rested her back on the wall. "So go seize it."

"I wish we could. She wasn't home, so we called her to find out her whereabouts. She said she'd gone out for the day and didn't tell us where."

Cooper was astounded. Linda Webb was the most unhelpful, selfish, self-obsessed...

"Tech are tracing her phone signal, and we have ANPR requests for her plates. We'll have the car by the end of today, Coop. I promise."

She believed him. Her team could be like a dog with a bone at times. They did not take kindly to being messed about.

Cooper pushed open the door to the girls' toilets. There was a smell of bleach and cheap perfume. "Does Paula have any news?"

"Err, yeah. She mentioned some news from a couple of fancy-dress retailers. Want me to get her to call you? She's at the allotments with Hong."

"No, that's all right, Tennessee. I'll call her in five. I'll see you at HQ."

"Roger."

Cooper hung up and stared around the girls' toilets. She had a hunch the secrets of Tynemouth Academy could be found in here, and she wasn't disappointed. The walls of each cubicle were a maze of graffiti. Every ounce of gossip, every accusation, and every rumour was scrawled in marker pen. Cooper walked the length of the toilets, letting her eyes wander up and down the walls before dialling Keaton's number.

"Hey, boss." Keaton's voice was muffled.

"Are you eating?"

"One of the gardeners down here at the allotments, he grows the best apples I've ever tasted. The last of the season. Gave me a bunch to make a pie with. A bag full of quince too. He's helping us with our enquiries. Says the hole in the fence was definitely not there at the start of the week."

Cooper listened whilst she read the graffiti in the first cubicle. It didn't take long to spot the first musings that concerned the murdered girls: *Shelly deserved it.* Cooper put Keaton on hold and used her phone to take a photograph.

"Tennessee mentioned you had news from a fancy-dress store."

Will Harper is the hottest, was written in red pen. *Baby killer. Jasmin Lee had an abortion,* was written in black.

"Yes, boss." There were more chewing noises before Keaton swallowed. "A decent lead. An online retailer called the hotline. They received an order for three pope outfits to be delivered to a locker at Morrisons in Tynemouth. The buyer used PayPal."

"Do we have a name?"

Written in blue biro: *Xander is gay*. Scratched into the tiled floor: *Webb is a bitch.*

Cooper smiled at the last one. Then she saw *Hands off Dunk the Hunk. He's mine,* and worryingly, another line of graffiti that she couldn't turn her eyes away from.

"Just an email address," answered Keaton. "Tech have it. They'll see if they can get anything from it. Martin's working with the Royal Mail to coordinate when the costumes will be delivered. We'll get the locker number, and then we can post someone to keep watch. Intercept when he collects the parcel."

"Good work, Paula."

Cooper felt sick when she hung up the phone. She knew fine well that teenage girls were prone to gossip and spreading lies - she'd been one herself - but there was also a nagging doubt. Where there's smoke, there's fire. On the back of a toilet door, written in Tip-Ex was: *Rachel lifts her skirt for Paedo Pete.*

- CHAPTER 27 -

COOPER PRACTICALLY RAN ALONG the corridor. When she reached the school lobby she urgently banged her fist on the door to the school office. Behind the glass panel, the school administrator looked up from her keyboard. She had the office phone tucked between her ear and her shoulder and her fingertips moved at lightning speed over the keys. Cooper banged her fist again. The administrator looked around; she was red-nosed and angry-browed. She held up a finger in Cooper's direction, a signal for her to wait. Cooper was in no mood for whatever first-come-first-served system the administrator was operating, she marched into the office and pressed the phone's hold button.

"Brian Hutchins. I want to speak to him now."

A look of pure indignation formed on the woman's face. "He's in with the OFSTED inspectors, you'll have to wait," she said with a prim and put out voice.

Cooper took a step closer to the woman and invaded her personal space. She stared down at her, fury coursing through her. Around the woman's neck, hung a security pass bearing the name Norma Medford.

"Norma, I don't give a shit about the inspectors. He could be having tea with the queen for all I care. Go and fetch him."

Norma Medford huffed through her nose and got to her feet. "Well I never," she mumbled as she left the room. "Manners cost nothing, you know?"

It didn't take long for Brian Hutchins to appear. He was flustered, glancing back over his shoulder at the men in suits who had followed him out of his office.

"Norma," he whispered as he approached the administrator. "Could you take our guests to the staff room, please? see if they'd like a coffee and perhaps a tour of the science wing."

The school administrator bowed her head. "Yes, Mr Hutchins."

"Detective?" he turned to Cooper, shifting his weight from one foot to the other. "What's going on? Has someone else gone missing? Please tell me no one else has been hurt. I don't think I could bear it, I don't think any of the staff could, and as for the students—"

"Calm down, Brian." Cooper patted him on the arm and offered him Norma's seat but he shook his head. "What's going on?" he repeated.

"As acting head, you're now the senior child protection officer for the school, correct?"

He nodded.

"Have any complaints ever been made about Pete Parke?"

"Pete? Oh, I wouldn't have thought so. I've known him since I joined the school. Ten years ago now."

Cooper's mouth thinned. "That's not what I asked. I don't want to know if you think anyone has raised concerns about Pete Parke. I want to know for definite. Where do you store the school's welfare concern reports?"

"They're locked in a filing cabinet in my office, detective, but they're confidential. I can't just let you go through them. I think you'd need a warrant or—"

"Brian!" Cooper's voice was tense. She was doing all she could to hold herself together. She didn't have time to go back to Nixon and request a warrant. It would waste time she just didn't have. Who knew when the killer would strike again and if Parke was involved she had to find grounds to arrest him and get him out of the school and away from these kids as soon as possible. Every second counted. Letting out the tiniest of grunts, Cooper grabbed Hutchins by the elbow and frog-marched him along the corridor and into the girls' toilets.

"Staff aren't supposed to enter the student toilets," said Hutchins. "It's a safeguarding issue."

Safeguarding issue, thought Cooper, staff entering the student toilets is the least of these girls' concerns when it came to safeguarding. Cooper grabbed the door to the first cubicle and swung the door open with enough force that it bounced back on its hinges. She didn't need to say anything, she simply pointed at the accusation scrawled on the back of the door in Tip-Ex.

"Think we can take a look at that filing cabinet now, Brian?"

Hutchins pulled a key from his desk drawer and unlocked the bottom drawer of a filing cabinet.

"Here. This is where we store any reports." He pulled out a plain brown box file. "This file is for the current school year, and this one is for last year." He handed Cooper the two files.

"How far do your records go back? she asked.

"Five years. Then we move them to storage." Hutchins added three more files to the pile Cooper held in her arms and she watched his face crease.

"I seriously doubt there's anything about Pete in there. Most of the pink slips concern children with unexplained bruises, kids turning up to school hungry or in dirty clothing, that sort of thing."

Cooper dumped the box files on Hutchins's desk and took a seat in his chair. She opened the uppermost file and began to sift through the pieces of paper. Cooper was careful to keep the files in order, laying each pink slip face down on top of its predecessor so she could return them to the box in the exact order as they had been. Hutchins had been right about the contents of the slips; most were completed by teachers who were concerned about their pupils' home lives and it didn't take Cooper long to find a slip concerning Rachel Pearson. Catherine Grainger had completed a form after asking Rachel about the number of bruises on her arms one day. According to the slip, Rachel had told her the bruises were from playing with her neighbour's dog. Cooper handed the sheet of paper to Hutchins. "Was this ever followed up?"

The new headteacher adjusted his glasses and held the sheet at arm's length. He frowned and shook his head. "I'm not sure. It was reported to Linda Webb. If it was a one-off, she'd be inclined to believe Rachel, if not, it may have been reported to Child Protection Services."

Cooper made a note of the slip's number and placed it on the pile to her left and continued making her way through the pile on her right. A number of slips expressed concern over William Harper and comments that were overheard by teachers about his mother. And a student named Lola Greens confided in Todd Carpenter about Jasmine Lee and the pressure she was under from home to achieve good grades in her GCSEs. Greens had suggested Lee had developed anorexia from the stress. Again, Cooper noted the slip number and continued. Eventually, she stopped, stared at one of the pink slips for a long while and slid it across the desk to Hutchins.

"Were you aware of this?"

Hutchins propped his elbows on the table and Cooper watched his eyes shift left and right as he read.

"It says," started Cooper, "that on the eighth of September, two students complained about Pete Parke entering the boys' changing rooms after football practice and that he was carrying his smartphone. I'm guessing that if staff aren't supposed to enter the student toilets, they're also not supposed to enter the changing rooms?"

Hutchins nodded. "That's right, not unless we think bullying is occurring or a student is in need of first aid."

"And is it normal practice for staff members to have their mobiles on them?"

"Definitely not. We leave our phones in the school office during lessons and can check them at lunchtime and at breaks. Also," he rubbed his brow, "the changing rooms are classified as no phone zones. All the students know they can't take their phones out of their bags in the changing rooms. It's an instant detention. Not that we can really enforce it."

"And as a staff member, Pete Parke would be well aware of this?"

"Of course, look, these boys that complained, they were probably miffed that a teacher broke the no phone rule when they'd get disciplined for it."

"Or, they were rightly concerned that someone who should know better, entered the changing room when they were getting undressed and that he was carrying a device that can take images and record film." Cooper got to her feet. "Please excuse me for a moment."

Alone in the corridor, Cooper placed a call to Superintendent Nixon.

"Cooper?"

"Sir, I'm at Tynemouth Academy. I'm going to bring one of the teachers in for questioning. A man named Pete Parke. His car's currently at the lab. I heard it was very recently valeted, which is suspicious enough, but I found graffiti concerning him and Rachel Pearson in the girls' toilets here as well as a report about a safeguarding violation."

"Be more specific, Cooper."

"Yes, sir. The graffiti implied Parke and Rachel had a sexual relationship, and a report made by two boys accused Parke of bringing his smartphone into the changing rooms. I think this, combined with the fact he drives an estate car, is enough—"

"Bring him in," said Nixon. "Do you need assistance?"

"Kowalski and Andrews are stationed here. I'll have them escort him to HQ."

"Okay. But Cooper, don't arrest him unless it's necessary. Try to get him to come in voluntarily. That way, we can run some background and give the lab time to work on the car without eating into the twenty-four hours we'll get if we arrest him."

"Good shout, sir. I'll see what I can do." Cooper knew she might not have a choice. If Parke refused to leave the school or suspected something was up, he'd be unlikely to come to the station voluntarily. It was worth a shot, though. She hung up and dialled Sam Sutherland's number.

"Boss?"

"Hey, Sam. You got a minute?"

"For you, I have two. Keaton and I are putting together a plan for tomorrow. We're going to find out who ordered the three pope outfits."

"Great, let me know what you decide. Anyway, you spent the most time with Rachel Pearson's diary, didn't you? Did you find anything about the school's PE teacher in there?"

"Parke? Not that I can recall. Want me to go back through it?"

"Please. Can you ask tech about her phone, too? See if there was any romantic communication between her and anyone other than Will Harper."

"Aye, no worries. What's going on? You suspect the PE teacher?"

Cooper sneezed and hoped she hadn‘t caught something. ”Yeah. I‘ll have him in HQ within half an hour. Can you do me a favour and ask Tennessee to run a background check on him and have him pull up the guy‘s latest DBS check?"

DBS stood for the disclosure and barring service and was the standard check used in the UK for individuals working in schools and organisations where children and vulnerable adults were present.

"Aye. Anything else I can do you for?"

"No, that's it. I'll see you in a bit."

She hung up and re-entered Hutchins‘s office. ”Brian, I‘m going to ask Mr Parke to accompany me to the station."

"Good God. Are you arresting him?"

"Not yet. I understand he's teaching at the moment. Can you take me to him?"

A look of worry passed over the man‘s face. Having a member of his staff escorted off the premises while OFSTED were present was all he needed right now. He nodded, got to his feet and silently guided Cooper out a side door and across the school field to the sports hall known as the shed.

A basketball lesson was in full swing with rows of teenage boys and girls taking turns to dribble their balls up to the various hoops fastened to the walls and take their shots.

"Mr Parke," said Cooper as she approached. The man's eyes narrowed, and he wiped his palms on his Adidas joggers. Cooper spoke quietly so as to not attract too much attention from the class. "I'd like to ask you a few questions. Would you please accompany me to the station?"

"Now? I'm teaching a class."

"Mr Hutchins will have someone cover for you."

"But... Wait, am I...?" He looked around nervously. "Am I...?"

"You're helping us with our enquiries," suggested Cooper. "You want to help us, don't you?"

"Well, yes, of course."

"Then follow me."

The sound of basketballs being bounced off the wooden floor came to an abrupt stop, and thirty pairs of eyes followed Pete Parke as he shuffled out of the shed.

Cooper walked ahead and had a quick word with PC Kowalski before turning back to Parke. "This is Mr Parke; he's kindly agreed to help us with our enquiries. Could you drive him to HQ?"

Kowalski nodded and held the door to his squad car open. Parke's posture shifted, he swallowed nervously. Cooper wanted to keep him onside as long as she could so she adopted a softer voice and tried to put the man at ease, even though every instinct she had told her to cuff him.

"Mr Parke, this is PC Kowalski and PC Andrews. There'll give you a lift to the station and make sure you're comfortable. If you want tea, coffee or anything while you wait for me, just ask. We really appreciate your help. She laid a hand on his arm and the gentle gesture was enough to persuade Parke to get in the squad car.

Cooper kept Parke plied with tea and chocolate digestives for over an hour while Tennessee worked his magic trawling various databases. The first thing he noticed was that Parke's latest DBS check should have been renewed two and a half years ago but it hadn't.

"What else can you tell me?" asked Cooper.

"Peter James Parke, aged fifty-two, married to Heather Parke, three children, two girls and a boy, youngest is sixteen, eldest is twenty-four. He left school at sixteen and played cricket professionally for Durham and Yorkshire, has two caps for England."

Cooper pulled a mildly impressed expression. "Go on."

"He retired from cricket at twenty-one after a rotator cuff injury - I got that from Wikipedia - before going back to college to train to become a teacher and has been at Tynemouth Academy for the last fifteen years. No criminal record, couple of speeding fines and police have been called to his home in Cullercoats a number of times over an ongoing dispute with his neighbour."

"What's the dispute about?"

"Anti-social behaviour. Loud music, keeping a Shetland pony in the back garden and letting it shit everywhere, throwing fag ends over the garden fence—"

"You're talking about the neighbour, right? Not Parke."

Tennessee laughed. "Yeah, the neighbour. Have you heard from Atkinson about the car yet?"

Cooper's chest warmed at the sound of Atkinson's name. She checked her phone and shook her head. "They're doing their best, but it takes time. Shall we pay our guest a visit then?"

Cooper and Tennessee headed to interview suite four where they found Parke dunking a chocolate biscuit into his tea. Around his mouth was a thin circle of dark chocolate. Cooper handed him a tissue and sat down opposite him.

"Thanks again for coming in and helping us, Mr Parke. This is DS Daniel. I hear you were quite the cricketing wiz? Played for England no less."

Parke studied Cooper. "Have you been running some sort of background check on me?"

"Not at all," she lied. "Leroy MacDonald mentioned it earlier while I was chatting to him."

The answer seemed to placate him and he returned to his packet of biscuits.

"What was it like teaching Rachel Pearson?"

Parke sighed. "It could be challenging. I mean, you know about her accident, right? I had to adapt a lot of the lesson plans so that she could still join in. We'd play walking football sometimes and I'd give her easier alternatives for some of the exercises."

"That's very inclusive of you."

"Well, I didn't want her to feel left out, you know."

"Did you ever give Rachel one-on-one training?"

He shook his head, the circle of chocolate was back around his lips.

"I saw on your desk that you have pictures of the netball and athletics teams. You must be very proud of their achievements."

"Oh yes." The man's eyes lit up. "Very proud. Well, you'll know how well the netball team are doing. Tina's one of the best wing attacks I've ever had the pleasure of coaching. So quiet off the court and so aggressive on it."

Cooper wanted to slap the man and tell him to keep her daughter's name out of his mouth. Tennessee must have sensed a change in Cooper because he took over the questioning.

"Shelly Smith was also on the netball team, wasn't she?"

"Yes, she was. Poor soul. Very talented girl, very talented. She was the team captain. Really understood tactics."

"The last time I spoke to you, you called her bitchy."

The corners of Parke's mouth turned down, and he lowered his eyes. "Yes, I did, didn't I? I'm not proud of that. Even if she could be that way inclined, it's no way to speak about a student, especially after what happened to her."

"And what about Jasmine Lee?" continued Tennessee. "You must have spent a lot of time with her?"

Again, his face lit up. Parke clearly loved talking about his prize athletes. Was he living vicariously through their achievements or did he enjoy talking about these girls for other reasons?

"Jasmine didn't run. She flew. She was like a comet. I called her The Bullet. She was devastated to only place second in the county trials. A real perfectionist, she was. Second was just never good enough for that one. I know she didn't apply herself as well as she could in some of her other subjects but she was an angel when it came to PE and games."

Cooper crossed her legs and smiled as if she was sharing the memories with Parke. "You must be very proud of what Jasmine and Shelly achieved?"

"Yes, of course I am. When Shelly joined Tynemouth she couldn't catch a ball to save her life, but by year ten she was captaining the school team."

"Is that why the photos are on your desk?"

Parke met her eyes and scrutinised her as if he wasn't sure if she was accusing him of something or not. Cooper kept her face neutral and waited to see how he would react.

"Yes," he answered with a questioning look. "I am extremely proud of the kids on the sports teams. Some of these kids, they're not good at academic stuff, struggle with maths and science and the like. If I can help them excel in sports, it gives them a sense of achievement that they're otherwise lacking. A purpose, if you will."

Cooper nodded in agreement and slid her phone across the desk. "I took this photograph earlier today. It's from the girls' toilets on the ground floor corridor."

Parke's face flushed beyond red. His cheeks turned to a purplish-blue. "I... I..." He swallowed. "I heard I was this year's punching bag, but I'd... I'd never..."

"What do you mean by punching bag, Mr Parke?" asked Tennessee.

"It's just kids being kids. You know what teenagers are like; there's always one teacher who gets more than their fair share of rumours being spread about them. It's obviously my turn."

"Obviously," repeated Tennessee, not letting an ounce of sarcasm slip into his voice.

"It was Catherine they went after last year. The rumour was that she was a lesbian. She's not, but she's not homophobic either, so when she brushed off the rumours and showed she wasn't bothered the kids must have got bored and moved on to me."

"Paedo Pete," said Cooper. "Not a good nickname to find yourself with. Do you think these rumours started after you took your smartphone into the boy's changing rooms?"

Parke slid his chair back a few inches and shoved his mug of tea away. "That was dealt with internally. How do you know about that?"

"Why did you have your phone on you, Pete? The changing rooms are designated no phone zones, correct?"

Parke looked from Cooper to Tennessee and back again. "Do I need a lawyer?"

"You're not under arrest."

"Well, it feels like I am." Parke stood up and took a step towards the door but found his exit blocked by Tennessee. Cooper now had no choice. If an individual helping police with their inquiries wanted to leave at any point they must be allowed to. If the police tried to stop said person from leaving, they must arrest him or her and let them know their rights.

"Mr Parke, I am arresting you on suspicion of four counts of murder. You do not have to say anything. But, it may harm your defence if you do not mention when questioned something which you later rely on in court. Anything you do say may be given in evidence."

Parke's mouth hung open, and he made a futile attempt to manoeuvre around Tennessee. Before Parke even knew what had happened, his hands had been cuffed behind his back.

"I want a lawyer!" His voice quivered between a snarl and a sob.

"And you are entitled to one, Mr Parke," said Tennessee. "I'll take you to the custody officer, who will brief you on your rights."

It took Parke's lawyer two hours to arrive and a further hour to be fully briefed by his client. Cooper used the time to check in with Sutherland and Keaton about their plan to intercept a delivery of pope outfits the next day. They'd been assigned a handful of PCs, had been in communication with the Royal Mail and seemed to have the whole thing under control. She grabbed a sorry-looking sandwich and a packet of salt and vinegar crisps from the canteen and called Atkinson from a quiet corner of the incident room.

"Erica."

"Hey, Justin. I'm just calling to keep you in the loop. We've arrested Pete Parke. I'm hoping you have some news regarding his car."

"I do, actually."

Cooper‘s heart raced.

"The car was thoroughly cleaned. I'd say it underwent two back-to-back valets given the amount of cleaning solution we found. Anyway, I can tell you that the tyre prints don't match any of the ones we found at Priors Haven."

"Shit."

"But," he continued, "I did find a long dark hair trapped between the cushions on the back seat."

"Jasmine Lee had long dark hair, so did Rachel Pearson."

"We're checking against the DNA samples we took from Jasmine and Rachel to see if they match."

"Any chance we can get those results in the next twenty hours?"

Atkinson made a sound as if stifling a laugh.

"It was worth a try," said Cooper. "Keep doing what you do and call me if you find anything else. Okay?"

"Naturally. Oh, and Erica?"

"Yes?"

"I'm really looking forward to this evening."

Cooper‘s heart raced again and she glanced around the room to make sure no one had noticed her Cheshire Cat grin.

"Me too."

Across the room, Keaton waved to her and called out, "Boss, the lawyer wants you."

Cooper picked up her files and made her way back to the interview suite, making sure to sweep the crisp crumbs from her suit jacket. She recognised Zach Hodge at once. He was a squat, mousy-haired man who spoke with a lisp and walked with a cane.

"I'm afraid this has been a waste of both of our times, DCI Cooper. Had you asked the most important question first, you'd know my client's alibi is airtight and you must release him at once."

Cooper felt as if she'd been sucker punched. She rested her back against the wall and cursed at her feet. "Go on then," she said, inviting Hodge to pass over the information he had gleaned. He was probably going to relish it as well.

"At the time of Rachel Pearson's murder on Tuesday the thirteenth, my client was at home with his wife and three kids. At the time of Michelle Smith's murder, he was, as you can probably guess, already at work. The school operate an electronic signing-in system. His time of arrival will be logged on the system."

"And on Monday night? I know he was involved in the search party. What about before and after?"

"My client was coaching an inter-school football match when he heard Jasmine and Reuben had gone missing. He went straight from the game to the search, where he helped until ten p.m. Afterwards, he had a drink in the Salutation Inn on Front Street. He's confident the barman will remember him as not many men drink rosé wine. He was back with his wife by ten fifty."

A string of expletives exploded in Cooper's head. The lawyer was right, this had been a massive waste of time and instead of bumbling on about photographs and graffiti, her first port of call should have been to establish any alibi. Zach Hodge's cane tapped against the floor as he waited for Cooper's response. No doubt his lawyer buddies would get a good laugh out of the stupid female detective who was letting her standards slip.

"He's not leaving until I can confirm his version of events with his wife, the school and the Salutation Inn. You're welcome to wait."

Hodge scoffed. "I have better things to do, detective. However, I will be calling to check up on my client. If he hasn't been released by four p.m. I will be back, and I will be very annoyed."

Cooper turned so he couldn't see her rolling her eyes.

- CHAPTER 28 -

AFTER A REFRESHING SHOWER and a liberal application of aromatherapy oils, Cooper joined Tina in the dining room where she found her daughter stirring a pot of massaman curry whilst simultaneously flicking through the Tarot Card Killer's case file.

The scent of lemongrass and coriander crashed over Cooper. "It smells like heaven in here," she said, taking the file from Tina. She stopped short of chastising her or even giving her a reproachful look. Tina was inquisitive by nature and telling her off for reading the file whilst she was cooking up a storm on her behalf would be ungrateful at best and shitty parenting at worst.

"It tastes like it too." Tina offered the spoon and Cooper took a slurp.

"Jesus. That's quite possibly the best curry I've ever tasted. You seriously taught yourself to make this?"

Cooper placed the file in her briefcase and lowered her eyebrows. She was certain she'd left the file locked in there. Time for a new access code, she thought, and this time she'd choose something less obvious than Tina's birthday.

Tina shrugged at the compliment as if whipping up a curry from scratch was no big deal. "I had a little help from YouTube."

Cooper's mind drifted back to a few summers ago when she and Tina had visited Cooper's parents in Lanzarote. An eleven-year-old Tina had read that Lanzarote was a Spanish Island and within two weeks had taught herself conversational Spanish. Sadly, she'd been too shy to utter a word of it to anyone outside her immediate family.

Tina nibbled on a cube of beef and tilted her head to the side for a moment as she considered the balance of ingredients. "I read about Mr Parke. The stuff written about him in the toilets; no one really believes it. Hell, Rachel probably wrote it herself."

"So, he's never made you feel uneasy?"

"God no," answered Tina as she double-checked the list of cooking instructions she'd scrawled down on a spiral-bound notepad.

"Because if he has, in any way, you know you can tell me?"

"I know, but he hasn't. Mr Parke's a great coach. Those rumours were made up by bitchy girls with nothing better to spend their time and energy on."

Cooper placed a hand on Tina's back. "As long as you're sure."

"I am. But Mum, it says in the file that you want to examine Linda's car. She's not a suspect as well, is she?"

"Well, we have a number of persons of int—"

persons of interest," she finished on Cooper's behalf while she made air quotes with her fingers. "I'm not a journalist; I'm your daughter. You can't really think Linda had anything to do with this. I mean, I know she's annoying and everything, and God knows what she and Dad see in each other..." Tina paused to look her mother up and down. "Is that what you're wearing?"

Cooper pulled a face and stared down at her jumper dress and leggings. "What's wrong with what I'm wearing?" She was comfortable and - most importantly - warm.

"It's a bit... No offence... Mumsy."

Cooper snorted. "News flash, Tina. I am a mum. Have been for fourteen years."

An eye roll of epic proportions followed as a pinch of salt was thrown into the pan. "You're also a badass detective with a pair of skinny jeans in your wardrobe that haven't seen the light of day for over six months." Tina glanced at her watch then pointed to the living room. "Go. Skinny jeans. Heels. Lose the wig. I'll set the table."

Cooper sighed and once again looked down at her outfit. Perhaps she was playing it a little too conservatively. "Okay," she conceded. "I'll change, but the wig stays."

Tina stuck out her lower lip. "Have it your way, but the buzzcut suits you better. Way more rock and roll. Anyway, go. He'll be here any second."

The scent of lemongrass followed Cooper to her bedroom. The skinny jeans had been relegated to the back of the lowest drawer in her dresser. They were creased and Cooper didn't have time to iron. She pulled off her leggings and tried the jeans. To her amazement, they still fit. She posed in front of the mirror; the creases were hardly noticeable now that the fabric had stretched over her thighs.

She slipped her feet into a pair of nude heels and gave herself an approving nod. Not bad. No Kate Moss. But she scrubbed up all right.

Cooper grabbed a Guns and Roses t-shirt and sat down in front of the mirror. She took a long, deep breath and noticed that butterflies had started having a party in her stomach. She sat and stared at her reflection for over a minute. Anxiety built up in her gut until she thought, "Sod it," and pulled the wig from her head. She applied a layer of red lipstick and repeated the words *total badass* three times before heading back downstairs.

She can't have been out of the room for more than five minutes, but Tina had set the table, lit scented candles and dimmed the lights. Jazz played quietly in the background and tall, intelligent Justin Atkinson was staring longingly into the pot of massaman.

"Mum tells me you work in forensics," said Tina. Her voice was soft and quivered slightly.

Atkinson nodded. "That's right."

"That must be really interesting," said Tina. "I want to do something like that when I go to uni. Maybe not forensics but definitely something science-based."

Cooper was impressed. She understood how hard it was for Tina to strike up conversations with strangers; she was clearly pushing herself, and Cooper thoroughly appreciated the effort.

"Well, if you want any advice," started Atkinson before he noticed Cooper in the doorway. His jaw literally dropped. "Erica! You look... Well... Wow."

Cooper looked down self-consciously. "Thanks," she replied, colour flooding her cheeks. "It's all Tina's doing. She wouldn't let me wear what I picked out."

"That's because what you picked out made you look like a Sunday school teacher." Tina opened a bottle of wine and poured three glasses. When Cooper raised an eyebrow, she answered, "What? I was just telling Justin how you've been slaving over this meal for hours." Then she smirked.

There it was: Tina's craftiness. She'd make out Cooper was a domestic goddess in exchange for a glass of Gavi. It was a deal.

"Anyway," continued Tina. She dished out a portion of rice and spooned a large dollop of curry on top. "I'll leave you to it." She grabbed a knife and fork and turned to Atkinson. "It was nice to meet you."

Tina scurried off to her bedroom, and Cooper heard the faintest hint of the theme tune from a Netflix show start to play from upstairs. There was an awkward pause between Cooper and Atkinson. An undercurrent of chemistry kept in check by nerves and trepidation.

"So," began Cooper, shifting her weight and lifting her glass. "Cheers."

Atkinson clinked his glass against hers. "I hope you don't mind, but I have two rules for this evening."

Cooper took a sip and smiled. "Please tell me one of them is absolutely no work talk. The whole debacle with Parke today has me totally riled. "

"Bingo. No work talk."

"Well, I'll drink to that." Cooper took another sip and began to serve up two plates of food. "And the second?"

"No talk of exes." He ran his free hand through his hair and shook his head. "Elspeth's been on the blower today, yapping on about the boys needing to repeat a year at Edinburgh. Honestly, that woman. She wasn't concerned about their grades when she did a runner with that paella-eating toy boy of hers in the middle of their A-levels, and oh, see I've already broken the second rule."

He slapped his palm off his forehead and muttered something under his breath.

Cooper extended an arm and motioned for Atkinson to sit. She'd never met Elspeth Atkinson but she was picturing someone who looked rather like Margot Swanson. "If it helps," she said, "I'd be delighted not to hear the names Kenny, Neil, or Russell, or Aiden, or... Well, the less said about that, the better."

Atkinson sat. He looked rather dashing in the candlelight, and free from his white coveralls, he appeared much leaner.

"You've put my casserole to shame," Atkinson mused as he swallowed a mouthful of beef.

Cooper's mouth twitched with guilt, and she pushed the charade from her mind. She could confess to her culinary ineptitude another day. For now, she could be the chef in high heels.

"I like your t-shirt," he added between mouthfuls. "I remember buying Appetite for Destruction at the old HMV store in town. That must have been, Jeez, eighty-eight?"

"It came out in eighty-seven," said Cooper. "Great album. I've got it on vinyl. Nothing to play it on, of course, but I can't bring myself to chuck it out."

Atkinson was shovelling curry as if his life depended on it. Cooper couldn't blame him; it was beyond scrumptious. "Were you even born in eighty-seven?" he asked.

"Barely."

"How you managed to raise a teenager and rise to DCI by your age, I'll never know."

Cooper put down her fork for a moment. "I didn't have much of a choice. I was seventeen, Megadeath had just reformed, and I had Slipknot's Subliminal Verses playing on loop. One night I was flicking through my study diary to check when my next A-level module was due and I noticed something else was due. I was three weeks late."

Atkinson blew out a long sigh. "I can't imagine how scary that must have been at seventeen."

"I wasn't half as scared as Kenny. He was nineteen and, well I'd be breaking our rules if I talked about him so I'll move on. My parents helped me with Tina until I finished sixth form, but the second I got my results, they left for the Canaries, and I moved in with my gran. It had been their dream for as long as I could remember to open up a bar somewhere in the sunshine. I didn't want to be the one to stop them, so I told them I'd be fine and sent them on their way. I was eighteen, unemployed, living with a sixty-two-year-old and I had an infant to care for."

"Top up?" asked Atkinson, but he poured before Cooper could answer. "I'm beginning to see how you became so resilient."

"Gran was taking care of Tina one evening. I was out clubbing on the Quay Side with my best friend, Cynthia Howes. I used to call her Cindy. Anyway, it was my first night out clubbing since having Tina and we had a great time. It was three in the morning and when we left the club, I stopped by the curb to tie the laces on my boots, and I looked up just as she got into an altercation with a group of bikers over who was next in the taxi queue. One of them shoved her, and she fell off the quay and drowned in the river."

"Oh, Erica." Atkinson looked horrified. "And you were eighteen?"

"Yeah. Just a kid myself really. They never caught him - the man who pushed her. I described the man until I was blue in the face, told them which street he'd run off on and everything. There must have been fifty people in that taxi queue but they never caught him. I spent night after night crying to Gran about how it was criminal that the police hadn't charged anyone. In the end, she got so sick of my moaning, well I was grieving to be fair, but she told me, 'They're doing their best. If you think you can do better, go join the police.' So I did."

"AHEM."

The little cough woke Cooper from her dream. She blinked through sleepy eyes and tried to get her bearings. Tina was standing in the middle of the living room staring at her with her arms folded over her chest. She was dressed in her school uniform and had her bag ready to go.

Cooper assessed the situation. She'd fallen asleep on the sofa with her head resting on Atkinson's lap. He was still sound asleep and snoring softly with his head lolled backwards and his lips parted. It wasn't his best look.

"Could be worse," whispered Tina. "At least you're both dressed."

Cooper flashed her a look. "Boundaries," she hissed.

Her head was foggy and a quick glance around the room explained why. There were two empty bottles of wine on the mantlepiece and a couple of tumblers on a side table looked to contain whisky or brandy. After pouring her heart out and telling her life story to Atkinson, he'd reciprocated and they'd turned the sorry event into a drinking game. Sip every time someone mentions a former lover. Sip every time someone mentions work.

She pushed herself to seated and rubbed her hands over her face. She felt grubby and her jeans had dug into her waist, leaving a painful red line. A dawning realisation pulsated behind her eyes; she was about to spend another day hunting a sick psychopath, and the thought of it made her stomach churn. Would all the children of Tynemouth make it safely to their beds this evening?

"Tina, listen. I'm not sure I want you going to school today. How about you come to the station instead? Hang out in the family room?"

"But it's Wednesday."

"And?"

"And Wednesdays are the best. I have maths and double art. And I can't miss chemistry if I'm going to do it at A-level. Mr Price said I need eights and nines if I want to do a science subject at uni."

Cooper could still taste chillies. Bits of rice were caught in her teeth and she had a headache forming behind her eyes. She remembered kissing Atkinson last night. Oh God, they'd kissed - a lot - and all the time she had nuggets of rice in her teeth. Big, sloppy, tongues-down-each-other's-throats, rice-in-their-teeth kisses.

Classy, Erica. Very classy, thought Cooper. She turned her eyes back to Tina, "I'd just prefer it if you had a day off and came to the station."

"Locked in the family room? Sounds more like I'm the one under arrest." Tina's words were still whispered, but her voice was increasing in pitch.

"Is there any chance I can get you to think of it as being under police protection?"

Tina threw herself into an armchair and huffed. "You can't seriously be concerned about Linda? Just tell the guys you have guarding the school not to let her in if she shows up. Besides, I promised Josh I'd help him with his biology—" She paused and mulled something over for a moment. "I'll come to the station if Josh can come too."

Cooper got to her feet. “Nice try. Give me ten minutes and I’ll drive you in. I want texts between every class, and I’ll have your dad pick you up.”

“But—“

“No buts. Now be an angel and make some coffee.”

- CHAPTER 29 -

"I AM SPEAKING TO the people of Tynemouth and North Shields. If you know something, say something. If you suspect something, you need to say something."

Cooper lifted her chin and spoke into the television cameras and flashing bulbs of press photographers. It was early afternoon and her stomach was starting to rumble. Hopefully, the microphones wouldn't pick it up. She sat behind a row of tables with the parents of Rachel, Shelly, Jasmine and Reuben, as well as Oliver Martin and a horse-faced member of the press office named Blair Potts. Behind her, a backdrop of royal blue was emblazoned with the badge of Northumbria Police and the slogan 'Proud to protect.'

Lisa Smith and Lou Pearson had delivered tearful statements whilst journalists from the length and breadth of the country took notes or held out microphones. Jasmine and Reuben's parents were too distressed to read their statements so Blair Potts read them on their behalf. For the entire duration Sally Pearson gripped her husband's hand so tightly it caused her arm to shake. She was glassy-eyed and still had the not-quite-present look of someone taking a lot of sedatives.

"We wish to speak to anyone who was near the Spanish Battery at half seven on the evening of Tuesday the thirteenth of November," continued Cooper. "Whittingham Road on the morning of Thursday the fifteenth of November; or on Front Street at five-thirty p.m. on Monday the nineteenth of November."

Cooper lowered her eyes for a moment, then closed her file and tucked it under her arm. "The smallest detail, no matter how insignificant it may seem, could hold the key to solving these murders. Someone is targeting our children. He is someone's son, someone's husband, or someone's father. If you know something, say something. Thank you."

Cooper stood, bowed her head and walked away to a flurry of camera flashes. Blair Potts tapped her microphone, cleared her throat and read out the number for the confidential hotline.

"Sir." Cooper chased Superintendent Nixon along a corridor. He was a lanky man with a paunch that hung over his belt, and his skin had the unhealthy greyish quality of someone who spent little time outdoors. As Cooper caught up with him she saw he was on the phone.

"We're chronically understaffed, dammit," he huffed. "Got at least half a dozen bleeders on maternity."

Cooper's eyes formed into thin slits. Nixon thought calling female officers 'bleeders' was nothing more than harmless banter. He felt the same way when he referred to the newest recruits as fresh meat or his elderly secretary as a coffin dodger. He was of the generation where referring to females on the force as women, ladies - or God forbid - officers, was political correctness gone mad, and no amount of sensitivity training was ever going to change that.

When he hung up, Nixon seemed surprised to see Cooper by his side. "How long have you been there?"

"Long enough," she responded.

"Ah, right." He straightened up and looked down at her; he hadn't trimmed his nose hair in a while. "What can I do for you?"

"You wanted an update, sir. Keaton and Sutherland are staking out Morrison's in Tynemouth. Some pope outfits are due to be delivered to the In-Post lockers between two and half-past."

"Is it our man?" He opened the door to his office but didn't invite Cooper in. Behind him, Cooper spied Commissioner Begum sat in Nixon's leather seat and Chief Constable Davison sat to his right. They were deep in conversation; voices lowered and heads tilted towards each other.

"I'm not sure, sir. I don't know why he would order three of the costumes. Either way, we'll know soon enough."

"Vests?"

"Yes, and a couple of PCs."

Nixon stood aside so Cooper could get a better look at the men in his office. "DCI Erica Cooper, meet PCC Amir Begum and CC Henry Davison."

Cooper stood to attention and Nixon looked like the effort of not looking phased was about to make him burst into flames.

"CC Davison wishes to shadow the investigation today. I think it would be a good idea for him to accompany detectives Keaton and Sutherland to Morrison's. Get to know the team and the lay of the land."

Cooper's jaw clenched. She didn't have a choice here; she could tell by the tone of Nixon's voice that he wasn't to be pressed on the matter. He didn't want CC Davison interfering with the sting, but equally, Nixon didn't want Davison watching over his shoulder every second. Keaton was going to blow her top and Cooper couldn't blame her.

She slid her jaw from side to side to loosen it up. "I'll arrange an extra vest and a car to take him over there," she said reluctantly.

Nixon looked visibly relieved. He shut his door and muttered, "Good, good. Thank you, Cooper."

Cooper stared at the door for a moment before whispering, "My pleasure," and walking off towards CID.

Tennessee looked up from his computer screen. "Christ. You've got bags under your eyes big enough to carry my weekly shop. Been burning the midnight oil?"

"Lovely to see you, too," Cooper replied through pursed lips. "Actually, I had a friend over for dinner. I might have had a touch too much wine."

Tennessee wiggled his eyebrows but stopped short of pushing his luck with any form of innuendo. Instead, he pushed a cup of steaming coffee towards Cooper.

"Cheers. What's new?"

Tennessee sighed. "Not much. Hayley's got it into her head we should raise the baby vegan once he's weaned."

Cooper perched on the edge of the desk and scanned his computer screen. "Christ. Is that healthy for babies?"

"No idea. I'm going to look into it, though. If the doc says it's okay, then I'll not argue. Happy wife, happy life and all that. Can't promise I won't sneak him the odd BigMac now and again."

"I'd be disappointed if you didn't." Cooper tilted the screen so she could get a better look. "Still trawling through social media?"

"Trying to find any other links between the victims. Been at it all morning. I'm going through their recent check-ins."

"Anything promising?"

Tennessee shrugged. "A couple. They've all checked in at Crusoe's recently. You know, the cafe down on Long Sands beach. Jasmine and Shelly both checked-in regularly at the rugby club, they used the gym there, and they were all at the same beach party last month. There're pictures from Jasmine's secret Instagram account showing half the year elevens drinking and smoking down at King Edward's Bay."

"Was anyone in the photos taking drugs? Or did any of them appear high?" Cooper shifted her weight. "I'm wondering if there's a drugs connection; perhaps they owed money to the wrong people."

"Hard to say." Tennessee clicked his mouse a couple of times, brought up the account and zoomed in on a few pictures. "I didn't spot anything other than beer cans and a bottle of Absolut. I'll ask tech to enhance some of the snaps. See if the cigarettes really are cigarettes but to be fair, it's not like Tynemouth kids are short of a bob or two. They'd have to be ordering in some big amounts to be in any serious debt."

"The Pearsons weren't wealthy," answered Cooper, thinking of their dilapidated semi. "And Lisa Smith was raising Shelly on her own. Even with a military pension, that can't be easy."

Tennessee shrugged. "Aye. Maybe you're right."

Maybe she was, but something was niggling at Cooper. There was a doubting feeling at the base of her skull. It might be the hangover but she couldn't help feeling that she should have solved this case by now. Was she rusty from her absence? She must be or she wouldn't have made such a glaring error with Parke. Something was off. She was missing something, or going about the case in the wrong way. Cooper took a gulp of coffee and sneered. The coffee machine in CID was no Starbucks, that was for sure.

Opening the case file, Cooper turned to the notes she'd made about Rachel Pearson. "I knew it," she said. "We took details about Rachel's routine when we interviewed the Pearsons. She had weekly physio sessions for her back. The physio worked out of the rugby club."

Tennessee sucked in a lungful of air.

"Google the gym for me," Cooper asked.

Tennessee clicked and brought up a website. "What we looking for?"

"I'm not sure. Just keep scrolling."

The gym offered studio classes, a boot camp and a spin class. It was fitted with free weights, resistance machines and cardio equipment. Happy, stick-thin women with mega-watt smiles posed with muscle-bound Adonis wannabes. Their website was sleek and encouraged you to sign up at every opportunity.

"Stop," said Cooper. She pointed to the spinning timetable. "There."

"Spin class. Mondays, Wednesdays and Fridays at six-thirty with Duncan Clark." Tennessee's eyes flicked to Cooper's. "Dunk the Hunk?"

"Could well be." Cooper stood up and slopped coffee over herself. "Dammit." She dried her hands on her suit and turned to her DS. "Fancy a workout?"

- CHAPTER 30 -

A HERRING GULL WITH a gammy leg cawed in the face of an Alsatian that dared wander too close to the remains of a Subway sandwich which she was guarding. The sandwich was hers, and she'd defend it to the death.

DS Paula Keaton admired the bird. For some reason, it reminded her of herself in her rugby-playing heyday. She'd never been scared to take on the biggest women on the pitch. Usually, it was the opposite; she'd make a beeline for the burliest member of the opposition and stamp her authority down with a vicious tackle the moment the opportunity arrived. She'd quickly earned herself the nickname Pitbull Paula.

An L-shaped carpark wrapped two sides of Morrison's supermarket. Keaton was stationed at the sliding doors that marked the entrance to the lobby. She leant back against the wall and pretended to play on her phone. Her eyes continuously flicked between the wall of lockers and the sliding doors where she could still watch the lockers, only this time, in the reflection of the glass. Sam Sutherland was resting against the opposite wall. He was pretending to read the morning paper and perfectly took to the role of bored husband waiting for his missus to finish her shopping.

Keaton had the same nervous energy coursing through her veins that she used to feel before an important match. Her legs twitched and her heart rate skyrocketed. She prayed whoever opened locker sixteen was their man. Her competitive ego craved victory. She wanted to be the one to catch him, she wanted the thrill and adoration of catching the killer, but more than anything, she just wanted the sick son of a bitch off the streets and in HMP Frankland. As a killer of children, the Tarot Card Killer would be dealt with by the justice system of the other inmates.

If he were disembowelled with a rusty nail - as horrific a thought that it was - he wouldn't be the first.

Until the death of Reuben Jones, Keaton had managed to keep her emotions in check. Well, mostly she had. The killer appeared to only target girls until Reuben went missing. Reuben was the same age as Keaton's youngest brother - Riley - and he looked a bit like him too. She tightened her fist at the thought of someone laying a finger on her sweet, softly-spoken brother and swallowed down the rage that filled her.

Keaton, Sutherland and two PCs who were waiting in an unmarked car had been at the supermarket since one. The Chief Constable had flounced in at half past and had tried to take over. Keaton sweet-talked him back to the car and told him that everything was under control. What she'd wanted to say was that until she was instructed otherwise she would only take orders from Cooper, that this was her stakeout, and that she didn't need some geriatric in a fancy suit poking his beak in and ruining the sting.

The Royal Mail had delivered the package at ten past two and they'd been keeping an eye on the locker ever since. Keaton was becoming increasingly antsy and was struggling to stay still. She spent the last couple of hours flittering between anticipation and unbearable boredom. Her adrenaline levels had spiked shortly after three when an elderly lady approached the lockers and used a code to open locker twelve but there'd been no action since.

Sutherland turned a page of his newspaper; it was their code for 'heads up.' Keaton's eyes found a tall male in a black baseball cap, black hoodie and grey jeans. His feet were at least a size ten. He stopped in front of the lockers and took out his mobile. Keaton was between the man and one set of sliding doors. She faked a yawn and stretched her arms above her head, a signal to the officers in the car to stand by. Sutherland dropped his paper into a shopping trolley and moved in from the man's rear.

This is it, thought Keaton. Her chest heaved against the stab vest she wore under her coat, reminding her how dangerous this man could be. She felt like every nerve ending was primed and ready for action. Edging forward, she watched the man type in his access code. The screen changed and writing appeared: *Locker 16 is now open. Have a great day.*

Would he run? Would he fight? Was he carrying a weapon?

The moment the man reached in the locker to retrieve the pope outfits, Keaton clamped a heavy hand on his right shoulder. "Police," her voice boomed. "Don't move."

- CHAPTER 31 -

Cooper's Mazda smelled of McNuggets and it didn't take a detective to work out why. Tennessee finished his last chicken nugget in one bite and crumpled the box into an impossibly small ball. Fast food didn't compare to massaman curry but there was nothing quite like Mcdonald's when you needed to soak up last night's wine. They'd visited the drive-thru in the neighbouring retail park and eaten while they drove to LeanLife Gym at the local rugby club.

Cooper finished the box of fries she'd been balancing in her lap whilst watching snowflakes dance in front of the car's windscreen. The temperature had dropped again, and in the time it had taken her to finish her food, the thin dusting of snow that covered the gym's car park had thickened into a blanket. There was something very naughty about eating fast food in a gym car park and she wondered how many of LeanLife's members had done the same. When the last fry disappeared, Cooper checked her phone. She had three increasingly sarcastic texts from Tina as well as a text from Atkinson. He said he'd had a lovely time and hoped to do it again soon. He'd signed off with JA and a heart emoji.

Heat swept up from Cooper's chest to her cheeks. She suppressed a smile and filed the giddy feeling away for now. The sun was starting to set, and as much as she wanted to think about Atkinson, there was tension building in her stomach as the end of the school day approached. How many students would make it back to class tomorrow?

Tennessee walked slightly ahead and held the door for Cooper. A small reception area was staffed by a woman in a cropped top. Her bare belly was taught, tanned and pierced.

Dressing for the weather, thought Cooper.

"Welcome to LeanLife," beamed the receptionist. The woman took in the striking man who stood before her and she battered her - presumably fake - eyelashes at him. "Are you interested in membership?"

Beyond the reception desk, Cooper spotted the triangular frame of Will Harper. He was working out in the free weights area, grunting and gurning his way through a set of bicep curls. He put the weights down and puffed up his chest when he saw the detectives watching him. It was a silverback display by the runt of the litter.

"That damn kid is everywhere we turn with this investigation," said Tennessee. He turned to the receptionist and showed her his ID. "No, thank you. DS Jack Daniel and DCI Erica Cooper. We need to speak to the manager."

The woman's smile vanished - she wasn't about to sell two annual memberships - but the rest of her face held the paralysed look of someone who had recently used botox.

"I *am* the manager," she said with a hint of insult to her voice. She held out a hand. "Robyn Watson. What's going on?"

Tennessee glanced at Cooper to see if she wanted to take the lead. She gave him a subtle nod, encouraging him to continue.

"We're investigating the murders of some of your members: Rachel Pearson, Michelle Smith, and Jasmine Lee."

Robyn's hand flew to her mouth but her forehead didn't budge. "Oh my goodness. I thought I recognised the blonde girl from somewhere. Did... Did they all go here? You don't think... The killer... He's not?"

"That's what we'd like to find out," said Tennessee, reading what Robyn was trying to say. "Could you check your records? I'd like to know if Reuben Jones had a membership here."

She turned to her computer. Her long nails *tip-tapped* over the keys, then she turned the monitor to face them. "Three members named Jones, but no Reubens."

Will Harper was still peacocking around the gym and constantly turning back to the reception area to see if he was being watched. He was a tempestuous, possessive young man and Cooper didn't trust him as far as she could throw him. Why did all roads lead to Will Harper? He should be in school at this time of the day. Then again, so should over eight hundred other kids.

"Can you find out the last time the girls were in the gym?" asked Tennessee.

Robyn nodded. "The system logs everyone's attendance." She began searching the database and printed off a list of the girls' recent gym sessions.

Cooper scanned the list. "Shelly was here the night before she was killed. So was Jasmine. Do you have cameras here, Robyn?"

Robyn Watson's nostrils flared. Cooper pondered if she was annoyed at the intrusion or if she could smell the junk food on their breath.

"We do. We have two in the gym and one in the studio. We only keep the footage for a month unless there's a problem."

Cooper propped her elbows on the desk. "I'd like to see any footage you have from Wednesday the fourteenth of November." She checked the list that Robyn had given her. "From about four p.m.? That's when Shelly and Jasmine arrived."

LeanLife's manager pulled on a zip-up hoodie and finally covered her midriff. "We'll have to go to the back office. Follow me." She propped a *Back In Ten Minutes* sign on the counter and led Cooper and Tennessee to a dingy box room that smelled of deodorant, Mary Jane, and if Cooper wasn't mistaken, sex.

It didn't take long for Robyn to find the footage Cooper was after. The detectives watched as greyscale images of Jasmine and Shelly moved around the gym. The heads of a number of men swivelled as the girls walked past the weights area and climbed onto neighbouring exercise bikes.

"Do you recognise this man?" asked Tennessee. He pointed at a man who didn't just follow the girls with his eyes. He walked closely behind them and chose the elliptical trainer directly behind their exercise bikes.

"Hmm," said Robyn. "I think so. Can't think of his name off the top of my head, but if I take a look at the attendance log for that time and look at the photos we have on file, I'll be able to get a name for you."

"Thanks," said Tennessee. "If we could do the same for these men as well, that would be great." He pointed at a few others who hadn't been able to keep their eyes in their heads.

Cooper watched the footage as a man in a LeanLife polo shirt stopped and talked to Jasmine and Shelly for a few moments. When he left, the girls appeared to giggle and whisper something to one another.

"Who's that?"

"That's one of our instructors."

"Duncan Clark?"

"Yes," said Robyn. Her voice was suspicious, and had she been able to lower her brows, she would have. "How did you know that?"

"We need to speak to him. Is he here?" Cooper asked.

Robyn checked the clock on the wall. "He's leading a boxercise class. He'll be finished in five minutes."

It was almost fifteen minutes later when Duncan Clark appeared in the reception area. He wasn't the most attractive man Erica had ever laid eyes on. Still, he had an air of confidence about him, and his toned physique, strong jaw and dark skin tone reminded Cooper of the boxer, Anthony Joshua. She could quite see the attraction.

Duncan wiped his neck with a towel and acknowledged the detectives. "The boss said you needed to see me. Said you're detectives?"

Cooper showed him her ID. "That's right, Mr Clark." Then she showed him a picture of Rachel Pearson. "Do you recognise this girl?"

He took a long, hard look at the photograph. "Aye. She's called Rach. Comes here once, maybe twice a week. Haven't seen her recently, though. She's usually with Benji, our physio."

Cooper took out photographs of Jasmine and Shelly. "What about these two?"

Duncan laughed. "Those two are trouble."

"What do you mean?" asked Cooper, noting his use of the present tense.

"Terrible flirts. The pair of them. I guess it's an occupational hazard, having young women throw themselves at me."

Tennessee lifted his chin. "You sound proud."

"It's not like that," said Duncan. He raised his hands in surrender. "Honestly. If it were the other way round and I was a female instructor and those two were men..." He stopped himself. "Look, they're not my type. What are they? Like seventeen? Eighteen?"

"They're fifteen."

"Oh, shit." Duncan's mouth hung open, and his eyes doubled in size. "Is that what this is about? Have they accused me of something?"

Tennessee looked to be struggling to hide his incredulousness. "No, Mr Clark. They're dead. They were murdered. Rachel too."

He stepped backwards, shaking his head. "No. No, that can't be."

"I'm afraid it's true," said Cooper, "and they'd mentioned you in a number of messages. We're going to need to... Mr Clark? Are you all right? Do you need to sit down?"

Duncan Clark's eyelids fluttered, his irises rolled backwards and he collapsed onto the gym's laminate flooring.

"What do you think?" asked Cooper after Robyn Watson had moved Dunk the Hunk to the physio room for a lie-down.

"He's either a good actor or he's been living under a rock for the past week and a half. I can believe not watching the news or never reading a paper, but this story has been everywhere." Tennessee stopped to watch the local first-team run sprints across the rugby pitch. A bit of snow wasn't going to stop these guys from training. Incredibly they were still in shorts and t-shirts. "He voluntarily gave us his phone, and he had an alibi for Monday evening."

Cooper's jacket pocket began to vibrate. She retrieved her phone from her pocket and glanced at the screen. It was Keaton. Hopefully, she had good news.

"Paula?"

"Boss. The In-Post locker was a dud."

Cooper cursed under her breath and looked to the darkening sky. "You sure?"

"Pretty darn sure. The pope outfits were for a bloody tarts and vicars party."

"Tarts and vicars? Are you kidding me?"

Tennessee was pulling faces, so Cooper switched to speakerphone.

"The guy's name is Fin Hamilton. Twenty years old and the captain of Northumbria Uni's ultimate frisbee team."

"Ultimate what?"

"Frisbee. Apparently, it's a thing now. Anyway, Northumbria played Newcastle last week, and Northumbria won the fixture so they get to dress as the clergy at this social thing and Newcastle's team have to go in drag."

Cooper didn't know whether to laugh or cry. What a waste of their time and resources.

"When he realised why we'd cornered him, the kid started freaking out. Wet himself. I'm not joking. Bloody pissed all over Morrison's lobby. They had to get wet floor signs and everything. I'm going to call the universities and Hamilton's teammates as soon as I hang up here and make sure his story checks out, but I think we'll be letting him go within the hour."

"God damn it. I was hoping you had him."

"Me too, boss. Me too. How'd it go at your end?"

"We found Dunk the Hunk," Cooper said.

"And he fainted," added Tennessee. "Managed not to piss himself, though."

Keaton snorted out of the phone. "And he's not our guy?"

"I don't think so. We have a few things to follow up on but it's looking less and less like it. Hold on a sec, Paula, we're going to freeze to death." Cooper opened the car doors and she and Tennessee climbed in. The engine roared to life and

Cooper turned the heating up to its highest setting. "You still there?" she asked once her phone had synced to the car's Bluetooth.

"I am."

"So what the bloody hell are we missing?" asked Cooper. Kenny's name flashed on her phone's screen and she tapped a button to send him to voicemail. She couldn't stand the thought of going to bed that night not knowing if she might wake up to the news that some poor kid had been strangled to death and dressed up as a hierophant.

"Let's start at the beginning," said Tennessee. "Rachel Pearson, killed after her yoga class, dressed as a magician and left in a boat at Prior's Haven. A former gymnast who broke her cervical spine, had physio here at the rugby club and dated Will Harper."

Cooper drummed her fingers on the steering wheel. "Michelle Smith, known as Shelly, suffocated in her own home after her mother left for work that morning. Dressed as a priestess. Worked out at the same gym, captain of the netball team and was also involved with Will Harper."

"Then there was Jasmine and Reuben," said Keaton. "Taken after attending an after-school arts club and going for fish and chips with a friend. Killed in the early evening, Reuben was stabbed and Jasmine was strangled. They were kept somewhere until around four forty in the morning and moved to the track behind the park. A witness saw a dark-coloured estate car pick up Jasmine and Reuben and we have door-cam footage of what is presumably the same car."

"What other evidence do we have?" asked Tennessee. He clenched his fists and flexed his fingers in front of the heater vents a couple of times. "We have a print from Reuben but the killer isn't in the system. There was charcoal residue on Rachel and a hair that could belong to Jasmine in Pete Parke's car."

"But Parke had an alibi for the times of each of the murders," said Cooper. Frustration was taking hold, and she could feel the beginnings of a tension headache. "You know. When I visited Linda Webb on Tuesday she was making a smoothy. One of the things she put in it was activated charcoal."

"You're shitting me?" asked Tennessee. "And she's still giving us the run around?"

"But," said Keaton before Cooper could confirm. "We're almost certain that the killer's male. Based on the fact he crushed Rachel's windpipe and overpowered Reuben. He was also able to not only move the bodies but to dress and style them, and in Rachel's case, lift her into a sailing boat."

Cooper closed her eyes and sighed. "You're right. I'm not sure Linda Webb's strong enough to move those bodies, but she isn't the smallest of women either, and let's not forget she had no alibi for the time of Jasmine and Reuben's death, or the times their bodies were moved. What else do we have on the killer?"

"The tarot card obsession," said Tennessee, who was still warming his hands. "He, *or she*, is on some sort of a journey. Isn't that what the old woman told you, Coop? That he's killing young people to absorb their youthful energy in some bid for immortality."

"Or as I like to put it," said Keaton, "he's a few pasties short of a Greggs."

Tennessee took his warmed hands and cupped them over his cheeks. "Nutter or not, he has a flair for the dramatic. He's leaving bodies all over Tynemouth like it's some sort of grotesque sculpture garden."

Sculpture, thought Cooper before repeating it aloud. "Sculpture, sculpture, sculpture. You know, when Rachel's body was discovered, I described it as having been dumped in the boat but Atkinson corrected me, saying the body had been displayed."

"He wants the world to see his work," said Tennessee with a nod.

"Because this is, what, his art?" asked Keaton.

"Fuck," said Cooper. The inside of her chest began to thunder with heart palpitations. "Are you thinking what I'm thinking?"

Tennessee nodded. "And the charcoal residue on Rachel's skin. Keaton, are you by a computer?"

"Looking at one right now."

"Look up that PVP chemical. See if it's found in glue?"

"I can tell you now, it is. glue-sticks and spray adhesives, fixatives, hairspray."

"Fucking hell!" Cooper shifted into first gear and wrestled the old Mazda across the Rugby club's icy car park. "He's treating the bodies as art projects, and the victims had trace amounts of art materials on them. Brian Fucking Hutchins."

Kenny's name flashed on the mobile's screen again. Cooper placed Keaton on hold for a second. "Not now, Kenny. I'm following a lead," she snapped.

Kenny's voice was breathy and low, and his tone chilled Cooper to the bone. "Erica. I can't find Tina."

- CHAPTER 32 -

Now it was Cooper who felt like fainting. Not Tina. Not her baby girl.

"Kenny? What are you saying?"

"She's missing, Erica. I went to pick her up from netball club but it was cancelled. I must have called her fifty times. She's not picking up."

Cooper gasped for breath but none came. Had Tina been missing since half three? That was over an hour ago. She stammered but the words got caught in her breath. Tennessee's hand fell on her shoulder and he took over the conversation.

"This is DS Jack Daniel. Have you checked Cooper's home?"

"Yes. Yes. I've just come from there."

"I'll call it in. We're heading straight to the school. Kenny, are you okay to drive?"

There was a moment of hesitation. "Yes."

"Check everywhere you can think of. I've heard Cooper mention Tina going to Woods cafe and the library on Front Street. Check the boyfriend's house and call all of her friends. Then you need to go to Cooper's and wait there in case Tina shows up."

"Like hell am I waiting around."

Cooper manhandled the car onto Queen Alexandra Road. The parent part of her personality was battling with the detective part. The parent wanted to cry. She wanted her bright little girl back in her arms, but if that was to happen, she had to be the detective.

"Do as you're told, Kenny. Go to Front Street, call Josh and get back to mine."

She hung up and jumped into the driver's seat while Tennessee made some calls. She drove as fast as she could on the snowy roads and heard her DS request backup.

"Oliver, it's Jack. What car does Hutchins drive? A Mini? Right, check if any other cars are registered to his address or if he access to any other cars. Now, dammit."

The car skidded as it turned into Tynemouth Academy and bumped a Mini Countryman that was still in the otherwise deserted carpark.

"That's his car. He's still here," whispered Cooper.

"Thanks, Oliver," said Tennessee as he ended the call and turned to Cooper. "Hutchins lives with his mother. She drives a dark blue Volvo V60."

PCs Andrew Underwood and Nate Lewis met them at the car but Cooper barely noticed them. Her breath billowed around her face as she stepped out of the car and began running across the forecourt towards the sports fields and the gymnasium that the students liked to call the shed.

The men followed closely behind. Cooper could hear their boots crunching through the snow. She grabbed a lamp post and slid around it, bringing herself to a standstill.

"Wait," she said, extending an arm to her side and almost clotheslining Tennessee. She pointed to footprints in the snow. They were small and shaped like women's shoes. Some heeled, some flat, some with pointed toes.

"There. You see?"

Tennessee and the other officers turned their heads downwards and studied the snow-covered tarmac.

"The footprints, there're at least eight sets." Cooper pointed a finger and traced the route. "They get to the door, then they change their minds and turn towards the school gate."

"Not all of them, Coop." Tennessee pointed at a lone set of footprints that belonged to a pair of flats. The prints turned in the opposite direction.

PC Underwood approached the door to the shed and read a paper note that was pinned to the door. "Says here, *Netball cancelled this week. No* coach."

"I'm guessing Parke wanted a day off after we marched him out of here and accused him of being a paedophilic serial killer," said Tennessee. Snowflakes danced around his head and caught in his hair.

"*We* didn't do that. *I* did. It was my mistake." Cooper followed the lone set of prints around a corner and stopped when she saw them meet a larger set of prints. There were signs of a scuffle and handprints in the snow. Taking a torch from her keyring, Cooper illuminated the snowy ground and yelped at the sight of snow that had been tinged pink from blood.

"Here," grunted Underwood. He pointed to a rock that was about the size of his fist. It was covered in viscous red liquid.

"The prints lead back inside," Tennessee remarked. "It looks like she was dragged in."

Cooper made to run towards the school but Tennessee held her back. "Coop. We're dealing with a dangerous killer. We're not wearing vests. We can't just go—"

Cooper pulled away from him. There was no way she was waiting for backup. Not when it was her own daughter's life at stake. She slipped into the lobby, wincing as the soles of her wet shoes squeaked on the tiled floor of the lobby. She stopped to remove her shoes, wanting to stay silent for now. Tennessee followed suit and spoke calmly into his handheld radio. Cooper could hear Sutherland's voice crackle in response.

"I've just arrived at the school. The other units aren't far behind."

Cooper mouthed her instructions to Tennessee. "Tell him to surround the school and seal the exits."

She turned her gaze to a photo of Brian Hutchins, smiling down at her from a display of all the school staff. She wanted to punch a hole in it. Her endocrine system released a torrent of hormones and she felt like a lioness protecting her cub. Cooper would fight tooth and nail if that's what it took. Did Hutchins know Webb would jump ship when the bodies started to mount up? Surely his motivation for murder went beyond simply wanting her job? Cooper and Tennessee turned on the spot, four corridors branched off from the main lobby, and two sets of staircases led the way to the upper floors.

Tynemouth Academy was not a small school by any stretch of the imagination. The cuboid building had three floors of classrooms, offices, studios and laboratories. At full capacity, the school held over two-thousand pupils and over 150 members of staff. It served not only the village of Tynemouth but the neighbouring towns of North Shields and Whitley Bay. With a building of this scale, it was hard to know where to start.

Outside, Sam Sutherland hugged the external wall of the school building as he approached and he stuck to the shadows until he reached the lobby.

"Christ. Cooper, are you okay?"

It was a ridiculous question. She was far from okay. Her girl had been taken by a madman. A man she was supposed to trust and who had killed four of her classmates. How would Sutherland feel if it had been Caroline? No, was the answer. She was not okay.

Cooper pushed her negativity to the back of her mind. She had to stay in police mode. "What areas of the building have lights on?" she asked.

"We did a lap as we approached. Keaton's watching the doors on the western side of the building and Martin's not too far away. He's in a squad car with Nixon." He was out of breath and needed to take a second before he could continue. "The eastern side on the ground floor. There're a few lights still on there, the first floor too, almost directly above. There's a cleaner making her way along the top floor. She's turning off lights as she goes, and we think we saw someone still working in the labs."

Cooper looked down the corridor that led to the art department. The hallway headed east, towards the North Sea, and towards the illuminated windows. "Do we have numbers?" she asked.

"More arriving every second," said Sutherland.

"Have a team come in and clear any remaining staff. Keep everyone without a badge away from the art department."

"Roger." Sutherland spoke into his radio for a moment then followed Cooper.

She led Sutherland and Tennessee along the darkened corridor. They moved quietly, checking each abandoned classroom as they went.

Cooper's mouth was dry; her heartbeat pulsated in her ears. She was acutely aware that she was unarmed. They'd come straight from questioning a gym instructor, and there'd been no time to organise guns or even tasers. The three detectives got into formation when they reached the door they were looking for, the two larger men flanking their underweight chief. They listened for a moment but no sound came from the other side of the door. Cooper gave the nod and Tennessee charged in, followed by Cooper and Sutherland. It didn't take long to establish that the room was empty. No one was here. Instead, they were surrounded by freshly painted clay pots and some sculptures made of soda cans and tin foil.

"Fuck." Cooper was beyond terrified. "Where is she?"

"Let's head upstairs," suggested Sutherland. He pointed at the ceiling and then frowned, his eyes flicking back down to the floor. "I thought that was paint, but it's not. It's blood."

A breadcrumb trail of red droplets snaked across the tiled floor, and Cooper struggled to keep the panic at bay. For years it had only been her and Tina. No parents around, no Kenny, no siblings to act as aunts and uncles. If she lost Tina, she lost everything. Something primal surged through her and she let out an almighty roar. "TINA!"

They stood in silence, listening for any signs of life. Cooper could hear footsteps on the gravel outside, she could hear a faint droning noise of an industrial vacuum cleaner somewhere in the building, and there, a thumping noise. Rubber on metal. Thump, thump, swish. Thump, thump, swish.

"There," said Tennessee. He pointed to a store cupboard. The noise was definitely coming from inside.

"Police!" boomed Cooper. She tried the handle but it was locked. She slammed her weight against the door, once, twice... Tennessee shoved past her. There was no time for "Allow me, ma'am." He shoulder charged the door, knocking it off its hinges.

Tina Cooper was curled on the floor in the fetal position. Her mouth gagged, her arms and legs bound, masking tape covering her eyes. She thrashed violently; the thump, thump, swish coming from her shoes banging and sliding against the tiles. Cooper dived at her, relief flooding her body. Tina was alive.

Cooper scooped Tina's head in her hands and soothed her. "It's me, Tina. It's Mum."

She gently removed the gag and peeled the tape from her daughter's eyes as her own eyes filled with tears. Tina flinched and turned her gaze away from the fluorescent lighting in the art studio. "It's Hutchins, Mum. It's Hutchins!"

Sutherland had found a pair of scissors and was working around Cooper to sever the cable ties on Tina's arms and legs. The plastic had cut into her flesh, leaving it raw and painful. Once freed, Tina flung her arms around Cooper and repeated herself. "Hutchins."

"We know." Cooper delicately pushed Tina's hair from her face. "Where did he go?"

Tina's jaw moved up and down, but words didn't come out at first. "Drama," she eventually managed. "Drama department. He... he said he needed a costume."

Cooper had to prise herself from Tina's grip. "Get her out of here, Sam."

"Mum! No!"

"Tina, sweetheart, go with Sam. He'll keep you safe. I'll be back soon, I promise."

Sutherland pulled Tina to her feet. She was sobbing uncontrollably. Tears stained her cheeks, and she struggled to catch her breath. Cooper recognised the beginnings of a panic attack, and it broke her heart to move away from Tina when she just wanted her mother to hold her.

"Which way?" she asked her daughter. "Come on, Tina. Focus, sweetheart. Which way?"

Tina pointed to the ceiling.

"EYES ON." Tennessee's radio crackled. "We have a runner."

Tina broke free from Sutherland's protective arm and pressed her face up against the window. Brian Hutchins's bleached hair was visible in the moonlight. He sprinted across the carpark and fumbled with his keys. The squad cars illuminated as half a dozen men ran towards him.

"That way," said Tina, her arm extending to point at an emergency exit.

Cooper and Tennessee barged through the emergency exit and gave chase. Hutchins had made it to his car. The engine was starting as Cooper reached the edge of the carpark. In her socks, she slid on the ice and fell head-first onto the curb. Tennessee faltered but chose to pursue Hutchins. It was the right choice. Cooper pushed herself back to her feet and wiped blood from her forehead.

The Mini Countryman surged forward and knocked a PC off his feet. Thankfully, he rolled out of the way before the car's tyres could roll over him. Sirens blared. The Mini collided with the first squad car, spinning in circles on the slick ground, almost taking out another officer.

Another squad car moved into position at the end of the road, cordoning off the street. Young Oliver Martin jumped from the vehicle as Hutchins fell out of his driver's side door, making a run for it. Keaton sprinted across the school field, the grass gripping her boots better than the road ever would. She was gaining on them. Cooper's heart was in her mouth as she watched Keaton overtake Martin and tackle Hutchins to the ground. She let the full force of her fullback's frame slam into him; the sound of the man's ribs cracking could be heard from twenty metres away.

Cooper sank to her knees and burst into tears. She didn't give a damn if anyone thought it was unprofessional. They had him. It was over.

Keaton held Hutchins in place by digging her knee into the small of his back and pinning his shoulders with her hands. Tennessee, Martin and at least ten PCs caught up and surrounded him.

Tennessee looked over to Cooper. "Want the honours?"

Cooper shook her head. Sutherland was carrying Tina into the back of an ambulance and wrapping a blanket around her shoulders. Keaton could have the pleasure of cuffing Hutchins and reading the bastard his rights. Cooper had a daughter to comfort.

- CHAPTER 33 -

The Northumbria Emergency Care Hospital was a short ambulance ride north on the A19. Due to the winter vomiting bug, visiting hours had been reduced to just one hour per day and limited to immediate family only. Poor Josh had turned up with flowers and a box of Tina's favourite chocolates, only to be sent away by a stern-looking nurse with crow's feet deep enough to swipe a credit card through. Cooper took the gifts from Josh and gave his hand a squeeze.

"Tina will love them, Josh. I'll have her call you."

The young lad's cheeks flushed and his eyes dampened. "I was so scared," he said.

"She's going to be all right. You don't need to worry anymore."

He nodded and shuffled his feet, toeing the shoelaces of one trainer with the other. "It was definitely Mr Hutchins?"

"Definitely. But it's over now. He's going to jail for a very long time, probably the rest of his life," she assured him.

Cooper bid Josh farewell and followed the same nurse to ward four. Tina sat up in bed when she saw her. She smiled but there wasn't much emotion behind it. Cooper kissed her forehead and handed her the gifts.

"From Josh. He's a sweet one, that lad."

"Can you tell Dad that?" she sniggered and it was nice to see a hint of Tina's usual sass.

Cooper pulled a curtain around the bed to give the pair of them some privacy. She wished whoever was in the neighbouring bed would turn their television down or have the decency to use headphones. She didn't think her daughter should need to listen to the swear-laden Sopranos or whatever mob drama he was watching after her ordeal.

"The nurse said your wrists and ankles will heal before long."

Tina examined the bandages on her wrists. "They itch like crazy." She opened the box of chocolates and stuffed three into her mouth before offering one to Cooper. "Don't shake your head. You need the calories too."

Cooper chuckled and did as she was told. "These are great," she said with her mouth full. She swallowed and continued. "I've arranged for a trauma counsellor—"

"Ah, Mum, no. I can't."

"I know you hate talking to strangers, sweetheart." Cooper rested her hands over her heart in a pleading fashion, "but she's an expert in this sort of thing. She'll be able to help you in ways I won't."

Tina drew her hands up as if she was going to slam them on the bed in protest. She paused and folded her arms over her chest instead. "I'd rather not." She turned her head back and forth several times, then added, "but I will if it makes you happy."

Cooper sighed. What a relief. "It will. Thank you, Tina."

Tina took another chocolate and unscrewed the lid off a bottle of water from the side of her bed. "You know what was weird? He kept apologising."

"Hutchins?"

"Yeah. We had art in the afternoon. He'd barely done any teaching since taking over from Linda, but the substitute was sick, so I guess he didn't have a choice. We were finishing up our sculptures and Hutchins wasn't paying any attention to the class. He was properly distracted with his own project. The class was basically running riot. Anyway, his fingers were all blackened because he was sketching a charcoal drawing and I remembered reading something about charcoal residue in the file you had on Rachel. So, I turned to Josh and whispered a joke about Hutchins being the Tarot Card Killer. I didn't mean it. I didn't really think he was and I didn't think I'd said it loud enough for him to hear me but when I looked back at him he was staring at me. And you know how I misread facial expressions all the time? I couldn't tell if he was angry with me for making the joke or if he was panicked because I was right. Either way, he gave me the creeps."

"Oh, Tina."

"The bell rang, and I got out of there as fast as I could. I was going to call you from the toilets in the shed when I got to netball."

"Only netball was cancelled, and the shed was locked."

"Yeah. The other girls decided to go get hot chocolate at Woods and I... I didn't. I thought it was best to call Dad and have him pick me up early. So, I walked back towards the school and that's when he grabbed me and hit me over the head with something." Her hand instinctively went to the back of her head to feel the scab that had formed in her hair.

Hearing the story sent chills down Cooper's spine. All the fear and pain she'd felt not knowing if Tina was alive or not came back to her. If she'd just kept her off school, none of this would have happened.

"He wasn't making any sense." Tina lowered her voice and her mother had to lean in to hear what she was saying. "He apologised over and over. Kept saying sorry and jabbering on about how I wasn't part of the plan. That I was a good student."

Tina shrugged and took another swig of water.

"Then he started saying that I wouldn't look right. That he didn't have the right clothes with him and how he'd have to make do with whatever he could find in the drama department."

Cooper swallowed. Her imagination was forcing images of a dead-eyed Tina dressed as a hierophant to the forefront of her mind. White robes and a pointed hat, blood oozing from a deep cut in her chest and coating the robes in scarlet. Cooper swallowed again but her mouth had dried up. She pictured a laminated card reading *The Lovers.* She wouldn't have been able to handle losing Tina. She'd been through a lot in her life but there was no way she'd be able to come back from that.

Cooper scooted Tina to one side of the bed so she could lie down next to her. "I think he was telling the truth, Tina. I don't think you were part of the plan. But if he suspected that you knew..." She paused for a moment and rolled onto her side to look at Tina. "If only you'd gone with the other girls. Safety in numbers and all that?"

Tina shrugged and began to play with the edge of her bedsheet. "I wasn't invited. I never am. I'm weird little Tina Cooper."

Cooper wiped a tear from her eye. "To hell with those girls," she said. "As far as I'm concerned, you're perfect little Tina Cooper.

The answer comforted Tina like a bowl of hot noodles on a cold day but it did nothing to ease Cooper's guilt. She'd been one of the popular girls during her own time at high school. She was the first to be invited to parties, she had the most fashionable friends, and boys paid her a lot of attention. Looking back, it was no surprise she'd been knocked up before she could finish sixth form. The ugly truth was that the Erica of old would not have been friends with someone like Tina; the Erica of old wouldn't have known she existed.

BRIAN HUTCHINS LICKED HIS lips and blew bubbles through the film of saliva. He did it over and over, creating a rhythm of pop, pop, pop noises. His glasses were askew and the brown stubble that covered his jaw didn't match his bleached head. He'd removed his shirt and was sat tethered to his seat in just a vest. Hutchins's entire upper body was covered in a spiderweb of tattoos. Cooper counted at least twenty pentacles from where she stood behind a sheet of one-way glass. As well as the pentacles, he was decorated with a handful of seeing eyes and the number 666. Down his arm, in cursive script, read, *He who drains the power of the youth will dine with Satan and know his truth.*

"So, the old woman was right," mumbled Cooper to herself as she read his tattoo. "Is he talking?" she asked Tennessee.

"Not since we last spoke." Tennessee twirled his mobile between his fingers. "They have a doctor coming to assess if he can be held in general population or if he needs a bed in the loony bin."

Cooper shot him a sideways glance. "Been taking vocabulary lessons from Nixon?"

He smirked. "I say we dump him in gen. pop. I won't shed a tear if he doesn't make it to trial."

"Agreed," said Cooper, "but the families might. They deserve to see him sentenced. Did we hear back from Martin?"

"We did. The mother's car's with forensics. I'd bet my house it's what he used when he picked up Jasmine and Reuben."

Cooper turned her back on Hutchins and rested against the window. "Even if forensics can't find anything, we have all the evidence we need. I just spoke to Keaton. Hutchins's house was crammed to the rafters with fortune-telling hooey, voodoo dolls, books on witchcraft, devil worship stuff. You name it, they found it. His diary's going to make interesting reading; he'd convinced himself that each time he took a life, it brought him closer to the devil."

Tennessee shook his head as if he could wake himself from this bizarre dream. "I heard they found a bunch of fancy dress costumes too."

"Yeah, they did. And drawings. The bastard had a list of who he wanted to kill and sketches of how he wanted to display the bodies. He was saving the fool until last. That card was marked out for none other than Linda Webb."

Tennessee blinked in disbelief. "Dare I ask?"

"She was destined for the ninth hole at Tynemouth golf club."

"And Tina?"

"She wasn't on the list. Neither was Reuben."

"So we were right about him only taking Reuben as a means to get Jasmine. How is Tina? She doing all right?"

Cooper dipped her head. "I can bring her home tonight. She's milking it. Demanding we get a Chinese takeaway."

"Good shout. Might have to head home via the Silver Moon myself." He switched his phone to his other hand and resumed his twirling.

Cooper tilted her head back, indicating Hutchins. "He and Linda Webb both went for the head teacher position when it became available last year. Linda got the job and twisted the knife by diverting funding from his department. He knew she'd flake the second the shit hit the fan. I checked her employment record and she looks to have a history of it. If all went according to plan, he'd get to kill her off and play the hero who saved the school. But, if it all went wrong and he got caught, well, he'd still be closer to his beloved Satan and his murderous art exhibition would make sure he went down in the history books as the most notorious killer of the century."

"The Tarot Card Killer," mused Tennessee to himself. "He's going to be infamous."

The pair stood in silence as they contemplated the loss of life over the previous few weeks. The sad truth of the matter was that the press office was already inundated with writers wanting to pen Hutchins's biography. His name would be forever etched into the British psyche, but by the time the case came to trial, no one would remember the names of the victims. Say the names: Mary Ann Nichols, Annie Chapman, Elizabeth Stride, Catherine Eddowes, or Mary Jane Kelly and faces turn blank. Say the name Jack the Ripper and everyone nods in recognition.

Cooper's mind was still in nineteenth-century London when Tennessee's phone rang loudly. She jumped and clasped her hands to her chest. Tennessee was equally shocked as he dropped the phone and cursed as it bounced off cheap, wiry carpeting.

"DS Daniel," he said, retrieving the phone and pressing it to his ear. "Really?" he asked, taking in a sharp inhalation. "Jesus. Okay. I'll be right there."

Tennessee fumbled with the phone again and slid it into his pocket.

"Jack?" asked Cooper, concern forcing her to use his real name for a change. "What's wrong?"

Tennessee was halfway out the door when he turned back. "Nothing's wrong." A look of merry wonder passed over him. "That was the mother-in-law. Hayley's gone into labour." He grabbed Cooper and kissed her on both cheeks before she could protest. "Baby Alfie's on his way. I'm going to be a Dad!"

- CHAPTER 34 -

KENNY ORDERED ENOUGH CHINESE food to feed an army. Plastic cartons formed a jigsaw pattern over the dining table and bowls of spring rolls, spare ribs and fortune cookies spilt over onto the kitchen worktops. A *welcome home* banner stretched from one corner of the ceiling to the other and the living room appeared to have been turned into a botanical garden, such was the number of flowers that had been delivered.

"Dad," laughed Tina when she walked through the door and took in the scene. "I've only been gone two nights."

Kenny wrapped his arms around Tina and shrugged. "Did I go overboard?"

"You went overboard, swam up the Tyne and started racing the salmon."

Cooper gave Kenny a friendly punch on the arm. His over-the-top gesture stank of overcompensation, but if Tina liked it then that was all that mattered to her. "You should have brought Linda," she said, thinking the former headteacher would want to celebrate that Hutchins was off the streets and that she was no longer a suspect. "Justin'll be here in five. Josh too."

Kenny checked his watch and his head lolled from one side to the other. "We kind of broke up?"

"Kind of?" Cooper gave him a sceptical look.

"When I told her Hutchins was the killer, that he'd been caught but that..." he lowered his voice to a whisper and looked back at his daughter, "that another five minutes and Tina might have been killed. Well, the first thing she said was how the governors would be begging her to come back to work. It made my blood boil. I couldn't believe it."

Cooper shook her head. "I can believe it. I know you liked her Kenny, and I'm sorry, but she was the most self-involved person I've ever met."

Before Kenny could agree or disagree, the doorbell chimed and announced the arrival of Josh. Tina opened the door and planted a sloppy kiss on her boyfriend's cheek. Josh chewed his own lip and tried to avoid Kenny's eye.

"Come on in, lad." Kenny's friendly tone caught the youngster off guard and the can of cool lager he was handed almost finished him off.

"Erm, thanks, Mr Roberts." He opened the can as if it was a test; he probably thought Kenny was about to rip it from his hands and announce that no daughter of his would date an underage drinker.

Tina was about to close the door when Justin Atkinson trotted up the front path waving a bottle of Champagne.

"Justin, Kenny. Kenny, Justin," introduced Cooper.

There was a brief awkward moment where the two men sized each other up. One, obviously the brains; the other, the brawn. One, the past; the other, the present. Atkinson would never be able to haul breeze blocks like Kenny could, and Kenny couldn't use a dictionary if it came with instructions and a helpline.

Atkinson broke the silence first. "Good to meet you," he said, his voice a few bars lower than normal.

Kenny responded with a grunted "Aye, same to you," and a handshake that probably crushed Atkinson's fingers, not that the forensics expert showed it.

Cooper ignored them and grabbed Champagne flutes for those not drinking lager. She took the bottle from Atkinson, popped the cork and poured three glasses. "We have a lot to celebrate," she said with a genuine smile. "My brilliant daughter is back from the hospital."

Everyone clinked their glasses and toasted, "To Tina."

"My brilliant mother caught the demon headmaster," said Tina.

Clink. "To Erica."

"And our colleague welcomes new life to the world," said Atkinson.

"To baby Alfie," Cooper toasted and they all clicked their glasses once more before taking a drink.

After an hour of overindulgence where Tina experimented with just how much crispy duck she could fit into a pancake and Josh opened fortune cookie after fortune cookie until one vaguely predicted Newcastle United would win their next match, Cooper began to clear the plates. She changed into skinny jeans, boots and a slinky top, and applied bright red lipstick.

"Are you sure you don't mind us going out?" she asked Tina who was trying to stop her father from showing Josh her baby photos.

"Of course. Go celebrate solving the case. You've earned it... Dad! Stop it. No, I don't look cute. I look like a Cabbage Patch Doll."

"Kenny?"

"We'll be fine." He pulled another album from a shelf. "Oh, look at Tina's little dimples."

"DAD!"

Atkinson put his arm around Cooper's shoulders. "Where are you taking me, anyway? You've been very mysterious."

"We're going to a gig. There's a band I've wanted to see for ages but they've only just started touring again. They're called The Screaming Dolls."

Justin's lips pinched in confusion. "Right. That sounds rather shouty."

"Oh, I hope so," said Cooper, taking her wig off and tossing it into the kitchen bin. She didn't want to hide behind it a second longer. "I haven't moshed in forever."

Atkinson pulled her in close and kissed the top of her head. "Part of me hopes you're joking."

"Just part?"

"Yeah," he shifted his weight and tucked his free hand into his pocket. "The other part is telling me to shut up right now and not jinx this."

Cold air flooded the house as they walked arm-in-arm into the chilly Tynemouth night. Kenny took a long swig of his sixth beer and marvelled at how stunning his ex had looked as she left. It had been a lifetime since they were together but she hadn't aged a bit, not in his eyes. She'd been his first real love and no one since had come close to comparing, especially not Linda, that self-obsessed snob. He'd been a fool in letting Erica go. He'd been a bigger fool in not coming back until now. He took another drink and savoured the numbing effect of the alcohol. He let his head fall back and rest on the back of the sofa while Tina selected a film on Netflix for them all to watch. He'd win her back, he thought. One way or another, Erica Cooper would be his.

DCI Erica Cooper will return in Rock, Paper, Scissors.

Rock, Paper, Scissors

B Baskerville

Hyem Books

- Chapter 1 -

The city didn't look right to Macey Gallagher as she stumbled out of the club. The lights of the traffic left red and white snakes across her vision as if her brain was set on long exposure. Her eyes couldn't keep up with the world, and her body couldn't keep up with her brain. Every movement required meticulous concentration. Right foot. Left foot. Right foot.

A neon pink sign blinked at Macey, but she couldn't read it; the letters looked jumbled, and they didn't make sense. All around her, Newcastle's party people were enjoying their Saturday night. They hugged, kissed and danced, oblivious to the nineteen-year-old's worsening state. Pearl would be around here somewhere. She must be. Macey just had to find her.

"Watch it." A woman with an angry face and impossibly black eyebrows shoved Macey out of the way and into a brick wall. "Look where you're going."

The bricks grazed Macey's arm, and tiny globules of blood popped to the surface, turning her skin into a Lichtenstein artwork.

Where was Pearl? She didn't like feeling like this. She'd only had a couple of drinks. Hadn't she? Two glasses of wine with dinner before switching to Diet Coke in the club. It wasn't that much, but her head pounded and she desperately needed to pee.

It was April in Newcastle upon Tyne and bright, clear days gave way to chilling, teeth-chattering nights. In these parts, the locals declined to wear coats despite the nighttime temperature barely reaching five degrees.

"Coats are for southerners," Alison had told her on her first day at Newcastle University. "If you want to fit in, leave your coat at home. Besides, who wants to cover up an outfit as cute as yours?"

An ambulance raced past with its lights flashing and siren blaring. Macey covered her ears and closed her eyes. Everything was louder and brighter than it should be. She could hear people laughing, and paranoia told her they were laughing at her. Across the road, two squat men got into a fight. Their heavy fists flew at each other's heads in great arcs until a ginormous man in black with an earring in one ear separated them. One stormed towards the taxi rank; the other marched towards Macey.

Macey backed herself as far into the wall as possible, hoping to make herself invisible.

"Alreet, pretty lass?" His scowl turned to a smile as he edged closer. Macey tried to focus. He was old, not granddad-old, but probably mid-forties at least, maybe fifty. Lines carved across his forehead, and whilst his head was bald, his beard was mid-brown with patches of white. "Now, where've you been all my life?"

Macey clutched her bag to her chest. Her mouth was drier than the Sahara, but she managed, "For most of it, I wasn't born."

It was a mistake. The man's scowl returned. "Bitch," he spat, edging closer still.

It wasn't the first time Macey's mouth had got her into trouble. She was quick-witted, like many of her Dubliner compatriots, and while some thought of her craic as endearing, the insecure could react badly.

A slender woman with brown spiral curls walked by.

"Pearl?" Macey called. *Thank God.* She ducked under the man's arm and made a run for it, though it could hardly be called a run; a stagger would be more accurate. "Pearl?"

The woman turned and looked Macey up and down. She wasn't Pearl. "You all right, love?"

Macey rested her back against the wall and nodded. The gesture satisfied the woman, but Macey was far from all right. She wasn't well, the bald man was still staring at her, and her flatmate was nowhere to be seen. They'd promised to travel back home together, to share a taxi and order a dirty great pizza to finish off the evening. Pearl would be mad that Macey had gone home without her, but the doorman wasn't going to let her back into the club, and she couldn't stay out in the cold all night. She took two steps towards the taxi rank and teetered over in her heels. What a total waste of money. The shoes looked amazing, but they were nearly impossible to walk in, and God knows why anyone would design something so uncomfortable to wear. She tried again. Right foot. Left foot. Her ankle buckled once more, and Macey fell straight into the arms of the woman who wasn't Pearl.

"Oops. I've got you." She had a kind face and wore a fluorescent vest, the sort of one a workman would wear. "You don't look like you're doing so good. Do you need help?" The good Samaritan propped Macey back upright and supported her around her tiny waist. "What's your name, love?"

"Macey." The word didn't come easy to her. Her brain was becoming foggier by the minute, and her jaw wasn't responding as expected.

"Great accent. Where in Ireland are you from?"

"Dublin."

"Oh, fantastic." The stranger helped push Macey's blonde, wavy hair behind her ear. "I've been there for the odd boozy weekend. Great place. You here for uni?"

Macey nodded. She felt nauseous and bewildered and didn't want to be sick, not on the street.

"I'm with the Tyne Pastors," the woman said, pointing to a logo on her yellow vest. Did you have too much to drink, Macey?"

She shook her head. "No," she managed. "No, I— I don't think so."

"We work with the police. We help people who could do with a sit-down and a glass of water, or people who are lost, that sort of thing. We have a van across the road." She pointed to a dark van with sliding doors. "If you want to shelter from the cold, we have blankets and can make you a nice cup of tea while we try and get a hold of your friends. Sound good?"

The thought of a warm drink drew Macey over the street as if she were being pulled by a magnet. She was steered away from a kebab that had been dropped in the road and supported as she stepped up the kerb.

"Careful of your footing here." The stranger waved to an amicable-looking man holding a pile of fleece blankets. "This is Macey. I think she'd like some tea and to rest her feet.

"Hi, Macey," he said as he handed her a blanket.

Macey wrapped it over her shoulders and pulled the ends tight to her chest. Instantly, she felt comforted.

"Take a seat." The woman smiled and indicated a bench that ran the length of the van. A slim woman with mascara running down her face was sitting on the bench and sobbing into her mobile. She hiccoughed and continued crying. Between her feet, some strong-smelling coffee steamed into the cold air.

"Thank you." Macey smiled at her curly-haired new friend. She was blurry but gentle, and she had a familiarity about her. It was like talking to an aunt or a cousin.

"Where do you live? We usually stay out until four. If we can't reunite you with your friends by then we can give you a lift."

"H— Heaton," she stammered. Heaton was a popular suburb that sat to the east of the city centre and was only a short drive away. "Rothbury Terrace. Near... Near the mosque." Macey sat on the bench and tried to make herself comfortable. The bench was hard, but the fleece cushioned her bottom and she was already feeling warmer. She slumped back and closed her eyes for a moment, then looked at the screen on her phone and tried to make out the logos that no longer made sense. Pearl and Alison were probably dancing. Had they even noticed she'd gone?

"Here you go." The man handed her a mug of tea. He screwed the lid back on the flask and returned to the driver's seat. This would all be over soon, she told herself. Either Pearl would come and find her, or she could wait an hour and the pastors would drive her back home. She craved to be back in her bed. A trip to the medicine cabinet and a pint of water and she'd be right as rain.

Curls returned to the van. "Any luck with your boyfriend?" she asked the crying girl. The girl shook her head and tucked her phone into a pocket. "How about we stop this awful draught?" She reached behind her and slid the van door until it clicked closed.

The driver looked over his shoulder, and Curls nodded to him. The engine started and the van pulled away.

"Are you taking me home?" Macey asked.

The driver didn't answer. Nothing sobered a person up quite like the sickening knowledge that something awful was about to happen to them. For as Macey Gallagher's hands were bound with a cable tie, she realised all too late that these were not the Tyne Pastors and the good Samaritan was not so good.

- Chapter 2 -

DCI Erica Cooper stepped out of the Crown Court onto Newcastle's Quayside. It was a drizzly morning; the grey sky muddled with the grey Tyne, casting a usually vibrant part of the city into dullness. Around her, paparazzi gathered with their cameras trained on the revolving doors of the courts. They hoped to catch the families of The Tarot Card Killer's victims in their most vulnerable moment. *Vultures*, thought Cooper.

The only reason the scavengers were ignoring Cooper as she strode past them was because she'd brought a change of clothing. She'd learnt this tactic during the month-long trial of notorious gangster Eddie Blackburn. Unless Cooper needed to address the press, she preferred to escape unnoticed. Her coat of choice featured an oversized hood that covered not only the top of her head but also her forehead and eyes too.

Once a safe distance away, Cooper dropped her hood and tilted her head to the sky. Droplets of rain splashed against her number two buzzcut and helped cool the rage that had been building inside her. Brian Hutchins's defence team had been arguing a case of diminished responsibility. Cooper's self-control had been tested as she listened to their sob stories. Hutchins had taken the lives of four teenagers and had been minutes, possibly seconds, away from killing Cooper's daughter when her team had apprehended him. Tina had suffered from nightmares ever since, and although Cooper hadn't told anyone, so had she.

A little further along the quay, a stooped woman sold flowers from a cart. She wore her hair in curlers and tied a plastic bag around her head to protect it from the rain. "The usual, pet?" she asked Cooper in a friendly, northern voice.

"Please."

Cooper took the single yellow rose and followed the quay to the spot where she'd seen her best friend murdered. Thirteen years ago, some drunken lowlife had pushed eighteen-year-old Cindy Howes into the river, and she'd drowned before anyone could get to her. No one was ever charged.

"I still miss you," said Cooper in a whisper. She brought the flower to her nose and inhaled. "And I'm still sorry we never caught him." Cooper kissed the petals before tossing the flower into the river.

Cooper had parked in a multi-story near the courts, and by the time she got back to her car, the April showers had soaked her to the skin. She decided to nip home to change before returning to Northumbria Police Headquarters. Once in a dry suit and with a fresh layer of make-up, Cooper picked up an extra-large chicken supreme pizza from the retail park next to HQ. She knew from experience that her team worked best on a full stomach, and anything was better than the staff canteen or the vending machine.

"You're not listening to me." A young woman with a Yorkshire accent slapped her hand on the front desk.

"Miss, take a step back and calm down." The desk sergeant got to his feet. "We do not tolerate the abuse of our staff."

"Abuse? Abuse?" The woman shook her head in disbelief. She was slim, dressed in sporty lycra and had a head of dark chestnut spiral curls. "She'll die if we don't find her soon."

"Miss, please lower your voice. We'll have someone take your statement as soon as we can, but we're very busy today. There'll be a bit of wait." He pointed to some plastic chairs.

Tears began to roll down the woman's pretty face. "Something's happened to her. I know it."

Cooper didn't know what was going on, but she felt for the woman; she was clearly distressed. She approached the desk and placed the pizza on it. "It's okay, Davis. I'm free. I can take her statement. Can you send this up to CID? Tell them to save me a slice."

Davis looked longingly at the box before nodding.

Cooper turned to the woman. "I'm DCI Erica Cooper," she said by way of an introduction. "What's your name?"

"Pearl," she sniffed. She couldn't have been more than nineteen or twenty. "Pearl Baxter."

"Follow me, Pearl. We'll get you a glass of water, and you can tell me what's going on."

It took a few moments for Cooper to calm Pearl Baxter down. From what she could gather, Pearl's flatmate had gone missing after a night out.

"But you said she's been texting you?"

Pearl shook her head. "No. Someone's been texting me. But it's not Macey. She said she was going to stay at the flat that night, but when she wasn't there the next morning, I thought she must have hooked up with her boyfriend. They're at that totally loved up, can't keep their hands off each other stage in their relationship, so I wasn't worried when I didn't see her on Sunday morning. When I hadn't heard from her by Sunday afternoon, I texted her to ask if she was at Aaron's."

"Aaron is Macey's boyfriend?"

Pearl paused while a couple of officers raced past. "Yes, Aaron Quinn. I asked her if she needed anything from the shop, and she replied with *no thanks*. That's not like Macey at all. She'd ask for something ridiculous like a tamed baby walrus or a glow-in-the-dark dildo."

Cooper tried not to smirk.

"And she always signs her texts XOXO. Always. Look."

Pearl handed Cooper her phone and scrolled through the girls' messages. "I see what you mean," said Cooper as she scanned hundreds of messages, all ending with XOXO. "And you don't think she's really at Aaron's because..."

"Because Aaron showed up at the flat yesterday looking for Macey. He hadn't seen her since Saturday morning."

"Ah."

"All the time I thought she was at his, he thought she was with me."

Cooper's hand moved quickly across the page as she noted down Pearl's statement.

"She'd messaged Aaron too," continued Pearl. "Well, whoever has her phone did. It didn't sound like Macey. Aaron actually thought she was in a mood with him because of the one-word replies."

"Have you tried calling her?"

"Of course I have. Dozens of times. It just goes to voicemail."

"Has Macey ever done this before? Could she have met a new man? Be avoiding Aaron for that reason?"

"No," snapped Pearl. "That's not her style. Like I said, she was loved up. I know it's only been a couple of days, but none of our friends have seen or heard from her. I checked her wardrobe, and I don't think anything's missing. Her toiletries too. They're all still there. And her medicine."

"Medicine?"

"Insulin. She has a kit that she takes on nights out because alcohol sends her hypo, or hyper. I forget which. But she only took one night's worth with her. The rest is in the flat."

A chill ran down Cooper's spine, and she knew why Pearl feared the worst. If Macey hadn't taken her diabetes medication with her, she was high risk. Wherever she was, Cooper needed to find her. And fast. Cooper placed her hand on Pearl's arm. "I can see why you're concerned. This is more worrying. Have you spoken to Macey's parents?"

Pearl shook her head. "I don't have their details. Aaron might. I'm not sure. Our landlord should have them, though. We had to name guarantors when we signed the lease."

"Pearl, I'm going to take some more details and open an investigation into Macey's disappearance. Then I want you to go home, make yourself a nice cup of tea and call this number." She handed Pearl a pamphlet for Missing People, a charity that provides support and advice for the families and friends of missing persons in the UK. "They offer round-the-clock emotional support. You're understandably distressed. These people can listen. I'll pop over to see you later today, okay?"

Pearl's lip trembled again. She was on the verge of falling apart. "Thank you," she said, taking the pamphlet. "I just hope we're not too late."

- Chapter 3 -

CID smelled of pizza. Sadly, as Cooper stared into the empty box, she realised her request that the other detectives leave her a slice had gone unanswered.

"You seen Tennessee?" she asked Detective Neil Fuller.

Fuller, a squirrelly man whom Cooper was once romantically involved with, looked up from his computer. "I still can't get used to you with that buzzcut. Suits you, though. Makes you look more, you know, confident."

Cooper ran her hand over her head. She liked the feel of the super-short hairs against her palms. Last year, she'd lost her hair to chemotherapy and had worn a wig to cover the evidence, but thanks to her daughter's enthusiasm and insistence that she looked like a total badass, Cooper had begun to embrace the look. She ditched the wig and bought herself a pair of clippers. Fuller was right; it did suit her.

"He's over there," nodded Fuller, and Cooper followed his eyes to a desk at the far end of the department.

DS Jack Daniel, who had been known as Tennessee since he was a bairn, was taking a bite out of the last slice of pizza. Strings of cheese stretched from his mouth to his hand like strands of yellowy spiderweb. Cooper approached with stealth, grabbed what remained of the slice and shoved as much into her mouth as she could manage before handing the crust back to Tennessee.

"Urgh," he grimaced.

"Now, now," teased Cooper. "Eat your crusts, or your hair won't go curly."

Tennessee pulled a face and turned his eyes upward towards his mop of blond curls. "What you got?" he asked, pointing to the file in Cooper's hand.

"Missing girl. Nineteen-year-old student named Macey Gallagher, originally from Dublin. Reported missing by her flatmate Pearl Baxter. Hasn't been seen since a boozy night out on the eighth and doesn't have her insulin with her."

Tennessee sat up. "Since Saturday? How'd the flatmate not realise until now?"

Cooper shrugged. "She assumed she was staying at her boyfriend's, and her boyfriend assumed she was with the flatmate."

"Is that likely?"

"I'm not sure, but the flatmate's been receiving texts supposedly from Macey, only she's convinced the messages aren't really from her." Cooper stole a chair from a neighbouring desk and sat down.

"And that's why you haven't handed it over to Mispers?" Tennessee asked, referring to the common abbreviation for missing persons. "You smell a rat?"

Cooper drew her lower lip in between her teeth and slowly released it. "I smell a rat," she confirmed, "but I hope I'm wrong. Listen, there's not much of the day left, but I'm going to make a start by contacting the girl's landlord and getting her parents' contact details. Can you put a request in for the missing girl's phone records? And get a trace while you're at it. Hopefully, it's still switched on."

"Consider it done," he replied with a yawn.

Cooper frowned at the DS. "Another restless night?"

Tennessee took the name and phone number of the missing girl from the file and got to his feet. "Little Alfie woke up about twelve times last night. I mean, I want to be a hands-on dad, I don't believe in leaving all the baby stuff to his mother, but Hayley didn't even stir. I swear that woman could sleep through a bomb blast. Anyway—" he waved the phone number. "I'll be back in a bit."

Cooper watched him walk away while she dialled the number Pearl Baxter had given her for their landlord. The first five months of fatherhood had ravaged Tennessee's fashion-model looks. The man was drained. His skin was dry and colourless, apart from the skin under his eyes, which had been stained a sickly shade of purple.

"Hello?"

Cooper could hear chewing noises. "Mr Walker? This is DCI Erica Cooper from Northumbria Police. I'm calling about a tenant of yours. Macey Gallagher?"

There was more chewing. "Gallagher? Gallagher? Oh, yeah. Blonde girl, Rothbury Terrace. Let me guess, noise complaint? Always is with the student lets."

Quieter than the chewing noise but still audible was the sound of excitable sports commentary. "No, Mr Walker, it's nothing like that. I'm afraid Macey's been reported missing. I need the contact details for her parents; I believe you have them listed as guarantors?"

"Missing?" The television was turned down but not muted. "Er, yes, I have their details somewhere. Can I call you tomorrow? I have a lot of properties. It'll take me a while to dig them out."

"Sorry, but I'm going to need them now. Your horse race will have to wait."

Several seconds of silence was followed by a sigh and, "Fine. Hang on. I'll just pop you on hold."

Cooper drummed her fingers on the table for a moment and checked her mobile for messages. She had two. Tina had messaged to say that her father was taking her and her boyfriend, Josh, to the cinema and asked if she wanted to join them. Cooper declined. She and Tina's father, Kenny, had split up the moment they found out she was pregnant. They'd barely spoken for the best part of twelve years, but recently, they'd been making an effort with each other. *Maybe next time, T. Have fun, and don't eat too much popcorn.*

The second message was from Justin Atkinson, a highly skilled scene of crime officer, silver-haired environmentalist, and Cooper's new beau. *Berlin is beautiful. Great conference. The Germans are making huge strides in forensic podiatry. Fascinating stuff. Miss you. J.*

Cooper smiled to herself. Not many people would consider forensic podiatry fascinating, but that was what made Atkinson so brilliant at what he did. As a teen, she'd always been attracted to alpha males. Strong, silent types with biceps bigger than their brains. After falling pregnant at seventeen, joining the police at eighteen and dedicating herself to a career that could provide for her daughter, Cooper's romantic confidence took a tumble, and she ended up in a string of on-again, off-again relationships with men like Detective Neil Fuller. Thankfully, her thirties had awoken Cooper's dormant sapiosexuality, and she couldn't get enough of Atkinson's extensive vocabulary. His tall, lean body was a felicitous bonus.

"You still there?" Matt Walker was back on the line and had interrupted her thoughts about something else that was extensive. "I have the names and address you wanted."

Cooper shook herself back to the present and grabbed a pen. "Yes, okay, go."

"Iris and Sean Gallagher. Six Kildonan Avenue, Perrystown. You want their phone numbers?"

"Please."

Cooper noted the landline and mobile numbers for Macey's parents and thanked Matt Walker for his help. She was just about to dial the Gallaghers when Tennessee returned.

"Here," he said, handing her a coffee. "Phone records will be with us tomorrow or Thursday at the latest."

"Cheers. I was just about to inform the family. Want to do the honours?"

Tennessee's mouth twitched. "Ah, Coop, you know I hate that."

"And you know everyone hates it. You're a capable DS. If you can handle the domestic we saw the other night, you can handle this."

The younger man rubbed his jaw and went to take a sip of coffee before realising it was far too hot. "Fine. Give me the phone. What are their names?"

"Iris and Sean Gallagher."

Cooper picked up a second line to listen in and take notes.

"Hello? This is DS Jack Daniel from Northumbria CID. I'd like to speak to Mr Sean or Mrs Iris Gallagher, please."

There was sniggering on the other end of the phone. "Aye," came a deep, male voice, "and this is Mr Jim Beam hoping to speak to Captain Morgan. Good one. Who is this? Mikey?"

"Sir, this isn't a joke. This is Detective Sergeant Jack Daniel from—" There was more giggling, and Tennessee turned to look at Cooper.

"Fine," she mouthed. "Sir? Sir? DCI Cooper here, DS Daniel's colleague. We're calling about Macey."

The giggling came to an abrupt end, and his voice hardened. "Macey? Should I be sitting down?"

"Macey was reported missing by her flatmate today. She and her friends haven't seen Macey since the evening of the eighth. When was the last time you spoke to your daughter, Mr Gallagher?"

"Missing?" Strangely, Cooper thought she heard him laugh again. "I thought you were going to tell me she'd been shot or something. Well, thank God."

Cooper and Tennessee frowned at each other. Sean Gallagher didn't sound too concerned for his daughter's safety.

"The last time you spoke to Macey, sir?"

"Oh, it's been a while. A month at least. I'll check with her mother, but this is classic Macey."

"How do you mean?"

"Well, she's always running off, isn't she? Did it when she was ten. Jumped on the train to Galway to see her aunt without telling anyone. Sparked a massive search. It made the news and everything. At fifteen, she stole her sister's ID – double of each other they are – and she went off to Amsterdam with a boy from her school. Got high on pot brownies and stole a pedal boat. And at eighteen, after telling us she was going to Trinity College, she runs off to Newcastle. She's a wanderer. Always has been, and always will be. I'll ask around, see if anyone's heard from her, but if history's anything to go by, she'll show up when she's hungry or runs out of money."

"Mr Gallagher," interrupted Cooper. "Macey's flatmate doesn't think she took any of her belongings with her. She also left her insulin at the flat they share."

"Hmm," he was quiet for a moment. "Well, that's more unusual. She'll pick up an emergency prescription, though. She was always very good at remembering to do her injections. I'll speak to Iris and Kate."

"Kate?"

"Her sister. It's Katherine, but we call her Kate."

"When you spoke to Macey last month, how was she?"

"Besotted with some boy."

Cooper consulted her notes. "Would that be Aaron Quinn?"

"Yeah, that's him. She said he'd never been abroad before and she couldn't wait for the summer break to come around so she could show him Bangkok. She's probably with him. They'll be holed up doing what young lovers do."

Cooper took a deep breath. She wasn't sure if Mr Gallagher was indifferent to the danger his daughter could be in, whether she genuinely was the type to disappear and not tell a soul, or if he was hiding something. "She's not with Aaron," Cooper said. "He's just as worried as Macey's flatmate. I'll be speaking with him first thing in the morning. Thank you, Mr Gallagher. I'll be in touch regularly to update you on the investigation. In the meantime, could you call me immediately if you hear anything?"

"Of course."

Cooper recited her number and hung up. She sipped her coffee as she mulled over the conversation. She and Kenny would be beside themselves if Tina disappeared again, and Tennessee would be the same way with his infant son. Sam Sutherland, a DI, had been so concerned about his daughter, Caroline, during the Tarot Card Killer case that he'd pulled her out of school. Sean Gallagher did not appear to be cut from the same parenting cloth.

"What now?" asked Tennessee.

"Put in a request for her bank records and meet me downstairs in fifteen. We should visit Macey's flat before we finish for the day."

Tennessee saluted and grabbed his coat. "What did you think of Sean Gallagher?"

She ground her teeth before speaking. "I think Papa Bear's a little too laid back about his baby girl going missing."

- Chapter 4 -

Tennessee opened an umbrella and held it over his and Cooper's heads as they strolled through Heaton Park. The young detective was as physically protective of Cooper as Cooper was emotionally protective of him. He reminded Cooper of a younger brother who always looked out for his much smaller *big* sister. She was worried about him; he'd checked his phone eight times on the short drive over here.

Heaton Park was a beautiful oasis of greenery in a diverse and fashionable area of Newcastle. The suburb of Heaton was close to the city, with good schools, independent cafés and restaurants, as well as the usual chains. The rain pitter-pattered off the umbrella as Cooper and Tennessee strolled towards the park's exit. The trees lining either side of the pathway were blushed pink with blossom petals while blooms of yellow daffodils erupted in patches over grassy verges. Even on a miserable spring day like today, the park was alive with colour.

On Cooper's right, the ancient ruins of The House of Adam of Jesmond stood proud against the downpour. A knight and loyal ally of King Henry III, Adam de Gesmuth rose to Sheriff of Newcastle only to become hated by his community for extortion and embezzlement. Fearful for his safety, the king allowed Adam to fortify his home. After Adam's death during the crusades, the house fell into disrepair, but two walls remained defiant to seven hundred years of wind and rain.

"What's that smell?" asked Tennessee.

Cooper sniffed the air. "Wild garlic."

"Can you eat it?"

"You can. Some fancier restaurants forage down here and use it in their menus. Please don't ask me how. You know I can't cook for toffee."

Tennessee kicked a pebble with his boot. "Did I hear Sutherland was called to an armed robbery?" he asked, referring to detective Sam Sutherland.

"Yeah, some jokers turned over a pawnbroker's in the city. He's got Keaton and Martin with him. Bit of a hostage situation going on. I'm sure they'll fill us in once it's all over."

The pair left the park, passed the Islamic Centre and turned up Rothbury Terrace. On one side of the street, substantial Victorian terraces housed well-to-do families. On the other, smaller terraced houses had been converted into flats for the city's ever-expanding student population.

Cooper double-checked the door number of one flat before ringing the bell. A red-eyed Pearl Baxter opened the door and hurried the pair in. "Come in. It's pissing down."

"How are you holding up, Pearl? Did you call the number I gave you?"

Pearl nodded at Cooper. "Spoke to some lady. She said I can call back whenever I want to talk."

Cooper placed a hand on the young woman's shoulder. "That's good. Pearl, this is DS Daniel. Could you show us Macey's room, please?"

"This way."

Pearl led the pair to the back of the house. "Macey had the back bedroom. She wanted the smaller room as the rent was cheaper." She pushed open the door. "I've left everything as I found it," she added.

Macey Gallagher's room was a shrine to Ikea. Cooper recognised the Malm range of furniture from her daughter's bedroom as well as a free-standing mirror she'd admired on her last visit to the Swedish labyrinth of flat-packs and temper tantrums.

Tennessee picked up a hairbrush from Macey's dresser and slipped it into a paper evidence bag.

"What are you doing?" asked Pearl. The corners of her mouth turned down accusingly as if Tennessee were stealing from her flatmate.

He sealed the bag before answering. "The hair on her brush includes the root. We can take a DNA sample from it."

"In case she turns up dead?"

Tennessee's face tensed, and he nodded. It was enough for Pearl to leave the room.

"Poor kid," he said to Cooper.

"Can't be easy." Cooper slid a MacBook out from under Macey's bed and opened it. "Her laptop's here; password-protected, though. We'll take it to the techies."

Tennessee continued to scan the room. "I have to agree with the flatmate. It doesn't look like anything's missing. Nothing obvious anyway." He opened a drawer and closed it again.

Cooper opened a second drawer. "Here's her passport." She flicked to the photo page and took in the image of Macey Gallagher, a pale blonde with rosy cheeks and blue eyes that seemed too big for her face.

"So she hasn't left the country."

"Her father said she'd travelled on her sister's passport before. We should check with the sister. Make sure she still has her passport."

"Any sign of a diary?" Tennessee said, continuing his search.

"No. There's plenty of notepads here, though." Cooper flicked through the pages of a beige exercise book. "Uni notes by the looks of it. Personal notes in the margins. *Dentist two o'clock, buy bread*, that sort of thing."

"Worth taking them?"

Cooper nodded and slipped the books into a bag. "Martin can comb through them when he's finished at the pawnbrokers. See if anything stands out."

"He'll love that," Tennessee said with sarcasm.

"He doesn't have to love it. He just has to do it. Right, I think we're done here for now."

Cooper found Pearl on her living room sofa, gripping a bottle of Czech lager with both hands. When she saw the DCI, she lifted the bottle, toasted the air and took a long swig. "It's been a shitty, long day."

In front of the sofa, a coffee table was littered with photocopied posters of Macey's face under the words *Have you seen me?* Tennessee picked one up. "Did you make these?"

Pearl shook her head and took another swig. "Aaron did. He feels a bit helpless. Wants to stay busy. He's been up and down Heaton Road handing copies to all the cafés and shops. He's going along Chillingham Road tomorrow morning and then Osborne Road in Jesmond."

"Can you tell me what Macey was wearing on Saturday night?" Cooper pulled a pen and pad out of her coat pocket.

"I can show you." Pearl opened her phone and scrolled through images until she found a suitable one. "This is Macey," she pointed to a short, slender girl in the middle of a group shot. "She had on these new Kate Spade heels. Apparently, they hurt like hell. That's a French Connection wrap dress, and I don't know what brand her handbag was, but it was a black clutch with silver trim. She kept an insulin pen in there, make-up too, and the silver bracelet..." Pearl zoomed in on Macey's right wrist. "It's a medical alert bracelet. Says she has type one diabetes."

"That's great, Pearl. Can you send that photo to this number?" Cooper handed Pearl her card. "And these girls are the ones you mentioned to me at the station? Imogen and Alison?"

"That's right."

"Who's this?" asked Cooper, pointing to a man who stood close to the group whose eyes were trained on Macey.

"A friend of Imogen's. Nick, I think. It was loud in the bar. Might have been Rick."

"And did you see Nick or Rick after you noticed Macey wasn't with you anymore?"

Pearl's shoulders lifted for a moment. "I don't know. I was pretty out of it. Too many shots. Sorry, I know I'm useless."

A tear rolled down her cheek, and she tipped the remaining beer into her mouth.

"You're not useless," Cooper told her. "You're doing well. Don't be too hard on yourself. Now, is there anything else you can think of? Anyone Macey was scared of? Or a reason she might want to disappear?"

Pearl wiped the tear away and left a smudge of mascara on the back of her hand. "No. She was happy. She was enjoying her course, and Aaron doted on her."

Cooper closed her notepad and gave Pearl a sympathetic look. "Thanks, Pearl. Call us if you think of anything else. We'll see ourselves out."

LIKE PUPPIES ABANDONED BY their mother, the girls huddled together for warmth. They whimpered and whined. Annoying little bitches. He was sick of them. Especially the Irish one. She was nineteen, according to her ID. Older than his boss would have liked, but luckily, she looked younger. Her eyes were big for her head, giving a baby-like appearance that would fetch some big bucks. The driver had done well picking her out of the crowd, and the lure knew what she was doing, knew how to get them to trust her. It was a shame the Irish girl was so noisy. Where she was going, they didn't like noise and backchat.

"Please," she begged, her voice loud but quivering. "Please." Her wrists were secured in front of her with cable ties, and she held her palms together as if praying. "Please, I need my medicine."

"I told you to pipe down," he replied, pushing her away so she fell into the others. She needed to be quiet. Their location wasn't as isolated as he would prefer, but his bosses had picked it out, and he had to make do. If she kept making this racket, she could blow the whole operation.

"Please," she tried again, louder this time. Snot streamed from her nose, and tears ran under the blindfold and into her mouth. "I need insulin. If I don't get it—"

He cut her off with a swift kick to her ribs. "Quiet."

She curled up in the foetal position and squeezed her upper arms to her sides, trying to protect herself from further blows. He stood watching her for a second and relaxed in the blissful silence that followed. His violence has worked. He'd have preferred to punch her in her pretty little mouth; it would have given him more satisfaction, but it would have split her lip or knocked a tooth out. His boss would be furious. He liked them young, beautiful and unmarked.

He crouched down and could smell sweetness on her breath, brought on by high blood glucose levels. "Listen," he whispered, "I'll get you some fucking insulin, all right? But you need to keep your gob shut. Understand?"

She cowered further into the other girls. As if those skinny bitches could protect her. They were bound and blindfolded just as she was.

"Understand?" he asked again. Growling this time because he didn't like to repeat himself.

She nodded and wiped her tears.

"Good." He placed a bottle in her shaking hands. "Drink some water. It'll help. I'll be back with food and insulin later. But I swear, if the guard tells me you've made so much as a peep, I'll flush the insulin down the bog, and you'll be tossed in the fucking sea."

- CHAPTER 5 -

"HOW DID YOU MANAGE to burn porridge?" Tina Cooper furrowed her dark brows as she stared into the pot on the hob. What should have been creamy porridge oats was now a brown, dried-out mess.

"Sorry, T," said Cooper with an apologetic smile. "I got distracted reading the news. I'll make some toast instead. So, what are your plans for today? And what in God's name are the seagulls so worked up about?"

There was an almighty racket coming from the roof of Cooper's home. Seagull squawks were part and parcel of living near the coast, but the family of herring gulls that had made Cooper's chimney stack their home seemed especially agitated today.

"They've been like that since dawn," yawned Tina. "And yeah, I've got a metric tonne of homework to do. The Easter holidays are hardly going to be a holiday at all. I'm going to hang out at Dad's this morning while I finish up a biology assignment and an English essay, and then I'm going to Josh's this afternoon. We'll do maths together, then take a walk down Longsands."

"Nice," said Cooper. "The beach bit, anyway, not the homework." Truth be told, Cooper knew Tina was just playing a part, saying the words she thought she ought to say. If she knew her daughter, and she believed she did, Tina would be far more excited about ploughing into a maths paper than getting sand between her toes.

The toast popped out of the toaster, and Tina slathered a healthy amount of chocolate spread on two slices and began to devour them. "Here," she said, handing Cooper two slices and a jar of ginger jam.

"Don't worry about me. You have them. I'll eat at the station."

Tina rolled her eyes and gave her mother the *no, you won't* stare. She was probably right. When Cooper was worried about a case, her appetite seemed to disappear, and she was extremely worried about Macey Gallagher. The longer it took to find her, the more danger she would be in.

The doorbell chimed at ten past eight, and Tina opened the door for Kenny. He greeted Tina with a kiss on the top of her head and Cooper with a clumsy hug. "Got you a present," he smiled.

Cooper was sure he meant Tina, so she busied herself by making a flask of tea to take with her, but when Kenny dragged an A1-sized framed poster from a Metallica gig through the door, with a grin worthy of the Cheshire Cat on his face and proudly declared "Ta-dah," she knew the gift was for her.

"Recognise it?" he asked.

Cooper grabbed the frame and held it up at eye height. "Is this what I think it is?" Memories flooded back to Cooper. Her mind conjured images of cheap lager in plastic cups, bodies bouncing off one another, and music so loud your ears hummed for days. "Our first date."

Technically, it wasn't a first date. Cooper had met Kenny at the concert when she'd crowd-surfed over a tide of head-banging moshers and had landed in his big, strong arms.

"Where did you find this?" asked Cooper. She could smell Kenny's aftershave from that night and could still feel her best friend, Cindy, squeezing her arm in excitement as they waited for James Hetfield to take to the stage.

"On an eBay auction," replied Kenny. "I thought you'd like it. Got the frame at a charity shop. Thought it was quirky."

"It is." The frame was made up of pin badges and buttons of all shapes and sizes. The classic yellow smiley face badge - synonymous with the nineties rave scene - stood out the most.

"I brought my tool kit. Thought I'd hang it for you before I whisk young Tina away for a morning of studying."

Tina was still nibbling on her crusts. She grunted, "Fun times," as crumbs fell from her mouth to the kitchen floor.

Kenny didn't wait for approval; he lifted the poster from Cooper's hands, heaved it upstairs and looked around Cooper's room. It felt odd, having him in her room. It took her back to being a teenager and enjoying stolen kisses and naughty moments under the sheets when her parents were at work and she was supposed to be at school. She hoped this wouldn't take too long. She didn't want the smell of Kenny's aftershave to linger until Atkinson returned from Germany. Not that she'd done anything to feel guilty about.

"Above the fireplace?" asked Kenny. He extracted the correct drill bit from his tool bag and held it between his teeth while he found a corresponding wall plug. Cooper nodded; the poster would look great there.

Kenny was finished in less than a minute. Impressive work. It would have taken her three hours of measuring, double-checking and working out how to use the damn drill to achieve the same result, and it would still be wonky.

Kenny's hands rested on his hips as he admired his handiwork, and then his eyes flickered to the dresser where Atkinson's spare glasses were resting on a Yuval Noah Harari book.

"Does the Science Man like Metallica?"

Over the last few months, Kenny had stopped referring to Atkinson as Justin and had instead started calling him the Science Man. It didn't bother Cooper; the name was pretty apt.

"He doesn't dislike them."

Kenny shrugged his large shoulders and left the room. Cooper followed him downstairs, where she found Tina balancing a pile of textbooks in her arms.

"Ready to go, sweetheart?"

Tina nodded and gave her mother the briefest of goodbye hugs. Cooper grabbed a leather jacket and her keys and followed Tina and Kenny out the front door, only for her ears to be assaulted by a chorus of caws. Whatever was bugging the winged rats, Cooper hoped they'd get it out of their system by the time she got home. Before her backside could reach the driver's seat, her phone buzzed. Cooper glanced at the screen and saw that it was Detective Chief Superintendent Howard Nixon.

Oh, bloody hell. What had she done now? "Sir?"

"Cooper, I have the results of the phone trace for your missing-presumed-dead girl."

Relieved that she hadn't done anything to warrant one of Nixon's notorious bollockings, Cooper braved correcting her superior. "She's not presumed dead, sir."

"Diabetic lass, out drinking alcohol till the wee hours, wearing next to nothing, and no one's seen hide nor hair from her since? If she turns up alive, I'll eat my hat."

"How about, if I find her alive, you give me a raise?"

Nixon chortled. "That's a big if, but like my ma used to say: Shy bairns get nowt. Right, note this down. The phone's been switched off since Monday lunchtime, but its last triangulation point was fifty-four degrees, fifty-eight point four minutes north, one degree, twenty-seven point three minutes west."

Cooper keyed the coordinates into her sat-nav and found they led to Bede Industrial Estate in an area called Jarrow. "Thanks, sir. I'll be in touch."

Cooper hung up and collected Tennessee from the corner of Front Street and Percy Park Road in Tynemouth.

"Get in," she yelled over the noise of car horns from the traffic building up behind her. "And I hope your tetanus is up to date. We're headed for darkest Jarrow."

"Christ. What did we do to deserve that?"

Jarrow, on the south bank of the Tyne, had been a powerhouse of the ship-building industry. When the local shipyard closed in the 1930s, over eighty per cent of the working-age men found themselves unemployed. Without investment in the area, the local population continued to suffer more than their fair share of crime and unemployment.

"It's the last known location for Macey Gallagher's phone. Thought we should check it out. You sleep better last night?"

The detective sergeant picked some sleep from the corner of his eye and flicked it out the Mazda's window. "Got a whopping three and a half hours."

Cooper turned her Mazda onto the A19 and headed for the Tyne Tunnel. It didn't take long for them to reach their destination. Tennessee emerged from the car and scanned the road back and forth. "There's nowt here."

"There's a bus stop," said Cooper. She approached the stop and studied the timetable. "Only one route stops here. The number twenty-seven. Goes to South Shields."

"You think she got a bus from here?"

Cooper pulled a face. "I'm not sure she was even here, but her phone definitely was. Phones hold secrets. Photos, emails, private messages."

Tennessee shuffled along the road's edge, checking under shrubs and kicking his feet into long blades of grass.

"Here." Cooper pulled a pair of gloves from her field kit and handed them to Tennessee. "Make yourself useful," she said, pointing to a rubbish bin next to the bus shelter.

Tennessee's face wrinkled as he approached the bin and stared down into it. "Seriously?"

"Seriously."

The DS didn't argue. Piece by piece, he pulled litter from the bin and laid it on the ground.

"Anything interesting?" asked Cooper.

"Crisp packets, cans of Monster energy drink and something that resembles a dead mouse. Oh, shit, it *is* a dead mouse. Gross."

Tennessee held the creature by the tail, at arm's length, before dropping it next to a soggy copy of The Sun.

"But no phone?"

"No phone."

Cooper sighed. She wanted the phone. CID would have Macey's call and text history soon enough, but there were other things that her records wouldn't show, and those were the items Cooper was most interested in. Besides, any prints could be run through the system. If they matched with someone with a record, they could pay them a visit. She pulled her own mobile out and called the operator.

"Hello? Yes, put me through to South Tyneside council, please. Environmental services." She watched Tennessee place each item of rubbish back in the bin, peel off his gloves and chuck them in the bin as well. "Hi, this is DCI Erica Cooper from Northumbria CID. There's a bus stop on Jarrow Road. I need to know when its bin was emptied."

A woman with a high-pitched Geordie accent conducted a quick check on her system. "It would have been collected on Tuesday. Could have been anytime between six a.m. and five p.m. I can contact the team and try to narrow it down for you."

"No, that won't be necessary. Where did they take it? Great. Thank you."

Cooper hung up and winked at Tennessee before dialling DC Oliver Martin, the youngest and most image-conscious member of her team. She put him on speakerphone.

"Oliver, it's Cooper." She spoke quickly, not giving him a chance to protest. "I need you to get a team together, don a fetching white coverall and get yourself down to the tip at Boldon. Ask the site manager where the refuse collections from Jarrow Road were dumped on Tuesday and sift through the landfill until you find me Macey Gallagher's mobile. A Huawei Y7 in a red case. Cheers."

She pictured the young man's face as she pocketed her phone.

"You know he's losing his shit right now?" said Tennessee, suppressing a grin.

"Well, he keeps saying he wants us to let him get his hands dirty. It's not my fault if I interpret that literally."

- Chapter 6 -

It took fifteen minutes to drive to Heaton, during which time Tennessee told Cooper about the gurgles baby Alfie had been making at two in the morning and how he was convinced he was trying to sing along to Tennessee's rendition of Fog on the Tyne.

Aaron Quinn, Macey Gallagher's boyfriend, lived in a student let above a betting shop. Tennessee knocked on the door and was greeted by a young man with bloodshot eyes, a stubble-covered jaw and joggers worn so low on his hips that at least three inches of his boxer shorts were visible. Cooper had to restrain herself from going into Mum-mode and yanking his trousers back up to his waist where they belonged.

"Aaron Quinn? I'm DCI Cooper. We spoke on the phone. This is DS Daniel."

Aaron led the pair up the stairs and into his living room. Cooper did a quick scan of the room; it hadn't seen a duster or a vacuum cleaner in at least two months. Empty beer bottles and energy drink cans littered the dining and coffee tables, Playstation controllers lay on the sofa, a game of FIFA had been paused, and an ashtray overflowed with cigarette ends. On the arm of the sofa was a bundle of the same posters they had seen in Macey and Pearl's flat.

Aaron hastily cleared some space for the detectives and invited them to sit.

"Erm, you want a coffee or something?"

Cooper couldn't see the kitchen from where she sat, but judging by the living room's standards of hygiene, she decided to decline his offer.

"No, thank you. Aaron, can you tell me when you last saw Macey?"

"That was the morning of the eighth," he answered. "She'd spent the night on the seventh, and we had breakfast together. Then I drove her to her flat. It's not far but it was raining."

"And how would you describe her mood that day?"

His nose wrinkled as he considered the question. "Just normal I suppose. She was looking forward to going out that night."

"Aaron, I'm sorry to ask you this. I know it's difficult for you right now, but did Macey ever give you reason to think she may harm herself?"

Aaron's eyes widened as his gaze met Cooper's. "God, no. I appreciate you have to check, but Jeez, no, not Macey. She wasn't depressed or suicidal, if that's what you mean."

Cooper watched Aaron pace back and forth while she asked her next question. "Did you hear from Macey again once you dropped her off at her flat?"

He shook his head. "No. I told her to text me if she wanted to meet up later on or if she wanted to crash here."

"But she didn't text you?" asked Tennessee.

"No. Not until the next morning, but I don't think that was really her. Did Pearl tell you we don't think the messages are from her?" He stopped pacing and checked his mobile.

"She did," Cooper assured him. "What did you do for the rest of the day, Aaron, after you dropped Macey at her place?"

"Erm, God, let's see. I played some footy in the park, then came home and did some uni work."

"You said it was raining." Tennessee looked up from his notepad.

"It was. The rain doesn't bother us. Getting covered in mud's half the fun."

"And what did you do in the evening?"

Aaron stared at Tennessee for a moment. "Why do you want to know so much about what I was doing that night? Seems like a waste of time. Shouldn't you be finding out what Macey was doing?"

Cooper gave him a supportive smile. "We are, Aaron. This is all part of the process. We want to establish what everyone in Macey's circle did that day so we can piece together exactly where Macey was and when."

"Ah, okay then. Well..." He started to pace again and played with something in his pocket as he spoke. "Me and Mikey, he's my flatmate, we went to the Blue Bell on the other side of the park with the lads in the flat next door and played some pool and had a few beers. Then we walked back, stopped in The Chillingham for a few more and got an Indian on the way home. I played some FIFA, but when I hadn't heard from Macey by two, I decided to go to bed."

"Thank you, Aaron," said Cooper. The man seemed nervous and agitated. Not surprising, given his girlfriend had disappeared. "This is helpful. You're doing a good job. Can you tell me when you first became worried about Macey?"

Aaron seemed to relax a little. He sat down at his dining table and rubbed his jaw. "I wasn't worried at first because she was texting me. But she seemed pissed off, like I was bothering her or being a pest or something. Her answers were just one word. I thought she was being short with me. I was more worried that she was upset with me for some reason, or—" his voice cracked with emotion. "Well, I can be a bit insecure when it comes to Macey. She's so gorgeous, and I'm just a daft scruff. I was worried she'd met someone else. I got a bit panicky. I've never met anyone like Macey before. She's amazing." Aaron's eyes turned glassy. No doubt his mind was frantic; going over everything he'd said or done and hoping to God he wasn't the reason she'd disappeared.

"She said she wanted to take me to Bangkok this summer. We've been saving up for the flights. Anyway, I was freaking out that she'd met someone or was sick of me because I'm not interesting or exciting enough. I was proper paranoid. So I thought I'd pick up a little gift and go over and see her. I got pastries and a Frappuccino, but when Pearl answered the door and I said I was there to see Macey, her face sort of fell. She pulled me inside and started going on about how she thought Macey was with me, and I told her I thought she was there. Pearl tried to call her, but it went straight to voicemail. I tried as well but the same thing happened. That's when we properly started to fret. Pearl was hyperventilating. We rang everyone we knew but no one had seen her."

Cooper crossed her legs and tapped the end of her pen against her notepad. The way Aaron Quinn was pacing and constantly fidgeting had caught Cooper's attention. It would be perfectly natural for him to be anxious about his girlfriend's disappearance, but he was coming across as more nervous than worried. The traits were similar, but in all her years of police work, Cooper had learnt the difference.

"Aaron, do you mind if DS Daniel takes a quick look around while I finish up my questions?"

His eyes darted to the door leading to the hallway and bedrooms. "Why?" he asked. "Don't you need a warrant?"

Cooper kept her face neutral. "The hair sample we took from Macey's brush yesterday didn't have enough root to provide us with a DNA sample; I was hoping we could find something with Macey's DNA here." It wasn't a lie, but it wasn't the truth either. The hair sample was with the lab and she hadn't heard yet if the quality was good enough to extract DNA from. "And, we only need a warrant if you won't let us look around. Is there a reason you wouldn't want to cooperate?"

Back and forth, Aaron's eyes flickered between Cooper and Tennessee. "Okay, go ahead. Sorry about the mess though. Three lads under twenty. We're not the tidiest." He took a seat and immediately stood up again as Tennessee excused himself.

Cooper gave a little cough to bring his attention back to her. "Does Macey have any friends in Gateshead or South Tyneside?"

"Gateshead?" His expression turned to one of a man racking his brains. "South Tyneside? Don't think so. I mean some of her uni friends might be from there but not that she's mentioned."

"No relatives in that area?"

"No." He shook his head. "Her whole family's in Ireland. Why?"

"We heard from her network provider that her phone was in Jarrow on Monday." Cooper saw Aaron's pupils dilate. "That doesn't mean she was there, of course. Her phone could have been stolen, and I appreciate that you think Macey was in a good place, mentally, and that you don't think she would have harmed herself, but there's also the possibility that she left and doesn't want to be found."

Aaron's exterior toughened. "That's not her style," he said gruffly.

"Mr Gallagher, Macey's father, seemed to think Macey had a habit of running away or going AWOL."

A look of hurt passed over Aaron's face as he contemplated the idea. "She had no reason to run away. She loves me, and she loves Pearl. She's doing well at uni. She's happy. I promise you she's happy. You can't give up on her, we have to find her."

Cooper stood as Tennessee re-entered the room. "It's okay, Aaron. I'm not giving up on Macey. I promise. I don't think she would leave without her insulin and I'm going to do my very best to find her."

Aaron wrapped his arms around himself and let his chin fall to his chest.

"Call us if you can think of anything else, and be careful with those posters, Aaron. There's a lot of sick people out there and you'll no doubt get hoax calls, time-wasters and cranks."

His jaw slackened for a moment. He hadn't considered that.

Out in the cool breeze of Heaton Road, Cooper turned to the DS. "Find anything interesting?"

"Some alt-right literature and about fifty Adderall pills, but no sign of foul play if that's what you mean."

Cooper started walking back towards her car.

"But I need to see the photo of Macey again," added Tennessee.

Cooper unlocked her phone, opened the photo app and handed it over. As Tennessee studied the photograph Pearl had sent her, her mind drifted back to the night she and Kenny had met at the Metallica gig. Catching herself feeling all warm and fuzzy, she vigorously shook her arms out as if to free herself from such ridiculous thoughts. As Tennessee handed the phone back to her, she pushed Kenny from her head and glanced at her messages to see if Justin - sweet, intelligent Justin - had been in touch. He hadn't.

"What did you need the photograph for?" Cooper asked.

"I thought I remembered Macey being fairly slim, but I wanted to check. There was a bra in Aaron's room, under the bed. The label said thirty-eight D."

"There's no way that can be Macey's. Far too big."

"So, my theory is that Aaron Quinn and Macey Gallagher aren't as loved up as he wants us to believe."

Cooper raised her brows and looked up at Aaron's flat. Aaron's face was pressed against the glass, watching the two detectives on the street below. As soon as he made eye contact with Cooper, he disappeared behind the curtain.

Tennessee patted Cooper on the shoulder and pointed across the Metro bridge that connected Heaton with the ward of Byker. A pasty man in board shorts with scrawny, lily-white legs poking out of them reached into his pocket before shaking hands with a greasy-haired girl with a terrible bout of the shakes. "Look what the cat dragged in."

- Chapter 7 -

"Well, well, well," Tennessee smirked. "If it isn't my old acquaintance, Mitch Logan. How's my favourite petty criminal?"

"Oh, bugger off, will ya?" Mitch Logan stood no more than five-foot-four and wouldn't weigh more than eight stone if he was fully dressed and soaking wet. His shaved head reflected the sun, and his bare, pigeon chest was tattooed with a Sunderland AFC crest; a brave move in these parts.

"Boss, have you had the honour of dealing with this little toe rag?"

"Can't say I've had the pleasure. Mitch Logan, did you say? I'm DCI Cooper."

Tennessee folded his arms over his chest and grinned knowingly. "Did you hear the joke about the skinny chav who robbed a load of tools and paint from a building site?"

Mitch propped himself up on a low wall and pouted. "Oh aye, here we go. Never going to live it down, am I?"

"Well, the dummy dropped one of the tins of paint. It spilt on the ground, he stood in it, and left a trail of magnolia footprints right to his front door."

Cooper chuckled. "That was you? I remember that case. It won the Piece of Piss award at the department Christmas party last year because a three-year-old could have solved it."

"Aye, that was me. Sixty hours community fucking service. So what do you two want?"

"Ah, just a catch-up," teased Tennessee, "and to conduct a stop and search."

Mitch tensed. "You can't do that. I know my rights. You need reasonable suspicion."

Tennessee snorted. "I literally just watched you give something to a girl who was shaking so hard she'd register on the Richter scale. I am *reasonably suspicious* that you are dealing drugs. Now empty your pockets."

Mitch threw his arms out wide. "I gave her a stick of chewy. That's all."

Tennessee glanced at Mitch, his watch, then back to Mitch. "I'm waiting."

"Fine," he grunted after looking left and right and deciding that running wasn't a wise choice. He laid the contents of his pockets on the wall behind him one by one.

"So, what you driving these days?" asked Tennessee. "Still got that rust bucket of a Renault?"

"Nah," answered Mitch, laying a lighter, a ten-pence piece, three sticks of gum, a torn five-pound note, and a key on the wall. "Got a fourth-hand Audi. Nice paint job. Glacier white."

"And how's that handsome fella of yours? James?"

"Haven't seen him in months, mate. Met this six-three Jamaican lad called Harrison on Grindr."

"Good for you." Tennessee assessed the items on the wall and made Mitch turn his pockets inside out to be sure.

"Happy?" he asked with a smug grin.

"Ecstatic." Tennessee couldn't sound more sarcastic if he tried. "Now clear off."

Mitch Logan stuffed his things back in his pockets and sauntered away while muttering about police harassment.

Two large coffees later and Cooper was up to speed on all Tennessee's dealings with Mitch Logan. Having also nicked a load of designer gear from John Lewis, he was caught after bragging about it on Facebook. He'd even posted the links to the eBay auction where he was flogging it all.

"Sounds like he fell out of the stupid tree and hit every branch on the way down." Cooper fished her keys from her trouser pockets and unlocked the Mazda. "What's next on our to-do list?"

"I think it's time we visited the others who were out the night Macey disappeared." He checked his notepad. "Imogen West and Alison Sparks-Forster."

MACEY GALLAGHER'S FRIENDS LIVED in a purpose-built student facility five minutes from Newcastle University. A bald facilities manager buzzed Cooper and Tennessee in and scrutinised their warrant cards. He was about the same height as Cooper, which made him short for a man, and his brown beard was flecked with grey. He pointed the detectives toward the lifts and told them they needed the third floor. On their way to the lifts, they walked past a glass-fronted, state-of-the-art gym and an impressive social room fitted with a full-size pool table, air hockey and - Cooper couldn't believe it - a karaoke machine.

Tennessee's eyes were popping out of his head. "Man. University's changed since my time. I lived in the halls of residence at Sunderland. My room was smaller than a prison cell. Not exaggerating. And man, you should have seen the state of the toilets."

"I didn't go to uni," said Cooper as she pressed the button for the lift. "I had Tina. I needed a job."

Tennessee stole a sideways glance at his chief. Cooper suspected he was shocked to hear that she didn't have a university education, given that it was common knowledge in the department that she'd aced the detectives' exam. At that moment, the lift doors opened and a raven-haired woman in a stylish blouse emerged carrying a baby in one arm and a pile of textbooks in another. She can't have been more than nineteen or twenty. Cooper smiled at her and then at her baby. *Impressive*, she thought, before feeling a pang of jealousy that ripped through her and caught her off guard. If only those opportunities had been there in her day. The subjects she could have studied, the people she could have met. She'd still have wanted to join the force, but a first-class degree in a core subject could put a new recruit on an accelerated course for promotion.

Emerging on the third floor, Cooper knocked on the door to room three hundred and twelve. A Taylor Swift song was playing from within, so Cooper had to knock again to be heard.

"What's the password, *biatch*?" chirped a voice behind the door, followed by hysterical sniggering.

Cooper thought about answering *Northumbria Police* in her toughest voice, but she refused to answer to *biatch,* so instead, she knocked again and waited.

"Come in already." This time, the voice was impatient.

Cooper shrugged and pushed the door open to Imogen West's room. Imogen, whom Cooper recognised from the photos Pearl had shown her, was an hourglass of a woman with a waist so much smaller than her hips that Cooper suspected she'd fallen prey to the Kardashian-inspired trend of waist trainers. She was sitting at her desk doing her makeup in a magnifying mirror, and a curtain of long red hair flowed to her lower back. She clocked the detectives in the mirror and span on her swivel seat.

Her eyebrows lowered as she surveyed them with a mascara wand held delicately between manicured nails. “Yah? Can I help you?”

Yah? Cooper’s jaw tensed. “Northumbria Police. We’re here about Macey.”

“Oh, gawd. She hasn’t turned up yet?” Imogen turned back to her mirror, finished her mascara and returned the wand to its bottle. She stood, walked to the opposite wall and thudded the side of her fist against the plaster three times. “Get over here, Ali! The police are here,” she shouted into the wall.

Thirty seconds later, Alison Sparks-Forster sat on Imogen’s bed. She looked like a modern Snow White: sharp black bob, peaches and cream skin, and scarlet lips.

“Ladies,” started Cooper, “Macey’s been missing for over eighty hours now and we’re extremely concerned about her well-being. It’s imperative we get as much information as we possibly can. Even the smallest detail could be important.”

Imogen and Alison exchanged a look. “What do you need to know?”

“Everything that happened that evening,” Cooper said. “Start at the beginning.”

Alison picked up a stuffed toy and held it to her chest. “Christ. Right, let’s see. Pearl and Macey got the Metro into town and met us at this Greek place for dinner.”

“What Greek place?” Tennessee asked. Cooper knew he knew the answer from their interview with Pearl. He was testing that the girls’ stories matched. Clever.

“No idea how you pronounce it,” shrugged Alison as she pulled her phone out from her pocket. “I can find it on the map though.” Her fingers slid across the screen. “Here,” she said. “It’s this one.”

Tennessee made a note. “And how was dinner?”

“Oh, it was fabulous. We had this delightful meze platter—”

“I meant, how was the atmosphere? Did Macey mention anything to concern you? Anything out of the ordinary? Or did her mood seem out of character?”

“Ah,” Alison blushed, looking at Imogen who took over.

“Not really. She was as bubbly as ever. She was trying to sweet-talk the waiter into letting her smash some plates. He didn’t let us so Macey said we shouldn’t leave a tip. But we did anyway. All was forgiven after a glass or two of wine.”

“Can you remember the waiter’s name?” asked Tennessee.

She shook her head and pouted for a moment. “Another thing, she wasn’t talking that much about Aaron. I remember because she’s been like a broken record recently with all the lovey-dovey talk, but on Saturday, I remember Alison making a joke, you remember, don't you, Ali? You said it was a new record. That she hadn't said his name in over an hour."

"Do you think they'd had a fight?"

"Who knows? It was probably just a sign of the spark fizzling for the first time."

"Pearl told us that Macey didn't have much to drink on account of her having diabetes. Is that accurate?"

Alison and Imogen traded looks.

"Please be honest," said Tennessee. "If Macey drank more than usual, we need to know."

"It's not that," answered Alison. "Macey didn't need alcohol to have a good time. She had two, maybe three, glasses of wine, and she switched to soft drinks once we left the restaurant. When we met up with Nico, he bought a round of vodka shots. When Macey refused hers, I think, well I'm not certain, and I don't want to get him into trouble, but I think I saw him drop it in her soda." She hugged the stuffed toy harder.

Cooper showed the photo she had of the group on her phone to Imogen and Alison. "This man here," she said, pointing to the man Pearl had referred to as Nick, or Rick. "Is this Nico?"

"Yeah, that's our Nico."

"His full name?" Cooper asked.

"Nicolas Petite," Imogen replied.

"French?"

"Yah."

Yah? Seriously? "Lucky, Nico. Outnumbered four to one by you ladies."

"Alison thinks he likes boys because he's so well dressed, but I keep telling her all French guys dress immaculately. I used to summer in France almost every year, you see. Father owns a château and a handful of gîtes, so I'm fluent in French, and as Nico barely spoke English when he arrived here, I sort of adopted him."

"And the only French I know is *voulez vous coucher avec moi ce soir.*" Alison giggled to herself before parting her lips slightly and looking up through her long lashes towards Tennessee.

Give me strength, thought Cooper. "We'll need to speak to him. Does he live in this block?"

Imogen flicked her hair over her shoulder. "Yah, he does. But you're out of luck. He's gone back to Lyon for Easter."

"No problem. We'll get his details from Admissions. Let's go back to Saturday night. What time did you leave the restaurant? And where did you go afterwards?"

"About half eight, maybe nine-ish? Right, Alison? Yah. Nine-ish. We went to Jalou for about an hour and a half, then Tokyo, then Feisty's because Pearl wanted to dance."

"When did you notice Macey had gone?"

Imogen pulled a face. "I'm not sure exactly. I was having fun. I wasn't checking my watch every five minutes."

"By *having fun*, she means she was getting frisky with Colin the Cockney."

"Shut up, Alison." She threw a hairbrush at her friend and turned back to Cooper. "It was after one. Before four."

"Didn't you look for her?"

She shrugged and glanced at Alison, but Alison was leaning back and trying to get a better view of Tennessee's backside. "We'd queued for ages," Imogen said. It was a shoddy explanation, and she clearly knew it as she added, "We didn't know anything was amiss. We thought she'd snuck off to see Aaron and get her nightly fix of Geordie boy."

Cooper didn't think she would get anything further from Imogen West or Alison Sparks-Forster. Macey's so-called friends were more concerned with making eyes at Tennessee than with her welfare. They let a man sneak her vodka shots and didn't look for her when they realised she'd become separated from the group. Macey's Dad thought the whole thing was a joke and Aaron, Macey's boyfriend, despite his insistence that he loved her, had another woman's bra in his bedroom. Cooper wondered if she, Tennessee and Pearl Baxter were the only people in the world who were worried about the missing diabetic.

Cooper made a quick note to follow up on the waiter at the Greek restaurant and to find Nicolas Petite, the drink-spiking son-of-a-bitch. "Thanks for your time, ladies. If we need any further details, we'll be in touch. I'll leave you to your studying."

Alison snorted. "It's Wednesday, no one studies on Wednesdays. We're off to the new cocktail bar near Grey's Monument. Imogen knows the manager. Don't you, Mo? Said he'd get us some Champers on the house. You can join us if you like," she said to Tennessee while licking her upper lip.

"He's married," Cooper snapped before her DS could reply.

"To you?"

"No."

"Then why do you care?"

Cooper swallowed down her anger. She cared because Tennessee was a new dad, struggling with all the adjustments that came with that huge responsibility. She cared because she was his chief and friend and—

"DCI Cooper cares because she holds her team to the highest standards." Tennessee closed his notepad and stored it in his trouser pocket. "You were two of the last people to see Macey before her disappearance. It would be unprofessional for me to see either of you in a social setting." He moved to the door and opened it for Cooper. "And like she said, I'm married."

- Chapter 8 -

"It's gone five," Cooper told Tennessee when they were back at Northumbria CID. "Get yourself home to that beautiful baby of yours."

Tennessee shut the open browsers on his computer screen and gathered his things. He paused, hesitating.

"What is it?" she asked him.

He shook his head. "It's nothing. Don't stay too late. Follow your own advice and get back to Tina, okay?"

She brought her hand to the side of her head and saluted the DS. "Aye, aye, captain."

As Tennessee left the room, Cooper knew he was right; she should follow her own advice and get the hell out of there. There were two things she wanted to do first, however. One, finish her report of the information gathered from Aaron, Imogen and Alison, and two, find out if Oliver Martin had any luck at the dump. She typed up her last two sentences, shut her computer down and went in search of Martin.

After searching most of Northumbria Police headquarters and ringing Martin twice, only for her calls to go to voicemail, Cooper eventually found Martin coming out of the shower rooms. He was void of styling products and had a face like someone had pissed on his chips.

"There you are. Find that phone for me?"

"No, I bloody didn't." Martin was on the verge of having a tantrum of teenager proportions and as much as Cooper empathised she didn't appreciate being spoken to like that. Not by the newest recruit. She could take a leaf out of Nixon's book and give him a swear-laden dressing down, or she could keep it simple.

"It's *no, I bloody didn't, boss*. Or if you absolutely must, *no I bloody didn't, ma'am*."

Martin took a deep breath. "Yes, boss. Sorry, boss."

"Want to get it off your chest?"

He took another breath, deep enough for his chest to visibly expand and stretch the fabric of his t-shirt. "Sorry, ma'am. Six hours I spent in that rat-infested stink-hole with flies buzzing about my head and all we found were a couple of iPhones and a duffle bag of Russian rubles."

"You what?" That caught Cooper's attention.

"Rubles. Worked out at thirty grand's worth."

"Hmm. Interesting. Any indication of who or why—"

"Not a thing. Plain black bag, no labels, no nothing. It's intriguing all right but it's also not our problem. I handed it over to Fraud."

"Fair enough. You got the smell out of your nose yet?"

"Not quite." Martin squeezed his nostrils together. "I've tried vapour rub but it's still there."

"I'm not surprised. You live in Gosforth, right?"

"Yeah."

"Nip into Boots on the High Street and buy yourself a nasal rinse. It'll help."

"Will do. Thanks for the tip. Oh, and boss..." Martin ran his fingers through his hair before swinging his backpack strap over his shoulder. "Sorry for being a brat."

Cooper softened. She patted his upper arm and bowed her head. "We've all been there. Just don't let it happen again."

COOPER WAS PLEASED TO get home. She loosened the laces on the cherry Dr. Martens boots she'd been wearing, pulled them off, and wiggled her toes. What she would give for one of Atkinson's foot rubs right now. Cooper checked her watch. It would be almost seven o'clock in Germany. Atkinson would be getting ready for dinner. Probably donning a well-fitted shirt and a smart pair of jeans, maybe adding a squirt of aftershave. He'd sit down to a no-doubt excellent meal and converse all evening with Europe's best and brightest in the field of forensic sciences. Meanwhile, Cooper was about to reheat last night's leftover lasagne and watch the news for any developments in the trial of the Tarot Card Killer.

The kitchen was spotless. Cooper was certain she'd left it as if a bomb had hit it this morning. Tina must have cleaned. *She'll be after something*, thought Cooper, *and whatever it is, it probably costs a fortune.*

A shoebox sat on the kitchen table and scrawled on the lid, in thick marker pen, were the words *Not junk. Do not throw out.* Cooper lifted the lid expecting to see a pair of shoes or a bunch of old photographs. She did not expect to see a baby seagull.

"TINA!"

Tina's footsteps trotted down the stairs. She was wearing a t-shirt of a llama in sunglasses. "Ah," she said when she spotted the lid was off the shoebox. "I see you've met Steven."

"Steven? *Steven?* Christ, you've named it. Why is that disease-carrying ball of feathers in my kitchen?"

Tina walked over to the shoe box and scooped the hatchling into her hands. "He fell off the roof, poor thing. I found him in the backyard. That's why the gulls were making a racket this morning."

"Tina. You can't keep it, sweetheart. You need to put it back in the yard."

"No." Tina's features pinched, and she looked fixedly at her mother. "He won't survive in the yard. All the cats that live on this street? He won't survive the night and he's at least a month away from being able to fly."

"So you plan on raising him? You can't keep a wild animal. It's illegal." She removed the leftover lasagne from the fridge and slid it into the microwave.

Sitting down at the kitchen table and stoking Steven's feathers, Tina shook her head. "Nice try. It's perfectly legal to keep a wild bird if it's unfit for release as long as you meet its welfare needs and release it as soon as it's ready to survive on its own."

Of course, Tina had already formulated her counter-arguments and conducted the required research to back them up. She'd probably printed off the supporting documents and filed them ready for presentation to a sceptical mother.

"Surely you need a licence?"

"Nope." Tina was smug. "The only birds requiring a licence are ostriches and cassowaries. Schedule four birds such as eagles and buzzards need to be registered with the council, but that doesn't include seagulls."

Cooper had been completely outmanoeuvred. "Okay, counsellor. You say you need to meet its welfare needs. How do you plan on feeding it?"

"Steven. Not *it*. I got some scraps from the fish quay, blended them into mush and froze them in an ice cube tray. At feeding time, I defrost one, warm it up, pop it in a piping bag and squirt it into his mouth."

The little genius had thought of everything. "Right." Cooper had lost. There was no point in arguing. "So you're telling me that not only is a seagull now living in my kitchen but that our ice cube trays are full of fish scraps?"

"Yes."

The microwave beeped and Cooper dished two portions onto plates. "Fine. But wash your hands for goodness sake before you give us all E. coli, salmonella and who knows what else."

Tina popped Steven back in his box and went to the sink. She was grinning from ear to ear.

When Cooper left for work the next morning, Tina was busy piping fish into the mouth of a greedy gull and reading her physics study notes. Cooper grabbed a Starbucks en route, and upon arriving at HQ headed straight to see The Collector.

The Collector, real name Cedric Bell, was a Local Intelligence Officer whose windowless office was usually ripe with body odour and egg sandwiches. Cooper always tried to send lower-ranking detectives to do this job but as Tennessee hadn't shown up yet she had to do her own dirty work.

"Erica Cooper, what brings you to my lair?" Cedric Bell chuckled from behind his computer. He had sweat patches under his arms and was drinking Lemsip. His desk was cluttered, and as Cooper's gaze scanned over various files and papers, he hastily gathered them into a neat pile. She was almost certain she'd spotted a porn mag amongst it all.

"I have some updates for you from DS Daniel." Cooper wanted to get out of The Collector's office as soon as possible. The man was creepy. "Mitch Logan. Full name, Mitchell Peter Logan."

Bell's fingers jabbed away at his keyboard. His fingernails were dirty and he had a frayed plaster fastened around his thumb. "Found him. What you got for me?"

"No longer driving a Renault. He has a white Audi now."

Bell entered the information into his database. "Anything else?"

"Yes," Cooper said. "Known associates. He's dating a Jamaican man named Harrison. No surname, but I'm sure it won't be too hard to find out."

More jabbing at the keyboard. "And how about yourself?" Bell asked. "Is it true you're off the market?"

Cooper felt ill. Everything about Bell and this room made her want to run. "I'm off the market, and you're inappropriate for asking." She turned, opened the door and left.

"Don't leave it so long next time, Erica, darling. I've missed you."

Cooper walked past the shower rooms. If she didn't have work to get on with she'd go in and wash Bell off her. Macey Gallagher was still missing. Nico Petite had possibly spiked the diabetic's drink with vodka and was one of the last people to see her. Cooper needed to speak to him as soon as she could. She looked up the number for Newcastle University's Admissions Office and waited for someone to pick up. She introduced herself and explained that she needed the home address and telephone number of Nicolas Petite.

"Oh, I'm afraid I cannot give out that information," replied the woman on the other end of the phone.

"Cara, was it? One of your students hasn't been seen since Saturday evening. She's an Irish national, and the man I want to speak to in connection with her disappearance is a French national. If Macey dies because I can't get insulin to her in time, it will be news across the entire continent, and I will not hesitate to let the press know that you slowed down our investigation. I want his home address and phone number, and I don't want to waste hours getting a warrant."

There was silence. Enough silence for Cooper to wonder if she'd been put on hold or hung up on, but eventually the admissions officer came back to the phone. "Sixteen Rue De Reims, Lyon." She followed with the phone number.

"Thank you, Cara," Cooper said. "You did the right thing."

Cooper wasted no time in ringing the number. With no knowledge of the French language beyond *bonjour* and *au revoir,* Cooper hoped the Petites would speak English. She would have to wait to find out as, despite twenty minutes of trying, no one was picking up.

Cooper typed the address into Google Maps and zoomed in to a pretty, suburban street where it looked as if one in every three homes had a swimming pool. She rolled her mouse back and forth over the surrounding streets until a little orange icon appeared with a knife and fork on it. "Petite Boulangerie," she read aloud. A Google search and a few trips to Google Translate later and Cooper's suspicions were confirmed. The bakery was run by a local family who were named Petite. She found the phone number for the business and gave it a call.

"Bonjour? Madame Petite? Je suis DCI Cooper. Je suis, erm..." That was the limit of Cooper's French. "I need to speak to Nicolas. Is he there?"

"I am sorry. I do not speak English," came the reply, ironically in perfect English.

The line disconnected and Cooper stared at her handset. Rude. She'd try again later. She wasn't going to give up that easily. Besides, she had translators at her disposal. She'd book one for later that day.

"Hey, stranger."

Cooper looked up to see Sam Sutherland pulling up a chair. If Tennessee was Cooper's CID brother, then Sutherland was her CID father. Older than her but junior in rank, Sutherland used slang from the seventies and occasionally dressed like it was still the eighties. His BMI was on the wrong side of twenty-five, but luckily he usually worked with ex-rugby star detective Paula Keaton. If anyone needed chasing, Keaton had it covered.

"How's it going?" asked Cooper, "and whoa! Look at that bling." She grabbed Sutherland's wrist and admired a sparkling Rolex that looked like it was worth more than her car.

Sutherland blushed. "An anniversary present. Twenty-five years. Doesn't seem like two minutes."

"Nice," said Cooper, still admiring the watch. It wasn't her style, but it was still mighty impressive.

"I screwed up, though."

"Don't tell me you bought Sue a new vacuum cleaner."

"Not quite that bad. I got her favourite flowers and these chocolates she likes from a patisserie in Edinburgh and some other small gifts. All the stuff I knew she'd love, but still, nothing on par with a Rolex."

Cooper raised her eyebrows. "So, you're sleeping on the couch, right?"

"Nah, I managed to swing it back by telling her I'd booked us a week in the Maldives. As soon as I stop for lunch, I need to get straight to a travel agent and book it before Sue asks any more details."

"Smooth. And what about Caroline? Has she settled in at Westfield?"

Sutherland loosened his tie. "Truth be told, no, not really. She likes the teachers, and they have a trampoline club which she's loving, but she's not making many new friends. Her grades are up, so Sue's pleased, but I just want her to be happy."

Cooper could appreciate that. She never had to worry about Tina's grades, but she was always worried that the bullying that had plagued her daughter's first few years at secondary school would start again. "We're having a bit of a party for Tina's fifteenth if you want to bring Caroline over. She won't have seen Tina since November. I know she's a few years younger, but it will be nice for them to catch up. Bring Sue. Atkinson will be there."

Sutherland's face glowed. "That's very kind of you, Erica. I'm sure Caroline will jump at the chance. What's the date? I'll have to check with the missus."

"The twenty-third. Easter Sunday."

"Great. Don't think we have anything on. Sue'll probably go to mass in the morning, but it's not my scene. So how's the missing girl case going? Heard it's a tricky one."

Cooper closed her eyes and shook her head. "I'm very worried. My gut tells me she's still alive, but..."

"But you don't have long?"

"I really don't."

"Well, if you need any help just give me and Keaton a shout. The armed robbery was open and closed - Muscovites connected to the Red Skulls - and this matricide in Benwell we were just handed is pretty straightforward. Eight kids. She changes the will to leave it all to the youngest, and three days later, she collapses at bingo. Ingested rat poison." He looked pointedly at Cooper. "We know the little swine did it; we just need to prove it. I'll have him in the cells by the end of the week. So, as I said, if you need a hand, just say."

Cooper gave an appreciative smile. "I might just do that. Oh." Tennessee had just arrived. "You made it in?"

"Yeah," he said with a yawn. "Sorry I'm late. Hey, Sam. Alfie's got a cough. Had to get him to the GP. Then Hayley... Oh, and I saw Nixon on the way in." He held up some papers. "I have Macey's phone records."

Cooper turned her chair to face him, her interest piqued. "And?"

"And, if you look to Saturday evening, there's a bunch of incoming calls that go unanswered. This number is Pearl Baxter, this is Aaron Quinn and this," he pointed to another number," is an unregistered pay-as-you-go phone. I've called it, and there was a foreign dial tone, but no answer. I also tried Pearl Baxter to see if she recognised the number but she doesn't have it in her contacts."

"Nico Petite?"

"Maybe. I can check with Imogen and Alison but..."

"But you don't want to be sexually harassed?"

He sat down and handed the phone records to Cooper. "Exactly."

"I'll do it."

"Thanks. But here's the interesting thing." He motioned to the records. "All those incoming calls, probably Pearl and co trying to find where Macey had disappeared to, but only one outgoing call."

Cooper ran her finger down the list until she found what she was looking for.

"Recognise the number?" Tennessee asked.

Cooper frowned. Should she? Then she saw it. A double seven, a double three and another double seven. "Matt Walker. The landlord. Now, why oh why did our missing girl call her landlord at three a.m.? And why didn't he mention it when I spoke to him?"

- Chapter 9 -

"So this is Great Park?" asked Tennessee. He wound the window down on Cooper's Mazda and stuck his head out to get a better view as she idled along a suburban street. Given his blonde curls, he was a panting tongue away from resembling a labradoodle. "Bit soulless, isn't it? What's with all the balconies and roof terraces? And is that a palm tree? They know this is Newcastle, right?"

It was a clever move on the part of the developers. Selling the dream of al fresco dining and barbecues in an area with an average temperature of eight degrees. Then there was the promise of a town centre, village stores and community spirit. Eighteen years after the houses went up, there still wasn't a supermarket or restaurant in sight.

Cooper knocked on the door to number eighty-four. Through the front window, she could see a man of average height with shaggy hair watching horse racing on a curved, wide-screen television. He turned to look and reluctantly got to his feet to answer the door.

"Yeah?" he asked, looking at Tennessee and barely glancing at Cooper. He had bright green eyes, a tan and a physique he was obviously proud of, given how tightly fitted his t-shirt was.

"Mathew Walker?" Tennessee introduced himself and held up his warrant card. Cooper did the same.

"You the one I spoke to on the phone?" he said, addressing Cooper with wandering eyes. "You don't look like a detective."

Cooper should have known better, but she took the bait nonetheless, "Then what do I look like?"

"I divint nah. Hair that short and a leather jacket? A neo-nazi? A tattoo artist? Both?"

Cooper's lips pulled inwards and she cocked her head. "I can assure you, I am neither of those things. Now, can we come in, Mr Walker? We have some questions."

Walker shrugged and moved aside. After leading Cooper and Tennessee into his kitchen he opened his fridge and got himself a beer.

Tennessee caught Cooper's eye as Walker's back was turned. "This place is immaculate," he whispered.

"Smells it too," she replied, noting the distinctive aroma of bleach.

As Walker opened his can it made a whooshing noise and foam bubbled from the top. He slurped it off the aluminium and grinned at Cooper. "I'd offer you one but yee lot aren't meant to drink on duty, are ya? That's the good thing about being self-employed. You set your own hours. I think I'll clock off right about now." He popped his hips to the side and leant against a faux marble worktop.

Cooper tried not to scowl. "How long have you known Macey Gallagher, Mr Walker?"

"Since August. All my student lettings run from August to August."

"And are you regularly in contact with her?"

"Nah. Not really. I carried out an inspection in December to make sure they weren't trashing the place, but they keep the flat in good nick. If anything needs doing it's usually the other one who gets in touch."

"Pearl Baxter?"

"Aye, that's her. Hair like she's stuck her finger in a socket."

Cooper's dislike for Matt Walker was growing by the second. She pinched the bridge of her nose and counted silently to three. "When did you last see Macey?"

"Ages ago. Would've been February time. I went round to install a new washing machine."

"And that was the last time you spoke to her?"

Walker took a long drink of beer, burped with his mouth closed and released the gas slowly through pursed lips. "Aye."

"So, then why, Mr Walker, did Macey phone you at three a.m. on the night she went missing?"

There was a palpable change in the atmosphere as Walker stayed motionless for a good ten seconds. "Did she?"

Cooper snorted. "Yes, she did. You know she did. Why did she call?"

"I don't know. I didn't pick up. I put my phone on silent overnight." His voice was quickening and he took brief sips of his drink between each sentence. "Was probably just a pocket dial. I didn't see it until the next morning."

"You didn't return her call?"

"No. It was from three in the effin' morning. I told you, I thought it was a pocket dial."

Tennessee folded his arms and lifted his chin. "Mr Walker. I'm only going to ask this once, so be honest, were you and Macey in a relationship?"

"God, no. Nee chance. I'm single, me." Walker finished his beer, rinsed the can under the tap, squashed it down to a disk using his bare hands and tossed it into a bin marked for recycling. "Would be unprofessional, wouldn't it? Improper. You don't have me picked as the sort of landlord who reduces the rent for sexual favours, do ya?"

"Of course not," lied Cooper. She didn't know what to make of Matt Walker, but a squeaky-clean landlord he was not. She'd bet her right leg on it. "Could I use your bathroom?"

Walker's nose wrinkled but before he could refuse, Cooper added, "Lady problems."

"Ah, alreet. Top of the stairs." He nodded his head back towards the hallway.

Cooper excused herself. As she climbed the stairs she could hear Tennessee asking Walker if he had a cleaner. Walker's bathroom was like the rest of his house, sparkling clean with a whiff of peroxide in the air. Cooper didn't need the toilet, nor did she have *lady problems;* she did, however, want to snoop around. She opened a mirrored medicine cabinet and scanned the shelves. A single toothbrush, a Wilkinson Sword five-blade razor, a box of paracetamols, shaving gel, caffeine shampoo, and a Nivea Men roll-on deodorant. If Macey had been in a relationship with Walker, she hadn't left any trace in the bathroom. No spare insulin kit, tampons or toothbrush. To Cooper, this looked one hundred per cent like a bachelor bathroom. That was until she spotted a Kirby grip on the floor behind the toilet.

Cooper crouched down and took a photo of the hairpin with her phone before pulling a clear evidence bag from her pocket and bagging the grip. It still had a hair attached to it. Dark blonde or light brown, it was hard to tell, but if the lab matched it to the hair sample they'd taken from Macey's hairbrush, it would be proof Macey had been here and that Walker was a lying piece of shit.

"Whose hair grip is this?"

Walker's head whipped around to the doorframe where Cooper was standing. "What?"

"This hair grip." She held the bag up in front of her and jangled it like a child does with a bagged goldfish from the fair. "If you're single, who does it belong to?"

"I divint nah. My sister's, maybe." Walker pushed his weight off the worktop and began walking back to his front door, trying to shepherd the detectives from his home.

"Oh, and one more thing," started Cooper. "Do you have voicemail?"

Walker's jaw clenched. "Yeah. Why? I told you it was a pocket dial. Just muffled night-out noises."

Cooper stood firm despite Walker's attempts to manoeuvre her to the door. "Play it for me."

Walker groaned and looked to the ceiling. "Fine. Don't even know if I still have it." He pushed his phone to his ear and cycled through a couple of messages before thrusting the phone at Cooper. "Here."

Cooper switched the speakerphone on and listened to what did indeed sound like a pocket dial. The message lasted three minutes and Cooper played it four times before giving up. She couldn't make out anything other than the noises of traffic and music. Tech, on the other hand, might be able to salvage something from it.

Cooper walked out of Walker's house and approached her car.

"Hey," he called after her. "My phone."

"You can have it back in a second, Mr Walker." Cooper opened her boot and pulled out a black canvas bag. She unzipped the bag and produced a black device that looked like an old Gameboy from the nineties. She selected an iPhone attachment and plugged the two devices together.

"Hey!" Walker had moved within a foot of Cooper. Tennessee moved within a foot of Walker. "What do you think you're doing?"

"I'm extracting your data," explained Cooper.

A furious look coloured Walker's face. "You can't do that. Not without my permission."

"Actually," started Cooper with half a smile. "I can."

- Chapter 10 -

Mobile phone extraction - more commonly referred to as a digital strip search - required neither a warrant nor a suspect's consent. The devices were a quick and easy way to download a person's call history and messages, as well as their communications using social media and apps. Digital strip searches had hit the headlines in recent times after forces began to use them on victims of crime, particularly in cases of rape, to establish the nature of any prior relationship between the accuser and the accused. Rights groups were campaigning to have this process more tightly regulated, but for now, Cooper had a great tool at her disposal. If Walker had so much as sent a Snapchat to Macey Gallagher, she would know about it.

"Play it again," asked Tennessee as he and Cooper strolled back into Northumbria Police HQ.

Cooper played the recording from the voicemail message again, shutting her eyes to try and focus her senses on the sound.

"You hear that? Like a swoosh and thud?"

Cooper opened her eyes and looked at Tennessee. He was pointing into thin air and swiping his finger in time with the noise. She heard it too, a swoosh and a thud, followed by a swoosh and another thud. "What is that?"

"I'll tell you what that is," said Tennessee. "That's a sliding door on a van or a people carrier."

"You're right." Cooper played it again just to be sure. "So what does this mean? Did Macey take a taxi? We've already sent her picture to all the major firms."

"They haven't all got back to us though. I'll chase them up. Now that we have a specific time of three a.m., they should be able to narrow down which drivers were in the city centre then."

"What if it wasn't a taxi? She could have accepted a lift from someone else?"

"And either that someone, or a taxi, took her to Jarrow and dropped her off at a bus station in the arse end of nowhere? To take a bus to South Shields for no reason that we can work out."

Cooper took a deep breath and thought things through for a moment. Macey Gallagher couldn't just vanish off the face of the planet. She was either hiding somewhere, being held somewhere or - and Cooper didn't like this option - she was lying dead somewhere. "Right," she said, "You follow up with the taxi firms and make some enquiries about the thirty-seven bus that runs from Jarrow Road to South Shields. If you have time, book a translator for us. Madame Petite is pretending she doesn't speak English. I'll drop the hair grip with evidence and take the extraction device to Tech, see if there's anything to link Walker to this, and then I'll start work on a press release. We need Macey's face in every newspaper. Someone must have seen her after she got separated from Pearl and the others."

Tennessee stifled a yawn. "I'm on it," he said before walking towards the lift. "I'll come and find you when I'm done."

COOPER HAD COMPLETED ALL but one of the errands and was hurrying through HQ on her way to the press office when she spotted a familiar face: Kenny Roberts was chatting to the desk sergeant.

"Kenny," she gasped, a wave of panic threatening to take over her. There was only one reason for him to be here. "What's happened? Is Tina okay?"

Despite his lack of social intelligence, Kenny registered the alarm in her voice. "Nothing's happened, Erica. Tina's fine. Last I heard, she was at the library."

Cooper almost collapsed into his arms. Ever since the Tarot Card killer had taken Tina, Cooper had been on edge. It was exhausting. Just when she thought she was getting over the trauma, something would set her off and she'd assume the worst. She closed her eyes momentarily and placed a hand over her heart. It was beating at over a hundred beats per minute. "Then why..." she opened her eyes and slapped Kenny on the arm, "...are you here? You gave me a heart attack."

Kenny chuckled and held up a paper bag. "I brought lunch. You still love Thai, right? Tina said she was worried you were losing weight with the Science Man being away."

Cooper flashed him a suspicious look.

"And I was in the area," he added.

She kept staring.

"And I thought we could discuss Tina's birthday. It's coming up and I don't have a blooming clue what to get her."

Cooper hadn't realised she was holding her breath until she finally exhaled. Of course he didn't know what to buy Tina. He'd only been around for two birthdays and Christmases. At least he was trying to make up for lost time, she thought, and by God, the Thai food smelled irresistible.

"Follow me," she said, letting her heart rate lower and a smile return to her face. "We can eat in the break room."

- Chapter 11 -

He pulled the girl to her feet. It was Friday morning, and she was a mess. A whimpering, shivering, snot-dribbling, pathetic mess of a girl. "This way," he growled, and she shuffled her bound feet, struggling to keep up with him. Struggling because she was blindfolded and he was not. The high-pitched snivelling was driving him mad. She sounded like a whippet begging his master for a scrap of lamb fat. It was enough to make him want to slap her.

"No funny business," he said as he cut her cable ties, "or I swear to God, I'll knock you out before you can blink. And you don't want to know what the lads'll do to you once you're unconscious." Her entire body shook like the last leaf of autumn. "Do I make myself clear?"

The girl nodded and squeaked a yes through her gag.

"The bucket's behind you. Be quick about it."

Women and their bloody bladder shyness. The last thing he wanted to do was hang about here for ten minutes while she worked up the courage to piss. If the little bitch didn't go now she'd have to hold it until lunch, and lunch was five hours away. She could piss herself; the other one had. Stunk the whole damn room out. Dirty cow. He'd had to clean her up because he was the only one the boss trusted not to get carried away. It was hard not to do anything that would get him a kicking, given how fucking fit she was. He'd sprayed her with a hosepipe and taken great pleasure in watching her flinch from the cold water. Not as much pleasure as he'd taken in drying her. He'd used a thin towel and could feel everything. He savoured the memory.

"Finally," he grunted when the tinkling came and the girl relieved herself in the plastic bucket. He handed her a few sheets of bog roll and waited while she wiped and dropped the paper into the bucket. Within seconds, he'd bound her hands and was roughly pushing her along the corridor and back to the rat-infested so-called bedroom.

He'd managed to get a syringe yesterday. He was going to prick her himself but he didn't want to fuck it up and kill her by injecting an air bubble into her veins. He'd have got a right hiding for that. Instead, he let her do it herself. He stood behind, so she couldn't see his face when he removed the hood and blindfold and held a knife to her throat in case she tried anything stupid with the needle. She didn't. Of course, she didn't. He could tell she wanted to fight, wanted to try, but she was in self-preservation mode and she wanted to live. To live meant following his orders.

He watched her settle into her corner of the room and try in vain to get comfortable. Impossible on a concrete floor. Maybe he'd bring them some blankets, a reward for not screaming all day. Or maybe he shouldn't. Can't be going soft now. The lads would rip him to shreds. She pulled her knees to her chest and looped her bound arms around them. Then her head tipped forward and she let out a barely audible sob.

He slid the heavy door closed and secured the padlock. The insulin he'd stolen would do for now. It was enough to keep her alive until she wasn't his responsibility anymore. He hoped.

"Come on, one more." DS Paula Keaton stood behind the weights bench in the gym at HQ. "Push. You can do it." Her dark hair was scraped back into her usual short, tight ponytail. She was rosy-cheeked from her workout, and from where Cooper lay on the bench, she could see straight up her upturned nose.

Cooper pushed with all her might as she finished the last repetition in a set of bench presses and was relieved when Keaton took the bar and secured it safely in the rack.

"My arms are shaking," she said, watching the tricep muscles on the back of her upper arm twitch rhythmically.

Keaton loaded the bar with an additional twenty-five kilograms and rattled out her set without so much as a gurn. Cooper would ask if she wanted her to spot her but she knew it would be pointless. If Pitbull Paula Keaton couldn't lift it, there was no way Cooper could.

Keaton caught the impressed look on Cooper's face. "I've been lifting weights since I was in primary school."

"I don't think I'll ever be able to lift what you lift," Cooper said.

"And you shouldn't." Keaton wiped her forehead with a sweat rag and took a swig from a metal water bottle. "We train for different reasons. I want to maintain my rugby body and have quads that could kill a man. You though, we're just undoing the shit that cancer did to you. Get you some strength back, a little bit of toning, a little bit of fast-twitch. Baby steps." She held up a palm for Cooper to high-five. "Good workout, boss. I'm going to hit the showers. I'll see you back upstairs."

Cooper was exhausted, but it was a good feeling. A satisfied feeling. Whatever she ate for lunch today, she'd feel like she'd earned it. Cooper had been working out with Keaton for a few months now, and she was already seeing some changes. She was still a scrawny wee matchstick but the first hint of curves were beginning to return to her thighs and her shoulders. The squats and presses were paying off. She could bound up the stairs without huffing and puffing, and she didn't have to ask Justin or Kenny to carry things for her anymore. She was beginning to feel like she had pre-the-big-C.

Back upstairs in CID, showered and dressed in a grey suit and white shirt, Cooper was about to call the Petites, and failing their cooperation, call the local police department in France and have them round Nico up on her behalf. Her plans were scuppered when Chief Superintendent Nixon coughed and called Cooper to his office. *Christ on a bike*. Cooper's stomach lurched and she prayed to herself. *Tell me she hasn't been found dead*. She got to her feet and trotted along the hall, her boots click-clacking on linoleum tiles, and entered Nixon's office only to find Neil Fuller in there, slumped in a chair and picking something from under his nails.

"Before you go off it, it's not my fault," he said with a wary look in his eyes.

Cooper's heart rate instantly raised and she met his eyes with distrust. "What do you mean it's not your fault?"

Nixon coughed again. "Settle down, you two. Nothing to fret about Cooper. Just some reshuffling."

Cooper didn't like the sound of that. If Nixon was about to tell her she'd been partnered up with Fuller, she'd hit the roof. There was no way she was working side by side with that weaselly, coward of a man-child.

Cooper's eyes remained narrowed, and she folded her arms across her chest. The muscles in her chest cried as she did so. In a slow, sceptical tone, she said, "Define reshuffling."

Nixon closed the door to his office and inched his way into the old wood and leather chair behind his antique desk. "I'm taking you off the Gallagher case."

"No."

"Yes," he barked before she could fly into a torrent of reasons why not. "I'm not wasting my best talent on a missing, presumed dead case. Chances are that girl got pissed, got emotional, and jumped in the river. Fuller can handle it."

Fuller took the insult on the chin and said nothing. Cooper, despite being called his best talent, was about to protest. She hated being transferred off cases. She liked closure. Anything less was unacceptable, and as far as she was concerned, Macey Gallagher was worth fighting for. Even if no one else was fighting for that poor girl.

"She's still alive, sir."

"God willing," said Nixon, though his voice suggested otherwise. "But I need you on a suspected hate crime. Keep the PC brigade off my back."

Cooper bristled. PC brigade meant one thing and one thing only. "I'm not your token female," she said, almost snarling.

"Don't forget part Arab."

Cooper's mouth hung open. "I'm like five per cent Persian, sir. Ninety-five per cent white British. You can't parade me as—"

"You need to solve the case before I can parade you as anything. Sit down. Fuller, take Sam Sutherland and Oliver Martin. Sam's suspect in the matricide case made a full confession. Pick up where Cooper left off on the Gallagher case."

Fuller ran a finger and thumb over his moustache and left the room under a cloud of humiliation.

"Question the French boy," Cooper called after him. "Get on the next flight to Paris if need be. It leaves at eleven forty." The door clicked shut and Cooper turned her attention back to the superintendent. "I'm keeping my fingers in that pie."

"Keep your fingers where I can see them," he warned. "Fuller will be fine. Too many cooks and all that. Anyway, this case." He dropped a file on the table. It was light and clearly new. "Omar Ali, Egyptian national, brought into the RVI this morning," he said, referencing the Royal Victoria Infirmary that resided in Newcastle's city centre. "A dozen stab wounds and beaten half to death. Left for dead in Weetslade."

"Weetslade? That's the park just off the A189, right? Former colliery."

"Aye. That's the one. Found by a dog walker in the early hours. Given the recent marches from the English Defenders and the White Rights Party, there's been an increase in violence against Muslims. Not to mention that far-right prick from Manchester bringing up the Rochdale sex abuse ring every five minutes."

"You mean Dominic Jefferson, acclaimed Member of Parliament?"

"Indeed I do. Specky, chinless, Mancunian twat."

Cooper hid her astonishment.

Nixon thrust the file into Cooper's hand. "You get Daniel and Keaton. Now get your skinny arse down to the RVI and speak to the victim before he bleeds to death. I want a UKIP-voting skinhead in custody before the loony lefties string me up by my left bollock."

Cooper took the file and closed her eyes for a moment. At least, she told herself, at least Nixon was equal opportunities when it came to offending people.

- CHAPTER 12 -

COOPER DODGED A TEAM of paramedics wheeling a patient into the trauma centre of the Royal Victoria Infirmary. A robust woman with tension alopecia at the temples was sat astride the patient, the heels of her hands thrusting into his chest as a pale, panicky-looking man squeezed a bag valve mask and tried to keep pace with the trolley. Cooper waited for the commotion to die down before she approached the young man monitoring the main desk. He was a pretty boy with lipstick smudges on his neck and a twinkle in his eye. His face hardened when she presented him with her ID and he escorted her to the room that housed Omar Ali.

Cooper's step faulted as she took in the scene. Doctors and nurses buzzed around the bed at such speed that Cooper could barely see Omar. The movement of their blue and indigo scrubs moulded them into a sea of bodies. Machines beeped, wires and tubes protruded in all directions and pads of white gauze blossomed with red blood. She approached the bed cautiously, not wanting to get in the way of the people doing the most important work right now; keeping him alive. She caught Omar's eye. His mouth and nose were covered with an oxygen mask and his dark eyes were wet with fear and confusion. His lips quivered and his finger twitched.

"Omar," she whispered in his ear. "My name's Erica. I'm a detective with Northumbria CID and I'm going to do my very best to find the people who did this to you." She didn't want to question him while he was in this state. Her intention was only to let him know she was on the case, that the police knew he'd been attacked and that they cared. She moved out of the way while a doctor applied pressure to a wound on Omar's chest. His finger twitched again, beckoning her back to the side of his bed. "What is it, Omar?" She leant in as close as she could.

"Ba— Da—"

She didn't understand.

His arm was swollen and bruised with great grazes along the length of his forearm and blood oozing from his elbow. He managed to lift it, hook a finger under his oxygen mask and try again.

"Bad dog," he said.

"Bad dog? What do you mean, Omar? Were you attacked by a dog?"

Omar's eyelids flickered, and his irises rolled back into his beaten skull. The rhythmic beeping of the machines turned frenetic and all hell broke loose.

"We're losing him."

A pair of electrodes were pressed to his chest.

"Clear."

As Omar's body convulsed, a nurse with blood-stained scrubs dragged Cooper from the room.

"Will he make it?" she asked.

The nurse sucked her lips in and looked to the floor before answering. "He's in a terrible way. But he's tough. We revived him once already."

"Before he..." Cooper couldn't find the word. "He said bad dog. Those wounds on his chest. Are they bite marks?"

The nurse shook her head. "No. They're definitely stab wounds. Scissors, he told us when he first came in."

"Scissors," she repeated to herself. Then what did *bad dog* reference? "What else did he say? Was it a gang attack?"

"Sorry." The nurse shrugged. She didn't know any more than that. "I'd better get back in there."

Whoever attacked Omar, they had left him for dead and Cooper worried that when word got out he was still alive, they might pay him a visit to finish the job.

"Sir," she called her superintendent. "Omar Ali flatlined. They're working to revive him, but it looks touch and go. I want a uniform stationed at the RVI, outside our assault victim's room. As far as I'm concerned, this is attempted murder. If Omar wakes up and the perp comes to finish what he started—"

"Say no more. I'll have two uniforms in rotation outside his room."

"Thank you, sir. I appreciate it."

Cooper waited at the hospital for an hour. The nurse was right about Omar being tough. They'd brought him back, but he was in a coma. She watched doctors and nurses come and go. Watched them stitch up the stab wounds, clean and dress the grazes and ice the bruises. She couldn't do anything for Omar sitting around waiting for him to wake up so she thanked the man with the lipstick-covered neck and walked out into the brilliant sunshine of a chilly April day in the north. She might not be able to do anything for Omar Ali right now, but she was in town, and she could perhaps do something for Macey Gallagher. Feisty's, the last bar Macey was definitely in, was only a fifteen-minute walk away.

A Greggs bacon butty later and Cooper was hammering on the door of Feisty's.

"We're not open," came the reply.

"Northumbria police," Cooper stated. It was an answer guaranteed to get a response, and within seconds the door was yanked open and a woman with rollers in her hair and a dripping mop in her hand greeted her with an up-and-down stare.

"There's no drugs dealt in here, love. The doormen are top at keeping the dealers out," she said in a rough local accent.

"I'm not here about drugs," Cooper reassured her, "but I would like a quick chat. Can I come in?"

The mop was shoved back into its bucket and the door opened enough for Cooper to squeeze through.

Nightclubs without people and music always seemed sad to Cooper, like a seedy ghost town. Without the disco lights and foggy vision of alcohol consumption, the cracks of the place showed. Stained floorboards, peeling wallpaper, and rips in the upholstery. In the harsh light of the day, the roped-off area that she had been led to looked more DIY than VIP.

"Misha Rudd," the woman extended her hand. "I'm the owner-manager of this money pit."

"Business not good?" Asked Cooper.

"Not since the bar next door was featured on Geordie Shore. Now every Charlotte Crosby wannabe has to been seen in there instead of here." She sighed and adjusted a roller that wasn't cooperating, pinning it back in place.

"I'm here about Macey Gallagher." Cooper brought up a picture of Macey from her phone.

Recognition showed on Misha's face. "She was on the news last night. Missing?"

"That's right. She was here the night she disappeared. The eighth. This was the last bar we know she visited. Could I speak with anyone who was working that night? And I'll need to take a look at your CCTV."

Misha looked in two minds but pointed to a girl polishing glasses behind the bar. "Dora was in. You can speak to her, but," she paused, "our cameras are on the blink. Have been for weeks. I can't afford to have them fixed. I know it's not proper, but it's that or be able to pay the staff their wages."

Cooper seethed. Camera footage could have been key. She thanked Misha through gritted teeth and approached a mousy girl in huge round glasses. "Dora? I'm DCI Cooper with Northumbria police. Your boss tells me you were working on Saturday the eighth."

Dora nodded. "I work most Saturdays. Is there a problem?"

"This is Macey Gallagher, she went missing last Saturday and was last seen in here." She displayed the photo of Macey and her friends and zoomed in so that Macey's image filled the screen. "Do you recognise her from that evening?"

Dora nodded and her glasses slid down her nose; she pushed them back up with her middle digit. Cooper hoped that wasn't her veiled way of giving her the finger. "She's been in a few times. I recognise her friend. She was... yeah she was in a bad way, like. Wobbly on her feet."

"Did you see anyone hassling her or looking at her funny?"

"She's a pretty girl in a little dress. Lots of guys were looking at her."

Cooper picked up a hint of resentment. "Tell me more."

"There were some guys in the club that night playing pub golf. About forty of them, all in golf jumpers. They looked like right pillocks. Anyway, I think I saw her chatting with four or five of them for a while. She stumbled about a bit, and they had to help her stay upright. I think one of them fetched her a glass of water at one point, but I didn't serve him, it might have been a gin and tonic for all I know."

"Did you see her leave?"

"Yeah, she was hurled out."

"Hurled out?" Cooper leant in.

"She was sick on herself. Not a lot. Not like projectile or owt. More of a hiccough that turned into a little bit of spew. Anyway, the bouncer saw, and he had her outside in under a minute."

When Cooper got her hands on Nico Petite, she was going to wring his—Nixon's warning rang in her head. She shouldn't even be here. "Who was the bouncer?"

"Tiny McGown. He works a day shift outside the jewellery shop on Pilgrim Street."

Cooper tried her best to get descriptions of the boys playing pub golf from Dora but they all sounded alike. Preppy, barely old enough to drink but acting like they ran the entire city.

Back in the daylight of the main road, Cooper put a call into Neil Fuller.

"Erica?"

"You in France yet?" A snorting noise confirmed he was not. "I just spoke to a barmaid from Feisty's who was working the night Macey went missing. "She was chatting to some guys who were playing pub golf."

"The barmaid?"

"No, you idiot. Macey was. They might have plied her with more alcohol. Find them and see what the deal is." Cooper's temper was being tested. "And get to Newcastle Jewellery Co. on Pilgrim Street. Speak to a security guard named Tiny McGowan. Something tells me he's not so tiny. He was on duty at Feisty's that night and he chucked Macey out after she threw up on herself."

"Erica..."

"Yes?"

"Thanks for the intel, but Nixon warned me you'd do this. This isn't your case anymore. Let me get on with it and let it go."

Hanging up and thrusting her phone into her pocket with unexpected aggression, Cooper marched up and down the street, avoiding the wrath of mums with pushchairs, commuters dragging wheelie cases towards the train station, and death-wish delivery cyclists who shouldn't even be on the bloody path. She scanned the street until her eyes came to rest on a camera bubble above a doorway to an office building. A few minutes of sweet smiles and Cooper was sat in front of an accountancy firm's security footage.

"Perfect," purred Cooper. The image was grainy but it clearly showed Macey leaving Feisty's, trying to re-enter and being denied. As predicted, Tiny was easily six-three. Cooper watched Macey walk along the street, stumble and continue. It was a chaotic Saturday night and it was hard to keep track of Macey in the crowd. Cooper tried to take in all the details. Countless Uber cars, an ambulance whizzing by, a topless man dancing in the middle of the road, a dark van driving past, a skinny boy losing his pizza to a bald man with a beard. The bald man getting into a fight. The bald man approaching Macey before she ran down a side street. "Who is this prick?" she muttered, thinking he looked familiar. "I need a copy of this."

A most obliging man with pink cheeks and even pinker ears burnt the footage onto a USB stick and handed it over. Cooper thanked him with the sort of smile that would last him all day and headed for the side street she'd watched Macey disappear into. A cat café selling crepes and overpriced coffees to people wanting a side order of fur with their food had a camera over the door. The Japanese waitress wasn't sure if the owner would want her letting someone into the office but Cooper had her call the boss in question. She let him know that as his camera pointed onto the street, she was entitled to look at it and if he made her come back with a squad car and a bunch of uniforms it would be very bad for business.

Scanning the files for the previous Saturday, Cooper clicked on footage that had been taken between two thirty and three thirty and sat back in her chair and waited until she spotted Macey run into the arms of a woman who resembled Pearl Baxter. She was a little taller and a little paler, and though the footage was in greyscale, she appeared to be wearing some form of worker's vest over a jumper. They chatted for a little while. The ambulance was visible in the distance; it appeared at the end of the street for less than a second as it made its way to its destination. A van slowed as it passed the two ladies, and the bald guy came back into the frame. He walked behind Macey, keeping his distance. The woman with the curly hair pointed further down the street. They linked arms and strolled out of shot, followed by the bald guy. Cooper rewatched the footage four times, pausing and playing, pausing and playing. She was sure she recognised the bald man with the beard, she just wasn't sure where from.

In a lay-by off the A696, Cooper avoided paying for airport parking as she waited for Justin Atkinson's flight to land. Man, she had missed her favourite scene of crime officer. Missed his conversation, missed his warmth, his humour, his tender kisses that made her giggle like she was five years younger. Whilst she'd been in town, after visiting Omar Ali and viewing CCTV of Macey Gallagher, she'd let off steam by nipping into John Lewis's lingerie department and picking up a lacy bra and knicker set from Elle McPherson's collection. It fit perfectly, and she couldn't wait to slide out of her clothes and show them to her man. She heard her phone buzz, and she reached into the Mazda's glove box to retrieve it. Her hopes that it was Atkinson saying he was at baggage reclaim were dashed when she saw the message was from Fuller. *I'll follow up on Curly and Baldy. But seriously, Erica, stop stepping on my toes. Don't make me go to Nixon.*

Cry baby. Cooper checked her reflection in the mirror. Her make-up was on point, and she didn't have to check her hair. Since clipping it, she knew there was nothing to check. Heels, skinny jeans and an AC/DC t-shirt with rips up the sides. She was ready for a night on the tiles with the man she adored.

The flight was late and Cooper waited in the lay-by for over an hour until she finally got the text she'd been waiting for. Thank God, there were only so many times a woman could scroll through the BBC news or check the Newcastle

Evening Chronicle for updates on the Tarot Card Killer's trial. Apparently, a scuffle had broken out in the viewing gallery between Hutchins's brother and the first victim's father. Igniting the engine and pushing the gearstick into first, Cooper joined the duel carriageway, turned right at the roundabout and made her way into Newcastle International Airport. She found a space just as Atkinson emerged from arrivals, pulling his suitcase behind him. He looked handsome in the sunshine in cargo pants and a designer t-shirt with his glasses tucked into his breast pocket. His silver hair accentuated the slight tan on his early forties skin. Cooper leapt from the car and into his arms. Her heart swelled as she felt the reassuring but understated strength in his arms.

"Oh, how I've missed you," he whispered, his hand folding around the back of her head and holding her into his chest.

"I missed you too. Woo. Even if you do smell like a brewery. Must have been a good night?" Cooper beamed at him and took the case, guiding it to the car. "And boy, do I have a night planned for us." Atkinson slid into the passenger seat and let out an almighty yawn. Cooper jumped in the driver's seat and headed for the barriers before her parking rate increased. "There's a taxi booked at seven, a table for two at Blackfriars... Four quid? Are they having a laugh? Bloody airport parking. Anyway, Blackfriars. If you've never been, get the pork belly. Then we're off to The Cluny. Hush In Hell have a set at nine. And..." she turned to wink at Atkinson before telling him about her new underwear, only Atkinson was covering his mouth with his hand and all the colour had drained from his face.

"Pull over," he urged.

Cooper hit the hazard lights and drew the car up on a grass verge just before the duel carriageway. Atkinson opened his door, leant over and emptied his stomach. He spluttered and heaved again for round two, round three, round four.

"Jesus, I'm sorry, Erica." He wiped his mouth with his hand. His glasses had slipped from his pocket and into the puddle of vomit. He bent to retrieve them, only to bring up round five.

Cooper shook her head. "How much did you have?" She felt all her excitement fall away; there was no way he was going anywhere near a bar or restaurant that evening.

"Not that much. Shared a few bottles of wine. I think the chicken was under-done."

Cooper felt like slapping him around the head. The chicken, indeed. He'd wanted to let off steam after all those days at the convention. It was understand-able he'd want to socialise, network, and have a good time. But throwing up on the junction to the A696 and filling Cooper's Mazda with the stench of bile? No. That was not okay.

"I'm sorry, Erica, darling. I think I need an early night. Could you just drop me at mine?"

Cooper didn't know what to say. The night she'd planned was ruined, and although it might be childish, she felt abandoned. He should have wanted to spend time with her, his girlfriend.

"Fine," was all she could muster.

The drive back to the coast was spent mostly in silence. Atkinson only broke the awkwardness to mumble that maybe it wasn't just wine he had had, that he had a vague memory of drinking shots of Sambuca.

"Sambuca? Why would you drink that stuff? It's deadly." It was hardly his style.

"Kenny recommended it last time I saw him."

"Kenny? My Kenny? Well, not *my* Kenny, but you know what I mean. Why would you listen to him? He's a flat-Earther, for goodness sake."

Atkinson managed not to vomit for the remainder of the journey. He apologised profusely when Cooper dropped him at his home. Cooper was too sad to be angry. This wasn't the Atkinson she was expecting to meet at the airport.

It wasn't long until Cooper was home alone, all dressed up with nowhere to go. Tina was at Kenny's. She'd shipped her daughter off to her father's - along with that bloody seagull - so that she wouldn't have to keep the noise down when they'd returned to the bedroom, but as that wasn't happening either, Cooper was at a loss.

"Sod it," she said aloud. She'd have her own party. Cooper stripped to her pretty new underwear, grabbed a cool beer from the fridge and played Hush In Hell's latest album on her phone. She danced the night away in her bedroom. Bouncing and waving her arms around her head, occasionally stopping to admire herself in the mirror. Her body anxieties from the previous year were beginning to fade away, and it was about time too. She peeked under the lace fabric of the bra and found the small blue dots that had been tattooed on for the oncologist to target her radiotherapy treatment. It wasn't the most rock and roll tattoo in the world. Although Tina would no doubt tell her that it was a symbol of her survival and that was as badass as it could get, sweet thing that she was. Between the lumpectomy scars and the blue dots, Cooper had felt reluctant about taking her top off in front of Atkinson. Unless the lights were off, she kept her top on in bed. That was until tonight. Tonight, she'd been ready. But he'd been hungover. She took another swig of beer, removed her bra and checked out her reflection. For the first time in a long time, she didn't look away or immediately cover up.

Maybe it was the beer talking, or maybe it was the fact that the lead singer of Hush In Hell was tattooed from top to bottom, but Cooper fancied some artwork.

- CHAPTER 13 -

ATKINSON USED HIS CULINARY skills to work his way back into Cooper's good books over the weekend. A mammoth Sunday roast for her and Tina had done the trick. Besides, Cooper rarely stayed mad at anyone for long, Fuller being the exception. Atkinson had been a perfect partner up until that point. He'd been reliable, patient, and had got to know Tina at a pace that had suited her. As Cooper mopped up the last of his delicious gravy with a crisp Yorkshire pudding, she decided he was more than forgiven.

Tina cleared the plates away. "Can I introduce Steven to Justin now?"

Cooper nodded. "If you must."

Tina's face spread into a wide grin. "Great." She raced up to her room and returned with the shoe box.

Atkinson looked curious. "Been getting a hamster?"

"Not quite," Cooper said as she started the dishwasher. "Doctor Doolittle here rescued a seagull hatchling that fell off the roof."

The three of them crowded around to look at the fluffy bird. Cooper didn't want to admit it, but he was rather cute. About the size of a tennis ball, with big black eyes and pale brown feathers. He plodded clumsily about on his stick-thin legs and looked up at them expectedly. She'd been impressed with Tina's dedication. She was an excellent seagull mother and hadn't complained once about Steven cheeping away in the middle of the night when he was hungry.

Atkinson reached down and scooped the little bird into his hands. "Hello, Steven Seagull. Oh! I get it. Steven. Sea. Gull. Very witty, Tina."

Tina blushed and Cooper bit her lip. She didn't get it. She was about to ask when Steven pooped all over Atkinson's hand and sent the two Cooper ladies into fits of giggles. As Atkinson furiously scrubbed his hands at the kitchen sink, Tina set about feeding her surrogate chick his evening meal.

"Did Mum tell you she wants a tattoo?"

Atkinson and Cooper's eyes met. She hadn't told him. Last night, she and Tina had scoured the internet for ideas. Hours they'd spent on Google Image Search, saving their favourites into a folder as they dipped crisps in a fancy beetroot dip that she'd bought from Marks and Spencer. There were some amazing floral designs, and Cooper had narrowed it down to three.

"No," answered Atkinson with heavy brows. "She didn't tell me that." He moved closer to Cooper. "Erica?"

Cooper opened her laptop and brought up the images. "To cover my scars."

His face softened. "Your scars? You don't need to do that. You're perfect just the way—"

"I know I don't *have* to. But I want to." She wrapped her jumper around herself without thinking. "It's not like I hate my body. I'm happy with how I am. But... but I could be happier. They really are works of art. Look at this one." She brought up an image of an intricate bouquet of black and grey flowers formed from mandalas.

"Hmm." Atkinson's mouth twitched from side to side, running the inside of his lips over his teeth. "I'm not sure that's a good idea. Shouldn't we discuss this? You should think it through before you permanently—"

"It's Mum's body," said Tina in a defensive tone. She squeezed the pipette and deposited fishy mush into Steven's beak. "She can do with it what she likes."

Cooper maintained a poker face.

"I mean, Mum doesn't tell you to dye your hair, does she?" The poker face slipped and try as she might, Cooper couldn't put it back. Her laughter had put an abrupt end to the conversation. *Thank you, Tina.*

ON MONDAY MORNING, COOPER called the Royal Victoria to check on Omar's status. She was told by the prim-sounding lady on the phone that he was still in a coma and the doctors were working to reduce the swelling on his brain. She then called PC Frankie Ingram, currently on guard duty, to check that no one had come to visit the victim or that no one had been lurking around his ward. So far, they had not.

"Right," she said, addressing Keaton and Tennessee. "The dream team, back together again. Let's find the bottom feeder who did this to Omar Ali." She pinned a picture of the victim to the board.

Tennessee leant over his desk and flipped through his notepad. "Here's what I have so far. Forty-four years old. Lives alone on Kendal Street in Byker. His landlord describes him as being a great tenant. Bills paid on time. No complaints from neighbours. No problems with the property. Has lived there for a year and a half."

"Family?" Cooper asked.

"A wife, Salwa, and two sons back in Cairo. His boys are fourteen and twelve. The wife's flying out tomorrow morning. I've arranged for an Arabic speaker to meet her at the airport."

"Good. Have the translator meet us at the hospital, too. I want to know what she knows. Did he have any enemies, any debts?" She turned to Keaton. "Work?"

"An eye doctor. Works in the opticians on Shields Road. The branch manager had only good things to say about him. Said not turning up to work was highly out of character. Apparently, the bloke never took a sick day, boss. He was a no-show on Wednesday, so they called his flat, but there was no answer. They put it down as an irregularity and called in someone to cover for him. The same thing happened on Thursday. This time they called the number of his next of kin but the number was disconnected. On Friday morning, they reported him missing, and that's when he was discovered at Weetslade."

"So he's been gone since Tuesday night or Wednesday morning?"

Keaton nodded. "Looks like it. Lives and works in Byker but was found six miles away, covered with stab wounds."

"And what was that bad dog reference about?" Tennessee asked.

Cooper looked at the photograph on the board. "No idea," she sighed. "The nurse was adamant he didn't have any bite marks."

"Bad dog?" Keaton brought up a map of Weetslade on her computer. "Yeah, I thought so. There's a doggy daycare centre a stone's throw from where he was found. My mum leaves her greyhound there sometimes."

Cooper got to her feet and looked over Keaton's shoulder. "Huh. Well, I know where I'm starting my inquiries. Can you two arrange some door-to-doors?" It wasn't really a question. "Tennessee, you take Byker. Talk to his neighbours. See if there's been anything suspicious going on or if they heard any commotion, especially Tuesday night or Wednesday morning." He saluted. "Keaton..."

"Around the park, boss? The roads leading into it and the surrounding businesses? I'll check traffic cams too."

"Perfect. Let's reconvene at lunch."

SCENE OF CRIME OFFICER Hong Evanstad met Cooper at the entrance to Weetslade Country Park. A North Korean by birth but Norwegian by adoption, Hong had the looks of his motherland and the accent of his adopted parents.

"Good morning, DCI Cooper," he greeted her, removing his gloves to shake her hand. "Are you looking for Justin? He's not assigned to this case."

"No, no. I came to see you," she assured him. "Justin's up near Rothbury today. Two poor souls were found drowned in the bogs up on the Simonside hills."

"Might be the duergar." Hong chuckled to himself and handed Cooper some white coveralls so she could join him beyond the police tape that marked the area where Omar Ali's dying body had been discovered. With over forty hectares of walking trails, woodland and wildflower meadows, Weetslade was a tranquil oasis and a far cry from its former life as a colliery. Atop the hill at the centre of the park, three giant drill bits paid homage to the park's past and on a brisk, bright day like today, they sparkled like beacons.

"What's a duergar when it's at home?" Cooper asked, struggling to wiggle into the paper outfit.

"Us Scandis aren't the only ones with tales of magical creatures roaming the countryside. You Brits have some folklore of your own. The duergar are dwarves that live on Simonside and use their lanterns to lure travellers to their deaths. Either by pushing them off the cliffs or into the bogs."

"Fascinating," said Cooper, truthfully. She'd never heard of the duergar; her knowledge of local folklore extended no further than the Lambton Worm.

Beyond the tape, Hong gave Cooper a quick rundown of his findings so far. There were no signs of the scissors used in the attack or any weapon for that matter. Some dirty needles and blackened spoons were found beneath some nearby trees. There was an extensive amount of disturbance to the meadowland, indicating that Omar had either been dragged through the area or had crawled through it on his knees, probably trying to reach the car park to find help.

"Over here," said Hong, "we found a wallet. Don't get your hopes up though. I'd say it's been there months given the water damage. Belongs to a Bryce Morton of Hayes Walk in Wideopen."

"That's just on the other side of the park. I'll have a couple of uniforms swing by and question him. If he walks here regularly, there's a chance he noticed something or saw something."

Hong nodded. "Worth a shot. There were a lot of footprints around here, as you might expect. A lot of hikers, dog walkers and bird watchers come through here. I ran some of the clearer prints through the database and found a match that was rather interesting. A pair of Yeezy Boosts."

Cooper looked blankly at him.

"That's Kanye West's brand. People queue up for days when new designs are launched. Even second-hand, a pair can fetch over two grand."

"Two grand? For trainers?" Cooper's eyes almost burst from their sockets.

"I know. Ludicrous. Now what sort of person would wear trainers worth that kind of money through a muddy country park?"

"An excellent question," mused Cooper. What sort of person indeed? One with more money than brains at the very least. Cooper gave the area one last look over, bid Hong Evanstad farewell and asked him to call her if anything else came up. She left the scene and took a walking trail towards the doggy daycare centre. A row of trees protected Cooper's head from the spring sunshine, and she took a moment to appreciate the birdsong surrounding her. Her boots crunched on patches of dry grass and without realising it, Cooper was taking deep inhalations of clean air.

When the smell of woodland gave way to the smell of traffic, Cooper had reached her destination. Dolly's Place was built on the border between the park and some industrial land. A cartoon of a small, black, fluffy dog greeted clients at the entrance and Cooper watched as a woman in kickboxing shorts and a vest wrestled an overly energetic Welsh terrier into her car.

After introducing herself to a minuscule woman whose ponytail almost reached the back of her knees, Cooper asked if she was aware of the assault that occurred in the park on Thursday night.

"Oh yes," she replied. "Word travels fast around here. The lady who found him, Patty, she brings her dogs here when she needs to pop into town for a few hours. Never likes to leave her babies unsupervised, you know. Very responsible dog owner."

Cooper's eyes wandered over the reception area as the loquacious manager continued.

"We've known Patty since this place opened. Dolly - my girl - loves her. She's a poodle cross. Just the most affectionate creature I've ever met. Would you like to meet her? She's playing with her friends in the outdoor area."

"No, thank you," said Cooper, hoping not to offend but registering the look of disappointment in the woman's eyes. She certainly loved her dog. "I'd rather know more about those cameras." Cooper motioned to a television screen that showed four different camera angles around the centre.

"Ah, our webcams. When clients leave their dogs with us, we give them a code, and they can log in and watch their dogs from work or wherever they happen to be. Builds trust, you see. I know when I'm not here, I'm always logging on to see what Dolly's up to."

"Do they capture any footage from outside the centre?"

"No, I'm afraid not. Just the inside of the enclosures. Besides, they're turned off when we close at half six. Turned back on at seven in the morning."

Cooper let out an audible sigh. That wasn't good news. She'd been hoping for otherwise, hoping to spot a clue. A man in mud-covered Yeezies sniffing around after dark with a pair of scissors in his hands might have been wishful thinking, but any clue would have done.

"Do you recognise this man?" Cooper showed her a photo of Omar that Tennessee had sent over from his place of work. It showed Omar in a shirt and tie, a wide smile and eyes that crinkled in the corners. It was a far cry from how Cooper had last seen him.

She shook her head. "No. Is that him? The man who was attacked?"

"Yes," said Cooper. "I'd like to talk to your other staff, see if they recognise him, or have seen or heard anything suspicious around here."

She pulled on a gilet and tidied her desk. "Follow me," she beamed, beckoning Cooper towards an indoor enclosure labelled *Puppy Playroom*, "hopefully someone can help. Just awful having something like that happen around here. I hope you catch them. Hope he gets what's coming to him. Okay, watch your feet. The young ones aren't toilet trained. The dogs, I mean, not the staff." She sniggered to herself. "Oh, hello Archibald. This is Archibald, our German shepherd pup. And little Cookie the Lab, and oh, isn't Buddy the cutest pug you've ever seen?"

Cooper found herself surrounded by eight to ten puppies all scrambling up her jeans and sniffing at her boots.

"I'll go find Leslie. He was working all last week, and Beth as well, our work experience girl. Perhaps they can help you generate a lead. Pardon the pun. Ha!"

She trotted off, and Cooper was certain that if the woman had a tail, it would be wagging.

- Chapter 14 -

Keaton proudly held up three brown paper bags as she sauntered into the lobby of HQ. The unmistakable aroma of a McDonald's takeaway floated over to Cooper's nostrils.

"Diet of champions," Keaton said with a grin.

"Darts champions, maybe."

"Oh?" Keaton forged a look of mock insult. "So you'll not want any? More for me and Tennessee in that case."

Cooper laughed and took a bag from Keaton. "Nice try." She opened it up and had a handful of soggy fries in her mouth before they'd even reached the lifts.

"Six o'clock," said Keaton and Cooper spun a one-eighty to look back at the glass doors. Detectives Neil Fuller, Sam Sutherland and Oliver Martin escorted a man into the building. Cooper recognised him as Aaron Quinn.

"That's Macey Gallagher's boyfriend," she explained to Keaton, her eyes never moving from Quinn. "Tennessee and I thought he was a bit twitchy when we went to see him."

Quinn's jogging pants were once again halfway down his backside and his cream-coloured hoodie was speckled with yellow stains. Curry, most likely. His face had the sheen of someone who hadn't washed so far today and his stubble was coming through in patches.

"Fuller," Cooper called. Neil Fuller broke away from the group and instructed Sutherland to get the young man into a cell until an interview suite became available. "What's going on?"

Fuller blew his nose on a tissue and looked to his left for a moment. Cooper wondered if he was considering telling her to mind her own business.

"I stopped by his flat with Sutherland. We were asking some routine questions, you know, following up where you left off, and we spot a baseball bat hidden behind his sofa. Not a big deal I thought at first; he's a sporty kid, might be on the university team, or maybe he wants it in case his flat gets broken into, but when we asked him about it, he freaked out. Started demanding a lawyer."

"That's a bit of a red flag." Cooper's gaze flicked back to Quinn; he had dark circles under his eyes and was demanding someone call his mother.

"Exactly. So we brought him in and asked forensics to take a closer look at the bat and his place."

"Christ," said Keaton, before taking a large bite of her burger and getting mayonnaise all over her chin.

Cooper shook her head. "All those posters. All the canvassing. He was the one really pushing the search for her."

"Aye, well, he wouldn't be the first guilty party to play the role of concerned lover. We'll see what the labs come back with." Fuller shrugged and walked away.

Cooper's heart was heavy as she pressed the button on the lift to take her to CID. She didn't like Quinn, didn't trust him, but she hoped he hadn't killed his girlfriend. She was still hoping Macey was alive somewhere.

Tennessee must have smelled the McDonald's coming because he was at the lift waiting for it to open. "Sweet," he said, taking a bag and tucking in without pausing for breath.

Cooper made space on one of the desks in the incident room and the three spread out their feast, sharing chicken nuggets between bites of burgers.

"Right." Cooper clapped her hands together when they had finished. "Tennessee, clear the table, and Keaton, you're up first. What you got?"

Tennessee crunched the rubbish into a tiny ball while Keaton opened her notepad. "Not a lot, to be fair. Door-to-doors are still ongoing. Seeing as we have no witnesses, I figure the attack happened in the middle of the night. I don't think he was lured to the park and then hit with a surprise assault because Omar was missing for a few days prior to his attack. So, I figure he was either staying with someone or was being held by someone during that time."

"That's what I thought," confirmed Cooper. "But we don't know if he was brought to the park then attacked, or if the attack occurred elsewhere and he was dumped in the park. Hong's taken soil samples to assess the blood content around where Omar was found. If the content's high, it's likely the attack occurred in the park. How are the door-to-doors coming along so far?"

"We started on the side of the park where the car park is. Around Clarks Terrace and Weetslade Crescent."

"Good shout."

"But no one has anything for us so far. A few of the older residents have pointed the finger at each other. Baseless, of course. Number twelve leaves his wheelie bin out, so he's obviously an axe murderer, and number thirty-two's conifers cast a shadow into number thirty-four's garden, so she's worse than Hitler."

"Traffic cams?"

"Well, as you can imagine, the roundabout on the A189 is stupidly busy. Always has been. But I've started with cars exiting the roundabout for Great Lime Road between one and four a.m. We can extend the time frame if nothing comes from what I have so far. Only three cars took that exit: a red Vauxhall Astra, a dark green Honda Civic, and a black Nissan Qashqai. I have the names and addresses of the registered owners and can give them a visit."

"Good start, Paula. Jack?"

Tennessee sat up straight in his chair. "I have footage of him getting off the Metro at Byker at eleven p.m. on Tuesday and heading towards his home. However, none of his neighbours can recall hearing him come home, including a busybody who lives next door on the left and seems to know everyone's comings and goings. According to her, Omar Ali stuck to quite a rigid schedule. Left for work at seven forty-five on the dot and returned between six and six thirty each day."

"This neighbour, did you get a stalker vibe at all."

"She's like ninety years old. She's not stalking anyone and certainly too frail to do what was done to Omar. She's just bored."

Cooper wiped the residual grease from her fingertips with a serviette and mulled it over. "He broke his schedule on Tuesday then. Where was he coming from so late? Tennessee, can you contact Nexus, try and find out where he got on the Metro? Cheers. Now, what happened after he got off the Metro? We can assume he never made it home. Was he taken? Lured away? What other cameras are in the area?"

Tennessee shrugged. "Frighteningly few. The climbing centre might have one. I can check and take a look for cars matching the ones Keaton described."

"Great."

"What about you, boss? What you got?" asked Keaton. "Do we have Omar's phone? And, did you get anything useful from the kennels?"

"No phone, unfortunately. And as for the kennels, no one's seen anything, no one's heard anything, no one knows anything."

Keaton blew a raspberry. "Balls."

"I had a good snoop around once I'd finished questioning the staff, but there were no signs of trouble. Still, I've asked Hong to sweep along the walking trail that links Dolly's Place with the park."

"Shame," said Keaton. "I really hoped *bad dog* was a reference to there."

"You mean…" Tennessee paused for dramatic effect. "We're barking up the wrong tree?" He laughed at his own joke until Keaton clipped him on the back of the head.

- Chapter 15 -

Margot Swanson stubbed her cigarette into a metal grate atop a bin and waved a perfectly manicured hand at Cooper as she approached the main gates to the Royal Victoria Infirmary. A group of junior doctors gave the Scottish pathologist an admiring look as they passed. Margot glanced down at her outfit, smiled, and undid another button on her blouse. Happy with her adjustments, she pulled out a compact mirror and checked her ruby-red lipstick.

"Margot." Cooper tried to disguise the tension in her voice.

"Great to see you, Erica. So, why have you summoned me into enemy territory?" Margot chuckled. She usually worked at the Freeman Hospital in Heaton.

"I have an assault victim. Omar Ali. He's in a coma..." Cooper's voice trailed away as she spotted the mountainous engagement ring on Margot's left hand. When she and Fuller had gone their separate ways, he had got together with Margot suspiciously quickly. Cooper was certain the pair had been having an affair behind her back. It didn't matter now. She was pleased to be shot of Fuller but the memory still stabbed at her and brought up all the feelings of inadequacy she'd tried to overcome. "Erm, where was I? Yes, he's in a coma and suffered multiple stab wounds. The nurse said he'd been stabbed with scissors, but I wanted your opinion on his wounds and other injuries."

With a dramatic click, Margot closed the compact mirror and dropped it into her designer handbag. "Well, I prefer to work with the dead. But I'll help if I can."

Cooper led her to Omar's room and introduced the pathologist, with her perfect hourglass curves, to the PC stationed on the ward. *Bless him*, thought Cooper, as Margot ran her eyes over his chest and arms. She'd have probably asked to squeeze his biceps if Cooper weren't standing next to her.

"Shall we?" Cooper opened the door and took a moment to steady herself. Besides the subtle rise and fall of Omar's chest, he barely looked alive. His bruising had developed further, mottling his skin with purples and greens and an IV fed nutrients into the crease of his elbow.

Margot took in a sharp inhalation of breath. "My goodness. They did a number on him."

"He has severe head trauma," said Cooper, "the doctor told me it's the swelling in his brain that's keeping him in the coma. They hope he'll regain consciousness when the swelling goes down. But the longer he's in a coma, the less chance he has."

"That's right," Margot said, in a tone that made Cooper think of a primary school teacher congratulating a child on reciting the alphabet for the first time. As if her tiny, detective brain couldn't comprehend a little medical knowledge. Margot put on some latex gloves, approached Omar and walked up and down both sides of his bed. As she examined him, Cooper glanced at her phone, hoping for news from Tennessee or Keaton. She had four missed calls from Tina from over an hour ago. *What's up?* She typed, with one eye on Margot. *Nothing. Doesn't matter now,* came the reply.

"He's been tied up at some point." Margot pointed to his ribs and arms. "He has friction burns over these linear bruises. I'd be inclined to suggest he was bound around the torso with his arms pressed to each side of his body. See the bruising stops at his flanks and continues onto the arms." She carefully lifted one arm to examine some of Omar's back. "It continues around his upper back. A rough rope by the looks of it."

Cooper quietly made notes, allowing Margot's thoughts to flow uninterrupted. A nurse assigned to Omar flinched as Margot rolled him further.

"It's okay, sweetheart. I won't interfere with his tubes," she assured her in her sweetest Highland accent. "The bigger wounds are on his back rather than his front. If he were dead I'd be able to get in there and estimate the depth, but as he isn't - thank goodness, of course - I only have the width to go on." She laid Omar flat again and peeled back a dressing on his chest. Again, the nurse flinched but Margot ignored her. "Not necessarily scissors, but most likely. Do you have photographs from when he was brought in? Before they stitched him up?"

"Yes." Cooper opened a file, pulled out a series of A4 photographs and handed them to Margot.

Margot's attention moved back and forth between Omar and the photographs. "There's a symmetry to most of the wounds. Ovoids with bruising around each one. Here, look. The attacker needed a lot of force to puncture the skin as the cutting blades are contained. These wounds aren't clean; they're ragged at the edges. But here, look closer. These parallel sets of puncture wounds are from when the scissors are open. The wounds are fishtailed in opposite directions and the entry points are much smoother. Yes. I'd say scissors with a shaft of, say ten to fifteen millimetres across. Probably just your everyday kitchen scissors."

Cooper straightened up from peering at Omar's wounds and rubbed her lower back. "Thank you, Margot."

"Oh, I'm not done yet." Margot moved to the top of the bed and examined Omar's neck.

Cooper put the gory photos back in her file and addressed the nurse. "Do you have the clothes he was wearing when he was brought in? We need them as evidence."

The nurse looked confused for a moment. "Clothes? No. He was naked when he was brought in."

"Naked?" Cooper's eyebrows lifted an inch, and she checked her notes. "No one told me that."

"His knees were caked in mud, his hands and feet too," said the nurse.

"He might have crawled away after the attack," Cooper mused. She scribbled down a note reminding herself to check with Hong about any clothing that had been recovered.

"This bruising is interesting," Margot said, capturing Cooper's attention once more. She pointed to Omar's neck.

"Strangulation attempt?"

"No. No, I doubt that. These aren't finger and thumb bruises."

"Rope? Like his arms?"

Margot's eyes narrowed. She straightened up, removed her gloves and placed a hand on her hip. "No, something smooth. Heavy too. It's been there a while, feasibly over forty-eight hours, and it's been pressed down on his clavicles and left bruising there as well. I don't know what, but he's had something clamped around his neck."

Cooper met her eyes. "Like a dog collar?"

"Yes," Margot said, "only much heavier. I suspect it was made of metal."

Cooper gulped and turned her head away. Margot had described a slave collar.

By the time Cooper negotiated city-centre traffic, picked up Atkinson, and made it back to the coast, dusk had arrived and Tynemouth's sky was an inky blue. Cooper took Atkinson's hand as they walked up to her front door. It felt nice. Warm. Soft but strong. After a day looking into Omar Ali's case and seeing the worst of what one human could do to another, it was grounding to feel the simple pleasure of walking hand-in-hand with the person she loved.

The smell of shepherd's pie hit Cooper before she'd even closed the door behind her. Tina was scrubbing a pan in the kitchen sink. She didn't look up when Cooper and Atkinson greeted her. She wasn't being rude. She was just being Tina.

Kenny raised a hand as he joined them in the kitchen. "Erica, Science Man."

"Of course he's here," muttered Atkinson, only loud enough for Cooper to hear. "He's always here."

Cooper huffed and looked up at him. "He's Tina's father. Play nice."

Oblivious, Kenny opened the fridge and handed Atkinson a beer. "Erica?"

Cooper nodded. "Hell, yes." She took a long drink of the cool IPA and savoured the refreshing flavour before peering into the oven to look at a layer of grated cheese bubbling atop creamy mash. "This looks amazing, Tina."

Tina still said nothing.

Kenny continued to busy himself in the kitchen, setting the table and humming a tune to himself. It was vaguely familiar. "Why can I smell peat?"

"That'll be me." Atkinson sniffed the shoulder of the fleece he'd been wearing and hung it up in the porch area. "A long day working in Simonside."

"Was it the duergar?" asked Cooper, her mouth curling at the corners.

"The what?"

"The dwarf things that live on the hills. Hong told me about them. Some local legend."

"Erica, two people lost their lives. They died awful deaths—"

"Jeez, just trying to lighten the mood." Cooper put her beer down and folded her arms over her chest.

Kenny began to dish up and continued to hum through the tension. Then it hit Cooper where she knew the tune from.

"That's Cerberus by Hush In Hell," she said, pointing a finger at Kenny. "That's so weird. I was just listening to that song the other night."

Kenny beamed. "No way? Spooky. Well, great minds think alike."

Tina slammed a cupboard door shut. "And fools seldom differ." She picked up her plate. "I'll eat in my room."

Her eyes were wet and her face painted with fury.

Cooper's mouth fell open. "Whoa. Tina, what's wrong?"

"Nothing you need to worry about."

Tina marched past her mother and headed for the stairs.

"Is it Steven? He's okay, isn't he?"

"Of course he is. He's a stupid bird. Looking after him isn't rocket science."

The sound of footsteps running up the stairs and Tina's door slamming left the three adults in stunned silence for a moment. They took their seats and Cooper turned to Kenny.

"What's going on?"

Kenny looked longingly at his forkful of food, put it down and ran a hand over his forehead. "Tina was at Josh's this afternoon."

"Oh God, Kenny. What did you do? You didn't give Josh a hard time again, did you?" She thought they'd worked past the over-protective-Dad stage. The man had been completely overbearing when Tina had started hanging out with Josh, and understandably, Tina thought he'd had no right.

"Me?" Kenny's eyebrows shot upwards. "I did my best. That's what I did. Tina called me after trying to get through to you for an hour."

Cooper's heart sank. "I texted her back. She said everything was fine."

"It wasn't. She was doing homework at Josh's house. Sat on his bed and she got her period. I don't know much about these things, but she was crying, said it came from nowhere, wasn't supposed to be that day and was super heavy. Niagara Falls, she called it."

Cooper rested her forehead in her palm. Her poor girl.

"She didn't know what to do. She'd bled through her clothes, so I came here, picked up a change of clothes for her and called in at Boots. Didn't have a clue what sort of, err, products she needed so I bought applicator, non-applicator, regular, super, towels, liners... You know they have organic tampons? What's that about? Anyway, I took them over with a box of chocolates and showed Josh how to use the washing machine." He took a sip of beer and shook his head. "I thought I'd done everything I could, but she's still upset."

Cooper reached across the table and patted Kenny's hand. To her left, Atkinson prickled, but she ignored him. She didn't have the energy for insecure egos right now. "You did do everything you could. She's not upset with you. She's embarrassed."

"But she didn't do anything wrong?"

"That doesn't matter. Being a girl... It's complicated. Look, we're only a generation or two away from when women were called dirty or unclean for having periods. In some parts of the world, it's still that way. That sticks with you."

Cooper covered her face with her hands. She hadn't been there for Tina when she needed her. She'd wanted her mum and she hadn't been there. Cooper had thought being a single, working mum would get easier as Tina got older. She'd been wrong. It was just going to get harder.

- Chapter 16 -

The Mazda's engine warning light illuminated just as Cooper slammed the brakes and brought the car to a stop in a car park on top of a cliff in South Shields. She'd narrowly missed a young girl of five or six who was carrying three pink balloons and holding hands with her mother. *Don't let it be her* she pleaded to the heavens as she emerged from her vehicle and raced to the cliff edge. *Don't let it be her.*

Down on the sand below her, uniforms were extending the police cordon as scene of crime officers worked to maintain the integrity of their evidence amidst a growing crowd of onlookers. Cooper ran as she descended the steep stone staircase that zigzagged down the cliff face, connecting green fields above to the grotto below. Her breath was haggard, and beads of sweat instantly formed on her forehead. Her feet maintained a steady rhythm, tip-tapping down the stone steps as fast as she dared. She didn't know how many steps there were, but she knew they weren't as many as Ropery Stairs in North Shields or King Edward's Bay in Tynemouth. When Tina was younger she would always count the stairs. It was a habit, or rather an obsession, that Tina must have grown out of at some point. Cooper was unsure when that had happened, and she felt sad for not noticing it sooner.

Marsden Beach was stunning. Ochre sand peppered with shells and pebbles faded to umber where the water lapped the shore. The odd piece of sea glass shimmered in the sunshine, and a towering monolith, the famous Marsden Rock, dominated the scenery. The rock stood one hundred feet tall and during high tide was completely cut off from the beach. Home to thousands of kittiwakes and cormorants, the rock had once been much bigger. Erosion had caused a large chunk of the rock to collapse into the sea, forming an impressive arch. It was postcard-perfect until the limestone above also fell victim to the saltwater.

Cooper continued running until she reached the police tape. Here, she found someone else who had fallen victim to the cruelty of the North Sea.

Atkinson met her at the tape as she flashed her identification at the officer in charge of logging all attendants.

"I had to call you," said Atkinson. He was dressed in the usual white coveralls. "I know it's not your case any more, but I know how invested you were."

"Thank you," she gasped, trying to regain her breath. "Is it her? Is it Macey?"

His eyes darted to the floor. "We're not certain. The water, well, you'll see for yourself, but I think so. She's female, the same height and hair colour. Approximately the same age."

Cooper felt like she'd been punched. The wind was suddenly gone from her sails. They were too late. "Can I see her?"

He paused for a moment. Cooper wasn't supposed to be there and he knew it. "Here," he said, "put these on. And be quick."

Cooper tried to lower her heart rate and steady her breathing before she entered the forensics tent. This wouldn't be the first victim that Cooper had seen pulled from the sea, but they never got any easier. She took a deep, slow breath, firstly to calm her nerves, and secondly, to fill her lungs with clean sea air.

"Shit." Cooper bowed her head in respect, and though she didn't consider herself religious, she hoped Macey was at peace and her soul was taken care of. The body was grotesque. She was bloated and barely recognisable as the smiling girl whose photograph Cooper had studied. She turned her head away to hide the tears forming in the corner of her eyes. It might not be professional, but dammit, she was sad; she'd let Macey down. "She's so swollen," she said in a voice so quiet she didn't even know if Atkinson had heard her. "Her face."

"That's the gas. When a human dies, the bacteria in the body, the gut especially, can go on living for some time, feeding on the sugar and protein in the body. As decomposition begins, gas is produced and the body swells."

Speaking of unrecognisable, Margot Swanson looked a shadow of her usual glamorous self. The white coveralls hid her curves, and the face mask she wore no doubt covered plump ruby-coloured lips. At least she couldn't pout at Cooper's man, not that she was ever interested in men over forty. "Erica," she greeted. "I'll have her transported from here as soon as possible. I'm sure Neil will arrange for the family to make a formal identification."

Cooper shook Margot's hand and forced her eyes back to the naked body of Macey Gallagher. "Who found her?"

"A boot camp coach," explained Margot. "He was setting out his cones and kettlebells when he spotted her in the shallows."

Cooper swallowed.

"She's been in the water at least thirty-six hours," said Atkinson, taking over. "Marine creatures had started to feed on her. That's why her eyes are gone, and parts are missing from the flesh on her stomach and thighs. Her hands were fastened together with a cable tie, and I think her legs had been as well."

"Jesus," hissed Cooper, her gaze moving down her legs as Atkinson spoke. "She's missing a foot. Someone cut off her foot?"

"I don't think so," said Atkinson.

"Me neither." Margot moved towards what was left of Macey's right leg. "She has marks on her left leg, around her ankle. And the way the flesh is pulled over here," she pointed to the stump, "I think her ankles were also bound with cable ties and that something heavy had been attached to them to weigh her down. They wanted her body to stay submerged for longer. But with the level of bloating and gas accumulation observed here, it's possible the upward force of her body caused the detachment."

Cooper was choked up but tried not to show it. Why would anyone want to do this? Why would anyone want to harm a beautiful girl who by all accounts was happy and friendly to everyone she met? "Was she alive when they did this?" she asked.

Atkinson shrugged. "We don't know. She has no gunshot wounds. No stab wounds. No signs of being beaten. And other than the missing foot she has no broken bones that we can tell. You said she was diabetic?"

Cooper nodded. "That's right."

"That might explain why her body bloated so quickly. If her sugar levels were elevated, it would be perfect conditions for the bacteria to feast. It's near impossible for us to know if she was killed by drowning or if she was already dead when she was dumped in the water. If she'd been discovered sooner, we might have been able to tell, but after being submerged for so long, her lungs would fill with water either way."

"There are tests," said Margot, "But they're unreliable. I might, however, be able to run some blood work and establish her insulin levels. It won't be perfect as the bacteria will have used the glucose in her body, but it might give us an idea of whether she slipped into a diabetic coma before this happened."

"Cooper," the voice was unmistakable, and it was angry. "What in the blue blazes are you doing here?"

"Sir," said Cooper, her voice squeakier than she would have liked.

Superintendent Howard Nixon's face was hard and his eyes furious. "You know damn well you were taken off this case. Fuller and Sutherland are on their way, how do you think they'll feel finding you crawling all over their crime scene?"

"I'm hardly crawling, sir." Cooper knew she was in the wrong, but her intentions were good. She just wanted to help. That was all she ever wanted to do.

"Hold your tongue, young lady. I'm not finished."

Cooper practically choked. "Young lady? Sir, human resources—"

"Fuck human resources."

"Hey!" Atkinson's voice was lower than Cooper had ever heard it. "Do not talk to her like that. Don't *ever* talk to her like that." He'd moved within six inches of Nixon, who looked like he was about to blow a fuse. He was visibly shaking and Cooper didn't know whether to love Atkinson for standing up for her or to hate him for, well, standing up for her. She almost always held her own with Nixon. Their relationship had never been the best, but she usually handled him okay.

"And just who do you think you are, addressing me like that?"

Atkinson pulled his shoulders back and lowered the mask covering his mouth. "I'm the senior scene of crime officer, and I have jurisdiction. No police, no detectives, no no one unless I say so. So get out of my tent and stop crawling all over *my* crime scene."

Nixon's mouth twisted. Cooper didn't think anyone had ever thrown his own line back at him before, and he couldn't argue with Atkinson's logic. He left the tent, giving Cooper a look that meant her life wouldn't be worth living.

"Bugger it," she sighed, throwing her hands up. "Bugger it all. I shouldn't be here. We both know that." She spun on the spot, hoping Nixon wasn't waiting outside the tent. "Here goes nothing. I'll see you at dinner, Justin." Cooper blew a kiss into the air and left.

In the few minutes she'd been in the tent, the crowd had grown exponentially, and television cameras had appeared on top of the cliffs. Out at sea, the Newcastle to Amsterdam ferry looked immune to the swell as it headed to the continent. Beyond it, on the horizon, storm clouds were moving in. Fast.

- Chapter 17 -

The oil warning and brake system lights illuminated orange. The power steering began playing silly buggers. Cooper didn't have time for this, but she didn't have much choice. She dropped the car at her local Kwik Fit and took an Uber into HQ.

The image of Macey's body wouldn't leave her. As she threw her handbag down next to a desk, she remembered the swollen, grey stump that was Macey's left leg. Exposed flesh, nibbled away at by fish and who knows what else. Cooper gagged. She clamped a hand to her mouth and raced to the toilets, desperately hoping to make it in time. She pushed open the door to the first stall and dropped to her knees. The top of her tibia slammed against the tiled flooring and she yelped in pain. She retched over and over again, but nothing came up. Panting, she placed a clammy hand back over her mouth and closed her eyes, but the image was still there. Cooper sat in the stall for over ten minutes. Only when she was certain she wasn't going to vomit over anyone did she emerge, red-eyed and pasty-faced.

Returning to her desk, she switched on her computer and began searching the database for crimes involving scissors or heavy collars until Tennessee arrived looking both harried and distracted. Cooper glanced at her watch. What time did he call this?

"I just passed Nixon in the hall. What's up his arse?" he asked, joining her at the desk.

"Me, mainly," she replied. She rubbed her eyes and turned back to the screen. "Margot confirmed scissors as the weapon used on Omar Ali. I'm looking for any matches in MO. We think he had some sort of heavy collar fastened around his neck too."

"A collar? Is that what the dog reference was all about?" Tennessee looked confused.

"We won't know until he wakes up." Cooper hesitated and added, "*If* he wakes up. He was probably delusional with pain. He could have said anything, but for now, it's a..." her voice faded away.

"You were going to say *lead*. Admit it."

"It's a line of inquiry."

After a few minutes of searching, Tennessee tapped his monitor. Nine years ago, homicide in Sunderland. Murder weapon was a pair of scissors. Toby Cresswell convicted... Oh, never mind, he's still in the can."

"Seamstress, Alba Fitz, attempted rape. Stabbed her attacker with sewing scissors. Self-defence. The assailant almost bled to death."

"Hmm." Tennessee leant back in his chair. "You don't think this could be something similar? Maybe Omar isn't the victim here. Maybe he's the perpetrator and some woman defended herself?"

Cooper snorted. "Omar attacks some woman and instead of running away, she somehow overpowers him, holds him captive for a few days, then beats him up and stabs him?"

Tennessee's posture shifted. He slumped forward in his chair, propped his elbows on the desk and rested his chin on his hands. "Sorry, stupid idea. Forget I said it."

He wasn't making eye contact. Cooper knew he wasn't right. He hadn't been right in days. "Jack," she said tentatively, "what's going—"

"What about this guy? Khush Patel. Convicted of GBH for stabbing someone with scissors. Served four years and now living in, would you believe it, Byker?"

Whatever it was, DS Jack Daniel didn't want to talk about it. Cooper bit her lower lip, and she bobbed her head. "Good. Let's shortlist him. We'll send a car over. In the meantime, keep looking."

Cooper kept scrolling and came across a case from ten years ago. "James Blake," she said. "Arrested after threatening a steward at St. James' Park with a pair of scissors. Blake and his girlfriend had turned up to the game in goth gear, and get this, the girlfriend was on a leash."

"No way?"

"Yes way. The stewards wouldn't let them in. Health and safety. Blake kicked up a fuss, said the collar and leash were a sign of trust and guardianship in the goth subculture. The stewards wouldn't budge, a scuffle broke out and Blake lunged at one of them with a pair of scissors he had in his pocket."

"Definitely on the shortlist."

The sound of Keaton's heavy boots plodding the corridors preceded her arrival. She greeted Cooper and Tennessee and shook her coat, leaving a small puddle by the door. Cooper turned to the window; the sky was black. Rain pelted the asphalt and paving outside.

Tennessee took in the state of Keaton. "I guess it's raining," he said sarcastically.

"You guess correctly." Keaton squeezed her small ponytail, adding more water to the puddle around her feet. "You know, with observation skills like that, you should be a detective."

"Now, now, children." Cooper picked up the phone and dialled for maintenance. She requested someone with a mop, a bucket and a wet floor sign pay a visit to CID. "Right, Paula, what's the latest from Weetslade?"

"The door-to-doors on the eastern side of the park aren't getting us any further forward, boss. On the western side, I've got a farmer who woke up at two a.m. on Friday when a car went past his house."

"Traffic cams on the western side?"

"None. But to get to the farm track you need to pass a retirement home. I have an appointment to view their CCTV later today."

Tennessee got to his feet and began pacing.

"What else, Paula?" Cooper asked.

"Well, I've contacted the owners of the cars we picked up on the traffic cams from the A189. The Astra owner, Vince Shepherd, Clarkes Terrace, was driving home from Bournemouth where he's been working. Was a crash on the M18 just south of Doncaster. Hence he was home so late. Checks out."

Cooper made notes while Keaton spoke. "And the Qashqai?"

"The Qashqai's owned by seventy-three-year-old Alice Faith. She'd been at a friend's bedside as she passed away." She made a sympathetic face before continuing. "And the Honda I traced to sixty-three-year-old Deanna Morton, who had no knowledge of her car being used at that time. She called her son who lives next door and apparently borrows it from time to time. He confirmed he'd gone for a drive because he couldn't sleep."

Tennessee scoffed. "He lives next door to his mother and uses her car? What are the odds she still cooks him dinner every night?"

"He's probably still breastfeeding," said Cooper. "What's the son's name?"

"Bryce." Confirmed Keaton.

Cooper tapped a finger on her lips three times before massaging her temples. "Bryce Morton," she said quietly to herself. "Hayes Walk, Wideopen?"

Keaton nodded. "That's the one. How'd you know?"

"Hong's team found his wallet near where Omar suffered the worst of his attack."

Keaton and Tennessee turned to look at her with furrowed, serious faces.

"Don't get excited. It had been there a long time. Doesn't prove anything, but that alibi was wishy-washy at best. We definitely need to speak to him."

Tennessee looked disappointed. He resumed his pacing and glanced at his phone again. He frowned, moved his thumb over the screen, and then frowned some more. "Sutherland says we should turn on the BBC."

Cooper, Keaton and Tennessee gathered around a small television in the corner of the room and Cooper scrambled for the remote. "How," she asked, "can this building be less than ten years old, but the television's from the Jurassic era?"

"Cutbacks," laughed Keaton. "Nixon probably bought it from Oxfam."

The screen flickered and eventually formed the red and white familiarity of the BBC news. The studio cut to a reporter at Newcastle International Airport sheltering under an umbrella that repeatedly threatened to turn inside out. "This morning a body matching the description of Macey Gallagher was discovered on Marsden Beach. Her parents, Sean and Iris Gallagher, are due to arrive in Newcastle shortly and are accompanied by their daughter, Katherine, as well as members of the Irish press and a representative from the TD of Dublin South-Central. They have issued the following statement: We are heartbroken at the thought of losing our beautiful baby girl. Macey was the sunshine in our lives and now that light has been extinguished. We are struggling to come to terms with what has happened to Macey, and we have many, many questions for Northumbria Police and Detective Neil Fuller. We ask for privacy during this difficult time."

"Oh, shit," said Keaton, "Fuller's in for it."

Cooper blinked back a feeling of shame. "He barely had that case two minutes. He never stood a chance. I failed that girl as much as he did, and now the press are going to tear him to pieces."

Tennessee placed his hand on Cooper's shoulder but she shrugged him away. "No one had seen her, Coop. No one had any clue where she'd gone or what had happened to her. We did our best. And as for her parents, they're redirecting their guilt. Her father didn't give a monkey's that she'd disappeared and now he feels shit about it so he's going after Fuller."

He might be right, but it didn't raise Cooper's spirits. She had questions of her own: Where was Nicolas Petite? Did the hair grip at the landlord's house belong to Macey? Why did Aaron Quinn get so upset when asked about the baseball bat? Was he released?

Tennessee's phone rang. He pressed it to his ear, pressing the volume button so neither Cooper nor Keaton could hear the other side of the conversation. "It's okay. I promise it'll be okay." He ran a hand over the back of his neck and spoke so quietly Cooper could barely make out his words. "I'm at work... I'll call Dr Worthington. Slow down and breathe. I'll call him. Is your mum there?"

While Tennessee hung up, Cooper and Keaton's eyes met. Keaton shrugged. She was as clueless as Cooper.

"Jack?"

Tennessee shook his head and looked away. "It's nothing, ma'am. It's fine."

"It's not fine." Cooper rose to her feet and approached him. His eyes had reddened, not that he would look at her. What had happened to the pristine man she once knew? She searched his face and asked again, "Jack? Talk to me."

"It's Hayley." His voice was barely audible. "She's struggling. Ever since Alfie was born. She loves him, I know she does but they're not bonding, and she's depressed, and sometimes she just stares into space for so long. It's like she's a statue of Hayley. She looks like her but isn't her... It's like she doesn't do anything for herself anymore, nothing that brings her joy. And... and I'm just worried she's going do something, you know, like hurt herself, or..."

"Jack." Cooper took Tennessee's phone from his hand and laid it on the desk. She took his hands in hers and looked at him until he finally looked back. "Go and be with Hayley and Alfie." Between not finding Macey in time, not being there for Tina when she'd needed her and not noticing what was going on in Tennessee's home life, Cooper's guilt levels were killing her. She squeezed his hands. "Go home. Take as long as you need."

"But Omar's wife, Salwa—"

"I'll take care of it," said Keaton.

"What about Morton and the others we shortlisted?"

"I've got it covered, Jack. Give Alfie a kiss from me."

A lightning bolt illuminated the sky and highlighted the worry lines on Tennessee's forehead. He nodded once, picked up his coat and left without saying goodbye.

- CHAPTER 18 -

THE INCIDENT ROOM REMAINED silent for several minutes after Tennessee's departure. No matter how hard Cooper tried to focus on her work, her brain kept returning to her failures. She was failing as a chief, as a detective, and as a mother. Eventually, without giving any explanation to Keaton, she got up and left in search of caffeine and a backbone. Feeling sorry for herself wouldn't do anyone any good, least of all the people she cared about.

The drinks machine at the end of the hall gurgled and spluttered until a plastic cup was full of cappuccino, or what was supposed to be cappuccino. Having tasted it, Cooper wasn't so sure. She blew on the frothy top as she walked up and down the corridor, cupping it with both hands and taking sips until she finished the drink. There was no backbone or magic cure in the bottom of the cup, but she'd used the time to give herself a pep talk, and by the time she got back to the incident room, she was ready to roll.

Keaton and her soggy coat were gone. She had initiative and didn't need Cooper to direct her every move. She'd be on her way to the retirement home on the western side of Weetslade before heading to the hospital to check on Omar and his wife. Cooper sat down in front of her computer and searched for James Blake. Nothing. She pouted and tried again, this time for Jimmy Blake. Again, the search didn't produce anything of use. There was a kinesiology lecturer in California by the same name and a managing director of a screen printing company in Alberta, Canada. Finally, she tried Jamie Blake.

"Bingo."

Jamie Blake worked as an art dealer and was based out of a gallery with the unusual name of The Biscuit Factory. Cooper zoomed in on the photograph of his face and squinted. She flicked back and forth between that and the photo she had on file from the incident at St. James' Park. They could be the same person, she concluded. His hair was lighter now; it must have been dyed black in his goth days. The earrings were gone, and he looked broader. But there were still many similarities: the thick brows, the shape of his ears and lips and the intensity in his eyes.

She wrote down his name, along with Khush Patel and Bryce Morton before reluctantly heading downstairs to visit the Collector.

"Erica. Two visits in the space of a week? I am a lucky boy."

Cedric Bell had half an egg sandwich open on his desk. The plaster on his thumb was now a disgusting shade of grey.

"And I am not a lucky girl," Cooper muttered, not caring if he heard or not. "I need you to bring up all known members of far-right groups within a thirty-mile radius of the city. I'm looking for Bryce Morton, James Blake and Khush Patel."

The Collector raised his eyes. "You think there's a Khush Patel in the White Rights Party?"

Cooper was silent. It was - admittedly - highly unlikely, but weirder things had happened.

"Suit yourself." The Collector shrugged and began typing with only his index fingers. After a minute or so, he printed a list of names and handed it to Cooper.

She scanned the list. "I don't see them. Can you run a separate search?"

His typing was painfully slow and Cooper hoped he wasn't intentionally dilly-dallying to keep her there longer than she needed to be.

"The only Bryce Morton I have in here lived in Hexham, was convicted on drug offences and died in HMP Haverigg. That your guy?"

Cooper shook her head. "Patel?"

"GBH? Four years?"

"That's the one."

"Living on Chirton Wynd, Byker. Arrested for drunk and disorderly in September 2016, but nothing else of note. No connections to radical groups on the left or right. Works as a refuse collector for Newcastle Council. As for Blake, his file hasn't been updated since his release." He picked a bit of green veg from his teeth, inspected it, and then ate it. "I have his address from the time and known associates. But it's ten years old. Shall I print it anyway?"

Cooper nodded and held out her hand with all the patience of a five-year-old. As soon as she had the printout, she was out of there.

As the garage was still performing open-heart surgery on the Mazda, Cooper borrowed a panda car and headed to Shieldfield. The Biscuit Factory was a converted warehouse from the Victorian era. Bare brick and white plaster, combined with glass and metal fixings, created a light and airy venue with a very modern vibe.

Unable to get a parking space at the gallery, she parked around the corner on the street. One of these days she'd sell her old girl and get herself an upgrade. Sutherland had recently got himself a shiny new BMW, and Nixon's Mercedes had caught her eye. It wasn't that she couldn't afford a new car; the Mazda had memories. She'd driven that rust bucket for over twelve years now. She hadn't been able to drive when she first joined the police but the walk to North Shields police station, where she'd been posted at the time, was only fifteen minutes at most. Once Tina was three and ready to go to nursery, Cooper bit the bullet and learnt to drive. She and the Mazda had been together longer than any relationship she'd been in. For richer, for poorer. In sickness and good health.

Despite the full car park, the art gallery appeared to be empty. A hum of excitement was coming from the brasserie, and Cooper concluded that some sort of function was going on. She wiped her boots on the mat, removed her wet coat and slung it over her arm. She cast a look around the place and decided to have a browse. A little culture would do her good.

An exhibition of animal heads on human bodies wasn't to Cooper's taste, but some humungous charcoal drawings of the local area took her breath away. What skill, she thought, until her mind turned to Brian Hutchins. The art teacher had been sketching with charcoal when Tina had made a joke that ultimately put her life in danger. Her stomach twisted as the memory of searching Tynemouth Academy for the Tarot Card Killer returned to her. She set her jaw and moved on to some sculptures made of old motorcycle parts. Some were vast and filled their alcoves. Others were small and set on pedestals. One in particular caught Cooper's eye. It was about the size of her fist but was made to look like a dragon. It would look great in her living room, or she thought it would until she saw the price tag.

"Quentin Herbert's work is masterful, don't you think?"

Cooper jumped and turned around. He was tall, just shy of six feet, and muscular too. He clearly worked out but not to bodybuilder standards. His eyes were the brightest green, his hair tidy and the colour of sand. A sling supported one arm, and he was, without a doubt, Jamie Blake.

"Very talented," she replied.

"Are you looking to make a purchase today?" He smiled at her with a mouth of bleached teeth and stood closer than Cooper was comfortable with.

"Oh, I was just browsing," said Cooper, "and sheltering from the rain." She gave him an innocent shrug. "Besides, I can't afford six grand on a tiny sculpture, no matter how masterful the artist is."

She wasn't sure if she should show her cards and introduce herself as a detective. All she had to connect Blake to Omar Ali was a pair of scissors and a mumbled comment about a dog by a man about to slip into a coma.

Blake chuckled and seemed to move even closer. "Well, I can't blame you for seeking shelter. It's teeming down out there." He touched her upper back and guided her to the left. "And six grand is pretty steep. Although, we did have Xanthe Lewis in here last week. You know, the girl who won Love Island a few years back then went on I'm a Celeb? She spent over ten grand on a single painting. Hideous thing."

"The painting, or Xanthe Lewis?"

He laughed too loudly for the empty gallery, and his voice carried around the room. "The painting, of course. Although, those lip fillers... Here," he stopped manhandling Cooper and pointed to a stack of prints. "I might not be able to tempt you with a six-grand Herbert sculpture, but perhaps one of these prints will capture your heart."

Cooper felt very small, and there was something in Blake's eyes that she didn't like. It was as if he saw straight through her and knew exactly who she was. She wished Tennessee was here. Or Sutherland. Then she wished she hadn't had such an unfeminist thought. It was all in her mind anyway. A simple case of height-envy. "Thanks," she told Blake, "I'll take a look."

He was about to walk away, but Cooper couldn't help herself. "Your arm looks painful," she said.

Blake's eyes darted to the sling. "Car accident," he explained, though Cooper noticed he didn't walk with a limp or have any cuts and scrapes. What she did notice were the bruises on his knuckles.

With a print of North Shields's fish quay that cost her thirty quid, Cooper nodded goodbye to Blake and got the hell out of the gallery. She'd come back with Keaton once she'd collected more intel. Keaton could provide just as much muscle as Tennessee, probably more.

For now, time was getting on and she wanted to get home at a reasonable hour. After what had happened with Tennessee, she wanted to spend some time with her daughter, and she hoped Tina would like the print. She'd bought it for her and thought they could name the seagull in the top right-hand corner after Steven. She was going to make it a girls' night. Neither Kenny nor Justin were staying for dinner, so they'd get a takeaway and go on a Netflix binge. She'd pick up some ice cream on the way home and— "You're effing kidding me!"

Some toe rag from parking enforcement had slapped a ticket on the windscreen of the panda car.

"Cheeky swines."

- Chapter 19 -

Cooper hadn't slept well. She'd checked the time on her phone at least eight times since three in the morning when she'd awoken. It was now a few minutes past six, and she thought it was a good time to act as Bryce Morton's wake-up call. She left twenty pounds on the dining table, along with a note, telling Tina to take Josh for lunch and to have a great day. Last night had gone well; Tina had loved the king prawn pathia and coriander naans she'd ordered and all appeared to be forgiven. Two things had kept Cooper awake. The first was a feeling of dread for her DS. Tennessee hadn't texted or called, and Cooper didn't want to pry or invade his personal space by checking up on him. But every time she'd drifted off she dreamt of bad news coming in the form of a text message and awoke with the phone gripped in her sweaty palms. The second thing keeping sleep at bay was a thought she didn't want to consider. A nagging threat at the back of her mind that ate away at her and distracted her every attempt at focus.

Historically, Wideopen wasn't the wealthiest of areas, but Hayes Walk had a sense of pride to it. Well-presented semi-detached houses with bay windows stood proudly behind perfectly manicured lawns. The scent of flowers carried down the street, and not one piece of litter could be seen.

Without even checking her notes, Cooper knew which houses belonged to the Mortons. A set of semi-detached houses, painted in the same shade of jasmine white with sage masonry, had identical lawns with stone hedgehogs and other woodland creatures scattered around them. A Honda Civic was parked on one driveway. Cooper gave it a once over as she approached the neighbouring doors. The car had mud splatter on the hubcaps and a nasty dent on the front bumper.

She knocked on Bryce Morton's door three times and waited. Silence. She huffed and knocked again. When there was still no response she pushed her face to the letterbox, and using her fingers to hold it open, called, "Mr Morton? Wakey, wakey. It's Northumbria Police. I'd like a word."

"Can I help you?"

A fragile woman in her sixties was standing in the neighbouring doorway. She wore a thin nightgown and was barefoot.

"Deanna Morton? I'm DCI Cooper. I'm looking for your son."

"He's already spoken to your lot," she answered, folding her arms over her flat chest.

"I understand he's spoken to a colleague of mine, but I have a few questions of my own."

Deanna rubbed her hands on her arms. Goosebumps were forming on her pale skin. "Guess you'd better come in then. He's in the kitchen having his breakfast."

Of course he is, thought Cooper. She was expecting a man-child and she wasn't disappointed. Bryce Morton, in his late thirties, had slim shoulders and wobbly pipe cleaners for arms, but his hips and thighs were wider, giving him a pear-shaped frame that would be more suited to a female. A pair of Harry Potter style glasses had slid down his nose, and he wore plaid pyjama bottoms with a t-shirt sporting Marvel's Avengers.

"Mr Morton, Bryce, I know you already spoke to my colleague, but I need to ask you about Thursday night and Friday morning, specifically why you turned off the A189 in the direction of Weetslade Country Park."

He looked at his mother before answering. "I told the officer who was here. I told her I have insomnia and when I can't sleep I like to go for a drive. I find it peaceful when it's dark and the roads are clear."

Cooper hadn't been offered a seat but she took one anyway, sitting opposite Morton. His mother's kitchen was old-fashioned with floral tiles and beige-coloured units and worktops. The kitchen table was covered with a plastic tablecloth and on the windowsill, a framed photograph of a portly man was surrounded by fake flowers and battery-operated candles. A small plaque read: Rest In Peace Derrick Morton. Cooper crossed her legs and made eye contact with Bryce. "What keeps you awake?"

"Oh, you know. The usual." He gave a brief chuckle. "Work stress, money worries, this and that."

"You obviously know about the assault that occurred in Weetslade on Thursday night?"

He nodded and ate a spoonful of Sugar Puffs. A drop of milk dribbled down his chin. "The officer who was here last time told me about it. She wanted to know if I'd seen or heard anything."

"And had you?"

"No."

"It was a very serious assault, Bryce. Weapons were used and the victim may not survive. In that case, this investigation will escalate to manslaughter, maybe even murder."

His eyes flicked to his mother's and they exchanged a look that Cooper wasn't able to interpret.

"I didn't see anything," he added, taking another mouthful of cereal.

Cooper opened her notepad and asked Morton to describe the route he had taken that night.

"I drove south and left the estate to join Sandy Lane. Then I went up Great Lime Road, past Weetslade and then along Dudley Lane and back into Wideopen."

"That can't have taken very long." Cooper was visualising the route in her head. In rush hour it would be a nightmare, but in the middle of the night, it wasn't more than a fifteen-minute drive.

"No," he agreed. "Twenty minutes maybe. Just long enough to zone out. Driving can be a form of hypnotherapy, you know. People get into a sort of autopilot."

"Did you stop off in the park?"

He shook his head. "No. I told you, I just went for a drive."

"Did you see any cars in the car park when you passed it?"

"No. I don't think so."

"No one hanging about?"

"It was pitch black beyond the road. If there was, I wouldn't have noticed. I'm very sorry that that man got hurt but I can't help you. I don't know anything about it."

"So, the forensics teams won't find your tyre tracks in the car park?"

He looked from Cooper to his mother and back again. "I go into Weetslade a lot. My car, I mean Mum's car, is often there."

"When was it last there, Bryce?"

"Last night," he said, the colour seeping from his pasty face. "Around six. The park's open again now, all the tape's been taken down. I went for a walk." He patted his belly. "I wanted some exercise. Got to get ten thousand steps a day."

Cooper knew many perpetrators liked to return to the scene of the crime. Some got a kick out of it by reliving the moment in their heads. Others liked to snoop around, see if the police were still there. The most audacious would seek out the police, pretend they witnessed the event or saw someone suspicious. Bryce Morton seemed a bit wet, a bit too much of a Mummy's boy to overpower a man, hold him captive and beat the living shit out of him. Still, she didn't rule out the idea that this weak man-child thing he had going on was a convincing act.

She tilted her head to one side. "Did you hear we found your wallet near to where the attack occurred?"

"My wallet? I— I lost that months ago. Months." His eyebrows inclined towards each other and his chin tucked in, merging into his neck.

Cooper said nothing.

"I cancelled all my cards. There was eighty quid in it though. Do you know if the cash was still there?"

"I don't. I can ask forensics."

"Forensics? It's not, I mean, you're not using it as evidence, are you? I said I wasn't in the park on Friday night. I didn't hurt that man. That wallet's been missing for ages. Am I in some sort of trouble?"

"We're just trying to establish who was in or near the park at the time of the assault." She put her card on the table and slid it across to Morton. While his eyes watched the card, she scanned his knuckles and forearms; he had no defensive wounds or bruises to raise Cooper's suspicions. "Have a think, Bryce. If you remember anything. No matter how insignificant it might seem, call me."

She got to her feet and excused herself. She had somewhere else she wanted to be.

Cooper had the Mazda back, and eight hundred quid later, it had been given the all-clear. She put it into first gear and headed north. Once she joined the A1 she put a call into Keaton using speakerphone.

"Boss?"

"How's it going, Paula? Any news?"

"I've got Omar's wife settled in at the RVI. She's a mess, poor thing. Imagine not seeing your other half for almost a year and when you do see them, they're in a coma and... well, you know what he looks like."

"Have you heard from Tennessee?"

"Nothing. You?" When Cooper didn't answer, Keaton pressed again. "Boss?"

"Sorry, Paula. I'm a bit distracted. Driving. Erm, no. I haven't heard anything. I'm giving him some space."

"I'm feeling pretty shitty about not realising something was up."

"You and me both, Paula. Postnatal depression's a terrible thing. I hope Hayley gets the help she needs. Tennessee too. Seems like he's been shouldering this for a while. I wonder why he didn't talk to us sooner?"

"Because he's a bloke. And blokes aren't exactly the best at opening up, are they?"

"Times are changing. Mental health seems to be at the forefront of people's minds these days. Hopefully the next generation won't be as closed off as we are." The irony of what Cooper had just said wasn't lost on her. She wasn't distracted because she was driving. She was distracted because of something else, and she bit her bottom lip for a moment as she pondered sharing her own feelings.

"I heard from Nexus," said Keaton before Cooper could decide. "Omar got on the Metro at Monument in Newcastle. I followed the CCTV backwards and traced him to Times Square. He was coming out of The Eagle."

"The Eagle?" Cooper racked her brain as she drove. "I don't recognise the name."

"It's a gay bar."

"Huh." All this time, Nixon had thought the attack on Omar was racially motivated. Perhaps this was a hate crime of a different sort. Was his attack down to homophobia? "Does the wife know?" she asked.

Keaton snorted. "If she doesn't, I'm not telling her. Besides, you don't have to be gay to go to a gay bar. Maybe he was meeting a friend? Maybe he just likes the music. He was only in there for an hour."

As Cooper continued north, she left Newcastle's northern suburbs and her world became very green. Sheep and cattle grazed in open pastures. Copses of conifers stood tall on either side of the dual carriageway.

"We don't know of him having any friends," Cooper mused, mainly to herself. "His work colleagues said he kept to himself and from what the neighbour said, it didn't sound like he had much of a social life. Can you nip into town, Paula, and talk to the staff? See if anyone remembers anything or recognises him. Then take another look at the cameras. We know he was fine when he got on the Metro at Monument, and we know he was still fine when he got off the Metro at Byker. I want to know if anyone followed him. See who got on at the same station. Did anyone approach him?"

Keaton confirmed she'd follow those lines of inquiry and hung up. It was an overcast day and the sky was stony grey. The darkness above made the colour of the fields pop in vibrant shades of green, punctuated occasionally with the bright yellow of rapeseed. It was the sort of day made for baggy jumpers, hot tea and a good book but Cooper stood little chance of engaging in that sort of behaviour; she was approaching Morpeth.

No one agreed on where Morpeth got its name. Some said it was derived from Moor Path as the road, which was the main route connecting England and Scotland, traversed the Northumbrian moorlands. Others said it was derived from the more sinister Murder Path, after a brutal killing that had occurred on the road. What everyone could agree on was the fact that Morpeth was a beautiful market town with many structures still standing from the 1500s. Cooper was especially fond of a cuboid clock tower that dominated the town centre. She slowed the Mazda as she drove past to get a better look and to cast her mind back to days out with her parents. Morpeth Castle had always fascinated the feminist in her; it had been handed down the female line of numerous powerful families, until the 1980s when, disappointingly, it became a holiday let.

Cooper continued until she reached the opposite side of town and followed a quiet street lined with plush, detached homes that Cooper would describe as half mansions. Finally, she reached her destination. An impressive house stood at the end of the road, separated from the nearest homes by at least a hundred metres of scrubland on either side. It was Jamie Blake's house.

"So, this is what you can buy on an art dealer's salary?" she whispered to herself. She was in the wrong profession. Cooper looked left and right and couldn't see any other cars. Blake should be at work by now, but she wasn't taking any chances; the man was creepy and she wanted to make sure no one was around. She waited in the car for several minutes, watching the windows for movement, and when none came, she dialled the number for The Biscuit Factory.

"Hello, The Biscuit Factory. Leanne speaking, how may I help you?"

Leanne's voice was prim and fast.

"Morning, could I speak to Jamie Blake, please?"

"He's not in yet." Cooper's heart quickened. "Could I take a message?"

Cooper hung up and waited several more minutes before sliding into the back seat of the Mazda to change her clothing. She dispensed with the smart trousers and blazer she had worn to speak to Bryce Morton and pulled on a pair of baggy jeans, an unflattering hoodie and a pair of worn Nike trainers. It wasn't her greatest look. Frankly, she could pass for a prepubescent boy, but if the goal was to not look like a detective, she'd achieved it.

Exiting her vehicle, Cooper locked the car and wandered up to Blake's house. Immediately, a sign above the letterbox caught her attention: Beware of the dog.

Bad dog? she wondered, peering through the living room window and seeing a stylish, modern interior. Not a piece of chintz or clutter in sight. There was also no sign of the aforementioned dog. Not able to hear any barking or scratching, Cooper squeaked the front gate back and forth on its hinges for a few seconds. No German shepherds came running at the door and no Jack Russells thinking they're German shepherds came either. The sign might just be a decoy to dissuade potential burglars. Not that Cooper had any intention of illegally entering Blake's property. As long as she stayed on the public land that surrounded his house, she wouldn't be doing anything wrong.

Cooper followed the start of a bridle path that ran down the side of Blake's house and casually cast her gaze through his kitchen window. She couldn't see much, being on the short side, but she could see two ornaments on the windowsill: a matching set of porcelain cocker spaniels. Blake's garden was vast and shielded from view by seven-foot-tall fences. Cooper had no chance of being able to see over the top, but she could just see through the gaps between some of the slats. The lawn was well-maintained, short and neat. There were no flowers but there were numerous pots of herbs, including mint, thyme and chives. She couldn't see any rosemary, but she could smell it. A garden path with night lights on either side snaked towards a two-person sauna, a hot tub and an outdoor shower. Jamie Blake had some serious wealth. This was a man who could afford Yeezies.

Near the far end of the garden, but still at least three or four metres away from the back fence, was a green shed. The shed was reinforced with sheets of hardwood that had been nailed to the sides. A series of heavy padlocks secured the door.

It was protected like Fort Knox.

Having recently studied a case file on David Parker Ray, the American known as the Toy Box Killer, the shed gave Cooper an uneasy feeling, but before she could take a closer look, the sound of an approaching car made her jump. She pulled up her hood and did her best *boy walk* back towards her car, never looking back for fear of making eye contact with Jamie Blake.

It took twice as long as it should have to drive back to Wallsend. Some numpty had left a gate open and a flock of sheep had wandered onto the A1. Thankfully, no sheep or humans had been harmed. Back in Wallsend, Cooper stopped at the local McDonald's drive-through to pick up an Egg McMuffin and an Americano hot enough to melt glass. She struggled to eat the breakfast sandwich while she was parked outside the restaurant; her mouth was dry and no matter how much she chewed, each bite was difficult to swallow. Eventually, she gave up, throwing the remaining sandwich in the bin and heading back around the corner to HQ.

As she exited the car and slung her handbag over one shoulder, Cooper looked to the sky and saw the sun beginning to break through the grey. A beam of sunlight shone down upon her car. Perhaps it was a good omen for her afternoon? Or, maybe it was the patron saint of cars trying to take her old Mazda off to the afterlife? She picked up her coffee in one hand and her suit in the other and strode into the building only to be immediately clocked by Nixon.

"Cooper."

"Sir." She hoped he wasn't about to rant at her for being at Marsden Rock yesterday.

A line appeared between his brows as he scrutinised her. "Why are you dressed like a twelve-year-old chav?"

Cooper's jaw tightened and she held up the suit she was carrying. "Don't worry, sir. I'll be suited and booted before you know it."

"What's the latest on the Weetslade assault case? The Chronicle ran a story last night, and there was something on Look North about women being too scared to go jogging or walk their dogs because of the attack. Now the blinking RSPCA have released a statement about how terrible it is that dogs are being denied the exercise they need because we're not making the streets safe."

"What a load of old tosh," said Cooper. "Statistically, Northumberland and Tyne and Wear are—"

"No one cares about statistics, Cooper. They care about headlines and selling papers. So, what's the latest?"

"The net's closing in, sir." Cooper took a deep breath and could smell the aroma of her coffee as it drifted up to her nostrils. It might have been a cheap cuppa from the local drive-through but it was causing her to salivate. Even just the smell of it was waking her up.

"The victim was last seen on Tuesday the twelfth. He finished work at the usual time and in the evening he visited a bar near Times Square. He got on the Metro at Monument at ten-forty and alighted at Byker shortly after eleven p.m. None of his neighbours can recall hearing him come home, and he never made it to work the next day. We believe he was either taken on Tuesday night or was lured away somehow. The bar he visited is a gay bar, so we're considering that the attack could be homophobic in nature rather than racially motivated. Keaton is speaking to the staff today."

Nixon glanced at his watch but urged Cooper to keep going.

"The wounds suffered by the victim indicate he had some sort of metal collar attached to his neck and had been bound by ropes around the torso. He suffered multiple stab wounds, which are consistent with scissor attacks. I've found some previous cases with similar MOs. Cases involving collars or scissors. One of whom is of particular interest. James Blake. I've checked with local intelligence and have found no connection to far-right groups."

"Sounds like you've made a good start, Cooper. I need it wrapped up as soon as you can though. We're stretched beyond belief at the moment." He checked his watch again. "Anything else?"

Cooper could have gone into more detail. She could have mentioned the cars caught on traffic cams and the wallet found at the scene. She could have asked why she'd been taken off the Macey Gallagher case and enquired about the latest developments. Instead, she fished the parking ticket she'd received yesterday from her bag and thrust it into Nixon's hand.

"Yes, sir. Can you make this go away, sir?"

- Chapter 20 -

When Cooper entered CID in the early afternoon, she spotted Paula Keaton playing a game of rock, paper, scissors with Oliver Martin. Apparently, in this version, every time someone lost they had to do five push-ups. Cooper watched Martin do fifty push-ups before asking if they had work to be getting on with.

Martin, whose complexion was now somewhat dewy, scurried away. Presumably, he still had his tail between his legs after the scalding she'd given him over his attitude. Keaton dusted her hands on her trousers and picked up some files from her desk.

"Boss, I'm just about to head over to Byker. Going to check in with the guys canvassing the area and see what they have. See if Khush Patel's name has come up. He served time for attacking someone with scissors, and I think it's a good idea to find out where he was on Tuesday evening and Wednesday morning. The climbing centre returned Tennessee's call. They have a small camera that covers a stretch of the main road directly in front of the centre. I'm going to go and see if it's picked anything up."

Cooper's face lit up. This was good news. Hopefully, the cameras caught something of use. "Excellent," she said. "Keep in touch and let me know how you get on. I have somewhere I need to be later, but if I don't pick up, just leave me a message."

Keaton nodded and moved towards the door. She hesitated and then turned back. "Boss, I'll be near the big ASDA in Byker. Thought I might nip in and pick up some things for Tennessee and Hayley. Some posh fruit? A load of vitamins might do them some good. There's a couple of herbal teas from Clipper that might help them sleep. Their organic nettle infusion's the bee's knees." She tipped her head from side to side. "Or, do you think I'm best staying clear and keeping my nose out of things?"

"I think that's a lovely idea, Paula." Cooper wondered why she hadn't considered the idea herself, but she knew the answer, deep down, she knew the answer. "Tell Tennessee I'm thinking of him and give Hayley my best. I have something to take care of this evening but I'll give him a call tomorrow, see how things are."

Just as Keaton left, Neil Fuller and Sam Sutherland walked in.

The men tipped invisible hats to Cooper with perfect synchronicity and Cooper was at a miss as to when the two had become so close. Sutherland, like Cooper, had always considered Fuller a bit of a cowardly wet blanket, and now, Cooper wouldn't be surprised if Sutherland put his arm around Fuller's shoulders in a display of uncensored bromance.

"Erica," they said in unison before taking a seat on either side of her.

Cooper was sceptical. "Gentlemen," she said with a rising inflection. "What can I do for you?"

"Two things," Sutherland said. "Firstly, Caroline said she'd love to come to Tina's party."

"Excellent. It'll be lovely to see you all."

"Sue asks what we should bring."

Cooper itched the back of her head as she thought. "We're just ordering food in but something with a percentage would go down a treat. What's the second thing?"

"We thought you'd want to know the latest from the Gallagher autopsy," said Sutherland.

"Margot's finished already?"

"She put a rush on it. Put it to the top of the queue, given all the press."

"And why are you coming to me with this?"

Fuller shrugged. "Because you're Erica Cooper, and whether Nixon approves or not, you'll find out one way or another."

She tried not to smirk. "Well?" she asked. "What did Margot find?"

"The glucose levels in the DB's urine and blood were perfectly normal."

"Meaning wherever Macey was, she had access to insulin?"

"No. Meaning, whoever washed up on Marsden Beach, isn't Macey Gallagher."

Cooper leant back in her chair and folded her arms. "What? You're shitting me?"

"I shit not," said Fuller. "The visual ID from the parents was negative as well. Macey has a large scar on her right thigh from being burnt as a toddler. Add to that, the DB is an inch too short and had clear braces. Macey's dentist sent over her latest X-rays. They don't match and she wasn't undergoing orthodontic treatment."

Cooper didn't know what to think. There was a chance Macey was still alive and that gave her hope. But who the hell was this other girl? Why did they look so similar? Questions raced through her mind so quickly she hardly knew where to begin.

"Holy Shit. Where's Macey? Who's the DB?"

"We don't know," Fuller said. "Missing persons are trying to find a match. Her braces have a serial number. They're in touch with the manufacturers. They should be able to match the brace to the victim."

"She looked so similar to Macey. Do you think this is somehow connected?"

"Who knows?" Sutherland yawned. "Margot's doing what she can. We have fingerprints from the body, so between those and the dental work we should be able to get an ID sooner rather than later."

"I'm completely blindsided." Cooper shook her head. She didn't know what to think. "Speaking of Margot, I noticed the massive rock she was sporting on her ring finger. Congratulations."

Fuller shared a look with Sutherland before getting to his feet and walking towards the window.

"Something I said?" Cooper asked Sutherland.

Sutherland picked at his lip, gave Cooper a meaningful look and slightly shook his head as if to say, *it's a sore subject.*

When Fuller turned around, his eyes had a slight sheen to them. "I didn't put that ring there," he said. "Some other bloke did that. I was traded in for a younger model."

"Jesus," said Cooper, more out of shock than pity. "Well, that sucks. Sorry to hear that, Neil."

"It was so out of the blue," he sniffed. "One minute we're in love, the next minute she's telling me it's over and she doesn't see a future for us anymore. Within days I heard she was seeing some twenty-something, tanned, steroid muncher with a waxed chest. Apparently, he's besotted with her. Proposed within a month. Dumb fuck."

The saying *what goes around comes around* flashed in Cooper's mind's eye. Part of her felt sorry for the man, it just wasn't a very large part. No wonder he'd latched onto Sutherland. Fuller was craving a father figure in his time of crisis and Sutherland was always capable of playing that role.

"I told him to keep his head down, get stuck in at work and keep his mind busy. The pain will pass, but until then, he might as well direct his energy into something productive."

She shot a sideways look at Fuller and lowered her eyelids halfway. "Wait," she said. "Is that why Nixon put you on the Gallagher case? Because he wanted to keep you busy?"

"No," he said, stretching the vowel sound for several seconds. He looked deeply insulted. "I don't talk to Nixon about my love life, for goodness sake."

"Okay, okay, I just wondered." Cooper held up her hands.

"I don't. Whatever reason he had for the reshuffling, it's as much a mystery to me as it is to you."

Sutherland interjected, "I think Nixon's just trying to utilise his resources appropriately. My case was cut and dry, Fuller didn't have much on, and this Gallagher case was always going to end in tears. Nixon probably thought it made sense to free you up. You're his golden girl."

Cooper blew out a raspberry. "Golden girl indeed. You wouldn't be saying that if you heard the bollocking he gave me yesterday."

Fuller placed his hands on his hips. "Yeah," he said, "I heard you were down at Marsden."

Cooper gave a guilty shrug but didn't apologise.

"I also heard that forensic investigator of yours gave Nixon a piece of his mind." The left corner of his mouth curled up and he raised one bushy eyebrow into a dramatic arch. "Quite the set of balls he must have. Don't think anyone's spoken to Nixon like that since he was in a nappy."

"To be fair, the whole thing was my fault," conceded Cooper. "So where does your investigation go now? Did the SOCOs uncover anything of use?"

"We haven't heard yet but the lads who were playing pub golf on the night of Macey's disappearance have come forward."

"Yeah?"

"Yeah. The night out was organised by Northumbria University's Student Union. They were all first years. Bussed in from the dorms on Coach Lane and all bussed back out again at the end of the night. All present and accounted for. No one was missing according to the student union rep. We chatted to a few of them. Barely anyone can remember much from that stage in the evening. There was one lad who wasn't drinking, a Damien Blethens. He remembers seeing Macey take her shoes off to rub her feet before putting them back on. He said she seemed tipsy but otherwise fine. She complained about being really hot and some of the blokes made a joke about her being, well, hot in the other sense of the word. Blethens went to the toilet and when he came back, she'd gone. He assumed she'd headed off with her own group."

"Did you follow up with the men who called her hot?"

"Of course we did." Fuller's tone was tetchy, and if Cooper wanted to continue receiving information on the case she had to be careful. Handle him with kid gloves.

"Sorry," she said. "Of course you did. You really don't have much to go on though, do you?" asked Cooper. "It's like she vanished into thin air."

Sutherland let out a small sigh and Fuller shook his head. "I'm hoping the lab turns up some evidence on the baseball bat we found in the boyfriend's flat. Quinn claims he only has it for self-defence. Says the student flats are always targeted by thieves and he wanted the bat in case anyone who broke in was armed."

Cooper knew student flats were a hot target for criminals. Four to a flat often meant four laptops, four mobiles, four televisions and sometimes, four game consoles.

"What really got our attention," Sutherland started before being interrupted by his belly loudly rumbling. He rubbed his palm over it as if to soothe it. "Was Quinn's flatmate coming to see us. I don't know if he and Quinn fell out or what, but he told us Aaron Quinn and Macey Gallagher regularly had blazing rows. He also said he passed out on the sofa at around quarter past one in the morning, so he couldn't vouch for Quinn's whereabouts when Macey went missing at three.

"Sounds like he's your guy," Cooper said.

Sutherland's shoulders lifted and fell. "Might well be. You know as well as I do that the most logical explanation is usually the right one. It's almost always the partner or ex-partner. Time will tell. How about you? Your case progressing nicely?"

"Getting there. I have a theory, but I need a warrant before I can go any further... and I need a bit more evidence if I'm going to get the warrant."

A HALF-HOUR LATER, COOPER arrived at Denewood in the village of Forest Hall. Denewood branched into several cul-de-sacs like bronchi branching into bronchioles. Detached new builds with spacious gardens and off-road parking made Cooper crave more space at home. Her home in Tynemouth wasn't small, but it was a terrace, and the backyard wasn't suitable for much more than hanging out laundry. Sure, she was close to the sea, but a house like one of these would give Tina her own bathroom and space to study outdoors. She considered as she watched a young boy whiz past on a scooter that she might not be able to afford it on her own, but she and Atkinson together certainly would. Not that they were ready to move in together. He couldn't handle the idea of her getting a tattoo and still resented Kenny's presence in her life.

Kenny had acted like an idiot during the first twelve years of Tina's life; in total denial of the fact he had a daughter. But Cooper had to admit, now Kenny was back and had got his act together, he had made things a lot easier for her. He did the school run when she couldn't, even stocked the fridge when he knew she wouldn't have time. And the little gifts were sweet too. She smiled at the thought of the Metallica poster hanging in her bedroom with its bizarre pin button frame. Atkinson would have to deal with his feelings towards Kenny before they could even contemplate living together full-time.

Cooper pressed the doorbell on a midnight blue front door. Beyond the door, she could hear the sound of children playing and a radio broadcasting the weather forecast. It took a while, but eventually, a woman with poker-straight, red hair cut into a stylish bob answered the door and looked quizzically at Cooper.

"Georgina Hibbert?"

"Yes," she answered, her eyes looking beyond Cooper into the street and the afternoon sun.

"I'm DCI Cooper. Northumbria CID. I know you must be very busy but I'd like a minute of your time."

Georgina's body stiffened and she manoeuvred herself so that the door was half closed between her and Cooper. "What's this about?" she asked.

"It's about James Blake."

"Bloody hell," she exclaimed. "I haven't heard that name in forever." She manoeuvred herself again, this time moving towards Cooper and partly closing the door behind her so that it was only open an inch.

"You were his girlfriend? Back in 2009?"

"Yes, that's right."

"And you were with him the day he was arrested at St. James' Park?"

Her cheeks coloured a rosy pink and she cast a glance back over her shoulder before turning back to Cooper. "Yes, that was me, but I don't understand why you're here now, ten years later."

"I'm investigating a crime where a man was restrained by a dog collar of sorts. He was stabbed several times with a pair of scissors. The only other incident I can find of a crime taking place involving scissors and a collar is the one involving

James and yourself. I was hoping you could talk to me about it. Tell me the significance of the collar and leash."

Georgina blew out her cheeks very slowly and quietly clicked the door into place. In a hushed voice, she said, "My husband's home. He doesn't know about that and he doesn't like hearing about ex-boyfriends. He gets jealous, you know, and he really wouldn't want to hear about how James treated me."

Cooper lowered her voice to match Georgina's. "How did he treat you?"

"Great at first. We were both in the goth scene. He was more traditional: leather trench coat, pale face, black eyeliner. I used to like the gothic Lolita look." She laughed at herself and ran her fingers through her hair. "God, we thought we were so cool. A few couples in our group used to do the collar and leash thing. I thought it was just a fashion thing when James first suggested it but there's much more to it than that. It's a symbol of commitment and trust. Like a wedding ring, I guess. If you're collared, you're taken."

"Owned?"

Georgina shook her head. "That's more the BDSM community. It wasn't an owner-slave relationship. More an *I trust you not to tug on this leash too hard and not to lead me anywhere I don't want to go* sort of thing." She sucked in her lower lip and looked at the floor.

"But?" asked Cooper, suspecting Jamie Blake hadn't maintained Georgina's trust.

She sighed. "But... he did lead me places I didn't want to go. He liked taking me to non-goth places just to... I don't know, be stared at, ruffle feathers."

"Like St. James' Park?"

"Exactly. The pub, the library, anywhere for shock value. He said all football fans were saddos whose weekly happiness depended on the success of eleven over-paid jocks, and if we turned up to a Newcastle game in our best goth attire, we'd blow their narrow, little minds."

"You didn't get the chance though. Security stopped you from entering the stadium."

Georgina nodded. "I'd say it was probably for the best, but you know how it ended up. Actually, I broke up with James after that, so it was for the best in the end." She looked down and to the right as if recalling a memory.

"Would you say he made you uncomfortable, Georgina?"

"More than uncomfortable. I didn't trust him at all in the end, but I was too weak to say anything until he was arrested. If I broke up with James I'd be cast out of our circle and that meant losing my friends too. I was scared of being alone and I think that's why I let him..." She wrapped her arms around her chest and hugged her hands into her armpits.

"You can tell me," Cooper said. "I just want to get a feel for James. Work out what he's like."

"He had a violent streak. Most of us were meek and quietly spoken, but he was like our leader. He had an aura about him and he... he slapped me a few times. He had fetishes, too. God, I don't think I can...I'm not like that anymore, you see. I've moved on." She checked that the door was still closed behind her before whispering. "He made me bark, you know, during sex. Like a dog."

WHEN COOPER TURNED INTO the Freeman Hospital in Heaton, her mind was somewhere between gay bars, BDSM and the possibility that Omar went with Blake voluntarily as his submissive. He had been naked, after all. Only, something must have gone wrong, they fought, and he lost. Badly. It didn't really make sense, she told herself as she directed the Mazda towards a multi-storey car park at the rear of the hospital. Missing work was out of character, and why was he at Weetslade? Neither Omar nor Blake lived anywhere near Weetslade Colliery. Either way, she needed to have a chat with Blake. She'd call Keaton when she was done here and have her find out what sort of car Blake drove. She wanted to know where his car was when Omar disappeared and the night he was attacked.

Cooper turned off the engine when she found a space on the roof of the car park and sat quietly for a moment. Her hands had left sweaty prints on the steering wheel. She wiped them on her trousers before exiting the car and approaching the lift.

"Out of order? Unbelievable." She growled and slammed her palm into the metal doors. She was on the sixth floor and her heart rate was fast enough as it was.

She gripped the railing as she walked down over ninety stairs, crossed the road and entered the sliding glass doors to the Northern Centre for Cancer Care.

- Chapter 21 -

"We're going to die."

"We're not going to die. Don't say that." Macey Gallagher tried to soothe Nina, the girl to her left. She spoke quietly, fearing their keeper was just on the other side of the door. "Everything's going to be okay."

She didn't believe her own words. How could she believe them? She didn't have a bloody clue if they would be okay. She thought of her family, wishing she'd never left Dublin and stayed home to study. What were her mother and father doing now? Did they know she was missing? She ached to be back home with them. It was the simple things she missed, like watching her mother hang laundry on a windy day, laughing as her father got too invested in a game of Gaelic football, and braiding Kate's hair while they watched a film. She made fists to stop her hands from shaking as she wondered if she'd ever see them again.

"They killed Elin," Nina whispered.

"Elin tried to escape."

Elin had nibbled at the cable ties all through the night, slowly weakening them until they snapped. She removed her blindfold but kept her hood on so their keeper wouldn't suspect anything when he brought them their breakfasts. When he was bent over, laying the paper plates of unbuttered bread on the floor, Elin made a run for it. She reached the door only to be dragged back into the room. Unable to cover their ears, Macey and the other girls had to listen as Elin was kicked to death less than two metres from where they sat. They'd heard her last breath. He didn't have to kill Elin. He'd done it to set an example. *This is what you get if you mess with us.*

"Listen, Nina, as long as we do what we're told and we don't piss them off, we'll be fine." Her words were forced and laced with artificial positivity because Macey was worried she'd be next. Kicked to death for asking for insulin one too many times? The irony being, that if she didn't ask for it, she'd be dead regardless.

Macey fought back tears. Last night, she'd heard their keeper on the phone when he thought they were sleeping. She hadn't heard everything, but she had an idea of their intentions and a small voice at the back of her mind kept calling out, *You know, death might be the better option.*

"Erica Cooper?"

Cooper looked up into the warm face of a young nurse with a glowing complexion and a pregnancy bump of at least seven months.

"This way, Erica. I'll take you to Dr McDermott."

The nurse made small talk, but Cooper was barely listening, and when she reached Dr McDermott's consulting room, she noticed her hands were shaking and she was suffering from dry mouth.

"Good Morning, Erica," boomed Dr McDermott. He was a large man who seemed to fill up most of the room, though not in an intimidating way, more in a Santa Claus sort of way. His thick white beard certainly helped contribute to that image.

"How have you been in the three months since we last spoke? This is your six-month checkup, correct?"

Cooper nodded. "Yes. Six months now. I'm doing okay. Busy but okay."

"Yes, yes, I've been following the news. Dreadful thing that happened last November. Dreadful. They're sentencing him tomorrow, aren't they?"

"It's the verdict tomorrow," Cooper said, not really wanting to think about The Tarot Card Killer right now. "Sentencing is usually straight after, but the judge might delay. We'll have to wait and see."

He nodded and looked at his notes. "So, today's plan, Erica, is to have a mammogram, an ultrasound, and we'll take some blood to run a few tests. He paused and tapped his pen on the desk for a few moments. "I think we'll book you in with one of our dieticians, too. I don't have to ask you to pop on the scales to know you're still underweight, and I'd have expected substantially more hair growth by now."

Instinctively, Cooper's palms went to her scalp. She ran her fingers through the super short strands. "Oh, this?" she said. "This is a choice. Turns out I actually like it short."

Dr McDermott's face brightened. "Yes, I can see why."

"And it certainly saves time. No drying, brushing, straightening..."

The doctor, who happened to be bald as a coot, ran his left hand over his head. "I quite agree. Though my hairstyle is not through choice, it's through age." He chuckled. "Now, tell me, have you noticed any changes such as redness or swelling?"

Cooper shook her head.

"Any dimpling or changes to texture?"

"No."

"Any discharge or pain?"

Cooper shook her head again. "No, nothing that I've noticed."

"And you examine yourself regularly?"

"Yes," she said, though if she were honest with herself, she didn't do it as often or as thoroughly as she should.

"Good, good. Right, let's take some blood and then Alexa here will walk you to the radiographers for a mammogram."

Cooper rolled up her left sleeve. She was wearing a white shirt, and her first thought was that she didn't want to get bloodstains on it.

Dr McDermott tied a band around her arm and readied a needle. "I suppose you're used to the sight of blood in your profession. I don't expect you to faint."

Cooper gave an empty laugh. "You'd be surprised, doctor. Detectives aren't as hardened to the sight of gore as you'd expect. If you don't mind, I'll stare out the window while you stab me."

"No problem at all," he replied. "You'll feel a small scratch."

You'll feel a small scratch was bullshit. Cooper had been a human pincushion during her treatment, and a *small scratch* always felt like someone shoving a needle into her, which of course, they were.

It wasn't until Dr McDermott said, "There, all done," and he'd popped a cotton pad over the ruby droplet forming over the puncture site that Cooper turned her head away from the window. He took a few inches of micropore tape and secured the cotton pad in place. "Now, Erica." He sat back in his chair and folded his hands in his lap. "Do you have any questions? Is there anything you're concerned about?"

"No," she answered him. In her head, however, she had a million concerns. She didn't understand how a nineteen-year-old girl could vanish without a trace and her double wash up on a beach. She was worried Hutchins would somehow be found not guilty and would begin roaming the streets again. She was concerned about Tennessee, his wife and their beautiful baby boy. Insecurities told her Tina hadn't fully forgiven her, and part of her wondered if she'd ever find a way of balancing her daughter's needs with her career. Dark thoughts kept swirling in her mind until Dr McDermott broke the silence.

"Excellent. You know you can call us anytime if you're worried about anything or have questions." He reached a hand over the desk and Cooper shook it. "Take it easy. Don't overdo it."

Cooper let out a more genuine laugh. "I don't always have a choice, doctor. There's never a quiet day at CID."

Alexa showed Cooper back into the airy atrium and guided her towards the rooms used for mammograms. Being in the building made Cooper feel sick. Her body felt like she was back in chemo. It wasn't the doctors or nurses or the volunteers who fundraised in the gift shop. Everyone here was lovely. The facility was famous for its high level of cancer care. It was simply Pavlovian. The building itself made her feel ill.

Once the door was closed, Cooper removed her upper garments. She knew the drill. She adjusted herself in front of the machine and the upper plate lowered onto the top of her breast. It wasn't painful, but it was uncomfortable and Cooper would ache for a few hours afterwards. Once the radiographer had taken her x-rays, Cooper dressed and was moved on for her ultrasound, where she needed to undress again. She lay down and a cold gel was applied. As she stared at the ceiling, Cooper had a nagging doubt. She was ninety per cent sure her results would come back clear, but the remaining ten per cent was playing havoc with her. She hated the thought of taking more sick leave and being out of the game. And what about Tina? She was becoming a young woman; she should be enjoying her life, not caring for her mother. And, God, what if she died? Cooper was still in her mid-thirties; death wasn't something a normal thirty-something had to consider. What would Tina do? Would she move in with Kenny? Or, go to the Canaries and live with her grandparents? Cooper had no idea what the school, college and university standards were like in Lanzarote, or if there even was a university. It was a morbid thought, but she should probably plan for it. It had been foolish of her not to plan last year.

The sonographer handed Cooper a paper towel to remove the excess gel. "I'll finish my notes and hand them to Dr McDermott. Your results will be ready in a day or two. You should expect a call."

Cooper indicated that she had heard and began to pull her bra and shirt back on, careful not to disturb the padding on her arm. She thanked Alexa as she left and began the walk back to the sixth floor of the car park. She shouldn't feel tired; she'd done very little physical exertion that day, but her stress hormones had leaked into her muscles, and her legs felt like lead.

Up and up she climbed, holding her phone to her ear and listening to the two voicemails she'd received. The first was from Tina, who asked what was for dinner because she could call into Co-op on the way home from the library and pick up the tortellini they both liked. The girl was an angel.

She paused on the fifth floor to listen to the second message. This one from Fuller.

"Erica, it's Neil. Nixon said I should keep you in the loop so you don't feel you need to keep poking about. His words. Anyway, three things. First, the hair grip in the landlord's bathroom wasn't Macey's. Second, I have to meet with the Gallaghers tomorrow. Wish me luck. Christ, it's going to be a nightmare. And three, Macey's phone was switched back on."

Cooper's heart jolted. She grabbed the handrail.

"We have the coordinates. We're moving in on a flat in Byker. Rented by Tennessee's favourite waste of space, Mitch Logan."

Cooper almost had a heart attack. What the fuck was Mitch Logan, the pigeon-chested, toe rag of a dealer doing with Macey Gallagher's phone? She pocketed her phone. She wanted to make calls, ask questions and get answers, but it was after six and her daughter came first. She was going home to eat pasta, catch up with Tina and be grateful for being alive. Pushing open the door to the rooftop car park, Cooper filled her lungs with fresh air and looked at the sky which had an almost imperceptible hint of dusky pink to it. She wiped her still sweaty palms on her trousers and fished in her pockets for her car keys.

"Boo."

Cooper jumped. She turned to see who was behind her, but before she could do so, her arms were pinned to her sides and she was being manhandled towards a Ford Connect. She jerked her body right and left, thrusting her head backwards in an attempt to head-butt her assailant. It was useless. He was too tall. Her head only banged against his chest. She tried to scream, but just as in her nightmares, no sound escaped her mouth. She could only manage weak gasping noises. One of his arms was long enough to hold her still, and as she finally found her voice, his free hand pressed a cloth to her face.

Ether, she could smell ether. Panic filled her and she held her breath, kicking the back of her heels into his shins as he continued to push her forward. Her left shoe fell to the tarmac. Her body spasmed as she fought against her instincts to breathe. She shook her head, trying to angle for fresh air but only inhaling more anaesthetic. "No! No!" The chloroform took hold and darkness moved in. She tried to fight once more, one last feeble kick of her foot and desperate jolt of her head. Her eyes closed and the Ford's door clicked into place.

- Chapter 22 -

Sam Sutherland loosened his belt a notch as he waited outside a flat in Byker. He must start that diet soon. For all his well-intended promises to Sue, he still hadn't shifted even a single pound since they'd had their little chat. His wife was a fine-looking woman: slim and toned. She looked after herself with regular trips to the hairdressers and he knew there'd been the odd bit of filler here and the odd Botox injection there. But her body, that was all-natural. She ate her five portions of fruit and vegetables per day, never snacked between meals, never ate pudding and was in the gym at six thirty every Tuesday and Thursday morning. He didn't think he was in any danger of losing her. He knew she loved him, but he wasn't so sure that she was attracted to him any more. He didn't blame her. His coping mechanism for stress was to eat his feelings. He could always drown his sorrows in chocolate cake or a multi-pack of crisps, and boy did he have some sorrows and stresses.

The diet starts right now, he told himself. Sue had been quite clear that they should set a good example for Caroline. After her school had been the target of a serial killer last year, he'd seen some of the same behaviours in his daughter. He'd seen the empty chocolate bar wrappers she'd tried to hide in the bathroom bin. They'd moved her to a new school, a posh one in a good end of town and hoped that she'd feel safer there. They had good security, and the staff were vetted to the highest standards. He fastened the button on his jacket so he didn't have to look at his gut. Caroline meant the world to him. If he gave himself a heart attack, he wouldn't be able to provide for Sue or keep Caroline safe. They deserved a better version of Sam Sutherland and he would deliver it to them. Screw it. Tonight, he would do the unthinkable. He would go for a bike ride.

Neil Fuller marched Mitch Logan out of the front door. Mitch wore nothing but a white vest, a pair of Y-fronts that used to be white but were now grey, and some pink flip-flops.

"I asked him to get dressed," said Fuller. "Asked him three times, but he refused, so he's coming to the station like this."

Sutherland opened the back door to his BMW and shielded Mitch's head as he sat down and slid along the back seat.

"This is bullshit," Mitch muttered as Sutherland closed the door.

Fuller rolled his eyes dramatically. "Says he doesn't know anything about Macey Gallagher. Claims he's never even heard of her. Doesn't watch the news, apparently."

"What about the phone?"

"He says he bought the phone off - and I quote - some bloke down the boozer with a glass eye and a gimpy leg."

"This gimpy-legged bloke have a name?"

Fuller shook his head. "Not that he's telling me. We'll ask him again when we get him back to the station. All he's given me is that it was a bargain at fifty quid."

Two minutes ago a uniform had emerged with the Huawei and plugged it into an extraction device. The data would be ready for them to examine as soon as they got back to HQ, not that there would be anything of use. There was no way an idiot like Mitch Logan was involved in this. He couldn't get away with kidnapping. Mitch was the dumbest criminal south of the border. He'd claim the British title if it weren't for some Scottish halfwit who, after killing his wife, forgot to destroy his computer. His search history included, *how to hide a body*, and *how to dismember a body*. In his notes, he had a list of equipment he'd need, including plastic sheeting and a powered handsaw. His GPS tracked him travelling to the nearest B&Q, where he was seen on CCTV buying said plastic sheeting and powered handsaw and paying for them with his debit card. Mitch Logan wasn't quite at that level of stupid, but he wasn't far off. Sutherland knew he wasn't their man.

Only four streets away, DS Paula Keaton's excitement levels rose as she stared at the monitor. The cameras at the climbing centre had captured Omar Ali leaving Byker Metro station and walking in the direction of Kendal Street. So far, this investigation had been like the build-up to an important game: slow and methodical. But now the whistle had been blown, and the chase was on.

Omar stopped a few paces from the station and bent over to tie his shoelaces. After a few seconds, he stood upright and walked to his left. Behind him, a man called out, approached and said something to Omar. Omar pointed further down the street and signalled right and then left as if giving directions. Keaton watched the man give him a thumbs up in thanks. He checked the directions by mimicking Omar's gestures, then walked with him in the direction Omar had indicated. They left the camera's field of vision.

Keaton slapped her hands together and commandeered the footage. She called Cooper but she didn't pick up. She left a message and told her she'd see her in the morning. Leaning in closer so her upturned nose was a mere inch from the screen, she squinted at the man. He was taller than Omar by about six inches and was slim or athletic in build. It was hard to tell as he was wearing a padded coat. He definitely wasn't overweight. His arms and legs were covered and he wore a dark baseball cap which cast most of his face into shadow. From what Keaton could see of his hands and face she thought he was probably white. Who was he?

Nexus had provided footage from the cameras inside the Metro car Omar had been travelling on. She had taken a cursory glance through it and no one had approached or bothered Omar during his journey. No one had stood too close or appeared to be overly interested in him. But now she had a hat and coat to look out for. Her first task in the morning was to find the mysterious man on the Metro footage and try to get a better image of him. The Metro cars were well illuminated and would have better quality footage.

"Right, you bastard," she said, pointing at the grainy image of the man. "I'm going to find you." She looked at her watch. It was quarter past seven at night. She'd be in the office by seven a.m. "Start running, shithead. I'll give you a twelve-hour head start."

"Oh good, you're awake."

Cooper was stirring. She felt drowsy and disorientated; her mouth was dry and she could feel a draught on her skin. Her feet were icy cold.

"Where are my shoes?" she mumbled, still dazed. A weight pressing down on her clavicles caused her pain and made her hands rush to her neck. The metal slave collar was cool, heavy and tight. Cooper's eyes sprung open and she clawed at the edges of the terrifying thing around her neck. She searched for a release button, a catch, or a weak spot. She found none.

A thick metal chain was attached to the collar via a D-ring. Cooper's hands followed it to the wall where it was drilled into a breeze block. She thrashed at it, pulling the chain with both hands, wrapping it around her arm for a better grip as she threw her weight away from the wall, hoping to free herself.

"Careful you don't tire yourself out," came a drawling voice from the darkness. "You'll need your energy for later."

Cooper's breath came in short, sharp gasps. She could feel her vocal cords seizing up with fear. She tried her best to keep the surging panic at bay, but it hit her like a spring tide. At that moment she realised she was not only restrained, but she was naked.

She kicked at the floor, her bare heels bruising against the concrete as she backed herself into the corner of the room. She pulled her knees as tight to her chest as she could, one arm hugging them and the other fighting relentlessly at the collar around her neck.

"Relax," came the voice. "I don't want your body. Not in that way, anyway. You know, it's quite interesting having a female here; all my other pets have been males."

"I'm not your pet," she snapped.

"The female form is very different to that of the male. You're much smaller, weaker, too. You carry less muscle, but your waist-to-hip ratio isn't as pronounced as I would have expected."

Cooper looked around the room, trying to grasp where she was being held. A single spotlight illuminated her corner of the room. The rest was in darkness. She estimated one wall to be approximately ten feet. She had no idea of the other dimensions. Fluorescent tube lights were fixed to the ceiling, but they were switched off. Sheets of foam padding, shaped into peaks that reminded Cooper of the bottom of egg cartons, covered the breeze block walls.

"Where am I?" She demanded.

"Oh, darling. Isn't it obvious? You're in the doghouse." He chuckled and the sound of his laugh gave him away.

"Bryce Morton." It wasn't a question. It was a statement. She knew who her captor was. "Where am I?" she asked again, forcing a brave tone to her voice that she did not feel inside.

"I told you. You're in the—"

"No. Not the doghouse. Where am I? What part of the city? What part of the country? Am I even in Newcastle? How long was I unconscious?"

"So many questions. You need patience. You'll get to explore your surroundings later when I take you for your walk. I hope you walk better than my last pet did. He did not walk nicely at all."

"Why me?"

There was a shuffling as Morton moved in the shadows. "Because you were getting too close."

"Why Omar?"

"No family, no friends. No one was going to go looking for him."

"Was Omar the first?"

"Oh goodness, no. There have been others."

Cooper's mind raced through missing person cases. "How many others?" she asked.

"My favourite pet was Benji," he continued, ignoring her question. "He was such a good boy. A border collie. I trained him myself when I was just eight years old. He was my best friend. My only friend really. The other children at school didn't like me; they thought I was an oddball and wouldn't play with me. But every day I'd come home, my face streaked with tears, and Benji would be pleased to see me." His voice was soft as he reminisced about his childhood pet.

"What happened to Benji?" asked Cooper. She was stuck in this prison with a madman, but she hoped that in talking to him she could understand him and perhaps put herself at an advantage.

There was a deep, sorrowful sigh. "My father was a hard man. I was always a disappointment. He wanted a son who could box and play football, who he'd be proud to take to the match or down the social club on a Sunday after the game. But I was a gentle boy. I prefer books to sports. He'd get so mad, finding me with my head in a comic. Benji never got mad at me."

"Bryce," Cooper's voice was cautious. "Did your father hurt Benji?"

"One day, he came home in a foul mood. I hid in my room, but I could hear him yelling at Mother. He was drunk and slurring and slamming things." Cooper heard him sniff. "I couldn't hear what he was saying, but I heard Mother scream when he struck her."

"That must have been awful."

"Then Father dragged me from my room and said he didn't have a job any more and that he could barely afford to keep me, let alone the dog. He told me to walk as far as possible and lose Benji. Make sure he didn't follow me home."

"That's terrible." Although Cooper was terrified and hated talking to shadows, she somehow sympathised with Morton's childhood self.

"I pleaded, but he beat me with his belt. Then I wandered the streets for hours in the rain until it got dark. It took all night to lose Benji. He didn't want to leave my side. He loved me, you see. He was a loyal friend."

He appeared to be softening. Cooper hoped that boded well for her. She knew childhood trauma played out in adult life. Usually, it affected a person's relationships, such as how they communicate or how deeply they trust. She'd never witnessed or read of a case like this though. She suspected he was trying to recapture the days of his kinship with Benji through the bizarre means of kidnap.

"Bryce, you're an adult now. Why don't you get another dog?"

"I have you."

That turned Cooper's stomach but she tried to continue. "No. I mean a real dog, like Benji. Maybe even another collie? If you untie me, I could take you to a rescue centre I know."

"Mother won't let me have a real dog. She says I was too upset after Benji."

"But you don't need your mother's permission, Bryce. You're a—"

"No." His voice was firm, and it scared Cooper. "I have you. I don't need another pet as long as I have you." He took two steps forward and was, for the first time, illuminated in the spotlight. He wore a padded Barbour jacket and heavy walking boots, and most concerning, in his left hand, he twirled a pair of silver scissors with pointed blades. "Are you thirsty?"

Cooper wanted to say no, but she couldn't deny her dry mouth and fatigued body. She nodded to say yes. There was an awful screeching noise as something was pushed along the concrete floor by Morton's foot. To Cooper's horror, it was a metal dog bowl filled with water. She hesitated, but her thirst was too much. She picked up the bowl and brought it to her lips, only for Morton to snatch it back, spilling water over her face and left shoulder.

He slapped her cheek. "Bad dog! The bowl stays on the floor."

Rubbing her cheek, Cooper looked up at him. "If you think for one second, I'm drinking off the floor..."

"Please yourself." Morton placed the bowl out of reach before returning to her, cupping her chin in his hand and stroking her head. She swiped his hand away with more force than she knew she was capable of, and certainly more force than was wise in this situation. "Feisty," he said with a yellow smile. "I don't usually like it when my pets have an attitude," he paused, "but it does make it more entertaining when it's time to put them down."

A scream caught in Cooper's throat, but her mind returned to sitting in Deanna Morton's kitchen and a question she knew better than to ask formed at her mouth. "How... How did your father die?"

Morton took a step back. "Officially? He died in a house fire."

"And," her voice shook, "unofficially?"

"He was the first pet I had after Benji. He didn't seem so big and scary once I was fully grown. It was easy. It only seemed right after what he did to Benji. I wasn't kind to him, though. I'll be kind to you as long as you behave. Will you behave?"

Cooper's eyes bulged as she tried to take in as much of the situation as possible. She nodded.

"Good." He sighed. "I thought about taking Father to the woods so he'd get lost and feel abandoned like Benji. I should have done it that way. It would have been more fitting. I kept him for a week until I got bored with him, then I held him over the bath and slit his throat. When the blood stopped dripping, I dragged him to his bed, lit a cigarette and put it in his hands. Mother always used to warn him about smoking in bed, but he'd never listen."

How he spoke so casually about killing his father made it all the more real to Cooper that he'd have no qualms about killing her.

"What time is it?" It may have seemed a strange question, but the windows were boarded up; she didn't know if it was day or night, or how long she'd been unconscious, or how far she'd been transported. Would Tina, Justin or Kenny have realised she was missing by now? She hadn't told anyone about her appointment at the hospital, so the police wouldn't know where to begin looking for clues. *Typical, bloody stupid, Erica Cooper,* she chastised herself. *Keeping things to yourself and not wanting to bother or worry anyone and now look where you are. Chained up like an animal and at the mercy of a madman.*

Morton checked his watch. "I'd say it's dinner o'clock. Here you go." He pushed the scissors into a pocket, emptied a pouch of Tesco own brand dog food into a separate bowl and slid it across to Cooper with his foot. "I'll be back later for your walk. Mother's expecting me for dinner." He fished some keys from his other pocket and jangled them in his hand. He approached the wall and turned on a small electric heater. It hummed as it came to life. "If you're still cold, there's a blanket to your left. Oh, and don't bother screaming. I had this place soundproofed."

Shivering uncontrollably, Cooper reached for the blanket and wrapped it around her shoulders. Morton unlocked each of the bolts and padlocks that secured the door and turned back to Cooper. He gave her an appraising look, then pulled a cord attached to the ceiling. There was a click, and the spotlight went out.

- CHAPTER 23 -

JUSTIN ATKINSON HAD SUFFERED a long day. It started at dawn when he dragged himself out of bed for a morning run along Whitley Bay beach. He put in a good seven miles and hated every step before showering and heading off to work. Work that day consisted of a morning in the labs to examine the samples Margot had sent from the Freeman following the mystery girl's autopsy. In the afternoon, he'd been squatting in the rain, sifting through the remains of a gruesome pile-up on the A686 involving an articulated lorry and three cars carrying six children between them. There were five deaths, three of which were children. The deaths of children always hit him particularly hard, and he was grateful each day that his sons were fit, healthy and living life to the fullest.

Atkinson was painfully aware that his striking girlfriend hadn't returned his text messages all day. It was understandable. She was under a lot of pressure from that berk of a superintendent to crack her current case and make himself look better in the eyes of the good people of Tyneside, Wearside and Northumberland. But now the workday had ended and he still hadn't heard from Cooper. He donned his favourite jeans and a smart shirt, dabbed some aftershave on his neck and went in search of the Wine Chambers and a beautiful bottle of Valpolicella. They hadn't argued much of late, but Atkinson feared she was slipping away from him. Cooper was cool, far cooler than he was, though she'd never say it or even think it. She wore leather jackets and rocked out to bands he'd never heard of. She was happiest being tossed about a mosh pit, and he was happiest with a glass of brandy, a knitted jumper and a good book.

It was dark when Atkinson walked up Cooper's driveway. He rang the doorbell and was surprised when Tina answered the door.

"Hi, Justin," She said in her quiet voice. "Mum didn't say you were coming over." Her natural curls were held back in a bun by a couple of pencils. She had ink on her lip, and in her left hand, she held a copy of Astrophysics For People In A Hurry.

Atkinson apologised for dropping in unannounced; Tina wasn't a fan of the unexpected. He held up the bottle of wine, "Thought I'd surprise her." Then he held up a chocolate bar, "And for you, the future of British science."

Tina smiled and took the chocolate. She stood aside and let Atkinson in. "Thanks, Justin. Mum's not home yet, but you know you're welcome to wait. I've just put Steven to bed and was going to watch Stranger Things; I have a few episodes to catch up on."

Atkinson's brows lowered, and he looked at his watch. "Your mum's not home? It's gone nine."

He was concerned. If Cooper was ever late, she had Kenny watch Tina. She didn't like to leave her alone for too long after the events of last winter.

"Really?" Tina looked at her phone. A look of amazement formed on her face. "Wow. That's late even by Mum's standards."

"Have you called her?"

Tina scrunched up her face. "I texted her earlier to see if she wanted tortellini. She didn't reply, but these days, she doesn't always."

There was a moment of awkward silence as they both remembered Tina's outburst from dinner the other night.

Atkinson reached into his pocket, pulled out his mobile and called Cooper. It went straight to voicemail. He sat at the kitchen table while Tina made him a cup of turmeric tea and told him how she'd had to get Steven a bigger box as he'd grown so much under her care. After ten minutes, he called Cooper again. Still no answer. She could be on an important call, or her phone may have run out of juice. Atkinson didn't want to be the sort of boyfriend who checked up on his woman every time she didn't answer the phone but Cooper wasn't the sort of woman who left her fourteen-year-old unsupervised at this time of the evening. He paused for a moment, then called Paula Keaton.

WHEN BRYCE MORTON LOCKED the door behind him, Cooper sat frozen, waiting for the sound of the Ford Connect to start up and drive away. When no sound came, she put it down to the soundproofing. She counted to one hundred, then burst into action. She grabbed the chain that attached her to the wall and heaved with all her might, trying to tear it from its fixing. It was no use. She pushed her bare feet against the wall and yanked at the chain until it nipped at the skin on her palms. Blood blisters formed and seeped their warm liquid down her hands.

She pinched her fingernails against the screws, trying to loosen them but they were fastened tightly. She pushed her thumbnail in the groove of one screw and twisted, breaking her thumbnail down to the raw flesh that had never been exposed to air before. She tried the padlock that secured the collar to her neck, but the result was, excruciatingly, the same.

Cooper must have thrashed like a horse that refused to be tamed for over an hour. Eventually, she collapsed and began to cry. She cried angry tears for less than a minute, but it was enough time to release the pent-up fear and frustration that gripped her. It was time to focus.

She lifted the water bowl and drank all she could, hoping and praying that Morton hadn't laced the water with poison or sleeping pills, then she moved the bowls to one side and crawled around her surroundings. The room was dark, save for a dot of light coming through a keyhole in the door and an orange light indicating the electric heater was turned on. She found the blanket and wrapped it around her bare shoulders, tucking the edges under the collar to protect her neck from the weight of it. Her fingers crept along the floor, finding a magazine that she couldn't read in the dark. She prized the staples from the spine and stored them in her mouth. They had little use as weapons unless she could stab them into Morton's eyes. She was desperate, and it was an option.

Her best hope was to find her phone, but she doubted Morton was stupid enough to have brought it here. It had probably been switched off and tossed from the van's window. Still, she searched in the blackness until the sound of a key in the door made her insides turn to ice. She had time for one quick movement before Morton entered the room.

"How's my favourite girl?"

"JACK. I'M SORRY, I know this is shitty timing, but have you seen Cooper? I think something's happened to her."

Tennessee was in a dressing gown and slippers. He held baby Alfie to his chest and moved aside to let Keaton into his hallway.

She wiped her boots on the mat. "How's Haley? How are you?"

"She's sleeping. I'm... coping. What's going on?" He bounced the baby gently, making cooing noises and planting light kisses on his head.

"She hasn't been seen since shortly after one this afternoon."

Tennessee carefully manoeuvred Alfie and lifted his sleeve to take a look at his watch.

"She was following up on the cases you two shortlisted. She told me she had something to take care of this evening but didn't tell me what. Atkinson doesn't know where she is. Tina hasn't heard from her since this morning, and her ex, Kenny, he's none with wiser."

An older woman with long, silver curls and reading glasses poked her head around the doorframe to the living room. "Jack?"

"Mum, this is Paula, my colleague."

"Nice to meet you, dear," she said with a glance that swept over Keaton from head to toe.

"Mum, I need to go out. Can you hold the fort?"

She looked concerned. "Jack, Hayley—"

"Hayley's asleep. I'm sorry. It's important." He handed her the baby, kissed him on the head again and kissed his mother on the cheek. "I'll stay in touch. I promise."

Keaton waited in her car while Tennessee changed out of his dressing gown. She needed to stay calm and think rationally but was beginning to fret. Cooper could go rogue occasionally, going dark if Nixon was overseeing her work so closely she felt smothered or if she didn't have time to wait for the relevant paperwork and permissions. This was out of character though; she would usually divulge any plan to her or Tennessee. Where could she be?

Tennessee slid into the passenger seat. "Who else knows?"

"Nixon. He's putting a team together. I'm to brief them as soon as I get to HQ."

"Do you think it's connected to our case?"

Keaton pulled away while Tennessee was still fiddling with his seatbelt. The dark streets were emptying and traffic was light. "Maybe. There's the Gallagher case, too. She was still looking into that one. But let's be honest, mate, Cooper's put some dodgy people away in her time. There'll be some folk out there with vendettas against her."

"Right." Tennessee lowered the visor and checked his reflection in the vanity mirror. He tutted and tried to tame his hair. "First things first, we need to follow the breadcrumbs. Work out where she's been and who she's seen. I'll make a list of everyone involved in the shortlisted cases involving collars and scissors. We can take it from there."

Keaton's hands clenched around the steering wheel as she shifted lanes.

Morton closed the door behind him and padded around in the dark, the sound of his footsteps only slightly louder than the sound of Cooper's heartbeat. She swallowed, using her tongue to pin the staples she'd found to the roof of her mouth. In her hands, she held her only chance. She had to get this right.

"Are you ready for your walk?" he asked. Cooper estimated him to be two metres away. She needed him to be closer.

He took two steps. "I said—"

Now, she told herself. *Now or never*.

The three prongs of the plug dug painfully into her palms as she swung the electric heater with all her might. There was a whooshing noise as it missed Morton the first time but not the second. The heater crashed into his temple with an almighty thump, his knees buckled, and he crumpled to the floor. Cooper could barely see him. He was a black blur on a floor of darkest grey. His shoulder twitched. He was still conscious but only just. Cooper didn't have much time. She grabbed him by the ankles and dragged him closer to her. She pounced on his body, turning him face down and binding his hands behind his back with the electrical cord.

She patted him down like airport security, searching for his keys. When she found them, she tried each key in the padlock that held the collar around her neck. None of them worked. Tears began to spill down her face again. If this plan failed, she would surely be Morton's next victim. She took the keyring and tried the keys in the padlock that held the chain to the wall.

Success. The key fitted but was stiff and wouldn't turn. "No. Come on," she pleaded. Below her, Morton began to stir.

She tried to force the key but could feel it beginning to bend. Cooper tried to calm herself and gently jimmied the key back and forth, her hands slippy with blood and shuddering with adrenaline. The lock sprung apart. She was free. Cooper grabbed the blanket and wrapped it around her naked frame. She didn't dare stop to look for her clothes or phone. Morton was deceptively strong and could free himself at any moment. She burst from the door to Morton's compound and tried to get her bearings. She planted her feet for a moment and looked around what appeared to be an industrial lot. The sound of a car engine caught her, and she sprinted in its direction. She sprinted as fast as she could in bare feet, cursing every time her ankle rolled or her skin ripped against stones and pebbles.

"Please," she screamed. "PLEASE STOP!"

Cooper ran into the road, waving her arms and letting the heavy chain drag and clatter behind her. Her blanket wouldn't stay fastened; she was partly exposed in the moonlight. It didn't matter. What mattered was that the car would stop. It had to stop. She ran further into the road, blocking its path and as the car screeched to a halt, Cooper collapsed on its bonnet.

"Police. DCI Cooper, Northumbria CID. I need your vehicle," she demanded of the driver.

He was a pale man, sporting a flat cap above a lined brow. His concerned gaze wandered over Cooper, and she knew she looked like a lunatic.

"DCI Cooper. Northumbria CID," she repeated. "Where am I?"

Behind the windshield, he spoke with a thick Geordie accent. "Sandy Lane."

Cooper stopped and looked around. She knew exactly where she was.

"What— What happened? What's with the chain?"

Cooper didn't think he'd believe her even if she told him. "I need your vehicle. Call the police. Tell them I need assistance apprehending a suspect."

The man cautiously got out of his car. "I think I need to take you to hospital, miss. You're bleeding."

"No." She wobbled and placed her hands on his shoulders. "Killer. Dangerous man." Her voice shook. "Dangerous. We need— Call the police."

Her legs gave way.

- Chapter 24 -

Two hospitals in two days. It was Good Friday, and from what Cooper could tell, it was a beautiful spring morning. She could see a perfect blue sky and every time the wind blew, a branch covered in pink and white blossom moved across the window. She longed to be outside, basking in the fresh air and soaking up vitamin D. Instead, she was trapped in the Royal Victoria Infirmary. Her wounds had been cleaned and a doctor had checked her for signs of shock. He was happy for Cooper to go home, but the ward sister refused to discharge her until the slave collar had been removed from her neck. A locksmith had been called but so far he was a no-show and the longer the collar remained on, the more claustrophobic Cooper felt.

At some point during the night, a ginormous bunch of roses arrived and a nurse had placed them in a vase with some water. They smelled heavenly and Cooper couldn't wait to thank Justin. She'd given him and Kenny strict instructions to look after Tina and under no circumstances let her visit Cooper while she still had the metal monstrosity fastened to her neck.

"Knock, knock."

Cooper knew Tennessee's voice anywhere. "Come in, Jack."

Tennessee peaked around the curtain before entering Cooper's little corner of the ward. He didn't look as rested as she would have liked, but his posture had straightened, and some colour had returned to his cheeks.

"Bloody hell." His eyes swept over the collar and to a yellowing bruise on Cooper's cheek. "May I?" he gestured to the collar.

"Knock yourself out."

Tennessee examined the lock and felt the metal with his fingertips. "Fuck. This thing weighs a tonne. Is this what he used on Omar?"

"Yeah. And who knows who else? He said there had been others."

He shook his head in disbelief. "Freak. I spoke to Nixon. He wants you to take some time off."

Cooper snorted. "Nixon? *Howard Nixon?* As in, our boss Howard Nixon?"

"Yes, that Nixon. Come on, you know deep down he cares. I mean... really, really, really deep down."

"There's work to be done."

"There's recovery to be done."

Cooper let out a reluctant huff. He was right, and Cooper wasn't averse to being told what to do by her sergeant, not when he was right.

"Here," he said, holding up a bag. "I called at your place. Atkinson dug out some clothes for you. Didn't think you'd want to go home in a hospital gown."

Cooper took the bag and Tennessee moved to the other side of the curtain while she buttoned up a shirt and pulled on a pair of leggings. From behind the curtain, he added, "Someone handed your phone in at the Freeman. No sign of your handbag, though."

"Shit. Oh, well, at least I have my phone. I'll cancel my cards. You can come back in now."

Tennessee threw the curtain back. "Ma'am— Coop, They said it was handed into the Centre for Cancer Care. Erm, you can tell me to mind my own beeswax, but is everything all right?"

"Everything's fine. Just my six-month check." Cooper didn't know if everything was fine or not. She'd call the centre in a couple of days to find out the results, but she didn't want Tennessee worrying in the meantime. "Now, shall we get down to business?" She nodded at the chair next to the bed. Tennessee took a seat.

"You're on the sick," he said.

"And you're starting to push your luck. What's the latest?"

"Morton's done a runner. He's not at his home, his mother's home, or the industrial unit he rents next to Weetslade. There's an all ports warning out for his arrest, and ANPR are tracing his mother's Qashqai in case she knows where he is and decides to pay him a visit. The Ford Connect wasn't in his name. It's registered to the man who rents the next unit down. Keaton's grilling him as we speak."

Cooper nodded and adjusted some pads of cotton wool that she'd placed under the collar to stop it from hurting so much.

"Oh, and you're under protection until Morton's caught." Tennessee flinched in anticipation.

"What? I'm not going to be babysat. Who gave that order? Nixon? Give me my phone, I'll sort this out—"

"Actually, I gave the order, and Nixon agreed. I'm to stay with you until the cavalry arrive. You shouldn't have been chasing James Blake and Bryce Morton alone. I should have been with you."

"It wouldn't have made a difference, Jack," she said to appease his ill-placed guilt. "He grabbed me at the hospital."

"I know, but if I'd been with you the past couple of days, you would have told me where you were going, and then the alarm would have been raised sooner."

Cooper rubbed a clammy hand over her face. "I didn't tell anyone, Jack. And you had better not be feeling in some way responsible. Your priority is not me. Your priority is Hayley and Alfie, and it always should be, okay?"

He lifted his chin to acknowledge the point and looked away.

She nudged his arm and held out her open hand. "I'd still like my phone."

Light returned to Tennessee's face as he handed over her mobile. She ignored the umpteen missed calls and texts and dialled Fuller's number. "Hey, it's me. What happened with Mitch Logan? Yes, I'm fine...Yes, I know I'm supposed to be resting."

Cooper could hear the clinking of crockery in the background. "We arrested him. Sutherland and I spent all night interviewing him. He denies ever meeting Macey. Says he bought the phone from a man in the pub."

Cooper rolled her eyes. "Of course he did."

"Well, we have a name and Sutherland and a couple of uniforms are bringing him in. We'll soon find out."

Cooper hung up and filled Tennessee in on Fuller's half of the conversation until a worried-looking Atkinson turned up with a uniformed officer who saluted and positioned himself at the entrance to the ward.

"That would be my babysitter," said Cooper. "Get yourself home, Jack. Enjoy Good Friday. Go via the fish quay. It's not Good Friday without fish and chips."

"And mushy peas," he added, getting to his feet and shaking Atkinson's hand. "I'm going to nip over to intensive care first. Omar's awake."

"Really?" Cooper's face burst with emotion. She sat up in the bed. "That's brilliant."

"He's still in a bad way, so I'm not going to press him on giving a statement just yet. But I'll let him know that we know who hurt him and that we're after him."

Tennessee left, and Atkinson flooded Cooper with kisses and inspected her head to toe. "Oh, Erica," he said, tears in his eyes as he tugged at the collar. "Haven't they got this thing off you yet?"

"A locksmith's on his way. Apparently. I'd rather wait for him than have the fire brigade cut me out of it."

Atkinson slid into bed next to her and peppered her with more kisses. "I'm so glad you're safe. I don't know what I would have done..." He was quiet momentarily, squeezing Cooper's hand so tightly it hurt. "I've been an insecure idiot of late, and I'm sorry. It's coming up on my *divorceaversary*." He made air quotes with his fingers. "I haven't been feeling myself. Doesn't help that Elspeth got remarried to that barely-legal Spaniard, and she posted pictures all over Facebook bragging about it. I unfriended her. How juvenile does that sound? But the boys are tagged in all the pictures, so they just keep popping up on my feed. Bloody Elspeth, honestly. He's a step-dad to boys only two years younger than he is."

Cooper didn't resent Atkinson's ranting. In fact, she appreciated the subject matter being something other than what had happened to her last night. She'd given him the basics last night when she'd been telling him to stay with Tina. Obviously, he wanted to know exactly what she'd been through but she was too tired and traumatised to go into any detail. She was glad he was respecting that. She'd speak about it when she was ready.

She rested her head on Atkinson's chest. "Thank you for the flowers, by the way. They're gorgeous."

"Flowers?" Atkinson's head craned around to the side table. "Erm... They are gorgeous, but they're not from me."

"Oh." She paused awkwardly. "I just presumed. The department might have sent them."

"I got you a fridge full of pastries, and there's a bottle of wine on your kitchen bench."

"Even better," smiled Cooper, and she meant it. "You can't drink roses. Now, how about we watch some television while we wait for this locksmith?"

Atkinson pulled the television around, handed Cooper the remote and wrapped his arms around her as they got comfortable.

On the screen, a smartly dressed woman held a microphone to her mouth while chaos erupted behind her. "Amelia Clarkson, reporting from Newcastle Crown Court where The Tarot Card Killer, Brian Hutchins, has been found guilty of four counts of murder and handed a whole life sentence." Behind Amelia, the parents of two of his victims, Jasmine Lee and Reuben Jones, were escorted past a wall of journalists and press photographers. "In his closing comments, Judge

Justice Finch addressed Hutchins, saying 'You are an abhorrent individual who preyed upon those whom you stood in a position of power over. You abused their trust, and I believe you should never be eligible for release.' We're told Hutchins will be transported to HMP Frankland within the next few minutes."

- Chapter 25 -

Cooper was bored. Mind-numbingly bored. It was early afternoon on Saturday and Tina had just brought her yet another cup of coffee. She placed the cup on her bedside table along with two chocolate digestives and jumped onto the end of Cooper's bed and sat cross-legged.

"At this point, if you cut me, I'll bleed pure caffeine."

Tina looked hurt.

"Sorry, T. Thank you for the coffee. I'm just stir-crazy. There's a lot to be getting on with."

"No, there's not," said Tina. She grabbed a handful of her hair and started twisting it around her forefinger. "The laundry's in, the dishwasher's on, I cleaned the bathroom, fed Steven, I got the shopping in—"

"Jeez, Tina. You don't have to do all that. I'm grateful, but you should be doing your homework, not fussing over me."

"Homework's done. Finished it days ago."

"But I saw you studying last night," Cooper said.

"That was just for fun. I was memorising Latin names for different species of birds. I can recite over sixty now. Want to hear some?"

"I believe you," Cooper said with a laugh. Her daughter was so very different from how she had been at her age, and they had vastly different definitions of the word *fun*. It was hard to believe the six-pound bundle of mayhem that she'd brought into the world was going to be fifteen tomorrow. Where had the years gone? Tina turned Cooper's world upside down when she gave birth at just eighteen years old. She'd been scared, confused and lonely during her pregnancy, but Tina turned out to be the best thing to ever happen to her.

"Can I have a hug?" Cooper asked, feeling nostalgic.

"No," Tina replied. She wasn't being rude. Tina had never been one for too much physical contact, and Cooper had made it clear that she didn't have to make herself uncomfortable so that others wouldn't think she was ill-mannered. "You can have a high-five, though."

"Deal." Cooper sat up and slapped Tina's open palm.

"I'm going to take a shower. Do you need anything?"

Cooper shook her head, and as soon as she heard the hot water running, she jumped out of bed, threw on the first suit she found in her wardrobe and legged it out the front door.

"Ma'am! Ma'am!" The babysitter jumped out of his panda car and rushed towards Cooper.

"It's all right, Northcutt. I'm just running some errands."

Northcutt got to her before she could unlock the car. He was young and tanned and sported a unibrow. "You're not to leave unescorted. Superintendent Nixon's orders."

"I'll be fine, Northcutt. I'll be back within the hour."

"We both know Nixon will have my head if anything happens to you."

She turned her gaze upward and growled at the sky. "Fine. Shall we take your car or mine?"

Northcutt gave the Mazda a scathing look. "We'll take the squad car."

Cooper held out her hand for the keys but the young man just laughed and opened the passenger door. "With all due respect, ma'am. Not a chance." He settled himself into the driver's seat, fastened his seatbelt and asked, "Where to?"

"Frankland," she said. "HMP Frankland."

FRANKLAND, HOME TO SOME of the UK's most notorious serial killers and terrorists, was found eighteen miles south of Newcastle in County Durham, an area otherwise known for its prestigious university, picturesque castle and magnificent cathedral. Northcutt had insisted upon not waiting in the car like Cooper had requested and even threatened to call Nixon if she didn't abide by his rules.

"Have it your way," Cooper said, smoothing down the front of her suit jacket, "but if anyone asks, we were never here."

Cooper considered heading towards the visitor's centre, but she wasn't here to hold hands with a loved one and stare longingly across steaming mugs of tea. She directed Northcutt to the main reception.

"They probably haven't even processed Hutchins yet," he said as he parked the car.

"Who said I was here to see Hutchins?"

Northcutt gave her a searching look but didn't press the matter. Cooper held her ID up to a camera and was buzzed into the building where she was immediately funnelled into a metal detector and then forced to stand very still while a drug detection dog sniffed at her shoes, legs, and awkwardly at her crotch.

"Erica Cooper." A guard spread his arms in a welcoming gesture. "Long time no see."

"Bruiser." She smiled and walked towards the desk once the dog was satisfied she wasn't a cocaine mule. She slid the logbook towards herself and signed her name. "I'd like to see Eddie. Nothing formal, he has every right to say no, but I'd appreciate him speaking with me."

"Eddie?" asked Northcutt. "Eddie Blackburn? Newcastle's answer to Tony Soprano?"

"Who's this?" Bruiser asked, examining Northcutt's ID.

"My babysitter. It's a long story," she said with a shake of her head as she'd rather not get into the whole Bryce Morton stripping her naked, chaining her up and keeping her as a pet thing.

Bruiser closed the logbook, picked up a phone and made a call. "Right," he said after he'd hung up. "Room B. I'll show you the way. Someone's fetching Blackburn."

A few moments later Cooper slid into an orange plastic chair like the ones she used to sit on at school. Northcutt insisted on being in the room so Cooper insisted he sit in the far corner and not to make a peep unless she said so.

"Well, well, well." Eddie Blackburn shuffled in. His hands and feet were shackled. Cooper fought not to let her hand go to her neck as the memory of the collar was still as fresh as her bruises. "If it isn't my favourite copper."

"Who's your second favourite?"

Aside from the similar job description, Blackburn also shared an uncanny resemblance to the Italian-American gangsters of Hollywood and HBO. He was a large, barrel-chested man with dark features and a crease down the middle of his nose.

"There are no second favourites. You, I like. The rest of your kind can go fuck themselves. You're the only reason I struck a deal with the CPS and kept my eldest out of here. The rest of those pigs would have sent my whole family down."

"How is Theo?" asked Cooper as Blackburn struggled into a chair that was far too small for his frame.

The guards who had escorted Blackburn mumbled a few words to Northcutt and left the room.

"He's gone back to school, believe it or not. Enrolled in some adult education classes, business and the like."

"Good for him."

"It's brilliant is what it is. Inspired me to, erm..." he waved his hands around, looking for the right phrase, "better myself. Got a job in the library. Can read all day if I want."

"That's excellent, Eddie. I'm glad to hear it."

"But that's not why you're here, is it? You didn't come for a catch-up with ol' Eddie. You need something? Information?"

Cooper cast an eye over her shoulder at Northcutt, then leant across the table and lowered her voice to a barely audible whisper.

"Macey Gallagher."

"The Irish girl? Pretty young thing?"

"Yes. That's her. You know who took her?"

"Nah. Nothing to do with my lot. You know that's not our style."

"But have you heard anything? Whispers on the grapevine?"

Blackburn shrugged. "Sorry, darling. You know I'd help you out if I could, but no one tells me owt these days."

"I heard Fletcher was running the family business. He tell you anything?"

Blackburn propped his elbows on the table and rested his chin on steepled fingers. "The Blackburns run a taxi firm and a chain of pizzerias. We're just honest entrepreneurs trying to earn a living in today's competitive climate."

"Yeah. And I'm Kim Kardashian." Cooper sighed and looked to the table in disappointment.

"There's something else." Blackburn's eyebrows peaked in the middle as he read her face and took a butcher's into her soul. "What else did you want to ask me?"

Was she that obvious? Cooper leant even further across the table so she was close enough to smell his prison-issue porridge breakfast and considered the ramifications of what she was about to do. It was out of character, unprofessional, and it was criminal.

"Hutchins," she said.

Excitement flickered in Blackburn's eyes. The corner of his mouth twitched. "You want him killin'?"

Cooper quickly shook her head. "No. And I mean it. No."

"But?"

"My daughter was next. He would have killed her..."

He sat quietly for a moment, his eyes darting back and forth, imagining what he would do if someone harmed his own daughter. Not that anyone would dare. "And you want his stay at this fine, five-star establishment to not be the most comfortable?"

Cooper's hands gripped the edge of the table between her and Blackburn until her knuckles turned white. She wasn't a perfect detective, the sort who never broke the rules or slipped into the grey area between moral and immoral. She was human.

"I want him to know what fear feels like."

Blackburn surveyed her face. She was serious.

"Consider it done."

"Where have you been?" Tina had a face like a bulldog chewing on a wasp. She was standing on the front step as Cooper and Northcutt pulled up. Her hair was wet from the shower and she was dressed in pyjama bottoms and a vest.

"I just had to nip out, sweetheart. No need to worry?"

"No need to worry?" Tina's voice was so high Copper wondered if all their glassware was about to smash. "You were kidnapped by a madman! Who's still on the loose, I may add."

"It's fine, Tina." Cooper walked past her daughter into the kitchen and poured herself a glass of wine.

"It's NOT fine." Tina's face was red and blotchy, tears were about to spill onto her cheeks. "You, Dad and Josh have made sure I'm accounted for at all times. Never left alone. Escorted here, there, and everywhere. And you know what? It's been a right pain in the arse, but I've gone along with it because I knew it gave you peace of mind... and then..." A tear burst free. Tina wiped it away with closed fists. "And then when something similar happens to you, you just swan off without telling me and it..." Her voice caught in her throat.

"And it was a shitty, selfish thing to do." Cooper's heart melted. "You're right. You're so right. I'm really sorry, T." She held out her arms. Tina moved in for a quick hug before letting go and eyeballing the floor. "Can I make it up to you? It's your birthday tomorrow, how about we start the celebrations early? Invite Josh over. We'll get a takeaway, anything you want."

Tina considered the offer. "Bowling. Me, you and Josh. And a burger afterwards?"

"Absolutely." Cooper laid a coaster over her wine glass. It would keep for later. "The babysitter will have to come too. Call Josh and tell him we'll pick him up in twenty, and if he keeps us waiting, I'll get Northcutt to start the siren."

COOPER HADN'T BEEN TO a bowling alley in years, but it turned out she wasn't too rusty. She bowled three strikes and a handful of spares, but it wasn't enough to beat the teenagers. Josh opened the game with a turkey, and once Tina started applying her knowledge of trigonometry and physics to the activity, no one stood a chance. It was now half eight, and Tina and Josh were in Tina's room watching Netflix, or at least she hoped that's what they were doing; she'd told them to leave the door open but hadn't been upstairs to check. Cooper finally had her glass of wine back in hand and was sat at the kitchen table with her laptop open. She wasn't supposed to do any official work, but she could use Google as much as she liked.

Starting with a simple search relating to Feisty's club, she noted down every skirmish, complaint or newsworthy event she could find. Next, she dove deeper into Nicolas Petite with a little help from Google Translate. Nicolas Petite had been awarded a substantial grant for outstanding academic success. He had hit the local headlines for blowing it all in one hedonistic night of partying that involved buying all his graduating class Champagne and hiring a bunch of strippers - male and female - for his friends' entertainment. The local press had dubbed him irresponsible, ungrateful and a bad role model. Two years ago, he'd been part of a group that climbed Kilimanjaro, raising over twelve thousand Euros in sponsorship, which they used to buy supplies for village schools in the Machame area. Nico's social media was flooded with images of him with smiling, bright-eyed Tanzanian children. Then a headline caught Cooper's eye. *Baker's Son Arrested on Drugs Charges.* Nico had been accused of distributing poppers out of his parents' bakery. According to sources, his classmates would come to the bakery on Saturday mornings when they knew he was working, order a pastry, hand over extra money and Nico would pop the pill into the paper bag along with a mille-feuille or an éclair. The charges were dropped due to lack of evidence.

"Hmm." Cooper had such distaste for Nico Petite she had to take care not to blind her own judgement. Being a drug-dealing drink-spiker did not necessarily mean he was capable of rape, kidnapping, murder or whatever cruel fate had been bestowed upon Macey. He had done a runner to his homeland, the flight manifest confirming he was on the eleven forty AirFrance flight to Paris on the Monday after Macey's disappearance and had so far not reported to his local police station or returned any of Northumbria Police's calls. Cooper cast her mind back through the various statements and pieces of evidence that had been collected so far, the van was playing on her mind. It had been in the camera footage taken from the accountancy firm and the cat café. The sliding door of a van had been near enough to Macey to be captured on the voicemail she left Walker. She braced herself and called Imogen West.

"Yah?"

"Imogen? This is DCI Erica Cooper." Loud music was thumping in the background. Cooper raised her voice. "I need to ask you a couple of questions."

"Now?"

"Yes, now." Cooper could imagine Imogen and Alison seated in a swanky bar waiting for someone to buy them drinks. "Has Nicolas Petite been in contact?"

"No."

"Are you sure? I don't need to remind you of how serious this case is. If you protect him, charges will be made against you."

"I'm sure. I haven't heard a thing. I sent him a few texts but he never replied." Her voice became muffled but Cooper picked up, "No, a double, please. Vodka."

"One last question, Imogen. Does Nico drive? Or have access to a van?"

Cooper thought she heard a snort.

"Nico thinks there are two sorts of people in this world... Thank you, darling. It's Diet Coke, right?... Those who are meant to drive and those who are meant to be driven. You can guess which category he falls into."

Cooper hung up without thanking Imogen. The news Nico didn't drive was disappointing. She'd still check if he was the registered keeper of a van, but her chances weren't good. She dialled another number.

"Erica, it's Saturday night. It's the Easter weekend. This had better be good." Fuller was not amused.

"I'm bored. Humour me."

"Make it quick," he grumbled.

"The bouncer. Tiny, I think his name was. Did you talk to him?"

"Oh, Jesus. Come on, Erica, let it go. After what you've been through—"

"Please, Neil." She sipped her wine and listened to him let out a very long sigh. "Did he mention anyone hanging around the club, or any suspicious vehicles?"

He kept her waiting, sighing again. "Nothing suspicious. Just the usual mix of taxis, Ubers and the Tyne Pastors."

"You mean the Street Pastors?"

"No. It was the Tyne Pastors. Same idea, different uniforms."

"You spoke to them?"

"Yeah. Called them. They had nothing. Can I go now, Erica? There's a bottle of Brown Ale with my name on it."

When Fuller rang off, Cooper topped up her wine and did some more digging. Try as she might, she could find no online presence for any organisation matching the Tyne Pastors. There were the Street Pastors and the City Pastors, but no Tyne Pastors. They didn't exist on Google, Facebook, Twitter, anywhere. She wondered if she'd misheard and he'd said Town Pastors, or perhaps he just told her what he thought she'd want to hear. Anything to get her off the phone. She'd probably do the same if the roles were reversed. She opened a new tab on her browser and tried one last time, searching for *Feisty's, Newcastle, Pastors* and *Van.* She scanned three pages of nothing until Reddit gave Cooper her first nugget of information.

r/NewcastleUni. Posted by Giggles768. 11 months ago

Ladies, be careful. I was worse for wear coming out of Feisty's last night and two men tried to get me to go in their van. Said they were the Tyne Pastors. Seemed a bit suspect. They didn't have any ID and their van was creepy as owt. No logo or anything.

The back of Cooper's neck tingled with horripilation. Nico had been relegated to number two; the van was now her number one suspect. Macey had walked off with a woman with dark curls. Had they both been bundled into the van? She made a note to check in with Mispers for anyone matching the woman's description and remembered that the woman was wearing some sort of work vest. She may have been a good citizen helping out the lost and disorientated of Tyneside, or the fake pastors Giggles768 spoke of could have upped their game.

Cooper continued scrolling down the thread. Most of the messages expressed concern. Some complained that the city wasn't as safe as it used to be, others suggested buying a rape alarm and a can of pepper spray. Then a reply made Cooper's heart stop for a second.

r/NewcastleUni. Posted by PopTartBoy4. 11 months ago

Something similar happened to my girlfriend. She was coming out of the club next door when she was approached by a man who claimed to be police. He said she was arrested for dealing drugs (utter bullshit) and he told her to get in his van. She ran off and the van followed her all the way down to the Quay Side. Luckily, she lost him down a side street and made it back to my place. Be on the lookout.

Cooper downed her full glass of wine and got to her feet. It was time for Josh to go home and for her to go to bed. She had things to mull over.

- Chapter 26 -

"Do I look okay?"

Cooper was flabbergasted. Her daughter looked more than okay. She looked more grown-up than ever. How could her baby girl be fifteen already? Fifteen years flew through her mind's eye. Babygrows, bottles, dummies, hand-me-downs from other mums on the force, first proper shoes, first school uniform, first netball kit. "You look amazing, T."

Cooper couldn't remember the last time Tina had worn a dress. She used to wear a regulation knee-length pleated skirt to school, but ever since Lucy Parker in the year above was up-skirted and the photo circulated to every teenage boy in the borough, Tina had opted for trousers. Tina looked at herself in her mother's mirror and examined the fabric of her t-shirt dress. She was knock-kneed and adjusting her weight awkwardly as she tried to get used to a pair of heels. She'd even straightened her hair, which was a big deal for Tina. She hated brushing her hair, and the most Cooper could usually hope for was that it was secured into some semblance of a ponytail.

Cooper joined her daughter at her side and put an arm over her shoulder. "How'd you grow up so fast?"

Tina shrugged. "Listen, Mum. I wanted to ask you something. Technically, I don't need your permission, but..."

That didn't sound good. Cooper patted the bed, and they sat on the edge of the mattress. "What is it, T?"

"I want to go on the pill."

The wind was knocked clean out of Cooper. "Oh. Jeez, Tina." She suddenly felt very protective and wasn't sure how she viewed Josh anymore. Sweet, polite Josh, who was currently waiting downstairs.

"Don't panic, Mum. Josh and I aren't... You know. I just want to regulate my periods. If I go on the pill, I'll know exactly when I'm due, and I won't have any accidents."

The relief must have been etched on Cooper's face because Tina added, "You look weird."

"I'm just..."

"Glad I'm still a virgin?"

Cooper laughed. "Something like that. Listen, I never regretted having you in my life, not for one second, but I was so young, and I don't want—"

"Me to be a teenage mother? Surely, that's another reason I should go on the pill. So that when I am ready for... You know... I won't get pregnant."

"I can't argue with your logic," Cooper said, taking her daughter's hand in hers. "How about we don't mention this to your dad, though?"

Fear flashed in Tina's eyes. "God. Imagine? Yeah, best we don't say anything."

"Anyway." Cooper pulled Tina to her feet. "Your guests are waiting, birthday girl."

Tina gave a toothy grin, and she made her way downstairs, the heels causing her to teeter like Bambi on ice. A duet of *Happy Birthday*, sung by Kenny and Josh, filled the house.

Downstairs, Kenny had filled the living room with a hundred balloons, and silver confetti shaped like the number fifteen had been sprinkled over every table, mantlepiece and countertop. Josh greeted Tina with a kiss on the lips and a nervous glance in Kenny's direction before handing her a card and a small box that could only be jewellery.

Cooper joined Kenny on the sofa. "Thanks for all this," she said, motioning at the decorations.

He shrugged as if it was no effort. "She's worth it," he said with a slight blush. "You both are. I'm sorry I wasn't there for all of her birthdays. I was a selfish idiot."

Thinking back to all she'd been through as a single mother, Cooper bobbed her head from side to side and replied, half-jokingly, "Yeah. You were. But you're here now, and I'm glad you and Tina have the makings of a real relationship."

Tina shrieked as Josh secured a silver necklace around her neck. "Look, Mum! It's the molecule for serotonin." She held the pendant in her fingertips. "The happy hormone."

Josh turned purple and whispered a little too loudly, "All I want to do is make you happy."

Kenny rolled his eyes at Cooper. "Bloody millennials and their sentiments. No one talked to each other like that when we were their age."

"When we were their age, the standard chat up line was, *giz a snog.*" Cooper shuddered. She'd always hated the word snog and thought it was the most unappealing word for kissing ever invented. "Besides. They're not millennials. The millennials were born between seventy-seven and ninety-five. So I hate to break it to you - given your love of millennial bashing - but you, dear Kenny, are a millennial."

Kenny's mouth opened, closed and opened again. "No, that can't be right. The millennials are the young'uns who eat too much avocado, need twenty pronouns and are scared of handling raw chicken."

"You're a millennial, Kenny. Deal with it."

"So what are those two?" he asked, raising a can of lager in Tina and Josh's direction.

"Gen Z. Also known as iGen or the digital natives. They've never known a time without the internet."

Kenny relaxed back on the sofa. "A time without the internet? Man, I remember those days. Woah! That makes me feel old."

"Tell me about it," said Cooper, wondering how she could possibly be old enough to have a daughter who wanted to go on the pill.

Kenny looked down to the carpet. "No texting, no mobiles, no Spotify or Netflix."

"No cyberbullying, no sexting, no Twitter mobs, or online shaming."

The doorbell rang, signalling the arrival of Atkinson and the Sutherlands, closely followed by two of Tina's netball team and four friends who attended the same study group as Tina and Josh. The teenagers immediately set up camp in the kitchen as that, apparently, was where the cool people hung out. At least that was something that hadn't changed since Cooper's day. Cooper struggled to pick Caroline out of the sea of youngsters at first. She'd shot up in recent months and was now a young woman with her mother's dark blonde bob and her father's shiny grey eyes. She was immediately welcomed in by the group and Cooper caught the look of joyfulness on Sam's face.

Tinny pop music began to play out of someone's phone, and Tina embraced Atkinson in a rare hug. He added a present to the growing pile of gifts for Tina and enquired about Steven before the grown-ups retired to the living room to give the teens some privacy.

"So, Steven's moved to a bigger box?" he said as Cooper gave him a welcoming kiss and made room for him on the sofa.

"The fluffball's growing by the day. It's ridiculous."

"Steven?" asked Sutherland.

Cooper laughed as she poured Sue a glass of white and handed Sutherland a lager. "Long story."

Atkinson pulled a bottle of Carmenère from a plastic bag and poured himself a glass. He offered some to Cooper who raised her lager and said, "Thanks, I'll have some when I've finished this."

Atkinson cast his eyes around the room at the balloons, confetti, flowers and cards. "Did you find out who sent you the roses? My money's on that chief superintendent's secretary."

"Oh, they weren't from work. They were from Kenny."

Kenny shifted himself around on the sofa and gave an embarrassed nod. "Guilty as charged."

"Hmm."

Kenny's brows lowered. "What do you mean, *hmm*?"

"Forget it. It's nothing."

"It's not nothing. If you have something to say, say it, Science Man."

"Okay, okay." Cooper got to her feet, sensing a very quick change in the atmosphere. This sort of thing was bad enough when it was just the three of them, but she wasn't the only witness this time. She had a work colleague and his wife here too. "Kenny, why don't you check on the digital natives in the kitchen? See if they're hungry yet?"

Kenny lifted his bulk from the seat but didn't remove his eyes from Atkinson until he was at the kitchen door.

"For goodness sake." Cooper turned to Atkinson. "It's Tina's birthday. The last thing she needs is you two bickering and causing a scene."

"Sorry, Erica, but can't you see what's happening here?"

"He bought the mother of his child flowers after she was held prisoner by a murderer. I don't think that's anything to—"

"He's stalking you, Erica."

Cooper stared down at Atkinson, who was still seated, glass of wine in hand. "What?" she exclaimed. "That's... That's just not true. What a load of... Sorry Sam, Sue. Can I get you another drink?"

The Sutherlands looked embarrassed and held up their very full glasses.

"How many times has he texted you this week?" Atkinson pressed.

It was at least fifty, but they'd been discussing Tina's birthday and whatnot. "I don't know," she lied. "Not many, and that's really none of anyone's—"

"And how many gifts has he bought you recently? The framed picture, the flowers? Popping over to police HQ with lunch? What else?"

Cooper's blood pressure was rising. She couldn't believe that Atkinson was acting like this. They had company, and he was behaving like a jealous child. Was it so unreasonable that she and Kenny were, God forbid, getting along? Was he really so petty?

"Well?" Atkinson pressed. "What else?"

Cooper pinched her nose as she often did when stressed or frustrated with someone's attitude and hissed her answer, "A fruit basket and some chocolates. He knows I don't eat properly when I'm stressed and..."

"He wants you back, Erica. He's always sniffing around, and it makes me uncomfortable."

"Don't be daft. He's just being nice."

Atkinson slammed his glass on a side table. Red wine slipped over the lip and ran down the stem onto untreated oak. It would stain. Sue jumped and disappeared, returning a second later with a tea towel to mop at the spilt wine while avoiding eye contact with Cooper and Atkinson.

"I'm not daft." Atkinson got to his feet, towering over Cooper. "And he's not being *nice*. He's being a creep."

Cooper checked that the kitchen door was closed before hissing, "And you're being bitter and insecure. If he's making you so uncomfortable, maybe you should just leave."

Hurt painted Atkinson's face. He ran a hand over his jaw and shook his head in disbelief. He waited for a second, and when Cooper didn't retract her statement, he uttered, "Fine," and stormed from the house.

- Chapter 27 -

By Tuesday morning, the Easter holidays had ended and Tina was heading back to school. Cooper had had all the rest she could stomach and was ready to return to normality, regardless of what Nixon would say. Taking a bite of toast and fishing a fiver from her purse so Tina could buy herself some lunch, she answered the door to Kenny, who'd volunteered for today's school run.

"How're things?" he asked.

Cooper shrugged. She hadn't heard from Atkinson since their argument and she was too stubborn to text him. She wasn't even sure who was in the wrong. One of them had overreacted, and she was fairly certain it wasn't her. Atkinson was older than Cooper, and she didn't want him acting overly protective of her or treating her like a child. That wasn't healthy, and neither was a relationship where a man told his woman who she should and shouldn't spend her time with.

"Are the nightmares getting any easier?"

The corners of Cooper's mouth turned down and she flashed back to the night terror she'd suffered on Sunday night; the slave collar had tightened, and tightened, and tightened until she'd awoken in a cold sweat.

"Who said I was having nightmares?"

"Tina said something. Besides, who wouldn't have nightmares after something like that? We're still reeling from last year and with Hutchins all over the news...It must be hard."

Cooper took another bite of toast and wrinkled her nose. "I've only had a couple of nightmares. They're not bad and I'm sure they'll stop with time. If not, we have a therapist on staff. I can speak to her if need be."

He reached over and touched her shoulder. "If you need help, go and get it. There's no shame in it."

"Who are you, and what have you done with Kenny? I thought you said therapy was for fragile little snowflakes?"

Kenny put on his best look of innocence. "Yeah, but I also didn't know what a millennial was, so best not listen to me."

Cooper smiled for the first time since Sunday. Tina came rushing into the room, said "Morning" to her dad and was halfway out the door when Cooper called after her.

"Necklace!"

"Aww, Mum."

"You know the rules. No jewellery in school. You'll be put in isolation." It was hardly a threat against Tina, who would much prefer to study alone, but she held out her palm and waited for Tina to undo the catch on her necklace and hand it to her. The silver chain curled up on Cooper's hand like a Lilliputian snake as the noise of huffs and whispered insults filled the room. Tina shuffled out of the door and headed for Kenny's truck. Kenny shared a look with Cooper and followed.

Before heading to work, Cooper made two quick phone calls: one to her GP to make an appointment for Tina, and one to the Northern Centre for Cancer Care. She was kept on hold for a worrying amount of time, which did her blood pressure no good at all. Eventually, a nurse came on the line and told her that everything had come back clear and that she didn't have to visit the centre again for another three months, but if she was at all concerned about anything, to give them a call.

Cooper sunk onto a seat at the kitchen table, covered her face with her hands and waited until her vital signs returned to normal. It was a huge weight off her shoulders and the relief threatened to spill over into tears. Now all she had to worry about was her relationship with Atkinson, a murderer and kidnapper on the loose, and Macey Gallagher's disappearance remaining unsolved.

None of those problems would solve themselves, so she shelved the personal problem, jumped in the Mazda and headed to Wallsend, ready to work on the other two. But first, coffee.

At Starbucks, Cooper texted Keaton to ask what she wanted and to find out if Tennessee was back at work. She was told Hayley had the tag team help of both of Alfie's grandmas, so Tennessee was back, and he wanted a mocha-choca-something-or-other.

Later, when she arrived in the incident room with two venti cappuccinos and a grande caffè mocha, Cooper found Keaton and Tennessee drowning in a tidal wave of paperwork. They gratefully took their frothy coffees, removed the lids, inhaled deeply and sighed simultaneously.

"Reports, reports, reports," Keaton groaned. "As if we didn't have enough to be getting on with. I need to check in with Omar and give him a photographic lineup. See if he picks Bryce Morton's photo. Speaking of which, we need to go over your statement, boss. Then we've got interviews with Morton's known associates to try and work out where the fucker's most likely to be."

Tennessee got to his feet and approached a map of the northeast of England that was pinned to the wall. Tiny red, orange and yellow stickers dotted the chart. "The press room released Morton's image, warning the public not to approach but to call in with any sightings. There's been at least fifty possible sightings since Friday and we have units following up with the most likely ones."

Cooper scrutinised the map, looking for clusters and patterns. "Looks to be a lot of sightings around the edge of the national park," she said, indicating a large swath of green.

"We think he might be hiding out in that area, but the park's over four hundred square miles. It's going to take us a while to flush him out. But we will, Coop."

"I don't doubt it for a second," Cooper said truthfully. She knew they wouldn't quit, especially after Morton had gone after one of their own. "What else do we have?"

"Look North want one of us to speak on the lunchtime news," Keaton answered, "and as your neck's currently bruised to fuck, and Tennessee has bags under his eyes you could fit a weekly shop into, I guess I'll do it."

Cooper laughed and blew on her drink to cool it down. "Thanks, Paula. Just try not to swear on live television. Are we covering Morton's mother?"

"We have a unit keeping tabs on their homes."

"Good. And a case file has been opened for the murder of Derrick Morton? His father. His death wasn't accidental."

"Done," said Tennessee, "and we contacted the fire investigators so they can reopen their file."

Cooper sipped her drink. "Excellent. Looks like you two have it covered. How about I do the reports? I'm not supposed to do any fieldwork, and Nixon'll have a heart attack if I leave the building, so I may as well make myself useful."

Keaton shifted her weight back in her chair and swung her legs to plant her feet on the desk before thinking better of it. "Brilliant. You don't mind?"

"I'd rather be hunting Morton but that's not going to happen, so I'll crack on clearing this mountain of paper."

"Sweet. Thanks."

Keaton and Tennessee picked up their coffees and coats and headed for the door while Cooper made herself comfortable and typed her password into a computer. She spent the next three hours typing up Keaton and Tennessee's notes before sweet-talking Oliver Martin into grabbing her a bag of chips from the burger van on the corner. As per her instructions, he'd smothered them in ketchup and brought her a wooden fork. Chips just weren't the same with proper cutlery.

After refuelling, she sat back at her desk, ready to continue her typing, but three hours was all she could take. She wasn't a typist; she was a detective, and she wanted to investigate. There was an itch in desperate need of a scratch. She opened the database and began searching for the cases that were reported on Reddit. Nothing. That didn't mean the stories were made up, and they never happened. It just meant they were never reported to the police. It made Cooper sad to think of how many crimes went unreported because people either didn't trust the police, didn't think the police would believe them or didn't think they'd be able to help. Next, she looked for any cases with similar themes. Young women, the city centre, a van, men claiming to be the police.

"Bingo." Cooper grabbed a notepad and pen and began scribbling down the details. When the door opened and Fuller walked in with Sutherland and Nixon, Cooper switched the browser back to her reports, nodded her thanks to their greetings, and poo-pooed their concerns.

Sutherland waited for Nixon and Fuller to start talking football before taking a seat next to her and asking, "Were you okay after we left on Sunday?"

Cooper flushed with embarrassment. "I'm good, Sam. Sorry you had to witness that."

"Hey, if it's any consolation, I think the kids had a great time. Caroline keeps asking if Tina can come for a sleepover at half term."

"Well, that's something at least." She was glad some people had a good time at the party. She'd spent the remainder of the evening faking enthusiasm whenever Tina or one of her friends spoke to her. Inside, she'd been sullen and saturnine.

"Have you spoken to Atkinson?"

She ground her teeth together. "No."

Sutherland gave her a look he might give Caroline, then put his arm around her shoulders. It was a move only he could get away with. "Listen, people these days, they're all about saving face, not making the first move, not being the one to crack. When I was young... I know, when woolly mammoths still roamed, it was a good thing to make the first move. The one who apologised first was the bigger man, or woman in this case. Life's too short to be angry with the one you love."

Cooper nuzzled into his shoulder. "Right as always," she said with a smile.

"So you'll call him? Or text?"

She nodded. "Once I've calmed down. I'll say something I regret otherwise."

Sutherland gave her a squeeze and released her, getting to his feet with a groan. "You're kidding, right?" he said in Fuller's direction. "United won't stand a chance if we sell Barboza. I have ten quid on him scoring a hat trick this weekend."

Sutherland and Fuller ambled into a meeting room set aside for them, and Cooper waited until Nixon left the department in the direction of his office before she reopened the case she had found on the police database.

Two years ago, Inga Jānis, born in Riga, Latvia, accepted a lift from two men in a van outside of The River Palace. Cooper did a quick Google search and found The River Palace used to be on the same road as Feisty's. It closed nine months ago and reopened as O'Neills. When Inga realised the van was headed out of town, she opened the door and jumped from the moving vehicle. The men gave chase and she made it to the motorway only to be run over by a taxi. Cooper winced as she read the list of Inga's injuries. Cooper switched back to Google, searched for Inga Jānis, and found someone with the same name on Facebook. A pretty blonde with small features and long lashes smiled from her profile picture. Cooper flicked through a couple more photos. A recent shot taken with the Tyne Bridge in the background suggested she still lived in the area, and another shot, taken from further away, showed she used a wheelchair.

In a second case, Cooper read about Sandra Hagen. An Australian in Newcastle on a student visa. After a night out, she reported being directed towards a van by a man claiming to be a police officer. He accused her of soliciting, which she denied. Sandra kicked up a fuss and ran away, running into two real police officers who found her in a panicked state. When the police tried to trace the van, the only CCTV footage they unearthed showed the number plate was obscured with mud.

Pushing a USB stick into the computer, Cooper brought up the footage she'd taken from the accountancy firm. She paused when the van drove by and tried to make out the front number plate. The footage wasn't the best. She zoomed in, but it was too much of a blur, and she suspected it had been smeared with mud. It might be an N-reg. That was all she could tell. The footage from the cat café was largely the same. She could see the rear numberplate in this footage but it was coated in mud or dirt. The left side of the first digit was a long vertical line. That fitted with an N, but could also be a B, D or any number of letters.

Cooper got to her feet and began to pace the room, letting her brain process the patterns and parallels that were becoming apparent. She returned to her computer, bent over the desk and looked up Giggles768. Next, she found PopTartBoy4 and scrolled through his posts until she found something useful. When a photograph of him with his new wheels came up she entered the number plate into a separate database to find his name. She put that name into Facebook and again scrolled through until she found out who his girlfriend was. Clicking control and P, Cooper waited for the printer to vomit up images of all the girls involved: Macey Gallagher, Dublin; Inga Jānis, Riga; Sandra Hagen, Melbourne; Klaudija Moreno, Bucharest; and Angela Wilson, the Isle of Wight.

Cooper collated the photographs before spreading them over her desk. All blonde, all dainty, all with child-like features, and all from out of town.

"Whatever's going on," Cooper whispered to herself, "someone doesn't like to shit where they eat."

- Chapter 28 -

Cooper approached Nixon's secretary to see if she knew where the superintendent was. She'd already crept past his office and knew he wasn't in there.

"He's meeting with the commissioner, Ma'am. It's scheduled until four. I can get a message to him if it's urgent."

"No, nothing important. Thank you, Vivian."

Satisfied that Nixon wouldn't notice if she wandered off, Cooper decided to visit Inga Jānis once she'd checked in with her team. Just as she was about to dial, her phone lit up. Keaton's name appeared on the screen.

"Paula, I was just about to call you. There's been another sighting, this time on the outskirts of Otterburn. Someone matching Morton's description was seen walking along the river."

"Boss. Jack and I just finished speaking with some of Morton's colleagues." Her voice was harried.

"Go on."

"Morton's hobbies include shooting. He's a member of Roker Rifle Club in Sunderland and Elite Gun Club in Rothbury."

Cooper glanced at the map on the wall. "Rothbury's not far from some of the sightings. He must know the area. Hang on." Cooper logged into another database. "Shit. He has an SGC," she said, referring to a shotgun certificate. "Certificate states he owns a .410 gauge bolt-action. A Webley and Scott. Last inspection was eight months ago. All in order. Stored in a locked box in the loft."

"Christ."

"Right, Paula. You call the unit that's stationed at the mother's house. Have them check Morton's loft. I'll contact the units in Northumberland National Park and tell them to hold back until we know more."

"Roger."

Cooper hung up and immediately got hold of dispatch. "Tell all units in the vicinity of Northumberland National Park that suspect Bryce Morton is potentially armed. Use extreme caution."

Her mobile rang again within two minutes. "Go ahead, Paula."

"The gun case is empty, boss. We're headed to Otterburn. Armed response have been called."

"Oh, bloody hell." Cooper's heart rate doubled and her hand went to her bruised neck. Her mouth was dry and though she was certain she'd been ready to return to duty, she was scared. Undeniably scared. "Don't go to Otternburn until the armed response units arrive. Meet me in Bellingham. It's the nearest police station to our search area. We'll set up an incident room and coordinate the search from there. I'll bring vests."

"Are we sure he's here in Otterburn?" Tennessee asked. His head low against an April shower, water dripping from the ends of his curls onto a bulletproof vest.

"Pretty darn sure." Cooper slid her hands into the back pockets of her trousers to keep them warm. "Three calls in the last two hours linked him to this place. Plus, one call mentioned a navy Barbour jacket. We didn't mention that in our media pack, but it's what he wore when he took me."

Tennessee nodded. They were stood next to a patrol car on the outskirts of Otterburn. The small village in the Cheviot Hills derived its name from the Otter Burn that branched away from the River Rede. Ahead, they watched as a tactical team inched closer to a fishing hut on the banks of the Rede. The hut was sheltered from the view of the village by a copse of trees.

"Morton was spotted walking north from where the sixty-eight meets the Birky Gill," Cooper continued. "We placed a unit there to creep north and another unit in Elishaw to creep south."

Keaton squeezed rainwater from her short ponytail. "I arranged road stops on the sixty-eight and the six nine six. He's not getting out of here by car."

"He's not getting out of here full stop," Cooper said with a grunt. "Thermal imaging suggests someone's in that hut. Besides, look around." She wafted her arms about and took in the endless green fields that contained nothing but grass and sheep. "Where else is there to hide?"

At the sound of camera shutters, all three detectives turned their heads and were greeted by flashes of light as local press revelled in the hottest news story of the week.

Tennessee scowled. "Permission to move the cordon back another hundred feet?"

"Permission granted." Cooper gave him a wry smile and turned back to the hut. If Morton weren't armed, they wouldn't have hesitated in storming the hut. As it was, Cooper didn't want to take the risk. Slowly, slowly.

Time passed, rain fell and Cooper's body temperature continued to drop. As darkness approached, she sent a text to Kenny to ask him to take care of Tina until she could get home. His reply came within seconds. *Of course. It's my pleasure. Be careful, Erica. Let me know when it's all over.*

The message warmed her, but not for long, she felt icy all over as soon as Bryce Morton emerged from the shadowy doorway of the fishing hut.

"LOWER YOUR WEAPON!" The leader of the tactical team boomed his command over and over but his words washed over Morton, whose eyes were fixed solely on Cooper.

"LOWER YOUR WEAPON!"

"I want him alive." Cooper's voice was quiet but firm as she spoke into the handheld. "Repeat. We take him alive."

"Copy."

Morton took a step forward. The thin, downy hairs on the back of Cooper's neck stood on end. She could taste the tension in the air.

"LOWER YOUR WEAPON!"

"I will only speak with DCI Cooper."

Cooper's hands shook as she picked up a megaphone and moved behind one of the cars for shelter. "I'm here, Bryce. You can speak to me."

"No." He shook his head side to side, causing his weapon to shift left and right. "Not like this. We can't talk like this. You have to come here."

Swallowing hard, Cooper brought the megaphone back to her lips. She had to handle Morton carefully. She didn't want to spook him or anger him.

"I'm sorry, Bryce, but we can't speak face to face until you put the gun down. Can you put the gun down for me?"

Morton started to pace. Two paces left, two paces right, his gun still raised.

"What would you like to talk about, Bryce?" When he didn't answer, Cooper tried, "We can talk about Benji if you like?"

His eyes sparked and he raised his head. "Benji was a good boy."

"Yes, he was. And you miss him, don't you?"

Morton nodded and then his face crumpled. He began to cry angry sobs, the gun trembling in his arms as he realised his options were few.

"I know what it's like to lose someone you love. We can help you, but you have to help us first."

He wiped his nose on his shoulder. "It's too late for me. I'm going to prison because you know too much."

He was going to prison because of all he had done. Morton was a deeply damaged individual who needed help, but he was also a dangerous criminal and needed to be detained to pay for his crimes and for the protection of the public. With Omar and Cooper, he had made mistakes, and those mistakes had led him to this situation. There were only two ways out: Either he lowered his weapon or armed response would be forced to shoot. It was his choice.

Cooper tried one last time. "Bryce, would you like to meet one of our police dogs?" To Cooper's relief, the idea worked and he stopped pacing to look at the dogs. "Put them at ease," she hissed to the nearest handler. The Belgian shepherds sat on command and panted. Clouds of condensation billowed from long, pink tongues. "What's her name?" Cooper asked quietly.

"Nancy."

"Bryce. This is Nancy. She's lovely, isn't she?"

Morton smiled. The rain was coming down heavier now and it was causing Morton to glance back towards the shelter. Cooper wanted to keep him where she could see him.

"Nancy's very friendly. You can come and meet her if you like. But she doesn't like guns. If you want to give her a stroke, you'll have to put the gun down."

He smiled again and a dreamy look passed over him. He lowered the shotgun so the barrel pointed to the ground and took a step forward. Nancy's hackles raised, but she wouldn't move unless her handler told her to.

"Put the gun on the ground, Bryce," Cooper repeated.

Morton squatted and lowered the gun towards a muddy puddle. He paused, looking deep in thought, before standing and pointing the gun at Cooper.

- CHAPTER 29 -

COOPER STARED STRAIGHT DOWN the barrel of the bolt-action shotgun. She was frozen, paralysed with fear. It took Tennessee's full might to haul Cooper to the ground and shield her behind the body of the patrol car. A single shot rang out and Cooper gasped for air beneath Tennessee's weight as the sound of angry dogs filled the village of Otterburn. "No," she pleaded. "I want him alive." She pushed herself to her feet and assessed the scene.

Morton was on his back. Two dogs were biting his arms, pinning him down as the tactical team raced towards him. The shotgun was kicked from his reach, and MP5s pointed at the man's chest. Watery, red blood seeped from his shoulder into the mud and grass around him. "Clear," someone called out, and a medic ambled towards Morton, pulling dressings from a shoulder bag.

"Shoulder," said Tennessee. "He's alive. It was a good shot."

Relief overpowered Cooper. She wiped her face with her hands, coating her cheeks with muddy fingerprints. If the shot had been fatal, she may never find out who Morton's other victims were. A waiting ambulance backed up towards the hut. Its back doors opened.

"Come on," said Tennessee. "You get the honours."

They squelched through the wet ground as Morton was rolled onto a stretcher. Medics worked to stop the bleeding from both the bullet wound and the dog bites. Cooper wondered if he'd continue his infatuation with dogs now he'd been chewed up by two of them.

"Bryce Morton, I am arresting you for the murder of Derrick Morton, the attempted murder of Omar Ali, the abduction and assault of a police officer," Cooper hovered over him and made sure to look him in the eyes. "Carrying a firearm to resist arrest, possessing a firearm with the intent to endanger life, and arson. Did I miss anything?"

He smirked. The painkillers he'd been injected with were starting to kick in. "You've missed so, so much, dear. There's a lot you don't know. Lots of pets you don't know about."

She'd find out. She'd get justice for every single one of Morton's victims. Taking a pair of handcuffs from her pocket, Cooper played with them as Morton watched. She couldn't restrain him while the medics did their work, but she looked forward to seeing him in chains.

"It's a shame these won't fit your neck," Cooper said just before the ambulance doors closed and its engine started.

"They're taking him to the Royal Victoria," said Keaton. "I'll head on over and let Omar know we got his attacker."

"Thanks, Paula. Don't tell him they're in the same hospital. We don't want to give Omar any extra stress or worry."

Keaton nodded. "Sure thing, boss." She clapped Cooper on the arm. "Well done. That can't have been easy."

It hadn't been. Facing Bryce Morton had been more terrifying than she had anticipated. She wasn't impervious to fear; she was human, and she'd have to face him again soon. She'd question him day and night, twenty-four-seven until she found out exactly who he'd hurt and where their bodies lay.

BELLINGHAM POLICE STATION WAS dying down for the night. Armed response conducted their debrief and waited while forensics finished up at the site. Cooper removed her bulletproof vest and washed the mud from her face in the sink of the women's toilets. She stuck her head under the tap and let the warm water run over her scalp and the back of her neck. It took some contorting, but she angled herself under the hand dryer and stayed there until her skin was dry and she'd thoroughly warmed through. While her shirt and trousers dried on an old cast-iron radiator, Cooper called Kenny to assure him and Tina that everything was all right.

"Glad to hear it," he said. "There's a couple of beers waiting in the fridge for you. Thought you'd need them. Don't worry about Tina. She's busy teaching Josh how to memorise the periodic table."

"That's my girl," Cooper laughed. "I'll still be a while. Can you hold the fort?"

"Absolutely. Do what you need to do, Erica."

Cooper hung up and read her text messages. Tina had sent her a heart emoji, and Atkinson had messaged to ask if she was okay. She didn't have the energy. Not now. Atkinson could wait.

Once the last patch of dampness faded on her trousers, she dressed and met Tennessee in her car.

"Have you called Hayley?"

He nodded. "Everything's fine. She's had a good day, and I get the feeling the mother-in-law wouldn't let her watch the news."

"Probably for the best."

Tennessee's face spread into a genuine smile. "That could have ended so much worse. Makes you feel grateful to be alive, doesn't it?"

It did, but Cooper was just about holding herself together so she responded by giving him a soft punch on the arm and calling him a big softy.

"Back to HQ?" he asked. "Write all of this up? Or we could head to the RVI, but I doubt the docs will let us start interrogating Morton."

"Actually, I want to take a detour." Cooper typed an address into Google Maps and started the engine.

INGA JĀNIS LIVED IN an impressive house on the outskirts of Darras Hall, an area famed for housing footballers and the more successful reality TV stars.

"Why do we want to talk to this woman?" Tennessee asked after Cooper rang the doorbell. "Shouldn't we hand over your findings to Fuller?"

"We should. But we're not going to. Not yet." Cooper could hear noises beyond the door, and the door opened.

"Yes?" Inga had the impossible beauty of Eastern Europe. She was blessed with a great complexion, slender build and golden locks.

"Inga. I'm DCI Cooper. This is my colleague DS Daniel. Sorry to disturb you, but I was hoping to ask you some questions about what happened two years ago."

Inga's forehead wrinkled. "Did you catch them?"

"No. I'm afraid not. But a few cases fit a similar pattern to what you went through. I'm hoping you can help me."

Inga wheeled herself backwards and turned herself in the opposite direction. "Follow me."

Inga led the pair through an expansive lobby and into a modern living room decorated entirely in white.

"Amazing place you have here," said Tennessee.

"Thank you. But it's not mine. Not really. I tutor art and design to the local school children. It's well paid but not *this* well paid." She gestured around. "Tiago pays the bills."

Cogs whirled in Tennessee's head, then a lightbulb illuminated in his mind and his eyes widened. "Not Tiago Barboza?"

Inga looked coy. "Yes. My boyfriend."

"Wow." Tennessee looked around in all directions, hoping the star Newcastle United striker was home.

Cooper moved closer to her DS and hissed, "Don't go all fanboy."

"I play wheelchair basketball," Inga continued. "Tiago and some other players had visited our practice session as part of some community work. They were in chairs and giving it a go, but they were useless, which was hilarious because I got the feeling these guys weren't used to being outplayed by little women like me. Anyway, we hit it off." She shrugged as if to say *the rest is history*. She extended an arm towards a plush white sofa. "Please."

"We're a little muddy. I don't want to stain your sofa. Is it okay if we sit at your breakfast table?"

"Of course."

Once seated, Cooper began her line of questioning. "So, Inga, two men tried to abduct you when you left the River Palace?"

"That's right."

"And that was on July seventeenth?"

"Yes, the year before last. Around half two in the morning. I wasn't sure of the exact time."

"Can you tell me what you remember about that night?"

She took a deep breath and pulled her sleeves down, so they covered her hands and began fidgeting with the fabric.

"I'd got into an argument with my then-boyfriend and he walked off. I decided to stay in the club to finish my drink but the venue was emptying out fairly quickly. When I left, the street was almost deserted. A man was talking to someone in a black van, and he asked me if I wanted to share a taxi."

"A black van?" Cooper consulted her notes. "In your original statement, it says a blue van."

"No, that can't be right. It was definitely black. That must be a mistake. Anyway, I said it didn't look like a taxi, but he said it was freelance, like an Uber or something. We were both headed to South Gosforth, so I thought *why not?* I was so, so stupid."

"You were trusting. That doesn't make you stupid."

Inga gave Cooper a thankful look. "Thank you, but on this occasion, yes, I think I was stupid. Straight away, I knew something wasn't right. It drove off towards the Tyne Bridge. I went to open the car door, but the man next to me grabbed hold of my arm. I hit him in the face with my elbow and jumped out. You know the rest." She cast her eyes downward.

"Did the men address each other by name?"

"No. I don't think so. I think the man in the back just called him Driver."

Cooper sifted her papers around and pulled out some sketches. "These are the artist's impressions of the two men that were drawn up at the time." She handed them to Inga, who examined them with a sad expression.

"Would you say they are accurate?"

"They're not bad," said Inga. "But I would make some changes." She moved to a sideboard and retrieved a pencil. "May I?"

The image was a photocopy of the original. Cooper had no problem letting Inga sketch over it, and who would be better qualified than an art tutor? "Go ahead."

"The man who lured me in and sat in the back, he was a little gaunter than this." She shaded in the hollows of his cheeks and adjusted the shape of his jaw. "His brows were thicker too." She continued sketching and moved on to the driver. "He was older than he looks in the picture." Inga's pencil moved in arcs, reforming the shape of the man's cheeks and hairline before thinning his lips. "There," she said, "That is as good as I can do."

Reaching across the table, Cooper dragged the pictures and rotated them so they faced herself and Tennessee. She examined the pictures of the lure and the driver, turned her head to her DS, and they exchanged a long, hard look.

- Chapter 30 -

Cooper, Tennessee and Keaton huddled around an ancient computer monitor in CID. Keaton had made a FaceTime call to Tennessee and placed her phone in the corner of the hallway so it was partially hidden behind a bin. As long as they kept one eye on Tennessee's screen, they'd have at least a forty-second head start if anyone was going to disturb them.

"What am I looking for?" asked Keaton as she opened an internal search engine.

"Unmarked cars, registered here at HQ, North Shields or Whitley Bay."

"Okay. Got them."

"Narrow the search to vans, then sort by colour," Cooper instructed.

"Done."

"How many are black?"

"Four."

"How many are N-reg?"

"Two. Right, give me a second. I'll see where they were on the night Macey went missing. Here we go. One was getting into position for a dawn raid in Benton. Checked out at eight p.m. and returned the next day at seven thirty a.m. Peterson and Myers had the other one in Seaton Sluice. They were staking out a carwash on modern slavery allegations. Looks like all the Is are dotted and the Ts are crossed. Checked out at twelve noon. Back by six p.m."

Cooper folded her arms. "Good. That's one less thing to worry about."

"Can you imagine the press?" Keaton asked.

"That wouldn't bear thinking about."

Tennessee picked up his phone. "Nixon's coming."

Within seconds, the computer was switched off, Tennessee pretended to do paperwork, Keaton watched the news on the antique television, and Cooper examined the map of Northumbria that was still pinned to the wall.

"What now?" whispered Tennessee.

"For now, we do our jobs," said Cooper. "Later, we meet back up and take a little drive."

SNUGGLED BETWEEN TYNEMOUTH AND Whitley Bay, Cullercoats was a perfect crescent of golden sand, contained at each side by matching piers. The beach was favoured by the local kayaking community who, during good conditions, would kayak beyond the piers and head three kilometres south to King Edwards Bay for a hearty kipper breakfast at Riley's Fish Shack before paddling back to their starting point.

Tennessee gave a long, low whistle as he watched two kayakers drag a tandem back up the sands, their bare feet sinking deeper into the sand the further from the shoreline they walked. "A sea view? Very nice."

Behind him, Cooper and Keaton took in a double-fronted, terraced home with three storeys of bay windows. It was indeed very nice, idyllic even. "Come on," she said, checking her watch. "Let's take a look around the back."

Keaton cast furtive glances over her shoulder as they walked to the end of the terrace and took an alleyway to the rear of the expensive properties.

"Any sign?" asked Cooper.

"No. We're clear," she answered. "Doesn't mean no one's at home. Let's keep our heads down and our mouths shut."

Cooper stopped walking when she reached a double garage extension to the home they'd been watching, and her eyes immediately flicked to the windows. The windows were lined with newspaper, ensuring the owner privacy. Privacy was for hermits, people who didn't want to advertise their wealth, and people who were up to no good. She switched on a torch and raised herself onto her tiptoes, trying to angle a vantage point where some Sellotape had lost its adhesion and the paper had fallen away. "I can't see," Cooper grumbled.

"Allow me." Being much taller, Tennessee didn't have to stand on his tiptoes. He angled the torch around for a few seconds, stepped back, and wiped a hand over his brow. "Fucking hell."

"What is it?" asked Cooper.

"A black van. Tinted windows."

Cooper's mouth hung open as her worst fears were confirmed. She rested her back against the garage door, needing the support to stop her legs from wobbling. "I don't believe it."

"Me neither, boss." Keaton shook her head, disbelief written all over her face.

The three detectives stood in silence, trying to process the information, when a beeping sound preceded the garage door starting to roll upwards. They jumped, turning to face the garage and watching as the owner of the van rifled in a lockbox for a set of keys. He swung the keyring on his index finger before pressing the fob to unlock the van. It was then that he clocked his colleagues. Cooper's eyes met those of Sam Sutherland.

- Chapter 31 -

For a second that seemed to last forever, everyone remained motionless. Sutherland's gaze moved from Cooper to Tennessee, to Keaton. All of their faces were frozen, hard and serious. Sutherland dropped the keys and charged at Cooper, knocking her into Tennessee. He ran south along the back alley and Keaton gave chase.

Cooper was quickly back on her feet and she and Tennessee followed Keaton. Their legs pumped as fast as they could and although she and Tennessee were both quick off the mark, neither of them were any match for the star athlete of the department. Sutherland didn't stand a chance. Five seconds later, he was prostrate on the black tarmac of Grand Parade with Keaton sat astride him, wrestling his arms behind his back.

Cooper caught up and read Sutherland his rights. Tears formed in her eyes as she told the man she considered a father figure that he was arrested for the kidnap of Inga Jānis and Macey Gallagher. Angrily rubbing the wetness around her eyes on the back of her hand, she instructed Tennessee to secure him in the car and call for backup to transport him to the cells to await questioning.

"You're the driver." It wasn't a question, and she noted how Sutherland couldn't meet her eyes. "The house? The new BMW? Sue didn't get you that Rolex for your anniversary, did she? What was your price, Sam? What were those girls worth?"

"I think I'd like a lawyer."

"Damn right, you'd like a lawyer. You're going to need one. You're the reason I was pulled off this case. Aren't you?"

He lowered his head, his jaw resting on his heaving chest.

"Answer me!" Cooper was beyond furious at his betrayal. She'd trusted him, confided in him.

Sutherland just shook his head and repeated his request. "Lawyer."

"Who are you working for? What did you do with Macey?" No answer. "Goddammit, Sam! Get him out of my sight. Keaton, call for forensics. We need the SOCOs to check the van for Macey's DNA and any other evidence they can find. We'll start searching the property. See what we can uncover."

Keaton pulled her phone out of her jacket pocket. "On it, boss." She gave Sutherland a scathing look, shook her head and turned away.

Tennessee led Sutherland towards where they had parked and shoved him, heavy-handedly, into the back seat of Cooper's Mazda. Meanwhile, Cooper squatted to the floor and did everything she could to stop herself from screaming. Not Sam. Not Sam Sutherland whom she'd known for over ten years and had been there with her on every step of her journey to DCI.

A UNIT OF UNIFORMS arrived to help with the search. Cooper and Keaton started upstairs and began the painstaking process of rifling through every drawer and cupboard, under every bed and behind every dresser. Opening a drawer and discovering a second Rolex caused Cooper to fume with disgust. She slammed her hand on the wooden top, an attached mirror shook in its frame.

"Let's wrap up this room, boss. There's nothing to lead us to Macey. Just flash trinkets we can use as evidence of payment. I know he's a rung up the ladder on me, but there's no way I could afford all this crap on my salary. I imagine the same would go for him."

Cooper gave the room one last look over. Expensive sheets on the bed, designer clothes in the wardrobes. Even Sue's makeup bag was stocked with the top brands. Had she been in on it? Did she question her husband's income, or just innocently revel in all the lavish gifts? "Let's move on to Caroline's room."

"You don't think he'd hide anything in there, do you?"

Cooper shrugged. "Wouldn't be the first one. Remember that dealer in Blyth? He stored all that coke in baggies and stitched them into his daughter's teddy bears?"

Keaton held the door to Caroline's room open for Cooper to go in ahead of her. "Oh, shit, yeah, I remember that one."

Caroline's room was typical of a girl in her early teens. Magazines, school textbooks and young adult novels littered the floor by her bed. Clean, pressed school uniforms of pink and navy hung in her closet and makeup brushes endorsed by the hottest influencers filled a stand on her dressing table. Tina had been invited to a sleepover. Cooper could imagine the girls painting their nails as they listened to music and talked boys. That wouldn't happen now. Cooper didn't think her daughter would be welcome in the Sutherland home now Cooper had arrested its patriarch.

"You notice how much security this place has?" Keaton asked, pointing to sensors on the bedroom window.

"I saw the cameras downstairs and the keypad by the door."

"There were sound sensors in the kitchen too. I guess Sam has a lot of pricey shit to protect."

"That he does." Cooper searched through the room but concluded that Keaton had been right. There wasn't anything tying Sutherland to the abductions in the bedrooms. She bobbed her head sideways. "Come on. What's next?"

Keaton opened the next door that led from the hallway. "It's an office."

"Now we're talking." Cooper entered the room and went straight to the desk. She tried the top drawer and found it to be locked. She found the same thing with the two drawers below it. In the corner of the room, an old black safe with a brass handle served as a plant stand for a dying yucca. Scanning about, Cooper looked for a key. When she didn't spot one, she sent Keaton to go to the garage and see if the box of keys could give them any joy.

Keaton saluted, "Gotcha," and left the room.

The desktop was cluttered with the usual household paperwork: bills, mortgage statements and insurance renewals waiting to be filed away. Cooper arranged them into a neat pile for the forensic accountants to review later.

"Here we are." Keaton dropped the metal box on the desk and it gave a loud clattering noise as its contents jumbled against each other. "Forensics have arrived. They're taking samples from the van. Atkinson asked if you have two minutes for a chat."

Cooper paused, caught off guard. "Erm. No. He'll have to wait." She wasn't being childish; she wanted to find as much evidence as she could. She needed to be in the drawers and, more importantly, the safe. But that required a combination. Besides, she was still too irate and hurt about Sutherland to have any reasonable conversation with Atkinson.

One by one, Keaton and Cooper tried the keys against the various locks.

"Most of these look like house keys and car keys, boss." Keaton held up an old fob for a Vauxhall. "And these ones are labelled *Joyce and Gary*. These ones say *number fourteen*. I'm guessing they're the neighbours."

"Urgh." Cooper ground her teeth in frustration. "Think like Sam. Where would he keep the key?"

"It wasn't in his pockets. Tennessee searched him before taking him away. But he's old school. If there's anything worth hiding in the drawers, the key'll be in the safe."

She was probably right. Sitting cross-legged in front of the safe, Cooper drummed her fingers on her thighs and then spun the dial, searching for the numbers of Sam Sutherland's birthday. When it didn't work, she turned her face up to Keaton, who was searching a bookcase. "Call Sue, his wife. She's probably been informed by now. Ask for the combination. If she doesn't know it, find out the date of their anniversary and her and Caroline's birthdays."

Keaton pulled out her phone.

"And call a locksmith," Cooper added, "in case the dates don't work."

Next to the safe, a small wastepaper basket was full of crumpled junk mail and sheets of lined paper. Cooper turned it upside down, emptying its contents over the floor. Given that she'd already had Oliver Martin sent to the dump and Tennessee elbow-deep in a bus stop's rubbish bin, she could hardly complain about searching through scrunched-up flyers for the local Chinese takeaway. It wasn't exactly attracting flies. She smoothed out each piece of paper in turn; they were mainly adverts for tradesmen and restaurants. One torn-out page from a notepad was covered in sums. Cooper was surprised anyone did sums by hand these days, not when everyone old enough to have a phone had a calculator in their pocket, but Sutherland was a traditionalist. It might well be quicker for him to do long division with pen and paper.

Keaton hung up and joined Cooper on the floor. "Try thirteen, four, ninety-three. That's the day Sam and Sue got married."

Cooper spun the dial, anticipating a satisfying click as the safe unlocked, but none came. "Damn it. Sue's birthday?"

"Three, twelve, sixty-five."

"Nope. What about Caroline's birthday?"

"Sixteenth of August, 2006."

"Let's give it a try." She turned the dial. "Sixteen, eight, six. Shit. No, that didn't work either. Let's keep thinking. In the meantime, can you read this?" Cooper handed her a piece of paper from the bin. "His handwriting's worse than my doctor's."

Keaton squinted and held the paper at arm's length. "It's an address. Unit sixty-three, Jarrow IE."

The synapses in Cooper's brain sparked into life, illuminated with urgency and excitement. She was getting somewhere. "Jack," she shouted into her phone. "Is he speaking?... Huh? ...But a lawyer's on the way? Okay. Listen. Get a unit over to Bede Industrial Estate in Jarrow. Unit sixty-three. No, sixty-three. We found an address in Sam's office. He was referred to as the driver, and the last place Macey's phone pinged was the road next to Bede Industrial Estate. That might be where he delivered her to. Great. Keep in touch."

"What did Tennessee say?" Keaton unfolded her legs and stretched them out in front of her.

"That Sam's not saying much, but he's protesting his innocence. Saying it wasn't his fault, he didn't have a choice and so on."

Keaton shrugged. "We'll find out soon enough, I guess." She rotated her ankles from side to side, her boots chiming against the side of the safe.

Sam Sutherland wasn't a complicated man. Cooper didn't mean that as an insult. He was down to earth, basic, and liked to keep things simple. "Sam wouldn't pick a random number for this bad boy. It would have to be something he could easily remember. We've tried birthdays, his anniversary..."

Keaton's arm extended and her index finger pointed to the top shelf of the bookcase. "It might be staring us in the bloody face. Look. The first three books. Catch 22, Seven Years in Tibet, Orwell's 1984." She leant forward and turned the dial to twenty-two, back to seven, then to eighty-four."

Click.

"You beauty." Cooper slapped Keaton on the back but stopped short of hugging her. "Right. What we got here?"

Three rolls of fifty-pound notes rolled off a manila folder and stopped at Cooper's feet. She bagged them as evidence. If Sutherland's accomplices had handled the money, Atkinson could get prints from them. The folder contained sheets of un-ruled paper with handwritten notes. They all appeared to be abbreviations and codes that neither Cooper nor Keaton could make heads or tails of.

"There's a mobile here. Looks like it's from the dark ages." Keaton handed Cooper a Nokia 3210.

"Christ. I had one of these when I was in school." She pressed the power button and found it still had two bars of battery. She wasn't surprised. She seemed to remember playing Snake all day, every day, and the little brick could go a week without a charge. Opening the phone's call history, she tilted the screen towards Keaton. "Only one number... Only one number in the contacts too."

"Keeper," Keaton read. "So, so far we have a driver, a lure and a keeper."

Cooper got to her feet and walked to the window.

"What is it?" Keaton asked.

"Do we take the phone to tech, have them trace the keeper's number, and try to triangulate the most recent location? Or..."

"Or we call the number? Might tip them off. But, saying that, they might know already. Sam was about to head somewhere with that van. If he hasn't shown, they might suspect something's off."

Cooper made a decision. She'd hand the phone over to tech after she'd called the number. Under her latex gloves, her hands were sweating and beginning to shake. She sat back down in front of the safe, took a deep, calming breath and pressed the call button.

"Sam! About bloody time." The keeper's voice was angry, gravelly, and his accent was distinctly northern. "Where the hell have you been? I had to hire a fucking van. The girls are loaded up and departure's at six fifty-four."

Cooper said nothing but locked eyes with Keaton. *Girls*. Plural. Loaded where? She looked at her watch; it was six thirty-three. Twenty-one minutes.

"I'm guessing you couldn't find a replacement for the Swedish bird? They're gonna be pissed we didn't fulfil the order. They wanted four. I told you, Sam, don't mess about with these guys. Their threats aren't empty. They'll do it... Sam?" His tone changed from angry to worried. "Sam?... Sam?"

The line went dead. Cooper and Keaton jumped back to their feet and raced through the house to get back to the street.

"Has to be the docks," Keaton said.

"Call the airports just in case. Newcastle, Tees, see if there are any smaller airfields too." She called Nixon. "Sir. It's Cooper... I know, unbelievable, sir, but we don't have much time. I think Sam was the driver in some sort of people-trafficking ring. Transporting young women to a unit in Jarrow and then taking them to the docks to go who knows where. Macey Gallagher wasn't the only girl taken. I think the DB at Marsden was part of the same operation. She may have been Swedish. Macey and two others are about to be shipped off. I need canine units at both the north and south banks. I want the ports closed. All available units from North and South Shields to make their way over, and I need the coast guard. Departure's at six fifty-four. We can not let that boat leave the Tyne."

Cooper had nineteen minutes until departure. The port was twenty minutes away.

- Chapter 32 -

"You," Keaton shouted to a young officer standing next to a panda car. "Port of Tyne. South side. Let's go." She jumped in the back of the car, leaving the passenger seat for Cooper. The officer looked dumbfounded as his car was commandeered. "You deaf?" Keaton yelled. "Now. Lights on. Sirens on."

Doing as he was bid, the car sped into action. It was a twenty-minute drive to the river and through the tunnel to the south side of the Tyne. Cooper hoped they could blast their way through in under fifteen if the good people of Tyneside shifted their cars out of the way. She radioed the Tyne Tunnel and gave them a heads-up. The roads were still busy, and once in the tunnel, they wouldn't be able to overtake or weave their way through. "Hold the barriers until we're clear," she requested.

"There's going to be some pissed-off commuters," the officer at the wheel murmured as cars switched lanes ahead, making way for their approach.

"Well, they'll have a pissed-off me if they don't do as I ask."

Cooper called Tennessee, told him to secure the unit at Jarrow and to meet her at the docks pronto.

The world around them darkened like a solar eclipse as they sped into the tunnel. Panels that lined the walls whizzed past in pulses until a circle of light appeared in the distance, and they emerged onto a clear motorway. Collectively their eyes narrowed to slits as they blinked away the bright sunlight.

"Time?" she asked.

Keaton glanced at her watch. "We have seven minutes."

"We should be there in under three." The officer lowered his visor and leant forward as he drove.

"Make it two." Cooper didn't want to take any chances.

Her radio crackled. "Cooper, Cooper, this is Daniel, over."

"Go ahead."

"I'm onsite. The ship's still docked. It's the Libra. Must have at least five hundred containers on it. I can see units arriving from South Shields. Awaiting instructions."

"Can you see the Coastguard?"

"The RIB's approaching, the boat's not far behind."

"Wait for the units, then board the ship. Detain all crew members. One of them will know something. Make sure to get the cargo manifest."

"Roger."

Cooper and Keaton held their breath. Even though Tennessee had told her the ship was still in port and the Coastguard were moving up the Tyne, she still had an awful feeling she would pull up to an empty port and be too late. The squad car ripped around the last bend, its tyres screeching against the road, and coming to a rest next to cars from South Shields police station. The ship was there. Looming against a Newcastle backdrop, the Libra, with a dark red hull, laden with multicoloured shipping containers stacked four high. They reminded Cooper of a giant Jenga set or Lego pieces for the gods. A van pulled up next to them and a man led three excitable spaniels from the rear. Sniffer dogs, tails wagging and mouths panting, keen to do their job and please their master.

"Let's go." Cooper jumped from the car and directed the dog handler to search for humans. Alive humans, hopefully. She picked up pace and ran towards the Libra, all the time scanning her surroundings and taking in the scene. Towards the mouth of the river, an orange boat labelled Port of Tyne Authority was descending on the Libra. Two smaller RIBs, most likely Coastguard, had positioned themselves to the stern. Arching her neck upwards, Cooper spotted Tennessee on deck. He escorted two men towards the gangway where they were met by uniformed officers. He raised his hand to Cooper and beckoned her on board.

The gangway was steep. Cooper held the rail and half ran, half pulled herself up.

"Ma'am," he paused, "Coop. We've already rounded up most of the crew. Half of them don't speak English, or claim they don't speak English. The rest are saying they don't know anything about any women or girls being transported."

"That might be true." Not everyone on the Libra needed to know what it was being used for, but it was someone's job to check the manifest against the actual cargo, and that person was the captain. "Where's the skipper?"

"On the bridge, having a tantrum."

Cooper looked upstream towards the famous bridges of the Tyne.

"He means where the helm and all that is," explained Keaton. "Like in Star Trek."

"Of course. What an idiot." She shook her head at herself. "What's he saying?"

"That he has a schedule to keep. I told him he's not going anywhere until the ship is searched, and if we find anything untoward, he'll be coming to the station for a chat."

"And the manifest?"

"Sealed in an evidence bag."

The spaniels dragged their handler up the gangway, their leads tight, choking themselves and barking from the thrill of it. The handler unclasped their leads and watched as the dogs lowered their noses to the ground and sprinted away in three different directions.

"I'll follow the one with the blue collar," Keaton said.

"Good luck with that," said the handler. The dogs were already out of sight. He held out his hand for each of them to shake. "Jared VanZant," he said. "We're best waiting here. They'll bark if and when they find anything."

Cooper didn't know if she could stand waiting around. She'd rather be part of the search but she conceded that the ship was vast and her sense of smell was far inferior to those of the dogs. It would take her a week to open up every container.

"Where was she heading?" she asked Tennessee.

"Who?"

"The boat." At least she wasn't the only one caught out by nautical terminology.

"Ah. Cyprus."

She opened a map on her phone and zoomed in on Cyprus. "I wonder why Cyprus?"

"It's pretty central," Keaton mused. "Transfer them to a smaller boat, and then it's just a short hop to north Africa, Syria, Turkey."

"Syria?" Tennessee tapped his handheld against his leg nervously. "ISIS brides?"

"God knows. Poor girls," Cooper said. She raised and lowered her shoulders, looking around for further evidence. "We won't know until Sam starts talking."

A crew member shuffled by, speaking in broken English to an officer who escorted him off the ship and in the direction of a waiting panda car.

"Did you hear that?" Tennessee cocked his head. "A bark?"

Like members of the pack, Cooper and Keaton cocked their heads in the same direction.

"I hear it," Cooper said. Her heart thumped. She turned to VanZant. "Which way?"

"Follow me."

The three detectives took off after VanZant. Keaton radioed for assistance. They'd need bolt cutters, medics, and a few extra bodies in case the girls had a minder. Her heart thumped harder the further they ran. The Libra was a monumental labyrinth whose scale couldn't be appreciated from the shore.

"This way." VanZant spotted one of his dogs heading in the direction of the barking and they rounded a corner and came to a halt, almost falling over the other two dogs, which were sat perfectly to attention and barking at the doors to a rusty red shipping container.

"Where are those bolt cutters?" Cooper grumbled. She grabbed the heavy lock and felt the weight of the chain, dropping it again as a memory from the previous week returned to her. She froze in horror.

"Boss?" Keaton eyed her. "You don't have to be here. Tennessee and I—"

"I'm okay. Thanks, Paula, you too, Jack, but I'm all right. I just had a bit of a flashback."

"You look like you've seen a ghost. Oh, here we go. Did someone order bolt cutters?" Keaton took the cutters and played with them for a moment, snapping them shut a few times.

"You need quite a lot of strength," the officer who had fetched the cutters said. "It's not easy. Would you like me to—"

Cooper placed a hand on his arm and shook her head as a way of quieting him. He'd clearly never met Paula Keaton.

"Three, two, one..." Keaton squeezed, her bulky arms flexing against the fabric of her jumper. She scrunched up her face and grunted like a weightlifter.

Click.

The dogs were rounded up and clipped back onto their leads as two officers pulled at the doors. The doors creaked on their hinges; an eardrum-piercing squeak made Cooper shudder. Three torches illuminated dozens of cardboard boxes that were stacked neatly to the roof of the container. Cooper's hope began to slip away. Were the dogs wrong? She hoped the girls weren't already at sea on another boat.

Tennessee stepped forward and started to shift box after box. Keaton and the uniforms joined in, creating a new pile just outside the doors in the natural light.

"Hello?" Cooper called. "Is anyone there?"

No answer.

Tennessee could now see over the wall of boxes. "There is something there. At the back. I can't make it out."

Everyone picked up the pace. Moving boxes in a conveyor belt fashion, passing them back along a line of people. The boxes were heavy, easily five or six kilograms a pop. Finally, a doorway emerged and Cooper squeezed through and into the darkness. The gap in the boxes had allowed some light to enter, but her body caused a shadow and she still needed the torch to make out her surroundings. Crates of bottled water were stacked in one corner with what looked like boxes of canned goods. Two buckets the size of dust bins were fastened to a wall with a shower curtain set up around them. There was a stench of vomit mixed with something sweet, and in the opposite corner, Cooper saw a mound of blankets. She approached, Tennessee close behind her, and pulled at the corner of a raggedy blanket. It slipped away, uncovering three girls, all pale in the torchlight, lying on their sides and not moving a muscle.

- Chapter 33 -

"Hello? Can you hear me? Can you open your eyes?"

The first aid training Cooper was forced to take every three years kicked in and she knelt next to one of the girls. "Hello?" she tried again. "Can you open your eyes? Shit." She lowered her head to the girl's mouth, waiting for the sensation of breath on her cheek or the sight of her chest rising and falling. "Come on, come on, come on," she pleaded. The thought of coming this far only for the girls not to have made it was almost too much for Cooper. Acting on the instincts of her training, she gently rolled the girl onto her back, ready to start chest compressions when she saw the slightest exhalation. The girl's eyes flickered before snapping open.

Cooper felt a formidable sense of relief. "She's alive. Heavily sedated, I think, but alive." The girl blinked at her. "It's okay, we're here to help. Paula, she looks terrified, poor thing."

"This one too." Keaton pulled a second girl to her feet. She was petrified, resisting Keaton's help and backing herself further into the container.

"It's all right. My name's Paula." She spoke in soft tones. "I'm with Northumbria Police. You're safe now."

The girl didn't seem to understand.

"Police?" she tried again. Letting go of the girl's hands and giving her some space. "We'll need translators," she called back to the awaiting officers. The first girl stood up from where she was crouched and hugged her fellow captive. They were shivering and unsteady on their feet.

Tennessee moved forward to help. They flinched, their eyes somehow widening further, pupils magnified with whatever cocktail their smugglers had given them. "I'll wait outside," he said to Cooper. "I'll move the male officers away too. We don't want to overwhelm them."

She nodded to him and turned back to the girls. "Macey?" she asked gently.

One girl shook her head and placed a hand on her chest. "Nina." Her gaze dipped to the third girl, still curled in the blankets. "She is Macey."

"Macey?" Cooper crouched down and gave her shoulder a gentle shake. She was cold to the touch and looked to be sleeping, perfectly still, eyelids closed, not even flickering. She was thinner than in the photos she'd seen, her cheekbones protruding through dry skin. "Macey? Come on, sweetheart. Wake up. You're safe now. It's over." Cooper shook her harder, fear building inside her. *No*. She was too late. There was no change. Macey wouldn't wake. Cooper realised the sweet scent was coming from Macey's mouth.

"Medic!" Keaton called. "Medic. Now!" She turned to Cooper, "Have we lost her?"

Cooper held a shitty cup of vending machine coffee between her palms on Thursday afternoon. The erupting steam warmed her face and condensed on her chin. She sat in a plastic chair and watched through one-way glass as two detectives from West Yorkshire Police interviewed Sam Sutherland. She had wanted the task - but rightly - Nixon had told her to sit this one out. She was too close to Sutherland, and though she didn't want to say it out loud, she was still shaken up by her abduction. It was only right that impartial detectives be brought in from a different force. So far, they had achieved nothing much other than *no comments* and time was running out.

The three young women they'd rescued from the Libra were transferred to South Tyneside District Hospital. Nina, an Estonian, was being treated for dehydration and malnutrition. The other girl, although physically well, was in a state of shock and the doctors did not want to let her leave without a family member or close friend. Unfortunately, she was too shaken to speak to the doctors or the translators, so they were yet to establish her name or nationality. Macey Gallagher was in a diabetic coma due to advanced levels of ketoacidosis. The Gallagher family were at the hospital in time for her arrival and had fallen apart at the sight of their daughter being so ill and unresponsive. The hospital chaplain comforted the family overnight. He stayed up to pray with Iris Gallagher throughout the evening and into the early hours. The doctors were confident that Macey would emerge from her coma, but as they didn't know how long she'd been in that condition, they feared she was at risk of severe brain damage.

"Says here you have a daughter. Caroline? Right?"

Sutherland nodded at DI Eloise Wan. She had thick eyebrows and blue-black hair pulled into a long braid. Next to her, DS Darren Thompson was silver-haired and round-bellied. He could have been Sutherland's twin.

"Thirteen-years-old. That's a difficult age." Wan sat back in her chair and folded her slender arms over her chest. "When I was Caroline's age, I discovered my father was a criminal." She paused as Sutherland raised his head to look at her. "He was an assistant manager in a care home. It wasn't glamorous, but it was good, honest work. He and his team looked after the elderly, kept them safe, fed and warm. He wasn't a doctor or an engineer, something my grandmother would be impressed by, but I was proud of him. Then he disappeared one day. Prison. I was too young to be told why, but I overheard my brother talking to my mother when they thought I was sleeping. He had three of the carers stealing money from the residents. Quite a small fortune they acquired over the years." She sighed, just short of dramatically. "Anyway, I never forgave him. Never once visited him in prison. Do you think Caroline will forgive you?"

Sutherland wiped a hand over his face and gasped for air. She'd got him. *Well played*, thought Cooper. He shuffled his chair backwards and couldn't figure out what to do with his hands.

"Do you think Caroline will visit you behind bars?"

"You don't understand," he sobbed. "I did it *for* Caroline."

Cooper moved closer to the glass. Finally, he was talking.

"So you could pay for private school? Buy her pretty things so she'd love you?"

"No!" he snapped.

If his outburst had shocked Wan, she didn't show it. She didn't so much as blink.

"You don't understand." Sutherland rose to his feet and walked around in a small circle.

"Sit down," ordered Thompson, but he was quickly overridden by Wan, who didn't want her interviewee to stop talking now he had started.

"It's okay, Sam. If you'd rather stand, that's fine by me. What don't I understand?"

"It was Caroline or those girls. If I didn't help take them, they'd take Caroline." He looked to the ceiling, noticed he was staring straight into the bubble-covered CCTV camera, and looked away again. "When they approached me, they had photos of Caroline taken through her bedroom window. Photos of her walking to school, at the beach, at her fucking swimming club."

Wan poured a glass of water and slid it over the table to Sutherland. He took it and downed it in one.

"Then they showed me the auction." He gagged and asked for more water.

"What auction?"

"She was for sale. Online."

Tears formed in his eyes. One by one they burst from his lash line and snaked down his face. Beyond the glass, Cooper's eyes had done the same.

"Some Saudi bastard had bid three hundred grand for her. I was furious. Blind with rage. I grabbed that little Russian shithead, head-butted him and punched him in the gob. But I was outnumbered. They had weapons. I... I..."

Wan didn't push. She gave him time to gather himself.

"They knew everything about Caroline. Sue too. I became desperate. I bargained. I begged. I said I'd do whatever they wanted so long as they didn't touch them. He - the leader - said, *Good. We need a driver. Work for us for three years and Caroline will be considered off-limits.*"

"Who's they?"

He shook his head furiously. "I don't know. Russians? Romanians? I... I don't know."

"You could have gone to your colleagues."

"I was scared."

"I saw the security system you had installed. Your fear bought a lot of nice things. You weren't too scared to take their money."

Sutherland rested his weight against the wall and supported his head in his hands.

Cooper jumped as Keaton and Tennessee entered the observation room. She put a finger to her lips and motioned for them to sit with her.

"CPS are going to love you," Thompson said, his tone was dry and oozing irony. "Cop turned human-trafficker? Juries are famously nice to bent coppers. I bet you get off scot-free."

"You need to give us something," Wan added. "You know you're facing jail time. The best you can do now is be as cooperative as possible. Give us the ring leaders and we might be able to broker a deal."

"I don't know their names. I don't know anything about them."

Tennessee filled his cheeks with air and exhaled slowly. "Some detective," he glowered. Cooper agreed.

"I only met them once. After that, I got my instructions from the keeper."

Wan picked up her pen. "And who's the keeper?"

"I don't know. He's local though. Borough accent."

"And the lure?"

"I don't know. Fucking hell. I don't know anything. They knew my name. Insurance, I guess. I didn't get to know theirs. She was a thin girl with curly hair, big eyes and some scars on her arm. An ex-cutter, I'd say. She got the girls to trust her, then led them to the van. She replaced a bloke they had. I don't know what happened to him."

"You really don't know much, do you?" Thompson said scathingly.

Sutherland's chest fell in defeat. He had nothing to offer them. Nothing to save his skin.

"How long have you worked for these mysterious Eastern Europeans? You said they told you they'd leave you alone after three years."

"Two years and nine months."

"Ooh." Thompson pouted, mocking Sutherland. "So close. You nearly made it. Bet you thought you were home and dry."

Sutherland returned to his seat as if he didn't even have the energy to stand anymore.

"Who else is involved in this little operation? There's you - the driver - the keeper, the lure, the unnamed bosses."

"There's a guy who works at the docks. He's the keeper's contact. He makes sure the containers are loaded up, and if any crew ask too many questions, they get a backhander to keep quiet."

Wan pulled her braid over her shoulder and ran her hand down the length of it. "Do the boats always go to Cyprus?"

Sutherland shook his head. "Depends who won the auctions. Sometimes it's Cyprus and on to the Middle East and Persia. Sometimes it's Morocco and into northern Africa."

"How many?" Thompson leant forward, propping his elbows on the table.

"How many what?"

"Bent coppers does it take to screw in a lightbulb. Girls. How many girls did you ship off as sex slaves or wives to order, or whatever you want to call it?"

Shrinking back, Sutherland lowered his gaze. Cooper wondered if he was counting them up in his head. Wondered if he was seeing each of their faces in his mind's eye.

"Since I started... Maybe twenty."

"Fuck me." Wan wrapped her braid around her fist as if it were a silky knuckle duster. "You coward. You could have asked for help, but instead you did as you were told like a good little soldier."

"It might have started as cowardice," said Thompson, "but it finished as greed. Twenty young women's lives ruined so you could cash your cheques." He got to his feet. "Sam Sutherland, you will be taken downstairs and charged. You will either be remanded or released on bail."

Thompson continued to explain to Sutherland the procedures he was already familiar with, but his words faded in Cooper's head. She watched Sutherland rise to his feet and be escorted from the room and from her life.

Twenty young women. She wiped her eyes and drew her shoulders back. She had phone calls to make. The National Crime Agency would no doubt want a word. Interpol too. Then there was the press; she had to do some damage control. This was going to be a long afternoon.

- Chapter 34 -

THE WATER WAS WARM and comforting. Cooper slid down the bathtub until she was fully submerged. A bath bomb turned the water a purply pink, and the room smelled of passionfruit. Beneath the water, she held her breath as the events of the last few days played in her mind like a video stuck on a loop. She saw Pearl Baxter's worry and Omar Ali's bruised face. She saw Sutherland flashing his new Rolex and Elin Karlsson - the Swedish girl's - swollen body. She saw Bryce Morton's maniacal demeanour and the pair of scissors twirling between his fingers. She saw the man slamming his brakes as Cooper fled from Morton's bunker. The look on Tennessee's face when Inga altered the sketches. The look on Morton's face as he was rag-dolled by the Belgian shepherds. Sutherland's face when he realised she knew his secrets and the poor girls' faces, stained with confusion when she helped escort them out of the dark and into the sunlight.

She exhaled one bubble at a time until her lungs were empty. Her body twitched and fought against her mind, willing her to sit up. She held on. Heat filled her chest, and orange spots flashed in front of her closed eyelids. Only when she couldn't hold on a second longer did she erupt from the water and gasp for air.

She was alive. Cancer hadn't got her, and nor had Morton. She was alive and thankful for it. It didn't mean she was happy.

Cooper pulled herself from the bath. Her skin was red with heat but the cool air from the open window caused goosebumps to form over her entire body and the tiny hairs on her head prickled as they stood on end. She checked the time on her phone. Kenny and Tina would arrive any second and her solitude would be over. She wrapped a towel around herself and shuffled to her bedroom, where she examined her scars in front of the mirror again. Fuck Justin Atkinson. She didn't know where they stood with each other, but she knew that if she wanted tattoos, she should get them. She imagined a floral design she'd seen, applied body lotion and got dressed. She'd just about buttoned up her jeans when the noise of Tina, Josh and Kenny floated up the stairs. Kenny had taken the digital natives to play mini-golf after school and had promised to pick up some fish and chips on the way home. Judging by the smell of vinegar, he'd made good on his promise.

"Mum! I got a hole in one! Didn't I, Dad?"

Kenny grinned while dishing up his quarry. "She sure did. I'd say it was a fluke, but knowing Tina, she probably applied some advanced trigonometry and factored in the wind speed and direction, and accounted for the camber of the grass, and—"

"It was a fluke, Dad." Tina winked at her mother to show that it most certainly wasn't a fluke before squirting a huge dollop of ketchup over her chips.

"Loads of mushy peas and extra vinegar," Kenny said. "Just the way you like it."

She was impressed. She took her plate and sat down at the kitchen table.

"Beer?"

"Hell, yes."

"Can I have one?" asked Tina.

"Yeah, can I have one?" Josh added. He was growing in confidence. Once upon a time, he'd barely look at Cooper, let alone Kenny.

"On a school night? Nice try." Cooper clinked her bottle against Kenny's and felt her body relax as the three others recalled the game, telling her who flunked on the ninth and who aced the third. It was nice to focus on something outside of CID. Once the food was finished and the dishes loaded into the dishwasher, Tina and Josh went upstairs to watch some show everyone at their school had apparently been talking about. Kenny got her another beer.

"Just us millennials," he said with a sheepish grin.

"So you finally accept it?"

He looked awkward. Usually, his big frame made him look formidable. Awkward looked plain weird on him. "Are you okay?" he asked.

"Yeah. I'm good."

"Erica. I've known you for a long time. I know I was away for a huge chunk of it... but anyway, it's been a long time. I know when you're not quite right. Is it work?"

She picked at the label on her bottle. "I had to arrest a colleague. It hit me like a truck."

"Shit. Sorry, Erica. That's got to suck. Want to talk about it?"

Cooper shook her head. She did want to talk, sort of, but there were too many thoughts in her head right now to make sense of it all.

"Well, when you're ready, you know where I am." He reached over and placed his hand on hers. The pads of his palms were calloused from his manual job. They rubbed against the moisturised skin of her knuckles. It wasn't a bad thing. It was nice, protective even. Her eyes met his, igniting an invisible spark, one that she'd thought she'd buried many moons ago. "I mean it. You know you can talk to me, right?"

"I know."

He hesitated, then leant in to kiss her cheek, but Cooper turned her head and their lips touched. Muscle memory controlled her. She wet her lips and went back for more. It was the briefest of kisses. Soft, with trembling lips and over fifteen years of build-up. She bit her lip and pulled back.

"Sorry," he said.

"Don't be. You didn't do anything wrong."

They sat there, quite still, for a good minute, just holding hands and contemplating in the silence where they should go from there.

Kenny spoke first. "I know it's not the most romantic thing to say, but I need the loo."

Cooper laughed. "Not romantic at all. But better than wetting yourself."

He squeezed her hand before letting go of it and heading for the stairs. A few seconds after he'd left, a phone began to vibrate somewhere in the kitchen. Cooper scavenged the room and found Kenny's phone just as the caller rang off. She unlocked the phone; his code hadn't changed since they were teenagers.

What she saw made her heart stop.

She blinked, unsure if what she was seeing was really real. It was a colour feed of her bedroom. It was definitely her bedroom. Her bed, her books, her towel on the floor from the bath she'd just taken. Her breathing came quicker, in shallow bursts of disbelief. Kenny was in her room. He looked directly into the camera before pulling four circular batteries from his pocket. The screen went black for a moment and then burst back to life. The angle was facing the dresser and Cooper's bed. It could only be coming from the mantlepiece and the framed Metallica poster. One of the buttons on the frame had to be a camera lens.

Nausea swept over her. She raced to the sink, vomiting her fish supper into the stainless steel. She gagged again before more came up. She knew she hadn't mentioned the nightmares to anyone. He'd watched her. Watched her sleep. She ran the tap, but her sick clogged the plug, and the water began backing up.

Chunks of fish and potato swam in the cloudy water. She turned the tap off, wiped her hand over her mouth and turned her eyes back to the camera, though her brain willed her not to. Kenny opened a drawer in Cooper's dresser, removed a pair of French Connection briefs and slid them into his pocket.

As she raced back to the sink to finish emptying her stomach, all she could think was that he was right. *Justin was right.*

- Chapter 35 -

Friday morning at eleven a.m. on the dot, Cooper, bleary-eyed and sulky-mouthed, walked to the Gibraltar Rock, a pub overlooking King Edward's Bay, and dragged herself to the upstairs bar. Superintendent Nixon had ordered she take a mental health day. Actually, he'd ordered she take a mental health week, but she didn't know if she could handle that. Last night, a squad car had been sent to find Kenny after she'd thrown half the contents of her kitchen at him and chased him out of her house. He'd been arrested on stalking charges, and Cooper was beside herself with mortification and isolation. His phone and the photo frame had been seized as evidence, and officers would be, at this moment, looking at footage of her in various stages of undress, crying after returning from her abduction, drunk dancing to Hush In Hell, and making love to Atkinson. Her cheeks burned. The files would be handled with sensitivity and stored securely, but the fact remained that her colleagues would see her in her worst moments of vulnerability.

There was a table in the bay window that overlooked the North Sea. A couple enjoyed a morning stroll on the sand. A Yorkshire terrier fruitlessly chased a whippet. A surfer briefly caught a wave before falling into the numbing sea. She ordered a double vodka. Straight. No ice. She wanted desensitising. She wanted to forget. She craved a day of complete numbness.

Her finger circled the rim of the glass. It emitted a low hum that groaned through her bones as she dwelled on her situation. Cutting Kenny from her life meant cutting him from Tina's life. Her daughter deserved a father, but she deserved better than Kenneth Roberts. She'd alienated Atkinson and left herself exposed at work. She was alone, and the person she'd usually turn to for wisdom was locked up on human-trafficking charges. She watched the surfer paddle out beyond the break, turn and pop to his feet. She willed him to fall again. An elderly man on the adjacent table rose and finished his pint, leaving a copy of the Evening Chronicle. Cooper reached across and took the paper. The headline caught her eye: *Tarot Card Killer's Legs Broken. Brian Hutchins brutally attacked in own cell.*

A glass collector looked over her shoulder. "Couldn't have happened to a nicer bloke."

Cooper snorted and sipped her vodka.

"My little sister was in one of his classes. Hope his arms are next."

Cooper didn't reply. She downed the rest of the drink. She'd wanted to be alone with her thoughts. To stew in peace. Not make small talk with an adolescent.

"They reckon it was that gangster, Blackburn, who did it. But my cousin's ex-boyfriend's mate is in Frankland, and he said Blackburn doesn't get his hands dirty. He just gives the orders."

Cooper had to get out of there. She felt as if the walls were closing in on her. She stood. "Blackburn didn't give the order," she said, handing him her glass and turning away.

"Oh yeah? How'd you know?"

Because I did, she thought. When it came down to it, was she any better than Sutherland? She hadn't kidnapped anyone and sent them overseas to live a life of torture and slavery. She wasn't the reason Elin Karlsson was dead or the reason Macey Gallagher was showing signs of brain damage. But she had broken the rules. She was crooked.

She descended the stairs and emerged onto the street. She turned her face to a cloudless blue sky and let the sun warm her skin. She checked her watch; the tattoo parlour would be open.

DCI Erica Cooper will return in Roll The Dice.

Roll The Dice

B Baskerville

Hyem Books

- CHAPTER 1 -

THE YEW TREE IS a complicated plant. To some, a symbol of immortality; to others, an omen of doom. This is a tree that lives so long it must endure nine hundred years to earn the title of *ancient.* There are yew trees in England that took root in Neolithic times, and yet the Romans believed they grew in hell.

Harbingers of death, yew trees are associated with churchyards, the plague, and the longbow. The longbow, England's traditional weapon of choice, was almost exclusively made from yew and was responsible for ending lives from the Bronze Age to the Battle of Flodden.

It made sense that such a tree would grow in the grounds of Fletcher Blackburn's home, for he was a complicated man from a family whose roots, he was certain, began in hell.

This past winter had been cruel to Fletcher's old yew. It stood at the bottom of an expansive garden and cast almost no shadow now that the summer sun was high in the sky. Fletcher Blackburn didn't know how old the yew was, but he knew it had survived two world wars and that his grandma had told him she'd climbed right to the very top when she was a wee whippersnapper. Granny Blackburn had passed on over twenty years ago. Still, the memory of being able to climb trees like a worry-free child must have seemed like another lifetime to the arthritic shell she'd become in her final years. So frail and isolated.

Yes, winter had been cruel to the old tree, but not as cruel as this summer had been to Fletcher. He felt a great compassion for the yew, for he also knew what it felt like to be a shadow of one's former self, to be weak and helpless after a lifetime of standing tall, to be a victim of a force he had not seen coming.

In his early fifties and struggling to breathe, Fletcher didn't feel like himself. He still saw himself as a strapping twenty-something, third in line to the Blackburn empire and feared by all who met him. *He* had been the omen of doom. But as time went on and he ascended the throne, the closer he was watched by the authorities and the fewer people he found he could trust. That was the cruelty of life; the more power you had, the less you could use it.

They say lightning never strikes twice, but it had for the ancient yew, and it had for Fletcher Blackburn. The yew was scorched twice by lightning bolts during a terrible storm one violent night in January. Fletcher, however, had been hit twice by 10mm bullets fired from a Glock .29 less than a minute ago.

Shot with his own gun. In his own study.

Fletcher lay on the floor, his cheek pressed into the white carpet of his home office. His new wife had chosen the carpet. *She'll never get the stain out*, he thought, blinking warily at the yew through a floor-to-ceiling window. The yew, along with the lawn and the flower beds, was tinted yellow. Did the world turn yellow for everyone on their death bed? Had it for Granny? He could feel blood oozing from his chest, his heart slowing, his breathing becoming laboured. His lungs were filling with blood, but he lacked the strength to cough it up. He could feel himself drowning. He didn't have long.

The sound of Mo's standard-issue boots thundering through the hall was a comfort. Mo could handle this; he was armed and medically trained. The door swung open, but there was no sound as Mo checked the room. He moved slowly and silently with his weapon drawn. Reflected in the glass of the windowpane, Fletcher could see his attacker crouched under the desk, concealed from view. He tried to warn Mo. He began to speak but only spluttered blood. Mo crept further into the room, and a shot rang out. Mo fell, his body slamming to the floor like the yew's branch had when it was severed by lightning. No one could help him now.

Fletcher blinked again at the old yew. It was scorched and missing branches and its thick knotted trunk was split in two. But despite its injuries, the tree lived on. Blossom flowers had come and gone, and in a few months, the tree would produce tiny, red berries. The tree had outlived his grandparents and his parents, now it would outlive him. The symbol of immortality would endure. Fletcher Blackburn would not.

- Chapter 2 -

A diamond-white Mercedes convertible surged west on the B6431, a road that connects two of Northumberland's most impressive buildings: Cragside Mansion and Alnwick Castle. To the west, the home of scientist and philanthropist, Lord Armstrong, was the first in the world to be lit using hydroelectric power. Amongst his many esteemed guests were the Shah of Persia and the King of Siam. To the east, Alnwick Castle has, for at least seven hundred years, been the home of the earls and dukes of Northumberland. Though, perhaps it is best known for featuring in the first two Harry Potter films.

Between these two architectural masterpieces, lies another awe-inspiring building. Tucked away in dense woodland, where no one would think to look for it, Morshaw Manor has one foot in the past, one in the future. Constructed in 1901 and retaining many of its original features, Morshaw had been updated with the best in home security, from cameras and sensors to dogs and an armed guard. It was a fortress—or a prison—depending on who you asked.

The convertible slowed as a junction approached. Two women, a blonde and a brunette, finished belting out the latest Mark Ronson hit. The wind tussled loose strands of the brunette's wavy hair, and she fought to push them back behind her ears while the blonde concentrated on the road ahead.

"Thanks again for dinner," the brunette said, turning to face her step-mother who was at the wheel. "And the spa treatments."

"Thank *you* for suggesting it, Lily." Charlene Blackburn turned the car off the main road and onto an unmarked trail that headed towards woodland.

It was still a bright, sunny day, despite the clock reading seven forty-five. Darkness wouldn't arrive until well after ten and the sky would lighten again before four. Long summer days were one of the best things about living in the north, thought Lily. They were up there with the endless beaches and the magnificent castles that dotted the landscape. Lily Blackburn was no fool; she knew everyone thought of her as a materialistic princess. Perhaps part of it was true. But beneath the gel nails, designer bags and influencer status, she was a home bird who loved her little corner of Northumberland.

Charlene patted Lily's knee, "It's been nice to spend some time with you. I feel like we've been so busy; we've hardly had a chance to catch up."

Lily's body stiffened. She had nothing against Charlene, but something inside her twisted whenever she tried to go into step-mother mode. She was not, and would never be, her mother. She was only five years older than her for Christ's sake. Quite what her father saw in her, she'd never know. No, scratch that, she knew *exactly* what her father saw in Charlene. A bubbly demeanour, youthful complexion, and colossal tits. She was the polar opposite of Lily's birth mother, not that Lily considered Hazel to be much of a mother either. Hazel left when Lily was emerging into adulthood. When she'd needed her most. Her parents divorced, Hazel moved to Turkey, and Lily was left at Morshaw Manor with only her dad and older brothers for company.

Charlene may have sensed the change in Lily for she put her hand firmly back on the steering wheel. Pine-shaped shadows engulfed the car as they approached the edge of the wood. Charlene pressed a button on the dashboard, and the car's roof began to move back into place. "How was your head massage?" she asked.

"Heaven," replied Lily, though her tone was flat. "And the salmon blini were to die for."

Charlene let out an orgasmic groan. "Oh, the blinis were absolutely amazing, weren't they?"

"Blini," corrected Lily. "One blin, two blini."

"Huh?" said Charline. "Well, you learn something new every day."

Charlene continued to waffle on about how gifted her masseuse was and about the quality of Kir Royale the hotel had served, but as the car was enveloped by woodland, Lily's thoughts wandered beyond the trees to cloudless Antalya where she wondered if her birth mother would let her come and live with her. Even for just the winter.

Morshaw Manor loomed in the distance, gloomy and ivy-covered. Charlene slowed the car as they approached a set of tall gates. A security system registered the number plate, and the gates automatically opened for the two Blackburn women. Lily's eyes turned to the camera fixed on the gatepost. Usually, it would train on cars as they entered the property, but not today. Today, the camera remained stationary. Charlene parked the E-class cabriolet on the drive and lowered her brow. "Where's Mo?" she asked, staring at the spot where her husband's trusted security guard usually stood.

"Maybe he's on a break?"

Charlene checked her watch. "It's not prayer time." She bit her lip and added, "Did you notice the camera didn't move?"

"Yeah," Lily replied. "Like I said, Mo's probably just on a break?" The brunette gracefully emerged from the car and began to stroll towards the manor, but the blonde remained hesitantly by her vehicle.

"What if something's happened?"

"Like what?"

"Like someone came looking for your dad? An associate or something?"

There was something in the way Charlene said the word *associate* that made Lily pout and shake her head. "Dad runs a taxi firm and a chain of restaurants."

Charlene wavered again then murmured, "Sometimes you can be so naive."

"Look, if you're feeling spooked, I can call Dylan."

"No," Charlene snapped. Her eyes not moving from the front door. "Your brother's resting. He won't want us bothering him."

"You don't have to flinch every time I say Dylan's name, you know? He's not a monster." *Though he might look like one,* she added silently.

Lily huffed and walked back towards Charlene, she linked her arm in that of her step-mother's and walked her to the house. "I think you need something stronger than a Kir Royale. We'll get our PJs on and I'll fix us some brandies." She pressed her thumb onto a fingerprint reader and waited for the click. "We can drink them in the back garden and see if the vixen and her cubs make an appearance."

Lily pushed open the front door to Morshaw Manor, but her hands immediately sprang back to cover her ears. Charlene's scream pierced the air as she forced her way past Lily, skidding towards the door at the end of the hallway and the pool of blood that seeped out from under it.

- Chapter 3 -

Toponymy is the study of place names and their origins. In the United Kingdom, the suffix *ham*, as in Nottingham or Tottenham, refers to a farm. The suffix *wick*, as in Berwick or Keswick, represents a bay. The suffix *shaw*, as in Morshaw Manor, refers to woodland. This isn't a surprise given the thick greenery surrounding the home, but more unsettling is the prefix *mor*, which depicts death. The Blackburns live in Death Woods.

Lily couldn't get to Charlene in time. All the colour drained from the smaller woman's face as she raced along the hallway to the study door. Lily grabbed her hand just as she pulled open the door and the full horror of what lay within was revealed.

"Mo! Oh, dear God. Mo! He's been shot, Lily. He's been shot. Look at him."

Mo's Asian skin tone had faded to ashen and his eyes, though cloudy, were open and staring up at Lily. She shuddered and covered her mouth with her free hand. Blood had pooled from his chest, coating his white shirt with scarlet. There was blood under his head; his scarred fingers still wrapped around the grip of a handgun. The fabric of one trouser leg bunched up over his boot, revealing the lustrous titanium of a prosthetic leg.

The room looked as if someone had taken a pot of red paint and thrown it around like Jackson Pollock. Blood covered the white carpet, seeping into its plush pile and staining it all shades of red from darkest burgundy to palest pink. It dribbled down the walls, speckled the window and painted the air with the sickly smell of copper.

Charlene dived to Mo's side and she touched his cheek. "Mo. Come on, Mo." She pulled her jumper off and began pressing it onto the wound on Mo's chest.

Lily wrapped her arms around Charlene and heaved her back to her feet. "That's not going to help. It's too late." Her voice shook as she added, "We shouldn't touch anything. We should phone the police."

"Police?" Charlene laughed manically. "Police are not welcome in Fletcher Blackburn's home." As she spat the words, they became caught in her throat. "Where is Fletcher? FLETCHER?" she yelled to the ceiling. "FLETCHER?" Then they saw it. The body of the man they both loved lay lifeless and blood-soaked on the floor behind the desk. His head was turned to face the window and the garden he'd cared so much for. "Oh."

Charlene's knees buckled, along with Lily's, and they wailed into each other until a shadow formed over their shoulders. They turned to look, shaking as their eyes crept up the man of six-foot-four until they reached a face carved from a life of violence. His frame was imposing, and his aura suggested a man never to be crossed. His mouth formed a thin line as he looked around the room, then he slowly turned his gaze down to the two fragile women.

Detective Chief Inspector Erica Cooper was on her first real date in a long time. Lobo Rojo was buzzing. The Mexican restaurant on the fish quay of North Shields was alive with all manner of folk from groups of teens, to octogenarian couples, and every age in between. There was a hum of panting mouths as brave souls poured hot sauce on freshly prepared tacos and deep sighs as chilled margaritas soothed fiery tongues.

"How's the fish?" asked the man sat opposite Cooper. On paper, he should have been perfect for her.

"It's great," Cooper answered, dabbing her mouth with a napkin and taking another look at her date.

Olly Timms, at thirty-six, was close in age to Cooper. He worked as a lawyer in the city-centre and owned a semi-detached in Gosforth. Guardian of domestic abuse victims, Olly specialised in defending women who killed in self-defence and assisted in divorces where one party used or threatened violence against the other. A lot of his work was *pro bono;* the rest of the time he charged a fortune. He was intelligent, a fan of metal music, and he was yet to make a derogatory comment about Cooper's buzzcut.

"Though, given its location," continued Cooper, "if the fish was anything less than stellar it would be criminal."

Olly sipped a beer and nudged his knee against hers under the table. "Well, if you need to sue them... I know a good lawyer." He gave a coy smile then corrected himself. "But you've probably got it covered."

Cooper inched her chair back so their knees wouldn't touch. Olly was good looking. That was beyond doubt. With thick mahogany hair, cut into a professional style, and eyes so dark even the most hardened of people could get lost in them, he was a pretty boy. Cooper liked his looks, his taste in music and the fact he had an autistic younger brother whom he spoke so highly of. He was great, but there was one problem, and it was a major problem: he wasn't Justin Atkinson.

The truth pained her. She wasn't over Atkinson and as long as that was the case, dating was a waste of everyone's time.

Cooper adjusted her weight. "Listen, Olly..."

Her date's face read like a book. *Here we go.*

"Look, I've had a lovely time tonight but—"

"Yeah, *it's not you, it's me,*" he said, making air quotes. "Heard it before. Except it's usually bollocks."

"It's not bollocks," Cooper protested, taking a swig of Corona. "And it is actually me." Before she could continue, her phone rang. She'd have thought, *thank God*, but she'd left it on full volume, causing the entire restaurant to turn and eyeball her. "It's my boss," she whispered apologetically. "Sir?"

Cooper pressed her phone as hard as she could to her ear and jammed a finger in the other one to blot out the sounds of Mexican music, chatter and crockery. Detective Chief Superintendent Howard Nixon sounded worried. Something serious had happened. She got to her feet, mouthed *Sorry*, dropped two twenty-pound notes on the table and hurried from Lobo Rojo.

JUSTIN ATKINSON, ONE OF the most senior scene of crime officers in the region, stood outside Morshaw Manor and checked his watch; it was gone half-ten. Dressed in a white overall and blue plastic booties, he pulled the hood on his fetching outfit down and relished the cooling night breeze on his forehead and cheeks.

"Here." Hong Evanstad, fellow SOCO, handed Atkinson a cup of coffee.

"Thanks." Atkinson thought of the time and asked, "Is this decaf?"

"Absolutely."

"You're such a liar. I'll never sleep if I drink caffeine at this hour."

Hong blew his floppy fringe from his forehead and eyed his superior. "You honestly think you'll get to bed before lunchtime tomorrow?"

He had a point.

"Did you hear the latest?" Hong continued. "Seems we're being Americanised. Can't say I like it."

Atkinson shifted his weight to his other leg. The aches and pains from his pre-dawn run had kicked in and his legs were seizing up. Muscle soreness had never bothered him in his thirties; it had been more of a badge of honour then. If you weren't sore, you hadn't run fast enough. But lately, it wasn't just his muscles that ached; his joints were feeling the strain. When had he become so old? He knew exactly when. It was the moment he'd broken up with Erica Cooper. She'd made him feel young, and without her, he was back to being a greying, forty-something, divorcé who lived to work rather than worked to live. "What do you mean *Americanised*?"

"The higher-ups want a change of name. We're going to be CSIs."

Atkinson winced. "What's wrong with SOCOs?" he asked. He hated change for the sake of change. Next thing you knew, the Queen would be ousted, the Prime Minister would be President, inspectors would be sheriffs and we'd all be ditching tea in favour of— He looked down at his coffee and laughed at himself.

"Got to admit, CSI sounds cooler." Hong put on his best northern English accent, not an easy task when you were Korean by birth and Norwegian by adoption. "Previously on *CSI Newcastle*..."

Atkinson laughed and cast his eyes out over the driveway and surrounding woodland. Other than the glow from the house behind them and the lights from their mobile forensic units, the place was eerily dark. Trees blocked out most of the moonlight, and with the absence of street lighting, the area was imposingly black. "What time did they say this bloodstain expert was going to get here?"

Hong shrugged. "Can't be long now. We requested him as soon as we arrived on site." He checked a small spiral notepad that he kept in his trouser pocket. "Ronnie Rogers. Sounds like he should be in porn, not forensics. Anyway, he's the best Greater Manchester Police could spare."

"Well, we don't see many shootings in our neck of the woods—"

"Neck?" The Korean-Norwegian furrowed his brow.

"It's an expression. Though now I come to think of it, it doesn't make much sense, does it?" He sipped his rapidly cooling coffee. "What I meant was, we don't see many shootings around here, so I'm happy to bring in someone with more expertise in the field."

"Even if they're a stuffy old Oxbridge grad?"

"Even if he wears a tweed jacket with elbow patches."

In the distance, two white headlights pierced the darkness, and the rumble of tyres on gravel could be heard as a classic MG convertible grumbled up the driveway.

"I knew his car would be bottle green," Hong said with an eye roll.

Atkinson and Hong approached the car to welcome their new colleague from the west. The car door opened and they stopped in their tracks. Ronnie Rogers was no tweed-wearing, stuffy, old academic. A perfectly manicured hand extended towards Atkinson and a bright smile lit up the darkness.

"Veronica Rogers," she said through lips the colour of merlot. "But please, call me Ronnie."

"SHE SMELLS LIKE ROSEMARY and lavender and all things good in the world," said Hong in a whisper from behind his forensics mask.

"Behave," warned Atkinson, though he thoroughly agreed. Ronnie Rogers smelled like Eden.

"That raven hair. That milky skin..."

"Don't come crying to me if you're sacked for sexual misconduct."

Ronnie looked up from behind her camera. "Who's been sacked for sexual misconduct?" she asked.

"No one," they answered in unison.

Atkinson shoved Hong in the ribs as a warning to keep his hormones in check and approached Ronnie as she continued to work. She'd photographed the scene from every angle imaginable and was about to start placing little markers wherever she thought more examination was necessary.

"Who has the bodies?" she asked.

"They're at the morgue. Freeman Hospital in Newcastle. Margot Swanson will take care of them."

"She any good?"

"She's excellent," Atkinson confirmed.

"I'd like to see the photographs of the victims from when they were still in situ."

"Of course," he replied. "I have them on my laptop. We took 3D images as well."

Ronnie nodded. "Good. The victims were shot from different directions and different heights. I can tell by the forward spatter. That's the blood as it leaves the exit wounds, but you don't need me to tell you that."

She stood on her tiptoes and aimed an imaginary gun towards a section of blood-soaked carpet by the window. Then she turned and crouched, looking back towards the door where pink misting covered a part of the wall and a swipe mark ran to the floor. "Any sign of the gun?"

"No. We've done a basic sweep but will continue in the morning. We found 10mm casings. Winchester Silvertips."

She nodded again. "That makes sense," she mused, taking a closer look at how some blood trailed down a standing lamp. "The victim by the window was shot in the chest. The victim by the door was shot in the torso then the head."

With the absence of bodies, Atkinson wondered how she could know so much already. "Did Hong tell you that?"

"No," Ronnie said with a glint in her eye. "The blood did, and blood never lies."

- Chapter 4 -

Almost three and a half thousand police officers make up Northumbria Police, making it the sixth-largest force in England and Wales. Several of those three and half thousand had been awoken earlier than planned. They washed, dressed and assembled in the force's headquarters on Middle Engine Lane in an area called Wallsend.

Four a.m. and despite the yawns, heads resting on desks, and sleep being picked from eyes, the incident room was filled with a quiet buzz. This was a big one; they could all feel it. There was electricity in the air. Journalists were going to wake to one of the biggest stories of the year, and careers were going to be made—or broken—on how everyone involved played it.

DCI Erica Cooper looked vastly different to how she had just hours earlier. Gone was the Keith Flint t-shirt and leather trousers she'd worn on her date. She'd opted for a tailored grey suit and the highest heels she could wear without wanting to amputate her feet after four hours. Cooper wasn't a stranger to wearing casual clothes to work. She often opted for jeans and flats, so were the perks of being plain-clothed, but on certain days you had to look the part, and today was one of those days. She opened a manilla folder as the sounds of the room dimmed to hushed whispers and pinned two photographs to the murder wall.

"Thank you for coming in so early," she said, addressing the room as one. "Last night, Fletcher Blackburn, fifty-two, acting head of the Blackburn family, was executed in his own home: Morshaw Manor."

Almost everyone in the room adjusted their weight, or sat up straighter, or scratched an itch they didn't know was there until now. "SOCO worked through the night in Fletcher's home office—that's the kill site—and will continue with the rest of the house and the grounds today. They've also brought in a bloodstain analyst from Greater Manchester Police. The murder weapon, a handgun, has yet to be found. Now, none of you will need our oleaginous friend in local intelligence..." Cooper cringed at the thought of local intelligence officer, Cedric Bell, and saw that DS Paula Keaton was sporting a grossed-out expression of her own, "...to tell you that Fletcher's brother, Eddie Blackburn, was head of the Blackburns until a certain someone," she motioned to herself, "made him sing like a canary and found him a new home at HMP Frankland."

There was a wave of smiles across the room as they all flashed back with nostalgia. A lone hand shot up from the back of the room.

"Yes, Boyd?" Cooper asked, acknowledging the newest face in the department.

DC Saffron Boyd blushed as the eyes of the room turned to her. "I'm afraid I'm not familiar with the Blackburns, ma'am."

"Ah, yes. Lucky you." Cooper extended an arm towards the new DC. "Everyone, this is DC Boyd. DC Boyd, this is everyone. Boyd recently transferred from West Yorkshire. I'll get a file put together to bring you up to speed. In the meantime, let me sum it up as follows..." Cooper perched on the edge of her desk and took a deep breath. "The Blackburns are a crime family known for drug distribution, prostitution, dogfighting, gambling syndicates, and extortion. Did I miss anything, Paula?"

DS Paula Keaton stifled a yawn. "Bare-knuckle boxing and counterfeit handbags, boss."

Cooper nodded at the woman who was twice the size she was. "Now Eddie liked to keep his hands clean, laundering money through a chain of pizzerias and a taxi firm. The NCA were after him for years, then one day, a pub up in Amble called the Harbour Lights went up in flames, and it burnt to the ground with two people inside it. Well, it fell into my lap, but the NCA were tripping over their dicks trying to take the case off me. Eddie's son was implicated, but I kept Theo out of it on the condition that Eddie told us everything he knew about the Daytons. The Daytons, for those of you who aren't familiar, are another criminal family and plague to the north-east. Eddie went to jail, and the NCA got a boatload of intel. Win, win. With Eddie safe and sound in Frankland, baby brother Fletcher rose to head of the family." Cooper pointed to his photograph. "Right, get your pens ready."

Everyone in the room opened their notepads and sat poised like good little schoolboys and girls.

"Fletcher Blackburn's manor home is situated in the woodland northeast of Cragside. Two hectares of land surrounded by eight-foot walls and security cameras. There's one road in unless you want a mile trek through the undergrowth and can climb like Spiderman. He's on his second marriage. Married to twenty-six-year-old Charlene Blackburn."

Cooper pinned a photo of a Barbie-like blonde next to the one of Fletcher. Murmurs about trophy wives and gold diggers floated through CID until Cooper coughed loudly. "He has three children from his first marriage: Dylan, George and Lily. I've never had the pleasure, but from what I hear, Dylan is the brawn, George is the brains and Lily is the beauty."

DS Jack Daniel folded his long legs and held his pen above his head of dark blond curls. "Who found the bodies?"

"That would be Lily and Charlene. They came home just before eight. Dylan appeared when he heard the screaming."

"You mean he was at home?" asked the detective known as Tennessee due to his distinctive name.

"Indeed he was."

Tennessee shrugged. "This seems pretty open and closed."

"Looks that way," Cooper confirmed, "but there are plenty of people who'd like to harm the Blackburns. Rivals, former employees, vengeful relatives of cannon fodder. We'll need to do some brainstorming."

"So who's that guy?" Tennessee pointed with his pen at the photograph of the second victim.

Cooper turned to Keaton. "Want to take this?"

Keaton cleared her throat, though there was no need; when Keaton spoke, people listened. "Ibrahim Moradi. Known as Mo. Born and raised in Bradford. Parents own a restaurant, brother owns a carpet shop. Ibrahim's ex-army. He served two tours in Afghanistan before being medically discharged after losing his foot to a landmine. Competed in the Invictus Games in 2018, winning bronze in the shot-put. Even got to shake Prince Harry's hand."

No one looked impressed. His achievements were tarnished by any association to the Northumbrian mafia.

"From what I've been told by the first responders, Lily and Charlene confirmed that Ibrahim worked as Fletcher's security guard. He monitored the front gates by CCTV and basically made sure no one came to the house without permission. Fletcher's inner circle was very small by all accounts. Few people were allowed in the house unless it was by prior arrangement."

"Any sign of forced entry?" Tennessee asked.

"None."

"So someone with access, presumably Dylan, overpowered Ibrahim to get to Fletcher?".

"That seems the most likely," Cooper answered.

"Okay. So what's the plan?"

Cooper closed her file and surveyed the room. "Tennessee, you're with me."

The younger DS smiled. He was usually at Cooper's side and didn't like it any other way.

"We'll head to Morshaw, speak with forensics and have a walkthrough of the scene. I want to know everything. Keaton and Martin, I need you two to head to Budle Bay. The family are staying in a property they own. Have a chat but handle them with kid gloves. These people hate the police. We're the enemy and they won't trust us. Keep it friendly and chatty. Get alibis in the most informal, relaxed way you can. If we push too hard, they'll shut us out, decide on their own who's guilty and hand out their own form of punishment."

Keaton saluted and turned to the young DC on her left. Oliver Martin liked to take care of his appearance. Even at this ungodly hour he'd styled his hair and dressed in the best suit he could afford. He looked back at Keaton and gave her a fist bump.

"Boyd, meet Elliot Whyte."

Nixon had given Cooper some extra manpower. She'd have preferred to have picked her own team, but beggars couldn't be choosers. Boyd and Whyte were free, so Boyd and Whyte were who she'd ended up with.

Saffron Boyd twitched a nervous smile at a large man in his thirties. He had heavy, dark brows and an aquiline nose. Boyd, conversely, was rather mousy in her appearance with light brown hair and wide eyes. Whyte looked like he could swoop down and carry her off to his nest at any moment. There had been many a rumour about Boyd since her transfer from West Yorkshire less than a week ago. Cooper didn't know if any or all of them were true, nor did she care. If Boyd had been sleeping with the superintendent, it was none of her business. As someone who had suffered more than her fair share of rumours spread about her, Cooper had no interest in discussing the matter. Whyte, on the other hand, she had known from way back in the day. Cooper and he had been on the same intake. That didn't mean she liked him.

"Elliot's new to CID but he's been with Northumbria Police since he was twenty-one. He knows the lay of the land. I want you two to speak to the neighbours, granted they're at least a mile away, but see if anything unusual happened last night."

"Yes, ma'am," Boyd replied, her face stony and all business.

Keaton leant back in her chair, balancing it on its two back legs, and in a stage whisper said, "The boss hates the M-word. Stick with Coop or boss if you don't want to end up doing all the grunt work."

Boyd's creamy complexion flushed red. "Sorry, boss."

"Paula," Cooper warned. "Stop scaring the new kids. As for the rest of you, what are you waiting for? You know what to do."

THE WESTGATE UNIT WITHIN HMP Frankland was a prison within a prison. Deep behind the walls and razor wire, beyond the patrolling guards and hefty German shepherds, lay a unit for the demons of society. Westgate was one of only four DSPD units in the country and catered for the nation's prisoners who displayed Dangerous Severe Personality Disorders.

Prison Officer Gareth Finch tapped on a heavy door and peered through the bars of its small window.

"What?" came the sullen reply.

"Sorry to wake you, Eddie," Gareth said in hushed tones. Why did he have to draw the short straw? *Shit*. Talk about shooting the messenger. "You have a phone call. You should take it."

Eddie Blackburn rolled to his side and threw his blanket to the floor. He stood, displaying his naked body to Gareth without any hint of shame. "What time is it?" he asked.

"Almost five."

"Fuck me." Eddie ran a hand over his face and pulled on a pair of orange trousers. Meanwhile, Gareth fumbled with the lock to his cell and tightly held his baton. At the slightest hint of trouble, the cavalry would come running, not that it made him feel any better. He'd served in Westgate for three years now and knew how much damage could be caused in only a few seconds given the right prisoner.

EDDIE WALKED AHEAD AND lifted a handset from one of the telephones mounted to a wall in the communal area. He hated this fucking place with every fibre of his being. He hated the cells, the so-called gym, the other inmates and the bloody screws. At least the screws had the good sense to treat him with an ounce of respect. Some of the inmates were a few too many fries short of a Happy Meal to know what was good for them. He didn't belong here with the murderers, rapists and terrorists. Eddie wasn't any of those things. Okay, he'd killed before, but in his defence, he'd been provoked. He wasn't one of these fruit cakes who shat up the walls just for the stinkin' hell of it.

"Hello?" he said as the line connected.

Eddie listened to every word as a panicked voice squealed down the phone. He noted the screw moving a few steps away from him. Eddie remembered his little brother as an innocent five-year-old when they'd snuck out to the department store to sit on Santa's knee and ask for Pa to stop hitting Ma. He thought of his little brother on his wedding day, blissfully happy at the thought of being shacked up with that miserable bitch, Hazel. Then he thought of Mo. He knew Mo and trusted him. No one got into Morshaw Manor without Fletcher's say so, not even Eddie. This was a betrayal.

Eddie replaced the handset and walked back to his cell without saying a word. As the door locked behind him, he slid his hand into his trouser pocket and felt the sharp edge of the shank. Betrayals were only handled one way in the Blackburn family.

- Chapter 5 -

THE SUN HAD BEEN up for an hour by the time Cooper and Tennessee arrived at Morshaw, and it still wasn't close to breakfast time. Cooper parked a few meters from the police tape and stared ahead at a forensics unit. The shiny BMW she now drove had once belonged to a former colleague. DI Sam Sutherland had been sentenced to eleven years for kidnapping and people trafficking, and the only good thing to come out of the whole sorry affair was Cooper's ability to buy his car at auction for a fraction of its worth. She missed her old colleague. He'd been a father figure, a shoulder to cry on, and a good detective. But she couldn't forgive him, nor would she ever visit him in the category C prison to which he'd been sent. Her actual father meanwhile, was living the high life in Lanzarote. Cooper hoped to visit him and her mother at Christmastime. By the time December got here, she'd be in dire need of some vitamin D and one of her father's famous sangrias.

"Things still awkward?" Tennessee asked.

Cooper blinked then followed his gaze. He was nodding his head towards where tall, silver-haired Justin Atkinson was balancing two hot drinks on a tray.

"Oh," she said, pushing fathers, real and surrogate from her mind. "Very."

"You know, if you want, I can—"

"Don't even think about it," Cooper said, cutting across him. Her heart was suddenly racing. "If you think for a second I'm going to ask you to take over the running of this walkthrough so that I don't have to make uncomfortable small talk with my ex you are wildly mistaken."

"Sorry, Coop." Tennessee looked terrified of the tiny ball of fury sat next to him. "I didn't mean you weren't capable of doing your job or owt, I just thought I'd save you the weirdness."

"Weirdness? I'm DCI. My work is twenty-four-seven weirdness. If I palmed off every task I didn't want to do, I'd never do anything."

"Sorry, Coop," Tennessee repeated.

"Ah. Forget it. I'm not angry at you. I'm angry at..." Her voice trailed away as she buried her frustrations. Why did Sutherland have to go and do what he did? If he'd just come to her for help, he'd still be on the team, and Elliot Whyte would still be under whatever rock he'd crawled out from. Cooper swallowed and checked her reflection in the car's vanity mirror. She looked good. Well, she looked average, but that was good for someone who'd been up all night and was fostering a great deal of resentment. At least she didn't have to see Justin Atkinson while looking like a complete emotional mess. She snapped the visor back into place and exited the car with a false pep in her step. She rounded the forensics van to find Atkinson giggling away with a woman who had the striking dark features and grace of a Jordanian princess. Cooper might look good all things considered, but she didn't look Jordanian-princess-good.

Atkinson and the beauty looked up from their pop-up stools, and Atkinson jumped to his feet, spilling tea all over his giggle-buddy.

"Erica," he greeted, ambling towards her.

"Justin. We must stop meeting like this." A shoddy attempt at light-hearted humour.

Atkinson laughed through his nose and shook hands with the two detectives.

"So, who's the new girl?" Cooper asked, casting a look beyond Atkinson's left shoulder.

"Girl? Well, woman, surely. She's thirty-six."

The woman was older than Cooper but had no lines or bags under her eyes. *Bitch.* Botox. It had to be botox.

"She's Veronica Rogers," Justin continued. "Head of bloodstain analysis for Greater Manchester. We needed more grey matter on this one."

Of course, she was also a genius. Cooper listened to her spiteful inner monologue and told herself to shut the hell up. She'd just told Tennessee she was capable of doing her job like a grown-up and yet, on the inside, she was acting like a catty sixteen-year-old.

"Shall we?" she asked, nodding towards the house. It pained Cooper that illegal activities and exploitation could buy such a breathtaking home. Up and down the country people were working long, hard days in honest jobs for minimum wage. Many of them struggled to get a foot the housing ladder.

Atkinson handed her and Tennessee protective clothing and shoe covers and led the way through a swarm of men and women in similar outfits. When he reached the door to Fletcher's home office, he pushed it open and waited for their reactions.

"Christ," was all Tennessee could mutter. His eyes flicked around the room, darting from one drop of blood to the next, and his lip curled at the sight of something congealed on a lampshade.

"That's brain tissue from the second victim," Atkinson explained. "If you were wondering."

The colour drained from the DS's face, so much so he looked almost green. "I wasn't, but thank you."

Cooper wasn't as squeamish as Tennessee, but she was still taken aback by what she saw. In her years in CID, she'd seen many a murder scene but very few shootings, and even fewer where brain matter had blown out the back of a victim's head.

"Fletcher was here," Atkinson said, pointing to a taped off area of carpet next to the window. "And Ibrahim was over here."

Cooper looked past the tape, into the garden. A tree that had seen better days looked like it had been set fire to at some point. A flower bed with snapdragons, delphiniums, peonies and foxgloves caught her eye; a colourful and cheerful distraction from the horror indoors. She looked around the room again and frowned at the mayhem that was the home office. Files were strewn about the place, a tub of pens had been upended and a chair lay on its side. A vase was shattered on the floor and though the water it contained had since dried into the carpet, the peonies it had held, presumably from the garden, were left to wilt on the floor. She stuck her head back into the hallway and scanned about. In contrast to the office, everything was as you would expect. Nothing seemed out of place. She wandered further down the hall and peered into a lounge area and an impressive kitchen. Nothing broken. No sign of a struggle.

She returned to Tennessee's side. "We were wrong about Ibrahim being overpowered to get to Fletcher. There's no suggestion of anything untoward anywhere but in here."

"That fits with what Atkinson just told me," he replied, looking to the SOCO to repeat himself.

"Ah, yes, as I was saying. Ronnie, that's Veronica, found blood spatter from Ibrahim that extended over the trousers of Fletcher." He pointed to a trail of blood droplets that cut through the carpet from near the lamp to the window. "If Ibrahim had been killed first, his blood would be under Fletcher's body, not over it. Fletcher was killed first."

"So, our killer either snuck past the security detail, or they had permission to be here?"

"Like the son who was supposedly asleep upstairs?" Tennessee asked.

Atkinson took a closer look at a book that had fallen off the bookcase. "I can't help you with that. But I can tell you Fletcher was shot from a height, roughly about here." He stood on his tiptoes and aimed his fingers as if they were a gun towards the desk. "Fletcher was shot once here, just above the desk. He was either sitting on it or standing in front of it. Then he either fell over it or was pushed off it, and as he was lying on the carpet over here, he was shot again."

Cooper scribbled down notes as he spoke.

"Ronnie will string the room up once we've finished collecting our samples and she'll be able to give you a much more accurate idea of height. Almost the opposite happened with Ibrahim. He was shot from low to high."

"The killer was hiding under the desk?" Cooper asked.

"Perhaps. It's a pretty big desk. I'd fit under it quite comfortably."

Tennessee bobbed his head as he often did when trying to visualise something. "Okay. So our killer is in here with Fletcher. There's a scuffle. He shoots him on or near the desk, then again when he's on the floor. The guard hears the commotion and the gunfire and comes running. The killer hides under the desk or is crouched next to Fletcher, and he shoots Ibrahim as he enters the room. Any prints?"

Atkinson chuckled. "Loads. I've taken prints from the wife, daughter and two sons. We'll start by eliminating them and see what's left."

"Footprints?" Cooper asked, her eyes turning down to the floor.

"Yes and no."

"What do you mean?"

"Someone stepped in Fletcher's blood. Presumably, it was the killer as Ibrahim didn't get that far into the room. They scrubbed it though, so it's just a blurry, bloody mess. We can't gauge shoe size or even type from it."

"What did they scrub it with?" Cooper asked.

"I don't know. We haven't found any bloody rags yet. If I had to guess, I'd say he stepped in the blood as he was climbing out from under the desk, then removed his shoes and tiptoed out of here."

Cooper pouted. "What about toe prints? Are they unique like fingerprints are?"

"Yes, they are indeed. But, the killer was most likely wearing socks, and even if he weren't, I can't lift a toe print from carpet. Hardwood, yes, but most of the house is carpeted."

Cooper huffed through her pouted lips. She'd hoped for something more concrete. "Right, Tennessee, get on to the first responders. They seized the tapes from the CCTV. I was told the tapes were wiped, but get them over to tech and see if they can work a miracle for us. Justin, I assume you've dusted the monitors?" He looked insulted. "Of course you have. Okay, let me know what turns up."

A blast of noise erupted from above them, and all three heads turned to the ceiling.

Hong's voice rang out. "I found a gun!"

- Chapter 6 -

Cooper waited on the upstairs landing. She had to give the scene of crime officers space to work and didn't want to accidentally contaminate any evidence. Still, from the hallway, she had a decent view into a sumptuous bedroom. A wardrobe was open, and numerous suits hung from padded hangers. A framed photograph of Fletcher and Charlene on their wedding day was set on a bedside table along with a copy of a romance novel, a book on landscaping, a Stephen King, an empty wine glass and some expensive-looking hand cream. It was clearly the master bedroom.

A short scene of crime officer with thick glasses pushed past on her way into the room. Cooper pressed her back into the wall to make space. The SOCO was holding a pad of tiny orange stickers and immediately got to work popping them on all surfaces that harboured potential evidence, including the rim of the wine glass.

Another SOCO held a heavy Canon camera and was taking photographs of a dresser. He moved closer so he could angle the camera into one of its drawers. A box was removed which was photographed, opened up and photographed again. Hong removed the gun from the box, slipped it into an evidence bag and carefully labelled it. When he was finished, he turned to another colleague and asked him to get it to the lab as fast as possible for print and DNA analysis.

"Put a rush on it," he added.

Cooper waved at Hong; he saw and motioned for her to enter the room.

"Where did you find it?" she asked.

"In a jewellery box, hidden at the back of Mrs Blackburn's underwear drawer," he held up a microscopic g-string that still had its price tag attached. He peered at it as if examining an alien species. "How come the smallest things cost the most?"

"Beats me." Cooper pulled her phone from her pocket but struggling to operate the touch screen through her gloves, she opted to leave the scene. Finding a gun in Charlene Blackburn's jewellery box was a massive red flag and one she had to deal with straight away. Once outside in the fresh, pine-scented air, she put a call into DS Paula Keaton.

"Boss?"

"What you up to, Paula?"

Keaton's voice was hushed. "We're over at Budle Bay. Been having a chat with the wife. She won't stop crying."

"Charlene? Where is she?"

"She's just nipped to the loo. I told her I'd make a cup of tea while she washes her face. Then I'll try to get her to open up some more."

"Is Martin with you?"

"He's right here."

"Forensics found a gun in Charlene's jewellery box."

Cooper heard what sounded like a teaspoon being dropped on a counter. "Shit. Right, We'll bring her in. See you back at HQ?"

Cooper confirmed then read the messages that had come through on her phone since the morning briefing. Olly Timms, her date from last night, had seen the news and asked if that's why she'd run off in such a hurry. She didn't want to ghost Olly, he was a nice guy, but at the same time, she hardly knew him and didn't owe him a detailed response. She sent a brief reply: *Sorry, can't discuss the case*. He'd understand; he was a lawyer.

She looked up from her phone and turned her attention to Atkinson. He had a laptop set up on a foldable table and was squinting at the screen. Cooper felt a bubble of sadness form in her gut. She should have listened to him when they'd been together. He'd tried to warn her about Tina's father, but she'd been too proud and too stubborn to hear. It was her own damn fault she felt this way.

She forced a smile and approached him. "I'm off now. Thanks for your help." She hoped her voice wasn't too obviously cheery.

He shut the laptop. "Just doing my job."

Cooper swallowed. "It's going to be a long day. Think I'll need a beer when it's finally home time."

"You're telling me."

Did she dare? She did. "Do you have plans?"

Atkinson's mouth opened, then his eyes flicked to where Ronnie Rogers was zipping herself into a forensics suit.

Cooper felt her cheeks burn. How stupid of her.

"Actually... Ronnie asked me to a talk at the City Library. There's a former New York CSI turned best-selling author giving a speech on the true cases that inspired his fiction."

Idiot. "Sounds great," Cooper said with a stammer. She felt like a prize fool and couldn't get out of there fast enough. Luckily, she now had a speedy BMW at her disposal. "Enjoy."

"HOW MANY TIMES DO I have to say it? I've never seen that gun before in my life."

Charlene Blackburn's voice was high-pitched and childlike. It reminded Cooper of Lisa Simpson's voice, had the Simpson's been set in the UK. Charlene didn't look anything like the glamorous image that Cooper had pinned on the murder wall earlier that day. Save for some mascara stains running down her cheeks, Charlene was make-up free. Her thick blonde hair was pulled back in a pony-tail, and wispy baby hairs poked out at all angles from her hairline. She was dressed in a velour tracksuit that, although hideous, probably cost a fortune. Her skin was blotchy from crying and she'd picked away at her gel nails and the surrounding flesh until her fingers were red raw.

Cooper maintained silent eye contact and waited for her interviewee to speak again.

Charlene sniffed and looked back at a photograph that lay on the table in the interview suit. "I told you. I don't recognise that gun. It's not Mo's. Mo uses a... Oh, what did he say it was? A Sig something?"

"A Sig Sauer P320."

"Yes. It's not his. He was— He was still holding the Sig when Lily and I found them." She dabbed the corners of her eyes with her fingertips then squeezed her eyes shut. "I can't get the image out of my head."

Cooper tapped the photograph, causing Charlene to open her eyes again and follow the sound. "This is a Glock .29. The bullet casings match the ones found at the scene. This was the gun used to kill Ibrahim Moradi and your husband, Fletcher Blackburn—"

"And I don't know whose it is—"

"Then why was it hidden in your underwear draw?"

"I don't know! Okay? I don't bloody know!" Her voice was shrill and quivering. "Whoever shot Fletcher must've put it there. They must want to make me look guilty. But I swear to God—" She slammed her hand on the table. "You won't find my prints on that gun."

Charlene was getting irritated; angry people made mistakes.

"Because you wiped it clean?"

"NO!" She slammed her hand down again.

Cooper looked to her left and stroked her cheek with two fingers. It was a coded message to anyone in the observation room that she wanted a coffee. One finger for tea, two fingers for coffee, and three fingers for *someone switch places with me before I lose my shit.*

"Okay, I'll humour you, Charlene." Another comment meant to wind her interviewee up. "Let's make-believe and say you've never seen this gun before and that you've no knowledge of how it could possibly end up in your underwear drawer."

"I haven't."

"Let me finish." Cooper was in no mood for interruptions. "Who would? And why would they want to frame you?"

Charlene looked down at her hands and pulled at a loose bit of cuticle until it snapped and began to bleed. She put her finger in her mouth and sucked it as she spoke. "I… I guess I'm the easiest one to pin it on. I know what they say about me."

"What do they say?"

"That I'm a gold digger."

"Who says that?"

"Well, everyone. But D-Dylan mostly."

"Fletcher's eldest?"

"Yes. That man hates me. He hates everyone. Has a right nasty temper as well."

The door opened, and Oliver Martin entered with coffee in a plastic cup. He placed it on the table and left before Cooper could request a biscuit.

"Why does Dylan hate you?"

Charlene shrugged and cowered into her chair. She examined her finger and balled it inside a fist.

"Do you need a plaster?"

"No, thank you."

"Then I'll ask again. Why does Dylan hate you?"

"I can't blame him. I'm younger than he is. Imagine having a step-mother who's younger than you are. It's got to be weird for him. And after Hazel left, that's Fletcher's ex, he probably thought as eldest he'd... you know... inherit Fletcher's money."

"How do you get on with Fletcher's other children?"

"George and Lily? They're all right. We get on. Well, we do most of the time. They don't call me any names, not to my face anyway. George doesn't say much to me. Half the time, if I walk into a room, he'll walk out. And as for Lily, I don't know, sometimes we're close, like sisters or friends, other times I can tell she wishes Hazel never left, but I... I think George and Lily understand."

"Understand what?" Cooper asked.

"That I love Fletcher. That I'm not with their father for his money. I don't want his stinking money. I just... I just want him back." She opened her hand. Her palm was smeared with blood, and the sight of it caused fresh tears.

Cooper gave her a moment to compose herself again before pressing on. "Charlene, I want to go over everything else that happened that day. You said you'd been for some spa treatments?"

"Yes. At Doxford Hall. Lily and I went for massages. I got my nails done as well." She stopped and looked at the sorry state her manicure was in now. "Then we had dinner and got home at around half eight."

Cooper knew Doxford Hall. She and Atkinson had spent New Years there. They'd walked through snowy woodland until they couldn't feel their toes then returned to sip a delicious red while sharing a warm bath. She couldn't think about that right now.

"And what did you do earlier in the day?"

She looked puzzled. "Erm... It's a bit of a blur really. I slept in, woke up after nine. Paulo was waiting for me."

"Paulo?"

"My pilates instructor. He was waiting in the back garden."

"Full name?" Cooper asked.

"Oh. I'm not sure. I just know him as Pilates Paulo. That's what he goes by on Facebook."

Cooper would check. "Go on."

"We trained for an hour. Paulo left. Then I made a smoothie and had a shower."

"Was anyone else around?"

"George was at home. He was in the kitchen and wanted the blender after I'd finished with it. Fletcher was busy in his office. Mo was watching the cameras. I'm not sure about Lily and Dylan."

Cooper made a note. "And after you showered?"

"I spent a few hours on housework then went shopping."

"Morshaw's a big house. You don't have a cleaner?"

She shook her head. "I don't mind playing house. I find cleaning rather therapeutic."

Cooper stared but said nothing.

"Fletcher doesn't like unnecessary people at Morshaw. He just about tolerates Paulo. He'd never approve of a cleaner."

Cooper cast her mind back to the murder scene. Other than the office, the rest of the house was spotlessly clean. She wondered if the lab would find the gun to be just as clean. "Where did you go shopping?"

"Jesmond. I parked on Acorn Road and went to Peak Boutique then walked to Clayton Road for Designer."

"After that?"

"After that, I drove into town and spent some time in Fenwick, got a latte at Starbucks, then Lily called and we arranged to go for some treatments."

Cooper would have Martin check in with the two Jesmond boutiques as well as the large department store in the city centre. She'd also have him run her plates against the city centre ANPR cameras.

There was a knock on the door to the interview suite. Keaton popped her head around the door. "Got a moment, boss?"

Cooper shuffled her papers back into their file and tucked it under her arm. She picked up her coffee and followed Keaton into the hallway. "What you got?" she asked, knowing Keaton wouldn't interrupt an interview without good reason.

"Two things." She leant against the wall and folded her thick arms over her chest. "Atkinson called, they found a copy of Fletcher's will as well as an entry in his diary that might be of interest."

"Will first," Cooper said, bringing the plastic cup to her lips and taking a sip. The coffee was still scorching. She'd told Martin a thousand times that he should add a touch of cold water to it. The boy needed more training.

"Charlene gets the lot."

"The lot? Nothing goes to the kids?"

"Not a penny," Keaton confirmed, one eyebrow raised high.

"The house is worth over two and a half million, and he's got a life insurance policy valued at six hundred grand."

Cooper whistled. "Nice."

"The restaurants and taxi firm go to Theo, his nephew."

"Yeah. That's Eddie's son."

"Dylan, George and Lily were only entitled to the money if he and Charlene divorced."

Cooper gently blew on her coffee. She'd been up all night and needed the caffeine to be able to function. "Hmm. If the kids knew about the will and were pissed that they wouldn't inherit anything..."

"Then they'd kill Charlene," Keaton suggested.

"Exactly. Why kill their father and frame their step-mother, leaving his estate tied up in legal knots for an age? It doesn't make sense."

Keaton pulled a face. "The things people do never make sense. You know that."

She was right. "So, what was in the diary?"

Keaton unlocked an iPad she was carrying and showed Cooper a photograph that had been emailed to her. Cooper studied the pages of Fletcher Blackburn's diary. It showed a weekly journal spread over two pages.

"*Sunday sixteenth. Drop off dry cleaning. Speak to George regarding Jamison account. Gym at five. Wayne Hanson at six. Call the witch regarding George's birthday.* Who's the witch?"

"I'm guessing the ex-wife," Keaton said with a chuckle. "I'll call Lily or George Blackburn and see if they can confirm."

Cooper continued scanning. "*Monday seventeenth. Family meeting at nine-thirty. Tennis at eleven. Wayne Hanson at two.*" Cooper tried her coffee again; it was just about drinkable. Downing the whole cup and feeling the caffeine hit her system, she widened her eyes and stood up a little taller. "Charlene hasn't mentioned a family meeting on the day her husband was killed."

"He could mean *family,*" Keaton said, making air quotes as she said the word family.

"As in the mafia? As in only those who need to know?"

She shrugged. "It's one explanation."

"And who's Wayne Hanson?" Cooper's brain was firing on all cylinders again; she was sure she knew the name from somewhere. "He met with Fletcher the day before and the day of his murder."

"I'll run the name," Keaton said.

"Good. Something tells me his name will come up in our database."

Keaton locked the iPad's screen and headed for the incident room. Cooper crushed the plastic cup and tossed it in a recycling bin before re-entering the interview suite. She found Charlene Blackburn sobbing into a dirty tissue, her eyes even redder than they had been just minutes before.

"Mrs Blackburn, if you're found not guilty, and that's a big *if* given the murder weapon was in your underwear drawer, you're going to be a seriously wealthy woman." She sat opposite Charlene and waited for her to look up. "Tell me what you know about Fletcher's will."

- Chapter 7 -

The tide was in at Budle Bay, and expansive mudflats were coated in a shallow film of water that shimmered under the summer sun. Sandpipers waded in the brackish water of the estuary where the Waren Burn met the North Sea. An oystercatcher dipped its bright orange beak below the surface and emerged with a mussel.

"I love it up here," Tennessee said as he looked out of the car window. They were driving north, approaching Budle Bay from Bamburgh. Bamburgh was a small village that despite its modest size, was blessed with a gargantuan castle and a beach that seemed to go on forever. It was something that had to be seen to be believed. "Hayley and I used to come hiking here a lot before Alfie was born."

"I heard there's an old World War II bunker around here somewhere?" Cooper glanced left and right as she drove.

"Yeah, it's just up that way on the right," Tennessee answered, pointing towards the sands. "Would have housed a large field gun back in the day to take out any approaching enemy forces." He blushed, then added, "I had sex in there once."

"No!?"

"Yes."

Cooper laughed. "You dirty little bugger."

"Don't tell Alfie, but he might have been conceived there. Was that or the lime kilns on Holy Island."

"And I had you pinned as the gentleman of CID." Cooper shook her head. Then, because she wanted to change the subject, asked, "How is Haley?"

"Some days are better than others. I told you the mother-in-law lives with us now?"

"You did. How's that working out?" Cooper rounded a bend and pulled the car into the driveway of a large barn conversion. Earlier in the year, Hayley Daniel has suffered a crippling case of postnatal depression. Tennessee had been worried she could hurt herself and had taken time off to look after his new family.

"In theory, it's great. Pat gives Hayley the support she needs while I'm working. Plus, Alfie loves her, and it gives Pat something to focus her energy on since her husband passed."

"And in practice?"

Tennessee gave her a look.

Cooper chuckled. "In practice, you're living with your mother-in-law. Say no more."

Cooper's phone began ringing; she selected speakerphone before answering. "Paula?"

"Boss. I've got the info on Wayne Hanson."

"Go on."

"Well, you were right about knowing his name. He's basically Gateshead's version of Blackburn, controlling everything in the triangle between Blaydon, Washington and Jarrow. Nowhere near as prolific as the Blackburns but still dangerous."

"Ah. I know the ones you mean," Tennessee chimed in. "They're big on cockfighting."

"And human cockfighting. Someone died at one of their underground boxing matches last year. The venue owner went down for it in the end. They couldn't prove Hanson had anything to do with it and no one would name the other fighter. Remember Athena Fox? Little blonde fighter from Shields? Helped solve the Tyneside Prowler case?"

"Yeah, I remember," said Cooper. It had been one mighty embarrassment for the force. Numerous young women were assaulted, the police were clueless, and in the end, they had a woman who smiled like an angel but fought like a demon to thank.

"Myers and I investigated a break-in at her home back when I was a DC. Rumour has it, the other fighter was one of the heavyweights from her old gym. Nothing to back it up though. When those guys close ranks, it's like getting blood out of a stone."

"Thanks for doing the research," Cooper said. "You and Martin going to pay Hanson a visit?"

"Already en route."

"Okay. Be careful, Paula."

Cooper heard a grunt before Keaton hung off.

Tennessee exited the passenger side door and took in the barn conversion. It was high-spec, modern, and it obviously cost a pretty penny. "Charlene gets this property as well?"

"Yeah. The two properties up here, an apartment in London, another in Ibiza, as well as all the cars. Course, she doesn't get a penny if she's guilty."

As Cooper and Tennessee approached the house they were greeted by whom Cooper presumed was Lily Blackburn. Luckily for her, she didn't inherit her father's looks or build, but she did have a strong Blackburn jawline and their trademark dark brown, almost black hair. Lily was reading in the courtyard; she looked elegant in a long-sleeved silk shirt and flowing trousers. Cooper suspected that behind her oversized sunglasses, were the blood-shot eyes of a young woman who'd just lost her father.

"Who are you?" asked the dark-haired woman.

"Lily?"

She nodded reluctantly.

"I'm DCI Cooper, Lily. This is DS Daniel." She nodded at Lily's book. "Reading anything good?"

Lily shook her head. "No. Well, maybe. I can't concentrate on it. Just trying to keep my mind busy." She closed the book and laid it on a patio table. "Where's Charlene?"

The door to the house opened and two men approached the detectives. They were both tall, six-foot or thereabouts, but that was where the similarities ended. The slimmer of the two had medium brown curls and wore round glasses. He moved awkwardly, shading his eyes from the sunlight and looking to the other man to take the lead. The broader man had an august build and hands that looked like wrecking balls. His facial features were misshapen, and hair the colour of black coffee was cropped close to a deformed skull. From what she had heard, Cooper assumed the broader man to be Dylan, Fletcher's eldest, and the slimmer man to be George, the middle child.

She introduced herself, then said, "I'm very sorry for your loss."

George snorted and took a seat next to Lily, who repeated herself. "I asked where Charlene was."

"We're detaining her for now," Cooper said.

George's forehead creased. "You don't think she did it?"

Dylan plodded towards his siblings. "That gold-digging bitch? She's guilty as sin. Of course she did it."

Cooper watched Lily watching Dylan. Even behind the shades, she could tell she wasn't taking her eyes off her older brother.

"Charlene wouldn't kill Dad," George said. "She doesn't have it in her. She's... sweet."

"You would say that," growled Dylan, his body casting a shadow over his siblings.

"Yeah, mummy's boy," Lily added, a teasing tone to her voice. "But," she turned to Cooper, "Charlene's no gold digger. She earned a fortune in her old job." She got to her feet. "I fancy a glass of anything that'll take the edge off. George?"

George nodded and followed his sister. Dylan's jaw tensed. "I'm guessing you're here to speak to me?" he asked. He placed a giant hand on the back of a chair and gripped it, his knuckles changing colour. Cooper had to crane her head upwards. She didn't want to appear intimidated, so she picked up a cushion from where Lily had been sat, fluffed it, then took her seat. Dylan's head was asymmetrical; his skull sloped down sharply on the right-hand side, and his right eye socket sat slightly lower than his left.

"I understand my colleagues questioned you at Morshaw Manor yesterday. But given the circumstances, I'd like to go over things again." Cooper pulled a notepad from her jacket pocket and clicked the top of a pen. "In case you've remembered anything else or want to add anything to your statement."

"You mean if I want to confess to killing my dad?"

"If you did, then confessing would make our lives a lot easier," Cooper said.

"And why would I want to make your lives easier?" Dylan half smiled and took a seat opposite Cooper. "Go on then, ask away."

Cooper steadied herself. There was such darkness and anger in his eyes. The man looked like a cobra that could strike at any moment. "Dylan, you told Sergeant Coombes that you were at home when your father was killed."

"That's right. I was asleep upstairs. I'd been in bed most of the day."

Cooper was sceptical but tried to keep her face neutral. "You slept through four gunshots?"

Dylan shrugged and pointed to the right side of his head. "Deaf in one ear. Have been since birth. I had an earplug in the other one and had taken some pretty lethal sleeping pills."

"Why did you spend the day in bed?" Tennessee asked.

"I was ill. Migraine attack. Had them all my life. Pain killers do fuck all, so I just knock myself out with sleeping pills and hope that when I wake up it's all over."

"I use sleeping pills from time to time," Tennessee added. "The sound of my six-month-old crying can wake me. I'd think gunshots would still wake most people."

Dylan gave Tennessee a searching look and sized him up. "I'm not most people. Nowt wakes me when I've had those pills. I'm like a tranquillised rhino. Besides, where we live, we're surrounded by woods and farmland. The woods are full of deer, rabbits, pheasants... And there's a clay pigeon range not far away. Our cousin, Theo, used to go. You often hear shotguns going off. It's nowt unusual." He paused before adding a rather sinister, "Someone's always shooting something."

"What time did you take to your bed?" Cooper asked.

"Quite early. Eleven maybe. Probably earlier. Half ten? I woke up at seven that evening with major stomach cramps. Had epic shits."

Cooper did her best not to grimace. He'd probably said it to see her reaction; she didn't give him the satisfaction.

"Probably sat on the bog for over forty minutes." He shifted his ample frame and puffed his chest out. "Then I heard Lily and the gold digger screaming. Brought my headache back in an instant."

"Then what?"

"Went downstairs and found them wailing and covered in blood. Looked around and I saw why."

"And what happened earlier that day? Your father's diary said there was a family meeting."

"Aye. George went over the accounts for this quarter. He's the numbers guy. Dad's talking... or rather he *was* talking, about opening up another two branches of *Gustoso Gustoso*. I imagine that'll fall by the wayside now."

"Who else was there?"

"Just me, Dad, George and Theo."

"Did your father seem different?" Cooper asked.

Dylan thought for a moment. "Nah. He was the same grumpy bastard he always was."

"Not worried about anything, or more stressed than usual?"

Dylan chewed on the end of his thumbnail. "If he was, I didn't notice."

Tennessee raised his hand to his forehead to shade his eyes from the sunlight. "And after the meeting?" he asked.

"I was supposed to do my collections—" He cut himself off.

Tennessee dropped his hand and squinted. "What were you collecting?"

"Just what we were owed."

"Protection money?" Tennessee tried.

"No."

"Loan repayments?"

"No." Dylan rose to his feet. Cooper didn't want the DS to push him too far, so she stepped in, softening her voice in the process.

"Dylan, we know what your father did and why you might want to keep things to yourself, but you don't have to protect him from us. We just want to find out who's responsible for his death."

Dylan didn't sit back down, but he didn't walk away either. "Look, some bars owed us money. I don't know why. It's not my job to know why. It's my job to ask for the money and to get a little heavy-handed if they don't pay up."

Cooper gave him a slight smile, enough to let him know he'd done the right thing in opening up to her, not enough for him to think of her as a friendly little girl. "But you couldn't do your collections because the migraine had started?"

"Dad was pissed. I mean proper veins pulsating at the temples pissed. He grabbed me by the throat and called me a fucking lazy retard."

"I'm sorry," Cooper said as she started to build a picture of Fletcher Blackburn before his death. She was surprised anyone had the balls to grab the beast who sat in front of her by the neck. But if anyone did, it would be another Blackburn.

Dylan huffed. "Don't be. I'm used to it. Been called far worse than that before."

"Your father was a violent man?"

"My father was Fletcher fucking Blackburn. You do the math. So, yeah, I was meant to go into Newcastle, but I can't drive when my head's splitting like that. I can't see properly. I get these visual disturbances, grey patches and flashing lights. Dad said he and Mo would go because, let's face it, George isn't going to get money out of anyone."

"Couldn't someone else have gone? Surely your father had a lot of people working for him?"

Dylan licked his teeth. "It was a bit late notice. The crews have their own business to attend to, and Dad didn't trust the youngsters much. He thought they we are much use as tits on a nun. Besides, he kept a precise schedule when it came to money. If he said Monday morning, someone had to be there to collect on Monday morning. Can't let people think we don't collect a debt when it's due."

"What about Theo? Could he have gone?"

"He'd already left by then, and he wasn't picking up." His shoulders rose and fell. "What can I say? Dad was an *if you want owt done properly, do it yourself* sort of man."

Cooper made a note. She wanted to know if Theo was the sort of person who'd be welcome at Morshaw and therefore get inside without Mo intervening. She also wanted to know where he'd been if he hadn't been answering his phone that morning. "Were Theo and your father close?"

"Yeah, I'd say so. With Eddie doing time I think dad sort of adopted Theo. Not that he needed it. He's old enough and ugly enough to look after himself."

"Did he come to Morshaw often?"

Dylan considered the question. "Few times a week. Family meetings, the odd dinner..." He sucked his lips in, reluctant to add anything further.

"If you can give me a list of the bars you were due to visit, Dylan, it would be really useful. It might help us track down anyone your father encountered that day."

He seemed in two minds, shifting his weight and folding and unfolding his arms. "Fuck it. There's eight of 'em."

Cooper's pen hovered over her notepad.

"Feisty's, McDermott's, LOL, The Silver Mirror, erm... Stilettos, Vixen, Bambi Bar and Bubbles."

Cooper hadn't heard of half of them. "Bubbles?"

"Yeah. They have a bubble machine," he said flatly. "Have foam parties. That sort of shit."

"Are these all in Newcastle city centre?"

"Aye. Most of them are in Grainger Town; the others are over near the station."

"Thanks, Dylan," Cooper said. "Two final things. Have you seen this gun before?" She handed him a photograph of the gun found in Charlene's drawer."

Dylan barely glanced at the photo. "No."

"Please look again."

His jaw clenched before he grudgingly turned his eyes back to the picture of the gun. "Was this the one used to shoot Dad?"

Cooper confirmed that it was.

"Don't recognise it."

She didn't believe him. His body language was giving off multiple signals that he was concealing something. He chewed his jaw, his arms twitched, he shifted his weight.

"Okay, Dylan, last question for now. Did anyone check on you after you went to bed? Or did anyone other than your father and Mo know that you'd taken ill?"

"You want to know if anyone can corroborate my story?" He filled his lungs, expanding his already impressive chest and clenched his hands in boulder-like fists. "Listen, love—"

Cooper squirmed, not from his use of *love*, but from the menacing stare he was directing straight at her.

"If I'd wanted to kill my father... I wouldn't need a fucking gun to do it. Do I look like I need a gun?"

- CHAPTER 8 -

DS PAULA KEATON SNORTED at DC Oliver Martin. He had a light dusting of icing sugar over the tip of his nose and most of his chin. She couldn't decide if he looked more like a baby covered in talcum powder or a lawyer covered in cocaine. She picked up a napkin from the table of the mom and pop café they were in and dabbed at his face.

"Stop squirming," she said.

"Stop babying me."

It was a quaint little place with checkered tablecloths and copper kettles, bone china and cheese scones the size of cantaloupe melons. A woman in her early sixties took a photo of her scone and said something to her husband about a blog. "Not as good as Penshaw Butchers, better than Cresswell. I'd give it an eight and a half out of ten."

Everyone needs a hobby, Keaton thought, then she wiped the last of the icing sugar from Martin's chin.

"The food's supposed to go in your mouth, not all over your face. The sooner you learn that, the sooner I can stop cleaning up after you."

Martin swiped her hand away. "Pack it in. Look." He nodded to a grand house opposite the café, where a pair of icy-blue, his-and-hers Audis were pulling up the driveway. A stout man in a designer suit emerged from the bigger car, and a slender woman in a teal dress, clutching a teddy bear and a basket of fruit, emerged from the smaller one. The man pulled the woman to him and kissed the top of her head. He lowered himself to whisper something in her ear before guiding her to the front door.

Martin mumbled, "Finally," and got to his feet, only to be yanked back into his seat by Keaton.

"Hold your horses."

"What? The Hansons are home. Let's go talk to them."

Keaton shook her head. "Patience, Grasshopper. Tell me what you see."

Martin frowned and ran a hand through his dark, gelled hair. The residual icing sugar on his fingers left a white streak. Keaton considered telling him, but it was more fun to leave him be. Besides, he looked like a badger. It was cute.

"Okay, okay. What do I see? I see high-end cars with custom alloys, a well maintained front garden, the exterior of the house looks like it's recently been painted and their wheelie bins are hidden behind bamboo screens. I'd say the Hansons like to keep up appearances. They're wealthy without being tacky, and they don't mind everyone knowing it."

Keaton smiled. "Good. What else?"

"They're security conscious. There's no ghastly gate at the end of the drive, but there're sensors and motion-activated lights. They have shutters on the windows, and I heard a bark when they opened the door."

"Sounded like a Dobermann," Keaton added.

Martin's eyes fixed on her. "You can identify a dog breed by its bark?" he asked incredulously.

"You mean you can't?" Keaton teased. She stood and paid their bill, grinning to herself and wondering how Martin hadn't spotted the window decal on Mrs Hanson's car for Dobermann Rescue UK.

The pair left the café with its sweet smell of freshly baked goods, crossed the road and walked up the driveway to the Hanson home. It was a beautiful home in a place called Rowlands Gill. Situated in Gateshead's green belt, the village had once been part of Country Durham but joined Tyne and Wear in the seventies. It was a picturesque spot famous for red kites and being the home of one of the Hairy Bikers, though Keaton could never remember which one. A house like Hanson's, in a village such as this, was the sort of place Keaton wished to have one day. Peaceful. Away from the hubbub of the city and the busier neighbourhoods, but still within an easy commute of HQ. April would like it too, she thought, thinking of her partner. Plenty of room for her blasted cats.

The door swung open before Martin could even knock. One of the sensors must have alerted Hanson to their approach.

"Christ. What do you lot want?" Wayne Hanson asked. Up close, his hair was flecked with grey, and he had innumerable wrinkles around his eyes. Probably from giving so many of his lackeys threatening looks over the years.

"I think you know," Keaton said, holding up her ID. There was a deafening series of barks and the rumbling of weighty dog paws from somewhere behind Hanson. Keaton took a step back and felt for the retractable baton she carried.

"Sit, Gazza. SIT!" Hanson's command brought the stampeding Dobermann to a standstill. It lowered its bottom to the floor and waited for further instructions. "Bloody Blackburns. Nothing but trouble. From behind bars, from beyond the fucking grave... Bloody trouble. Right, best you come in. Don't pet the dog."

Keaton gave the dog a wide berth as she and Martin followed Hanson. Gazza had a docked tail, clipped ears and a shifty look in his eye. Whilst he looked to weigh half of what Keaton did, she didn't fancy her chances.

"Put the kettle on, Traci," Hanson boomed through an open door before turning back to the detectives. "Right, let's have it then. And before you start, the dog looked like that when we adopted him. Cutting an innocent animal's ears off? Barbaric is what it is. Illegal for a reason. His previous owners should have been hung drawn and quartered."

Keaton had read everything she could find on Hanson. When he was thirteen, he served three years in a YOI for taking a knife to a classmate's ear. It appeared his hatred of mutilation didn't extend to his fellow humans.

Hanson's living room was surprisingly chintzy with floral prints on the walls and upholstery. Above a wide fireplace, a family portrait hung showing Hanson and Traci with whom Keaton presumed were his mother and three children. Two older boys and a much younger girl. A jade-coloured urn sat on the mantlepiece. It was labelled *Mam*. In the corner of the room stood an impressive globe in sepia colours. Keaton suspected it opened up into a liquor cabinet.

"Mr Hanson, I'd like to ask you about your relationship with Fletcher Blackburn."

"What relationship?"

Here we go. "How do you know each other?"

Hanson sat down on his floral sofa. "Who says I know him?"

Keaton could feel her hormone levels rising. "Don't treat me like an idiot, Mr Hanson. You know why we called. Fletcher Blackburn and Ibrahim Moradi were shot dead, and you were one of the last people to meet with them."

Hanson took a slow breath before calmly answering. "We're just golf buddies. That's all."

Keaton tilted her head to the side and eyeballed Hanson. "Aye. And I'm a SlimFast shake away from being a supermodel. Let's start with your meeting with him on Sunday and don't fob me off, it's listed in Fletcher's diary, and they have you on camera turning up at Morshaw."

Something changed in Hanson's posture. The camera footage had been wiped from Monday morning onwards, but Hanson would only know that if he'd been the one to erase it. Had he intended to wipe the footage from earlier on? He said nothing.

Martin cleared his throat. "Mr Hanson," he said in a much more soothing tone than the one Keaton had been using. "We don't work for the National Crime Agency. We work for CID. We investigate murders, rapes, assaults and armed robberies. We only want to solve the murders of Fletcher Blackburn and Ibrahim Moradi. I promise you, how you make a living is of no interest to me. Help us to rule you out."

Hanson clearly appreciated the softly, softly approach because he relaxed further into his sofa. The rattling of teacups on saucers preceded Traci Hanson's arrival. She walked into the room with dainty steps and placed a silver tray of tea and biscuits on a side table. She avoided looking at anyone, including her husband, then retreated again. Keaton clocked her red eyes and bitten fingernails.

"Okay," Hanson conceded. "I met Fletcher on Sunday."

Martin sighed. "Thank you. I'm curious why the meeting was at Morshaw. I was under the impression that family were the only ones allowed in Fletcher's home."

He shrugged. "Kings recognise kings."

"So, it's a respect thing?" Martin asked. "As heads of powerful families, you're expected to show hospitality to one another?"

"That's right."

Damn, Martin was doing well. Whether Hanson didn't appreciate her manner, or he simply didn't appreciate being asked questions by a woman, it didn't matter. Martin had stepped in at the ideal time with the perfect attitude.

Martin handed Hanson his cup of tea, and Hanson pointed at a box on top of the mantlepiece. "Hand me that, would you?"

If Martin was put out, he hid it well, handing Hanson the box with a smile. Hanson opened the box, pulled out a cigar, cut the tip and lit it.

"We won't be much longer, Mr Hanson. I'd like to know why you met with Fletcher two days in a row? What brought you back yesterday?"

A plume of smoke formed in front of Hanson's face, then it dissipated into a wispy line of white. "I didn't meet him yesterday."

"His diary says you did." Keaton countered.

"His diary's wrong. We met on Sunday."

There was another puff of smoke. Keaton hated the smell, it was going to seep into her clothes and her hair. She'd taste it on every bite of food she'd have that day. As an athlete, her lung capacity had been legendary. She never tired, never faded. The thought of that poison filtering into her lungs made her want to pull her shirt up around her mouth and form a makeshift mask.

"I was busy yesterday. All day."

"Where were you?" Martin asked.

"The hospital. Been there most of this morning too. My little girl's sick. Measles."

"I'm sorry to hear that," Martin said while Keaton made a note.

"Which hospital?" she asked.

"The RVI," Hanson answered. "She'll pull through. She's tough. She's a Hanson." He pointed to the family portrait. "Millie. My baby girl."

Martin hesitated then asked, "Why did you meet with Fletcher on Sunday?"

"You know I'm not going to incriminate myself, boy."

"Come on, Wayne."

Nice touch, thought Keaton. Switching to his first name after all that sycophancy. It caught Hanson off guard.

"I don't want to bring you in. My colleague here would love to drag you to HQ and parade you in front of the press as our number one suspect, but I don't want that. I also don't want to have to do a Capone and start sifting through every tax return you've ever submitted."

"But you will?" Hanson growled with narrow eyes.

Martin leant closer. "Help me help you."

He groaned and puffed on the cigar again. "Let me put it this way. We have a joint venture. Or we did. The enemy of my enemy is my friend. That sort of thing."

"Who's the shared enemy?" Martin asked.

Martin was met with silence while Hanson mulled over whether he should answer or not. Martin didn't press him; instead, he picked up two biscuits and handed one to Keaton. They nibbled away while they waited.

"The Roker Boys," he finally answered. "Bloody Mackems getting too big for their boots. Neither us nor the Blackburns can take them down on our own."

The word *Mackem* is a nickname given to people from the City of Sunderland. Where Newcastle and Gateshead are severed by the River Tyne, it's the Wear that flows through Sunderland. Tynesiders and Wearsiders, whilst neighbours, had always been rivals.

Martin asked the obvious question. "But together you could?"

"Exactly. The plan was to out muscle them. Then the Blackburns would have Roker, Fulwell and Southwick. I'd manage Pallion, Thornhill and Hendon."

Martin caught Keaton's eye. They were thinking the same thing. If the Roker Boys had got wind of Fletcher's intentions, they wouldn't have hesitated in protecting their interests. Had someone blabbed?

- Chapter 9 -

IT TOOK THE BEST part of half an hour for Cooper and Tennessee to walk back from Bamburgh to the Blackburns' barn conversion in Budle Bay. In the interests of their health, they'd opted to leave the car and take a leisurely stroll to a restaurant called The Potted Lobster. They'd been lucky to get a seat; the sunshine had brought the hikers and the twitchers in droves. Cooper found a small table in the corner and they ordered two bowls of mussels with crusty bread and shared a portion of truffle and parmesan fries.

With full bellies, they tackled the walk back along a country road that was lined with thickets and nettles. Lacking a pavement, they occasionally had to dodge traffic and walk on the grass verge. Cooper walked barefoot, carrying her heeled shoes. The road was smooth and warm, having been heated by the midday sun. Every hundred metres or so Cooper would turn her head and look back towards Bamburgh to see if she could still see the castle looming in the distance. She could. Now and again they would pass a gate between bushes and could look in on fields of oblivious sheep and nosy cows.

Tennessee passed the time by trying to convince Cooper that she should sign up to a charity relay triathlon that the commissioner had organised in a bid to boost public relations. Northumbria Police versus the Tyne and Wear Fire Service. Cooper was less than enthusiastic. For one, Tennessee had bagsied the cycling leg and Keaton, as the former professional full-back, had been nominated to do the running leg. That would leave Cooper with the open-water swim. In the North Sea? No, thank you. Secondly, she could see it now. For every member of the public cheering them on there'd be someone jeering that they should bloody get back to work.

Both Cooper and Tennessee were rosy-cheeked when they arrived back at the barn, hoping to speak to Lily Blackburn. They found Lily propping up the kitchen island with a glass of something sparkling in her hand.

"To Dad," she said, toasting the air. "Hope you don't mind, but I thought I'd get the weekend started early.

Cooper didn't want to judge; the girl had just lost her father. But she was thrown by Lily's choice to wear sunglasses indoors because as far as Cooper was aware, only two types of people wore sunglasses indoors: the blind, and celebrity arseholes.

"As you're aware, Lily, we have your step-mother in custody—"

"Urgh. Don't call her my step-mother: she's Charlene. And George is right, she wouldn't hurt Dad. Besides, she was out with me. You should have seen her when we found... when we found them." Lily paused, her lower lip quivering. "She was beside herself. When are you going to let her come home?"

"As soon as we can establish if she handled the gun that killed your father," Cooper said. "What I was wondering, was how your mother felt about your father's marriage to Charlene?"

Lily shook her head and let out a shallow laugh. "If you mean, did she approve, then no, of course not. Charlene's only five years older than me. When I was born, she was still learning to use a knife and fork."

"So, she's more like a big sister?" Tennessee asked.

"Urgh," she grunted again. "Yeah. Maybe. If you say so. Sometimes we were close, but it was weird. I mean, she was Dad's wife."

Cooper looked to a pair of bar stools next to the marble-topped island. "May we?"

Lily shrugged, so they took their seats. Cooper looked down and saw that Tennessee's feet rested on the floor, whereas hers dangled a good six inches away. She felt like a child taking a seat at the big table.

"I know Ibrahim was well-regarded by your father. Would he allow your mother into Morshaw?"

"Oh, no. Not at all," Lily said, shaking her head. "She tried once: a year after the divorce. She was drunk as a skunk and driving this way and that, yelling through the intercom... Anyway, Mo let the dogs out, so she took off."

"And your mother lives in Turkey?" Cooper asked.

"Last I heard. She hasn't answered my calls since all this happened. I don't know if she's even heard yet."

Cooper gave Tennessee a look. They'd developed a good level of telepathy over the years, so she didn't have to glance at his notepad to know that he was writing, *check H. Blackburn is not in the country.*

"Who is allowed through the gates?" Cooper continued.

"Well... family, obviously. Me and the boys. Charlene, Theo—"

"That's Eddie's son?"

"Yeah." She wet her lower lip and took a sip of Champagne. "Then there's Pilates Paulo. You know about him?"

Cooper confirmed that she did.

"We have a chef on weekends too. He cooks for Dad and Charlene on Saturday nights. It's like their date night thing." She pulled a face. "Then he stays in the guest room and makes breakfast and lunch for us the next day. Dad likes us to eat Sunday lunch together as a family."

"That sounds nice," Cooper said.

Lily's mouth curled down. "It can be. Depends on what mood Dad and Dylan are in. And it's not like Dad had much of an appetite lately; he was pretty much on a liquid diet. Gross health drinks in the morning and whiskey in the afternoon. I suppose you'll want the chef's details?"

Cooper nodded. Lily jotted down a name and handed it to her: *Darren Ray.* She finished her glass and stifled a burp before opening the fridge and getting herself a top-up.

"Charlene mentioned you don't have a cleaner."

"No. Apparently, that's a woman's job." She closed the fridge and swayed slightly. "I know Charlene doesn't mind cleaning. I mean, it's not like she was busy doing much else, other than riding Dad or working on her tan. But I work. I have no intention of cleaning up after the men all day. It's a tad 1950s."

"What do you do?" Tennessee asked.

"I work in a beautician's. Nails, waxing, that sort of thing. I'm still learning the basics, but I plan on running my own salon one day. Maybe a boutique too. I'm into fashion, and I have an online presence. I'm a bit of an influencer. I get sent stuff to promote." She tapped the side of her designer shades.

Okay, Cooper thought. Three types of people wear sunglasses indoors: the blind, celebrity arseholes, and wannabe celebrity arseholes.

"Nice," Tennessee said when Cooper failed to respond. "And I'm sorry to ask. But can you tell us where you were on Monday?"

"I was out with Charlene. We went to Doxford for dinner and massages. We've already been over this?"

"Yes, but I meant earlier in the day."

Lily sighed. "I'm getting tired, and there are arrangements to be made... I haven't slept." A tear rolled down her cheek, and she turned away to dab under her glasses with a sheet of kitchen roll. "But fine, I was at home until ten, maybe quarter past, then I went into work for a few hours." She steadied her voice and turned back to face them. "And between clients, I got my nails done, curled my eyelashes and got everything waxed," she paused to look at Tennessee. "Everything."

THE RIOT IN HMP Frankland began at eight p.m. precisely, just as he'd asked. The guards and their riot shields struggled against the sea of men holding them back. One-on-one with a guard was an impossibility; they had shields, sprays, batons and dogs. But like ants, when the inmates worked as a team, they could achieve great things, and right now, they were holding off twenty guards. In the distance, Eddie Blackburn could hear the German shepherds preparing for battle. The faintest barks over the constant drone of sirens.

Like a king surveying his lands from a mountain citadel, Eddie Blackburn watched the chaos unfold. Heath held the man still while Blackjack jammed the shank into his ribs three times. He was their second target; the first lay dying under a pile of plastic chairs. The man crumpled to the floor only to be trodden on in the stampede of approaching inmates. J-wing had heeded the call and were coming to join in the fun. Blackjack hauled the man out of the chaos, grabbed his left arm and pulled it violently, dislocating it at the shoulder. He screamed and raised his right arm to defend himself, only to have his elbow kicked—and probably broken—by Heath. Blood pooled around him, and he begged for his life like a child begs not to go to bed early.

Eddie never took kindly to begging: it only made him angrier.

Blackjack cleared some space. "He's all yours, Eddie."

Eddie approached slowly. He was in no hurry. He could watch the riot all night; it was likely to last that long anyway, and it was the best entertainment he'd had in a long time.

The man was crying, sobbing even. "Please. Please, Eddie. You don't have to do this. It wasn't me, you know it wasn't."

Eddie bent over him and lowered his lips to his ear. "I know it wasn't, but this is war," he whispered. "Wars have casualties."

The man bucked and flinched. "No. Eddie. No." His arms were useless, flopping by his sides, unable to protect him.

Eddie dragged the tip of the shank over the lens of his eyeball. The man screamed, but his sounds barely carried over the noise of mayhem.

Eddie grinned. "An eye for an eye."

The shank plunged through the iris and into the vitreous body. The scream that followed was one Eddie would never forget. He pulled the shank free and admired the eyeball impaled on the end of it. He wanted to keep it as a trophy but knew no good would come from that, so he pulled it free and let it roll through the bedlam until it was trampled by Fat Matt from G-wing.

Eddie walked back to his cell and stood in his doorway. The citadel that was his cell was calm and secure. All he had to do was close the door behind him. He took one last look at his soldiers as they did his bidding then returned to his bed. It felt good to be the king.

- Chapter 10 -

Forensic pathologist Margot Swanson finished her pre-work cigarette while strolling around the small lake in Paddy Freeman's park. She savoured this moment each day; it was her *above-ground time*. Margot kept this routine regardless of the weather. Still, she especially liked days like today when the sun was bright, the sky was blue, and the green heads of the mallards on the lake shimmered in the sunlight. She stubbed out her cigarette at the bin near the entrance to the park then headed into the Freeman to start her shift. Margot nipped to the ladies room, swilled with mouthwash and moisturised her hands. She didn't like to look at her hands, so she kept her eyes on the reflection in the mirror. Dermatitis and age had ravaged the backs of her fingers. She could colour her roots, get fillers every six months and keep as much pep in her step as she could manage, but her hands would always give her away.

"Relax," she purred to her reflection. "You're only as old as the man you feel... and Tony's twenty-six."

She smiled as she thought of the athletic young man to whom she was engaged. She hadn't expected them to last: they rarely did. The novelty usually wore off after a couple of months, and one or both of them would move onto pastures new. This one had been different. He'd seen past her age, and she'd seen past his youth. They connected. It sounded like such soppy tripe, but the words *soul mates* kept coming to mind. Margot rubbed the inner edge of her engagement ring with her thumb and headed back to the morgue, keeping thoughts of dissection at bay with thoughts of being cuddled up on the sofa with the man she'd fallen for. She fancied watching a film tonight. Something spooky so they could cuddle even tighter during the scary bits.

The morgue in the bowels of the Freeman was sterile and chilly, with white and avocado-green tiles that reminded Margot of her parent's bathroom where she'd grown up in Elgin. Margot covered her lab coat with a transparent apron with sleeves and got to work. She'd finished the autopsy of Ibrahim Moradi last night and was ready to get to know Fletcher Blackburn. His body was wheeled from storage and his ankle barcode scanned. Margot opened the file she'd received from radiology and examined the x-rays that had been taken on intake. The x-rays showed two old breaks, the first was to the left radius and the second to the right tibia. According to his medical history, these both occurred when Fletcher was in his late teens. The radial break was from fighting with his older brother, and the tibial break occurred after he jumped out of a tree. A bright oval of white, clearly visible in the x-ray, indicated a bullet remained in the body.

"Good morning, Fletcher."

Admittedly, it was an odd custom to greet the dead, but it was a custom Margot had continued from her old mentor at the University of Edinburgh.

"Let's get you more comfortable," she said as she began to undress the body. Some pathologists were rushed and handled DBs like rag dolls. Margot preferred a slower, more respectful manner. Fletcher's shirt, suit jacket and trousers were removed, folded, bagged and sealed as evidence. She didn't like to cut clothing unless absolutely necessary. His wallet, keys and watch were placed to one side for his next of kin. As she did this, Margot paused to think of the family and the grief they would be experiencing. The cold, naked body that lay before her was once a living, breathing human, and he was worthy of being handled with dignity.

"Fletcher Blackburn, fifty-two," she said, pressing record on a dictaphone. "Wednesday nineteenth of June, ten-forty a.m. Commencing anterior external examination... Loose skin on the arms and abdomen suggests recent weight loss. Slight jaundice to the eyes and skin. Two entrance wounds consistent with gunshots to the torso. One appears to be through the fourth rib on the left-hand side, just proximal to the costal cartilage. The second wound is through the sixth rib on the right-hand side. There are bruises to the right shin."

Margot applied an ink roller to Fletcher's fingertips and pressed each finger in turn against a piece of card. She then collected samples from under his nails and gently rolled the body over. "Posterior external examination reveals an exit wound to the left of the lumbar spine," she said before turning Fletcher back. She took a scalpel and made a Y-shaped incision from his shoulders to his sternum and down to the groin. "Exposing the ribs confirms the location of the wounds to left four and right six."

Margot's next job was to remove the front of the ribcage to give her access to the organs. To do this, she needed rib cutters: pruning sheers for the human body. She removed the lungs, photographed the position of the remaining bullet, retrieved it and bagged it for the investigating team. Next, she weighed the lungs and took samples of lung tissue. She collected samples of urine, blood and bile, labelled the vials and put them to one side for analysis.

Removing the stomach to examine its contents was one of the worse aspects of her work, and never a task Margot enjoyed. She weighed the stomach, braced herself and made her incision.

Margot paused and lowered her head to get a closer look. She picked up some pieces of purple and green with a pair of tweezers and held them up to the light.

"Well," she said, removing her gloves and picking up the morgue's telephone. "This just got interesting."

- Chapter 11 -

Yesterday had been one hellish long day. Cooper had returned home in the early evening to find her home abandoned save for the baby seagull that was now living in her kitchen. Steven Seagull had outgrown his shoebox and was now housed in a straw-filled crate that sat in the corner of the room between the bin and the fridge. Cooper's first task of the evening was to disinfect the kitchen floor because try as she might, Tina hadn't been able to toilet train the winged beast. Her second task was to text Tina and find her whereabouts. Her fifteen-year-old was having dinner at her boyfriend's and promised to be home before dark. True to form, Tina arrived two minutes before the official sunset time. Cooper threw a ready meal in the microwave and ate it straight from its plastic tray.

As night fell, Cooper did everything she could to give herself the best chance of a good night's sleep. She showered, applied lavender body lotion, drank camomile tea and played relaxing music as she pulled on some pyjamas. After the events of April, Cooper was never sleeping naked again. She curled up and tried to create an environment of sensory deprivation by using earplugs and an eye mask. Unfortunately, the earplugs couldn't block out her thoughts, and her mind continuously circled back to Atkinson and his glamorous bloodstain analyst. They were no doubt sharing a delicious bottle of red while they discussed all things forensics. The regret and jealousy that raged inside her kept Cooper awake until four a.m., which is why, when she arrived at CID, she looked like morning breath personified.

Cooper had barely crossed the threshold when Chief Superintendent Howard Nixon summoned her to his office.

"Don't sit. This won't take long."

Cooper stood awkwardly and wished she'd stopped for coffee on her way in. Facing Howard Nixon while in a decaffeinated state was never a wise move.

"Andre Spence and Charlie Mellor. Those names mean anything to you, Cooper?"

"Should they?" Cooper looked Nixon up and down. He was well dressed, as always, but his skin was oddly pale for this time of year, and his greying hair was thinning at the temples. He was stressed.

"They're two of Wayne Hanson's crew. Murdered last night during a riot at Frankland."

Cooper's shoulders sagged as she considered the implications. "Shit."

"Shit? Shit doesn't begin to cover it. Spence was hit on the back of the head, his eyeballs removed, then stabbed multiple times. Mellor had both arms broken, eyeballs removed then stabbed and kicked to death."

Cooper felt faint. She could actually feel the blood draining from her head and had to place a hand on Nixon's doorway to make sure she didn't collapse. "*An eye for an eye?* Bloody hell. Sir, last I heard from Keaton, she didn't think Hanson had anything to do with this. I don't have all the details yet, but she said the Hansons and the Blackburns were working together on something."

"Didn't anyone tell Eddie this?"

"Probably, sir. He must have thought they'd been stabbed in the back. We're going to have a war on our hands."

"Blackburn, Moradi, Spence and Mellor. That's four." He held up four fingers on his right hand to force home the point. "I'd say the war has already started. Wouldn't you?"

"Yes, sir."

He gestured towards the door, but Cooper needed something first. Once she was sure her legs wouldn't give way, she told Nixon what she needed. "As you know, sir, we have Charlene Blackburn in custody. The gun was found in her underwear draw. We're still following up on her alibi, but I haven't heard back from the lab yet. I'm hoping they'll find a print or some DNA on the gun that can tie this to Charlene but our twenty-four hours are almost up. I need an extension if I'm to hold her any longer."

Nixon nodded and turned his attention back to his computer monitor. He didn't have to say anything; the extension to thirty-six hours would be approved.

"Coffee?"

DS Paula Keaton was a mind reader. She held a cardboard tray containing four steaming cuppas in one hand and carried three ring binders in the other. Cooper took one of the coffees and headed to a table in the corner of CID where Tennessee and Martin were sat. She'd just got off the phone with her mother. They didn't speak often, but that didn't mean there was any bad blood. Her parents were living their lifelong dream of running a bar in the sunshine. Benji's Bar catered to the British and Irish crowd. During the summer the place was packed with tourists and brought in the big bucks, but it was the quieter winter months that Julie and Ben Cooper enjoyed the most, when the local ex-pat community gathered in the bar and swapped stories about the previous season. Cooper and Tina tried to visit every other year, and they always received a warm welcome from the bar's regulars. She wondered how they'd react to her new hair—or lack of it—when she and Tina made the journey this Christmas. Julie, her mother, had droned on for a good while about her friends, the Smalls, and had told a fifteen-minute story about a taxi driver that didn't seem to go anywhere. The story, not the driver. It was towards the end of the conversation that Julie had mentioned Ben's tight chest and shortness of breath for the past day or so.

"Mum! You need to take him to A&E."

"Always, such a worrier. It will have been that giant surf and turf he ate on Monday. Trust me."

"I trust doctors more."

"Well Dr Diaz will be in later; he's always in on a Wednesday night. I'll have a chat—"

"Mum!" Cooper had to stop herself from snapping at her. "Dr Diaz is an orthopaedic surgeon. You need to speak to a cardiologist. Do it today. Please."

It had taken ten minutes of persuading to convince Julie that it was worth shutting the bar for an afternoon to be sure and to put their daughter's mind at rest. *Family.*

Keaton took a seat next to Cooper. "Tennessee tells me you're up for swimming in the relay triathlon."

"Did he now?" Cooper flashed him a scathing look. "I'd rather scratch my eyes out. Speaking of which, I'm sure you've heard what went down last night?"

They all nodded, looking serious.

"And as for the swim, Martin can do it."

Martin coughed. He was looking even more well-kempt when usual. His shirt had been ironed to within an inch of its life, and he was definitely wearing a new aftershave. "Sorry, boss. I'm already in a team with Boyd and Whyte. We don't stand a chance, but it's for a good cause."

Keaton pressed her palms together in prayer and tried to give Cooper the puppy dog eyes. "Please," she said in a voice that was high-pitched and girlie and didn't suit her one bit. "I neeeeed to compeeeete."

"Urgh. Fine. Just never pull that face again."

Keaton punched the air jubilantly and folded her legs so that her left foot rested on her right knee. Her eyes flicked to the doors as Saffron Boyd and Elliot Whyte arrived. *Great.* Cooper's mind was suddenly in the past, hiding around the side of North Shields Police Station, crying her eyes out and hoping none of her colleagues saw.

Boyd and Whyte took their seats and nodded hellos to the rest of the team. Martin sat up a little straighter and couldn't mask his joy that Boyd had chosen the seat next to him. *That explained the aftershave.* Keaton pointed a finger in Whyte's face and said, "Morning Ell-i-ot," as if she was E.T.

Whyte, though lower in rank, didn't hesitate to swipe her finger away. Martin chuckled and mimicked Keaton's teasing. "Ell-i-ott."

"All right, pack it in," warned Cooper. "We have work to be getting on with. Tennessee, you're up first."

"Right. Fletcher's ex-wife, Hazel, also known as *the witch*..."

Keaton and Martin giggled.

"...is not in Turkey."

"She's not?" Cooper leant in.

"There's no evidence that she's in the UK, but she boarded a flight to Barcelona from Istanbul two and a half weeks ago and hasn't returned yet."

"Date?" Cooper asked.

"Second of June. She's been posting prolifically on social media. Several posts per day to both Facebook and Instagram since at least three days before Fletcher and Ibrahim were murdered. It's almost like—"

"Like she wants the world to see she has an alibi," Cooper finished for him.

"Exactly." Tennessee interlaced his fingers and stretched his arms above his head. "But she messed up." Five sets of eyebrows lifted around the table and he presented a printout from Hazel Blackburn's Facebook page. "This leathery-looking lady is Hazel Blackburn. According to Facebook, she was reclining on this sun lounger with a mojito at quarter past three on Monday afternoon, however, see this little detail?"

"Published by Hootsuite," Cooper read. "What's Hootsuite?"

"It's a social media management platform. It allows users to schedule posts in advance. Hazel could have taken that photo an hour before, or a week before."

Cooper leant back in her seat and savoured her coffee while she mulled things over. "Interesting. Find out what hotel she's supposedly at and give them a call."

The DS nodded.

"Keaton, you're next."

Keaton sat up tall and began to fill the team in on her and Martin's trip to Rowlands Gill to speak with Wayne Hanson.

"Martin managed to get some quality intel out of Hanson. He and Fletcher Blackburn were working together to muscle the Roker Boys out of Sunderland. They were after their territory. He admits to being at Morshaw on Sunday but flat out denies being there on Monday. Say's the diary entry is wrong and that he never saw Fletcher again after their Sunday meeting."

"Alibi?" Cooper asked.

"At the RVI most of the day with his sick daughter. I've spoken to the ward in question and have the names of some of the nurses who were on duty at the time. I'll nip over today and speak to them."

"Good. Tennessee, remind me to check with George Blackburn when we speak to him. See if he knows anything about another meeting.

Tennessee nodded and made a note.

"Okay," Cooper continued. "In case anyone hadn't heard, two of Hanson's crew were killed in Frankland during a riot last night. I'll spare you the gory details, but the photographs are in this file if any of you want to have nightmares. I'm not daft enough to put this down to coincidence. This is Eddie's work. He clearly thinks Hanson's to blame, either by killing Fletcher or by tipping off the Roker Boys."

"Do you think it'll escalate?" Boyd asked in her quiet voice.

"I'd say so," Tennessee answered. "I imagine Hanson will be pissed. He'll probably retaliate. We should probably tail him."

Cooper agreed. "Can't be you two though," She directed at Keaton and Martin. "He'll recognise you, and by now he'll know I'm heading the investigation. I'll have to arrange for—"

"He won't recognise me," Boyd suggested. "Or Elliot."

Whyte dipped his chin and looked to Cooper. My God, she hated his face. It had aged since their time together at North Shields, but his face still represented the way he'd made her feel all those years ago.

"We can tail him," he said. "We've spoken to all the nearest neighbours, and there's absolutely nothing worth following up. We're free to do it."

"All right. Be careful," Cooper said, looking at Boyd in particular, "and keep a good distance."

"What about the Blackburns?" Keaton asked. "Do we offer them protection?"

Tennessee snorted. "Waste tax payer's money protecting vermin? Besides, they can protect themselves."

Cooper was in two minds. She agreed with Tennessee's summation, but she also didn't want any blood on her hands. "One squad car," she said. "We'll post it on the road between their barn conversation and Bamburgh. Close enough to see any comings and goings, not so close that the Blackburns feel suffocated and do a runner somewhere we won't find them. I still want to keep them on side. Which leads me to this situation with the Roker Boys."

"Whether it was Hanson who tipped them off or not," Keaton started, "If they knew, they could well have done this to protect themselves."

Boyd shuffled and lifted a finger. "Erm, boss?"

"Yes?"

"I ran a background check on the private chef Lily told you about. Darren Ray, forty-three, squeaky clean, no record. I checked his website and social media accounts and found he was born and raised in Chester-le-Street. He trained at a catering college in Sunderland before moving to London to work with Marco Pierre White. He stayed there for over ten years, then returned to the northeast to set up his own business." She nibbled at a nail before adding. "He trained in Roker Boy territory. I wondered if he knew them back in the day."

"And that he might do them a favour by knocking off Fletcher?" Cooper finished for her.

She shrugged. "Just a thought."

"It's a good thought," Martin said with a smile. "Coop likes it when we spitball ideas. Don't be scared to share a theory with her." He looked to Cooper.

"Martin's right, and we should keep his name in the mix for now. I don't think Fletcher would be foolish enough to talk business in front of the chef, but there is a small chance the Roker Boys recruited him. It doesn't explain how he got access to Morshaw on a Monday. Lily said he was only there Saturday and Sundays."

"Maybe he left something on purpose so he had the excuse of going back to collect it?" Boyd said in her quiet voice.

Cooper wasn't so sure, but she didn't want to put Boyd off when she was so shy already. "Okay, well you know the drill. Trace, interview, eliminate. If you get anything, great. If not, don't worry. Let's not dwell too long on this though, we don't even know if the Roker Boys knew anything about the Blackburns and the Hansons. It's all speculation right now."

Martin's lips slid back and forth over his teeth as he mulled something over. "It's not like we can even ask the Roker Boys. I mean, imagine it, *Hi Guys, quick question. Did you know the Blackburns and Hansons were teaming up to muscle you off your turf?*"

"Because if they did know, they wouldn't tell us," said Tennessee.

"And if they didn't..." Cooper considered. "Well, we'd have a three-way war on our hands," She gulped down what remained of the coffee and got to her feet. "Tennessee, we have a meeting with forensics. Boyd, Whyte, you two tail Hanson and arrange for the car to monitor the Blackburns. Keaton and Martin, follow up on Hanson's alibi and pay a visit to Cedric in Local Intelligence. Find out all you can on the Roker Boys: the big players, known associates, latest addresses, likely locations."

Keaton nodded at Martin, they pushed their chairs out and stood up. Before leaving, Keaton pulled Cooper's file across the table and flicked through until she found the photographs from Frankland. She gagged. "Oh, Jeez. That's disgusting."

"Don't say I didn't warn you."

- Chapter 12 -

Justin Atkinson and Veronica Rogers both displayed the slow gait and exaggerated yawns of people who had been up past their bedtimes. Despite this, Atkinson still looked his tall, dashing self with a sprinkle of the Milky Bar Kid geek-chic that made him all the more adorable. Veronica, or Ronnie as she preferred to go by, was rosy-cheeked and without a hair out of place.

"Morning," Cooper greeted the pair as they joined her and Tennessee in the meeting room. "How was the talk?" she braved asking.

"Fabulous," Ronnie gushed, shooting a look of admiration in Atkinson's direction. "But dinner was better. Justin took me to Peace and Loaf. Have you been there? I had scallops with rhubarb and sea lettuce. It looked like a work of art, I almost didn't want to ruin it by eating it."

Of course Cooper had been there. She'd been there with Atkinson and had ordered the bloody scallops. Ronnie was right about it being delicious, but Cooper's stomach twisted at the thought of them there together. Had they ate at the lovely table by the kitchen that gave you a view of the highly skilled chefs at work? Had he ordered her the same wine he'd introduced Cooper too?

Pushing jealous thoughts aside, Cooper simply got down to business. "You said you had some updates?"

Atkinson cleared his throat. "Erm, yes. There were no fingerprints on the gun, not even a partial print. No DNA, no nothing. Someone took great care to make sure that gun was clean. They also cleaned the doorknob on the door to the bedroom and wiped clean the handle on the draw where Hong found the gun."

Cooper's shoulders sagged in disappointment. "That wasn't what I'd hoped for."

"I might be able to put a smile on your face," Ronnie said, spreading her glossed lips into a wide smile. She laid a file on the table, opened it and spread crime scene photographs out in a fan shape."

Cooper told herself Ronnie was probably a lovely person and it wasn't her fault she and Atkinson weren't together. Still, she couldn't help the bitchy feeling that bubbled up inside. She needed to get a grip. She was a Detective Chief Inspector after all.

"I'm certain our shooter was hiding under the desk when the second victim entered the room. Justin's team found gunshot residue on the underside of the desk. It's highly unlikely to have got there had the gun been fired above the desk," Ronnie said.

"And we also found trace evidence of gunshot residue on the hands of Dylan, Lily and Charlene," Atkinson added.

Cooper knew from experience that gunshot residue didn't equal guilt. Lily and Charlene were the ones to discover the bodies. They most likely touched the victims to confirm they had died or to try to come to their aid. Residue can travel up to five feet, so anyone who'd touched furniture or surfaces in the vicinity would have been contaminated.

Ronnie singled out two photographs and pushed them across the table. These are relevant to when Fletcher was shot the first time. You can see the damage where the bullet exited the body and hit the edge of the desk. When combined with what Ms Swanson, the forensic pathologist, has told us, I would estimate the bullet was travelling downwards at an angle of one hundred and forty degrees. There are also void marks on the wall behind where the shooter was stood."

Before Cooper could ask for that in plain English, Ronnie added, "Void marks indicate an absence of blood, where the spatter has been blocked by the body of the shooter. When he was shot the second time, Fletcher was on the floor. The bullet remained in the body, again that's backed up by Ms Swanson, and we have expirated bloodstain patterns on the floor where Fletcher coughed up blood before death."

Cooper winced but signalled to Ronnie to keep going.

"The second victim was shot in the chest first. Justin recovered the bullet from the wall." She handed Cooper another photograph. "The angle of the spatter tails is further evidence that the shooter was under the desk when this occurred. The victim slid down the wall, hence these swipe marks. He was then shot in the head, causing these high velocity spatter patterns mixed with brain matter."

Cooper glanced at Tennessee; he was looking a little rough. She frowned at the two forensic experts. All that information was interesting and helped paint a clear mental image of what happened, but she was unsure which part of the gruesome details was supposed to make her smile.

Reading her mind, Atkinson waded in. "Which brings us to our good news." He smiled at Ronnie then turned back to Cooper. "Without Ronnie, I wouldn't have been able to give you anything more specific than the killer was tall. But, Ronnie is an expert in her field, between her angles and formulas and algorithms, she's narrowed the shooter's height down to five-foot-ten to six-foot-two."

Cooper let out a long sigh and looked to Tennessee. He pulled the mug shot that had been taken of Charlene upon her arrest out of the file.

"Five-two," he said.

Cooper slumped and rested her head on the table. "Damn it." She appreciated that having a good estimate of the shooter's height was useful; it would help them narrow the field. Still, given the turf war implications, it would have been easier on everyone if the wife had done it.

- Chapter 13 -

Dylan Blackburn had one of his headaches. He tore into a fresh box of paracetamol and threw the information leaflet in the bin. Two tablets every four hours? As if that dose would even take the edge off. He took three, along with a higher than recommended dose of ibuprofen. He didn't have time for a headache; there was work to be done. Business didn't stop just because his father was dead.

Dylan stalked towards the stairs, briefly stopping to peer into his sister's room. Lily was lying on her bed, her thumbs busily tip-tapping away at her phone.

"I'm going into town," he said when she looked up.

"Bamburgh or Newcastle?"

"Newcastle."

Lily sat up and crossed her legs. She must have applied her make-up with a trowel this morning. She looked like a fucking drag queen. "You meeting Theo?"

Dylan sniffed. Wouldn't she like to know? "I'll be back later," was all he said.

His sister grabbed a pillow and threw it towards the door, causing it to slam in his face. *Brat.* Precious little Lily. Always annoyed at being sidelined. She didn't know how good she had it. If she'd had to work day in, day out with the likes of his father and his uncle she'd soon change her tune. She didn't understand the sacrifices he'd had to make to keep her safe. He continued downstairs and fished a black bin liner from under the sink. He opened the tumble dryer and stuffed the items into the bag. George was in the living room with his nose in a book. Dylan grunted at him. It was brother speak for: *see you later.*

It took an hour to drive into Newcastle. Dylan parked in the first pay and display spot he came across, pulled the bin liner from the boot of his car and walked until he found a charity shop. He didn't bother greeting the shop assistant;

he didn't care for small talk. Instead, he tossed the bin bag in the sheepish man's direction, mumbled, "Donation," and left, heading towards a street named Bigg Market.

The Bigg Market was once an important trading post for the buying and selling of barley on the Great North Road. Now, it was known for its nineties themed bars, dodgy takeaways and fights in the taxi rank. The street made national news when five hundred drunken Newcastle fans rioted after their defeat to Manchester United in the 1999 cup final. Phone boxes were smashed up and trees uprooted. All because one group of overpaid wankers could kick a ball better than another group of overpaid wankers.

Speaking of overpaid wankers... Dylan found Theo five minutes later in a seedy basement bar with topless barmaids.

Theo was a younger version of his father. Tall and powerful with a round face, a hairline that showed the first signs of receding, and dark, shoulder-length hair secured in a ponytail. He walked with a swagger, thought he was smarter than he was, and the way he talked about women fawning over him: he thought he was Jason fucking Momoa. He clocked Dylan as soon as he entered the bar and finished the few inches of lager left in his pint glass. It wasn't even lunchtime.

"It's five o'clock somewhere," he said, reading Dylan's questioning look. He raised two fingers at the barmaid and practically drooled as he watched her pull two more pints. "You know, cuz, if this is too much for you... I can handle business. If you'd rather be at home with your grieving family."

He didn't look like he could handle business. He looked like he was a few slurps away from slurring his speech. Drinking to forget? What was Theo Blackburn's conscience feeling guilty about?

"I think Dad would feel better knowing his assets were being taken care of by immediate family," Theo continued.

Dylan's lip curled. He knew this would happen. With Uncle Eddie behind bars, Theo saw Fletcher's death as his cue to take the throne. He'd always hated playing yes man to Fletcher when he considered himself the rightful heir.

Dylan moved closer to Theo and watched his face stiffen as he tried not to look intimidated by Dylan's malformed appearance. "I don't take orders from you. Until I hear different from Uncle Eddie, and only Uncle Eddie, business continues as usual. I do my collections, and you do... whatever it is you fucking do." He took one sip of his pint and placed the drink back on the bar. It tasted of warm piss. "When's Hurls getting here?"

Theo checked the expensive watch on his wrist, making sure he lifted his shirt sleeve long enough for the barmaid to see he was wearing at least twelve grand of

Swiss engineering. "Any minute now. I hope you lighten up before dinner cuz. I don't want your snarling face mean mugging me while I try and enjoy some lovely pasta."

Dylan bristled. "You're coming to the barn for dinner?"

"Lily invited me. Would be rude not to." He leant closer and whispered, "She's making a lasagne."

The smugness on his face was hard to stomach. "You're fucking disgusting," Dylan said as Hurls entered the room with his minder. Why he had that steroid monkey follow him around everywhere, Dylan would never know. Sure, he looked intimidating to those uneducated in combat, but he'd last less than a minute against someone like Dylan.

Paddy Harlow-Hurley preferred to go by Hurls. Double-barrelled names sounded a bit wank in the sort of circles they were used to. "Boys," he greeted them, "let's get this over with."

A pint was placed in front of him without asking. Dylan eyed him with suspicion. Why call them *boys?* The sons of Eddie and Fletcher Blackburn were not to be infantilised. Were the capos planning on making a move?

"First things first. When's the next shipment due? Decker's crew's running low, and my guys are onto the dregs."

Theo inflated his chest. "Some lads arrived in from Malaga yesterday. They're at the safe house in Craster until—"

"I'm not talking that small fry shit," said Hurls, folding his arms. "There's only so much coke a group of chavs can swallow or stick up their arses. We need kilograms, not milligrams."

"Friday," Dylan answered. "Six kilos coming into NCL from Tenerife by way of Sierra Leone."

That got his attention. Had he thought Dylan had been sat around on his arse since Monday? No, it was business as usual.

"You've got it coming direct?"

"Why give the Scousers a cut when we can bring in our own?"

Hurls pursed his lips. "Who you using?"

"AJ and Maggie." Andrew James Peters and Margaret Peters were two of their best mules. No one suspected a couple in their sixties who looked like university professors. Maggie was a genius when it came to smuggling coke in her luggage. Not only did she do things like hide smaller baggies inside sanitary towels and empty shampoo bottles, but she would surreptitiously drip sardine oil onto the suitcases of other passengers on their flight. The sniffer dogs couldn't resist.

Hurls nodded his approval. "And the cleaners?"

"Fully vetted." AJ and Maggie would collect their luggage from baggage claim and visit the toilets before immigration. There, they would strike up a conversation with the hard-working cleaners and drop their supplies into the cleaning trolleys when no one was looking. The cleaners would remove the drugs from their trolleys before finishing their shift. AJ and Maggie would walk through immigration clean as whistles.

If Dylan didn't know better, he'd say Hurls was disappointed. He'd wanted him to fail.

"Anything else," Dylan asked, getting to his feet. He had collections to tend to.

"Yes, actually." Hurls folded his arms and his minder mimicked him. *Monkey see, monkey do.* "I have a problem, which means Morrison has a problem."

Morrison worked directly for Fletcher; he was on the second top rung of the ladder.

"One of the boys we have working over in Arthur's Hill hasn't been handing over all that we're owed. I know he's had clients round the clock—we've been watching the house—but he's only forking over two-thirds of what it should be. Been going on for months."

"What do you want me to do about it?"

Anger flickered in Hurls's eyes. "I want you to scare the shit out of him, that's what. We're owed a couple of grand. Find out where it is. Morrison will meet you on Thursday. He's busy until then."

Dylan ground his teeth. "Theo can do it."

Theo's mouth flopped open. "Careful, cuz. Morrison asked Hurls to ask *you*. Besides, I'm busy Thursday." He said it flippantly and with a wave of his arm as if the idea of shaking down a rent boy was beneath him.

Dylan hated taking orders from Hurls, but he hated taking orders from Theo more. He knew what his cousin wanted. One poxy business course at the college—which he failed—did not mean he could run this family.

COOPER PLACED A CHOCOLATE muffin and a cup of lukewarm tea in front of Charlene Blackburn.

"Thank you," she said, tucking straight into the muffin.

Charlene was a mess after a night in custody, but the news that she was no longer a suspect due to her short stature had brightened her complexion.

Despite her relief, Charlene's face was still marked with grief, and she hadn't stopped crying since they'd brought her in.

"Tell me more about Fletcher's boys," Cooper asked. "I met them yesterday, they're both tall, just like their dad."

"All the Blackburn men are tall. Lily must take after her mother."

"Should we start with George?"

Charlene hugged the cup of coffee in both hands. "Well, George isn't like the other Blackburns. If he didn't have Fletcher's height and eyes, I'd say he was adopted."

"What do you mean?"

"He's nice," she said with a half-smile. "I mean, Fletcher was nice, when he wanted to be, but firmness and hostility came naturally to him. George is meek and quiet; he doesn't have a violent bone in his body. Even Hazel had a vicious streak. I never met her, but I heard she'd raise her hands to the children."

Cooper couldn't help but show her repulsion in her expression. She couldn't imagine raising a hand to her daughter. Cooper's parents had smacked her from time to time under the guise of discipline. It was normal in those days she supposed. *In those days?* It was only the nineties. Still, to Cooper, smacking was nothing more than lazy parenting and an abuse of trust.

"George isn't like them," Charlene continued. "He's not cut out to do what Dylan does. He's not built for it. I mean, he's tall, but he's scrawny. He couldn't intimidate anyone. He's too sensitive."

"What did Fletcher think of that?"

Charlene sighed. "He would tease him. He'd call him..." Her voice faded away. "He'd call him names that we're not supposed to use anymore. Fletcher was from a different generation. He didn't go in for any PC stuff."

"I know a few people he would have got on with," Cooper said, thinking of Superintendent Howard Nixon.

"George is a bright boy. He's a bookworm and always has been. He's good with numbers too. That's why Fletcher had him do the accounts."

Cooper nodded. "What about Dylan?"

She flinched.

"You know," Cooper continued, "you cower every time I say that name. Are you scared of Dylan?"

She played with a silver bangle on her left wrist.

"Charlene?"

"Everyone's scared of Dylan. You've seen him." Her voice was shaky. "Can't believe I used to feel sorry for him."

"Why?"

Charlene rubbed her mouth with her hand. "Do you know why his head is shaped like that?"

Cooper shook her head.

"Because of Fletcher." She looked ashamed just for saying it. "He kicked Dylan... When he was still in Hazel's womb. When he was born, his skull was misshapen.

Cooper had to work hard not to grab Charlene and ask her why in God's name she could fall for a man who'd kicked his pregnant wife in the stomach. She found herself agreeing with Dylan's appraisal of Charlene. The only explanation was money.

"I didn't know," Charlene said, by way of an explanation. "I didn't know that story when I married Fletcher. I don't know if he mellowed with age or if he and Hazel were simply a toxic match, but he never put his hands on me. Not once. The Fletcher I knew was a gentleman."

"How did you meet?"

"I was a dancer. At Stilettos."

In other words, she was a stripper. "Ah," said Cooper, recognising the name of the bar from the list Dylan had given her.

"Fletcher would come in once a week."

"To collect protection money?"

She shrugged. "I guess so. I didn't know that at the time. This was before Eddie went to jail and I just thought of Fletcher as a regular. He could easily have someone else do it, but he had an eye for the ladies. I think he liked coming to the clubs. He'd come in every week and we'd chat. He'd always buy me a drink, but he never asked for a lap dance or say anything lewd. We'd just chat for ages. I told him I was a fan of Hemingway, and the next week he came in with a first edition of *The Old Man and the Sea* for me. It was a few months before he asked me out. After that, I never worked there again."

Cooper gave her a supportive smile. That was quite the fairytale.

"I know people think I'm a gold digger, but I was earning good money dancing for rich idiots—really good money. I had a lot saved up. Dylan has me all wrong."

"And you're too scared of him to set him straight?"

Charlene gave a nervous laugh. "George told me he was sent to a special school because everyone assumed he was slow... because of his head. Dylan would fall asleep at his desk because he couldn't sleep at home due to Hazel and Fletcher's arguing. The nuns who ran the school didn't take kindly to him sleeping in class so they'd beat him. Then, because of how he looked, he was a target for bullies and would get beaten up by the other kids at lunchtime."

"It doesn't sound like he had an easy life."

"You don't know the half of it. The nuns would tell Hazel he'd been naughty at school and then Hazel would give him the belt. All he ever knew was violence. Then one day, his growth spurt kicked in, and he realised he was big enough to fight back. So he did. He never took crap from anyone again once he knew his fists could protect him. Fletcher, Hazel, those bloody hypocrite nuns... They created a monster."

- Chapter 14 -

While Cooper chatted to Charlene Blackburn and tried to find out any more details that might help the case, Tennessee travelled into Newcastle to talk to the owners of the eight bars who Fletcher Blackburn had been due to visit on the day he died. The young DS parked near Central Station and jogged across two lanes of heavy traffic to nip into a branch of Greggs. He bought a chicken bake, a sausage roll and a beef and vegetable pasty. His haul would hopefully keep him going until lunch. *If* he got lunch. It wasn't guaranteed these days, and devastatingly, any food waiting for him when he returned home was bound to be vegan.

Finding a bench, Tennessee tucked into his sustenance and fought off a couple of aggressive pigeons. A techie with an eye for detail had done him a solid favour and identified the hotel where Hazel Blackburn was supposedly staying. According to Tripadvisor, there were almost two thousand hotels in Barcelona, and because Hazel hadn't tagged the hotel in any of her posts, they'd had to use some detective work to narrow it down. The hotel had a rooftop bar; that narrowed it down to a more manageable one hundred and thirty-one. In the background of some of Hazel's photographs, four spires from the *Sagrada Familia* could be seen rising into a perfectly blue Spanish sky. Gaudi's unfinished basilica couldn't have been far away. They estimated it was within a mile and that brought the list down to only five hotels. They could have stopped there and simply looked through the photographs of each hotel until they found the one they wanted, but the techie had noticed that the basilica was to the south of the hotel, and that brought their list down to one: *Hotel de Tranquilidad*.

Tennessee made the call and prayed that whoever was staffing the desk spoke English. To his surprise he was greeted by Zara, a Geordie lass having a gap year in Catalonia.

"And you're sure? Ms Blackburn is definitely staying there?" he asked.

"Definitely. I saw her at breakfast. I can try her room, but I'm ninety-nine per cent sure I saw her get on the tour bus to Montserrat this morning."

"No, that's okay, Zara. Could you tell me if you saw Ms Blackburn on Monday the seventeenth of June?"

There was one direct flight from Barcelona to Newcastle per day, but it was also possible to go via Paris or Amsterdam. Technically, Hazel could nip into Newcastle, kill her ex-husband and be back in Barcelona in time for happy hour.

"Oh, goodness. Erm... I can tell you I've seen her most mornings. She likes to get to breakfast early so she can get one of the seats in the sunshine, but I don't know if I've seen her every single morning."

Tennessee thought for a moment about what Ronnie Rogers had told them earlier. "Would you say Ms Blackburn a tall lady?"

"No. She's smaller than me, and I'm five-one. Should I ask her to call you when she gets back?"

He told her not to bother. Hazel had a decent alibi and was even shorter than Charlene was. With his mind at ease, he shooed yet another bloody pigeon away and returned his focus to whatever Fletcher had been up to on the morning of the day he died.

Bambi Bar was tucked away down a side street called Pink Lane. The bar was situated on the upper floor above a nail bar and Thai massage parlour. If you didn't know it was there, you'd never spot the entrance. A small sign on an unremarkable door showed a picture of a young deer next to a flourished letter B. Tennessee checked he didn't have any crumbs on his shirt then pressed a buzzer and stared into a camera.

"Members only," came the reply.

The DS held up his ID. There was a pause and a stifled swear word before the door clicked open. A man in a cheap suit, with thinning hair and bird shit on his left shoe, met Tennessee at the top of the stairs.

"DS Daniel. Northumbria Police. Are you the manager?"

"Frank. Frank Ashman. And, yeah, you could say that."

Tennessee could smell stale cigarette smoke coming from fabric-covered chairs and barstools. A couple of ashtrays backed up his theory that Bambi Bar didn't observe the smoking ban. The venue was one long main room with doorways branching off to other rooms. A metallic bar was in the centre, staffed by suspiciously young women in cropped tops and booty shorts. A lone customer sat huddled over a pint glass with a tatty newspaper. He adjusted his posture so Tennessee couldn't see his face.

"I'd like to ask you some questions about Monday."

Frank's shoulders stiffened. "I don't care what you've heard. None of our barmaids are on the game."

Tennessee thought Frank doth protest too much. He suspected that behind the closed doors to the other rooms, he would find beds, and God knows what else.

"I'm sure they're not," he said dryly. "Now cut the bull. I'm here about Fletcher Blackburn."

Frank looked suddenly nervous.

"When did you last see him?"

Frank rubbed his neck. "Not in a long time. Years."

"He wasn't here on Monday?"

"No. His son is a regular though."

Tennessee sighed. "I said cut the bull. Dylan's not a regular. He comes here to collect protection money, right?"

"Erm..." A bead of sweat formed in the centre of Frank's forehead.

"Relax, Frank. It's not like I'm going to tell him you snitched. Dylan gave me the list of bars he was going to visit on Monday voluntarily. He was due to come by, wasn't he?"

A single nod.

"But he didn't?"

Another nod of agreement.

"And Fletcher came instead?"

"No. I told you. I ain't seen him in years."

"What about his bodyguard?" Tennessee pulled up a picture of Ibrahim on his phone.

Frank studied it then shook his head. "No. Ain't seen him either."

"Did anyone representing the Blackburns come in that day?"

Frank led Tennessee away from the bar and his only customer. "No. Dylan was in the month before. As usual. He's like clockwork. But business has been slow lately, which meant I was light by fifty quid. I was expecting a bit of a kicking, was beyond relieved when he didn't show."

Tennessee noted it all down. "So, to be clear, you haven't seen any Blackburns in over a month?"

"Swear to God."

"And you were here on Monday?"

"Yeah. From about ten in the morning to..." He thought about it. "To probably just after midnight."

"Can anyone corroborate that?"

Frank looked even more worried than he had a moment ago. "The barmaids. Gilly and Lola were working Monday. They're not in again until Friday. I can give you their numbers?"

Tennessee waited while Frank scribbled down two phone numbers. Bambi Bar was truly a depressing place. No wonder business was slow. It needed a deep clean and a visit from vice. As he descended the stairs, ready to walk the short distance to McDermott's, Tennessee couldn't help but contemplate what he'd heard. Fletcher hadn't been to Bambi Bar to collect his money. Had he gone to any of the other venues? And if not, where the bloody hell had he been?

JUST OVER A MILE away, Paula Keaton was reversing into a rare parking space at the Royal Victoria Infirmary. She locked the car and approached the Great North Children's Hospital.

"Good morning. DS Paula Keaton." She flashed her ID at the woman sat at the desk. "I called yesterday. I need to speak to..." She pulled a notepad from her pocket and double-checked the name. "Danielle Cutmore."

The woman's eyes moved back and forth between Keaton's face and the image of her on her ID card. Satisfied, she put down her pen and asked Keaton to take a seat. "She's assisting a patient right now. I'll let her know you're here."

Keaton's boot tapped loudly against pale flooring as she waited. She wasn't impatient, she just hated hospitals, and the name *Cutmore* made her uneasy. Who would want a nurse or a doctor with that surname?

"Detective?"

Keaton jumped to her feet and shook hands with a diminutive woman with white curls and a broad face. "I'm Sister Cutmore. I was told you wished to speak with me about Millie Hanson." She led the way down a corridor to what looked like a break room. "I hope you understand that I can not give out any information that would jeopardise patient confidentiality."

"Actually, it's not Millie I need to ask you about: it's her father."

The ward sister's brows lowered. "I don't follow, dear."

Keaton glanced out the window at a group of men who were smoking in the car park. They were hooked up to IVs, and two of them needed canes to walk. Illness and immobility weren't going to come between them and their nicotine hit. "I'm investigating a serious crime that occurred on Monday. Mr Hanson is helping us with our inquiries. He told me his daughter was being treated here for measles."

"For complications related to measles, yes. We wouldn't treat her in this ward if she was still contagious. There are too many sick children with weakened immune systems. Any outbreak would be devastating."

Keaton didn't know if Hanson's daughter hadn't been vaccinated on medical grounds or if her parents believed the conspiracy theories surrounding childhood vaccinations, but either way, she hoped Millie made a full recovery.

"Mr Hanson told me he was here all day on Monday, but I noticed while I was sitting in the waiting area that visiting hours are only two till four and six till eight. Is that right?"

"Yes, and no," she replied. "Those are the official visiting hours, but it's really at the discretion of myself or the doctors. Millie's pneumonia has been severe; naturally, her parents have been anxious to stay by her side. He arrived at about ten in the morning. I remember because two women were arguing over whether the television in the family area should be showing *Homes Under the Hammer* or the *Teletubbies*." She rolled her eyes at Keaton. "He stayed with Millie until lunchtime then he nipped out for a half-hour and came back with a stuffed toy and a meal deal. When Mrs Hanson arrived with their sons in the afternoon, he left for an hour, maybe two."

Keaton paused. Half an hour was nowhere near enough time for Hanson to drive to Morshaw Manor, kill Fletcher and Ibrahim, hide the gun and return home, but two hours was doable. Forty minutes there, forty minutes back. Probably more like thirty-five minutes; he didn't seem the sort to obey the speed limit. That left fifty minutes to fire four shots, clean up and get out. It was possible. Keaton didn't know if Hanson had done it, but she knew one thing: he was a liar. He'd told her and Martin that he'd been at the hospital all day.

"What time did he leave in the afternoon?

Sister Cutmore sighed. "I'd say half two. I can't be certain."

"And he returned between half three and half four?"

"Yes. It was before I finished my shift at five."

Keaton thanked Sister Cutmore and left under a haze of annoyance. She should have known Hanson was hiding something. She knew he was a lying piece of dirt, but now he was a lying piece of dirt with no real alibi.

It wouldn't have taken long to get back to HQ, but Keaton somehow hit every red light on the way. The traffic gods were not her side today. When she entered the lobby, Martin was waiting expectantly.

"How'd it go at the hospital?"

"His alibi's a crock of shit," she muttered, taking the stairs to CID. "He told us he was at his daughter's bedside all day, didn't he? He didn't tell us he popped out for a few hours in the early evening."

Martin was out of breath at the top of the stairs. "Don't look at me like that."

"Do your teammates know you've got the stamina of an asthmatic sloth?"

Martin put his hands on his hips and took a deep inhalation. "I'm fit as a fiddle."

"Aye, looks it," Keaton laughed. She pushed open the double doors and claimed a table at the far end of the department.

"The thing is," Martin started, "If Hanson was guilty of killing Fletcher and Ibrahim, why would he doctor the diary to make it look like they'd had a meeting? It doesn't make sense."

Keaton frowned. "What do you mean doctored?"

"Look." Martin opened a cardboard folder and removed some photographs. Keaton recognised them as the photographs she'd shown Cooper of Fletcher Blackburn's planner. He'd owned a leather-bound journal with lined paper that had been open on his desk at the time of the shootings and was, as a result, covered in red blood spatter.

"This is Monday's entry," he said, jabbing his finger at the image.

"Yes. I know. *Monday seventeenth. Family meeting at nine-thirty. Tennis at eleven. Wayne Hanson at two.*"

Martin's face spread into a smirk. "I didn't say read. I said *look*."

What was he on about? Keaton pulled the images closer and squinted. "It doesn't say two o'clock. It says fourteen hundred hours."

"Exactly."

Keaton continued to scan through some other photos, images taken from various pages in the diary, not just of the day when Fletcher was killed. "He always uses the twelve-hour clock. Ten a.m., eleven a.m., three p.m. I don't see a single other entry using the twenty-four-hour clock."

"I've been through all the photographs," Martin said. "That's the only one. Add to that, the handwriting doesn't match. Now, before you say anything about handwriting analysis being largely debunked, hear me out because there are noticeable differences."

Keaton hunched over the photographs as if she was shortsighted and needed to be within three inches of the prints to read anything. "The looped Y in Wayne?"

"Do you see any other looped Ys? Or Gs, or Js?"

Oh, he was a clever boy. Keaton grinned at Martin. "I think you're onto something. I don't think Fletcher wrote this."

He pushed a rogue strand of hair back into place. "So, who did? Who would use military time?"

"Ibrahim would. He was in the army." Keaton folded her arms. "But why would he want to frame Hanson?"

"It's not framing someone if they're really guilty. We still don't know where Hanson was when he said he was at the hospital."

"You're right," Keaton said. "There's a gaping hole in his alibi and he either killed Fletcher or someone wants it to look like he did."

"Or someone left us a clue?"

Keaton gathered up the photographs. "We need to speak to Coop."

- CHAPTER 15 -

COOPER REMOVED HER SHOES and walked barefoot across Longsands beach towards a spot Keaton and Martin had picked out. It was a mile of golden sand and award-winning clean water. To outsiders, it was a spot of postcard-worthy beauty. To natives of the northeast, it was just one speck on the one hundred mile stretch of stunning coastline that they'd been blessed with. Best not make a song and dance about it though. The longer the rest of the country thought it was *grim up north*, the longer the locals could keep it for themselves.

Martin waved a wooden fork above his head when he spotted Cooper's approach. A few steps further and she could smell the vinegar of their fish and chip lunch.

"Get 'em while they're hot," Martin said with a mouthful of fish.

The sun was high in the sky, beating down on the top of Cooper's head. She pulled a baseball cap from her bag to protect her scalp while Keaton dished up one more portion of grub.

"Don't say a word," Cooper said as they collectively looked at the odd combination that was a cap with a smart suit. "The last thing I need is a sunburned head."

The four detectives weren't the only ones taking a moment to appreciate the baking hot June day. In the northeast, whilst you were always guaranteed a winter, you weren't always guaranteed a summer. It made sense to get outdoors and enjoy the vitamin D while you could. Mums with children too young to go to school were building sandcastles. Teenagers queued up outside Crusoe's café to grab a bite on their lunch breaks and hold hands as they strolled through the shallows.

Dog walkers were confined to the north end of the beach, and a lone windsurfer was optimistically trying to right his sail despite the lack of wind.

"The water looks nice," Keaton said as she handed Cooper a cardboard tray of cod and chips with extra batter. "You looking forward to swimming in the triathlon?" There was a soupçon of sarcasm to her voice that indicated she knew fine well what Cooper's answer would be.

"About as much as I'd look forward to dancing naked on the Tyne Bridge." Cooper's heart suddenly darkened. What was supposed to be a silly quip dredged up memories from the spring. She didn't know if anyone from her team had seen the footage captured on the hidden camera Kenny Roberts had placed in her bedroom, but the embarrassment still stung. She hadn't done anything wrong, apart from being naive and trusting, but still, she felt like a prize fool. At least no one in the team seemed to notice her shift in mood. The conversation about the upcoming triathlon continued without her input until Tennessee arrived and nudged her shoulder.

"Isn't that Tina?"

A group of girls in school uniforms walked arm-in-arm, their giggles carrying far and wide. Tina was on the end of the row, and her free arm dragged her school bag through the sand, leaving a trail that looked like a giant snake had slithered through it. Tina usually spent every free moment she had with Josh, and their usual lunchtime hangout was the library. Josh was nowhere to be seen, and whilst Cooper was happy for Tina to widen her social group, she was worried she was missing something. Had they had a fight? She also wondered about the girls. Tina stayed clear of popular girls; she'd been burnt before by fake friendships, rumour mills and bitchiness. Cooper considered waving, but she didn't want to embarrass her daughter, especially if she was making new friends and even more so because she was wearing a baseball cap with a smart suit. These looked like trendy girls with overly straightened hair, HD brows and skirts rolled over at the waistband. Just as she was about to turn back to her lunch, Tina spotted her. She didn't look horrified, in fact, she beamed at Cooper, ran over, said *hi* to everyone, stole a handful of chips and scampered off again.

"Who are they?" asked the girl in the middle of the chain.

"That's my mum and her team," Tina answered.

"The detective?" one asked. She appraised the team as they sat in the sand.

"Yeah." Tina pulled in her lips as she often did when she was nervous.

"Hey, Ms Cooper!" another girl called out. "Thanks for locking up Mr Hutchins. I heard you lifted him above your head like a wrestler and slammed him on the school car park so hard his head exploded."

Cooper let out a laugh. "Actually, I slipped on the ice, and it was *my* head that was bleeding. DS Keaton here was the one who tackled him to the ground."

The girls made a collective, "Cool." Without an invitation, they sat down and bombarded the team with questions about the Tarot Card Killer.

After ten minutes, Tina checked her watch. "We have to go. Biology starts in five."

While the girls picked up their things, Cooper mouthed to Tina, "Everything okay?"

Tina shrugged. "I'll see you at home. Will you be back for dinner?"

Cooper wondered what that answer meant. "I'll be back by six. I promise."

With the teenagers trudging back up the beach with less pep in their steps than had been there earlier, talk returned to their current caseload.

"Why would Ibrahim put a fake entry in the diary?" asked Tennessee. "Did he want Fletcher to think he was meeting Hanson?"

"I don't think he did. I think someone just wanted it to look like Ibrahim wrote it," Martin said.

Cooper wrinkled her nose, and for a second, she resembled a bunny rabbit. "Perhaps it's neither. The killer might have written that entry in to throw our attention on to Hanson but didn't take the time, or have enough time, to mimic Fletcher's handwriting that closely."

Keaton picked up a handful of sand and let it filter through her fingers. "You don't think Ibrahim was working for the Roker Boys on the side, do you? Perhaps he put the entry in the diary on their orders but ended up getting killed himself."

"To leave no witnesses?" Martin added.

"That's really the only explanation we'd have for the Roker Boys gaining access to Morshaw," Cooper replied. "Even without the armed guard, the place was well protected. High walls, electronic gates, dogs, cameras..."

Keaton continued to play with the sand. "We should collect handwriting samples from the family."

Cooper nodded. "I want authentic samples. Things they've written at home when they've been relaxed, without a detective looking over their shoulders. When the SOCOs are finished with the house, we'll have a mooch around and look for notepads, shopping lists, diaries. Anything like that."

Everyone agreed.

"Tennessee, what did you get from the bars? And you said you wanted to rule Hazel Blackburn out?"

Tennessee finished a mouthful of fish and cleared his throat.

"Yeah. She's still in Spain. The receptionist recalls seeing her each morning for breakfast. Now it's possible to fly to Newcastle, murder two people and fly back to Spain in the course of a day, but it's a long shot. Also, she's shorter than Charlene, and I don't see how she'd get past the guard after what Lily told us."

"Fair enough," Cooper said. "What about the bars?"

"I don't know who the owners are more frightened of, us, or the Blackburns. Probably the Blackburns to be honest. I spent most of the morning trying to get them to admit that they were being extorted let alone tell me when they last saw Fletcher or Dylan." He pulled his notepad from his pocket and flicked the pages around a spiral wire until he found the information he was after. "Fletcher got to Feisty's first. The owner, Misha Rudd, told me he got there at quarter past twelve on Monday. He didn't hang around and was out the door as soon as he had his cash."

Cooper nodded. She knew Feisty's and its owner from a troubling case she'd worked earlier in the year. A case that saw her having to arrest her own colleague.

"Approximately ten minutes later, he was at the Silver Mirror. It's a pole dancing club. Fletcher bought one of the girls a drink and stayed for a while. The girl's called Sarah Lewis but goes by Sasha. She says he was a gentleman and left her a fifty quid tip. Doesn't recall seeing anyone going by Ibrahim's description. He may have waited in the car, might have been watching the exits. Who knows. It was twenty past one when he got to LOL. It's a nineties theme bar. The manager said Fletcher was looking a bit peaky but otherwise didn't have anything to report."

"What did she mean by peaky?" Cooper asked. "Nervous? Ill?"

"I asked, but she couldn't really say. Said she'd met him a handful of times and he'd always come across as a strong, larger than life character, but on Monday he didn't seem himself. It was about twenty to two when he got to Vixen. Vixen calls itself a gentlemen's club, but it's just another strip joint. Aleksei Pavlovich, the owner, said he introduced Fletcher to a redhead named Darcy Houston. He and Darcy flirted for a while but then his mood shifted and he wanted to leave. He got his money and left."

Cooper raised a brow. "She turned him down?"

"Perhaps. I haven't spoken to her yet. After that... I'm at a loss because Fletcher didn't make it to McDermott's or Bambi Bar."

"I wonder why?" Cooper pondered out loud while Keaton and Martin scrunched up the rubbish from their fish and chips into a ball. "Something made him go home. Did he get a call to lure him back to Morshaw?"

"I'll get onto the phone companies," Keaton offered.

"Thanks, Paula. And while you're at it, find out where Hanson actually was. You and Martin go and have a chat with him. Tell him we know there's a gap in his alibi that coincides with the time Fletcher's movements became unaccounted for. He can either tell us what the bloody hell he was up to, or we can arrest him for murder—his choice. Tennessee, we'll head back to Budle Bay and speak with George Blackburn. He's the only immediate family we haven't really spoken to yet."

Tennessee nodded. "And Theo. We should speak to him."

Cooper agreed. "And won't that be something to look forward to?"

"Like a hole in the head."

- Chapter 16 -

Tennessee used the drive to Budle Bay as an opportunity to call his wife, Hayley, and check in on her and little baby Alfie. Cooper couldn't hear Hayley's half of the conversation, but she picked up a happier tone to her voice than she'd heard of late. It was a good sign. Hayley put Alfie on the phone to speak, or gurgle, to his Dad and Tennessee sang a number of nursery rhymes to his son while he and Cooper zipped through the Northumbrian countryside. When they arrived at the Blackburns' barn conversation, they found Lily in the garden reading a copy of Marie Claire. She cut a stylish figure in a pair of bug-eyed shades, skinny jeans and a floaty, bat-wing jumper. Inspired by Tennessee's concern for his loved ones, Cooper sent a quick text to her mother. *How's Dad?*

Lily lowered her shades for the briefest of seconds and asked, "Where's Charlene? Why are you still holding her?"

Cooper and Tennessee shared a look. "Actually," Cooper said, making sure to keep her voice neutral, "New evidence came to light and Charlene is no longer considered a suspect. She was released this morning."

Lily looked put out. She pulled her phone from a designer handbag and marched towards the house. "Charlene? The police said you'd been released... You have! About time too. Where are you? Do you need a lift?"

The door to the barn closed and Cooper and Tennessee were left in the courtyard twiddling their thumbs until George emerged with a tray of drinks.

"Sparkling water?" he asked. The ice cubes chimed against the glasses as he walked. He placed the tray on the patio table and took a seat. "I assume it's my turn to *have a little chat*. I overheard Lily. Is it true? Is Charlene free to come home?"

Cooper nodded; he seemed relieved.

"I never thought she was capable of something like that."

Cooper and Tennessee sat opposite George. Tennessee removed a notepad and pen and waited for Cooper to begin.

"George, I wanted to ask you about your relationship with your father."

George scoffed and ran his finger up the edge of his drink, snaking a trail through the condensation that was forming on the outside of the glass. "What relationship? It certainly wasn't one of father and son. We were employer and employee." He paused to look at the sky. "Actually, I didn't have much of a choice in the matter so it would be more accurate to say we were master and slave. I used to be jealous of other families. I knew my family was wealthy, and I was supposed to be grateful, but I was always jealous of the poorer kids at school. They'd come in on a Monday and talk about what they'd been up to with their families. Building a den in the woods with their dad. Making a pie with their mum. Putting the sofa cushions on the floor and camping out in the living room. We never did anything like that. In Morshaw, it wasn't a case of children should be seen and not heard, it was a case of children should stay the hell out the way at all times. Until we were old enough to be useful, that is."

Cooper felt terrible for him. There was clearly an unhealthy dynamic to the Blackburn clan.

"Yesterday," she started, "when I said I was sorry for your loss, you snorted. Did you doubt my sincerity, or are you glad your father is dead?"

George leant back so that the sunshine covered his face while he considered the question. He stayed like that for a good twenty seconds before adjusting his posture again. "My dad was a bad man," was all he said.

"I heard what happened to Dylan when he was younger. From what I've been told, it sounds like your father was a violent man."

"That's putting it mildly."

Cooper considered placing a hand on his arm as a comforting gesture but thought it might be overkill and reconsidered. "Tell me more," she said.

"He created a monster. You just have to look at Dylan to see that. Beat the shit out of him so he'd beat the shit out of others."

A monster. That wasn't the first time Cooper had heard that phrase used to describe Dylan.

George removed his glasses and placed them on the table. His eyes looked smaller without the glass lenses to magnify them. He pressed the heels of his palms into his eyes for a moment before continuing. "If you ask me, I'd say Dylan snapped. It's the cycle of violence, isn't it?" His voice trailed away as he gulped at his water.

Cooper noted that the young man's eyes were reddening at the edges and he didn't look like he'd had a good night's sleep in a while.

"And as for Lily," he paused to look over his shoulder, "Dad controlled every aspect of her life. The precious little princess. You know, until this happened, I'm not sure Lily even knew what Dad and Uncle Eddie did for a living. The baby girl sheltered from the big bad world. Dad didn't even like her dating. Apart from the Hanson boy. Practically whored her out to broker that deal."

"Which Hanson boy?" Tennessee asked.

"The eldest. He's called Richard. Dylan and I just called him Dick."

Tennessee's mouth twitched.

"Theo couldn't stand it. Understandably. Called Dad a dirty old pimp. Course he's the only one who could talk to Dad like that and get away with it. He basically has immunity being Eddie's son."

Cooper's forehead creased into three lines. "Why couldn't Theo stand it?"

George rolled his eyes. "Because he and Lily are a thing. It's disgusting. They're cousins. They think no one knows, but they're not that subtle, and we're not idiots." He shook his head and rolled his eyes again. This time they looked like they'd disappeared back into his skull. "So, coming back to your earlier question. Am I glad my father is dead? The answer is yes. He beat on Dylan before he was even born, he never let Lily grow up, and as for me..." He stopped himself.

"What did he do to you?" Cooper asked.

George's eyes narrowed. "I don't want to talk about it." He picked up his glass of sparkling water and threw it with all his might against the wall of the barn. The glass shattered into hundreds of tiny pieces that scattered around the courtyard. Ice cubes slid across the paving stones, and a slice of lemon came to rest by George's foot. "My dad was a bastard. The devil incarnate. He deserved to die."

Cooper had been caught off guard by George's outburst. She'd heard he was the quiet, bookish one of the Blackburn family, but perhaps that was just when he was viewed in comparison to the likes of Dylan and Fletcher.

"George," Tennessee said, his voice calm but firm, "is there anything you'd like to tell us?"

"Like if I killed my father? No. I did not. And as for Mo, I didn't want him dead. He was good to us. Excuse me for a moment. I need to wash my face." He got to his feet, picked up his glasses and walked away.

While George composed himself, Cooper put a call into Whyte, and Tennessee stroked the belly of a tortoiseshell cat that had wandered into the courtyard.

"What's the latest on Hanson?"

"Bugger all, Erica—"

"Ma'am," she corrected him.

There was a pause. "I was under the impression you hated being called ma'am."

"You're new to my team. Until we have the level of familiarity and trust that I have with the others, we'll be using the formal means of address." What Cooper didn't add was that she didn't think he'd ever reach that stage. He'd shown his true colours when they'd joined the force. "If you don't like ma'am, chief is also fine. Now, what do you mean by bugger all?"

"We've been watching him since ten or ten-fifteen. He left his home to walk to the local shop, bought a paper and some Rizlas. Didn't leave home again until noon, when he, his wife and son headed to the RVI, which is where we are now, ma'am."

There was a tension in his voice when he added *ma'am*.

"Okay. Keaton and Martin want to speak to Hanson again. Call Keaton and let her know where she can find him. Don't talk to them when they arrive. I don't want Hanson making you or Boyd. Let me know if he meets any associates."

Cooper hung up and Tennessee eyed her. "What's the deal with you and—" He cut himself off when George returned. She wondered if he thought Whyte was a former lover and things had ended badly. She trusted Tennessee and would explain her coldness to Whyte, but for now, they had more questions for George Blackburn.

"George, are you okay to continue?"

He nodded and sat down. "Sorry about that. I'm usually more controlled."

"It's a difficult time for all of you," Cooper said softly. "I'd like to take you back to Sunday when your father met with Wayne Hanson. Were you there for the meeting?"

"Yes. It was me, Dylan and Dad. Theo was there and Mo too. Hanson brought a heavy with him, but it was all very amicable. Dad and Hanson were working toward the same goal."

"Taking out the Roker Boys."

His body tensed. "Who told you that?"

"It doesn't matter," Cooper said. "So, you're saying the atmosphere was good? There was no tension between your father and Hanson?"

"It was fine. They'd been meeting regularly. They agreed on the plan."

Cooper wiped a hand over the back of her neck; she was going to burn if she wasn't careful. "What was the plan, George?"

He flashed a knowing smile. "No comment."

He wasn't silly. He didn't want to incriminate himself or his remaining family. As he wasn't under arrest, he had no motivation to share that information.

"Did your father arrange for Hanson to return on Monday?"

"No." He shook his head. "We arranged to meet again in a week's time."

"How did you spend Monday?"

He glanced sideways, recalling the day his father died. "Erm, let's see. In the morning I walked the dogs. I took them up to Keilder and hiked a five-mile trail. I got back to Morshaw at about noon, had a shower, chatted to Charlene. She wants to redesign the garden. She wanted my input—"

"You like Charlene?" Cooper asked. She'd picked up on Lily's *mummy's boy* comment.

"What do you mean *like?*"

He was sensitive to it. When no teasing remark followed, he continued.

"She's the only person in my family who never made fun of me for liking books and stuff."

"What did you do in the afternoon?"

His cheeks reddened. "I had a date."

"Who with? Where did you go?"

"Her name's Rose Watson. We met at about two next to Grey's Monument, ate at Wagamama's in Newcastle then went to the cinema in the Gate. We had a few drinks afterwards."

To her left, Cooper saw Tennessee note down the name of the restaurant. "What did you see?" he asked.

"The new Tarantino."

"Is it any good?" Tennessee asked, lifting his eyes from the notepad.

George shrugged. "It was all right. Took a while to get going."

A rumble of car tyres on gravel caused all three pairs of eyes to turn to the driveway. A silver Mercedes rolled to a stop, and a towering man with a dark ponytail and eyes the colour of coal emerged. Cooper immediately recognised him as Fletcher's nephew, Theo Blackburn. That saved Cooper the job of tracking him down. He'd come to them.

"Erica Cooper, long time no speak," he said as he approached. He extended an arm and shook Cooper's hand. He stank of beer and was most likely over the limit. "I liked you better with long hair," he said as if Cooper cared. "You know, I think Dad had a thing for you. Pretty ladies were always his weak spot. It's the only explanation for him dishing on the other families. The Blackburns aren't rats. I bet he thinks about you while he's tucked up in bed in that cell of his. If you know what I mean."

Cooper knew exactly what he meant. It was nonsense. Eddie Blackburn did not have a thing for her, nor did she consider herself the sort of pretty lady a Blackburn boss would go for. Theo had only said it to unsettle her. It wouldn't work.

He turned to George. "Your sister at home?"

George glared at him, blinked, then tilted his head towards the barn.

As Theo walked away, Cooper placed a photograph on the table. "Do you recognise this gun?"

George swallowed. "Is this what..."

"Yes, that's the gun that was used to shoot your father and Ibrahim Moradi."

"Em..." He looked back at the house and rubbed his forehead.

"What is it?" Cooper asked.

"It's nothing. No. No, I don't recognise it."

"You do, George. I can see it in your eyes. There's no point lying to me."

He glanced at the house again and shook his head in resignation. "That's Dad's gun," he said. "He kept it hidden in his office."

Finally, they were getting somewhere. They knew who the murder weapon belonged to. Now to work out who'd used it.

Tennessee leant forwards. "Who else knew about the gun?"

George turned his head back to look at Tennessee. "Hardly anyone. Dylan, Theo, Mo and well, me. And even though we knew he had it, we never knew where to find it."

"You said he kept it in his office," Cooper reminded him.

"Yes, in his office, but beyond that, I couldn't tell you. Dad was a paranoid man. He trusted few people and to be honest, I don't think he even trusted those. I mean... look what happened. The bastard was right, wasn't he? Three times I saw that gun. Once he pulled it out of the desk drawer and stuck it in my face because I'd put a decimal point in the wrong place. Completely messed up our calculations for the new restaurant. Another time it was in a book, a fake book, one of those ones where the pages have been hollowed out."

"What had happened on that occasion?"

George turned his palms to the ceiling. "Some little chav kid from Blyth. Don't ask me his name—I have no idea—but I know he was part of Cannon's crew."

"And who's Cannon?" Cooper asked.

"He erm, he works for someone who works for Dad."

"So Cannon's a soldier?"

"Call him what you like." George was momentarily distracted by the tortoise-shell cat as it jumped on to his lap and purred loudly. He shoved it off his knee and wiped his hands on his trousers. "Allergies," he explained. "Yeah, this chav kid was selling... let's say, sweets."

"Sweets?" Cooper asked, making air quotes.

"Yeah, sweets. Anyway, he lost a bag of these *sweets*, said they'd been stolen, but Canon thought he'd kept them for himself. He owed Canon, which meant he owed Peters, which meant he owed Dad. He didn't shoot him. Just scared the crap out of him. I don't think the gun's ever been used, not until..."

"When was this?" Cooper asked, wondering if the unnamed chav kid could have been feeling vengeful.

George stared into space for a moment and exhaled. "Got to be at least three, four years ago."

Cooper concluded that unless the kid wanted his revenge served ice cold, he probably wasn't involved. "And the third time you saw the gun?"

"I saw it hidden behind the bin. I think he thought if he kept moving it, no one would be able to grab it before he could."

He'd been wrong. Someone had managed it.

Cooper got to her feet; she had all the information she needed for now. "Thank you for your time, George. I'd like to speak with Theo. Where would I most likely find him."

George rubbed his brow. "He's either raiding the liquor cabinet or doing something unspeakable to my sister."

Cooper hoped it was the former.

- Chapter 17 -

Theo Blackburn was what Cooper would describe as a workie-ticket. Nixon would say he was a good-for-nowt-piss-taker with an ego the size of St. James' Park. When Cooper asked Theo for a word, he picked up a copy of the Evening Chronicle and said. "Give me five minutes, sweetheart. I need to take a dump."

Charmed, Cooper waited outside the downstairs loo for five minutes, then she waited five more. When Theo still hadn't returned after forty minutes, she banged several times on the bathroom door.

"Can't a man shit in peace?" His voice was low and gravelly, but it cracked a few times. He wasn't angry. He was stifling a laugh and wasting her time.

Tennessee looked like he was ready to kick the door down, which gave Cooper an idea.

"Theo. You've been in there a long time. I'm becoming concerned for your safety, and as a member of law enforcement, I can legally enter a room to conduct a welfare check. If you don't want us to see you with your pants around your ankles, I suggest—"

The toilet flushed and the door opened.

"See," he said, zipping up his fly. "Alive and well."

Cooper hid her face in the crook of her elbow. "But we won't be if we stand here much longer," she muttered.

"That'll be last night's chilli."

"You don't say." Cooper's eyes were beginning to water. "Now, Theo. I need to discuss—"

"Shower first. Discussions later." He pushed past Cooper and headed for the stairs.

"Theo?" He was trying her patience.

"Come on, you know you have to have a shower after taking a shit."

Tennessee shot his arm out and blocked the stairwell. "Nice try. Now go back to the kitchen, sit down and answer our questions or—"

"Or what exactly?" Theo's expression turned from class clown to evil clown. Cooper had seen it time and time again with these alpha males. Tennessee had the height, clear skin and cheekbones of a runway model and men like Theo Blackburn didn't take kindly to being challenged by pretty boys. To be fair, they didn't take kindly to being challenged by anyone, but attractive men really seemed to get them riled up. Cooper knew exactly how to bring him back into line. She pulled out her phone and started dialling.

"What you doin'? Askin' for back up?"

Cooper smiled. "Nope." She pressed *speakerphone*.

"Westgate Unit. HMP Frankland."

Theo's expression changed again. This time from evil clown to little boy.

"This is DCI Cooper, Northumbria CID." She recited her badge number. "I'd like a word with Eddie, please."

Theo shook his head. "All right, all right. Hang up. You made your point."

As Theo skulked off to the kitchen, Cooper winked at Tennessee. He winked back.

"Let's start with an easy one. Where did you go after the family meeting on Monday morning?"

Theo already had a can of Coors in his hand. It whooshed as he pulled the tab and he gulped down the foam before it overflowed.

"Out and about. Here and there."

"Dylan called you that morning. He said you weren't picking up."

"I was driving. You're not supposed to use your phone and drive at the same time. It's illegal. Isn't it, detective?"

Dick, Cooper thought. "Where were you driving, Theo? Start talking or I hit redial."

"All right, don't get your panties in a twist. I drove home, parked up and I went into Newcastle for a few hours then got the Metro to Sunderland. If you're looking for an alibi, I'm bound to be on camera getting the train from Haymarket to Pallgate."

"Why in God's name..." Cooper stopped herself from asking why in God's name he'd want to go to a place like that. Some of her school friends had taken places at Sunderland University and had been housed in student accommodation in Pallgate. She'd visited once or twice when her gran had offered to look after Tina, and whilst she was sure the place had improved in the last fifteen or so years, she had no desire to go back based on what she'd seen at the time. She rephrased it. "Why were you in Newcastle, and why did you go to Sunderland?"

He drank, then he drank some more. "I fancied a few drinks."

"On a Monday?" Tennessee asked.

"It's as good a day as any."

Tennessee shrugged at Cooper. He couldn't argue with that. "So, these bars and pubs you visited in Newcastle, they wouldn't have been part of your collection racket?"

"I wouldn't know anything about a collection racket."

"Course you wouldn't," Tennessee said with a wry smile. "What about in Sunderland? We know you don't control that area."

"Went to see a friend. Walked towards the centre and had a pint in Fitzgeralds before heading back."

"Isn't that a good half-hour walk?" Tennessee asked before Cooper asked the more pertinent question.

"Which friend?"

Theo put his can on the kitchen bench. "More like twenty minutes when your legs are as long as mine, and as for the other question... No comment."

"Did you meet the Roker Boys?" Cooper asked.

"Who?"

He was playing innocent.

"Come off it, Theo. We know you know who they are. Okay, humour me for a second. Your uncle and Wayne Hanson were going after their turf and you were pissed off because you weren't going to get a slice of the pie, or the slice you were getting wasn't big enough for you?"

"That's a nice theory, DCI Cooper, but my response is still *no comment*." He looked at his can of Coors but didn't take another drink. Perhaps he thought it was best to stay sober, or relatively sober. "If you want more from me, I'll be needing my lawyer."

Cooper nodded. Fair enough. She could talk to him at the station if needed. For now, she'd wait and see what alibi Wayne Hanson came up with.

"We'll be off now," she said. "Take care, Theo. Give your father my best when you speak to him. Oh, and Lily's a lucky girl."

He met her gaze. "What?"

"Lily. She's obviously in bits about losing her dad, and not having a mother around, that's tough... I bet she's grateful to have you and her brothers to turn to."

ONCE BACK IN COOPER's shiny new car, Tennessee turned the radio on to mask their conversation while they pulled away. "Did you see how he froze up when you asked about Lily."

"He knew we'd be watching his body language, so he stayed still. Too still. He was like a statue."

"If Theo is in love with Lily..."

"And Fletcher wanted Lily to stay away from Theo and date the Hanson boy..."

"That gives Theo a motive... And he knew there was a gun in that office." Cooper turned out of the street and lowered the radio. "Do you know how bloodlines work in families such as the Blackburns?"

Tennessee shook his head. "Not really."

"Power goes from father to son unless the son isn't of age. We're not talking the age of consent or old enough to drink or vote. In families like this, they like a little more maturity. You usually need to be at least twenty-five to be head of the family."

"So when Eddie went to jail, the family passed to Fletcher because Theo would have only been, what, twenty-one?"

"Exactly. Now, are you thinking what I'm thinking?"

Tennessee slapped his hands off his thighs in a rhythm. "I'm thinking nine out of ten murders come down to sex or money. If killing Fletcher meant Theo could take the throne and be free to be with Lily, then it looks like he has twice the motive. His alibi isn't great either."

"The Metro? A little convenient. He could have killed Fletcher and Ibrahim then purposely went somewhere he knew would have cameras."

Cooper's phone rang. She fished it from her pocket and handed it to her DS. "Answer that, will you?"

"It's Nixon... Daniel here, sir. Yes, she's driving. We're heading back to HQ... Okay. Will do, sir."

"What was that about?" Cooper asked as she turned left and joined the A1.

"We need to go straight to the Freeman. Margot wants to see us ASAP."

- Chapter 18 -

As Cooper waited for the red light to change at the junction to enter the Freeman Hospital, she could feel her chest tightening. She gripped the steering wheel so firmly that the pads of her fingers began to throb. The lights turned green, but her foot remained frozen on the brake pedal. The driver behind her beeped their horn and Cooper lurched the car forward while it was still in second gear, causing it to stall. A group of young men in fluorescent vests who were waiting at the bus stop pointed and laughed.

"Coop? You okay?" Tennessee asked.

Cooper fought with the car and got it moving again. She circled the open-air car park three times. There had to be a space. There had to be. She couldn't face the multi-storey car park. Not today. Not after what happened. Was there a fucking convention on? Why wasn't there a God-damned space in *this* car park?

"Coop?" Tennessee touched Cooper's arm and she jumped. "Listen." His voice was soft but anxious. "Why don't you get out here and I'll park? I'll meet you in the morgue."

Cooper stopped the car and ran her hands over her face, they were shaking and clammy. This had happened before when she'd come to observe an autopsy on a prominent priest who'd died under mysterious circumstances. On that occasion, she'd been alone. No one had been there to witness her panic attack. She swallowed and turned to the DS. "Thank you," she said. Her mouth was dry. "I'll see you inside."

Cooper pulled herself from the vehicle and left the door open for Tennessee as he switched seats. She could barely put one foot in front of the other, and although she was outdoors and there were no walls to close in on her, she felt claustrophobic all the same. She forced herself to take slow breaths. Her abductor was miles away, in a secure unit, and could do her no harm. Still, she felt frightened. She pulled at her shirt, loosening it around the neck. She unfastened two buttons and didn't care if it was an unprofessional look that risked showing her bra, she couldn't stand the feeling of anything on her neck.

When she reached the hospital doors, she stopped to steady herself, aware of concerned looks on the faces of people coming and going and wondered what they must think of her. She wasn't here as a patient or relative. No one had given her life-changing news. She had to get it together. Cooper blinked back a tear and followed her usual unmarked route to the morgue.

Tennessee caught up with her at the bottom of a flight of stairs. "Hey. Erm, I can handle this if you want to stay above ground."

Cooper smiled at him. He'd always had her back. "That's twice you've tried to step in to protect my headspace during this case. If it was anyone else, I'd be giving them an ear full."

"But as it's me?"

"As it's you, I'll give you a pat on the arm and tell you I'm fine."

"You sure? You still look a little green around the gills."

"Well we're about to go into the morgue, so I'm probably going to look greener than the Tyne Bridge in a minute. You ready?"

Tennessee was notoriously weak around the dead.

"As I'll ever be."

He pushed open a set of double doors and led the way along a corridor and into an observation room. The temperature, which usually chilled Cooper to the bones, was a pleasant relief from the heatwave occurring outdoors.

From the observation room, they watched forensic pathologist Margot Swanson at work. She was elbow deep in a man who must have weighed over two hundred kilograms. She lifted out the man's heart, set it on an electronic scale, noted the weight and caught sight of her guests.

"Oh, hello there," she said. "Give me a minute to clean Mr Warner up, and I'll be right with you." She concluded what she was doing, removed her gloves and apron and placed them in a specialist bin before removing her face mask and goggles. She approached a filing cabinet that was set in the corner of the room and fingered her way through it until she found the file she was after. "Do you want to come through?" she asked.

Cooper and Tennessee shared a look, then they shook their heads synchronously and beckoned Margot to come to them instead. Otherwise, there was a chance some poor orderly would have to clean up Tennessee's vomit, or her own, or both.

"Let's get down to business, shall we?" Margot started in her melodic Highlands accent. She opened her file and handed Cooper her report. "Ibrahim Moradi. Homicide. Cause of death was loss of brain function due to a gunshot wound to the head. Fletcher Blackburn. Homicide. Cause of death was cardiac arrest due to gunshot wounds to the chest."

Cooper and Tennessee waited. This was one of those *no shit, Sherlock* moments. You didn't need a degree in forensic pathology to work that out. Margot was teasing them. She was holding something back—but what?

"But?" Cooper pressed.

"But, I thought you'd like to know that Fletcher was already dying."

"Well, he was getting on in life," Tennessee said. "I doubt he lived a very healthy lifestyle."

"He was only fifty-two," Margot snapped, "and there was nothing wrong with his cardiovascular system."

He'd touched a nerve and Cooper tried not to smirk.

"I was curious after I spotted yellowing in Fletcher's optical media and even more so after I examined his stomach. I sent some samples to toxicology, and as suspected, he displayed high levels of digoxin."

Cooper straightened up. "And what's digoxin when it's at home?"

"It's used fairly commonly in heart medications. It's usually prescribed as digitalis and is used to treat atrial arrhythmias and congestive heart failure. Low levels of digoxin would suggest Fletcher was using one of these medications but, as I said, his cardiovascular system was in fine working order. His medical history showed no prescriptions made for such a medicine."

"But you said Fletcher displayed high levels of this digoxin."

"Exactly," Margot said, pulling her soft curls free from a hair tie and running her fingers through the locks.

"Which means?"

"Which means Fletcher Blackburn was poisoned."

- Chapter 19 -

DS Paula Keaton wanted to get back to April, open a bottle of red wine and snuggle on the sofa. They'd been together for over a year now, and April had pretty much adopted Keaton's youngest brother like he was her own child. They had become their own little family. When Keaton was all sports, crime-fighting and sullen moments, April was a bubbly, ray of light who understood her demanding role at Northumbria CID and could make the best fried chicken this side of the Atlantic. Riley, Keaton's brother, had turned up on her doorstep late last year with a black eye, a suitcase and his piggy bank. He'd stayed with them ever since.

Keaton and Martin had just left a trendy little flat in a part of Gateshead named Low Fell. "What do you think?" she asked Martin.

"I say she's telling the truth. She did give us a frightening amount of detail."

Keaton shuddered, pushed the disturbing visual away, and called Cooper. "Boss, we've just left Hanson's alibi's place."

"Back up a second," came the reply.

"Ah, sorry, boss. Martin and I visited Hanson at the RVI after Whyte called to say he was there. We took him to one side, so we wouldn't freak out his daughter, and told him we knew his alibi was bullshit and that he was not at the hospital all day like he'd told us."

"Go on."

"Well, he fessed up that he'd been with his bit on the side. A woman named Natasha Cleveland who lives in the Fell. He obviously didn't want his missus to find out."

Cooper sounded distant. She must be using speaker phone. "And the bit on the side confirmed this?"

"Yes, she backs his story."

"She would though," Cooper added. "I mean, if Wayne Hanson tells you to lie to the police, you lie to the bloody police. Unless you want your thumbs broken."

Keaton slid into the driver's seat of her car and waited for Martin to jump in the passenger side after he'd stopped to tie his laces. "We believe her. She didn't spare us the details so expect to see inches, costumes and positions in my write up."

Keaton heard a snort before she asked how Cooper was getting on.

"We've just left the morgue. Margot wanted to see us."

"You mean she wanted to see our dashing DS Daniel."

Keaton could hear Tennessee saying something in the background but couldn't make it out.

"There's been an interesting development, Paula. I'll fill you all in at the morning briefing. In the meantime, could you follow up on George and Lily's alibis? Lily said she was working at Rachel's Beauty Retreat on Pilgrim Street and George said he was on a date. He went to Wagamama's and then saw the new Tarantino at the cinema in The Gate."

"You got it, boss."

Keaton thought of April. She'd have been home for over an hour now and would have no doubt already fed the cats, picked up Riley from band practice and done some laundry. She'd be waiting for Keaton and choosing what to have for dinner. She pulled over to send a text. *Don't worry about dinner. I'll bring in Wagamama's.* Within thirty seconds, Keaton had received a string of heart-shaped emojis as the reply. She truly loved that woman.

FREEMAN HOSPITAL WASN'T TOO long of a drive from Tynemouth, perhaps fifteen minutes on a good day and with a flagrant disregard for the fifty zone on the Coast Road. Sadly, today was not a good day, and as well as hitting rush hour, there were several camera traps set up on Benton Road. Cooper had promised Tina she'd be home at six and it was ten past when she crossed the threshold. She found Tina mopping the kitchen floor while Steven squawked at her for his next feed. His cute baby cheeps were long gone, and now he cawed as loud as his little lungs would allow.

"You're late," Tina huffed without looking up.

It was only ten minutes, but she'd have been a fool to think Tina wouldn't have noticed. "I'm sorry, T. I'm working a challenging case at the moment. I'm just pleased to have got home before midnight." She dropped her bag onto a chair at the kitchen table and watched Steven spread his wings and give them a tentative flap. "Hey, that's new. Does that mean he'll be able to fly soon?"

Tina stopped mopping to gaze upon her feathered baby. "From what I've read, I don't think he'll be ready to fledge until August."

August? That meant Cooper had to put up with at least another five weeks of Steven living in the kitchen. He had grown on her, but now he was out of his adorable, fluff ball stage, Cooper was looking forward to having her kitchen back. Not that she ever used it for more than microwaving packets of rice or reheating takeaways.

"I let him explore the back yard earlier. Thought I should get him used to the local smells. I made sure to scare next door's cat away first."

"Good idea," Cooper said, giving Tina a quick squeeze and looking in the freezer for something simple for dinner. "Pizza?"

"I made a hot pot," Tina said. "It'll be ready at seven."

Cooper appreciated Tina's efforts to help around the home. Her natural instinct was to worry that between cooking and caring for Steven that Tina's homework and grades would suffer. of course, Cooper knew there was little chance of Tina allowing that to happen. Still, there was a heaviness to Tina's voice that Cooper didn't like. Something was troubling her, and she wondered if it had anything to do with her new friends.

"What's with the new crowd?" she asked. "You and Josh haven't fallen out, have you?"

"No, Mum." Tina's tone had the aural quality of eye-rolling. "I'm just trying to widen my circle. Not put all my eggs in one Josh-shaped basket. If Josh and I did split up, I'd have no one."

"You'd have me."

"You don't count. No offence." Tina peered into the oven to check on the hotpot for a moment.

"So, who are they? Are you in the same classes?"

"The little redhead is Sarah, and the tall, skinny one is Lana. They're on the netball team. Sarah plays centre and Lana's goal attack. The other's are Lana's friends. They're all in the top sets."

"You've never hung out with your teammates much before."

Tina huffed. "That's because the team used to be made up of Shelly Smith and her friends. They all dropped out after Shelly... died."

A shiver ran down Cooper's spine. Shelly Smith hadn't simply died—she'd been suffocated.

"Anyway, we have new players now," Tina said. "I'm going to make a start on my English homework. This'll beep when it's done."

Cooper smiled. Her daughter was wise, but she wasn't entirely buying it. Tina had never liked having a lot of people in her life. She'd always had one intense friendship at a time, and until recently, that had been Josh. He was both best friend and boyfriend. She scrutinised Tina then nodded, "Okay. I'll call you when dinner beeps."

While Tina picked up her school bag and headed for her room, Cooper poured herself a cold glass of Estrella and sat down at the kitchen table. She hadn't heard back from her mother yet, but that wasn't unusual. The bar could be busy, and Julie and Ben couldn't pause the pulling of pints to reply to every text message. Still, she hoped her father was feeling better, so she sent a follow-up text. *Hey, Dad. Hope you're doing okay. Call me. E xxx.*

Her phone rang while it was still in Cooper's hand, and a quick glance at the screen told her it was Elliot Whyte. For a brief moment, she considered ignoring the call, but that wouldn't be appropriate. That was something Whyte would do. Instead, she took a deep breath and closed her eyes as she answered.

"Ma'am." To Cooper's relief, it was Saffron Boyd on the other end of the call. "Sorry. We're just across the road from the Hanson residence."

"What's the latest?"

"He's been cool as a cucumber all day. Even after Keaton showed up at the hospital to question him."

Cooper suspected there was a *but* coming.

"But..." *There it was.* "He's just blown his top."

"Why?" Cooper asked, sipping her Estrella and wondering if she was going to be called away from her beer and hotpot.

"Sorry, ma'am, no idea. We can see in his living room. The shutters are open. His phone rang a minute or so ago, and something's set him off. He's angry, like apoplectic with rage. Pacing back and forth. We couldn't hear what he was yelling from here, but he's properly pissed."

"Thanks, Saffron. I'm guessing word just got to him about the attack in Frankland last night. Can you and Whyte stick to him until nine? Let me know if he goes anywhere. I'll arrange for someone to replace you for the nightshift."

Boyd agreed and hung up. She called dispatch to have some plainclothes officers ready to replace Boyd and Whyte later that evening then checked the landline for any messages. There was just the one.

"Ms Cooper. This is Gus Laing from Redheugh Solicitors. Our client, Kenneth Roberts, has asked us to reach out to you regarding visitation rights with his daughter."

Cooper's heart felt like it had stopped. She'd had a restraining order slapped on Kenny within twenty-four hours of his arrest. He couldn't come within a hundred feet of her or make contact with her by phone, text or email. Sadly, those rules didn't extend to his lawyer. Cooper listened to the rest of the message then spotted the time it had come in: five-thirty. Tina must have heard the message. Did that explain the dourness in her voice? Perhaps. Whilst Kenny had never made Tina feel uncomfortable in his care, Tina felt betrayed by him. She'd let him into her life, bonded with him and finally formed a father-daughter relationship. Then one night this spring, Tina and Josh overheard Cooper yelling and came running down the stairs just as she was phoning the police.

The timer on the oven showed there was still at least thirty minutes until dinner was ready. Cooper took a long sip of beer to calm her nerves—Kenny had a way of making her skin crawl—and opened her laptop. She had research to be getting on with. She began with a simple Google search on digoxin. It didn't take long before she found that digoxin and digitalis were derived from foxgloves.

"All parts of the foxglove plant are poisonous," she read out loud. "Symptoms of foxglove poisoning include visual disturbances, headaches, nausea, vomiting and diarrhoea. Muscle weakness and tremors." If someone had been trying to poison Fletcher Blackburn, had they become impatient and shot him instead? Cooper hadn't spent long at Morshaw Manor and struggled to remember what plants were in the garden and surrounding flowerbeds. She swallowed her pride and called Justin Atkinson.

"Erica? Is everything okay?"

He sounded concerned. *He still cares, even after you treated him the way you did.*

"I'm okay, Justin. Sorry for disturbing you. It's actually a work thing." She listened for any sign of disappointment but could only hear the rattle of cutlery and din of chatter. He was in a restaurant.

"Oh. All right, go on."

"I spoke to Margot earlier, and she thinks Fletcher was poisoned. Digoxin."

"Foxgloves?"

"Yes." His intellect never ceased to amaze her. In the background, a female voice asked if he wanted a top-up. You didn't need to be a detective to work out that he was having dinner with Veronica Rogers. Again.

"Small doses over a long period of time lead to hallucinations. People who have ingested it report yellow halos and their vision can become tinted as if wearing yellow glasses. There's actually a hypothesis about Van Gough using digitalis, and that's why a lot of his paintings have a yellow hue to them."

"Really?"

"Yes. It's quite evident in Starry Night and The Night Café."

Cooper suspected Atkinson was enjoying the chance to discuss art. She typed The Night Café into Google and had to agree with the theory. There was an abundance of yellow in the oil painting. The felt of the billiard table was chartreuse in colour and around the ceiling lights, dabs of yellow in concentric circles implied dancing, golden halos.

"Listen," she continued. "You've spent more time at Morshaw than I have."

"And you're wondering if foxgloves grow in the garden?"

"I am."

"They do. Purple and white ones. You can see them from Fletcher's office."

Cooper nodded though Atkinson couldn't see. "Interesting."

"Very. I'll catch up with you tomorrow. I have to go. Ronnie's headed back to Manchester tomorrow morning, so the team wanted to take her out to dinner. I'm being anti-social."

The team. Cooper's mood lifted. It wasn't just the two of them, and even better, she was leaving.

- Chapter 20 -

Oliver Martin and Paula Keaton pulled up in the car park of a complex known as The Gate. The Gate housed a cinema, a casino and host of bars and restaurants. It wasn't everyone's idea of a good time, but Martin had met his first, and only, serious girlfriend there. In a German-themed pub named Wonderbar, no less. He'd always been shy around women and couldn't believe his luck when this stunner approached him and began flirting. After a stein too many he said something about her wearing a Wonderbra in the Wonderbar and immediately regretted it. Luckily, Steph saw the funny side, and after making fun of him for ten minutes, she leant in and kissed him on the cheek. He'd been on cloud nine all night after that. He and Steph had a whirlwind nine months until she took her dream job in Australia and made it clear she didn't expect him to go with her. Never mind.

Keaton and Martin arrived at the cinema just as a couple of ushers were struggling to evict a group of teenagers for throwing popcorn. Keaton flashed her badge; the teenagers suddenly remembered they were upstanding citizens, straightened their backs, closed their mouths and left without further trouble.

Keaton approached a tired-looking usher and asked to speak to a manager.

"Can I ask what this is about?"

Keaton didn't beat around the bush. "A murder."

The colour seeped from the usher's face, and she ran off in search of a supervisor. Keaton smirked.

It didn't take long for the shift manager to introduce himself and find evidence of George Blackburn having been at the cinema on Monday. He had a booking reference for the four-thirty showing under G Blackburn and the cameras caught him and a slender woman with strawberry blonde hair arriving at four-twenty.

"One down," Martin said. "How about we split up and save ourselves some time? I'll take the restaurant; you can take the beauty retreat?"

Keaton stared at him.

"What?"

Still, she said nothing.

"Fine," Martin sighed. "I'll go to the beautician's."

"Good boy. Now, remember you're there on official business. If you want HD brows or lip fillers do it on your own time."

If he didn't know that being taken the piss out of at every opportunity was part of the job and that Keaton had a heart of gold under all that muscle, he'd probably hate her. As it was, he thought she was ace.

"I'll bring you back a price list," he joked as he walked away. "I know how you like to look after your nails."

Martin didn't turn around to check, but he was sure Keaton would be flipping one nail in particular in his direction.

Rachel's Beauty Retreat was tucked away on Pilgrim Street in the heart of the city centre. Martin climbed a set of stairs and was transported from a dusty street suffering under the exhaust fumes of countless busses to an island paradise. Tropical ferns, which may or may not be plastic, filled every spare inch of floor space. Murals depicted sunny beaches and crystal water. Sounds of waterfalls and birdsong filled the room, and there was a heavenly scent of sandalwood and vanilla. A popping noise caught Martin's attention. Two young women were being served glasses of Champagne while they waited for their treatments. Behind them, Martin spotted a massage table in an empty treatment room. Tempting. Very tempting.

"Good evening, welcome to Rachel's Beauty Retreat. Do you have an appointment?"

Wow, she was beautiful. Sunkissed skin, shiny hair and lashes that were too long to be natural but not so long they looked fake. Pretty freckles, light brown hair, cupid's bow lips. She looked… just like Saffron Boyd. He knew he had a thing for the new member of the team. He'd felt it the second he'd laid eyes on her. But what would she want with someone like him? He wasn't experienced; he'd only had one proper relationship. Nor was he in a position of power, which was her thing, apparently. He still lived with his parents, and with the rate at which he was managing to save for a deposit on his own home, he would be living with them for some time.

"Hello. No, I don't have an appointment—"

"Well we are open until nine and can squeeze in a few walk-ins. Were you after a teeth whitening treatment?"

What was wrong with his teeth? "No. I'm here about Lily Blackburn." He showed her his badge.

She gasped. "Wasn't it awful what happened? Poor Lily."

"Yes. It's very unfortunate. I was hoping you could help me with something... No, not my teeth... I want to know if Lily was working on Monday."

"Oh, well, that's easy." She swiped left on an iPad, tapped her finger on the top left corner and seconds later a printer spat out what looked like a timetable. "This week's shifts and appointments," she explained.

She placed the sheet of paper on her desk and ran her finger down a column. "Here we are. Yes, Lily was in on Monday. She had clients from eleven until three-thirty."

"Thank you...erm?"

"Peyton."

"Thank you, Peyton. Could I have this?" Martin asked, picking up the timetable.

"Sure. Is there anything else I can help you with?"

His eyes went to the massage table again. Keaton would kill him if he kept her waiting. "No, thank you. Maybe next time."

Back out on Pilgrim Street, Martin found himself craving the birdsong and sandalwood of the spa. He arrived back at Keaton's car just as she did. She was carrying a large paper bag.

"Everything check out?" she asked, pressing a button on her key fob to unlock the car.

"She was working. What about the restaurant?"

"CCTV. They arrived at three-fifteen. He had chicken katsu; she had firecracker prawns."

A loud noise grumbled out of Martin's stomach. "You're making me hungry."

Keaton opened the paper bag and tossed a smaller bag in his direction. "Good job I got you some steamed buns."

Ace. He thought Keaton was ace.

TINA'S HOTPOT HAD DONE the trick. There was something about warm, comfort food that never failed to elevate Cooper's mood. Even in the heat of a summer's day, the best meals were the same ones Cooper craved in the dead of winter: hotpots, mince and dumplings, a vat of chilli, or a blow-your-head-off curry. Tina had remained quiet over dinner and hadn't wanted to talk about her father, though she did say something about Josh and how he thought she should at least meet with Kenny to hear what he had to say. Cooper didn't push it. She'd talk if and when she wanted to and hounding her wouldn't help things. Cooper made herself a cup of herbal tea and headed up to bed. Her brain was awash with questions, thoughts and theories and she doubted she'd be able to switch off at any time soon. And it wasn't just the case that was bothering her, it was the call from Kenny's lawyer, Atkinson and Ronnie, Tina, her father, Whyte. The list went on.

At midnight, Cooper gave up on her third attempt at counting backwards from three hundred as her way of falling asleep and instead turned to the Audible app. She downloaded an album entitled *Hello Sleep* and listened to the soothing tones of the narrator. He had her within an inch of drifting off when a memory forced its way into her consciousness.

She was stood outside of North Shields Police Station, her long hair—for it was really long back then—danced in the wind. Across the road, two children and their father played on the swings in the play area, and a man walked by with five dachshunds. She remembered it like it was yesterday. Her shift had ended. She'd taken a moment to enjoy some fresh air after an afternoon dealing with a bunch of teens who smelled like a brewery. A brewery that had been dipped in sweat and rolled in tobacco.

Whyte came jogging after her.

"Hey. Wait up, Erica."

He had fewer lines in those days. Tanned from a recent holiday and with dark brows and a downturned nose, he reminded Cooper of a Roman soldier.

"Listen, erm... It's Friday and after a shift like that... I was going to nip to the Bell and Bucket." He looked coy. "I wondered if I could buy you a drink."

It was a chilly evening, and the idea of a cool pint in a warm, old-fashioned pub appealed to her. Not to mention that socialising with people her own age would do her some good. She lived with a baby who couldn't talk and a pensioner who did nothing but talk. But there lay the problem.

"I'd love to," she told him, "but I can't tonight—"

"Tomorrow?"

Cooper tightened her coat around her. The wind was picking up. "I can't tonight, or any night really. I have a little girl at home. My gran takes care of her while I'm at work, but I don't think it's fair if I leave her with her more than necessary."

His eyes widened. "You're a mum?"

"Yeah."

"But you're..."

"Young. I know."

He nodded. "Ah well, no harm in asking, was there? Maybe in the future?"

Cooper nodded back. "Yeah, maybe." It felt nice being asked out for a drink. Even if she couldn't take him up on the offer."

They went their separate ways, with Whyte heading back into the station and Cooper beginning her walk home. She'd got about ten paces when she realised she'd forgotten her purse. Heading back into the station, her ears pricked up when she passed the break room and heard her name.

"Whyte struck out! Shit, I had twenty quid on you. Right, who's next?"

"Jameson's next." It was Whyte's voice.

"That wet blanket? I'll give him odds of fifty to one. Doesn't stand a chance."

"None of us stand a chance." It was Whyte again. "You know she's got a bairn?"

"Nee way?"

"I'm telling ya. A baby girl apparently. Has to get home to breastfeed it or something."

"She's only nineteen."

"I know." There was a pause. "Slapper."

The break room exploded with laughter; every synonym for slapper was thrown about. Called such names because she *hadn't* gone out with him. It was illogical, stupid, insulting, infuriating...

"Tell you what, let's all go to the Bucket. I'll buy you a commiseration drink."

Cooper fled before they could see her. Tears in her eyes, she hid around the side of the building until their voices faded. Whyte had been her friend—she'd enjoyed her shifts with him—and he'd hit on her as part of some silly game of who-can-bed-the-new-girl. Cooper wiped her eyes and turned to walk home. The guys were a good thirty metres away when Whyte turned his head to glance back. He saw her crying. She could tell by his expression that he knew why, and yet he never apologised. Not once.

Cooper rolled onto her other side and stopped the track from *Hello Sleep*. It was useless. She wasn't going to sleep tonight. She might as well get her laptop and do some more research. See what she could dig up on the Roker Boys.

She crept downstairs, poured a generous shot of whiskey into a tumbler and opened her laptop. Cooper had barely typed anything into the search bar when her eyes flicked to her phone. It had been switched to silent mode, but the screen was illuminated with an incoming call.

"Dad?"

"It's me, dear."

"Mum?"

There was silence, which was usual for two reasons: Julie Cooper filled almost every moment of silence with small talk; and, at this time of night, the bar would be noisy. She should hear gregarious ex-pats singing the theme to *Only Fools and Horses,* or pint glasses being collected in, or stag groups chanting *Super Leeds, super Leeds, super Leeds United*.

"Mum? It's gone midnight. What's wrong?"

"It's your father, dear. His chest pains... I took him to the hospital, like you said, and... they got worse."

She stopped to blow her nose, and Cooper knew instinctively that something awful was coming. "Erica, he had a heart attack."

- Chapter 21 -

The first thing Cooper noticed when she entered the incident room on Thursday morning was a foil tray scattered with dark brown crumbs. Someone had brought in chocolate cake, and the gannets had demolished it before the clock had struck eight. The second thing she noticed was the huddle of men and women, some suits, some uniforms, gathered around Paula Keaton. She was sat at a table holding court.

"Silk scarves? Ooh, kinky!" Cooper heard someone say.

Curiosity got the better of her, and she forced a gap between a young uniform and Tennessee to take a look at Keaton's notes from her interview with Natasha Cleveland. "French maid's outfit?" she asked, eyebrows peaked. "A little cliché?"

"Keep reading," Keaton urged.

Cooper scan read as childish giggles filled the room. "Oh! Wait. *He* was wearing it?"

Keaton nodded, a sly smile on her face. "It gets worse."

"I believe you." Cooper didn't need to read all the ins and outs—so to speak—she already had a pretty horrific mental image that she was trying to shake. "Okay people," she said, raising her voice to take command of the room. "Let's try our best to focus. Paula, put that file away before anyone vomits." She found her place next to the whiteboard and made eye contact with as many people as she could. "There have been a few developments. Firstly, as we've all read, Hanson has an alibi for the time of the murder." She took a red pen and drew a line through his name on the whiteboard.

"Dirty old perv," someone called out.

"Quite. Said dirty old perv was tailed all day yesterday. Saffron?"

Saffron Boyd swallowed and stood up. She wrung her hands together and spoke quietly. Was she nervous, or did she simply not like it when everyone looked at her? Cooper didn't know.

"Ma'am, em, boss. There was nothing to report until the evening when Hanson received a call and became increasingly angry. After the call in question, he paced for a while, and it was only once his wife left to take the dog for a walk, that he made a series of other phone calls, all similar in tone. He didn't leave the family home."

"Do we know who called?" Cooper asked.

"I'm waiting for the phone company to get back to me."

"Well chase them. We don't have time to waste."

"I will, boss."

Tennessee raised his hand to get Cooper's attention. "If he waited for his missus the leave, he was probably talking to the mistress. He knew we were going to speak to her, but he probably didn't count on her on giving quite so many details. Might explain his anger?"

"It could." Cooper paused, hugging a beige coloured folder to her chest. "Or, word reached him about what went down in Frankland."

"You're right," Tennessee said. "I wouldn't be surprised if he fired back in some way."

"I can guarantee he'll want revenge. We need to act quickly. Before Nixon gives himself a heart attack—" The word caught in her throat and she struggled to fight back the tears. Ben was undergoing bypass surgery to improve blood flow to his myocardium. She wouldn't be able to speak to him for hours, possibly days, so for now, she had to battle on. "Is Hanson still at home?" she directed at Boyd.

"As of twenty minutes ago. That's when I called the team who took over from us last night."

"Which brings us to the other developments." Cooper filled her lungs with air and exhaled slowly. "Regarding the murder weapon. Both Dylan and Charlene deny having ever seen the Glock. However, George tells us that not only did the gun belong to his father, but that Dylan knew about it and therefore lied to us. Now according to George, Theo would have also known that a gun was stashed in the office at all times, and Dylan told us Theo used to go clay pigeon shooting. I had someone check the SGC records; Theo Blackburn was the registered keeper of a Blaser F16 from 2016 to 2018. Prior to that, he had a Beretta DT11. His licence has expired, but young Theo was quite the marksman. He was a regional champion at fourteen and national champion at sixteen."

Around the room, people exchanged glances at the news that Theo knew how to handle guns much bigger than a Glock. 29.

"But here's the real kicker," Cooper continued. "Fletcher Blackburn may have died from gunshot wounds to his chest, but he was also poisoned."

A murmur floated through the incident room like a Mexican wave, moving from Cooper at the front to the officers right at the back. Heads turned, shoulders shrugged.

"A chemical derived from foxgloves was found in his system during the autopsy. It's highly toxic, and chances are that Fletcher was either very ill or indeed dying when he was shot."

Martin shuffled in his seat and caught Cooper's eye. "Didn't the man who owns LOL say Fletcher was looking peaky?"

Tennessee spoke in the affirmative. "Yeah. Said he was sweating and tugging on his collar."

Cooper nodded. "That makes sense."

Keaton was wiggling her pen around in the air.

"Paula?"

"Are we thinking someone got bored waiting for the poison to kick in?"

"That's what I was wondering. I've already taken the liberty of printing off the search histories from the laptops and tablets the SOCOs removed from the Blackburn residence. Printouts are in your files, but I've seen nothing to suggest any of the Blackburns were researching poisons."

"Surely they would have wiped their search history."

"I would have thought so," Cooper said. "But regardless, nothing is ever truly deleted. Tech will update us if they find anything at all relating to foxgloves or poisons. Tennessee, Keaton and Martin, we're going to Morshaw. I want handwriting samples for each member of the family. The fake entry in the diary is still a key piece of evidence. Whyte and Boyd, stick to Hanson like glue. He probably knows he's being tailed and therefore won't get up to much."

"What about the Roker Boys?" Whyte asked. "Shouldn't we put them under surveillance?"

Keaton pulled a file from within another file. "Here's what we got from Local Intelligence. No top guy as such. It's a four-way partnership. Toby Beck, Richie Boyer, Alex Deacon and Kayla Dunn."

"Kayla?" Whyte looked doubtful.

"You heard. Despite their name, the Roker Boys are shattering the glass ceiling for female mobsters everywhere."

"Go feminism," Cooper said dryly. "Nixon's not going to approve much or anything in the way of surveillance. Budgets are tight, overtime is a thing of the past, and we don't have anything to justify a warrant, let alone a phone tap. The best we can do is talk to them and get alibis for the time of the murder. Can you action it, Whyte?"

Whyte nodded. "I'll get the locals on it. Do we have the names of their capos and soldiers?" he asked using the mafia terms for those below boss-level on the mob family tree.

"All in the file," Keaton said, handing it to Whyte. She stood up and popped on a pair of sunglasses. "Right then. It's a lovely day, let's go catch a killer."

- Chapter 22 -

Dylan Blackburn knocked on the door of a house in Arthur's Hill. The house had no door number, not that it mattered, it never received any post because officially, no one lived there. When no one answered within ten seconds, he began to knock harder and harder. A constant thunder of fist against wood until it was opened by a small, undernourished man with a haircut that made him look like a toilet brush. Dylan Blackburn was not the sort of man to wait for an invitation. He forced his way in, picked the man up in a vice-like grip and carried the starveling to the kitchen where he dropped him onto a plastic chair.

"Here, man, Dylan. There's nee need for this."

Behind him, Dylan could hear Morrison following him in and shutting the front door.

"Quiet," Dylan said. He pulled a length of rope from his back pocket and began securing the man to the chair.

"Dylan! Dylan!" His voice was filled with fear. "Whatever he's told you, it's bollocks. I swear, it's bollocks."

Morrison lurked in the doorway to the kitchen. "Where's the money, Pickett?"

"What money?"

Dylan had no patience for Pickett. He was a dirty rent boy who should be grateful. Most little shits in his line of work lived on the street. They'd sheltered him, given him a safe place to sleep in exchange for a fair share of the profits, and because Pickett—who was nineteen or twenty—looked about thirteen years old, there was always plenty of profit. Dylan didn't take any joy in hurting skinny weaklings, especially if they'd never raised a hand to him first, so he gave the scrote one last chance.

"Truth or dare?"

Pickett stopped squirming and looked up. He had a sore on his mouth and what was either terrible acne or a suspicious-looking rash across one side of his face and down his neck. "Huh?"

Dylan repeated himself, more slowly this time. "Truth or dare? Truth, you tell me where the money is, or dare, you pull out one of your teeth with these."

He slammed a pair of pliers on the kitchen table so hard that Pickett jumped in his seat and let out a squeal like a rusty hinge. "Nee way. Come on, Dylan, I didn't take any money. I didn't. I didn't."

He started to cry. Man, he hated it when they cried. The criers reminded him of himself when he was seven or eight, when the other kids would form a circle around him in the schoolyard and take turns spitting on the weird-looking kid. Dylan knew what was at stake here. Morrison was a capo and wouldn't usually concern himself with these matters. He should have left it with Hurls to divvy it out to one associate or another. Still, Morrison—one level down from Fletcher—had told Hurls to tell Dylan. It was a test; Dylan had to show strength. He had to show he was unflappable and capable of handling anything. He was Fletcher Blackburn's eldest son and the throne should go to him. He'd fucking earned it, unlike Theo, who caused nothing but trouble. He had to show he was a leader before this whole enterprise went to shit.

"Don't want to play truth or dare, Pickett? That's fine, you can take the forfeit instead."

"Nah, nah. Dylan, listen... Listen, mate—"

"I'm not your mate."

"Sorry. Sorry, Dylan." He tried to hold up his hands to apologise, but because of the rope, couldn't lift them more than a centimetre from his thighs. "It's not that I don't want to play. Truth. I pick truth."

Dylan scraped a second chair across the linoleum floor and sat facing the thin, frightened man. "All right." Dylan leant in so that his face was less than three inches from Pickett's and yelled, "WHERE IS THE MONEY?"

More tears ran down his face. "There is no money. I haven't been lifting. That's the truth, Dylan. That's the truth. Hurls has just got it in for me."

Dylan could feel the rage building as it had done so many times before. He struggled to keep it at a simmer. "I'd think carefully about insulting someone like Hurls."

He couldn't kill him. Well, he could—easily. But dissolving their under-sized earner isna vat of hydrofluoric acid wouldn't get them their money back, and it would cut their future income.

"I wasn't insulting him. I was just—"

Dylan looked at Morrison. He didn't look impressed. *Shit*. It was time to get serious.

"Just nothing," Dylan growled. "I've had enough. You get the forfeit. Time to say goodbye to your legs."

He stood, grabbed both of Pickett's legs and placed his feet on the chair from which he'd just stood. He raised his own foot and hovered it above Pickett's left knee joint.

"No, no, no, no, no, no. Not my legs. Please, please, I need my legs."

Tears flooded from his eyes.

"You're a fucking low life, addict, rent boy. You don't need legs; you only need your gob and your arse."

Dylan stomped his leg downwards. Through the thick soles of his boot, he still felt the snapping of Pickett's fibula and tibia.

The scream that followed was bound to trigger a migraine; it would kick in in an hour or two. It was a good thing they'd soundproofed this place.

Saliva poured from Pickett's open mouth as he writhed in the chair. Dylan raised his foot again, this time hovering it over his right leg.

"WAIT," he bellowed, closing his eyes. "Under... the bed... Loose floorboard."

Bingo.

Dylan kept his leg raised and primed while Morrison went to check. When he returned, he was waving a wad of cash.

"Three g's."

Dylan placed his foot back on the floor and looked down on the snivelling thief.

"Please... I need an ambulance."

Morrison had barely taken his phone from his pocket when Dylan slapped it from his hand. The phone skidded across the dirty floor and came to a stop by an overflowing bin. Morrison looked like his spleen was ready to blow.

"We need the lad fixing up so he can see punters again," he growled.

"You mental? Bringing the flashing blue lights round here?"

"I was going to leave him in the street," Morrison said through clenched teeth.

Dylan walked right up to Morrison and towered over him. "Still too close for comfort. Drop him by the phone box in the park." He pushed past him. "And have someone follow him to the hospital. Make sure he doesn't nick off."

Dylan needed to get home and take a beta-blocker before his vision started to cloud, but despite his sore head, Dylan smiled as he strode away. He'd just given a capo an order. What did that make him?

IN ANOTHER AREA OF Newcastle, Aleksei Pavlovich unlocked Vixen. He deactivated the gentlemen's club's alarm system and picked up his post from the doormat. He shuffled the letters together into a neat pile and thumbed through them one by one. Electric bill, tax demand, flyer for Indian food, bank statement and, oh joy, a letter from the water company to say his rates were going up. Again.

Aleksei switched on the lights and shielded his eyes as the bulbs stuttered and flickered into life. What had become of his baby? His club had been the talk of the town when he opened in 1995. Lawyers brought clients here for a light lunch, to butter them up and seal the deal. Accountants came after work to celebrate having saved their bosses millions by making a thousand hard-working, blue-collar guys redundant. Footballers came to throw their money around and party the night away. He had the prettiest girls in town and the money they attracted meant Aleksei had been able to buy the most exquisite things for the club. It had been opulent. Now, his baby was depressed, like a faded photograph or a wilting flower. It made him sad just to be there. Lad culture was discouraged in big businesses; shareholders had no interest in indiscretions that could land their firm on the wrong side of a Twitter mob. And the footballers stayed away, instead choosing to spend time with their families. What was the world coming to?

Aleksei opened the dishwasher and found two glasses hadn't survived the wash cycle. *Wonderful. More things that need replacing*. There'd been a leak in the bathroom for three weeks now, and he couldn't afford a plumber. His favourite blonde had quit after getting herself pregnant, the graceful brunette with legs up to her armpits hadn't shown up in days, he was behind on his car payments and he was sure one of the bouncers had his fingers in the till. And now, to top it off, Fletcher Blackburn was dead.

Aleksei was no fan of Fletcher Blackburn, nor was he a fan of his ogreish son. Coming round every month demanding their *pizzo*. That's what the Italians call it: a *pizzo*. Aleksei called it extortion. At least Fletcher had been consistent, the pizzo hadn't been raised since the turn of the millennium. Just shy of a monkey each and every month. Four hundred and fifty fucking quid. It was money Aleksei could have used to fix the leak, to pay his car off, to put towards his mounting credit card debt. Now Fletcher was gone Aleksei was worried about who would take his place, because someone would definitely take his place. And when they did, how much would the pizzo be then?

There was a noise in the back alley. The damn cat must have got in the bins again. He thumbed through the pile of letters once more and let out a long sigh at his electric bill. Choosing the ostrich approach of burying his head in the sand, Aleksei dropped the pile of letters in the bin. They could wait until next month's reminder.

Years ago, Aleksei had tried to rally the other bar, club and restaurant owners in this and the surrounding streets. He'd heard of the *addiopizzo* movement in Sicily and hoped to start something similar in Newcastle. A union of sorts. But people were nervous about going against the Blackburns. Venues had been trashed for refusal to pay, people had been hurt, maybe even killed. Aleksei poured himself an apple juice and leant over to rest his head on the bar; it smelled of cleaning products. Perhaps, now that Fletcher was dead, it would be a good time to try and form his *addiopizzo* union again. He closed his eyes and wondered if such a thing could work on Tyneside, then he was distracted by another noise.

Aleksei froze, focusing his hearing towards the dressing room that the girls used. There was a rustling and a crackling, followed by a whooshing noise. It wasn't the damn cat, and it wasn't in the back alley.

- Chapter 23 -

Forensics thought they'd collected all they needed from the Blackburns' home in rural Northumberland, but given the news about Fletcher's digoxin poisoning, they pulled their bunny suits back on and scattered themselves around the grounds of the manor home in search of more clues. With the SOCOs dressed in identical white all-in-ones, complete with hoods and boots, it was impossible to distinguish one from the other. Atkinson could be any of them. Cooper had her team record their attendance in the crime scene log book, then they pulled on their own PPE to protect the scene and got to work looking for handwriting samples. The grounds, study and kitchen were bustling with activity, so they began upstairs in the bedrooms.

"This is the master bedroom," Cooper said, pushing open a heavy, solid wood door. It was exactly how they had left it on Tuesday. That was only two days ago and yet so much had happened. It was one of those weeks when you were so busy that time slipped away from you and days ended before you even felt like they had begun and yet the week passed at a snail's pace. Despite the slow pace, Cooper loved the hunt, not in the visceral way that Keaton loved it, but in the problem-solving sense. This was a logic puzzle that needed to be unlocked. Unfortunately, as much as Cooper wanted to see the case through to the end, there was the matter of her father and her need to see him as soon as possible. When Ben Cooper came out of surgery, he'd be kept in intensive care, be monitored for arrhythmia and pumped full of drugs to thin his blood. Part of her craved stability. Wouldn't it be nice to have the sort of job where you could take leave whenever it was required? To work the same hours each day, knowing exactly what was expected of you and what needed doing for each shift? *No,* she thought, stopping by the dresser drawer where Hong Evanstad had found Fletcher's gun. *Absolutely not.*

Unable to do anything for Ben right now, Cooper turned her attention back to the search. "Anything with handwriting on it is useful," Cooper told the team. "This is the room Charlene shared with Fletcher. We've removed Charlene from our list of most likely suspects based on her height and the evidence from our hired help from Greater Manchester, but let's be thorough. Find something she wrote just to back that up."

Tennessee took a sniff of the wine glass that had been abandoned on the bedside table and wrinkled his nose. "Smells like vinegar." He picked up a romance novel with a fancy lace bookmark hanging from it and read the title. "Summer in Sicily: A Mobster Romance? I guess Charlene Blackburn has a type."

Keaton suppressed a laugh. "My mum used to read that type of book. Western romance, billionaire romance, bad boy romance, reverse harem. You name it, it's out there."

"What the hell's reverse harem?" Martin pulled a spiral-bound notepad out of a junk drawer and flicked through the lined pages. "Blank," he added.

Keaton found an old Valentine's card in a shoebox at the back of Fletcher's wardrobe. "One woman, lots of boyfriends. What other books does she have over there?"

Tennessee put *Summer in Sicily* back down on the bedside table."She has eclectic tastes. There's Hemingway, Wilde, a Stephen King novella and... Oh, what do we have here? *Gardening Through the Year.*"

Cooper looked over. "George told us Charlene was redesigning the garden."

"You don't need to be six-foot-two to poison someone," Tennessee added. "Maybe Charlene stumbled across toxic plants during her research. We might have been too quick in releasing her."

"You're right." Cooper took the book as evidence. "But let's stay on track for now. I want handwriting samples."

Keaton handed the Valentine's card she found to Cooper, who examined the pink, glittery writing. "*I love you with all my heart*...Looped tails here on the Y of *you* and again on the Y of *my*."

"Different structure overall though," Keaton said. "Too round compared to the diary entry." She held a copy of the page in question. "This is more oval based and very slanted. Like it's written in italics."

Cooper agreed. The two samples were very different. "Shall we move on?" The team followed her from the master bedroom, past a bathroom and a home gym, to the next room along the hallway. She stopped to check a room plan from her file. "This should be Dylan's room." She entered and cast her gaze around. "Now before any of you smart arses make a joke about Dylan Blackburn not being able to read or write, remember looks can be deceiving. Charlene told us people assumed he was slow, but we all know what happens when you assume things."

Tennessee nodded. "It makes an *ass of you and me*... It's like an opium den in here. Blinds closed, curtains closed, low watt bulb."

"He suffers from migraines. It probably helped to keep his room in darkness." Cooper began to work her way through the room. She watched Keaton open the wardrobe and drawers and noted the amount of camo print clothing he had. What struck Cooper most was how little the room told her about Dylan. There was no indication of who he was as a person; no photographs of loved ones, no signs of a hobby, no books or DVDs. Not that anyone bought DVDs these days, she corrected herself. Dylan's room appeared to be a functional space for sleeping and dressing, nothing more. All the surfaces were clean and dust-free, and nothing was strewn about. The only sign of life was a dehydrated peace lily in a terracotta pot. Had the nuns beaten this level of discipline into him?

"I've got something," Martin said, holding a scrap of paper. "A phone number. Doesn't say whose it is."

Cooper took it and they continued their search, finally finding a sudoku book tucked under Dylan's pillow.

Keaton opened the puzzle book and pulled a face. She scanned through a few more pages and pulled an even stranger face.

"What is it?" Cooper asked.

"I've never been able to finish these bastards. Could never get my head around them. But this son of a bitch has finished loads of them. In fact, I can't find a single one that he's started and not finished. You might be right about looks being deceptive, boss."

Cooper chuckled as she took the sudoku book. "What me?" she said sarcastically. "Be right about something? Never in the world."

The room next door belonged to George Blackburn, and it couldn't have been further in style to that of his brother's. Whilst it was also impeccably clean with no sign of mess, the room was warm and bright, decorated in shades of white, stone and cornflour blue. It reminded Cooper of a boutique hotel with its floor-length curtains and reading chair by the window. George was an avid reader by the looks of his bookshelves. A quick look in his desk drawer told her he was into art: a set of watercolour pencils, a putty rubber, and a pad of artist's paper.

"Bless, he still keeps his pyjamas under his pillow," Keaton joked as she checked around the bed.

Martin frowned. "Doesn't everyone do that?"

The team stopped to stare at him.

"That's where my mum puts them when they've been ironed—" he stopped himself too late. "I'm not going to live that down, am I?"

Keaton shook her head and patted him on the back. "Not for a long time, kiddo."

"Well, well, well," Tennessee said, bringing their focus back to the investigation. No shortage of handwriting samples for Georgie Boy. He's an aspiring poet." Tennessee held up a satin-backed notepad that he'd recovered from the bookshelf. "Listen to this... *Golden hair and aqua eyes, angel wings and butterflies. Gentle soul with slender wrists, she fears the man and fears his fists. Angel run away, fly free, angel run away with me.*" He blew a raspberry. "Blimey. That apple fell a long way from the tree."

Cooper tried not to giggle as she took the book of poems. This was George baring his soul, something he probably couldn't do verbally with a family such as his. Cooper wondered if he'd ever shared his love of art or poetry with any of his family. If he had, he'd probably been mocked for it. "Oval structure," she mused as she examined the shapes of the letters. "What do you think?" she asked, showing the book to Keaton.

Keaton squinted and gave Cooper a subtle nod.

Five minutes later and they were in a lilac-coloured, princess-themed room complete with crystal chandelier, four-poster bed and a dresser that housed more make-up than a branch of Boots. The name Lily was written in fairy lights across a wall, and stuffed toys, mostly pink, peered at Cooper from a window seat.

"Let's find a diary or something sharpish," Cooper said. "Those cuddly bears are giving me the creeps. I feel like they're watching me."

It was a feeling Cooper was experiencing more and more. Every button, bulb or bubble could be a hidden camera as far as she was concerned.

"This whole room gives me the creeps," Tennessee added. "I feel like if I stay in here too long, I'll need testosterone replacement therapy."

"I thought Hayley painted Alfie's room purple?" Cooper asked.

"She did," said Tennessee, "but the decorating fairy turned up one night and painted it blue."

Cooper snorted as she opened Lily's wardrobe and examined her designer handbags. "Does the decorating fairy have blond curls and a Geordie accent by any chance?"

He grinned at her. "Ah divint knaa what ya on aboot, pet."

"Bingo." Martin had a notepad in his gloved hand. "Looks like handwritten notes on gel versus acrylic manicures."

"Excellent. That should do it." Cooper let her eyes float over the rest of Lily's wardrobe and her expansive shoe collection. Cooper's black boots with sturdy soles were boring and androgynous in comparison to the array of shoes on display. Jewel encrusted ballerina shoes, stylish court shoes, shoes with see-through heels, shoes with glittered soles, pink trainers and designer flip-flops.

"Erica?...ERICA?"

Justin Atkinson's voice was tense and urgent. It caught her completely by surprise. "We're up here," she called, leaving the room to peer over the bannister.

Atkinson pulled his hood down and removed his protective mask. "Erm... The television in the lounge is on." He thumbed towards one of the downstairs rooms. "One of the guys wanted to check last night's footie scores..." He shrugged and rolled his eyes. "Anyway, the news is on. You should come down and see for yourself."

The scene reminded Cooper of earlier that morning when everyone had huddled around Keaton's desk. Now the SOCOs had gathered around the television in a semicircle, a hum of shocked chatter drowning out the news presenter's voice.

"Quiet." Cooper's solitary word did its job, and the wall of white fell into silence.

The studio cut to Newcastle city centre where a glossy-lipped correspondent addressed the camera. "Shocking scenes in Newcastle today as firefighters struggle to control fires at three bars. The western end of Westgate Road, the Cloth Market and Stepney Lane have all been evacuated."

"Jesus," Keaton muttered. "What's going on?"

"My eyes are stinging from smoke," the correspondent continued. "We're being asked to vacate the area. You can see behind me that the sky, which was cloudless only half an hour ago is now black with smoke. I... Yes, we'll move in two minutes... We're live on air... Authorities have confirmed that the fires started in McDermott's, The Silver Mirror and Vixen. Back to the studio."

Cooper switched the television off. "Everyone back to work."

Once the bunny suits disbanded, she turned to Tennessee, Martin and Keaton. "They're all Blackburn controlled bars. Shit. This is heavy. It's broad daylight."

"Hanson?" Tennessee asked.

"Of course it's Hanson. Get onto Whyte and Boyd. Find out what they know and see if the phone company has got back to Boyd yet. Martin, have someone protect the daughter at the RVI. The Blackburns *will* retaliate."

Tennessee wiped his face nervously. “Eddie has a lot of contacts. Between him and Dylan, I think they’ll blow up half of Gateshead if they think they need to.”

Cooper looked to the floor to gather herself. It was all going to shit. On her watch. “I know. That’s what I’m afraid of.”

- Chapter 24 -

Justin Atkinson had stopped to smell the roses. Literally. Cooper observed him double over, stick his nose in the rose bushes and inhale deeply. Next to him, an old yew blackened from a lightning strike was struggling to hold on. Patches of green spine-shaped leaves grew on the branches that hadn't been damaged, and the sun filtered through, speckling the lawn and flowerbeds with dots of light and shade. Cooper's phone vibrated; she removed it from her pocket to look at the screen. It was Olly Timms asking if she'd eaten yet because he was near Wallsend and could bring her some lunch. No, she hadn't eaten yet, the rumbling in her stomach confirmed that, but she was also nowhere near HQ and she was staring at the man she really wanted to have lunch with.

Right on cue, Atkinson looked up. Cooper hastily shoved her phone back in her pocket, pulled her shoulders back and flashed a smile.

He nodded his head towards another flowerbed, and they ambled towards it, their steps in sync with one another. In a parallel universe, Cooper and Atkinson would be hand-in-hand, walking through the manicured grounds of a different stately home. Belsay Hall, Longframlington Gardens, it wouldn't matter as long as they were together. Instead, they were walking at a respectful distance from one another, through the scene of a double murder.

"The foxgloves are over here," Atkinson told her.

"They're pretty," Cooper commented as she looked at the spires of purple and white bell-shaped flowers that reached for the sky.

"Pretty, but deadly," he smiled, "I've known a few women who can go by that description."

Cooper looked away. "It's definitely the nicest murder weapon I've seen. Any chance you can lift prints from the flower petals?"

"It hasn't rained, so yes, there is a small chance. It'll be difficult, but I'll try. That's assuming our killer wasn't wearing gardening gloves. You can see here that this plant has been pruned recently." He pointed to where a stem had been clipped and leaves removed.

"So Ronnie's gone back to Manchester?"

"Yes, she headed back this morning. What a talent. Watching her work was really something."

"Are you going to visit her?"

Atkinson looked confused. "Why would I do that?"

Cooper lifted her shoulders and put her hands in her pockets. "Because you seemed to hit it off."

"Well, she is great, and we have a lot in common, but I'm not looking for a long-distance thing."

The warmth of the sun felt good on Cooper's skin. She pushed the sleeves of her shirt up so her forearms could benefit too.

"Manchester's only three hours away," she said before she could stop herself. What was she doing? If Cooper could have slapped herself, she would've done.

"Why would I want a long-distance relationship when the perfect woman lives a ten-minute walk from my house?"

Hopes dashed, Cooper had to accept that Atkinson had moved on. She could hardly blame him. She began to pick at the skin around her thumbnail until a lightbulb slowly illuminated in the darkest corner of her mind. Didn't *she* live a ten-minute walk from Atkinson's house?

"Me?"

"Yes, you." He laughed. "It's always been you."

Cooper didn't know quite what to do. She had hurt him terribly; she'd pushed him away when all he was trying to do was keep her safe. "I'm far from perfect," she mumbled.

"That's the thing about perfection," he said, picking a snapdragon from the flowerbed and handing it to Cooper, "like the beauty of a flower, it belongs entirely in the eye of the beholder."

Before Cooper could ask him to dinner, or simply extend her arm and stroke her hand against his, she spotted Keaton moving quickly in their direction.

"Coop, the fire at McDermott's has been extinguished. No casualties. The Silver Mirror is under control, and three people have been transferred to the RVI due to smoke inhalation."

"Thanks, Paula. What about Vixen?"

"They're struggling to contain it. Some sort of accelerant has been used—probably petrol. It's spreading to the office building next door." She paused and looked back and forth between Cooper and Atkinson. "Everything okay? You look weird, boss."

Cooper hoped that if she was blushing she could at least pass it off as sunburn. "I'm fine. What's the consensus on the handwriting samples? Are we all in agreement?"

"We are, and if I'm being honest, I'm not shocked."

Atkinson clapped his hands together. "You have a theory?"

The right corner of Cooper's mouth turned upwards, and she popped her hands on her hips. "I do. I just need more evidence. Which is where you two come in. Paula, can you find out where the three nearest libraries are and pay them a visit? I want to know what books the Blackburns have been checking out. If they haven't been using their laptops or phones, they've been getting their research from somewhere."

Keaton nodded and walked away, calling over her shoulder, "Consider it done."

Checking to make sure no one was around, Cooper moved closer to Atkinson and let her little finger brush against his forearm.

He sighed. "I really want to kiss you right now."

Cooper's stomach flipped over, and she gave him a coquettish look.

"And we have a lot to talk about," he added.

He was right. There were reasons beyond Kenny Roberts that had caused her and Atkinson problems. Kenny had just been the tinderbox. "We can talk... and kiss, as much as we like, but only once this case is out of the way," she teased. "Right now, I need you to test the following items from the kitchen, office and bedrooms..."

THE INFERNO HAD SPREAD to a pair of offices above Vixen. The sky was stained a dark grey, and tiny, ashy, scraps of paper floated towards the pavement like paper raindrops. It reminded Watch Manager Jed Coles of a show he'd watched about Chernobyl; thankfully, nothing here was radioactive. Now that the orange flickers and popping noises had subsided, the crowds had thinned and dispersed, only a few nosy buggers remained. One of his men emerged from the strip joint and began to remove his breathing apparatus. Even in full gear, Coles knew he was looking at Pinkman. He could recognise all of blue watch by either their frame, posture or gait.

"It's out, gaffer," Pinkman said. "Was a right ball ache getting it under control. Fucker poured petrol all round the back before setting the place alight. When the flames reached the bar, the alcohol only worsened it."

"And the two on the stairs?"

"The smoke got them before the flames. Poor bastards must have panicked, forgot about the external fire escape and tried to come out the front entrance. The stairwell's above the bar area; it was thick with smoke. Would've been disorientating."

Cole ran a hand over the back of his neck. Usually, commercial fires were easier to deal with than residential fires, emotionally speaking at least. You didn't have to sift through the charred remnants of a family's possessions: cherished memories, photos from once in a lifetime holidays, portraits of departed loved ones, baby teeth, locks of hair and ticket stubs from first dates to the cinema. But bodies were bodies. Didn't matter if they were in a home or a business—they were never easy to deal with. Two people had gone to work this morning and would never return home.

"Thanks, Pinkman," Coles said. "Give the station manager a bell and update him."

"Aye," he replied.

"And thank the crews from Byker for their assistance," Coles added. Central had been unable to handle the three simultaneous fires on their own and crews from Byker and Gosforth had been called in to assist. "This was a tough one. Tell the lads I'll be in the Vic tonight if anyone fancies a pint."

Pinkman nodded and headed towards one of the engines. Across the road, a smallish woman with a slight frame and hair shorter than his was speaking to Gibson. She held up some form of ID and was allowed through the cordon.

"Watch Manager Coles? I'm—"

"DCI Cooper. Yes, I was expecting you. I'm afraid the situation has worsened."

"Really? I heard the fire had been extinguished."

"It has." Coles looked around and conducted a silent headcount of his men and women. He always wanted to know how many were in and out of a building at any one time. "But it was hard going, and it was definitely started deliberately. I have no doubt about that. Two fatalities and a casualty."

Coles watched Cooper's face. She had the same look he did when confronted with death. She was saddened. She didn't know the two people who had perished in the blaze, but it affected her all the same.

"No identification for the DBs yet, but I can tell you they were descending from the upstairs offices. The surviving casualty is the owner of the bar. He suffered burns and minor smoke inhalation. He's been taken to hospital as a precaution."

"Did he see the arsonist?"

Coles shook his head. "Not really. Saw the back of his head as he legged it out the back door into the alley. Male. Medium height. Medium build. Brown hair."

"That narrows it down," Cooper said with dry sarcasm. She folded her arms over her chest. "I'll find out if there are any cameras covering the back lane, but I imagine it's just a waiting game until the investigation team can tell us more."

Coles smiled.

"What?" She asked, her eyes narrowing.

"Follow me." Coles strode away at a quick pace, forcing the shorter woman to practically break into a jog to keep up with him. He turned when he reached the end of the street where tents for collecting evidence were already erected. Coles stuck his head into the first tent and emerged seconds later with a clear plastic evidence bag. "Thought this might come in useful."

COOPER COULD HAVE HUGGED him. "Where was it found?"

"In the back alley. It was dropped by our medium-height, medium-build male."

Cooper clasped her hands together as if thanking a deity. Sometimes the CID gods threw her a bone, and today's bone was shaped like a Google Pixel XL mobile phone. With Atkinson busy in the lab and Keaton traversing between rural libraries, Cooper finally had something tangible, something she could grasp with two hands and present as evidence.

"You're a star."

Coles shrugged sheepishly. "It's likely a burner. Pardon the pun."

"It's a pretty swanky phone for a burner. I'll get it straight to our tech team. If there's a trail, they'll find it."

Cooper high-tailed it the short journey to Byker Police Station where the digital forensics lab was located and handed the clear evidence bag to Rebecca Hogg. Rebecca Hogg was affectionately known as Becky the Techie and whilst she might look innocent enough in her beanie hat, large, wire-framed glasses and oversized jumper, rumour had it she also had two side hustles on the go. She was both a qualified skydiving instructor and was selling her urine over the internet. Some people might want clean urine to pass mandatory work-place drug tests, but others just liked buying pee from young women. It took all sorts.

Within ten minutes, Becky had already confirmed that the phone was registered as stolen and that our genius arsonist hadn't been too careful.

"He signs his texts as JR," Becky told her. She kept scrolling. "Has a girlfriend by the looks of it... Oh, here we go, she calls him Johnny."

"Surname?"

She pushed her glasses up until they rested on top of her grey beanie. "Not that I can see. Leave it with me. I'll run some programmes and see what I can come up with. Pop back in an hour?"

Cooper thanked Becky and decided to use her hour to tidy up a bit of home admin. She walked the short distance to Morrisons and picked up a few staples as her cupboards were looking worryingly bare. She got pasta, rice, tinned tomatoes, tinned fish and other basics that most people always had in, as well as sunscreen, insect repellant and some new razors. When queuing for the checkout, she called her mother. No answer.

Once her shopping had been deposited in the BMW's boot, Cooper used her remaining time to check the flight schedule between Newcastle International and Lanzarote. The next flight wasn't until Sunday, meaning she had no choice but to swim in Saturday's triathlon.

"Tell me you have a name," Cooper pleaded when she returned to Becky the Techie's desk.

Beckie took a long slurp from a KFC drink and kept drinking until the gurgling noise indicated the cup was empty. "You want the good news, the really good news, or the *really really* good news?"

"The good news first."

"I have a name: Johnathon R. Kane. Here's his email."

"And the really good news?" Cooper asked.

"I know what he looks like. Here's a selfie he took just last week."

Cooper drew back in horror. "A trigger warning would have been nice."

Beckie laughed. "Sorry. Here's one where he's wearing clothes."

Cooper concluded that like detectives, digital forensic technicians probably had a sick sense of humour. When half their job entailed finding evidence of child abuse, if the techies didn't know how to make a joke every now and again, they'd go crazy.

"This is better," Cooper said, holding the printout Beckie had given her. "And dare I ask, what's the *really really* good news?"

"Genius Johnny didn't fully disable location services."

"Meaning?"

"Meaning I've looked for patterns and clusters in his location history and I can tell you exactly where he'll be tonight."

- Chapter 25 -

Two o'clock had been and gone before Cooper had her first meal of the day. There was a canteen and a host of vending machines to choose from at HQ, but craving some peace and quiet, the team took a short drive to the Shiremoor House Farm, a pub less than three minutes away by car. Almost seventy-two hours had passed since the shooting of Fletcher Blackburn and Ibrahim Moradi, and CID was a rat's nest of pandemonium. After the escalation in violence between those loyal to Blackburn and Hanson, Nixon had put out an appeal to the public and calls were coming into the hotline faster than they could be answered. Officers were busy sifting through the bullshit in the hope of finding something useful. Sadly, the public didn't grasp that the police only wanted information concerning the shootings at Morshaw Manor and the arson attacks in the city centre; they had little interest in the he-deserves-its and the I-knew-he-was-troubles. Alibis had to be checked and double-checked. Everyone in the inner circle, apart from Dylan and Theo, had a reasonable to good alibi for the time of the murder. Dylan had, by his own admission, been tucked up in bed since lunchtime. It seemed ridiculous to Cooper, but if he were guilty, wouldn't he have thought of a better lie to spin than that? Theo was annoyingly allusive, only giving up that he was in both Newcastle and Sunderland that day. They'd yet to find CCTV footage of him on the Metro, and he'd given them no indication as to what he'd been up to or who he'd met when he'd got there. There was a chance he'd gone behind his uncle's back to meet with the Roker Boys, but in doing so, he'd also have gone against his father's wishes. No wonder he didn't want Cooper to speak to Eddie.

Tennessee went to the bar and ordered her a half pint of IPA and a bowl of cheesy chips. Cooper found a seat and took a moment to zone out and calm her mind. She breathed slowly and pictured a circle expanding and contracting in time with each breath, just as the mindfulness app had taught her during chemo. By the time Tennessee joined her, she'd managed to stave off the headache that had been threatening her since she saw the news that morning.

Full of fats and carbs, Cooper felt better as she walked back into Northumbria Police HQ. Tennessee had scoffed not only a plate of fish and chips but also a chicken parmo under the guise of carb-loading for the relay triathlon. Back in CID, Cooper cleared the incident room; she and Tennessee had calls to make, and they wanted some space to work without the current volume levels.

"I'll start with Rose Watson. Can you call the beauticians?"

Tennessee affirmed and opened a file to find the number he was after.

"Rose? Hello. This is DCI Erica Cooper from Northumbria Police. Sorry to disturb you but I wanted to ask you a few questions about a date you had with George Blackburn on the seventeenth of June?"

Rose was silent.

"Have you spoken to George since Monday?"

"No. What's this about? Did something happen to George?" Rose had a soft, child-like tone to her voice.

"George's father was shot that day."

There was a gasp. "Oh. Wow. I don't know what to say. I mean, I hardly knew George. We met online. But still, that's terrible."

Cooper quickly glanced over the report Keaton had given her. She could see Wagamama's had CCTV footage of George and Rose entering the restaurant at quarter past three, and Cineworld had confirmed they attended the half four showing of the latest Tarantino flick. "George told me he met you at two o'clock on Monday afternoon—" She was about to ask where the pair had been between two and quarter past three when Rose cut her off.

"No. That's not right."

"It's not?"

"No. We were supposed to meet at two, but George was late. I waited for ten minutes and decided to go shopping. I popped into Waterstones and got a couple of books then went to French Connection. He eventually showed up at three."

Cooper was taken aback. "He was an hour late?"

"Yeah." She sighed. "It was a nice date in the end, but I wasn't sure if I'd want a second one. I was pretty miffed at being kept waiting so long, and to be honest, I don't think he was that into me."

"Just one more thing, Rose. What was George like that afternoon? Can you tell me anything about his behaviour?"

"He was fine. A little quiet, I suppose, but he had perfect manners, other than being late. Wait. Why would you ask that? You want to know if he seemed shifty, don't you?"

Cooper had a feeling Rose was going to want a second date after all. In Rose's mind, George had gone from being a quiet gentleman, to a damaged boy who'd lost his father, to a potential murderer in the space of a brief conversation. Some girls couldn't resist a project; other girls couldn't resist a bad boy—someone who would change if only you could love them enough. Cooper wanted to tell her to run for the hills and stay as far from the Blackburns as she could, but alas, it was none of her business. She thanked Rose, hung up and turned to Tennessee. He was sat with his arms folded over his chest.

"George was an hour late," she told him. "So, he has no alibi until three o'clock. Not two o'clock like he told us."

"And get this. Martin spoke to a temp when he called in at the beauticians. She told him Lily had been scheduled to work that day, she was on the rota..."

"But?"

"But, I just spoke to the boss, and she told me Lily only popped in to get her legs and bikini line waxed. She'd actually swapped shifts with another girl. Said she'd told them she had somewhere else she needed to be."

Cooper was incensed. "This entire family is made up of liars and people who don't care if they look guilty. I should lock up every last one of them."

"Please do," Tennessee said. He raked his fingers through his curls and gave himself a brief head massage, his eyes closed as he processed things.

What Cooper wouldn't give for a massage right now.

"Right, let me get this straight," he continued. "We have two bodies at Morshaw and two bodies in Frankland. That's four murders and one attempted murder if you count Fletcher's poisoning."

"Which we do," Cooper added. "Plus we have three arson attacks and two people who died in the fire at Vixen."

"Charlene is too short to carry out the shooting, but she knows her way around a garden and would have known foxgloves were poisonous. Then there's George, who wasn't where he said he was, and Lily, who wasn't where she said she was. There's Dylan, who lied about knowing about the gun and has no alibi. And Theo, who won't give us a bloody alibi. Not a good one anyway."

"And Hanson who has way too much of an alibi," Cooper chimed in. "That's six suspects with six motives. They all stood to gain from killing Fletcher. Charlene gets money, yes she already had money, but not like this. Hanson would get power. With Fletcher and Eddie out of the way, I'm not sure the youngsters have enough clout with the soldiers to keep them onside. They'll desert a sinking ship and go work for Hanson or the Daytons or the blooming Roker Boys."

"Dylan's motive is revenge," said Tennessee. "What his parents put him through... I'd be surprised if he didn't off the mother as well. Lily gets the freedom to see who she wants, even if it is that arsehole cousin of hers."

"And that leaves George, who gets justice for the people he cares about, and Theo, who gets the keys to the Blackburn empire. But like I said, if he can hang on to it remains to be seen."

Tennessee got to his feet and bent over to stretch his back. "Sex and money," he mused. "It always comes down to sex and money. Six suspects, six motives. We may as well roll a dice and choose one." He straightened up and began stretching sideways.

Cooper laughed. "You think I need to roll a dice to solve this one?"

He met her gaze. "You said you were going to have to lock them all up."

"No. I said I *should* lock them all up. I have my favourites. I just need to hear from Keaton." Cooper's phone began vibrating. "Speak of the devil."

"You won't be calling me the devil when I tell you what I've got," Keaton answered.

"Hang on, I'll stick you on speaker phone. Okay, go."

"I'm in the bustling metropolis of Wooler," she said sarcastically.

Wooler was a small town in Northumberland with pretty stone buildings and the beautiful backdrop of the Cheviot hills.

"Two books were checked out of Wooler library on June the sixth and returned on June eleventh: Death In The Garden and Plants That Kill."

"Who checked them out?" Cooper asked.

"That would be our good friend Theo Blackburn."

"Theo?" *Interesting.*

Tennessee pointed at her and mouthed, *Told you so. Sex and money.*

"Confirm with CCTV, Paula, and see what else is on his reading list of late. Get ahold of the books as well. I want them in the lab tonight. If someone else has checked them out, find them."

Cooper hung up and called Atkinson.

"Hey beautiful," he whispered.

"Hey you." She could hardly say *Hey handsome* with Tennessee sat next to her. Not that it mattered, he was making kissy faces anyway. Cooper covered the receiver and hissed at her DS, "Remember what I said about transferring you to Sunderland?"

Tennessee held his hands up in defeat.

"Make yourself useful and go and check the start times for that stupid triathlon thing... Okay, Justin, give me some good news."

"I tested the item you were interested in. Trace evidence of digoxin."

Cooper punched the air. "Yes! Paula will be bringing some books your way. Death In The Garden and Plants That Kill. I need to know whose prints are on what pages."

"That sounds time consuming."

"But you'll do it for me, right?"

"Well, as it's you... Anything else I can do for the great DCI Erica Cooper?"

"Yes." Cooper had checked the flight schedule between Newcastle International and Lanzarote and knew she wouldn't be able to see her father until Sunday afternoon at the earliest. She planned on using her time between then and now as best she could by not only solving the Blackburn case, but by winning back Atkinson. With the spirit of *who dares, wins*, she asked the burning question.

"Will you have dinner with me on Saturday night?" Cooper held her breath while she waited for the answer. It may be too soon and asking him the second Ronnie left the region was probably a touch desperate, but she hadn't been able to help herself. He hadn't answered yet. Why hadn't he answered yet? The pause went on and on, and when he finally responded, his voice was trembly.

"I'd love to."

Thank god.

"But on one condition. I cook. No offence but—"

Cooper's insides were dancing. "I know, I know... I can burn water."

Keaton struggled to get comfortable on a swivel chair as she watched and rewatched a segment of CCTV footage. The armrests of the chair dug into her thighs and pinched her glutes. It must have been made for a child or one of those eight-stone, size six women she wanted to force-feed. That, or Keaton had been overdoing the squats of late. Nonsense. There was no such thing as too many squats. She scooted her weight to the left and almost toppled the chair. Once her heart calmed down, she rewound the footage and watched it again.

She was watching Theo Blackburn walk into the library, browse the science aisles, select a number of books, flick through them, choose two and check them out. She rubbed her eyes and moved her face closer to the screen. He was the right height and build, but the baseball cap he wore was doing her head in; she didn't have a single second of footage with a clear view of his face. It was probably Theo, but she could just as easily be looking at Dylan or George. Heck, it could have been Fletcher himself. *No*, she thought to herself, *Fletcher wouldn't wear camo print shorts... But Dylan would.*

Dylan's wardrobe had been filled with camouflage print when she'd seen it as part of the search. Had he taken Theo's library card? He could have done.

On the desk, a clear evidence bag contained a copy of Plants That Kill. The other book, Death In The Garden, had been checked out by someone who lived three streets away. She'd pay the elderly man a visit when she was done here and get both books to Justin. She wondered if it would be Theo or Dylan's prints he'd find.

Keaton squirmed. Unable to handle it any longer, she stood and slid the chair away. She retrieved a USB stick from her pocket and downloaded the video footage for Cooper to take a look at later. Next, she logged back into the library's system. Theo Blackburn's account was only two months old, and prior to that, he hadn't checked out a single book. Not surprising. He seemed the sort to watch Fast and Furious films on repeat. Chances were, he only set up the account so that he didn't have to look up information on poisons on his phone or laptop. She was about to log off when something caught her eye, and she scanned down the info attached to Theo's account. Slowly, very slowly, a huge grin spread across her face, and she laughed so loud a man in a tweed jacket hushed her.

"Sorry," Keaton whispered, though she wasn't sorry in the slightest. She hit the control and P keys on the computer's keyboard and waited while an ancient printer spewed up what she'd been looking at on the monitor. Still unable to stop smiling, Keaton called Cooper.

"Boss. The good news is that I've got one book in my possession and I know where the other one is. I'll have them both in the lab within an hour. Ninety minutes tops."

"And the bad news?"

"The CCTV system here is a bobby dazzler. Instant results and good quality footage. I have video of a man checking out the books in question. Same height and build as Theo but for two reasons I can't be one hundred per cent sure it's him. First, he's wearing a baseball cap that covers half his face. I don't have a single frame that we can realistically use."

"Shit."

"Don't despair," said Keaton with a teasing tone to her voice.

"Why?" asked Cooper. "What was the second reason?"

“His account was only set up two months ago. He registered online, and you’ll never guess in a million years what his password is.”

- Chapter 26 -

Cooper called Aleksei Pavlovich for the fifth time. There was one piece of information she needed to unravel this web of lies, and she was sure it lay in the hands of Vixen's owner. An offhand remark by one of the younger Blackburns had niggled at the back of her brain for a while. Something had interfered with Fletcher's plans that day. There must have been a reason for him to go home after collecting his money from Vixen rather than moving onto McDermott's or Bambi Bar. The phone company had confirmed he hadn't received any calls during the timeframe they were looking at, so something had either angered him, scared him, or tempted him away. Cooper thought she knew which.

No answer. She tried again, this time leaving a disgruntled message about how she understood how busy he was, what with his bar burning to the ground, but if he didn't call her back within the hour someone would start checking visas.

Cooper then issued messages to the team that she wanted them all back at Northumbria Police Headquarters by nine p.m. for a meeting. When Elliot Whyte called asking if it couldn't wait until the morning briefing, she almost bit his head off.

"There isn't going to be a morning briefing, Elliot. Instructions tonight; action tomorrow. Be here at nine or don't be here at all."

There was silence on Whyte's end of the call. Cooper could picture him biting his tongue. "Ma'am," he said eventually with all the fake politeness in his voice that he could muster.

While Cooper waited, she checked on Tina who was alone and waiting for Josh to come over to do homework. Or, at least that's what she told her mother they were going to be doing.

"That's fine. No alcohol though."

Tina gave one of her trademark huffs before sulkily replying, "No, Mum. I told you, we're doing homework."

"I believe you, but put my mind at ease and tell me you've been taking your pill every morning."

"Oh, sweet baby seagulls! Yes, mum!"

"At the same time each day? Because if you take it late or—"

"Mum!"

Cooper stopped to laugh at herself. She didn't mean to hassle Tina. Her daughter had proven herself to be trustworthy and honest, but the higher Cooper's adrenaline levels climbed, the more she fixated on those she held dear. All she had ever wanted from the moment Tina was born was for her to have the chances Cooper had never had; for her to be sheltered from the side-glances and insults that had come Cooper's way when her baby bump had begun to show at such a young age.

"Sorry T. I'm a little on edge."

"You don't say."

Cooper ran a hand over her head to the back of her neck where she began massaging her trapezius muscles. Tina was very fond of her grandfather. Cooper wasn't sure how she'd react to the news of his heart attack. When she'd told her about her breast cancer diagnosis, Tina had clammed up and stopped talking for almost a month. Selective mutism was what the doctor called it. The shock and worry had overwhelmed her, and she'd been unable to express herself verbally. Knowing her mutism was causing her mother anxiety had only added to Tina's guilt and made the situation worse. Cooper had been forced to find a way to carry on as if everything was normal, including communicating through pen and paper, nods and shakes, thumbs up and thumbs down, until Tina could relax.

"I'm going to be late. It'll be at least ten when I get in." Cooper said. She'd have to tell Tina tonight and hoped some junk food would lessen the impact. "Fancy a late supper? I can bring in a takeaway?"

Tina didn't hesitate. "Salt and pepper ribs and duck in plum sauce."

"Okay. Stay safe and lock the doors."

Another huff.

Cooper got to her feet when the line went dead and wandered in search of coffee. *Sweet baby seagulls?* That was a new one. She opted for a black Americano from the vending machine. She almost dropped it on herself when Vixen's owner finally returned her call.

"Mr Pavlovich, I'm texting you a photograph. I want to know everything you know."

IT WAS GONE EIGHT when suspected arsonist Johnny R Kane was dragged into HQ. Becky the Techie had been right about his habits. She'd told Cooper he'd been in the Tanners Arms every Thursday night since he acquired the phone. The Tanners was a popular pub near Newcastle's train station. Cooper hadn't been in years, but she had fond memories of their Sunday lunch. According to Kane's data, Becky predicted he'd arrive between half-five and six and would stay until half-ten. Two of Whyte's contacts from Newcastle City Centre Police Station had picked him up just as he was about to tuck into a pie and a pint and brought him to Wallsend. SOCOs immediately took his prints and DNA as well as various swabs. They'd look for traces of accelerants and other evidence that he'd started the fires rather than just being in the wrong place at the wrong time.

By the time Cooper got her hands on him, it would be closer to eight-thirty. With the team arriving at nine, she hoped she could get what she needed from him quickly. Aleksei Pavlovich described the arsonist as medium-height and medium-build, but looking at the selfies Becky had picked out, Cooper would describe him as more on the scrawny side. She paced the corridor while Tennessee rested his back against the wall and thumbed through photos of his young son on his phone. It gave Cooper an idea.

"You got his file there?" she asked.

He handed it over. "What do you need to know?"

Cooper continued pacing as she read. "Family."

"Easy. Father died last year. Mum's in a home with dementia. Unmarried, but lives with a woman named..." He scrunched up his face as he tried to remember. "Laura Something. Laura has two daughters, the youngest is Kane's."

Cooper closed the file. She hardly needed it after that. "Nice."

An officer emerged from interview suite six and gave them a nod. "He's ready for you. Says he needs a piss, but I reckon he can wait."

Cooper hoped he couldn't. People talked faster when their bladders were full. She and Tennessee entered the room and turned on the recording device.

"Thursday the twentieth of June. Eight twenty-seven p.m. I am DCI Erica Cooper, also present is DS Jack Daniel. Please state your name and date of birth."

He swallowed. "Johnathon Richard Kane, August sixth, erm 1980."

"Pleased to make your acquaintance," Cooper said sarcastically. "Right. I'll make this quick. Our scene of crime officers are top-notch, and our lab is world-class. You can shower, scrub your hands, whatever you like, but if you started those fires, and I believe you did, there will be trace evidence on you. We found your phone at Vixen and location services tracked it to the scene of the other two fires. This isn't looking good for you, is it?"

Kane blinked and mumbled, "No comment."

Tennessee snorted. "You know, you don't actually have to say *no comment*. You can just... not comment."

"Come on DS Daniel," Cooper said. "Give him a break. He left his phone at the scene of a crime; he's not the brightest. Mr Kane, How old is your daughter?"

Kane looked up, he seemed confused. "How did...? She's six."

"Nice age," said Cooper. "Young enough to still worship her father but old enough to feel abandoned when he goes to jail. I wonder what will become of her? A young girl with no father figure around. She might fall in with the wrong crowd, start drinking too young, a bit of weed here, a line of coke there, next thing you know—"

"Don't talk about my girl," he snarled.

She kept her face relaxed, but on the inside, Cooper was smiling. She crossed one leg over the other and decided to push another button. "And your poor mother. She'll never see her pride and joy again."

"Stop it."

Cooper wouldn't stop it. Not yet. She stood up and walked around the desk to get a better view of him. She made a big show of looking him up and down and added, "Don't take this the wrong way Mr Kane, but you're not built for jail. You're too slim to hold your own in a fight, and as for those long eyelashes and full lips, well, I think someone will take a shine to you. Oh, don't look so worried, I'm sure they'll be gentle."

"STOP IT!"

Cooper sat down. "Sentences for arson vary depending on the severity of the damage caused. Considering we're looking at double manslaughter, I think it's safe to say you'll be getting life."

If she didn't have Kane's attention before, she did now. The colour drained from his face as he asked, "Manslaughter? What do you mean, manslaughter?"

Tennessee took this one. "Manslaughter is defined as murder without premeditation."

"I know that." Kane was beginning to flap. He wiped his hand over his mouth, then raked his fingers through his short brown hair. He didn't know where to look. “I mean, I know what manslaughter is, but, b-but why are you talking about manslaughter?”

“Well, Mr Kane, we haven’t told the press yet because we’re still tracing the families,” Tennessee began, “but two office workers died in your little bonfire. That’s three counts of arson and two counts of manslaughter. That’s life. You’ll never see the outside of jail again.”

Kane continued to pale. He looked like he could faint at any moment. There was no bravado left in the man, not that there’d been much to start with.

“Laura will visit,” Cooper assured him. “She will at first anyway. Then the excuses will begin and she’ll miss the odd visit. Then she’ll miss two in a row. Then you’ll hear on the grapevine that she’s seeing someone new; someone who can provide for her girls. Only he’s not a good egg. Has a thing for the young ones.”

Cooper stopped. She could smell something, and when she looked at Tennessee, the look he gave her meant she hadn’t imagined it. Urine. They both slid their chairs back twelve inches.

Tennessee pressed a button. They’d have to pause while Kane got cleaned up.

While they waited for assistance, Cooper leant forward and softened her tone. “Look, Johnny, we both know you didn’t wake up this morning and decide to burn down three city-centre bars. Someone told you to do it. Give us the bigger fish, and I’ll see what I can do about reducing the charges.”

He gawped at his sodden groin. Scared and humiliated. Cooper could see him weighing up his options. What was better, grassing someone in and risking their wrath, or a lifetime behind bars with the nightmares she’d just implanted in his brain?

A big, fat tear rolled down his cheek. She was right; he wouldn’t last five minutes in the slammer. Two officers arrived to take Kane to change into a paper boiler suit. When he got to the door, he turned back and met Cooper’s gaze. “Hanson,” he said. “He’s called Wayne Hanson.”

Cooper let out the sort of sigh where every last ounce of breath left her lungs. Tennessee slapped her on the back. “Nice work,” he said, checking his watch, “and nice timing.”

Cooper spoke into the recording device one last time. “Interview terminated eight-fifty p.m.”

Uniformed officers and detectives alike sat straight-backed despite their stifled yawns and itchy eyes. They were tired. It had been non-stop since the moment Cooper had taken the call about Fletcher Blackburn and Ibrahim Moradi's shooting on Monday evening. Meals had been missed, sleep had been sacrificed, and families had been neglected. It was time to put an end to their suffering.

Keaton was the last to arrive. Her usually neat ponytail was askew but the grin she was wearing told Cooper she'd tracked down the books and had taken them to the lab. She approached Cooper and patted her on the arm. "I waited while Hong ran the prints. Thought you'd want to know straight away."

"And?"

Keaton's face spread into a wide grin. "As suspected."

Relief filled Cooper's heart. She hadn't assembled everyone for no reason. She reached up and cupped Keaton's face in her hands. "You star," she said. "Now do what you do best."

Keaton turned to face rows of her colleagues. "Right, peeps. Switch your phones off and switch your brains on. Court is in session." The room fell silent as eyes turned to Keaton and Cooper. "God gave you two ears, but only one mouth so hush up and listen up."

Cooper had to marvel at the way Keaton commanded her peers. Years of playing and captaining team sports had given the woman a confidence and swagger Cooper could only dream off. Erica Cooper wasn't a wallflower by any stretch of the imagination, but her self-esteem had taken a beating over the last few years between some disastrous relationships and her illness.

Keaton took a seat between Boyd—whom she dwarfed—and Tennessee, who turned to her and whispered, "Decent. A solid eight out of ten. Had to deduct a point for *peeps*."

Cooper had the floor. She perched herself on the edge of a desk and shuffled her weight until she was sat on it. Crossing her legs, she picked up a folder and pulled out her notes. Within half an hour, everyone knew the theory, the evidence that backed it up and what was still conjecture.

"As for Hanson, the phone found at the scene of one of the bar fires led us to Johnathon Kane. He's given up Hanson and will no doubt give us more details once he's dried off and put on some big boy pants. Whyte, Boyd, you two have been tailing Hanson, so it's only right you get the honour of putting him in cuffs. Speak to Kane and arrange some back up for the morning. Grab him at six a.m."

Whyte nodded; Boyd bit her lip.

"I need someone to tail Theo Blackburn," Cooper continued, turning her attention to the back of the room. "I want to know where he spends the night.

If he's at Budle Bay, leave him be. Otherwise, drag him out of bed at the crack of dawn."

No one volunteered.

"I'll speak to Nixon about overtime."

Two hands shot up from the back row. *Typical.*

"Thank you," Cooper said to the volunteers. "The rest of us will meet at the outskirts of Budle Bay at five forty-five a.m. Not a second later. We have an early start, so get home and get to bed. Drink some warm milk, or some camomile tea, or screw it, have a wee dram. Whatever works."

She sighed. They'd done it.

"HELLO, STEVEN."

Cooper stepped over the baby herring gull and let out a hearty sigh as she placed a takeaway for three on the kitchen table. Her legs felt heavy, but not as heavy as her eyelids. Tina and Josh emerged, sniffing the air and drooling as they clawed at the paper bags. It was late; they must be famished. Tina grabbed some cutlery, dished out three portions and headed towards the dining table.

"Did you get your homework done?" Cooper asked the teenagers as she sat.

They nodded, mouths already full of spare ribs.

"Finished maths and chemistry," Josh said between bites. "Then, we started watching *Riverdale* on Netflix."

Cooper hadn't heard of it.

"It's a murder mystery!" Tina said.

Josh tore another strip of spare rib meat from the bone. "You only like it because the main character's always taking his shirt off."

Tina kicked Josh under the table. Cooper didn't see it, but she heard him grunt, "Hey! Ouch."

Josh's father picked him at half-ten, and Cooper chose that moment to talk to Tina about her grandfather.

"Listen, T. I have some bad news."

"Is it Dad? Because I've been thinking about it and I don't care what Josh says—"

"It's not your father."

"Good, because I'm not interested—" Tina's eyes suddenly widened, and she made pointed eye contact with Cooper. A rarity. "The cancer's back?"

"No. No, it's not that, T."

Tina collapsed back in her chair. "You scared me."

"Sorry. I didn't mean to scare you, but it's your grandfather. He's really not well. He had a heart attack and needed surgery."

Tina sat very still while she processed that information. "Is he going to die?"

Cooper pinched her nose. She'd tried to push the thought away all day. "No, he's tough as an ox. He'll be fine."

"Are you sure?"

"I hope so."

"Me too. I like Grandad Ben."

"And he likes you. He loves you."

Tina began to tidy the table and prepare Steven's evening meal.

Cooper braced herself because she knew how Tina felt about disruption. "I think we should go and visit him."

Her daughter froze with a syringe full of mashed fish in her hand. "When?"

"As soon as possible."

"Would I be in trouble at school?"

Tina had taken time off school to recover after the events of the last winter. She'd had perfect attendance otherwise. "You won't be in trouble. *I* might be. There'll be a fine to pay but as far as I'm concerned it'll be worth it to have you with me."

Tina scooped Steven up and placed him on her knee. He lifted his beak upwards and began to beg. "How long for?"

"A week. Maybe two. If you need to come home sooner because you miss home or your studying is suffering, we can probably arrange it."

Tina concentrated on Steven for a few moments. "You know me. I can study anywhere."

Cooper got to her feet and kissed Tina on the top of her head. "I was hoping you'd say that. The next flight is Sunday morning. Should I book it?"

Tina nodded. "But we have a problem." She motioned towards the bird on her lap. "A seagull-shaped problem."

The bird would need taking care of. He'd been Tina's project since he fell off the roof as a hatchling and she was determined to give him the care required until he was ready for release.

"We can't ask Dad," Tina said. "He only does nice things if there's something in it for him.

"What about Josh?"

"His Mum's a clean freak."

"Your netball friends?"

Tina shook her head. "No. I don't want them to know how weird I am yet."

"Don't talk like that. You're not weird."

Her daughter stared at her. "Mum, I'm hand-rearing a baby seagull."

Cooper narrowed her eyes. "Okay, you have a point."

"So, what do we do? He can't fledge yet."

She couldn't ask Atkinson. Not when they weren't officially back together yet. She reached over and stroked Steven's feathers. He was unbelievably soft. It would have to be someone from the team. It would be unethical to ask a personal favour of the two newest members, not that she'd ask Whyte anyway, and she didn't know Martin well enough to ask this of him. It had to be Keaton or Tennessee. Keaton would probably make a joke about roasting him with some Maris Piper potatoes, and Tennessee would say yes because he was the sort to always help others and always go the extra mile. It was in his nature. However, Tennessee had an infant at home, a wife struggling with parenthood and an elderly mother-in-law. They could do without a creature that, if you weren't careful, would give you a nasty bout of salmonella.

Cooper sighed. "I'll ask Paula."

- Chapter 27 -

Half four and the first blush of pink was creeping over Tynemouth's horizon. A hint of blue sky penetrated the darkness before the pink gave way to burnt orange and stained wispy stratus clouds with rose gold. Moments later, the sun burst free, dissipating the thinnest clouds into nothing. Cooper drained her coffee and headed for the door, her mind torn between Northumberland and the Canaries. Upstairs, a restless Tina had given up on sleep and had instead begun typing a list of caregiving instructions for Steven. In a nearby suburb, Hayley Daniel clutched her baby to her chest as she watched her husband leave for work. A familiar dread crawled into her stomach, as it had done every time he left since Alfie was born. Twenty miles south, Eddie Blackburn clenched and relaxed his fists over and over. It had started to sink in that his little brother would not be visiting him this month, or next month, or ever again. His anger had been like a thick fog that he was unable to navigate through. But over last night's dinner, depression had started to nibble away at the anger, started to dull it. He had to be careful. Depression couldn't regain an empire, but anger could. Sixty-five miles north, Eddie's niece and nephews lay awake, staring at their respective ceilings. His son slept soundly.

A lone light was on at the Blackburns' barn conversation in Budle Bay. As Cooper and her colleagues approached, Charlene Blackburn could be seen hunched over their large kitchen island, a cup of something hot clutched in her hands. They tiptoed up the gravelled driveway before knocking gently. Charlene jumped and clutched her chest. It took a moment for her to relax and come to answer the door.

"Is everything okay?" she asked nervously.

Cooper was keen to bring this whole dreadful business to a close. "Could you wake the others, please? I'd like everyone in the kitchen."

Charlene glanced from Cooper to Tennessee, then to Keaton and Martin. Her eyes caught sight of another officer waiting in the driveway. She wouldn't know about the vehicles stationed at either end of the B1342: one in Bamburgh, and one at Waren Mill. No one was jumping in their flashy car and making a run for it. Fletcher's second wife nodded silently and padded from the hallway towards the stairwell.

Ten minutes later and three of the Blackburns, still in their nightwear, gathered around the large kitchen island. Charlene tightened her silk robe and sipped fresh coffee. To her left, George cleaned his glasses on plaid print pyjamas and Dylan, in grey camouflage shorts, folded his arms over his bare chest. The kitchen was fitted with spotlighting that accentuated Dylan's indented skull and cast his eyes in shadow. "This had better be good," he grumbled, checking his watch.

"Where's your sister?" Tennessee asked.

Dylan snorted. "The princess is still in bed."

"And your cousin?"

Dylan's look darkened. "In the princess's chamber," he growled.

"Are my ears burning?" Theo Blackburn pushed open a heavy oak door and joined the group in the kitchen. Baggy joggers trailed on the floor, his bare chest bore red fingernail scratches and his hair was loose with dark waves skimming his collar bones. He typed on a mobile as he walked. "Lily's in the shower. She said there'd better be coffee on the go. So what's so important we had to—" He looked up, his eyes narrowing upon Cooper. "Ah fuck, what do you want at this hour? You know, if my father was here we'd be given the fucking respect of a lie-in."

Cooper cut him off. "If your father were here, you'd be the one in jail. We all know he took the fall for your freedom." She stopped, briefly thinking of her own father. Thank goodness she'd be with him soon. She and Tina would go straight from baggage claim to the hospital and shower Ben in affection. Cooper pushed the thought aside and returned to Theo. "You'd be serving time for arson, you little pyromaniac, manslaughter too. So I suggest you stop whinging. Now, as for why I wanted you all here, I thought you'd like to know who killed your uncle."

Theo stopped, put his phone in the back pocket of his joggers and smirked at Dylan. The big man met his gaze with daring intensity, challenging him to say something. Anything.

Tennessee positioned himself between the Blackburns and their kitchen door. "In respect to the attempted murder of Fletcher Blackburn—"

"Whoa. Hang on a minute." Theo addressed the elephant in the room. "What do you mean *attempted*?" He made air quotes with his fingers. "My uncle is dead and rotting in the morgue. I mean, I didn't *see* the body, but—"

"*I* saw the body," Charlene snapped. Her eyes were filling with tears, and she looked like she could throw her scalding coffee over him. "I saw the body of my husband. The man I loved. He was shot. Show him some damn respect."

Theo gave her a condescending smile before opening the fridge. "What? No beer?"

Charlene stood up, unable to stay still any longer. "My husband was shot, DS Daniel. Twice. There was no attempted murder. He was murdered."

"Actually, Mrs Blackburn," Tennessee began, "before he was shot, Fletcher was poisoned. His autopsy showed high levels of digoxin, a poison derived from foxgloves."

The Blackburns looked at each other, perhaps visualising the impressive gardens at Morshaw Manor, its flowerbeds adorned with white and purple foxgloves amongst snapdragons and peonies.

Keaton stepped forward, she placed a file on the kitchen island and removed some images from it. "On Thursday the sixth of June, two books were checked out of Wooler library: Death In The Garden and Plants That Kill." She pointed to pictures of the two books. "They were checked out using your library card, Theo."

All eyes turned to Theo Blackburn, who froze for a moment then raised his hands. "No. No way. Don't bloody drag me into this. I don't even have a fucking library card."

"Oh, but you do." Keaton tweaked her ponytail. "It was applied for online using your name and details. Don't take this the wrong way, Theo, but I take you to be the sort of man who'd use the word *password* as his password, or maybe *one, two, three, four*. Whoever applied for this library card must have been in a hurry because they didn't choose a password that any average Joe would pick. They chose something that only they would know and that they'd easily remember. It was, all-one-word, *angel wings and butterflies*."

George jumped from his seat. "Shit."

The room erupted. George resembled a cornered animal, wide-eyed and looking for a way out. Charlene was the first to speak, crying out a pained "No!" She reached out and firmly grabbed his arm. "George? No. I— I don't believe it."

"Believe it," said Keaton. "Funny you used the word *shit* there, George. Because that's exactly how I'd describe your poetry, of course, I'm not your target audience. I like dance music, anything fast that I can workout too. The chief here, she likes rock music and a bit of metal. This handsome fella is a cheesy pop kind of guy, but he'll deny it—"

"Focus, Paula," Cooper said with a smirk while Tennessee grumbled something about cheese.

"*Angel wings and butterflies* is a line from a poem you wrote," Keaton continued. "A poem we believe is about Charlene."

Charlene immediately let go of George's arm. "What?"

George turned away, unable to look at her.

"Your Oedipus complex is none of my business, but the evidence is." Keaton pointed to the pictures of the books from Wooler library. "Your prints are on the covers of both books, and I'm willing to bet my house that your prints are all over pages seventy-five to seventy-eight in Plants That Kill and page thirty-three of Death In The Garden. Those are the pages that detail foxgloves."

Cooper leant forward. "Your father had a health shake every morning, didn't he?"

George nodded.

Placing another photo on the island, Cooper continued. "The foxgloves at Morshaw were pruned recently, as shown here and here. You took the leaves and stems and blended them with kale and spinach after your step-mother used the blender on Monday morning."

He swallowed but said nothing.

"You should have cleaned it more thoroughly because the lab found digoxin on the blades. The family meeting began, and you handed your father his death smoothie."

"You bastard," Charlene cried. She ran at George, pumping her fists into his chest over and over. George didn't fight back or even try to defend himself. Theo did nothing to stop her. He seemed to find some sick humour in his cousin trying to frame him for murder. Keaton gently wrapped her arms around Charlene and guided her back to a seat.

"I don't regret it," George said. "He deserved it. Everyone will be happier now he's gone." His chest heaved. He extended his arms, palms up, and awaited the cuffs. Keaton, who was nearest, obliged. "You'll be happier," he said, turning to

Charlene. "You will. Trust me. I tried to warn you about him, but you didn't listen. I could see it in his eyes. He was starting to look at you the way he used to look at Mum. Like you were, I don't know, some sort of pet. A pretty little creature that he could crush the second he got tired of it, or the second it dared to disobey him. He would have gone on to abuse you like he abused everyone else. I couldn't let that happen, though. And you're young enough to escape all this. I saw his will in the office. You'll be set. You don't have to be a part of any of this. You're free now."

Charlene's face was set like stone. "I didn't want to be free," she said, barely moving her lips. "I didn't need saving, and you had no right... no right to play God like that."

George's glasses slipped down his nose. He nudged his face against his shoulder to try and push them back up. "I tried a few times. A petal here, a petal there. I was trying to use as little as possible, and I knew it was working because his eyes had started to turn yellow over the last few days and he'd stopped eating. I used a little extra on Monday, added some leaves and stems, then I put the smoothie on Dad's desk, but Dylan said he was thirsty and took a sip. I tried to stop him." He blinked slowly, as if his eyelids were suddenly heavier.

"Hang on," Dylan rubbed his temples. "Is that why my head was killing me all day?"

Cooper nodded. "I think so. You injuries mean you're more susceptible to headaches. The poison affected you very quickly. A few sips wouldn't be enough to kill you, but it was enough to make you very ill."

Dylan moved towards George, but nothing about his demeanour seemed angry. He hugged his little brother, and that's when Cooper scrutinised his expression. It was pride. Admiration almost.

George allowed Keaton to peel him away from Dylan and take him by the arm. She guided him through the door to the courtyard where officers waited to escort him to HQ.

Dylan called after him. "I didn't think you had it in you."

George's face cracked. "No one ever did."

THE DOBERMANN WENT BERSERK at the sound of Elliot Whyte pressing Hanson's doorbell. It was quarter to six in the morning, and the only other sign of life in Rowlands Gill was a baker delivering goodies to the café across the road. He paused to take a gander at Whyte and Boyd as they stood on Hanson's doorstep but scarpered as soon as the door began to creak open.

Hanson's voice could be heard from behind the door. "Gazza! Bugger off will you."

The Dobermann was possessed. Barking and clawing to get to the intruders. Boyd took a step backwards and looked to Whyte for support. She always looked so vulnerable with those big eyes and something about her appearance made him think of a deer or a bunny from a Disney film. She was capable though, she proved that by finding the chef, interviewing him, following up on his alibi and eliminating him from the investigation. She had a good head on her shoulders. Twice he'd tried to subtly ask if she was single—twice he'd bottled it. He didn't want a repeat of the Cooper incident. That was going to haunt him till the day he retired. Best stick to civilian women. Besides, Martin clearly had a thing for Boyd. The atmosphere may always be strained between him and Cooper, but he didn't need to add to it by becoming anyone's love rival. Whyte flashed Boyd a reassuring smile and clutched his retractable baton. He gestured to one of their back up units to keep their distance, then signalled to another to move around the back of the property.

Eventually, the barking subsided. It sounded as if the Dobermann was being dragged to another room and given a stern, "Stay!"

Hanson appeared in his dressing gown. "Fucking hell," he moaned when he saw the panda cars. "Bring the whole squadron, did you? What in God's name do you want? I already spoke to that Martin fella and the hefty woman." His brows quickly lowered. "Wait. I know you. You were at the hospital," he said, pointing at Boyd. "On the children's ward. And you," his finger moved to Whyte, "you were at the Shell garage... and Tesco." It dawned on him. "You fuckers have been tailing me."

"Glad you could catch up," Whyte said dryly.

"What's this all about?" He checked his watch. "I have a sick daughter who I'm supposed to be having breakfast with at seven."

"The only person you'll be having breakfast with is Harrison Pace."

"And who the bloody hell is he?"

Whyte and Boyd's back up moved to either side of them. Four against one—if you didn't count the massive dog.

"He's a known troublemaker who my colleagues picked up last night on drug-related offences. He'll be your cellmate when we return to the station. Big guy by all accounts and I hear he has a thing for French maids."

Boyd tried to suppress a laugh, but it escaped as a snort and she quickly looked away from Hanson who's face had turned beetroot with rage. His posture changed to one of aggression: chest inflated, shoulder's rounded, jaw clenched. It was his eyes that gave him away: they flickered with fear.

"What do you mean *cellmate*? I didn't touch Fletcher. Didn't lay a finger on him. I have an alibi, don't I? I swear you're making a big mistake, lad."

If Whyte didn't approve of being called *lad*, he didn't show it. "I'm not making a mistake, and I know you didn't kill Fletcher."

Hanson was incandescent, his voice loud enough to wake the neighbours. "Then why the fuck are you wasting my time?"

Whyte didn't answer straight away. He was enjoying watching him squirm. "On Wednesday evening, you received a phone call that made you very angry. We know what number that call came from."

Boyd rattled off the number. "That number is registered to a little old lady who lives in Berwick."

"I don't know any little old ladies from Berwick," snarled Hanson.

"I believe you," Whyte said. "She reported her phone as stolen back in May. Some arsehole mugged her on her way back from doing her weekly shop. The wise guy who's been using said phone—and I use the term *wise guy* in an ironic sense—forgot to fully disable location services. Yesterday morning, that phone was on Westgate Road at eight minutes past eleven, the Cloth Market at twenty-seven minutes past eleven and Stepney Lane at twelve-oh-one. Do those locations mean anything to you?"

Hanson glowered. "Should they?"

"Stop bullshitting me. Two people died. They're the locations of McDermott's, The Silver Mirror and Vixen."

"That doesn't prove anything."

"No" Whyte conceded. "But the testimony of the man who was using that phone does. My colleagues picked him up in the Tanners Arms last night and he's singing like a karaoke-lovin' canary. McDermott's, The Silver Mirror and Vixen have been paying the Blackburns for aeons. I believe you ordered the fires as payback for the murders of your associates in Frankland. You wanted to hit them in their wallets, where you knew it would really hurt."

Hanson looked back over his shoulder. Whyte didn't know if he was considering making a bolt for the back door or if he was about to release Gazza.

"Don't even think about it," Whyte urged, covering both bases. "Mr Hanson, I am arresting you for arson and manslaughter."

The two back up officers moved in and wrestled a struggling Hanson into handcuffs while Whyte finished reading Hanson his rights.

As he was led away to an awaiting patrol car, Whyte turned to Boyd. "You want to give him the good news?"

She brightened and opened her mouth but quickly changed her mind, fear getting the better of her. "I'll let you," she told Whyte.

Whyte would spend time later wondering why she was so skittish, but for now, he relished passing on some information to Wayne Hanson.

"Mr Hanson, a lovely lady from the National Crime Agency can't wait to meet you. She took an overnight train and will be at the station in time for your arrival."

As well as the NCA, a team from the North East Regional Special Operations Unit—who went by the rather rubbish acronym NERSOU—would also be waiting. Still, they weren't the only ones who wanted a piece of Hanson. News vans from the BBC, ITV, Sky and Channel Four would be clamouring for the best view of the front of HQ. Someone bearing an uncanny resemblance to Saffron Boyd had tipped them off.

- Chapter 28 -

George grinned as he was led away. Cooper had seen her fair share of Cheshire Cats in cuffs. Some smiled in bravado, a way of covering their fear of jail and what awaited them. Others gave evil smirks, trying to force fear upon the arresting officer. "Wait until I get out. I'll have some fun with you," one predatory man told Cooper back when she was new to the force and Whyte had left her alone with a suspected rapist to chase down his accomplice. And some smiled because, frankly, they were off their rockers. George's smile was new to Cooper and she strongly suspected it was a smile of relief. He'd done what he had to do to protect Charlene and his family, and now they were free of their overbearing father, and he was free of the secret he'd been carrying. Nothing about jail could scare him as much as his father had.

Once the car pulled away and the sound of its engine faded to nothing, Cooper pulled her attention back to the remaining Blackburns. There were looks of shock on all their faces.

"I don't believe it." Charlene was holding a folded tea towel over her face and breathing through it as a way to stop herself from hyperventilating.

"The scrawny geek's got some balls on him," Theo said. "But that was attempted murder. You said so yourself," he turned to Cooper. "George didn't shoot anyone. His balls aren't that big. He hated guns. Almost pissed himself when I took him on a pheasant shoot when we were teenagers."

Cooper pulled her lips in and looked to the floor. Part of her didn't want to do this, but a more significant part knew it was her job and the right thing to do. "You're right. George didn't shoot Fletcher." She looked up. "I think it's time we got Lily out of the shower."

Theo froze, his mouth slightly ajar and his eyes narrowed to slits. "What? You're joking?" He shook his head.

"I'm sorry. I'm not." Cooper asked Tennessee and Martin to wait with the others while she and Keaton, as the female detectives, followed the sound of running water.

The stairwell was a mix of modern and old. The original stone steps were adorned with a handrail made of chrome and glass. The walls were decorated with Georgia O'Keefe prints in black frames with thick white mounts. All lilies, Cooper noted.

"Lily?" Cooper knocked on a bedroom door. "Lily, it's DCI Cooper. I'm coming in with DS Keaton." Lily's room at Budle Bay was markedly different from her room at Morshaw. At Morshaw the room was fit for a princess. Girlie. This room was more for a queen; it was tasteful and grown-up. The room was neutral with accents of teal. It featured a king-sized bed with a padded headboard, its sheets still crumpled from last night's activities. A velveteen chaise longue was pointed towards a window with a sea view, and an antique dresser sat flush against the opposite wall.

"Nice," Keaton muttered.

"Lily?" Cooper called again. She stood at the door to the en suite. It was ajar and swirls of steamy air were pouring through the gap. She glanced through the opening. The glass surround of a large shower cubicle was speckled with water droplets, but beyond the glass, as steamy as it was, there was no movement.

"Shit." Cooper burst into the en suite, knocking over a bottle of perfume and tripping on a pile of clothes. The perfume bottle shattered, sending its over-powering fruity scents into the air. Cooper raced to the window where two words were scrawled onto the pane in rose-coloured lipstick: *I'm sorry*.

"She's gone," Cooper growled. She lowered the toilet lid and climbed up, using it as a step. Pushing open the window as wide as she could, she scanned the surrounding country lanes, fields of sheep and grass-covered dunes. "LILY!" she yelled, but there was no sign of the youngest Blackburn.

In the bedroom, Keaton pulled her handheld radio from her belt and quickly dispatched instructions to the units in the area. She looked out the bedroom window, angling her head to the courtyard. "The cars are still there."

"She went on foot," Cooper said as she jumped off the toilet lid and raced toward the stairs, skidding in the pool of perfume and gagging as the fragrance found its way into her mouth and eyes. "There's a tree branch under the window. Easily thick enough to take her weight." When she reached the kitchen, Theo was her first target. "Where is she?"

"What?" Theo looked taken aback.

"Lily. Where did Lily go? Tell me now or—"

Cooper didn't get to finish her threat.

"What do you mean, *where is she?* She's upstairs." He pointed to the ceiling.

"No, she's not."

Theo ran towards the stairs to check for himself. Satisfied that the upstairs of the house was empty, he returned and made for the front door.

"Not so fast," Cooper warned. "Stay here with DS Daniel. Jack, find out what he knows. Martin, you're with me."

"I— I don't know anything. First, you tell me Lily killed Uncle Fletcher. Now you're saying she's run off and I that know where—"

Cooper ignored Theo and scrambled to the courtyard where a handful of officers awaited her. Dylan Blackburn followed, pulling a pair of grubby trainers onto bare feet and sliding his thick arms into the sleeves of a knitted jumper.

"Stay with your cousin, Dylan."

"Not a chance." He locked eyes with Cooper, and she knew in an instant he wouldn't be persuaded without the use of force, and she would need a truckload of force to restrain a man like Dylan Blackburn. "My Mum's gone, my dad's dead, brother's going to jail. I need to hear from Lily what happened."

She nodded—like he would take any other answer—and called for Keaton. "Paula, the units in Waren Mill and Bamburgh?"

"Roadblocks are ready. They have Lily's description and will radio if they see anyone who even remotely looks like her. There are local units on their way to provide assistance as well. I've sent a photo of Lily to their sarge."

"Good. Have them check the caravan sites and campgrounds. Right, she's probably avoiding the main road. Paula, Martin, take four men and head inland. The rest of you, Dylan, we'll follow the coastal route. Leave no stone unturned."

Keaton instantly took charge of her team. They took off at a quick pace and split into pairs to cover the trails that Keaton pointed out.

"Dylan, are there any outhouses on the property? Sheds? Somewhere Lily could hide?"

He scanned about. "Yeah, there's a shed in the back garden and an old den we made when we were younger."

Cooper pointed to one of the uniforms. "Go check them out."

The rest of them headed down a country lane towards the sea. They peered over stone walls and squinted into dense bushes. Cooper constantly surveyed the horizon, her eyes programmed to pick up the first hint of movement. Not wanting to spook Lily, she moved quietly and refrained from calling her name.

"How's your relationship with Lily?" she asked Dylan as they reached the edge of the dunes.

"I call her a spoiled brat; she calls me a dickhead. But," he paused, looking about, "I try to look out for her, and she doesn't talk to me like I'm a fucking idiot."

"Is she scared of you?"

He shook his head. "No. She might be the only God-damned person in the world who sees past what I look like."

Cooper's eyes started to sting. She blinked back a tear. Now was not the time to feel sorry for a criminal, even though that was precisely how she was feeling. "Call for her," she whispered. "She might show herself for you."

Dylan moved through the dunes calling Lily's name. Not too loud, not too urgent. His heavy feet sank into the sand as he walked and even Cooper, who was considerably lighter, felt her legs being sapped of energy with each step that she took in the loose sand. When they reached the beach, Dylan turned to her. "North or south?"

Picturing a map of the area in her mind, Cooper tried to place herself in Lily's shoes. "The tide's in. If she went north, she'd either have to cross the estuary or stick to the roads. Either way, the unit at Waren Mill will spot her. I say we head south. Keep covering the dunes and move towards the holiday cottages, she could be sheltering there."

They turned south, spreading out to cover as much ground as they could. "Tucker?" she called to a uniform. "Head down to the beach. Check any caves. There's a couple of boats down there too. Give them a once over."

"Ma'am," he replied, turning away and heading to the shore.

The worn path had shrubs to one side and dunes to the other, but even the heady scent of salty air mixed with heather couldn't cover the perfume seeping through Cooper's clothing. It made her feel sick. She pulled her jacket off, discarded it on a rock and shivered, for although the sun was up, it had yet to warm the sea breeze. Dylan continued to call for his sister, leaving long gaps between calls so they could listen for a reply or the sound of footsteps. Tucker neared a stone pier that jutted out into the estuary and looked up the steep bank to Cooper. She pointed towards the pier, wanting him to check both sides as well as the pieces of rock that had crumbled away.

Where was she? The only signs of life were the seagulls above and the wading birds below. Cooper withdrew her radio and touched base with Keaton. "Any luck?"

"Nothing yet, boss."

Ahead, a flat area of concrete was partially consumed by green ferns and nettles. It looked out of place amongst the unrelenting natural coastline that surrounded it. As Cooper approached, it dawned on her that it wasn't simply a flat piece of concrete: it was a roof. A structure was built into the dunes with small, circular openings drilled into otherwise solid grey walls. She'd found the World War II gun encampment. Cooper and Dylan exchanged a look, nodded to each other and approached the entrance. The building was small, only a few metres across, and it was slowly being reclaimed by nature. Patches of grey concrete were turning green from microscopic plant life.

"Lily?" Dylan whispered. "Lily, are you in there?"

They entered the dark space. The only light came from a panoramic hole that framed a perfect view of the estuary and its pristine white sand. In the distance, Holy Island towered out of the waves of the North Sea. A circle of round metal pegs poked out of a mounting plate where an enormous gun would have once sat, protecting the northeast from invading forces. Cooper turned around in the gloomy room. Under a solid concrete shelf, a shivering Lily Blackburn crouched, holding a broken bottle to her neck.

- Chapter 29 -

The sharp edge of the bottle pressed into Lily's pale flesh. It hadn't cut through a major vein or artery, but it had pierced the skin. A rivulet of scarlet blood ran down her neck and chest. Her face was deathly white, except for some yellowing under one eye and on her jaw. Her pupils were twice the size they'd normally be. The youngest Blackburn shivered, wearing only a thin set of silky pyjamas and white socks that were now soaked through and stained with mud and grass. Cooper spied further cuts and grazes on her shins and forearms.

"Stay back," Lily blurted, pressing the glass firmly into her neck, causing the blood to flow quicker.

"It's okay, Lily." Cooper spoke calmly and took a step back to avoid crowding the frightened girl. "You look cold. I can get you a blanket."

Lily shook her head and sniffed, "I want Theo."

Not wanting Lily to harm herself further, or end up taking her own life, Cooper radioed for Tennessee and asked him to bring Theo as quickly as he could. "Arrange an ambulance," she added quietly. "No sirens."

"Is he coming?"

"He's on his way," Cooper assured her. "Please, Lily. You're freezing. Do you want your brother's jumper?"

Lily's eyes darted back and forth between Cooper and Dylan. Eventually, she nodded. "But stay there," she warned him.

Dylan stayed where he was, removed his jumper and tossed it onto the floor a foot or so from where Lily sat. She pulled it towards her using her foot. "I don't want to go to jail. I can't."

"Your family will do everything they can to stop that happening, Lily." Cooper kept her distance but crouched down so she could be eye-level with Lily.

Dylan nodded. "Of course. Whatever happened, we'll fix it."

The Blackburns had good lawyers. They needed to with the sort of things Eddie and Fletcher had got up to over the years.

"And if I'm right about what I think happened," Cooper continued, "I'll try my best to help you as well."

Lily looked surprised.

"I'm serious. I'm not here to frame you or paint you in a bad light. I promise you that. I only want the truth. I'll be fair, and importantly, so will the judge."

The bottle moved ever so slightly. There was a noise at the entrance to the bunker before Theo edged his way in. For someone who was usually so cocksure and arrogant, he looked nervous.

"What happened, babe? Jesus, you're bleeding."

He moved forward, saw her shaking arm holding the bottle to her neck and froze. He raised his hands and stepped back.

Dylan wrapped his arms around himself. "You wanted Theo. He's here now. So how about you put the bottle down and he can give you a hug and then we can get you somewhere warmer."

Lily wavered, but the glass remained pressed into her skin.

Cooper looked up at Theo and Dylan. From her crouched position, they looked even bigger than usual. "She needs medical attention, but we can't do anything while she has a weapon. I can't risk her hurting herself."

Theo looked like he wanted to say something but couldn't find the right words. Dylan took a deep breath. "Come on, Lil. Put the bottle down. You heard the detective; she wants to help you."

"That's right," Cooper said. "I'm not going to rush over and arrest you." She looked back to Theo. "Has the ambulance arrived?"

He nodded.

"Could you ask for some blankets?"

Theo left. Cooper was freezing, Lily more so, and now Dylan had given up his jumper, Cooper suspected he was also suffering from the cold of the morning. When Theo returned, he was carrying a pile of green fleece blankets. Cooper reached up and took two. One for herself and one for Lily. "Here, put this round you."

Cooper shuffled a little closer to Lily and tilted her head at Dylan. Slowly, he joined them and sat himself down next to his sister. He opened his hand and she slipped her free hand into his. It looked so tiny, almost doll-like, in Dylan's shovel-sized palm. He closed his fingers around hers and squeezed gently.

"No one's going to rush you, Lily," Cooper told her. "No one is going to grab you or try to wrestle the bottle from you. I don't want you or your brother to get hurt, okay?"

Lily blinked but said nothing. Tears began to stream from her eyes; a translucent version of the red that flowed down her neck.

"Right, I'm going to start at the beginning, and I want you to stop me if I go wrong." Cooper swallowed nervously. "You had a very sheltered upbringing. You couldn't date who you wanted to," her eyes flicked to Theo, "you couldn't work where you wanted to. You were expected to cook and clean and take care of the men in your family. But that wasn't the life you wanted. You wanted...fame? Fortune?"

"No," Lily said with a sniffle, lifting her eyes from the grubby floor of the bunker. "I didn't want to be a celebrity or anything. Not really. I just wanted... more."

"But nice clothes and likes on social media made you feel good? They validated you."

She nodded. "I guess." Further tears snaked down her flushed cheeks.

"That's nothing to be ashamed of. It's normal. But a part-time job at a beautician's didn't pay for the labels you like to wear. I know you call yourself an influencer, and I might be older and more out of the loop than people your age, but I'm no dinosaur either. I had a look at your account; you have less than a thousand followers. I doubt anyone is gifting sunglasses worth over eight hundred pounds to an account with those numbers. You bought those glasses yourself, didn't you?"

Lily wiped her face on the back of her hand, wincing as she touched yellow flesh near her eye. "Yes."

Cooper was glad Lily was talking, and she seemed to be warming up slightly. Her shivering was less pronounced. "You didn't really know what your father did for a living, did you?"

She shook her head.

"But you knew what Charlene used to do. She didn't hide it. You knew she earned great money, and you wanted some of that, so, you took a job at Vixen."

"YOU WHAT?" Theo's attitude changed in an instant from that of a concerned boyfriend to an angry abuser. "You danced for dirty old men?" he spat, stepping forward to tower over the weeping Lily.

Lily flinched, cowering further into the corner. "I— I just danced. I didn't strip or anything, Theo."

"Back off," Dylan warned, his teeth bared at his cousin.

Theo ignored him. "You little slapper."

Rage coursed through Cooper. The word stung her as much as it stung Lily. "Out," she commanded, pushing Theo in the chest. He didn't budge. She saw Tennessee and Tucker lurking in the shadows, ready to assist if needed. "Do I need to remind you, Theo, that I can reopen the Harbour Lights case any time I damn well like? Now get out." He looked at her as if she wouldn't dare and when she raised her right brow to challenge him, he ground his jaw, folded his arms and walked away.

Cooper let out a sigh and realised her hands were shaking. She wiggled her fingers for a few moments while she calmed down before continuing to talk to Lily. "The money was good at Vixen. You worked the quiet afternoon shifts as it meant you could juggle it with your job at the beautician's, and you always made it home for dinner. No one would be suspicious. No one would know. You had no idea your family charged protection fees to the owner."

Cooper faced Dylan, who was massaging his temples. His hands were so large he could rub both sides of his head with one hand. "Dylan, the owner of Vixen—Aleksei Pavlovich—told me you never go in the bar."

"Yeah. I... I make the girls nervous. I can see it in their faces. They don't like to look at me."

Cooper felt for him. He was a brute all right, but he was also the product of his upbringing. She'd been sneered at when she pushed a pram while wearing her school uniform, and kids had pointed when the wig she used to wear would slip. But she'd never know what it was like to be Dylan, to wear the damage of abuse so obviously.

"Aleksei said you'd go to the back door and wait for one of the bartenders to bring out the cash. Then you'd take off."

"Yeah. I didn't like to hang around."

"But you were ill on Monday. Poisoned. So Fletcher did the rounds himself. He wasn't going to let the fact he was nauseous and probably seeing double come between him and his money."

"Not when he'd already called me every name under the sun for taking a sick day."

"Do you think your father was the sort to just go to the back door of a gentleman's club?"

He shorted, but not out of amusement. "Not a chance. There's no way he'd go to Vixen or Bambi Bar, or any of those clubs, and not go in to take a look at the girls."

Cooper carefully leaned forward and patted Lily on her knee. "Aleksei said your father's mood suddenly changed. He described your father as happy but sickly-looking one minute, then like he was ready to kill someone the next. He saw you, didn't he?"

Lily's mouth opened, and she gasped for breath, her eyes pleading with the ceiling as if asking for forgiveness. It took several minutes and a lot of soothing words from her brother before she was able to speak through the panic.

"I came out of the dressing room and got on the stage. He was sat there, drinking whiskey and... and... our eyes met. I panicked. I didn't know what to do. He stormed out of there so fast. I just jumped off the stage and ran back to the dressing room. I couldn't go back on after that. I couldn't do anything."

"Where did he wait for you?" Cooper asked.

"The back alley." She doubled up. Her shoulders rounded, head bowed, legs crossed in front of her. She looked half the size she was; like someone who wanted to be so small that they'd disappear. "I put my jacket on. I wanted some fresh air because it was like I couldn't breathe. I grabbed a packet of cigarettes and went out the back to have a smoke, but my hands were shaking so much I couldn't light it. His... his car came screeching round the corner. He got out and dragged me into it."

Dylan formed his free hand into a fist and cracked his knuckles.

"He raced home. Speeding. I was sure we were going crash into a tree and go up in flames. I was crying, and he was calling me all sorts. I told him that he never called Charlene those names, but it made him even madder. He said it was different, that I was his daughter and I was an embarrassment. He grabbed me by my hair and dragged me into the house."

Terror gripped Lily, she squeezed her eyes shut, grabbing Dylan's hand so tightly the ends of his fingers turned pink. Her other arm slammed downward, shattering the bottle against the concrete floor. Shards of green glass ricocheted off the wall next to her; the bottleneck, with its knife-like edges, remained clasped in Lily's hand.

"Take your time," Cooper said as calmly as she could. "There's no rush."

"I kept asking Mo to help me. I begged him."

"But he'd never go against his employer?"

She shook her head from side to side. "It was like he couldn't even hear me. Dad— Dad dragged me into his office and slammed the door. He was slapping me, punching me." She took her hand away from Dylan's and touched the tender skin around her eye. "I fell to the floor and curled up. I wrapped my hands around my head to protect myself... but he started kicking me instead."

Dylan winced. The story of abuse all too familiar to the eldest of Fletcher's children.

"He wouldn't stop. He just kept kicking me, over and over. I tried to crawl under the desk to get away from him... and I saw the gun, taped under there... I thought... I thought he was going to kill me."

"I believe you," Cooper said. "You grabbed the gun. Then what?"

"He backed away for a second, long enough for me to clamber to my feet and move towards the door. I wanted to make a run for it. I was going to pack a bag and go to Theo's." She grimaced, perhaps recalling how Theo had just spoken to her. "Then Dad lunged at me and the gun went off. I... I don't remember pulling the trigger. He fell over the desk and onto the floor. Then I shot him again. That time, well, I suppose that wasn't an accident. I had to make sure he didn't get back up. I killed him. Oh, God. I killed Dad." She screamed, pulling her blanket open and stabbing the bottleneck into her thigh, once, twice—

Dylan lunged, grasping her hand in his. "Stop, Lily. I won't let you do this."

He pulled the make-shift weapon free and tossed it from the bunker's window. Cooper heard it shatter. Dylan quickly folded a blanket and pressed it to Lily's leg, stemming the flow of blood, but only for a moment; a circle of red was already blooming on the green fabric.

"It's okay, Lily. It's okay."

"Time to get her out of here," Cooper said. She motioned for Tennessee to get a paramedic, but Dylan had already scooped her up and was carrying her towards the exit. The three of them blinked as they emerged into the sunlight. Two paramedics helped Dylan lay Lily on a stretcher in the back of the ambulance. The shorter of the two cleaned her wounds while the other secured her to the bed ready for transport."

"Berwick?" The shorter one asked, referring to the nearest big town.

The taller one shook his head and tightened a strap around Lily's legs. "Too much blood loss. We'll take her to Cramlington. We need to floor it."

"Dylan," Cooper called. "Go with DS Daniel; he'll follow the ambulance. I don't have time to argue. We need to go now."

Thankfully, he did as he was asked and jumped from the vehicle. Tennessee already had the door to a squad car open and ready for him. As the doors shut, Cooper asked how she could help.

"Hold this."

Cooper pressed clean gauze against Lily's neck. She looked even paler.

"I didn't want to shoot Mo," she said, her breathing shallow but rapid. "I was frightened, and I knew he was armed. I thought he'd shoot me if he saw me with the gun, so I just... You know."

Stroking her hair, Cooper tried to relax Lily as the ambulance raced south along the A1. When they arrived at the Specialist Emergency Care Hospital, they were met by a team of surgeons and nurses who wheeled Lily away through double doors. It was four and a half hours before Cooper saw her again.

Cooper didn't think Lily was a danger to the public, but following protocol, she had to arrange for officers to monitor the ward at all times. Regardless of Lily's reasons, she'd still need to be taken into custody for the time being, and Cooper couldn't risk her doing another runner.

Greeting a pair of officers, Cooper and Tennessee briefly spoke with Lily's surgeon before following him onto the ward. There were only two patients in the eight-bed ward, and they had been placed in opposite corners of the long room. The doctor pulled back a curtain and busied himself with charts, heart rates and blood pressure readings. Next to the bed, Dylan snored loudly in an uncomfortable-looking chair.

Cooper smiled at Lily. "How are you feeling?"

"She'll be woozy for a while," answered the doctor on Lily's behalf. "And Lily, you didn't react too well to the anaesthetic. If you continue feeling nauseous, just press this button."

She blinked wearily but brightened when she saw Dylan next to her.

"You'll have to go over all of this again later, but I hoped you could clear a few things up for us," Cooper said.

She lowered her eyes, then nodded once.

"What were you wearing when your father dragged you back to Morshaw?"

"Erm... a bikini, a red one, with a denim jacket and heels."

"These heels?" Cooper showed her a photo that had been taken of the inside of Lily's wardrobe.

Another nod.

"We had an expert bloodstain analyst assess your father's study. I released Charlene and initially dismissed you as a suspect because our expert told me the shooter had to be between five-foot-ten and six-foot-two. How tall are you?"

"I'm five-five."

"Even in a pair of high heels, you'd still only be five-eight, five-nine at a push. But these..." she tapped on a pair of shoes with see-through heels that had caught her eye during the search for handwriting samples. "These are eight-inch perspex platform heels. Otherwise known as..."

"Stripper heels," Lily answered with a sigh.

"Which means, on Monday, you were six-foot-one."

Dylan stirred. "Hey, you're awake," he said with a smile. It was the first time Cooper had seen him look happy.

Something was troubling Cooper. She asked, "Why did you write Hanson's name in your father's diary?"

"I didn't know who he was at first, but I kept hearing his name around the house—the Hanson meeting this and the Hanson deal that. Dad made me go out with his son, Richard, a couple of times and he kind of creeped me out. I didn't like him. He was really cagey about his family and how they knew ours... and I knew the boys hated him. Theo told me he was a... well a bad person, so I... I thought it would help, or at least buy me more time. I wasn't thinking straight. I wiped the diary with my jacket; under the desk too. Then I got out of there, but I still had the gun and... Oh god, you have to tell Charlene I'm sorry. Promise me, Dylan. Tell her I'm so sorry."

"Why hide it in her jewellery box?" Cooper asked.

"I knew it locked. And Charlene kept the key in the nightstand. I got cleaned up, cleaned the gun and got out of there. I was going to go back later and get it, but I thought *what if someone's found them already?* What if Dylan or George found them and the police are already there? So, I called Charlene and arranged to spend the day with her. I thought it would give us both an alibi. I tried to make it right. I didn't mean to frame her. I tried to tell you she wouldn't do that."

Lily was becoming increasingly anxious, and her doctor looked like he was ready to throw Cooper and Tennessee out of there.

"Try to relax," she told her.

Dylan stood, moved to the bed and sat on the edge so Lily could nuzzle into him. "The long sleeves and heavy make-up. You've been hiding the bruises he gave you, haven't you?"

Lily's head bobbed in and out of his chest. He protectively stroked her black hair and addressed Cooper. "It was self-defence."

"I know that," Cooper said. "But she'll still be charged." She felt for the young woman, and though she hoped the CPS would be lenient, forgiving even, she knew Lily's life would never be the same. She was going to have to live with this forever. "I'm sorry, Lily. Dylan, you should call your lawyer. He'll know what to do."

He shook his head. "I'll get someone new. Dad's lawyer was a tax and finance specialist. I wouldn't trust him with this. Not with you, Lily. I'll get you the best."

Cooper looked at Tennessee. He returned her stare with a bob of his head; it was time to let the young woman get some sleep and recover from her surgery.

Before leaving, Cooper thanked Dylan for his help while they'd been in the bunker. She couldn't know how it would have played out without him, but she knew he'd acted swiftly when they'd needed to carry Lily out of there. Thanks to him, Lily hadn't bled out. Tennessee held the curtain for Cooper. As she left, she reached into a pocket, retrieved a small white card and placed it on the corner of the bed.

WHEN DYLAN BLACKBURN WAS sure his sister had fallen back to sleep, he picked up the piece of card that the detective with the short hair had left, and walked to the window for some fresh air. He felt heavy with the weight of a crumbling family on his shoulders, but it was a weight he was determined to bear. He would save his siblings and breathe new life into the Blackburn name.

He took in the view of a fan-shaped car park and waited until the two detectives reached their car and drove away. Glancing down at the piece of card in his hand, Dylan turned it over. It was a business card: *Oliver Timms, Defence Lawyer.*

- Chapter 30 -

Gentle waves lapped at the shore. Bands of white were pushed up the golden sand by the enduring power of the North Sea. The sky was cloudless and bright, the sea, aquamarine with hints of grey. Longsands beach looked glorious. To the south, the ruins of Tynemouth Castle and the Priory loomed over the cliff face, and to the south, the steeple of St. George pierced the sky.

Cooper watched the water, almost hypnotised by the rhythm it held. In, out, in, out. A never-ending force. As sure as the Earth kept spinning, the tides would keep moving. Just like crime. One case in, one case out. As soon as one investigation came to a close, you could be damn sure another would emerge. With various Blackburns either dead or in custody, and with Hanson facing life for arson and manslaughter, Cooper hoped that organised crime in the region would take a dive. That was wishful thinking at best and pure naivety at worst. The Roker Boys or the Daytons would move in and battle over the remnants like scabby seagulls fight over chips. If she was lucky, there'd all take each other out and leave the city mob-free, however, she'd never been the lucky sort. Now that the Blackburn / Moradi case had drawn to a close, Cooper was feeling refreshed and physically lighter. She worried about Lily and what awaited her. She'd wanted to hunt a cold-blooded killer but had instead found a scared little girl who feared for her life.

A staging area had been set up at the south end of Longsands, next to Crusoe's café. Commissioner Begum from Northumbria Police and Chief Fire Officer Spence delivered speeches while spectators gathered for the charity triathlon. A representative from the Fishermen's Mission, a charity that provides welfare and support for fishermen as well as running services for lost seafarers, thanked Begum and Spence. He took the microphone, spoke about the important work of the Mission, and expressed his gratitude to those involved in today's fundraiser.

Cooper pulled her dressing gown tighter around her. Underneath it, she wore a plain black bathing suit that didn't entirely cover the impressive black and grey chest tattoo she'd recently acquired. The design of roses, complete with leaves and thorns, perfectly hid her lumpectomy scars and covered not only her breasts but some of her upper chest and shoulders.

The relay triathlon would soon begin. Cooper took her place on the starting line with all the other poor sods who'd been strong-armed into doing the swimming leg. All body types were represented, from hulking firemen to more heavy-set women who were giggling with each other to cover their nerves.

Elliot Whyte took the spot next to Cooper. "Good luck, ma'am." He removed his robe and added it to a growing pile. Cooper did the same. "Fuck me. It's colder than I thought. I'm freezing my fucking tits off." Suddenly his jaw fell. "Ah, shit. Sorry."

"Relax. It's just a phrase, and besides, I didn't have a mastectomy."

"Oh. Well, good." He looked away, fixing his gaze on the grey-blue that awaited them.

Cooper thought he looked uncomfortable so she couldn't resist making it worse. "And since when were you worried about hurting my feelings?"

Before Whyte could answer, a bell rung to signal the start of the race. Cooper didn't waste a second, she sprinted towards the sea, all the time wondering what the hell she was doing there. How had Tennessee convinced her to do this? Her feet met the shallows. *Jesus*. The water was icy cold. High-pitched squeals filled the air, and once the water reached groin level, the men felt their prized possessions rapidly start to shrink. Cooper tried to block out the cold, telling herself she'd been through worse, that cold water was nothing compared to chemo. The tactic worked and Cooper was soon deep enough to dive forward and begin swimming. She followed the route marked by buoys, concentrating on her breathing and maintaining a steady pace. The cold began to seep beyond her skin and chilled her to the bones. She'd kill Tennessee when she got her hands on him. He owed her big time. Sod it, he could look after Steven Seagull instead of Keaton.

Cooper had no idea how long she'd been in the water. Time seemed to slow down. Salty water got in her mouth and splashed up her nose, she spluttered and floundered but found her technique again. As she reentered the shallow water and her feet found the sand, she counted the people ahead of her. There were maybe six or seven, meaning she was in the first third. She couldn't see Whyte. Was she beating him? She hoped so.

Cooper ran up the beach, though waded or even plodded would be a better way to describe it. There was nothing glamorous about trying to run through shallow water or over soft sand, despite what the opening credits of Baywatch led you to believe. The sand clung to her cold, goose-pimpled skin, and each step she took was laboured. She was gasping for air. Tennessee was waiting at the end of the road that led to the beach. His arm outstretched, waiting for her to high-five him.

"You owe me a beer," Cooper said, panting as she slapped his palm with hers.

Tennessee jumped on his bike. "I'll buy you two," he said as he furiously began to pedal up the hill and onto the promenade.

"Make it three," she called after him.

Tennessee had to follow the road to the very top of Whitley Bay and back to the opposite end of Longsands where he'd find Keaton waiting for him. Keaton would then sprint back along the beach to the finish line.

Now she'd stopped exercising, the chill really took hold, and her body began to shake. Despite her coldness, there was a great atmosphere on the beach. A steel band were playing, and a sandcastle competition was in full swing. Some of the sculptures were amazing. A huge coiled snake made of sand was so intricate the artist must have begun work in the wee hours, a fairytale castle decorated in shells stood taller than most of the children gathered around it, and a great sand sailing boat was beginning to take shape. Lifeguards were performing CPR demonstrations and encouraging members of the public to have a try on the dummies. All in all, the organisers had done a great job, and it was for an excellent cause.

Whyte appeared at her side, gasping and holding two dressing gowns.

"Thanks." Cooper grabbed her fluffy robe, shook it free of sand and wrapped it around her body.

"Listen, about what you said earlier. I know what you were referring to and I guess I deserved it. I should have had your back, but I didn't. I was a..."

"A prize dickhead?"

"Em, yeah. You know I don't really think like that. It was the environment. The station was a bit of an old boy's club back then."

"Translation, the station was a hive a misogynistic twats, and because you wanted to fit in, you threw me under the bus. I was fair game."

He scratched his head. "I regret it... Oh, Martin's overtaking someone. Where's Tennessee?"

"He's near the front. You can't miss him; he's wearing bright pink." But almost as soon as Cooper said it, Tennessee disappeared from view. He'd be back in around fifteen to twenty minutes.

"Mum!" Tina and Josh were running down the beach and had to dodge a boy of eight or nine who was having a massive tantrum. "I'm all packed! Can't wait to see Granny and Grandad. We'll need to weigh my bag though, it's full of textbooks. I might need to leave a few behind."

"Take as many as you like," Cooper reassured her. "We'll find space in my suitcase if need be."

Tina smiled. "Cool, thanks. I blended some fish to make enough feed for Steven for the next two weeks and got it portioned up and in the freezer. And I booked our taxi to the airport, and checked our travel insurance was still valid, and got some Euros, and... Oh yeah, we brought you some hot chocolate." She brandished a stainless steel flask.

Cooper hugged her daughter. "You angel. Hi Josh, how're things?"

Josh gave a nervous, mumbly answer that Cooper didn't understand a word of. Her hands were too cold to open the flask, so she asked Tina to pour her a cup. She gripped the lid as Tina filled it up with piping hot liquid. It smelled mouthwateringly good. It obviously wasn't the one calorie per cup crap.

"You were brilliant, Mum. We watched from the old pool."

The boy having the tantrum was now running away from his mother and trying to kick over every sandcastle that he passed.

It wasn't long before the first cyclists came back into view. The leading pack was about five strong and Tennessee's bright pink t-shirt was amongst them. Cooper bounced with excitement and began cheering for him, not that there was any chance of him hearing her. Tennessee leapt from his bike and ran down the bank that led onto the north end of Longsands. A group of runners jostled on the starting line, waiting for high-fives from their teammates. Cooper couldn't tell which blurred dot in the distance was Keaton, but she knew she wouldn't hesitate in barging a burly fireman out of the way if it meant giving herself a competitive edge.

The running leg of the race was just under a kilometre in length, but the soft sand would make the journey much more tiring than had it taken place on tarmac or grass.

"There's Paula," Tina said, pointing up the beach. "She's gaining on the man in third."

Keaton's legs pumped hard, causing plumes of sand to billow behind her as she ran.

"Come on, Paula!" Cooper cupped her hands around her mouth and yelled as loud as she could. "Yes, she's caught him. She's in third."

"The man in second is slowing," Tina said. "That, or Paula's getting faster."

A beefy man in too-tight shorts crossed the finish line to rapturous applause from the gathered spectators.

"They're neck and neck... Oh, come on, Paula. SPRINT... YES!" Keaton overtook the man in second and powered over the line. She didn't even look that out of breath. Cooper, Tina, Josh and Whyte ran over to her and showered her in congratulations.

One by one, more runners crossed the line, running into the arms of their teammates. Tennessee didn't take long to jog along the beach and reunite himself with what he had dubbed the Dream Team. His wife, Hayley, pounced and showered him in kisses. The action made Cooper smile; she hadn't seen Hayley so happy in a long time. A few feet away, Hayley's mother cradled little Alfie and chatted to Keaton's partner and brother.

"Well done," Hayley gushed at them all. "And Erica, I can't believe you went in the sea!"

Cooper was halfway through insisting that Tennessee and Keaton take all the credit when Tina handed her her mobile. "Mum, it's Granny."

Cooper took the phone and walked away from the group, covering her other ear with her free hand. "Hi, Mum."

"Hello, Erica. I'm just at the hospital." Julie's voice was distant.

"How's Dad? Flights are booked and bags are packed. Tina and I are due to arrive just before two tomorrow afternoon." She looked at Tina who was bouncing up and down, telling Keaton how to feed a juvenile seagull while the bratty boy destroyed the sand sailboat? *Where was his mother?* Her daughter had been through a lot. Some time in the sun would do her good, even if it wasn't under the best of circumstances.

"Oh. That's..."

"Do you want me to bring any goodies over? Yorkshire Tea? Marks and Spencer's chocolate?'

"Erica dear..."

Cooper could sense it before Julie had even said it. "I'm sorry, darling. There were complications with his surgery. The doctor said something about a clot breaking loose and causing another heart attack. He— He didn't make it."

Tears flooded Cooper's eyes. "What?" she asked. It didn't make sense. It just didn't.

"He died, darling. He passed about twenty minutes ago."

Cooper span to face the sea, not wanting the others to see the shock and pain on her face. Though she'd only seen her father a handful of times since he moved away, she always loved him, always missed him. The father-daughter bond had suddenly been snapped in two and the hole it left in her gut ached. Cooper felt as if she was falling.

"Oh, Mum." Her voice quivered then broke. She hadn't made it. She'd been too late and would now never get to say goodbye or tell him one last time that she loved him. What was wrong with her? She should have booked an earlier flight. She could have flown from Manchester or Leeds. She should have handed the case over to another DCI and been on the first flight out of the country the second Julie mentioned chest pains. She'd regret her decision until the day she died.

Sobbing into the phone, apologising over and over for not being there, Cooper felt more out of breath than she had done during her swim. She couldn't breathe. Behind her, an announcement was booming over a loudspeaker. *No. Not now.*

"And in second place, from Northumbria CID, congratulations to DCI Cooper, DS Paula Keaton and DS Jack Daniel."

"Boss?" Keaton saw the look on Cooper's face and tapped Tina on the arm. Tina instantly read her mother's mind and ran to her.

"She can't go up there," Tina urged.

Tennessee grabbed Keaton. "I'll go up. You stay here."

Tennessee took to the stage and collected an enormous silver cup and shook hands with Commissioner Begum and Chief Fire Officer Spence. He thanked his team, thanked Superintendent Nixon and tried to say something witty. Regrettably, no one was listening or watching Tennessee. Cooper's pained wails had attracted the attention of the crowd; her despair was too raw to stifle. Tennessee jumped from the stage to make way for the winning team from Tyne and Wear Fire and Rescue, but as his feet hit the sand, a scream filled the air. A scream loud enough to drown out Cooper's cries. Then another. And another.

All eyes turned to the undisciplined boy. He was staggering backwards, away from the sand sculpture of the snake. His eyes were wide; his mouth a perfect oval. He'd kicked a great hole in the side of the snake, and something protruded from the crumbling mound of sand. It was pale and bloated, and it was unmistakably a human arm.

DCI Cooper will return in Northern Roulette.

- Also by B Baskerville -

The DCI Cooper Series:
Cut The Deck
Rock, Paper, Scissors
Roll The Dice
Northern Roulette
Hide & Seek
Finders Keepers

Stand Alones:
The Only Weapon In The Room
Dead In The Water

- Be Sociable -

Facebook: B Baskerville - Author
Twitter: B__Baskerville
TikTok: B_Baskerville
Instagram: B_Baskerville_Author

Newsletter: You can subscribe to the B Baskerville newsletter using the form on BetsyBaskerville.com. You'll mainly hear from B when she has something to share, such as a pre-order going live, a new book release or sale etc.

Milton Keynes UK
Ingram Content Group UK Ltd.
UKHW021523250724
1035UKWH00042B/595

9 781739 244569